PENGUIN BOOKS
THE PENGUIN BOOK OF VAMPIRE STORIES

Alan Ryan lives in New York. As well as writing novels and short stories, he has edited several anthologies. His story *The Bones Wizard* won the 1985 Film Fantasy Award for the Best Short Story of the Year. Alan Ryan has won and also judged the World Film Fantasy Awards and is a member of the National Book Critics Circle. He writes reviews and articles on literature and travel and regularly contributes to the *Washington Post*, *USA Today*, the *Smithsonian* and *Travel and Leisure*, among other newspapers and journals.

THE PENGUIN BOOK OF VAMPIRE STORIES

Edited by Alan Ryan

Bloomsbury Books
London

PENGUIN BOOKS

Published by the Penguin Group
Penguin Books Ltd, 27 Wrights Lane, London W8 5TZ, England
Penguin Books USA Inc., 375 Hudson Street, New York, New York 10014, USA
Penguin Books Australia Ltd, Ringwood, Victoria, Australia
Penguin Books Canada Ltd, 10 Alcorn Avenue, Toronto, Ontario, Canada M4V 3B2
Penguin Books (NZ) Ltd, 182-190 Wairau Road, Auckland 10, New Zealand

Penguin Books Ltd, Registered Offices: Harmondsworth, Middlesex, England

First published in the USA,
under the title *Vampires: Two Centuries of Vampire Stories*,
by Doubleday & Co., Inc., New York, 1987
Published by Penguin Books 1988
This edition published by Bloomsbury Books, an imprint of
Godfrey Cave Associates Ltd, 42 Bloomsbury Street, London WC1B 3QJ,
under licence from Penguin Books Ltd, 1991
1 3 5 7 9 10 8 6 4 2

Selection and Introduction copyright © Alan Ryan, 1987

The acknowledgements on pp. xi and xii constitute an extension
of this copyright page

Printed in England by
BPCC Hazell Books
Aylesbury, Bucks, England
Member of BPCC Ltd

ISBN 1 85471 006 0

Like everything else,
this book is dedicated
to Marie

Contents

ACKNOWLEDGMENTS

Grateful acknowledgment is made to the following for permission to reprint their copyrighted material. Every reasonable effort has been made to trace the ownership of all copyrighted stories included in this volume. Any errors that may have occurred are inadvertent and will be corrected in subsequent editions, provided notification is sent to the Publisher.

"A Rendezvous in Averoigne" by Clark Ashton Smith. Copyright © 1931 by Popular Fiction Publishing Company; copyright © 1942 by Clark Ashton Smith. Reprinted by permission of Arkham House.

"Shambleau" by C. L. Moore. Copyright © 1933 by Popular Fiction Publishing Company; renewed 1961 by C. L. Moore. Reprinted by permission of Don Congdon Associates, Inc.

"Revelations in Black" by Carl Jacobi. Copyright © 1933 by Carl Jacobi. Reprinted by permission of Arkham House.

"School for the Unspeakable" by Manly Wade Wellman. Copyright © 1937 by Popular Fiction Publishing Company; renewed 1965 by Manly Wade Wellman. Reprinted by permission of Kirby McCauley, Ltd.

"The Drifting Snow" by August Derleth. Copyright © 1948 by August Derleth. Reprinted by permission of Arkham House.

"Over the River" by P. Schuyler Miller. Copyright © 1941 by P. Schuyler Miller. Reprinted by permission of Mary E. Drake.

"The Girl with the Hungry Eyes" by Fritz Leiber. Copyright © 1949 by Avon Books. Reprinted by permission of the Author.

"The Mindworm" by C. M. Kornbluth. From *The Best of C. M. Kornbluth*, edited, with Introduction by Frederik Pohl. Copyright © 1976 by Mary Kornbluth, John Kornbluth, and David Kornbluth. Reprinted by permission of Ballantine Books, a Division of Random House, Inc.

"Drink My Blood" by Richard Matheson. Copyright © 1951 by Richard Matheson; renewed 1979 by Richard Matheson. Reprinted by permission of Don Congdon Associates, Inc.

INTRODUCTION

Judging from the vampire fiction written in the last two hundred years, there seem to be as many different kinds of vampires as there are kinds of cats in T. S. Eliot's poetic catalogue: every sort from lyrical to satirical, from categorical to metaphorical.

Because of the large number of movies about these creatures of the night, our visual image today of the classic vampire tends to bear a striking resemblance to various actors who have played the role on the screen: Max Schreck, Bela Lugosi, Christopher Lee, or Klaus Kinski, for example, or George Hamilton, Frank Langella, or even Catherine Deneuve.

But vampires had been appearing in fiction for more than a century before they began starring in movies.

As early as 1800, a vampire story called "Wake Not the Dead" was published in England. It was by Johann Ludwig Tieck who, like other German romantic writers of his time, often used legends as sources for his stories. Sixteen years later, the great romantic poet Lord Byron was toying with the idea of writing a vampire tale. And three years after that, Dr. John Polidori, a former friend who had quarreled with Byron, wrote and published a story called "The Vampyre." Not surprisingly, the evil figure of the vampire, named Ruthven in Polidori's tale, bore more than a little resemblance to Byron himself.

In 1845 a new novel called *Varney the Vampyre, or, The Feast of Blood* began appearing in England in weekly parts, each costing a penny. This was not literary fiction, by any means, but rather a cheap and popular entertainment, offered in a form and at a price that the average person could afford. The author, James Malcolm Rymer, managed to stretch out his lurid tale for two years and 109 parts. In fact, *Varney* proved so popular that it was reprinted in 1853.

By that time, the image of the vampire—a combination of Polidori's Ruthven and Rymer's Varney—was taking on a cohesive form in people's minds. The vampire, everyone knew, was monstrously evil and hideously ugly, though he bore a human form.

That human form may be the key to understanding the "popularity" of vampires, both in the nineteenth century and now. Their form, though recognizably human, is seen in a grotesquely distorted version, making them all the more horrible. In physical features, they are repulsive: long nails that curve like claws; skin showing a deathly pallor, except when it is flushed with blood after feeding; eyes often described as "dead"; and ratlike fangs designed for attack. Psychologically, they are repulsive too: they are evil, devoid of any moral code; they stand outside, and therefore threaten, all normal society; they drink blood; they kill; and, even worse, they make their victims like themselves.

Looked at from a commercial angle, the vampire's human form was wonderfully convenient. Since the vampire had the shape of a human being, it could be represented on a stage by an actor, and the middle years of the nineteenth century saw many productions of plays about vampires staged both in England and on the Continent. Furthermore, for sheer entertainment value, it didn't hurt that vampires seemed to have a special interest in attacking beautiful and vulnerable young women, a symbol for all that was good and holy in Victorian England.

Toward the end of the nineteenth century, an Irish writer and theatrical manager named Bram Stoker, working in London, developed an interest in European vampire myths and their origins. He began doing serious research that culminated in his greatest work, the novel *Dracula*, in 1897.

There is nothing in literature quite like *Dracula*. It is a tense and compelling novel, filled with suspense and an unsettling mood of dread throughout. It has a terrible figure of overpowering evil in the vampire Count Dracula. Just as important, it has a cast of sympathetic characters. Aided by Professor Van Helsing and all the powers of modern science, they muster their courage when they are forced by circumstances to do battle with a terrifying and unknown enemy.

The novel was hugely popular and firmly fixed the vampire figure in the popular imagination: immortal, unholy, ruthless, intelligent, living only by night and shunning sunlight by sleeping in its coffin. It also clearly established the vampiric figure as an aristocrat, someone set apart from the common man.

It was only twenty-five years later, in 1922, that the first vampire movie was made. It was called *Nosferatu* (meaning "the undead") and used different names for the characters, but it was based on Stoker's *Dracula*. Only a lawsuit brought by Stoker's widow, who was receiving no royalties from this unauthorized adaptation, kept the movie from wide circulation. *Nosferatu* is readily available today, and even modern audiences, accustomed to marvels of special effects in the movies, are struck most powerfully by the hideous, ratlike appearance and strange bodily movements of Max Schreck, the actor playing the vampire.

And then there was Bela Lugosi. In 1931 the Hungarian actor repeated his Broadway stage role in *Dracula*. Opinion on the film is divided, with some critics calling Tod Browning's direction static and Lugosi's acting stylized. For many people, however, Bela Lugosi perfectly embodied the character of the vampire with his strange, balletic style of movement, his flashing eyes, his Hungarian accent, and his engagingly ominous way of delivering lines.

And then in 1958 the fine British actor Christopher Lee played the role of Dracula for the first of many times in Hammer Films' *Horror of Dracula*. No other actor before or since has captured all the subtleties and contradictions inherent in Stoker's character. Lee's Dracula is simultaneously both powerful and vulnerable, terrifying and attractive.

Since then, many other actors have played the role, from a suave and comic George Hamilton bewildered by modern life in New York City to, most notably, the German actor Klaus Kinski, who recreated the inhuman and repellent figure portrayed in 1922 by Max Schreck.

Inevitably, the power of these visual images affects the thinking of writers, just as the trends of literary tastes influence the making of movies. Tradition and innovation stand side by side in both vampire movies and vampire fiction.

Writers in the twentieth century have continued telling tales based on the traditional body of vampire lore. The details are familiar: vampires fear the sun, a crucifix, garlic; they cannot cross water; they must carry a little of their native earth with them wherever they go; they must always have an evil assistant to do their dirty work by day.

Other modern writers have preferred to explore the vampire myth in new ways, using only the core of the myth and the symbolic value of the vampire as a force of evil wreaking havoc in the world of mortals.

The variety of twentieth-century vampires is dazzling. In 1933 C. L. Moore placed a vampire in the fantasy world of a future Mars in "Shambleau." In 1939 August Derleth was seeing a vampire in the patterns made by "The Drifting Snow." There are male and female vampires. There are vampires that are invisible and vampires that can change their shapes at will; which kind is more frightening depends on the writer. And, going right to the central symbolism of the myth, there are vampires that do not suck blood at all from their victims. Instead, they steal things that are perhaps just as valuable to a human being, things like youth . . . and hope . . . and love.

Perhaps the vampire is so compelling precisely because he is so repellent. Perhaps he works so powerfully on our imaginations because he represents such a distortion of human nature, a reversal of everything normal. And perhaps—just perhaps—we are fascinated by him because, in our heart of hearts, we want to be just like him.

In any case, the stories that follow are filled with vampires. They're lurking here in all their variety, in all their horror, and in all their glory.

While preparing this book, I've profited from the advice of many colleagues. I wish to express my thanks to Robert Bloch, Ramsey Campbell, Suzy McKee Charnas, Charles L. Grant, Stuart David Schiff, Steve Rasnic Tem, Peter Tremayne, Karl Edward Wagner, Douglas E. Winter, and Chelsea Quinn Yarbro, all of whom suggested stories for consideration. Roger Anker kindly shared with me some of Charles Beaumont's unpublished letters. Mary Sherwin Jatlow and Ellen Asher at Nelson Doubleday Books were constantly supportive with their enthusiasm for the project and with suggestions and expertise. And as always I owe more than I can say to Marie Marino.

ALAN RYAN

VAMPIRES

GEORGE GORDON, LORD BYRON *(1788–1824), the great English roman-tic, did not confine his dark and often gloomy imaginings to his poetry.*

In 1816 Byron planned a trip across Europe, intending to visit Swit-zerland, where he would meet with his friends, Percy Bysshe Shelley and Shelley's wife Mary, and then the party would travel on to Italy. Byron's companion on the journey was Dr. John Polidori (1795–1821), uncle of the future Dante Gabriel and Christina Rossetti and the youngest man ever granted a medical degree by the University of Edinburgh. Polidori was selected partly because it was customary to bring along a doctor on such an extended visit to the Continent, and partly because of his bright conversation. But the two men quarreled often and tension was high by the time they reached Geneva and were united with the Shelleys on May 27. True to form, Polidori took an instant dislike to Shelley and sulked silently through the group's many conversations about poetry.

During a period of nasty weather from June 15 to 17, the group was staying at the Villa Diodati on the shores of Lake Geneva. To pass the time, they began reading some volumes of ghost stories translated from German into French. The circumstances and the mood came together, and one day Byron announced, "We will each write a ghost story."

Mary Shelley dreamed the idea for her novel Frankenstein, which she began at once and which was published two years later. Shelley, who had earlier written two Gothic novels that he'd published privately, lost interest quickly in the project and, apparently, wrote nothing. Byron wrote out a brief fragment of a story in his notebook. And "poor Polidori," as Mary Shelley later reported, "had a terrible idea about a skull-headed lady."

The quarrels continued and Polidori even challenged Shelley to a duel before Byron finally dismissed him at the end of the summer.

But Polidori was to be heard from again. The New Monthly Maga-zine for April 1819 contained a story called "The Vampyre," which was attributed to Byron. The next month's issue, however, contained a letter from Polidori, in which he claimed the story as his own work while admit-ting that it was based on the story Byron had begun and abandoned in Geneva in 1816. This seems to have been the truth, and Polidori's malice also seems clear, especially since the vampire Ruthven resembles more than a little the popular image of Byron current at the time.

Whatever its provenance, however, Polidori's "The Vampyre" was the first vampire tale of any substance in the English language, and the image of the vampire Ruthven would influence all treatments of the theme that followed it, including James Malcolm Rymer's hugely popu-lar Varney the Vampyre (1845), Le Fanu's "Carmilla" (1872), and

Bram Stoker's Dracula *(1897), and these stories in turn have influenced all the vampire literature that followed in the twentieth century.*

Both Byron's original 1816 "Fragment of a Novel" and Polidori's 1819 version of it follow here.

Fragment of a Novel (1816)
BY GEORGE GORDON, LORD BYRON

"June 17, 1816.

"In the year 17—, having for some time determined on a journey through countries not hitherto much frequented by travellers, I set out, accompanied by a friend, whom I shall designate by the name of Augustus Darvell. He was a few years my elder, and a man of considerable fortune and ancient family: advantages which an extensive capacity prevented him alike from undervaluing or overrating. Some peculiar circumstances in his private history had rendered him to me an object of attention, of interest, and even of regard, which neither the reserve of his manners, nor occasional indications of an inquietude at times nearly approaching to alienation of mind, could extinguish.

"I was yet young in life, which I had begun early; but my intimacy with him was of a recent date: we had been educated at the same schools and university; but his progress through these had preceded mine, and he had been deeply initiated into what is called the world, while I was yet in my novitiate. While thus engaged, I heard much both of his past and present life; and, although in these accounts there were many and irreconcilable contradictions, I could still gather from the whole that he was a being of no common order, and one who, whatever pains he might take to avoid remark, would still be remarkable. I had cultivated his acquaintance subsequently, and endeavoured to obtain his friendship, but this last appeared to be unattainable; whatever affections he might have possessed seemed now, some to have been extinguished, and others to be concentred: that his feelings were acute, I had sufficient opportunities of observing; for, although he could control, he could not altogether disguise them: still he had a power of giving to one passion the appearance of another, in such a manner that it was difficult to define the nature of what was working within him; and the expressions of his features would vary so rapidly, though slightly, that it was useless to trace them to their sources. It was evident that he was a prey to some cureless disquiet; but whether it arose from ambition, love, remorse, grief, from one or all of these, or merely from a morbid temperament akin to disease, I could not discover: there were circumstances alleged which might have justified the application to each of these causes; but, as I have before said, these were so contradictory and contradicted, that none could be fixed upon with accuracy. Where there is mystery, it is generally supposed that there must also be evil: I know not how this may be, but in him there certainly was the one, though I could not ascertain the extent of the other—and felt loth, as far as regarded himself, to believe in its existence. My advances were received with sufficient coldness: but I was young, and not easily discouraged, and at length succeeded in obtaining, to a certain degree, that common-place intercourse and moderate confidence of common and every-day concerns, created and cemented by similarity of pursuit and frequency of meeting, which is called intimacy, or friendship, according to the ideas of him who uses those words to express them.

"Darvell had already travelled extensively; and to him I had applied for information with regard to the conduct of my intended journey. It was my secret wish that he might be prevailed on to accompany me; it was also a probable hope, founded upon the shadowy restlessness which I observed in him, and to which the animation which he appeared to feel on such subjects, and his apparent indifference to all by which he was more immediately surrounded, gave fresh strength. This wish I first hinted, and then expressed: his answer, though I had partly expected it, gave me all the pleasure of surprise—he consented; and, after the requisite arrangement, we commenced our voyages. After journeying through various countries of the south of Europe, our attention was turned towards the East, according to our original destination; and it was in my progress through these regions that the incident occurred upon which will turn what I may have to relate.

"The constitution of Darvell, which must from his appearance have been in early life more than usually robust, had been for some time gradually giving away, without the intervention of any apparent disease: he had neither cough nor hectic, yet he became daily more enfeebled; his habits were temperate, and he neither declined nor complained of fatigue; yet he was evidently wasting away: he became more and more silent and sleepless, and at length so seriously altered, that my alarm grew proportionate to what I conceived to be his danger.

"We had determined, on our arrival at Smyrna, on an excursion to the ruins of Ephesus and Sardis, from which I endeavoured to dissuade him in his present state of indisposition—but in vain: there appeared to be an oppression on his mind, and a solemnity in his manner, which ill corresponded with his eagerness to proceed on what I regarded as a mere party of pleasure little suited to a valetudinarian; but I opposed him no longer—and in a few days we set off together, accompanied only by a serrugee and a single janizary.

"We had passed halfway towards the remains of Ephesus, leaving behind us the more fertile environs of Smyrna, and were entering upon that wild and tenantless tract through the marshes and defiles which lead to the few huts yet lingering over the broken columns of Diana—the roofless walls of expelled Christianity, and the still more recent but complete desolation of abandoned mosques—when the sudden and rapid illness of my companion obliged us to halt at a Turkish cemetery, the turbaned tombstones of which were the sole indication that human life had ever been a sojourner in this wilderness. The only caravansera we had seen was left some hours behind us, not a vestige of a town or even cottage was within sight or hope, and this 'city of the dead' appeared to be the sole refuge of my unfortunate friend, who seemed on the verge of becoming the last of its inhabitants.

"In this situation, I looked round for a place where he might most conveniently repose: contrary to the usual aspect of Mahometan burial-grounds, the cypresses were in this few in number, and these thinly scattered over its extent; the tombstones were mostly fallen, and worn with age: upon one of the most considerable of these, and beneath one of the most spreading trees, Darvell supported himself, in a half-reclining posture, with great difficulty. He asked for water. I had some doubts of our being able to find any, and prepared to go in search of it with hesitating despondency: but he desired me to remain; and turning to Suleiman, our janizary, who stood by us smoking with great tranquillity, he said, 'Suleiman, verbana su,' (i.e. 'bring some water,') and went on describing the spot where it was to be found with great minuteness, at a small well for camels, a few hundred yards to the right: the janizary obeyed. I said to Darvell, 'How did you know this?' He replied, 'From our situation; you must perceive that this place was once inhabited, and could not have been so without springs: I have also been here before.'

" 'You have been here before! How came you never to mention this to me? and what could you be doing in a place where no one would remain a moment longer than they could help it?'

"To this question I received no answer. In the mean time Suleiman returned with the water, leaving the serrugee and the horses at the fountain. The quenching of his thirst had the appearance of reviving him for a moment; and I conceived hopes of his being able to proceed, or at least to return, and I urged the attempt. He was silent—and appeared to be collecting his spirits for an effort to speak. He began—

" 'This is the end of my journey, and of my life; I came here to die; but I have a request to make, a command—for such my last words must be.—You will observe it?'

" 'Most certainly; but I have better hopes.'

" 'I have no hopes, nor wishes, but this—conceal my death from every human being.'

" 'I hope there will be no occasion; that you will recover, and——'

" 'Peace! it must be so: promise this.'

" 'I do.'

" 'Swear it, by all that——' He here dictated an oath of great solemnity.

" 'There is no occasion for this. I will observe your request; and to doubt me is——'

" 'It cannot be helped, you must swear.'

"I took the oath, it appeared to relieve him. He removed a seal ring from his finger, on which were some Arabic characters, and presented it to me. He proceeded—

" 'On the ninth day of the month, at noon precisely (what month you please, but this must be the day), you must fling this ring into the salt springs which run into the Bay of Eleusis; the day after, at the same hour, you must repair to the ruins of the temple of Ceres, and wait one hour.'

" 'Why?'

" 'You will see.'

" 'The ninth day of the month, you say?'

" 'The ninth.'

"As I observed that the present was the ninth day of the month, his countenance changed, and he paused. As he sat, evidently becoming more feeble, a stork, with a snake in her beak, perched upon a tombstone near us; and, without devouring her prey, appeared to be steadfastly regarding us. I know not what impelled me to drive it away, but the attempt was useless; she made a few circles in the air, and returned exactly to the same spot. Darvell pointed to it, and smiled—he spoke—I know not whether to himself or to me—but the words were only, ' 'Tis well!'

" 'What is well? What do you mean?'

" 'No matter; you must bury me here this evening, and exactly where that bird is now perched. You know the rest of my injunctions.'

"He then proceeded to give me several directions as to the manner in which his death might be best concealed. After these were finished, he exclaimed, 'You perceive that bird?'

" 'Certainly.'

" 'And the serpent writhing in her beak?'

" 'Doubtless: there is nothing uncommon in it; it is her natural prey. But it is odd that she does not devour it.'

"He smiled in a ghastly manner, and said faintly, 'It is not yet time!' As he spoke, the stork flew away. My eyes followed it for a moment—it could hardly be longer than ten might be counted. I felt Darvell's weight, as it were, increase upon my shoulder, and, turning to look upon his face, perceived that he was dead!

"I was shocked with the sudden certainty which could not be mistaken—his countenance in a few minutes became nearly black. I should have attributed so rapid a change to poison, had I not been aware that he had no opportunity of receiving it unperceived. The day was declining, the body was rapidly altering, and nothing remained but to fulfil his request. With the aid of Suleiman's ataghan and my own sabre, we scooped a shallow grave upon the spot which Darvell had indicated: the earth easily gave way, having already received some Mahometan tenant. We dug as deeply as the time permitted us, and throwing the dry earth upon all that remained of the singular being so lately departed, we cut a few sods of greener turf from the less withered soil around us, and laid them upon his sepulchre.

"Between astonishment and grief, I was tearless."

See note for Byron's "Fragment of a Novel" (1816).

The Vampyre
(1819)
BY JOHN POLIDORI

It happened that in the midst of the dissipations attendant upon a London winter, there appeared at the various parties of the leaders of the *ton* a nobleman, more remarkable for his singularities, than his rank. He gazed upon the mirth around him, as if he could not participate therein. Apparently, the light laughter of the fair only attracted his attention, that he might by a look quell it, and throw fear into those breasts where thoughtlessness reigned. Those who felt this sensation of awe, could not explain whence it arose: some attributed it to the dead grey eye, which, fixing upon the object's face, did not seem to penetrate, and at one glance to pierce through to the inward workings of the heart; but fell upon the cheek with a leaden ray that weighed upon the skin it could not pass. His peculiarities caused him to be invited to every house; all wished to see him, and those who had been accustomed to violent excitement, and now felt the weight of *ennui*, were pleased at having something in their presence capable of engaging their attention. In spite of the deadly hue of his face, which never gained a warmer tint, either from the blush of modesty, or from the strong emotion of passion, though its form and outline were beautiful, many of the female hunters after notoriety attempted to win his attentions, and gain, at least, some marks of what they might term affection: Lady Mercer, who had been the mockery of every monster shewn in drawing-rooms since her marriage, threw herself in his way, and did all but put on the dress of a mountebank, to attract his notice—though in vain;—when she stood before him, though his eyes were apparently fixed upon hers, still it seemed as if they were unperceived;—even her unappalled impudence was baffled, and she left the field. But though the common adultress could not influence even the guidance of his eyes, it was not that the female sex was indifferent to him: yet such was the apparent caution with which he spoke to the virtuous wife and innocent daughter, that few knew he ever addressed himself to females. He had, however, the reputation of a winning tongue; and whether it was that it even overcame the dread of his singular character, or that they were moved by his apparent hatred of vice, he was as often among those females who form the boast of their sex from their domestic virtues, as among those who sully it by their vices.

About the same time, there came to London a young gentleman of the name of Aubrey: he was an orphan left with an only sister in the possession of great wealth, by parents who died while he was yet in childhood. Left also to himself by guardians, who thought it their duty merely to take care of his fortune, while they relinquished the more important charge of his mind to the care of mercenary subalterns, he cultivated more his imagination than his judgment. He had, hence, that high romantic feeling of honour and candour, which daily ruins so many milliners' apprentices. He believed all to sympathise with virtue, and thought that vice was thrown in by Providence merely for the picturesque effect of the scene, as we see in romances: he thought that the misery of a cottage merely consisted in the vesting of clothes, which were as warm, but which were better adapted to the painter's eye by their irregular folds and various coloured patches. He thought, in fine, that the dreams of poets were the realities of life. He was handsome, frank, and rich: for these reasons, upon his entering into the gay circles, many mothers surrounded him, striving which should describe with least truth their languishing or romping favourites: the daughters at the same time, by their brightening countenances when he approached, and by their sparkling eyes, when he opened his lips, soon led him into false notions of his talents and his merit. Attached as he was to the romance of his solitary hours, he was startled at finding, that, except in the tallow and wax candles that flickered, not from the presence of a ghost, but from want of snuffing, there was no foundation in real life for any of that congeries of pleasing pictures and descriptions contained in those volumes, from which he had formed his study. Finding, however, some compensation in his gratified vanity, he was about to relinquish his dreams, when the extraordinary being we have above described, crossed him in his career.

He watched him; and the very impossibility of forming an idea of the character of a man entirely absorbed in himself, who gave few other signs of his observation of external objects, than the tacit assent to their existence, implied by the avoidance of their contact: allowing his imagination to picture every thing that flattered its propensity to extravagant ideas, he soon formed this object into the hero of a romance, and determined to observe the offspring of his fancy, rather than the person before him. He became acquainted with him, paid him attentions, and so far advanced upon his notice, that his presence was always recognised. He gradually learnt that Lord Ruthven's affairs were embarrassed, and soon found, from the notes of preparation in —— Street, that he was about to travel. Desirous of gaining some information respecting this singular character, who, till now, had only whetted his curiosity, he hinted to his guardians, that it was time for him to perform the tour, which for many generations has been thought necessary to enable the young to take some rapid steps in the career of vice towards putting themselves upon an equality with the aged, and not allowing them to appear as if fallen from the skies, whenever scandalous intrigues are mentioned as the subjects of pleasantry or of praise, according to the degree of skill shewn in carrying them on. They consented: and Aubrey immediately mentioning his intentions to Lord Ruthven, was surprised to receive from him a proposal to join him. Flattered by such a mark of esteem from him, who, apparently, had nothing in common with other men, he gladly accepted it, and in a few days they had passed the circling waters.

Hitherto, Aubrey had had no opportunity of studying Lord Ruthven's character, and now he found, that, though many more of his actions were exposed to his view, the results offered different conclusions from the apparent motives to his conduct. His companion was profuse in his liberality;—the idle, the vagabond, and the beggar, received from his hand more than enough to relieve their immediate wants. But Aubrey could not avoid remarking, that it was not upon the virtuous, reduced to indigence by the misfortunes attendant even upon virtue, that he bestowed his alms;—these were sent from the door with hardly suppressed sneers; but when the profligate came to ask something, not to relieve his wants, but to allow him to wallow in his lust, or to sink him still deeper in his iniquity, he was sent away with rich charity. This was, however, attributed by him to the greater importunity of the vicious, which generally prevails over the retiring bashfulness of the virtuous indigent. There was one circumstance about the charity of his Lordship, which was still more impressed upon his mind: all those upon whom it was bestowed, inevitably found that there was a curse upon it, for they were all either led to the scaffold, or sunk to the lowest and the most abject misery. At Brussels and other towns through which they passed, Aubrey was surprized at the apparent eagerness with which his companion sought for the centres of all fashionable vice; there he entered into all the spirit of the faro table: he betted, and always gambled with success, except where the known sharper was his antagonist, and then he lost even more than he gained; but it was always with the same unchanging face, with which he generally watched the society around: it was not, however, so when he encountered the rash youthful novice, or the luckless father of a numerous family; then his very wish seemed fortune's law—this apparent abstractedness of mind was laid aside, and his eyes sparkled with more fire than that of the cat whilst dallying with the half-dead mouse. In every town, he left the formerly affluent youth, torn from the circle he adorned, cursing, in the solitude of a dungeon, the fate that had drawn him within the reach of this fiend; whilst many a father sat frantic, amidst the speaking looks of mute hungry children, without a single farthing of his late immense wealth, wherewith to buy even sufficient to satisfy their present craving. Yet he took no money from the gambling table; but immediately lost, to the ruiner of many, the last gilder he had just snatched from the convulsive grasp of the innocent: this might but be the result of a certain degree of knowledge, which was not, however, capable of combating the cunning of the more experienced. Aubrey often wished to represent this to his friend, and beg him to resign that charity and pleasure which proved the ruin of all, and did not tend to his own profit; but he delayed it—for each day he hoped his friend would give him some opportunity of speaking frankly and openly to him; however, this never occurred. Lord Ruthven in his carriage, and amidst the various wild and rich scenes of nature, was always the same: his eye spoke less than his lip; and though Aubrey was near the object of his curiosity, he obtained no greater gratification from it than the constant excitement of vainly wishing to break that mystery, which to his exalted imagination began to assume the appearance of something supernatural.

They soon arrived at Rome, and Aubrey for a time lost sight of his companion; he left him in daily attendance upon the morning circle of an Italian countess, whilst he went in search of the memorials of another almost deserted city. Whilst he was thus engaged, letters arrived from England, which he opened with eager impatience; the first was from his sister, breathing nothing but affection; the others were from his guardians, the latter astonished him; if it had before entered into his imagination that there was an evil power resident in his companion, these seemed to give him almost sufficient reason for the belief. His guardians insisted upon his immediately leaving his friend, and urged, that his character was dreadfully vicious, for that the possession of irresistible powers of seduction, rendered his licentious habits more dangerous to society. It had been discovered, that his contempt for the adultress had not originated in hatred of her character; but that he had required, to enhance his gratification, that his victim, the partner of his guilt, should be hurled from the pinnacle of unsullied virtue, down to the lowest abyss of infamy and degradation: in fine, that all those females whom he had sought, apparently on account of their virtue, had, since his departure, thrown even the mask aside, and had not scrupled to expose the whole deformity of their vices to the public gaze.

Aubrey determined upon leaving one, whose character had not yet shown a single bright point on which to rest the eye. He resolved to invent some plausible pretext for abandoning him altogether, purposing, in the mean while, to watch him more closely, and to let no slight circumstances pass by unnoticed. He entered into the same circle, and soon perceived, that his Lordship was endeavouring to work upon the inexperience of the daughter of the lady whose house he chiefly frequented. In Italy, it is seldom that an unmarried female is met with in society; he was therefore obliged to carry on his plans in secret; but Aubrey's eye followed him in all his windings, and soon discovered that an assignation had been appointed, which would most likely end in the ruin of an innocent, though thoughtless girl. Losing no time, he entered the apartment of Lord Ruthven, and abruptly asked him his intentions with respect to the lady, informing him at the same time that he was aware of his being about to meet her that very night. Lord Ruthven answered, that his intentions were such as he supposed all would have upon such an occasion; and upon being pressed whether he intended to marry her, merely laughed. Aubrey retired; and, immediately writing a note, to say, that from that moment he must decline accompanying his Lordship in the remainder of their proposed tour, he ordered his servant to seek other apartments, and calling upon the mother of the lady, informed her of all he knew, not only with regard to her daughter, but also concerning the character of his Lordship. The assignation was prevented. Lord Ruthven next day merely sent his servant to notify his complete assent to a separation; but did not hint any suspicion of his plans having been foiled by Aubrey's interposition.

Having left Rome, Aubrey directed his steps towards Greece, and crossing the Peninsula, soon found himself at Athens. He then fixed his residence in the house of a Greek; and soon occupied himself in tracing the faded records of ancient glory upon monuments that apparently, ashamed of chronicling the deeds of freemen only before slaves, had hidden themselves beneath the sheltering soil or many coloured lichen. Under the same roof as himself, existed a being, so beautiful and delicate, that she might have formed the model for a painter, wishing to pourtray on canvass the promised hope of the faithful in Mahomet's paradise, save that her eyes spoke too much mind for any one to think she could belong to those who had no souls. As she danced upon the plain, or tripped along the mountain's side, one would have thought the gazelle a poor type of her beauties; for who would have exchanged her eye, apparently the eye of animated nature, for that sleepy luxurious look of the animal suited but to the taste of an epicure. The light step of Ianthe often accompanied Aubrey in his search after antiquities, and often would the unconscious girl, engaged in the pursuit of a Kashmere butterfly, show the whole beauty of her form, floating as it were upon the wind, to the eager gaze of him, who forgot the letters he had just decyphered upon an almost effaced tablet, in the contemplation of her sylph-like figure. Often would her tresses falling, as she flitted around, exhibit in the sun's ray such delicately brilliant and swiftly fading hues, as might well excuse the forgetfulness of the antiquary, who let escape from his mind the very object he had before thought of vital importance to the proper interpretation of a passage in Pausanias. But why attempt to describe charms which all feel, but none can appreciate?—It was innocence, youth, and beauty, unaffected by crowded drawing-rooms and stifling balls. Whilst he drew those remains of which he wished to preserve a memorial for his future hours, she would stand by, and watch the magic effects of his pencil, in tracing the scenes of her native place; she would then describe to him the circling dance upon the open plain, would paint to him in all the glowing colours of youthful memory, the marriage pomp she remembered viewing in her infancy; and then, turning to subjects that had evidently made a greater impression upon her mind, would tell him all the supernatural tales of her nurse. Her earnestness and apparent belief of what she narrated, excited the interest even of Aubrey; and often as she told him the tale of the living vampyre, who had passed years amidst his friends, and dearest ties, forced every year, by feeding upon the life of a lovely female to prolong his existence for the ensuing months, his blood would run cold, whilst he attempted to laugh her out of such idle and horrible fantasies; but Ianthe cited to him the names of old men, who had at last detected one living among themselves, after several of their near relatives and children had been found marked with the stamp of the fiend's appetite; and when she found him so incredulous, she begged of him to believe her, for it had been remarked, that those who had dared to question their existence, always had some proof given, which obliged them, with grief and heartbreaking, to confess it was true. She detailed to him the traditional appearance of these monsters, and his horror was increased, by hearing a pretty accurate description of Lord Ruthven; he, however, still persisted in persuading her, that there could be no truth in her fears, though at the same time he wondered at the many coincidences which had all tended to excite a belief in the supernatural power of Lord Ruthven.

Aubrey began to attach himself more and more to Ianthe; her innocence, so contrasted with all the affected virtues of the women among whom he had sought for his vision of romance, won his heart; and while he ridiculed the idea of a young man of English habits, marrying an uneducated Greek girl, still he found himself more and more attached to the almost fairy form before him. He would tear himself at times from her, and, forming a plan for some antiquarian research, he would depart, determined not to return until his object was attained; but he always found it impossible to fix his attention upon the ruins around him, whilst in his mind he retained an image that seemed alone the rightful possessor of his thoughts. Ianthe was unconscious of his love, and was ever the same frank infantile being he had first known. She always seemed to part from him with reluctance; but it was because she had no longer any one with whom she could visit her favourite haunts, whilst her guardian was occupied in sketching or uncovering some fragment which had yet escaped the destructive hand of time. She had appealed to her parents on the subject of Vampyres, and they both, with several present, affirmed their existence, pale with horror at the very name. Soon after, Aubrey determined to proceed upon one of his excursions, which was to detain him for a few hours; when they heard the name of the place, they all at once begged of him not to return at night, as he must necessarily pass through a wood, where no Greek would ever remain, after the day had closed, upon any consideration. They described it as the resort of the vampyres in their nocturnal orgies, and denounced the most heavy evils as impending upon him who dared to cross their path. Aubrey made light of their representations, and tried to laugh them out of the idea; but when he saw them shudder at his daring thus to mock a superior, infernal power, the very name of which apparently made their blood freeze, he was silent.

Next morning Aubrey set off upon his excursion unattended; he was surprised to observe the melancholy face of his host, and was concerned to find that his words, mocking the belief of those horrible fiends, had inspired them with such terror. When he was about to depart, Ianthe came to the side of his horse, and earnestly begged of him to return, ere night allowed the power of these beings to be put in action;—he promised. He was, however, so occupied in his research, that he did not perceive that day-light would soon end, and that in the horizon there was one of those specks which, in the warmer climates, so rapidly gather into a tremendous mass, and pour all their rage upon the devoted country.—He at last, however, mounted his horse, determined to make up by speed for his delay: but it was too late. Twilight, in these southern climates, is almost unknown; immediately the sun sets, night begins: and ere he had advanced far, the power of the storm was above —its echoing thunders had scarcely an interval of rest;—its thick heavy rain forced its way through the canopying foliage, whilst the blue forked lightning seemed to fall and radiate at his very feet. Suddenly his horse took fright, and he was carried with dreadful rapidity through the entangled forest. The animal at last, through fatigue, stopped, and he found, by the glare of lightning, that he was in the neighbourhood of a hovel that hardly lifted itself up from the masses of dead leaves and brushwood which surrounded it. Dismounting, he approached, hoping to find some one to guide him to the town, or at least trusting to obtain shelter from the pelting of the storm. As he approached, the thunders, for a moment silent, allowed him to hear the dreadful shrieks of a woman mingling with the stifled, exultant mockery of a laugh, continued in one almost unbroken sound;—he was startled: but, roused by the thunder which again rolled over his head, he, with a sudden effort, forced open the door of the hut. He found himself in utter darkness: the sound, however, guided him. He was apparently unperceived; for, though he called, still the sounds continued, and no notice was taken of him. He found himself in contact with some one, whom he immediately seized; when a voice cried, "Again baffled!" to which a loud laugh succeeded; and he felt himself grappled by one whose strength seemed superhuman: determined to sell his life as dearly as he could, he struggled; but it was in vain: he was lifted from his feet and hurled with enormous force against the ground:—his enemy threw himself upon him, and kneeling upon his breast, had placed his hands upon his throat —when the glare of many torches penetrating through the hole that gave light in the day, disturbed him;—he instantly rose, and, leaving his prey, rushed through the door, and in a moment the crashing of the branches, as he broke through the wood, was no longer heard. The storm was now still; and Aubrey, incapable of moving, was soon heard by those without. They entered; the light of their torches fell upon the mud walls, and the thatch loaded on every individual straw with heavy flakes of soot. At the desire of Aubrey they searched for her who had attracted him by her cries; he was again left in darkness; but what was his horror, when the light of the torches once more burst upon him, to perceive the airy form of his fair conductress brought in a lifeless corpse. He shut his eyes, hoping that it was but a vision arising from his disturbed imagination; but he again saw the same form, when he unclosed them, stretched by his side. There was no colour upon her cheek, not even upon her lip; yet there was a stillness about her face that seemed almost as attaching as the life that once dwelt there:—upon her neck and breast was blood, and upon her throat were the marks of teeth having opened the vein:—to this the men pointed, crying, simultaneously struck with horror, "A Vampyre! a Vampyre!" A litter was quickly formed, and Aubrey was laid by the side of her who had lately been to him the object of so many bright and fairy visions, now fallen with the flower of life that had died within her. He knew not what his thoughts were—his mind was benumbed and seemed to shun reflection, and take refuge in vacancy;—he held almost unconsciously in his hand a naked dagger of a particular construction, which had been found in the hut. They were soon met by different parties who had been engaged in the search of her whom a mother had missed. Their lamentable cries, as they approached the city, forewarned the parents of some dreadful catastrophe.—To describe their grief would be impossible; but when they ascertained the cause of their child's death, they looked at Aubrey, and pointed to the corpse. They were inconsolable; both died brokenhearted.

Aubrey being put to bed was seized with a most violent fever, and was often delirious; in these intervals he would call upon Lord Ruthven and upon Ianthe—by some unaccountable combination he seemed to beg of his former companion to spare the being he loved. At other times he would imprecate maledictions upon his head, and curse him as her destroyer. Lord Ruthven chanced at this time to arrive at Athens, and, from whatever motive, upon hearing of the state of Aubrey, immediately placed himself in the same house, and became his constant attendant. When the latter recovered from his delirium, he was horrified and startled at the sight of him whose image he had now combined with that of a Vampyre; but Lord Ruthven, by his kind words, implying almost repentance for the fault that had caused their separation, and still more by the attention, anxiety, and care which he showed, soon reconciled him to his presence. His lordship seemed quite changed; he no longer appeared that apathetic being who had so astonished Aubrey; but as soon as his convalescence began to be rapid, he again gradually retired into the same state of mind, and Aubrey perceived no difference from the former man, except that at times he was surprised to meet his gaze fixed intently upon him, with a smile of malicious exultation playing upon his lips: he knew not why, but this smile haunted him. During the last stage of the invalid's recovery, Lord Ruthven was apparently engaged in watching the tideless waves raised by the cooling breeze, or in marking the progress of those orbs, circling, like our world, the moveless sun;—indeed, he appeared to wish to avoid the eyes of all.

Aubrey's mind, by this shock, was much weakened, and that elasticity of spirit which had once so distinguished him now seemed to have fled for ever. He was now as much a lover of solitude and silence as Lord Ruthven; but much as he wished for solitude, his mind could not find it in the neighbourhood of Athens; if he sought it amidst the ruins he had formerly frequented, Ianthe's form stood by his side;—if he sought it in the woods, her light step would appear wandering amidst the underwood, in quest of the modest violet; then suddenly turning round, would show, to his wild imagination, her pale face and wounded throat, with a meek smile upon her lips. He determined to fly scenes, every feature of which created such bitter associations in his mind. He proposed to Lord Ruthven, to whom he held himself bound by the tender care he had taken of him during his illness, that they should visit those parts of Greece neither had yet seen. They travelled in every direction, and sought every spot to which a recollection could be attached: but though they thus hastened from place to place, yet they seemed not to heed what they gazed upon. They heard much of robbers, but they gradually began to slight these reports, which they imagined were only the invention of individuals, whose interest it was to excite the generosity of those whom they defended from pretended dangers. In consequence of thus neglecting the advice of the inhabitants, on one occasion they travelled with only a few guards, more to serve as guides than as a defence. Upon entering, however, a narrow defile, at the bottom of which was the bed of a torrent, with large masses of rock brought down from the neighbouring precipices, they had reason to repent their negligence; for scarcely were the whole of the party engaged in the narrow pass, when they were startled by the whistling of bullets close to their heads, and by the echoed report of several guns. In an instant their guards had left them, and, placing themselves behind rocks, had begun to fire in the direction whence the report came. Lord

Ruthven and Aubrey, imitating their example, retired for a moment behind the sheltering turn of the defile: but ashamed of being thus detained by a foe, who with insulting shouts bade them advance, and being exposed to unresisting slaughter, if any of the robbers should climb above and take them in the rear, they determined at once to rush forward in search of the enemy. Hardly had they lost the shelter of the rock, when Lord Ruthven received a shot in the shoulder, which brought him to the ground. Aubrey hastened to his assistance; and, no longer heeding the contest or his own peril, was soon surprised by seeing the robbers' faces around him—his guards having, upon Lord Ruthven's being wounded, immediately thrown up their arms and surrendered.

By promises of great reward, Aubrey soon induced them to convey his wounded friend to a neighbouring cabin; and having agreed upon a ransom, he was no more disturbed by their presence—they being content merely to guard the entrance till their comrade should return with the promised sum, for which he had an order. Lord Ruthven's strength rapidly decreased; in two days mortification ensued, and death seemed advancing with hasty steps. His conduct and appearance had not changed; he seemed as unconscious of pain as he had been of the objects about him: but towards the close of the last evening, his mind became apparently uneasy, and his eye often fixed upon Aubrey, who was induced to offer his assistance with more than usual earnestness—"Assist me! you may save me—you may do more than that—I mean not my life, I heed the death of my existence as little as that of the passing day; but you may save my honour, your friend's honour."—"How? tell me how? I would do any thing," replied Aubrey.—"I need but little—my life ebbs apace—I cannot explain the whole—but if you would conceal all you know of me, my honour were free from stain in the world's mouth—and if my death were unknown for some time in England—I— I—but life."—"It shall not be known."—"Swear!" cried the dying man, raising himself with exultant violence, "Swear by all your soul reveres, by all your nature fears, swear that for a year and a day you will not impart your knowledge of my crimes or death to any living being in any way, whatever may happen, or whatever you may see."—His eyes seemed bursting from their sockets: "I swear!" said Aubrey; he sunk laughing upon his pillow, and breathed no more.

Aubrey retired to rest, but did not sleep; the many circumstances attending his acquaintance with this man rose upon his mind, and he knew not why; when he remembered his oath a cold shivering came

over him, as if from the presentiment of something horrible awaiting
him. Rising early in the morning, he was about to enter the hovel in
which he had left the corpse, when a robber met him, and informed him
that it was no longer there, having been conveyed by himself and comrades, upon his retiring, to the pinnacle of a neighbouring mount, according to a promise they had given his lordship, that it should be
exposed to the first cold ray of the moon that rose after his death.
Aubrey astonished, and taking several of the men, determined to go and
bury it upon the spot where it lay. But, when he had mounted to the
summit he found no trace of either the corpse or the clothes, though the
robbers swore they pointed out the identical rock on which they had
laid the body. For a time his mind was bewildered in conjectures, but he
at last returned, convinced that they had buried the corpse for the sake
of the clothes.

Weary of a country in which he had met with such terrible misfortunes, and in which all apparently conspired to heighten that superstitious melancholy that had seized upon his mind, he resolved to leave it,
and soon arrived at Smyrna. While waiting for a vessel to convey him to
Otranto, or to Naples, he occupied himself in arranging those effects he
had with him belonging to Lord Ruthven. Amongst other things there
was a case containing several weapons of offence, more or less adapted
to ensure the death of the victim. There were several daggers and
ataghans. Whilst turning them over, and examining their curious forms,
what was his surprise at finding a sheath apparently ornamented in the
same style as the dagger discovered in the fatal hut;—he shuddered;—
hastening to gain further proof, he found the weapon, and his horror
may be imagined when he discovered that it fitted, though peculiarly
shaped, the sheath he held in his hand. His eyes seemed to need no
further certainty—they seemed gazing to be bound to the dagger; yet
still he wished to disbelieve; but the particular form, the same varying
tints upon the haft and sheath were alike in splendour on both, and left
no room for doubt; there were also drops of blood on each.

He left Smyrna, and on his way home, at Rome, his first inquiries
were concerning the lady he had attempted to snatch from Lord
Ruthven's seductive arts. Her parents were in distress, their fortune
ruined, and she had not been heard of since the departure of his lordship. Aubrey's mind became almost broken under so many repeated
horrors; he was afraid that this lady had fallen a victim to the destroyer
of Ianthe. He became morose and silent; and his only occupation consisted in urging the speed of the postilions, as if he were going to save

the life of some one he held dear. He arrived at Calais; a breeze, which seemed obedient to his will, soon wafted him to the English shores; and he hastened to the mansion of his fathers, and there, for a moment, appeared to lose, in the embraces and caresses of his sister, all memory of the past. If she before, by her infantine caresses, had gained his affection, now that the woman began to appear, she was still more attaching as a companion.

Miss Aubrey had not that winning grace which gains the gaze and applause of the drawing-room assemblies. There was none of that light brilliancy which only exists in the heated atmosphere of a crowded apartment. Her blue eye was never lit up by the levity of the mind beneath. There was a melancholy charm about it which did not seem to arise from misfortune, but from some feeling within, that appeared to indicate a soul conscious of a brighter realm. Her step was not that light footing, which strays where'er a butterfly or a colour may attract—it was sedate and pensive. When alone, her face was never brightened by the smile of joy; but when her brother breathed to her his affection, and would in her presence forget those griefs she knew destroyed his rest, who would have exchanged her smile for that of the voluptuary? It seemed as if those eyes, that face were then playing in the light of their own native sphere. She was yet only eighteen, and had not been presented to the world, it having been thought by her guardians more fit that her presentation should be delayed until her brother's return from the continent, when he might be her protector. It was now, therefore, resolved that the next drawing-room, which was fast approaching, should be the epoch of her entry into the "busy scene." Aubrey would rather have remained in the mansion of his fathers, and fed upon the melancholy which overpowered him. He could not feel interest about the frivolities of fashionable strangers, when his mind had been so torn by the events he had witnessed; but he determined to sacrifice his own comfort to the protection of his sister. They soon arrived in town, and prepared for the next day, which had been announced as a drawing-room.

The crowd was excessive—a drawing-room had not been held for a long time, and all who were anxious to bask in the smile of royalty, hastened thither. Aubrey was there with his sister. While he was standing in a corner by himself, heedless of all around him, engaged in the remembrance that the first time he had seen Lord Ruthven was in that very place—he felt himself suddenly seized by the arm, and a voice he recognized too well, sounded in his ear—"Remember your oath." He had hardly courage to turn, fearful of seeing a spectre that would blast him, when he perceived, at a little distance, the same figure which had attracted his notice on this spot upon his first entry into society. He gazed till his limbs almost refusing to bear their weight, he was obliged to take the arm of a friend, and forcing a passage through the crowd, he threw himself into his carriage, and was driven home. He paced the room with hurried steps, and fixed his hands upon his head, as if he were afraid his thoughts were bursting from his brain. Lord Ruthven again before him—circumstances started up in dreadful array—the dagger—his oath.—He roused himself, he could not believe it possible—the dead rise again!—He thought his imagination had conjured up the image his mind was resting upon. It was impossible that it could be real— he determined, therefore, to go again into society; for though he attempted to ask concerning Lord Ruthven, the name hung upon his lips, and he could not succeed in gaining information. He went a few nights after with his sister to the assembly of a near relation. Leaving her under the protection of a matron, he retired into a recess, and there gave himself up to his own devouring thoughts. Perceiving, at last, that many were leaving, he roused himself, and entering another room, found his sister surrounded by several, apparently in earnest conversation; he attempted to pass and get near her, when one, whom he requested to move, turned round, and revealed to him those features he most abhorred. He sprang forward, seized his sister's arm, and, with hurried step, forced her towards the street: at the door he found himself impeded by the crowd of servants who were waiting for their lords; and while he was engaged in passing them, he again heard that voice whisper close to him—"Remember your oath!"—He did not dare to turn, but, hurrying his sister, soon reached home.

Aubrey became almost distracted. If before his mind had been absorbed by one subject, how much more completely was it engrossed, now that the certainty of the monster's living again pressed upon his thoughts. His sister's attentions were now unheeded, and it was in vain that she intreated him to explain to her what had caused his abrupt conduct. He only uttered a few words, and those terrified her. The more he thought, the more he was bewildered. His oath startled him;—was he then to allow this monster to roam, bearing ruin upon his breath, amidst all he held dear, and not avert its progress? His very sister might have been touched by him. But even if he were to break his oath, and disclose his suspicions, who would believe him? He thought of employing his own hand to free the world from such a wretch; but death, he remembered, had been already mocked. For days he remained in this state; shut up in his room, he saw no one, and ate only when his sister came, who, with eyes streaming with tears, besought him, for her sake, to support nature. At last, no longer capable of bearing stillness and solitude, he left his house, roamed from street to street, anxious to fly that image which haunted him. His dress became neglected, and he wandered, as often exposed to the noon-day sun as to the mid-night damps. He was no longer to be recognized; at first he returned with the evening to the house; but at last he laid him down to rest wherever fatigue overtook him. His sister, anxious for his safety, employed people to follow him; but they were soon distanced by him who fled from a pursuer swifter than any—from thought. His conduct, however, suddenly changed. Struck with the idea that he left by his absence the whole of his friends, with a fiend amongst them, of whose presence they were unconscious, he determined to enter again into society, and watch him closely, anxious to forewarn, in spite of his oath, all whom Lord Ruthven approached with intimacy. But when he entered into a room, his haggard and suspicious looks were so striking, his inward shudderings so visible, that his sister was at last obliged to beg of him to abstain from seeking, for her sake, a society which affected him so strongly. When, however, remonstrance proved unavailing, the guardians thought proper to interpose, and, fearing that his mind was becoming alienated, they thought it high time to resume again that trust which had been before imposed upon them by Aubrey's parents.

Desirous of saving him from the injuries and sufferings he had daily encountered in his wanderings, and of preventing him from exposing to the general eye those marks of what they considered folly, they engaged a physician to reside in the house, and take constant care of him. He hardly appeared to notice it, so completely was his mind absorbed by one terrible subject. His incoherence became at last so great, that he was confined to his chamber. There he would often lie for days, incapable of being roused. He had become emaciated, his eyes had attained a glassy lustre;—the only sign of affection and recollection remaining displayed itself upon the entry of his sister; then he would sometimes start, and, seizing her hands, with looks that severely afflicted her, he would desire her not to touch him. "Oh, do not touch him—if your love for me is aught, do not go near him!" When, however, she inquired to whom he referred, his only answer was, "True! true!" and again he sank into a state, whence not even she could rouse him. This lasted many months: gradually, however, as the year was passing, his incoherences became less frequent, and his mind threw off a portion of its gloom, whilst his guardians observed, that several times in the day he would count upon his fingers a definite number, and then smile.

The time had nearly elapsed, when, upon the last day of the year, one of his guardians entering his room, began to converse with his physician upon the melancholy circumstance of Aubrey's being in so awful a situation, when his sister was going next day to be married. Instantly Aubrey's attention was attracted; he asked anxiously to whom. Glad of this mark of returning intellect, of which they feared he had been deprived, they mentioned the name of the Earl of Marsden. Thinking this was a young Earl whom he had met with in society, Aubrey seemed pleased, and astonished them still more by his expressing his intention to be present at the nuptials, and desiring to see his sister. They answered not, but in a few minutes his sister was with him. He was apparently again capable of being affected by the influence of her lovely smile; for he pressed her to his breast, and kissed her cheek, wet with tears, flowing at the thought of her brother's being once more alive to the feelings of affection. He began to speak with all his wonted warmth, and to congratulate her upon her marriage with a person so distinguished for rank and every accomplishment; when he suddenly perceived a locket upon her breast; opening it, what was his surprise at beholding the features of the monster who had so long influenced his life. He seized the portrait in a paroxysm of rage, and trampled it under foot. Upon her asking him why he thus destroyed the resemblance of her future husband, he looked as if he did not understand her;—then seizing her hands, and gazing on her with a frantic expression of countenance, he bade her swear that she would never wed this monster, for he—But he could not advance—it seemed as if that voice again bade him remember his oath—he turned suddenly round, thinking Lord Ruthven was near him but saw no one. In the meantime the guardians and physician, who had heard the whole, and thought this was but a return of his disorder, entered, and forcing him from Miss Aubrey, desired her to leave him. He fell upon his knees to them, he implored, he begged of them to delay but for one day. They, attributing this to the insanity they imagined had taken possession of his mind, endeavoured to pacify him, and retired.

Lord Ruthven had called the morning after the drawing-room, and had been refused with every one else. When he heard of Aubrey's ill health, he readily understood himself to be the cause of it; but when he learned that he was deemed insane, his exultation and pleasure could hardly be concealed from those among whom he had gained this information. He hastened to the house of his former companion, and, by constant attendance, and the pretence of great affection for the brother and interest in his fate, he gradually won the ear of Miss Aubrey. Who could resist his power? His tongue had dangers and toils to recount—could speak of himself as of an individual having no sympathy with any being on the crowded earth, save with her to whom he addressed himself;—could tell how, since he knew her, his existence had begun to seem worthy of preservation, if it were merely that he might listen to her soothing accents;—in fine, he knew so well how to use the serpent's art, or such was the will of fate, that he gained her affections. The title of the elder branch falling at length to him, he obtained an important embassy, which served as an excuse for hastening the marriage (in spite of her brother's deranged state), which was to take place the very day before his departure for the continent.

Aubrey, when he was left by the physician and his guardians, attempted to bribe the servants, but in vain. He asked for pen and paper; it was given him; he wrote a letter to his sister, conjuring her, as she valued her own happiness, her own honour, and the honour of those now in the grave, who once held her in their arms as their hope and the hope of their house, to delay but for a few hours that marriage, on which he denounced the most heavy curses. The servants promised they would deliver it; but giving it to the physician, he thought it better not to harass any more the mind of Miss Aubrey by, what he considered, the ravings of a maniac. Night passed on without rest to the busy inmates of the house; and Aubrey heard, with a horror that may more easily be conceived than described, the notes of busy preparation. Morning came, and the sound of carriages broke upon his ear. Aubrey grew almost frantic. The curiosity of the servants at last overcame their vigilance; they gradually stole away, leaving him in the custody of an helpless old woman. He seized the opportunity, with one bound was out of the room, and in a moment found himself in the apartment where all were nearly assembled. Lord Ruthven was the first to perceive him: he immediately approached, and, taking his arm by force, hurried him from the room, speechless with rage. When on the staircase, Lord Ruthven whispered in his ear—"Remember your oath, and know, if not my bride to day, your sister is dishonoured. Women are frail!" So saying, he pushed him towards his attendants, who, roused by the old woman, had come in search of him. Aubrey could no longer support himself; his rage not finding vent, had broken a blood-vessel, and he was conveyed to bed. This was not mentioned to his sister, who was not present when he entered, as the physician was afraid of agitating her. The marriage was solemnized, and the bride and bridegroom left London.

Aubrey's weakness increased; the effusion of blood produced symptoms of the near approach of death. He desired his sister's guardians might be called, and when the midnight hour had struck, he related composedly what the reader has perused—he died immediately after.

The guardians hastened to protect Miss Aubrey; but when they arrived, it was too late. Lord Ruthven had disappeared, and Aubrey's sister had glutted the thirst of a VAMPYRE!

Although his training prepared him to be a civil engineer, JAMES MAL-
COLM RYMER *(1814–1881) became one of the most prolific authors of his
time in England. His novels have such intriguing titles as* Ada the Betrayed *and* The Black Monk, *but his geatest work, for its immense popularity and its influence on later vampire fiction, was* Varney the Vampyre,
or, The Feast of Blood.

A novel of huge length, Varney *was first published, in the fashion of
the time, in 109 weekly parts, beginning in 1845 and ending in 1847.
Until recently, it was widely thought to be the work of Thomas Preskett
Prest (1810–1859), author of* The Calendar of Horrors *(1835), but recent scholarship has established Rymer as almost certainly the author.*

*The first edition was labeled simply "A Romance," but the title page
of an 1853 reprint, decorated with a full complement of bats, skulls,
skeletons, gravestones, a leering vampire, and a swooning damsel, called
it "A Romance of Exciting Interest." It is that.*

Varney the Vampyre *was the first vampire novel in English. Rymer
was a master of the sensational style popular in the "penny dreadfuls," as
these serialized stories were called by their critics, and his lurid melodrama fulfills all expectations. While the writing is not of literary quality,
Rymer's portrait of the vampire—loathesome, bloodthirsty, unkillable,
with dead eyes and dripping fangs—is, to say the very least, memorable.
Rymer succeeded in synthesizing all the most sensational elements of the
vampire legend and in fashioning a monster of evil whose characteristics
and features would live on in other fictional vampires down to the present
time. Writing of the novel's influence, Robert Bloch, screenwriter and
author of* Psycho, *has said that "Carmilla is as assuredly Varney's sister
as Dracula is his brother." Interestingly, Rymer's vampire develops a
degree of self-awareness as an evil creature; after hundreds of pages (and
two years of chills for the novel's first readers) he finally destroys himself.*

*Following is an excerpt containing Rymer's portrait of the vampire and
a representative episode.*

Varney the Vampyre, or, the Feast of Blood (excerpt) (1845)

BY JAMES MALCOLM RYMER

CHAPTER I

The solemn tones of an old cathedral clock have announced midnight—
a strange death-like stillness pervades all nature. Like the ominous calm
which precedes some more than usually terrific outbreak of the elements, they seem to have paused even in their ordinary fluctuations, to
gather a terrific strength for the great effort. A faint peal of thunder
now comes from far off. Like a signal gun for the battle of the winds to
begin, it appeared to awaken them from their lethargy, and one awful,
warring hurricane swept over a whole city, producing more devastation
in the four or five minutes it lasted, than would a half century of ordinary phenomena.

Oh, how the storm raged! Hail—rain—wind. It was, in very truth,
an awful night.

There is an antique chamber in an ancient house. Curious and
quaint carvings adorn the walls, and the large chimney-piece is a curiosity of itself. The ceiling is low, and a large bay window, from roof to
floor, looks to the west. The window is latticed, and filled with curiously
painted glass and rich stained pieces, which send in a strange, yet beautiful light, when sun or moon shines into the apartment. There is but
one portrait in that room, although the walls seem panelled for the
express purpose of containing a series of pictures. That portrait is of a
young man, with a pale face, a stately brow, and a strange expression
about the eyes, which no one cared to look on twice.

There is a stately bed in that chamber, of carved walnut-wood is it
made, rich in design and elaborate in execution; one of those works of

art which owe their existence to the Elizabethan era. It is hung with heavy silken and damask furnishing; nodding feathers are at its corners —covered with dust are they, and they lend a funereal aspect to the room. The floor is of polished oak.

God! how the hail dashes on the old bay window! Like an occasional discharge of mimic musketry, it comes clashing, beating, and cracking upon the small panes; but they resist it—their small size saves them; the wind, the hail, the rain, expend their fury in vain.

The bed in that old chamber is occupied. A creature formed in all fashions of loveliness lies in a half sleep upon that ancient couch—a girl young and beautiful as a spring morning. Her long hair has escaped from its confinement and streams over the blackened coverings of the bedstead; she has been restless in her sleep, for the clothing of the bed is in much confusion. One arm is over her head, the other hangs nearly off the side of the bed near to which she lies. A neck and bosom that would have formed a study for the rarest sculptor that ever Providence gave genius to, were half disclosed. She moaned slightly in her sleep, and once or twice the lips moved as if in prayer—at least one might judge so, for the name of Him who suffered for all came once faintly from them.

She has endured much fatigue, and the storm does not awaken her; but it can disturb the slumbers it does not possess the power to destroy entirely. The turmoil of the elements wakes the senses, although it cannot entirely break the repose they have lapsed into.

Oh, what a world of witchery was in that mouth, slightly parted, and exhibiting within the pearly teeth that glistened even in the faint light that came from that bay window. How sweetly the long silken eyelashes lay upon the cheek. Now she moves, and one shoulder is entirely visible—whiter, fairer than the spotless clothing of the bed on which she lies, is the smooth skin of that fair creature, just budding into womanhood, and in that transition state which presents to us all the charms of the girl—almost of the child, with the more matured beauty and gentleness of advancing years.

Was that lightning? Yes—an awful, vivid, terrifying flash—then a roaring peal of thunder, as if a thousand mountains were rolling one over the other in the blue vault of Heaven! Who sleeps now in that ancient city? Not one living soul. The dread trumpet of eternity could not more effectually have awakened any one.

The hail continues. The wind continues. The uproar of the elements seems at its height. Now she awakens—that beautiful girl on the antique bed; she opens those eyes of celestial blue, and a faint cry of alarm bursts from her lips. At least it is a cry which, amid the noise and turmoil without, sounds but faint and weak. She sits upon the bed and presses her hands upon her eyes. Heavens! what a wild torrent of wind, and rain, and hail! The thunder likewise seems intent upon awakening sufficient echoes to last until the next flash of forked lightning should again produce the wild concussion of the air. She murmurs a prayer—a prayer for those she loves best; the names of those dear to her gentle heart come from her lips; she weeps and prays; she thinks then of what devastation the storm must surely produce, and to the great God of Heaven she prays for all living things. Another flash—a wild, blue, bewildering flash of lightning streams across that bay window, for an instant bringing out every colour in it with terrible distinctness. A shriek bursts from the lips of the young girl, and then, with eyes fixed upon that window, which, in another moment, is all darkness, and with such an expression of terror upon her face as it had never before known, she trembled, and the perspiration of intense fear stood upon her brow.

"What—what was it?" she gasped; "real, or a delusion? Oh, God, what was it? A figure tall and gaunt, endeavouring from the outside to unclasp the window. I saw it. That flash of lightning revealed it to me. It stood the whole length of the window."

There was a lull of the wind. The hail was not falling so thickly—moreover, it now fell, what there was of it, straight, and yet a strange clattering sound came upon the glass of that long window. It could not be a delusion—she is awake, and she hears it. What can produce it? Another flash of lightning—another shriek—there could be now no delusion.

A tall figure is standing on the ledge immediately outside the long window. It is its finger-nails upon the glass that produces the sound so like the hail, now that the hail has ceased. Intense fear paralysed the limbs of that beautiful girl. That one shriek is all she can utter—with hands clasped, a face of marble, a heart beating so wildly in her bosom, that each moment it seems as if it would break its confines, eyes distended and fixed upon the window, she waits, froze with horror. The pattering and clattering of the nails continue. No word is spoken, and now she fancies she can trace the darker form of that figure against the window, and she can see the long arms moving to and fro, feeling for some mode of entrance. What strange light is that which now gradually creeps up into the air? red and terrible—brighter and brighter it grows. The lightning has set fire to a mill, and the reflection of the rapidly consuming building falls upon that long window. There can be no mistake. The figure is there, still feeling for an entrance, and clattering against the glass with its long nails, that appear as if the growth of many years had been untouched. She tries to scream again but a choking sensation comes over her, and she cannot. It is too dreadful—she tries to move—each limb seems weighed down by tons of lead—she can but in a hoarse faint whisper cry,—

"Help—help—help—help!"

And that one word she repeats like a person in a dream. The red glare of the fire continues. It throws up the tall gaunt figure in hideous relief against the long window. It shows, too, upon the one portrait that is in the chamber, and that portrait appears to fix its eyes upon the attempting intruder, while the flickering light from the fire makes it look fearfully life-like. A small pane of glass is broken, and the form from without introduces a long gaunt hand, which seems utterly destitute of flesh. The fastening is removed, and one-half of the window, which opens like folding doors, is swung wide open upon its hinges.

And yet now she could not scream—she could not move. "Help—help!—help!" was all she could say. But, oh, that look of terror that sat upon her face, it was dreadful—a look to haunt the memory for a lifetime—a look to obtrude itself upon the happiest moments, and turn them to bitterness.

The figure turns half round, and the light falls upon the face. It is perfectly white—perfectly bloodless. The eyes look like polished tin; the lips are drawn back, and the principal feature next to those dreadful eyes is the teeth—the fearful-looking teeth—projecting like those of some wild animal, hideously, glaringly white, and fang-like. It approaches the bed with a strange, gliding movement. It clashes together the long nails that literally appear to hang from the finger ends. No sound comes from its lips. Is she going mad—that young and beautiful girl exposed to so much terror? she has drawn up all her limbs; she cannot even now say help. The power of articulation is gone, but the power of movement has returned to her; she can draw herself slowly along to the other side of the bed from that towards which the hideous appearance is coming.

But her eyes are fascinated. The glance of a serpent could not have produced a greater effect upon her than did the fixed gaze of those awful, metallic-looking eyes that were bent on her face. Crouching down so that the gigantic height was lost, and the horrible, protruding, white face was the most prominent object, came on the figure. What was it?—what did it want there?—what made it look so hideous—so unlike an inhabitant of the earth, and yet to be on it?

Now she has got to the verge of the bed, and the figure pauses. It seemed as if when it paused she lost the power to proceed. The clothing of the bed was now clutched in her hands with unconscious power. She drew her breath short and thick. Her bosom heaves, and her limbs tremble, yet she cannot withdraw her eyes from that marble-looking face. He holds her with his glittering eye.

The storm has ceased—all is still. The winds are hushed; the church clock proclaims the hour of one: a hissing sound comes from the throat of the hideous being, and he raises his long, gaunt arms—the lips move. He advances. The girl places one small foot from the bed on to the floor. She is unconsciously dragging the clothing with her. The door of the room is in that direction—can she reach it? Has she power to walk?—can she withdraw her eyes from the face of the intruder, and so break the hideous charm? God of Heaven! is it real, or some dream so like reality as to nearly overturn the judgment for ever?

The figure has paused again, and half on the bed and half out of it that young girl lies trembling. Her long hair streams across the entire width of the bed. As she has slowly moved along she has left it streaming across the pillows. The pause lasted about a minute—oh, what an age of agony. That minute was, indeed, enough, for madness to do its full work in.

With a sudden rush that could not be foreseen—with a strange howling cry that was enough to awaken terror in every breast, the figure seized the long tresses of her hair, and twining them round his bony hands he held her to the bed. Then she screamed—Heaven granted her then power to scream. Shriek followed shriek in rapid succession. The bed-clothes fell in a heap by the side of the bed—she was dragged by her long silken hair completely on to it again. Her beautifully rounded limbs quivered with the agony of her soul. The glassy, horrible eyes of the figure ran over that angelic form with a hideous satisfaction—horrible profanation. He drags her head to the bed's edge. He forces it back by the long hair still entwined in his grasp. With a plunge he seizes her neck in his fang-like teeth—a gush of blood, and a hideous sucking noise follows. *The girl has swooned, and the vampire is at his hideous repast!*

CHAPTER II

(The house is aroused by the girl's screaming. Her mother, her brothers, Henry and George, and a "stranger" in the house come running to the girl's chamber, only to find the door barred.)

To those who were engaged in forcing open the door of the antique chamber, where slept the young girl whom they named Flora, each moment was swelled into an hour of agony; but, in reality, from the first moment of the alarm to that when the loud cracking noise heralded the destruction of the fastenings of the door, there had elapsed but very few minutes indeed.

"It opens—it opens," cried the young man.

"Another moment," said the stranger, as he still plied the crowbar —"another moment, and we shall have free ingress to the chamber. Be patient."

This stranger's name was Marchdale; and even as he spoke, he succeeded in throwing the massive door wide open, and clearing the passage to the chamber.

To rush in with a light in his hand was the work of a moment to the young man named Henry; but the very rapid progress he made into the apartment prevented him from observing accurately what it contained, for the wind that came in from the open window caught the flame of the candle, and although it did not actually extinguish it, it blew it so much on one side, that it was comparatively useless as a light.

"Flora—Flora!" he cried.

Then with a sudden bound something dashed from off the bed. The concussion against him was so sudden and so utterly unexpected, as well as so tremendously violent, that he was thrown down, and, in his fall, the light was fairly extinguished.

All was darkness, save a dull, reddish kind of light that now and then, from the nearly consumed mill in the immediate vicinity, came into the room. But by that light, dim, uncertain, and flickering as it was, some one was seen to make for the window.

Henry, although nearly stunned by his fall, saw a figure, gigantic in height, which nearly reached from the floor to the ceiling. The other young man, George, saw it, and Mr. Marchdale likewise saw it, as did the lady who had spoken to the two young men in the corridor when first the screams of the young girl awakened alarm in the breasts of all the inhabitants of that house.

The figure was about to pass out at the window which led to a kind of balcony, from whence there was an easy descent to a garden.

Before it passed out they each and all caught a glance of the side-face, and they saw that the lower part of it and the lips were dabbled in blood. They saw, too, one of those fearful-looking, shining, metallic eyes which presented so terrible an appearance of unearthly ferocity.

No wonder that for a moment a panic seized them all, which paralysed any exertions they might otherwise have made to detain that hideous form.

But Mr. Marchdale was a man of mature years; he had seen much of life, both in this and in foreign lands; and he, although astonished to the extent of being frightened, was much more likely to recover sooner than his younger companions, which, indeed, he did, and acted promptly enough.

"Don't rise, Henry," he cried. "Lie still."

Almost at the moment he uttered these words, he fired at the figure, which then occupied the window, as if it were a gigantic figure set in a frame.

The report was tremendous in that chamber, for the pistol was no toy weapon, but one made for actual service, and of sufficient length and bore of barrel to carry destruction along with the bullets that came from it.

"If that has missed its aim," said Mr. Marchdale, "I'll never pull a trigger again."

As he spoke he dashed forward, and made a clutch at the figure he felt convinced he had shot.

The tall form turned upon him, and when he got a full view of the face, which he did at that moment, from the opportune circumstance of the lady returning at the instant with a light she had been to her own chamber to procure, even he, Marchdale, with all his courage, and that was great, and all his nervous energy, recoiled a step or two, and uttered the exclamation of, "Great God!"

That face was one never to be forgotten. It was hideously flushed with colour—the colour of fresh blood; the eyes had a savage and re-markable lustre; whereas, before, they had looked like polished tin—they now wore a ten times brighter aspect, and flashes of light seemed to dart from them. The mouth was open, as if, from the natural formation of the countenance, the lips receded much from the large canine-looking teeth.

A strange, howling noise came from the throat of this monstrous figure, and it seemed upon the point of rushing upon Mr. Marchdale. Suddenly, then, as if some impulse had seized upon it, it uttered a wild terrible shrieking kind of laugh; and then turning, dashed through the window, and in one instant disappeared from before the eyes of those who felt nearly annihilated by its fearful presence.

"God help us!" ejaculated Henry.

(They give chase. Although Henry fires his pistol and hits the fleeing figure, the monster escapes, leaving no trace of bloodstains from a wound.

Henry watches all night by the bedside of Flora, whose neck displays two bloody bite marks. She sleeps only fitfully and cries out in anguish upon awakening. After hearing her confused account of the attack, he goes to take counsel with Marchdale.)

Henry proceeded at once to the chamber, which was, as he knew, occupied by Mr. Marchdale; and as he crossed the corridor, he could not but pause a moment to glance from a window at the face of nature.

As is often the case, the terrific storm of the preceding evening had cleared the air, and rendered it deliciously invigorating and lifelike. The weather had been dull, and there had been for some days a certain heaviness in the atmosphere, which was now entirely removed.

The morning sun was shining with uncommon brilliancy, birds were singing in every tree and on every bush; so pleasant, so spirit-stirring, health-giving a morning, seldom had he seen. And the effect upon his spirits was great, although not altogether what it might have been, had all gone as it usually was in the habit of doing at that house. The ordinary little casualties of evil fortune had certainly from time to time, in the shape of illness, and one thing or another, attacked the family of the Bannerworths in common with every other family, but here suddenly had arisen a something at once terrible and inexplicable.

He found Mr. Marchdale up and dressed, and apparently in deep and anxious thought. The moment he saw Henry, he said,—

"Flora is awake, I presume."

"Yes, but her mind appears to be much disturbed."

"From bodily weakness, I dare say."

"But why should she be bodily weak? she was strong and well, ay, as we; as she could ever be in all her life. The glow of youth and health was on her cheeks. Is it possible that, in the course of one night, she should become bodily weak to such an extent?"

"Henry," said Mr. Marchdale, sadly, "sit down. I am not, as you know, a superstitious man."

"You certainly are not."

"And yet, I never in all my life was so absolutely staggered as I have been by the occurrences of to-night."

"Say on."

"There is a frightful, a hideous solution to them; one which every consideration will tend to add strength to, one which I tremble to name now, although, yesterday, at this hour, I should have laughed it to scorn."

"Indeed!"

"Yes, it is so. Tell no one that which I am about to say to you. Let the dreadful suggestion remain with ourselves alone, Henry Bannerworth."

"I—I am lost in wonder."

"You promise me?"

"What—what?"

"That you will not repeat my opinion to any one."

"I do."

"On your honour."

"On my honour, I promise."

Mr. Marchdale rose, and proceeding to the door, he looked out to see that there were no listeners near. Having ascertained then that they were quite alone, he returned, and drawing a chair close to that on which Henry sat, he said,—

"Henry, have you never heard of a strange and dreadful superstition which, in some countries, is extremely rife, by which it is supposed that there are beings who never die?"

"Never die!"

"Never. In a word, Henry, have you never heard of—of—I dread to pronounce the word."

"Speak it. God of Heaven! let me hear it."

"*A vampyre!*"

Henry sprung to his feet. His whole frame quivered with emotion; the drops of perspiration stood upon his brow, as, in a strange, hoarse voice, he repeated the words,—

"A vampyre!"

"Even so; one who has to renew a dreadful existence by human blood—one who lives on for ever, and must keep up such a fearful existence upon human gore—one who eats not and drinks not as other men—a vampyre."

Henry dropped into his seat, and uttered a deep groan of the most exquisite anguish.

"I could echo that groan," said Marchdale, "but that I am so thoroughly bewildered I know not what to think."

"Good God—good God!"

"The Mysterious Stranger," translated from the German of an anonymous author, appeared in the magazine Odds and Ends *in England in 1860. The portrait of the grotesque vampire is not far removed from that in Rymer's earlier* Varney the Vampyre *(1845), and is still recognizable in Bram Stoker's vampire in* Dracula *(1897).*

The Mysterious Stranger (1860)

ANONYMOUS

> *"To die, to sleep,*
> *To sleep, perchance to dream, ay, there's the rub . . ."*
> *Hamlet.*

Boreas, that fearful north-west wind, which in the spring and autumn stirs up the lowest depths of the wild Adriatic, and is then so dangerous to vessels, was howling through the woods, and tossing the branches of the old knotty oaks in the Carpathian Mountains, when a party of five riders, who surrounded a litter drawn by a pair of mules, turned into a forest-path, which offered some protection from the April weather, and allowed the travellers in some degree to recover their breath. It was already evening, and bitterly cold; the snow fell every now and then in large flakes. A tall old gentleman, of aristocratic appearance, rode at the head of the troop. This was the Knight of Fahnenberg, in Austria. He had inherited from a childless brother a considerable property, situated in the Carpathian Mountains; and he had set out to take possession of it, accompanied by his daughter Franziska, and a niece about twenty years of age, who had been brought up with her. Next to the knight rode a fine young man of some twenty and odd years—the Baron Franz von Kronstein; he wore, like the former, the broad-brimmed hat with hanging feathers, the leather collar, the wide riding-boots—in short, the travelling-dress which was in fashion at the commencement of the seventeenth century. The features of the young man had much about them that was open and friendly, as well as some mind; but the expression was more that of dreamy and sensitive softness than of youthful daring, although no one could deny that he possessed much of youthful beauty.

As the cavalcade turned into the oak wood the young man rode up to the litter, and chatted with the ladies who were seated therein. One of these—and to her his conversation was principally addressed—was of dazzling beauty. Her hair flowed in natural curls round the fine oval of her face, out of which beamed a pair of star-like eyes, full of genius, lively fancy, and a certain degree of archness. Franziska von Fahnenberg seemed to attend but carelessly to the speeches of her admirer, who made many kind inquiries as to how she felt herself during the journey, which had been attended with many difficulties: she always answered him very shortly, almost contemptuously; and at length remarked, that if it had not been for her father's objections, she would long ago have requested the baron to take her place in their horrid cage of a litter, for, to judge by his remarks, he seemed incommoded by the weather; and she would so much rather be mounted on the spirited horse, and face wind and storm, than be mewed up there, dragged up the hills by those long-eared animals, and mope herself to death with ennui. The young lady's words, and, still more, the half-contemptuous tone in which they were uttered, appeared to make the most painful impression on the young man: he made her no reply at the moment, but the absent air with which he attended to the kindly-intended remarks of the other young lady, showed how much he was disconcerted.

"It appears, dear Franziska," said he at length in a kindly tone, "that the hardships of the road have affected you more than you will acknowledge. Generally so kind to others, you have been very often out of humour during the journey, and particularly with regard to your humble servant and cousin, who would gladly bear a double or triple share of the discomforts, if he could thereby save you from the smallest of them."

Franziska showed by her look that she was about to reply with some bitter jibe, when the voice of the knight was heard calling for his nephew, who galloped off at the sound.

"I should like to scold you well, Franziska," said her companion somewhat sharply, "for always plagueing your poor Cousin Franz in this shameful way; he who loves you so truly, and who, whatever you may say, will one day be your husband."

"My husband!" replied the other angrily. "I must either completely alter my ideas, or he his whole self, before that takes place. No, Bertha! I know that this is my father's darling wish, and I do not deny the good qualities Cousin Franz may have, or really has, since I see you are making a face; but to marry an effeminate man—never!"

"Effeminate! You do him great injustice," replied her friend quickly. "Just because instead of going off to the Turkish war, where little honour was to be gained, he attended to your father's advice, and stayed at home, to bring his neglected estate into order, which he accomplished with care and prudence; and because he does not represent this howling wind as a mild zephyr—for reasons such as these you are pleased to call him effeminate."

"Say what you will, it is so," cried Franziska obstinately. "Bold, aspiring, even despotic, must be the man who is to gain my heart; these soft, patient, and thoughtful natures are utterly distasteful to me. Is Franz capable of deep sympathy, either in joy or sorrow? He is always the same—always quiet, soft and tiresome."

"He has a warm heart, and is not without genius," said Bertha.

"A warm heart! that may be," replied the other; "but I would rather be tyrannized over, and kept under a little by my future husband, than be loved in such a wearisome manner. You say he has genius, too. I will not exactly contradict you, since that would be impolite, but it is not easily discovered. But even allowing you are right in both statements, still the man who does not bring these qualities into action is a despicable creature. A man may do many foolish things, he may even be a little wicked now and then, provided it is in nothing dishonourable; and one can forgive him, if he is only acting on some fixed theory for some special object. There is, for instance, your own faithful admirer the Castellan of Glogau, Knight of Woislaw; he loves you most truly, and is now quite in a position to enable you to marry comfortably. The brave man has lost his right hand—reason enough for remaining seated behind the stove, or near the spinning-wheel of his Bertha; but what does he do?—He goes off to the war in Turkey; he fights for a noble thought——"

"And runs the chance of getting his other hand chopped off, and another great scar across his face," put in her friend.

"Leaves his lady-love to weep and pine a little," pursued Franziska, "but returns with fame, marries, and is all the more honoured and admired! This is done by a man of forty, a rough warrior, not bred at court, a soldier who has nothing but his cloak and sword. And Franz—rich, noble—but I will not go on. Not a word more on this detested point, if you love me, Bertha."

Franziska leaned back in the corner of the litter with a dissatisfied air, and shut her eyes as though, overcome by fatigue, she wished to sleep.

"This awful wind is so powerful, you say, that we must make a detour to avoid its full force," said the knight to an old man, dressed in a fur-cap and a cloak of rough skin, who seemed to be the guide of the party.

"Those who have never personally felt the Boreas storming over the country between Sessano and Trieste, can have no conception of the reality," replied the other. "As soon as it commences, the snow is blown in thick long columns along the ground. That is nothing to what follows. These columns become higher and higher, as the wind rises, and continue to do so until you see nothing but snow above, below, and on every side—unless, indeed, sometimes, when sand and gravel are mixed with the snow, and at length it is impossible to open your eyes at all. Your only plan for safety is to wrap your cloak around you, and lie down flat on the ground. If your home were but a few hundred yards off, you might lose your life in the attempt to reach it."

"Well, then, we owe you thanks, old Kumpan," said the knight, though it was with difficulty he made his words heard above the roaring of the storm; "we owe you thanks for taking us this round as we shall thus be enabled to reach our destination without danger."

"You may feel sure of that, noble sir," said the old man. "By midnight we shall have arrived, and that without any danger by the way, if——" Suddenly the old man stopped, he drew his horse sharply up, and remained in an attitude of attentive listening.

"It appears to me we must be in the neighborhood of some village," said Franz von Kronstein; "for between the gusts of the storm I hear a dog howling."

"It is no dog, it is no dog!" said the old man uneasily, and urged his horse to a rapid pace. "For miles around there is no human dwelling; and except in the castle of Klatka, which indeed lies in the neighborhood, but has been deserted for more than a century, probably no one has lived here since the creation.—But there again," he continued; "well, if I wasn't sure of it from the first."

"That howling seems to bother you, old Kumpan," said the knight, listening to a long-drawn fierce sound, which appeared nearer than before, and seemed to be answered from a distance.

"That howling comes from no dogs," replied the old guide uneasily. "Those are reed-wolves; they may be on our track; and it would be as well if the gentlemen looked to their firearms."

"Reed-wolves? What do you mean?" inquired Franz in surprise.

"At the edge of this wood," said Kumpan, "there lies a lake about a mile long, whose banks are covered with reeds. In these a number of wolves have taken up their quarters, and feed on wild birds, fish and such like. They are shy in the summer-time, and a boy of twelve might scare them; but when the birds migrate, and the fish are frozen up, they prowl about at night, and then they are dangerous. They are worst, however, when the Boreas rages, for then it is just as if the fiend himself possessed them: they are so mad and fierce that man and beast become alike their victims; and a party of them have been known even to attack the ferocious bears of these mountains, and, what is more, to come off victorious." The howl was now again repeated more distinctly, and from two opposite directions. The riders in alarm felt for their pistols and the old man grasped the spear which hung at his saddle.

"We must keep close to the litter; the wolves are very near us," whispered the guide. The riders turned their horses, surrounded the litter, and the knight informed the ladies, in a few quieting words, of the cause of this movement.

"Then we *shall* have an adventure—some little variety!" cried Franziska with sparkling eyes.

"How can you talk so foolishly?" said Bertha in alarm.

"Are we not under manly protection? Is not Cousin Franz on our side?" said the other mockingly.

"See, there is a light gleaming among the twigs; and there is another," cried Bertha. "There must be people close to us."

"No, no," cried the guide quickly. "Shut up the door, ladies. Keep close together, gentlemen. It is the eyes of wolves you see sparkling there." The gentlemen looked towards the thick underwood, in which every now and then little bright spots appeared, such as in summer would have been taken for glowworms; it was just the same greenish-yellow light, but less unsteady, and there were always two flames together. The horses began to be restive, they kicked and dragged at the rein; but the mules behaved tolerably well.

"I will fire on the beasts, and teach them to keep their distance," said Franz, pointing to the spot where the lights were thickest.

"Hold, hold, Sir Baron!" cried Kumpan quickly, and seized the young man's arm. "You would bring such a host together by the report, that, encouraged by numbers, they would be sure to make the first assault. However, keep your arms in readiness, and if an old she-wolf springs out—for these always lead the attack—take good aim and kill her, for then there must be no further hesitation." By this time the horses were almost unmanageable, and terror had also infected the mules. Just as Franz was turning towards the litter to say a word to his cousin, an animal, about the size of a large hound, sprang from the thicket and seized the foremost mule.

"Fire, baron! A wolf!" shouted the guide.

The young man fired, and the wolf fell to the ground. A fearful howl rang through the wood.

"Now, forward! Forward without a moment's delay!" cried Kumpan. "We have not above five minutes' time. The beasts will tear their wounded comrade to pieces, and, if they are very hungry, partially devour her. We shall, in the meantime, gain a little start, and it is not more than an hour's ride to the end of the forest. There—do you see—there are the towers of Klatka between the trees—out there where the moon is rising, and from that point the wood becomes less dense."

The travellers endeavoured to increase their pace to the utmost, but the litter retarded their progress. Bertha was weeping with fear, and even Franziska's courage had diminished, for she sat very still. Franz endeavoured to reassure them. They had not proceeded many moments when the howling recommenced, and approached nearer and nearer.

"There they are again and fiercer and more numerous than before," cried the guide in alarm.

The lights were soon visible again, and certainly in greater numbers. The wood had already become less thick, and the snowstorm having ceased, the moonbeams discovered many a dusky form amongst the trees, keeping together like a pack of hounds and advancing nearer and nearer till they were within twenty paces, and on the very path of the travellers. From time to time a fierce howl arose from their centre which was answered by the whole pack, and was at length taken up by single voices in the distance.

The party now found themselves some few hundred yards from the ruined castle of which Kumpan had spoken. It was, or seemed by moonlight to be, of some magnitude. Near the tolerably preserved principal building lay the ruins of a church which must have once been beautiful, placed on a little hillock dotted with single oak-trees and bramble-bushes. Both castle and church were still partially roofed in, and a path led from the castle gate to an old oak-tree, where it joined at right angles the one along which the travellers were advancing.

The old guide seemed in much perplexity.

"We are in great danger, noble sir," said he. "The wolves will very soon make a general attack. There will then be only one way of escape:

leaving the mules to their fate, and taking the young ladies on your horses."

"That would be all very well, if I had not thought of a better plan," replied the knight. "Here is the ruined castle; we can surely reach that, and then, blocking up the gates, we must just await the morning."

"Here? In the ruins of Klatka?—Not for all the wolves in the world!" cried the old man. "Even by daylight no one likes to approach the place, and, now, by night!— The castle, Sir Knight, has a bad name."

"On account of robbers?" asked Franz.

"No; it is haunted," replied the other.

"Stuff and nonsense!" said the baron. "Forward to the ruins; there is not a moment to be lost."

And this was indeed the case. The ferocious beasts were but a few steps behind the travellers. Every now and then they retired, and set up a ferocious howl. The party had just arrived at the old oak before mentioned and were about to turn into the path to the ruins, when the animals, as though perceiving the risk they ran of losing their prey, came so near that a lance could easily have struck them. The knight and Franz faced sharply about, spurring their horses amidst the advancing crowds, when suddenly, from the shadow of the oak stepped forth a man who in a few strides placed himself between the travellers and their pursuers. As far as one could see in the dusky light the stranger was a man of a tall and well-built frame; he wore a sword by his side and a broad-brimmed hat was on his head. If the party were astonished at his sudden appearance, they were still more so at what followed. As soon as the stranger appeared the wolves gave over their pursuit, tumbled over each other, and set up a fearful howl. The stranger now raised his hand, appeared to wave it, and the wild animals crawled back into the thickets like a pack of beaten hounds.

Without casting a glance at the travellers, who were too much overcome by astonishment to speak, the stranger went up the path which led to the castle and soon disappeared beneath the gateway.

"Heaven have mercy on us!" murmured old Kumpan in his beard, as he made the sign of the cross.

"Who was that strange man?" asked the knight with surprise, when he had watched the stranger as long as he was visible, and the party had resumed their way.

The old guide pretended not to understand, and riding up to the mules, busied himself with arranging the harness, which had become disordered in their haste: more than a quarter of an hour elapsed before he rejoined them.

"Did you know the man who met us near the ruins and who freed us from our fourfooted pursuers in such a miraculous way?" asked Franz of the guide.

"Do I know him? No, noble sir; I never saw him before," replied the guide hesitatingly.

"He looked like a soldier, and was armed," said the baron. "Is the castle, then, inhabited?"

"Not for the last hundred years," replied the other. "It was dismantled because the possessor in those days had iniquitous dealings with some Turkish-Sclavonian hordes, who had advanced as far as this; or rather"—he corrected himself hastily—"he is *said* to have had such, for he might have been as upright and good a man as ever ate cheese fried in butter."

"And who is now the possessor of the ruins and of these woods?" inquired the knight.

"Who but yourself, noble sir?" replied Kumpan. "For more than two hours we have been on your estate, and we shall soon reach the end of the wood."

"We hear and see nothing more of the wolves," said the baron after a pause. "Even their howling has ceased. The adventure with the stranger still remains to me inexplicable, even if one were to suppose him a huntsman——"

"Yes, yes; that is most likely what he is," interrupted the guide hastily, whilst he looked uneasily round him. "The brave good man, who came so opportunely to our assistance, must have been a huntsman. Oh, there are many powerful woodsmen in this neighborhood! Heaven be praised!" he continued, taking a deep breath, "there is the end of the wood, and in a short hour we shall be safely housed."

And so it happened. Before an hour had elapsed the party passed through a well-built village, the principal spot on the estate, towards the venerable castle, the windows of which were brightly illuminated, and at the door stood the steward and other dependents, who, having received their new lord with every expression of respect, conducted the party to the splendidly furnished apartments.

Nearly four weeks passed before the travelling adventures again came on the *tapis*. The knight and Franz found such constant employment in looking over all the particulars of the large estate, and endeavouring to introduce various German improvements, that they were

very little at home. At first Franziska was charmed with everything in a
neighborhood so entirely new and unknown. It appeared to her so romantic, so very different from her German Father-land, that she took
the greatest interest in everything, and often drew comparisons between
the countries, which generally ended unfavourably for Germany. Bertha was of exactly the contrary opinion: she laughed at her cousin, and
said that her liking for novelty and strange sights must indeed have
come to a pass when she preferred hovels in which the smoke went out
of the doors and windows instead of the chimney, walls covered with
soot, and inhabitants not much cleaner, and of unmannerly habits, to
the comfortable dwellings and polite people of Germany. However,
Franziska persisted in her notions, and replied that everything in Austria was flat, *ennuyant,* and common; and that a wild peasant here, with
his rough coat of skin, had ten times more interest for her than a quiet
Austrian in his holiday suit, the mere sight of whom was enough to
make one yawn.

As soon as the knight had gotten the first arrangements into some
degree of order the party found themselves more together again. Franz
continued to show great attention to his cousin, which, however, she
received with little gratitude, for she made him the butt of all her fanciful humours, that soon returned when after a longer sojourn she had
become more accustomed to her new life. Many excursions into the
neighborhood were undertaken but there was little variety in the scenery, and these soon ceased to amuse.

The party were one day assembled in the old-fashioned hall, dinner
had just been removed, and they were arranging in which direction they
should ride. "I have it," cried Franziska suddenly, "I wonder we never
thought before of going to view by day the spot where we fell in with
our night-adventure with wolves and the Mysterious Stranger."

"You mean a visit to the ruins—what were they called?" said the
knight.

"Castle Klatka," cried Franziska gaily. "Oh, we really must ride
there! It will be so charming to go over again by daylight, and in safety,
the ground where we had such a dreadful fright."

"Bring round the horses," said the knight to a servant; "and tell
the steward to come to me immediately." The latter, an old man, soon
after entered the room.

"We intend taking a ride to Klatka," said the knight: "we had an
adventure there on our road——"

"So old Kumpan told me," interrupted the steward.

"And what do you say about it?" asked the knight.

"I really don't know what to say," replied the old man, shaking his head. "I was a youth of twenty when I first came to this castle, and now my hair is grey; half a century has elapsed during that time. Hundreds of times my duty has called me into the neighbourhood of those ruins, but never have I seen the Fiend of Klatka."

"What do you say? Whom do you call by that name?" inquired Franziska, whose love of adventure and romance was strongly awakened.

"Why, people call by that name the ghost or spirit who is supposed to haunt the ruins," replied the steward. "They say he only shows himself on moon-light nights——"

"That is quite natural," interrupted Franz smiling. "Ghosts can never bear the light of day; and if the moon did not shine, how could the ghost be seen, for it is not supposed that any one for a mere freak would visit the ruins by torch-light."

"There are some credulous people who pretend to have seen this ghost," continued the steward. "Huntsmen and woodcutters say they have met him by the large oak on the crosspath. That, noble sir, is supposed to be the spot he inclines most to haunt, for the tree was planted in remembrance of the man who fell there."

"And who was he?" asked Franziska with increasing curiosity.

"The last owner of the castle, which at that time was a sort of robbers' den, and the headquarters of all depredators in the neighbourhood," answered the old man. "They say this man was of superhuman strength, and was feared not only on account of his passionate temper, but of his treaties with the Turkish hordes. Any young woman, too, in the neighbourhood to whom he took a fancy, was carried off to his tower and never heard of more. When the measure of his iniquity was full, the whole neighbourhood rose in a mass, besieged his stronghold, and at length he was slain on the spot where the huge oak-tree now stands."

"I wonder they did not burn the whole castle, so as to erase the very memory of it," said the knight.

"It was a dependency of the church, and that saved it," replied the other. "Your great-grandfather afterwards took possession of it, for it had fine lands attached. As the Knight of Klatka was of good family, a monument was erected to him in the church, which now lies as much in ruin as the castle itself."

"Oh, let us set off at once! Nothing shall prevent my visiting so interesting a spot," said Franziska eagerly. "The imprisoned damsels who never reappeared, the storming of the tower, the death of the knight, the nightly wanderings of his spirit round the old oak, and lastly, our own adventure, all draw me thither with an indescribable curiosity."

When a servant announced that the horses were at the door, the young girls tripped laughingly down the steps which led to the coach-yard. Franz, the knight, and a servant well acquainted with the country followed; and in a few minutes the party was on the road to the forest.

The sun was still high in the heavens when they saw the towers of Klatka rising above the trees. Everything in the wood was still except the cheerful twitterings of the birds as they hopped about amongst the bursting buds and leaves and announced that spring had arrived.

The party soon found themselves near the old oak at the bottom of the hill on which stood the towers, still imposing in their ruin. Ivy and bramble bushes had wound themselves over the walls, and forced their deep roots so firmly between the stones that they in a great measure held these together. On the top of the highest spot a small bush in its young fresh verdure swayed lightly in the breeze.

The gentlemen assisted their companions to alight, and leaving the horses to the care of the servant, ascended the hill to the castle. After having explored this in every nook and cranny, and spent much time in a vain search for some trace of the extraordinary stranger whom Franziska declared she was determined to discover, they proceeded to an inspection of the adjoining church. This they found to have better withstood the ravages of time and weather; the nave, indeed, was in complete dilapidation, but the chancel and altar were still under roof, as well as a sort of chapel which appeared to have been a place of honour for the families of the old knights of the castle. Few traces remained, however, of the magnificent painted glass which must once have adorned the windows, and the wind entered at pleasure through the open spaces.

The party were occupied for some time in deciphering the inscriptions on a number of tombstones, and on the walls, principally within the chancel. They were generally memorials of the ancient lords, with figures of men in armour, and women and children of all ages. A flying raven and various other devices were placed at the corners. One grave-stone, which stood close to the entrance of the chancel, differed widely from the others: there was no figure sculptured on it, and the inscription, which on all besides was a mere mass of flattering eulogies, was here simple and unadorned; it contained only these words: "Ezzelin von Klatka fell like a knight at the storming of the castle"—on such a day and year.

"That must be the monument of the knight whose ghost is said to haunt these ruins," cried Franziska eagerly. "What a pity he is not represented in the same way as the others—I should so like to have known what he was like!"

"Oh, there is the family vault, with steps leading down to it, and the sun is lighting it up through a crevice," said Franz, stepping from the adjoining vestry.

The whole party followed him down the eight or nine steps which led to a tolerably airy chamber, where were placed a number of coffins of all sizes, some of them crumbling into dust. Here, again, one close to the door was distinguished from the others by the simplicity of its design, the freshness of its appearance, and the brief inscription: "Ezzelinus de Klatka, Eques."

As not the slightest effluvium was perceptible, they lingered some time in the vault; and when they reascended to the church, they had a long talk over the old possessors, of whom the knight now remembered he had heard his parents speak. The sun had disappeared, and the moon was just rising as the explorers turned to leave the ruins. Bertha had made a step into the nave, when she uttered a slight exclamation of fear and surprise. Her eyes fell on a man who wore a hat with drooping feathers, a sword at his side, and a short cloak of somewhat old-fashioned cut over his shoulders. The stranger leaned carelessly on a broken column at the entrance; he did not appear to take any notice of the party; and the moon shone full on his pale face.

The party advanced towards the stranger.

"If I am not mistaken," commenced the knight; "we have met before."

Not a word from the unknown.

"You released us in an almost miraculous manner," said Franziska, "from the power of those dreadful wolves. Am I wrong in supposing it is to you we are indebted for that great service?"

"The beasts are afraid of me," replied the stranger in a deep fierce tone, while he fastened his sunken eyes on the girl, without taking any notice of the others.

"Then you are probably a huntsman," said Franz, "and wage war against the fierce brutes."

"Who is not either the pursuer or the pursued? All persecute or are persecuted, and Fate persecutes all," replied the stranger without looking at him.

"Do you live in these ruins?" asked the knight hesitatingly.

"Yes; but not to the destruction of your game, as you may fear, Knight of Fahnenberg," said the unknown contemptuously. "Be quite assured of this; your property shall remain untouched——"

"Oh! my father did not mean that," interrupted Franziska, who appeared to take the liveliest interest in the stranger. "Unfortunate events and sad experiences have, no doubt, induced you to take up your abode in these ruins, of which my father would by no means dispossess you."

"Your father is very good, if that is what he meant," said the stranger in his former tone; and it seemed as though his dark features were drawn into a slight smile; "but people of my sort are rather difficult to turn out."

"You must live very uncomfortably here," said Franziska, half vexed, for she thought her polite speech had deserved a better reply.

"My dwelling is not exactly uncomfortable, only somewhat small —still quite suitable for quiet people," said the unknown with a kind of sneer. "I am not, however, always quiet; I sometimes pine to quit the narrow space, and then I dash away through forest and field, over hill and dale; and the time when I must return to my little dwelling always comes too soon for me."

"As you now and then leave your dwelling," said the knight, "I would invite you to visit us, if I knew——"

"That I was in a station to admit of your doing so," interrupted the other; and the knight started slightly, for the stranger had exactly expressed the half-formed thought. "I lament," he continued coldly, "that I am not able to give you particulars on this point—some difficulties stand in the way: be assured, however, that I am a knight, and of at least as ancient a family as yourself."

"Then you must not refuse our request," cried Franziska, highly interested in the strange manners of the unknown. "You must come and visit us."

"I am no boon-companion, and on that account few have invited me of late," replied the other with his peculiar smile; "besides, I generally remain at home during the day; that is my time for rest. I belong, you must know, to that class of persons who turn day into night, and night into day, and who love everything uncommon and peculiar."

"Really? So do I! And for that reason, you must visit us," cried

Franziska. "Now," she continued smiling, "I suppose you have just risen, and you are taking your morning airing. Well, since the moon is your sun, pray pay a frequent visit to our castle by the light of its rays. I think we shall agree very well, and that it will be very nice for us to be acquainted."

"You wish it?—You press the invitation?" asked the stranger earnestly and decidedly.

"To be sure, for otherwise you will not come," replied the young lady shortly.

"Well, then, come I will!" said the other, again fixing his gaze on her. "If my company does not please you at any time, you will have yourself to blame for an acquaintance with one who seldom forces himself, but is difficult to shake off."

When the unknown had concluded these words he made a slight motion with his hand, as though to take leave of them, and passing under the doorway, disappeared among the ruins. The party soon after mounted their horses and took the road home.

It was evening of the following day, and all were again seated in the hall of the castle. Bertha had that day received good news. The knight Woislaw had written from Hungary that the war with the Turks would soon be brought to a conclusion during the year, and that although he had intended returning to Silesia, hearing of the Knight of Fahnenberg having gone to take possession of his new estates, he should follow the family there, not doubting that Bertha had accompanied her friend. He hinted that he stood so high in the opinion of his duke on account of his valuable services, that in future his duties would be even more important and extensive; but before settling down to them, he should come and claim Bertha's promise to become his wife. He had been much enriched by his master, as well as by booty taken from the Turks. Having formerly lost his right hand in the duke's service, he had essayed to fight with his left; but this did not succeed very admirably, and so he had an iron one made by a very clever artist. This hand performed many of the functions of a natural one, but there had been still much wanting; now, however, his master had presented him with one of gold, an extraordinary work of art, produced by a celebrated Italian mechanic. The knight described it as something marvellous, especially as to the superhuman strength with which it enabled him to use the sword and lance. Franziska naturally rejoiced in the happiness of her friend, who had had no news of her betrothed for a long time before. She launched out every now and then, partly to plague Franz, and partly to express her own feelings, in the highest praise and admiration of the bravery and enterprise of the knight, whose adventurous qualities she lauded to the skies. Even the scar on his face and his want of a right hand were reckoned as virtues; and Franziska at last saucily declared that a rather ugly man was infinitely more attractive to her than a handsome one, for as a general rule handsome men were conceited and effeminate. Thus, she added, no one could term their acquaintance of the night before handsome, but attractive and interesting he certainly was. Franz and Bertha simultaneously denied this. His gloomy appearance, the deadly hue of his complexion, the tone of his voice, were each in turn depreciated by Bertha, while Franz found fault with the contempt and arrogance obvious in his speech. The knight stood between the two parties. He thought there was something in his bearing that spoke of good family, though much could not be said for his politeness; however, the man might have had trials enough in his life to make him misanthropical. Whilst they were conversing in this way, the door suddenly opened and the subject of their remarks himself walked in.

"Pardon me, Sir Knight," he said coldly, "that I come, if not uninvited, at least unannounced; there was no one in the ante-chamber to do me that service."

The brilliantly lighted chamber gave a full view of the stranger. He was a man of about forty, tall, and extremely thin. His features could not be termed uninteresting—there lay in them something bold and daring—but the expression was on the whole anything but benevolent. There were contempt and sarcasm in the cold grey eyes, whose glance, however, was at times so piercing that no one could endure it long. His complexion was even more peculiar than the features: it could neither be called pale nor yellow; it was a sort of grey, or, so to speak, dirty white, like that of an Indian who has been suffering long from fever; and was rendered still more remarkable by the intense blackness of his beard and short cropped hair. The dress of the unknown was knightly, but old-fashioned and neglected; there were great spots of rust on the collar and breastplate of his armour; and his dagger and the hilt of his finely worked sword were marked in some places with mildew. As the party were just going to supper, it was only natural to invite the stranger to partake of it; he complied, however, only in so far that he seated himself at the table, for he ate no morsel. The knight, with some surprise, inquired the reason.

"For a long time past I have accustomed myself never to eat at night," he replied with a strange smile. "My digestion is quite unused to solids, and indeed would scarcely confront them. I live entirely on liquids."

"Oh, then we can empty a bumper of Rhine-wine together," cried the host.

"Thanks; but I neither drink wine nor any cold beverage," replied the other; and his tone was full of mockery. It appeared as if there was some amusing association connected with the idea.

"Then I will order you a cup of hippocras"—a warm drink composed of herbs—"it shall be ready immediately," said Franziska.

"Many thanks, fair lady; not at present," replied the other. "But if I refuse the beverage you offer me now, you may be assured that as soon as I require it—perhaps very soon—I will request that, or some other of you."

Bertha and Franz thought the man had something inexpressibly repulsive in his whole manner, and they had no inclination to engage him in conversation; but the baron, thinking that perhaps politeness required him to say something, turned towards the guest, and commenced in a friendly tone: "It is now many weeks since we first became acquainted with you; we then had to thank you for a singular service——"

"And I have not yet told you my name, although you would gladly know it," interrupted the other dryly. "I am called Azzo; and as"—this he said again with his ironical smile—"with the permission of the Knight of Fahnenberg, I live at the castle of Klatka, you can in future call me Azzo von Klatka."

"I only wonder you do not feel lonely and uncomfortable amongst those old walls," began Bertha. "I cannot understand——"

"Why my business is there? Oh, about that I will willingly give you some information, since you and the young gentleman there take such a kindly interest in my person," replied the unknown in his tone of sarcasm.

Franz and Bertha both started, for he had revealed their thoughts as though he could read their souls. "You see, my lady," he continued, "there are a variety of strange whims in the world. As I have already said, I love what is peculiar and uncommon, at least what would appear so to you. It is wrong in the main to be astonished at anything, for, viewed in one light, all things are alike; even life and death, this side of the grave and the other, have more resemblance than you would imagine. You perhaps consider me rather touched a little in my mind, for taking up my abode with the bat and the owl; but if so, why not consider every hermit and recluse insane? You will tell me that those are holy men. I certainly have no pretension that way; but as they find pleasure in praying and singing psalms, so I amuse myself with hunting. Oh, away in the pale moonlight, on a horse that never tires, over hill and dale, through forest and woodland! I rush among the wolves, which fly at my approach, as you yourself perceived, as though they were puppies fearful of the lash."

"But still it must be lonely, very lonely for you," remarked Bertha.

"So it would by day; but I am then asleep," replied the stranger dryly; "at night I am merry enough."

"You hunt in an extraordinary way," remarked Franz hesitatingly.

"Yes; but, nevertheless, I have no communication with robbers, as you seem to imagine," replied Azzo coldly.

Franz again started—that very thought had just crossed his mind. "Oh, I beg your pardon; I do not know——" he stammered.

"What to make of me," interrupted the other. "You would therefore do well to believe just what I tell you, or at least to avoid making conjectures of your own, which will lead to nothing."

"I understand you: I know how to value your ideas, if no one else does," cried Franziska eagerly. "The humdrum, everyday life of the generality of men is repulsive to you; you have tasted the joys and pleasures of life, at least what are so called, and you have found them tame and hollow. How soon one tires of the things one sees all around! Life consists in change. Only in what is new, uncommon, and peculiar, do the flowers of the spirit bloom and give forth scent. Even pain may become a pleasure if it saves one from the shallow monotony of everyday life—a thing I shall hate till the hour of my death."

"Right, fair lady—quite right! Remain in this mind: this was always my opinion, and the one from which I have derived the highest reward," cried Azzo; and his fierce eyes sparkled more intensely than ever. "I am doubly pleased to have found in you a person who shares my ideas. Oh, if you were a man, you would make me a splendid companion; but even a woman may have fine experiences when once these opinions take root in her, and bring forth action!"

As Azzo spoke these words in a cold tone of politeness, he turned from the subject, and for the rest of his visit only gave the knight monosyllabic replies to his inquiries, taking leave before the table was cleared. To an invitation from the knight, backed by a still more pressing one from Franziska to repeat his visit, he replied that he would take advantage of their kindness, and come sometimes.

When the stranger had departed, many were the remarks made on his appearance and general deportment. Franz declared his most decided dislike of him. Whether it was as usual to vex her cousin, or whether Azzo had really made an impression on her, Franziska took his part vehemently. As Franz contradicted her more eagerly than usual, the young lady launched out into still stronger expressions; and there is no knowing what hard words her cousin might have received had not a servant entered the room.

The following morning Franziska lay longer than usual in bed. When her friend went to her room, fearful lest she should be ill, she found her pale and exhausted. Franziska complained she had passed a very bad night; she thought the dispute with Franz about the stranger must have excited her greatly, for she felt quite feverish and exhausted, and a strange dream, too, had worried her, which was evidently a consequence of the evening's conversation. Bertha, as usual, took the young man's part, and added that a common dispute about a man whom no one knew, and about whom anyone might form his own opinion, could not possibly have thrown her into her present state. "At least," she continued, "you can let me hear this wonderful dream."

To her surprise, Franziska for a length of time refused to do so.

"Come, tell me," inquired Bertha, "what can possibly prevent you from relating a dream—a mere dream? I might almost think it credible, if the idea were not too horrid, that poor Franz is not very far wrong when he says that the thin, corpse-like, dried-up, old-fashioned stranger has made a greater impression on you than you will allow."

"Did Franz say so?" asked Franziska. "Then you can tell him he is not mistaken. Yes, the thin, corpse-like, dried-up, whimsical stranger is far more interesting to me than the rosy-cheeked, well-dressed, polite, and prosy cousin."

"Strange," cried Bertha. "I cannot at all comprehend the almost magic influence which this man, so repulsive, exercises over you."

"Perhaps the very reason I take his part, may be that you are all so prejudiced against him," remarked Franziska pettishly. "Yes, it must be so; for that his appearance should please my eyes is what no one in his senses could imagine. But," she continued, smiling and holding out her hand to Bertha, "is it not laughable that I should get out of temper even with you about this stranger?—I can more easily understand it with

Franz—and that this unknown should spoil my morning, as he has already spoiled my evening and my night's rest?"

"By that dream, you mean?" said Bertha, easily appeased, as she put her arm round her cousin's neck and kissed her. "Now, do tell it to me. You know how I delight in hearing anything of the kind."

"Well, I will, as a sort of compensation for my peevishness towards you," said the other, clasping her friend's hands. "Now, listen! I had walked up and down my room for a long time; I was excited—out of spirits—I do not know exactly what. It was almost midnight ere I lay down, but I could not sleep. I tossed about, and at length it was only from sheer exhaustion that I dropped off. But what a sleep it was! An inward fear ran through me perpetually. I saw a number of pictures before me, as I used to do in childish sicknesses. I do not know whether I was asleep or half awake. Then I dreamed, but as clearly as if I had been wide awake, that a sort of mist filled the room, and out of it stepped the knight Azzo. He gazed at me for a time, and then letting himself slowly down on one knee, imprinted a kiss on my throat. Long did his lips rest there; and I felt a slight pain, which always increased, until I could bear it no more. With all my strength I tried to force the vision from me, but succeeded only after a long struggle. No doubt I uttered a scream, for that awoke me from my trance. When I came a little to my senses I felt a sort of superstitious fear creeping over me— how great you may imagine when I tell you that, with my eyes open and awake, it appeared to me as if Azzo's figure were still by my bed, and then disappearing gradually into the mist, vanished at the door!"

"You must have dreamed very heavily, my poor friend," began Bertha, but suddenly paused. She gazed with surprise at Franziska's throat. "Why, what is that?" she cried. "Just look: how extraordinary— a red streak on your throat!"

Franziska raised herself, and went to a little glass that stood in the window. She really saw a small red line about an inch long on her neck, which began to smart when she touched it with her finger.

"I must have hurt myself by some means in my sleep," she said after a pause; "and that in some measure will account for my dream."

The friends continued chatting for some time about this singular coincidence—the dream and the stranger; and at length it was all turned into a joke by Bertha.

Several weeks passed. The knight had found the estate and affairs in greater disorder than he at first imagined; and instead of remaining three or four weeks, as was originally intended, their departure was deferred to an indefinite period. This postponement was likewise in some measure occasioned by Franziska's continued indisposition. She who had formerly bloomed like a rose in its young fresh beauty was becoming daily thinner, more sickly and exhausted, and at the same time so pale, that in the space of a month not a tinge of red was perceptible on the once glowing cheek. The knight's anxiety about her was extreme, and the best advice was procured which the age and country afforded; but all to no purpose. Franziska complained from time to time that the horrible dream with which her illness commenced was repeated, and that always on the day following she felt an increased and indescribable weakness. Bertha naturally set this down to the effects of fever, but the ravages of that fever on the usually clear reason of her friend filled her with alarm.

The knight Azzo repeated his visits every now and then. He always came in the evening, and when the moon shone brightly. His manner was always the same. He spoke in monosyllables, and was coldly polite to the knight; to Franz and Bertha, particularly to the former, contemptuous and haughty; but to Franziska, friendliness itself. Often when, after a short visit, he again left the house, his peculiarities became the subject of conversation. Besides his odd way of speaking, in which Bertha said there lay a deep hatred, a cold detestation of all mankind with the exception of Franziska, two other singularities were observable. During none of his visits, which often took place at supper-time, had he been prevailed upon to eat or drink anything, and that without giving any good reason for his abstinence. A remarkable alteration, too, had taken place in his appearance: he seemed an entirely different creature. The skin, before so shrivelled and stretched, seemed smooth and soft, while a slight tinge of red appeared in his cheeks, which began to look round and plump. Bertha, who could not at all conceal her ill-will towards him, said often, that much as she hated his face before, when it was more like a death's-head than a human being's, it was now more than ever repulsive; she always felt a shudder run through her veins whenever his sharp piercing eyes rested on her. Perhaps it was owing to Franziska's partiality, or to the knight Azzo's own contemptuous way of replying to Franz, or to his haughty way of treating him in general, that made the young man dislike him more and more. It was quite observable that whenever Franz made a remark to his cousin in the presence of Azzo, the latter would immediately throw some ill-natured light on it or distort it to a totally different meaning. This increased from day to day, and at last Franz declared to Bertha that he would

stand such conduct no longer, and that it was only out of consideration
for Franziska that he had not already called him to account.

At this time the party at the castle was increased by the arrival of
Bertha's long-expected guest. He came just as they were sitting down to
supper one evening, and all jumped up to greet their old friend. The
knight Woislaw was a true model of the soldier, hardened and strengthened by war with men and elements. His face would not have been
termed ugly, if a Turkish sabre had not left a mark running from the
right eye to the left cheek, and standing out bright red from the sun-
burned skin. The frame of the Castellan of Glogau might almost be
termed colossal. Few would have been able to carry his armour, and
still fewer move with his lightness and ease under its weight. He did not
think little of this same armour, for it had been a present from the
palatine of Hungary on his leaving the camp. The blue wrought-steel
was ornamented all over with patterns in gold; and he had put it on to
do honour to his bride-elect, together with the wonderful gold hand, the
gift of the duke.

Woislaw was questioned by the knight and Franz on all the concerns of the campaign; and he entered into the most minute particulars
relating to the battles, which, with regard to plunder, had been more
successful than ever. He spoke much of the strength of the Turks in a
hand-to-hand fight, and remarked that he owed the duke many thanks
for his splendid gift, for in consequence of its strength many of the
enemy regarded him as something superhuman. The sickliness and
deathlike paleness of Franziska was too perceptible not to be immediately noticed by Woislaw; accustomed to see her so fresh and cheerful,
he hastened to inquire into the cause of the change. Bertha related all
that had happened, and Woislaw listened with the greatest interest. This
increased to the utmost at the account of the often-repeated dream, and
Franziska had to give him the most minute particulars of it; it appeared
as though he had met with a similar case before, or at least had heard of
one. When the young lady added that it was very remarkable that the
wound on her throat which she had at first felt had never healed, and
still pained her, the knight Woislaw looked at Bertha as much as to say
that this last fact had greatly strengthened his idea as to the cause of
Franziska's illness.

It was only natural that the discourse should next turn to the
knight Azzo, about whom everyone began to talk eagerly. Woislaw inquired as minutely as he had done with regard to Franziska's illness
about what concerned this stranger, from the first evening of their ac-

quaintance down to his last visit, without, however, giving any opinion on the subject. The party were still in earnest conversation, when the door opened, and Azzo entered. Woislaw's eyes remained fixed on him, as he, without taking any particular notice of the new arrival, walked up to the table, and seating himself, directed most of the conversation to Franziska and her father, and now and then made some sarcastic remark when Franz began to speak. The Turkish war again came on the *tapis,* and though Azzo only put in an occasional remark, Woislaw had much to say on the subject. Thus they had advanced late into the night, and Franz said smiling to Woislaw: "I should not wonder if day had surprised us, whilst listening to your entertaining adventures."

"I admire the young gentleman's taste," said Azzo, with an ironical curl of the lip. "Stories of storm and shipwreck are, indeed, best heard on *terra firma,* and those of battle and death at a hospitable table or in the chimney-corner. One has then the comfortable feeling of keeping a whole skin, and being in no danger, not even of taking cold." With the last words, he gave a hoarse laugh, and turning his back on Franz, rose, bowed to the rest of the company, and left the room. The knight, who always accompanied Azzo to the door, now expressed himself fatigued, and bade his friends good night.

"That Azzo's impertinence is unbearable," cried Bertha when he was gone. "He becomes daily more rough, unpolite, and presuming. If only on account of Franziska's dream, though of course he cannot help that, I detest him. Now, tonight, not one civil word has he spoken to anyone but Franziska, except, perhaps, some casual remark to my uncle."

"I cannot deny that you are right, Bertha," said her cousin. "One may forgive much to a man whom fate had probably made somewhat misanthropical; but he should not overstep the bounds of common politeness. But where on earth is Franz?" added Franziska, as she looked uneasily round. The young man had quietly left the room whilst Bertha was speaking.

"He cannot have followed the knight Azzo to challenge him?" cried Bertha in alarm.

"It were better he entered a lion's den to pull his mane!" said Woislaw vehemently. "I must follow him instantly," he added, as he rushed from the room.

He hastened over the threshold, out of the castle, and through the court before he came up to them. Here a narrow bridge with a slight balustrade passed over the moat by which the castle was surrounded. It appeared that Franz had only just addressed Azzo in a few hot words, for as Woislaw, unperceived by either, advanced under the shadow of the wall, Azzo said gloomily: "Leave me, foolish boy—leave me; for by that sun"—and he pointed to the full moon above them—"you will see those rays no more if you linger another moment on my path."

"And I tell you, wretch, that you either give me satisfaction for your repeated insolence, or you die," cried Franz, drawing his sword.

Azzo stretched forth his hand, and grasping the sword in the middle, it snapped like a broken reed. "I warn you for the last time," he said in a voice of thunder as he threw the pieces into the moat. "Now, away—away, boy, from my path, or, by those below us, you are lost!"

"You or I! you or I!" cried Franz madly as he made a rush at the sword of his antagonist and strove to draw it from his side. Azzo replied not; only a bitter laugh half escaped from his lips; then seizing Franz by the chest, he lifted him up like an infant, and was in the act of throwing him over the bridge when Woislaw stepped to his side. With a grasp of his wonderful hand, into the springs of which he threw all his strength, he seized Azzo's arm, pulled it down, and obliged him to drop his victim. Azzo seemed in the highest degree astonished. Without concerning himself further about Franz, he gazed in amazement on Woislaw.

"Who art thou who darest to rob me of my prey?" he asked hesitatingly. "Is it possible? Can you be——"

"Ask not, thou bloody one! Go, seek thy nourishment! Soon comes thy hour!" replied Woislaw in a calm but firm tone.

"Ha, now I know!" cried Azzo eagerly. "Welcome, blood-brother! I give up to you this worm, and for your sake will not crush him. Farewell; our paths will soon meet again."

"Soon, very soon; farewell!" cried Woislaw, drawing Franz towards him. Azzo rushed away and disappeared.

Franz had remained for some moments in a state of stupefaction, but suddenly started as from a dream. "I am dishonoured, dishonoured forever!" he cried, as he pressed his clenched hands to his forehead.

"Calm yourself; you could not have conquered," said Woislaw.

"But I will conquer, or perish!" cried Franz incensed. "I will seek this adventurer in his den, and he or I must fall."

"You could not hurt him," said Woislaw. "You would infallibly be the victim."

"Then show me a way to bring the wretch to judgment," cried

Franz, seizing Woislaw's hands, while tears of anger sprang to his eyes. "Disgraced as I am, I cannot live."

"You shall be revenged, and that within twenty-four hours, I hope; but only on two conditions—"

"I agree to them! I will do anything—" began the young man eagerly.

"The first is, that you do nothing, but leave everything in my hands," interrupted Woislaw. "The second, that you will assist me in persuading Franziska to do what I shall represent to her as absolutely necessary. That young lady's life is in more danger from Azzo than your own."

"How? What?" cried Franz fiercely. "Franziska's life in danger! And from that man? Tell me, Woislaw, who is this fiend?"

"Not a word will I tell either the young lady or you, until the danger is passed," said Woislaw firmly. "The smallest indiscretion would ruin everything. No one can act here but Franziska herself, and if she refuses to do so she is irretrievably lost."

"Speak, and I will help you. I will do all you wish, but I must know——"

"Nothing, absolutely nothing," replied Woislaw. "I must have both you and Franziska yield to me unconditionally. Come now, come to her. You are to be mute on what has passed, and use every effort to induce her to accede to my proposal."

Woislaw spoke firmly, and it was impossible for Franz to make any further objection; in a few moments they both entered the hall, where they found the young girls still anxiously awaiting them.

"Oh, I have been so frightened," said Franziska, even paler than usual, as she held out her hand to Franz. "I trust all has ended peaceably."

"Everything is arranged; a couple of words were sufficient to settle the whole affair," said Woislaw cheerfully. "But Master Franz was less concerned in it than yourself, fair lady."

"I! How do you mean?" said Franziska in surprise.

"I allude to your illness," replied the other.

"And you spoke of that to Azzo? Does he, then, know a remedy which he could not tell me himself?" she inquired, smiling painfully.

"The knight Azzo must take part in your cure; but speak to you about it he cannot, unless the remedy is to lose all its efficacy," replied Woislaw quietly.

"So it is some secret elixir, as the learned doctors who have so long attended me say, and through whose means I only grow worse," said Franziska mournfully.

"It is certainly a secret, but is as certainly a cure," replied Woislaw.

"So said all, but none has succeeded," said the young lady peevishly.

"You might at least try it," began Bertha.

"Because your friend proposes it," said the other smiling. "I have no doubt that you, with nothing ailing you, would take all manner of drugs to please your knight; but with me the inducement is wanting, and therefore also the faith."

"I did not speak of any medicine," said Woislaw.

"Oh! a magical remedy! I am to be cured—what was it the quack who was here the other day called it?—'by sympathy.' Yes, that was it."

"I do not object to your calling it so, if you like," said Woislaw smiling; "but you must know, dear lady, that the measures I shall propose must be attended to literally, and according to the strictest directions."

"And you trust this to me?" asked Franziska.

"Certainly," said Woislaw hesitating; "but——"

"Well, why do you not proceed? Can you think that I shall fail in courage?" she asked.

"Courage is certainly necessary for the success of my plan," said Woislaw gravely; "and it is because I give you credit for a large share of that virtue, I venture to propose it at all, although for the real harmlessness of the remedy I will answer with my life, provided you follow my directions exactly."

"Well, tell me the plan, and then I can decide," said the young lady.

"I can only tell you that when we commence our operations," replied Woislaw.

"Do you think I am a child to be sent here, there, and everywhere, without a reason?" asked Franziska, with something of her old pettishness.

"You did me great injustice, dear lady, if you thought for a moment I would propose anything disagreeable to you, unless demanded by the sternest necessity," said Woislaw; "and yet I can only repeat my former words."

"Then I will not do it," cried Franziska. "I have already tried so much—and all ineffectually."

"I give you my honour as a knight, that your cure is certain, but you must pledge yourself solemnly and unconditionally to do implicitly what I shall direct," said Woislaw earnestly.

"Oh, I implore you to consent, Franziska. Our friend would not propose anything unnecessary," said Bertha, taking both her cousin's hands.

"And let me join my entreaties to Bertha's," said Franz.

"How strange you all are!" exclaimed Franziska, shaking her head; "You make such a secret of that which I must know if I am to accomplish it, and then you declare so positively that I shall recover, when my own feelings tell me it is quite hopeless."

"I repeat, that I will answer for the result," said Woislaw, "on the condition I mentioned before, and that you have courage to carry out what you commence."

"Ha! now I understand; this, after all, is the only thing which appears doubtful to you," cried Franziska. "Well, to show you that our sex are neither wanting in the will nor in the power to accomplish deeds of daring, I give my consent."

With the last words, she offered Woislaw her hand.

"Our compact is thus sealed," she pursued smiling. "Now say, Sir Knight, how am I to commence this mysterious cure?"

"It commenced when you gave your consent," said Woislaw gravely. "Now, I have only to request that you will ask no more questions, but hold yourself in readiness to take a ride with me tomorrow an hour before sunset. I also request that you will not mention to your father a word of what has passed."

"Strange!" said Franziska.

"You have made the compact; you are not wanting in resolution; and I will answer for everything else," said Woislaw encouragingly.

"Well, so let it be. I will follow your directions," said the lady, although she still looked incredulous.

"On our return you shall know everything; before that, it is quite impossible," said Woislaw in conclusion. "Now go, dear lady, and take some rest; you will need strength for tomorrow."

It was on the morning of the following day; the sun had not risen above an hour, and the dew still lay like a veil of pearls on the grass or dripped from the petals of the flowers swaying in the early breeze, when the knight Woislaw hastened over the fields towards the forest, and turned into a gloomy path, which by the direction one could perceive led towards the towers of Klatka. When he arrived at the old oak-tree we have before had occasion to mention, he sought carefully along the road for traces of human footsteps, but only a deer had passed that way. Seemingly satisfied with his search, he proceeded on his way, though not before he had half drawn his dagger from its sheath, as though to assure himself that it was ready for service in time of need.

Slowly he ascended the path; it was evident he carried something beneath his cloak. Arrived in the court, he left the ruins of the castle to the left, and entered the old chapel. In the chancel he looked eagerly and earnestly around. A deathlike stillness reigned in the deserted sanctuary, only broken by the whispering of the wind in an old thorn-tree which grew outside. Woislaw had looked round him ere he perceived the door leading down to the vault; he hurried towards it and descended. The sun's position enabled its rays to penetrate the crevices, and made the subterranean chamber so light that one could read easily the inscriptions at the head and feet of the coffins. The knight first laid on the ground the packet he had hitherto carried under his cloak, and then going from coffin to coffin, at last remained stationary before the oldest of them. He read the inscription carefully, drew his dagger thoughtfully from its case, and endeavoured to raise the lid with its point. This was no difficult matter, for the rusty iron nails kept but a slight hold of the rotten wood. On looking in, only a heap of ashes, some remnants of dress, and a skull were the contents. He quickly closed it again, and went on to the next, passing over those of a woman and two children. Here things had much the same appearance, except that the corpse held together till the lid was raised, and then fell into dust, a few linen rags and bones being alone perceptible. In the third, fourth, and nearly the next half-dozen, the bodies were in better preservation: in some, they looked a sort of yellow-brown mummy; whilst in others a skinless skull covered with hair grinned from the coverings of velvet, silk, or mildewed embroideries; all, however, were touched with the loathsome marks of decay. Only one more coffin now remained to be inspected; Woislaw approached it, and read the inscription. It was the same that had before attracted the Knight of Fahnenberg: Ezzelin von Klatka, the last possessor of the tower, was described as lying therein. Woislaw found it more difficult to raise the lid here; and it was only by the exertion of much strength that he at length succeeded in extracting the nails. He did all, however, as quietly as if afraid of rousing some sleeper within; he then raised the cover, and cast a glance on the corpse. An involuntary "Ha!" burst from his lips as he stepped back a pace. If he had less expected the sight that met his eyes, he would have been far more overcome. In the coffin lay Azzo as he lived and breathed, and as Woislaw had seen him at the supper-table only the evening before. His appearance, dress, and all were the same; besides, he had more the semblance of sleep than of death—no trace of decay was visible—there was even a rosy tint on his cheeks. Only the circumstance that the breast did not heave distinguished him from one who slept. For a few moments Woislaw did not move; he could only stare into the coffin. With a hastiness in his movements not usual with him, he suddenly seized the lid, which had fallen from his hands, and laying it on the coffin, knocked the nails into their places. As soon as he had completed this work, he fetched the packet he had left at the entrance, and laying it on the top of the coffin, hastily ascended the steps, and quitted the church and the ruins.

The day passed. Before evening, Franziska requested her father to allow her to take a ride with Woislaw, under pretense of showing him the country. He, only too happy to think this a sign of amendment in his daughter, readily gave his consent; so followed by a single servant, they mounted and left the castle. Woislaw was unusually silent and serious. When Franziska began to rally him about his gravity and the approaching sympathetic cure, he replied that what was before her was no laughing matter; and that although the result would be certainly a cure, still it would leave an impression on her whole future life. In such discourse they reached the wood, and at length the oak, where they left their horses. Woislaw gave Franziska his arm, and they ascended the hill slowly and silently. They had just reached one of the half-dilapidated outworks where they could catch a glimpse of the open country, when Woislaw, speaking more to himself than to his companion, said: "In a quarter of an hour, the sun will set, and in another hour the moon will have risen; then all must be accomplished. It will soon be time to commence the work."

"Then, I should think it was time to entrust me with some idea of what it is," said Franziska, looking at him.

"Well, my lady," he replied, turning towards her, and his voice was very solemn, "I entreat you, Franziska von Fahnenberg, for your own good, and as you love the father who clings to you with his whole soul, that you will weigh well my words, and that you will not interrupt me with questions which I cannot answer until the work is completed. Your life is in the greatest danger from the illness under which you are laboring; indeed, you are irrecoverably lost if you do not fully carry out what I shall now impart to you. Now, promise me to do implicitly as I shall tell you; I pledge you my knightly word it is nothing against Heaven, or the honour of your house; and, besides, it is the sole means for saving you." With these words, he held out his right hand to his companion, while he raised the other to heaven in confirmation of his oath.

"I promise you," said Franziska, visibly moved by Woislaw's solemn tone, as she laid her little white and wasted hand in his.

"Then, come; it is time," was his reply, as he led her towards the church. The last rays of the sun were just pouring through the broken windows. They entered the chancel, the best preserved part of the whole building; here there were still some old kneeling-stools, placed before the high altar, although nothing remained of that but the stonework and a few steps; the pictures and decorations had all vanished.

"Say an *Ave;* you will have need of it," said Woislaw, as he himself fell on his knees.

Franziska knelt beside him, and repeated a short prayer. After a few moments, both rose.

"The moment has arrived! The sun sinks, and before the moon rises, all must be over," said Woislaw quickly.

"What am I to do?" asked Franziska cheerfully.

"You see there that open vault!" replied the knight Woislaw, pointing to the door and flight of steps; "You must descend. You must go alone; I may not accompany you. When you have reached the vault you will find, close to the entrance, a coffin, on which is placed a small packet. Open this packet, and you will find three long iron nails and a hammer. Then pause for a moment; but when I begin to repeat the *Credo* in a loud voice, knock with all your might, first one nail, then a second, and then a third, into the lid of the coffin, right up to their heads."

Franziska stood thunderstruck; her whole body trembled, and she could not utter a word. Woislaw perceived it.

"Take courage, dear lady!" said he. "Think that you are in the hands of Heaven, and that, without the will of your Creator, not a hair can fall from your head. Besides, I repeat, there is no danger."

"Well, then, I will do it," cried Franziska, in some measure regaining courage.

"Whatever you may hear, whatever takes place inside the coffin," continued Woislaw, "must have no effect upon you. Drive the nails well in, without flinching: your work must be finished before my prayer comes to an end."

Franziska shuddered, but again recovered herself. "I will do it; Heaven will send me strength," she murmured softly.

"There is one thing more," said Woislaw hesitatingly; "perhaps it is the hardest of all I have proposed, but without it your cure will not be complete. When you have done as I have told you, a sort of"—he hesitated—"a sort of liquid will flow from the coffin; in this dip your finger, and besmear the scratch on your throat."

"Horrible!" cried Franziska. "This liquid is blood. A human being lies in the coffin."

"An *unearthly one* lies therein! That blood is your own, but it flows in other veins," said Woislaw gloomily. "Ask no more; the sand is running out."

Franziska summoned up all her powers of mind and body, went towards the steps which led to the vault, and Woislaw sank on his knees before the altar in quiet prayer. When the lady had descended, she found herself before the coffin on which lay the packet before mentioned. A sort of twilight reigned in the vault, and everything around was so still and peaceful, that she felt more calm, and going up to the coffin, opened the packet. She had hardly seen that a hammer and three long nails were its contents when suddenly Woislaw's voice rang through the church, and broke the stillness of the aisles. Franziska started, but recognized the appointed prayer. She seized one of the nails, and with one stroke of the hammer drove it at least an inch into the cover. All was still; nothing was heard but the echo of the stroke. Taking heart, the maiden grasped the hammer with both hands, and struck the nail twice with all her might, right up to the head into the wood. At this moment commenced a rustling noise; it seemed as though something in the interior began to move and to struggle. Franziska drew back in alarm. She was already on the point of throwing away the hammer and flying up the steps, when Woislaw raised his voice so powerfully, and so entreatingly, that in a sort of excitement, such as would induce one to rush into a lion's den, she returned to the coffin, determined to bring things to a conclusion. Hardly knowing what she did, she placed a second nail in the centre of the lid, and after some strokes this was likewise buried to its head. The struggle now increased fearfully, as if some living creature were striving to burst the coffin. This was so shaken by it, that it cracked and split on all sides. Half distracted, Franziska seized the third nail; she thought no more of her ailments, she only knew herself to be in terrible danger, of what kind she could not guess: in an agony that threatened to rob her of her senses and in the midst of the turning and cracking of the coffin, in which low groans were now heard, she struck the third nail in equally tight. At this moment, she began to lose consciousness. She wished to hasten away, but staggered; and mechanically grasping at something to save herself by, seized the corner of the coffin, and sank fainting beside it on the ground.

A quarter of an hour might have elapsed when she again opened her eyes. She looked around her. Above was the starry sky, and the moon, which shed her cold light on the ruins and on the tops of the old oak-trees. Franziska was lying outside the church walls, Woislaw on his knees beside her, holding her hand in his.

"Heaven be praised that you live!" he cried, with a sigh of relief. "I was beginning to doubt whether the remedy had not been too severe, and yet it was the only thing to save you."

Franziska recovered her full consciousness very gradually. The past seemed to her like a dreadful dream. Only a few moments before, that fearful scene; and now this quiet all around her. She hardly dared at first to raise her eyes, and shuddered when she found herself only a few paces removed from the spot where she had undergone such terrible agony. She listened half unconsciously, now to the pacifying words Woislaw addressed to her, now to the whistling of the servant, who stood by the horses, and who, to while away his time, was imitating the evening-song of a belated cowherd.

"Let us go," whispered Franziska, as she strove to raise herself. "But what is this? My shoulder is wet, my throat, my hand——"

"It is probably the evening dew on the grass," said Woislaw gently.

"No; it is blood!" she cried, springing up with horror in her tone. "See, my hand is full of blood!"

"Oh, you are mistaken—surely mistaken," said Woislaw, stammering. "Or perhaps the wound on your neck may have opened! Pray, feel whether this is the case." He seized her hand and directed it to the spot.

"I do not perceive anything; I feel no pain," she said at length, somewhat angrily.

"Then, perhaps, when you fainted you may have struck a corner of the coffin, or have torn yourself with the point of one of the nails," suggested Woislaw.

"Oh, of what do you remind me!" cried Franziska shuddering. "Let us away—away! I entreat you, come! I will not remain a moment longer near this dreadful, dreadful place."

They descended the path much quicker than they came. Woislaw placed his companion on her horse, and they were soon on their way home.

When they approached the castle, Franziska began to inundate her protector with questions about the preceding adventure; but he declared that her present state of excitement must make him defer all explanations till the morning, when her curiosity should be satisfied. On their arrival, he conducted her at once to her room, and told the knight his daughter was too much fatigued with her ride to appear at the supper-table. On the following morning, Franziska rose earlier than she had done for a long time. She assured her friend it was the first time since her illness commenced that she had been really refreshed by her sleep, and, what was still more remarkable, she had not been troubled by her old terrible dream. Her improved looks were not only remarked by Bertha, but by Franz and the knight; and with Woislaw's permission, she related the adventures of the previous evening. No sooner had she concluded, than Woislaw was completely stormed with questions about such a strange occurrence.

"Have you," said the latter, turning towards his host, "ever heard of Vampires?"

"Often," replied he; "but I have never believed in them."

"Nor did I," said Woislaw; "but I have been assured of their existence by experience."

"Oh, tell us what occurred," cried Bertha eagerly, as a light seemed to dawn on her.

"It was during my first campaign in Hungary," began Woislaw, "when I was rendered helpless for some time by this sword-cut of a janizary across my face, and another on my shoulder. I had been taken into the house of a respectable family in a small town. It consisted of the father and mother, and a daughter about twenty years of age. They obtained their living by selling the very good wine of the country, and the taproom was always full of visitors. Although the family were well-to-do in the world, there seemed to brood over them a continual melancholy, caused by the constant illness of the only daughter, a very pretty and excellent girl. She had always bloomed like a rose, but for some months she had been getting so thin and wasted, and that without any satisfactory reason: they tried every means to restore her, but in vain. As the army had encamped quite in the neighbourhood, of course a number of people of all countries assembled in the tavern. Amongst these there was one man who came every evening, when the moon shone, who struck everybody by the peculiarity of his manners and appearance; he looked dried up and deathlike, and hardly spoke at all; but what he did say was bitter and sarcastic. Most attention was excited towards him by the circumstance, that although he always ordered a cup of the best wine, and now and then raised it to his lips, the cup was always as full after his departure as at first."

"This all agrees wonderfully with the appearance of Azzo," said Bertha, deeply interested.

"The daughter of the house," continued Woislaw, "became daily worse, despite the aid not only of Christian doctors, but of many amongst the heathen prisoners, who were consulted in the hope that they might have some magical remedy to propose. It was singular that the girl always complained of a dream, in which the unknown guest worried and plagued her."

"Just the same as your dream, Franziska," cried Bertha.

"One evening," resumed Woislaw, "an old Sclavonian—who had made many voyages to Turkey and Greece, and had even seen the New World—and I were sitting over our wine, when the stranger entered, and sat down at the table. The bottle passed quickly between my friend and me, whilst we talked of all manner of things, of our adventures, and of passages in our lives, both horrible and amusing. We went on chatting thus for about an hour, and drank a tolerable quantity of wine. The unknown had remained perfectly silent the whole time, only smiling contemptuously every now and then. He now paid his money, and was going away. All this had quietly worried me—perhaps the wine had gotten a little into my head—so I said to the stranger: 'Hold, you stony stranger; you have hitherto done nothing but listen, and have not even emptied your cup. Now you shall take your turn in telling us something amusing, and if you do not drink up your wine, it shall produce a quarrel between us.' 'Yes,' said the Sclavonian, 'you must remain; you shall chat and drink, too'; and he grasped—for although no longer young, he was big and very strong—the stranger by the shoulder, to pull him down to his seat again: the latter, however, although as thin as a skeleton, with one movement of his hand flung the Sclavonian to the middle of the room, and half stunned him for a moment. I now approached to hold the stranger back. I caught him by the arm; and although the springs of my iron hand were less powerful than those I have at present, I must have gripped him rather hard in my anger, for after looking grimly at me for a moment, he bent towards me and whispered in my ear: 'Let me go: from the grip of your fist, I see you are my brother, therefore do not hinder me from seeking my bloody nourishment. I am hungry!' Surprised by such words, I let him loose, and almost before I was aware of it, he had left the room. As soon as I had in some degree recovered from my astonishment, I told the Sclavonian what I had heard. He started, evidently alarmed. I asked him to tell me the cause of his fears, and pressed him for an explanation of those extraordinary words. On our way to his lodging, he complied with my request. 'The stranger,' said he, 'is a Vampire!' "

"How?" cried the knight, Franziska, and Bertha simultaneously, in a voice of horror. "So this Azzo was——"

"Nothing less. He also was a Vampire!" replied Woislaw. "But at all events *his* hellish thirst is quenched for ever; he will never return. But I have not finished. As in my country Vampires had never been heard of, I questioned the Sclavonian minutely. He said that in Hungary, Croatia, Dalmatia, and Bosnia, these hellish guests were not uncommon. They were deceased persons, who had either once served as nourishment to Vampires, or who had died in deadly sin, or under excommunication; and that whenever the moon shone, they rose from their graves, and sucked the blood of the living."

"Horrible!" cried Franziska. "If you had told me all this beforehand, I should never have accomplished the work."

"So I thought; and yet it must be executed by the sufferers themselves, while someone else performs the devotions," replied Woislaw. "The Sclavonian," he continued after a short pause, "added many other facts with regard to these unearthly visitants. He said that whilst their victim wasted, they themselves improved in appearance, and that a Vampire possessed enormous strength——"

"Now I can understand the change your false hand produced on Azzo," interrupted Franz.

"Yes, that was it," replied Woislaw. "Azzo, as well as the other Vampire, mistook its great power for that of a natural one, and concluded I was one of his own species. You may now imagine, dear lady," he continued, turning to Franziska, "how alarmed I was at your appearance when I arrived: all you and Bertha told me increased my anxiety; and when I saw Azzo, I could doubt no longer that he was a Vampire. As I learned from your account that a grave with the name Ezzelin von Klatka lay in the neighbourhood, I had no doubt that you might be saved if I could only induce you to assist me. It did not appear to me advisable to impart the whole facts of the case, for your bodily powers were so impaired, that an idea of the horrors before you might have quite unfitted you for the exertion; for this reason, I arranged everything in the manner in which it has taken place."

"You did wisely," replied Franziska shuddering. "I can never be grateful enough to you. Had I known what was required of me, I never could have undertaken the deed."

"That was what I feared," said Woislaw; "but fortune has favored us all through."

"And what became of the unfortunate girl in Hungary?" inquired Bertha.

"I know not," replied Woislaw. "That very evening there was an alarm of Turks, and we were ordered off. I never heard anything more of her."

The conversation upon these strange occurrences continued for some time longer. The knight determined to have the vault at Klatka walled up for ever. This took place on the following day; the knight alleging as a reason that he did not wish the dead to be disturbed by irreverent hands.

Franziska recovered gradually. Her health had been so severely shaken, that it was long ere her strength was so much restored as to allow of her being considered out of danger. The young lady's character underwent a great change in the interval. Its former strength was, perhaps, in some degree diminished, but in place of that, she had acquired a benevolent softness, which brought out all her best qualities. Franz continued his attentions to his cousin; but, perhaps owing to a hint from Bertha, he was less assiduous in his exhibition of them. His inclinations did not lead him to the battle, the camp, or the attainment of honours; his great aim was to increase the good condition and happiness of his tenants; and to this he contributed the whole energy of his mind. Franziska could not withstand the unobtrusive signs of the young man's continued attachment; and it was not long ere the credit she was obliged to yield to his noble efforts for the welfare of his fellow-creatures, changed into a liking, which went on increasing, until at length it assumed the character of love. As Woislaw insisted on making Bertha his wife before he returned to Silesia, it was arranged that the marriage should take place at their present abode. How joyful was the surprise of the Knight of Fahnenberg, when his daughter and Franz likewise entreated his blessing, and expressed their desire of being united on the same day! That day soon came round, and it saw the bright looks of two happy couples.

JOSEPH SHERIDAN LE FANU *(1814–1873), a grandnephew of Richard Brinsley Sheridan, was born in Dublin and educated at Trinity College. He edited several newspapers during his life and, most notably, the* Dublin University Magazine, *in which he published, often anonymously, most of his short fiction. After the death of his wife in 1858, Le Fanu became rather a recluse, writing ghost and horror stories in bed. He died in his Dublin home, which can be visited today in Merrion Square, of a heart attack in 1873.*

Le Fanu was a prolific and popular novelist. Uncle Silas *(1864) is regarded as his masterpiece. Among his other novels, many of which are still widely read, are* Wylder's Hand *(1864) and* Guy Deverell *(1865).*

As is the case with many authors included in this volume, Le Fanu's lasting reputation rests on his short fiction, most of which was rescued from obscurity and published early in this century by British author and scholar M. R. James. Several of Le Fanu's stories are classics of supernatural fiction, among them "Schalken the Painter," and "Green Tea," described by English author V. S. Pritchett as among "the best half-dozen ghost stories in the English language."

Nothing in Le Fanu's work, however, is as famous as "Carmilla," which is not only one of the best, but one of the most seminal stories in all vampire literature, and Bram Stoker admitted its influence on Dracula.

"Carmilla" deals openly, using both subtlety and gruesomeness, with the sexual content of the vampire myth. It provides unforgettably chilling scenes and compels the reader to return again and again to its mysteries. In 1970 it was filmed as The Vampire Lovers, *but there is nothing quite like Le Fanu's "Carmilla" itself.*

Carmilla (1872)

BY J. SHERIDAN LE FANU

PROLOGUE

Upon a paper attached to the Narrative which follows, Doctor Hesselius has written a rather elaborate note, which he accompanies with a reference to his Essay on the strange subject which the MS. illuminates.

This mysterious subject he treats, in that Essay, with his usual learning and acumen, and with remarkable directness and condensation. It will form but one volume of the series of that extraordinary man's collected papers.

As I publish the case, in this volume, simply to interest the "laity," I shall forestall the intelligent lady, who relates it, in nothing; and after due consideration, I have determined, therefore, to abstain from presenting any *précis* of the learned Doctor's reasoning, or extract from his statement on a subject which he describes as "involving, not improbably, some of the profoundest arcana of our dual existence, and its intermediates."

I was anxious on discovering this paper, to reopen the correspondence commenced by Doctor Hesselius, so many years before, with a person so clever and careful as his informant seems to have been. Much to my regret, however, I found that she had died in the interval.

She, probably, could have added little to the Narrative which she communicates in the following pages, with, so far as I can pronounce, such a conscientious particularity.

CHAPTER I

An Early Fright

In Styria, we, though by no means magnificent people, inhabit a castle, or schloss. A small income, in that part of the world, goes a great way. Eight or nine hundred a year does wonders. Scantily enough ours would have answered among wealthy people at home. My father is English, and I bear an English name, although I never saw England. But here, in this lonely and primitive place, where everything is so marvelously cheap, I really don't see how ever so much more money would at all materially add to our comforts, or even luxuries.

My father was in the Austrian service, and retired upon a pension and his patrimony, and purchased this feudal residence, and the small estate on which it stands, a bargain.

Nothing can be more picturesque or solitary. It stands on a slight eminence in a forest. The road, very old and narrow, passes in front of its drawbridge, never raised in my time, and its moat, stocked with perch, and sailed over by many swans, and floating on its surface white fleets of water-lilies.

Over all this the schloss shows its many-windowed front, its towers, and its Gothic chapel.

The forest opens in an irregular and very picturesque glade before its gate, and at the right a steep Gothic bridge carries the road over a stream that winds in deep shadow through the wood.

I have said that this is a very lonely place. Judge whether I say truth. Looking from the hall door towards the road, the forest in which our castle stands extends fifteen miles to the right, and twelve to the left. The nearest inhabited village is about seven of your English miles to the left. The nearest inhabited schloss of any historic associations, is that of old General Spielsdorf, nearly twenty miles away to the right.

I have said "the nearest *inhabited* village," because there is, only three miles westward, that is to say in the direction of General Spielsdorf's schloss, a ruined village, with its quaint little church, now roofless, in the aisle of which are the mouldering tombs of the proud family of Karnstein, now extinct, who once owned the equally-desolate château which, in the thick of the forest, overlooks the silent ruins of the town.

Respecting the cause of the desertion of this striking and melancholy spot, there is a legend which I shall relate to you another time.

I must tell you now, how very small is the party who constitute the inhabitants of our castle. I don't include servants, or those dependents who occupy rooms in the buildings attached to the schloss. Listen, and wonder! My father, who is the kindest man on earth, but growing old; and I, at the date of my story, only nineteen. Eight years have passed since then. I and my father constituted the family at the schloss. My mother, a Styrian lady, died in my infancy, but I had a good-natured governess, who had been with me from, I might almost say, my infancy. I could not remember the time when her fat, benignant face was not a familiar picture in my memory. This was Madame Perrodon, a native of Berne, whose care and good nature in part supplied to me the loss of my mother, whom I do not even remember, so early I lost her. She made a third at our little dinner party. There was a fourth, Mademoiselle De Lafontaine, a lady such as you term, I believe, a "finishing governess." She spoke French and German, Madame Perrodon French and broken English, to which my father and I added English, which, partly to prevent its becoming a lost language among us, and partly from patriotic motives, we spoke every day. The consequence was a Babel, at which strangers used to laugh, and which I shall make no attempt to reproduce in this narrative. And there were two or three young lady friends besides, pretty nearly of my own age, who were occasional visitors, for longer or shorter terms; and these visits I sometimes returned.

These were our regular social resources; but of course there were chance visits from "neighbours" of only five or six leagues' distance. My life was, notwithstanding, rather a solitary one, I can assure you.

My gouvernantes had just so much control over me as you might conjecture such sage persons would have in this case of a rather spoiled girl, whose only parent allowed her pretty nearly her own way in everything.

The first occurrence in my existence, which produced a terrible impression upon my mind, which, in fact, never has been effaced, was one of the very earliest incidents of my life which I can recollect. Some people will think it so trifling that it should not be recorded here. You will see, however, by-and-by, why I mention it. The nursery, as it was called, though I had it all to myself, was a large room in the upper story of the castle, with a steep oak roof. I can't have been more than six years old, when one night I awoke, and looking round the room from my bed, failed to see the nursery-maid. Neither was my nurse there; and I thought myself alone. I was not frightened, for I was one of those happy children who are studiously kept in ignorance of ghost stories, of fairy tales, and of all such lore as makes us cover up our heads when the door creaks suddenly, or the flicker of an expiring candle makes the shadow of a bed-post dance upon the wall, nearer to our faces. I was vexed and insulted at finding myself, as I conceived, neglected, and I began to whimper, preparatory to a hearty bout of roaring; when to my surprise, I saw a solemn, but very pretty face looking at me from the side of the bed. It was that of a young lady who was kneeling, with her hands under the coverlet. I looked at her with a kind of pleased wonder, and ceased whimpering. She caressed me with her hands, and lay down beside me on the bed, and drew me towards her, smiling; I felt immediately delightfully soothed, and fell asleep again. I was wakened by a sensation as if two needles ran into my breast very deep at the same moment, and I cried loudly. The lady started back, with her eyes fixed on me, and then slipped down upon the floor, and, as I thought, hid herself under the bed.

I was now for the first time frightened, and I yelled with all my might and main. Nurse, nursery-maid, housekeeper, all came running in, and hearing my story, they made light of it, soothing me all they could meanwhile. But, child as I was, I could perceive that their faces were pale with an unwonted look of anxiety, and I saw them look under the bed, and about the room, and peep under tables and pluck open cupboards; and the housekeeper whispered to the nurse; "Lay your hand along that hollow in the bed; some one *did* lie there, so sure as you did not; the place is still warm."

I remember the nursery-maid petting me, and all three examining my chest, where I told them I felt the puncture, and pronouncing that there was no sign visible that any such thing had happened to me.

The housekeeper and the two other servants who were in charge of the nursery, remained sitting up all night; and from that time a servant always sat up in the nursery until I was about fourteen.

I was very nervous for a long time after this. A doctor was called in, he was pallid and elderly. How well I remember his long saturnine face, pitted with small-pox, and his chestnut wig. For a good while, every second day, he came and gave me medicine, which of course I hated.

The morning after I saw this apparition I was in a state of terror, and could not bear to be left alone, daylight though it was, for a moment.

I remember my father coming up and standing at the bedside, and talking cheerfully, and asking the nurse a number of questions, and laughing very heartily at one of the answers; and patting me on the shoulder, and kissing me, and telling me not to be frightened, that it was nothing but a dream and could not hurt me.

But I was not comforted, for I knew the visit of the strange woman was *not* a dream; and I was *awfully* frightened.

I was a little consoled by the nursery-maid's assuring me that it was she who had come and looked at me, and lain down beside me in the bed, and that I must have been half-dreaming not to have known her face. But this, though supported by the nurse, did not quite satisfy me.

I remember, in the course of that day, a venerable old man, in a black cassock, coming into the room with the nurse and housekeeper, and talking a little to them, and very kindly to me; his face was very sweet and gentle, and he told me they were going to pray, and joined my hands together, and desired me to say, softly, while they were praying, "Lord, hear all good prayers for us, for Jesus' sake." I think these were the very words, for I often repeated them to myself, and my nurse used for years to make me say them in my prayers.

I remember so well the thoughtful sweet face of that white-haired old man, in his black cassock, as he stood in that rude, lofty, brown room, with the clumsy furniture of a fashion three hundred years old, about him, and the scanty light entering its shadowy atmosphere through the small lattice. He kneeled, and the three women with him, and he prayed aloud with an earnest quavering voice for, what appeared to me, a long time. I forget all my life preceding that event, and for some time after it is all obscure also; but the scenes I have just described stand out vivid as the isolated pictures of the phantasmagoria surrounded by darkness.

CHAPTER II

A Guest

I am now going to tell you something so strange that it will require all your faith in my veracity to believe my story. It is not only true, nevertheless, but truth of which I have been an eyewitness.

It was a sweet summer evening, and my father asked me, as he sometimes did, to take a little ramble with him along that beautiful forest vista which I have mentioned as lying in front of the schloss.

"General Spielsdorf cannot come to us so soon as I had hoped," said my father, as we pursued our walk.

He was to have paid us a visit of some weeks, and we had expected his arrival next day. He was to have brought with him a young lady, his niece and ward, Mademoiselle Rheinfeldt, whom I had never seen, but whom I had heard described as a very charming girl, and in whose society I had promised myself many happy days. I was more disappointed than a young lady living in a town, or a bustling neighbourhood can possibly imagine. This visit, and the new acquaintance it promised, had furnished my day dream for many weeks.

"And how soon does he come?" I asked.

"Not till autumn. Not for two months, I dare say," he answered. "And I am very glad now, dear, that you never knew Mademoiselle Rheinfeldt."

"And why?" I asked, both mortified and curious.

"Because the poor young lady is dead," he replied. "I quite forgot I had not told you, but you were not in the room when I received the General's letter this evening."

I was very much shocked. General Spielsdorf had mentioned in his first letter, six or seven weeks before, that she was not so well as he would wish her, but there was nothing to suggest the remotest suspicion of danger.

"Here is the General's letter," he said, handing it to me. "I am afraid he is in great affliction; the letter appears to me to have been written very nearly in distraction."

We sat down on a rude bench, under a group of magnificent lime trees. The sun was setting with all its melancholy splendour behind the sylvan horizon, and the stream that flows beside our home, and passes under the steep old bridge I have mentioned, wound through many a group of noble trees, almost at our feet, reflecting in its current the fading crimson of the sky. General Spielsdorf's letter was extraordinary, so vehement, and in some places so self-contradictory, that I read it twice over—the second time aloud to my father—and was still unable to account for it, except by supposing that grief had unsettled his mind.

It said, "I have lost my darling daughter, for as such I loved her. During the last days of dear Bertha's illness I was not able to write to you. Before then I had no idea of her danger. I have lost her, and now learn *all,* too late. She died in the peace of innocence and in the glorious hope of a blessed futurity. The fiend who betrayed our infatuated hospitality has done it all. I thought I was receiving into my house innocence, gaiety, a charming companion for my lost Bertha. Heavens! what a fool I have been! I thank God my child died without a suspicion of the cause of her sufferings. She is gone without so much as conjecturing the nature of her illness, and the accursed passion of the agent of all this misery. I devote my remaining days to tracking and extinguishing a monster. I am told I may hope to accomplish my righteous and merciful purpose. At present there is scarcely a gleam of light to guide me. I curse my conceited incredulity, my despicable affectation of superiority, my blindness, my obstinacy—all—too late. I cannot write or talk collectedly now. I am distracted. So soon as I shall have a little recovered, I mean to devote myself for a time to inquiry, which may possibly lead me as far as Vienna. Some time in the autumn, two months hence, or earlier if I live, I will see you—that is, if you permit me; I will then tell you all that I scarce dare put upon paper now. Farewell. Pray for me, dear friend."

In these terms ended this strange letter. Though I had never seen Bertha Rheinfeldt, my eyes filled with tears at the sudden intelligence; I was startled, as well as profoundly disappointed.

The sun had now set, and it was twilight by the time I had returned the General's letter to my father.

It was a soft clear evening, and we loitered, speculating upon the possible meanings of the violent and incoherent sentences which I had just been reading. We had nearly a mile to walk before reaching the road that passes the schloss in front, and by that time the moon was shining brilliantly. At the drawbridge we met Madame Perrodon and Mademoiselle De Lafontaine, who had come out, without their bonnets, to enjoy the exquisite moonlight.

We heard their voices gabbling in animated dialogue as we approached. We joined them at the drawbridge, and turned about to admire with them the beautiful scene.

The glade through which we had just walked lay before us. At our left the narrow road wound away under clumps of lordly trees, and was lost to sight amid the thickening forest. At the right the same road crosses the steep and picturesque bridge, near which stands a ruined tower, which once guarded that pass; and beyond the bridge an abrupt eminence rises, covered with trees, and showing in the shadow some grey ivy-clustered rocks.

Over the sward and low grounds, a thin film of mist was stealing, like smoke, marking the distances with a transparent veil; and here and there we could see the river faintly flashing in the moonlight.

No softer, sweeter scene could be imagined. The news I had just heard made it melancholy; but nothing could disturb its character of profound serenity, and the enchanted glory and vagueness of the prospect.

My father, who enjoyed the picturesque, and I, stood looking in silence over the expanse beneath us. The two good governesses, standing a little way behind us, discoursed upon the scene, and were eloquent upon the moon.

Madame Perrodon was fat, middle-aged, and romantic, and talked and sighed poetically. Mademoiselle De Lafontaine—in right of her father, who was a German, assumed to be psychological, metaphysical, and something of a mystic—now declared that when the moon shone with a light so intense it was well known that it indicated a special spiritual activity. The effect of the full moon in such a state of brilliancy was manifold. It acted on dreams, it acted on lunacy, it acted on nervous people; it had marvellous physical influences connected with life. Mademoiselle related that her cousin, who was mate of a merchant ship, having taken a nap on deck on such a night, lying on his back, with his face full in the light of the moon, had wakened, after a dream of an old woman clawing him by the cheek, with his features horribly drawn to one side; and his countenance had never quite recovered its equilibrium.

"The moon, this night," she said, "is full of odylic and magnetic influence—and see, when you look behind you at the front of the schloss, how all its windows flash and twinkle with that silvery splendour, as if unseen hands had lighted up the rooms to receive fairy guests."

There are indolent states of the spirits in which, indisposed to talk ourselves, the talk of others is pleasant to our listless ears; and I gazed on, pleased with the tinkle of the ladies' conversation.

"I have got into one of my moping moods tonight," said my father, after a silence, and quoting Shakespeare, whom, by way of keeping up our English, he used to read aloud, he said:—

> In truth I know not why I am so sad:
> It wearies me; you say it wearies you;
> But how I got it—came by it.

"I forget the rest. But I feel as if some great misfortune were hanging over us. I suppose the poor general's afflicted letter has had something to do with it."

At this moment the unwonted sound of carriage wheels and many hoofs upon the road, arrested our attention.

They seemed to be approaching from the high ground overlooking the bridge, and very soon the equipage emerged from that point. Two horsemen first crossed the bridge, then came a carriage drawn by four horses, and two men rode behind.

It seemed to be the travelling carriage of a person of rank; and we were all immediately absorbed in watching that very unusual spectacle. It became, in a few moments, greatly more interesting, for just as the carriage had passed the summit of the steep bridge, one of the leaders, taking fright, communicated his panic to the rest, and, after a plunge or two, the whole team broke into a wild gallop together, and dashing between the horsemen who rode in front, came thundering along the road towards us with the speed of a hurricane.

The excitement of the scene was made more painful by the clear, long-drawn screams of a female voice from the carriage window.

We all advanced in curiosity and horror; my father in silence, the rest with various ejaculations of terror.

Our suspense did not last long. Just before you reach the castle

drawbridge, on the route they were coming, there stands by the road-
side a magnificent lime tree, on the other side stands an ancient stone
cross, at sight of which the horses, now going at a pace that was perfectly frightful, swerved so as to bring the wheel over the projecting
roots of the tree.

I knew what was coming. I covered my eyes, unable to see it out,
and turned my head away; at the same moment I heard a cry from my
lady-friends, who had gone on a little.

Curiosity opened my eyes, and I saw a scene of utter confusion.
Two of the horses were on the ground, the carriage lay upon its side,
with two wheels in the air; the men were busy removing the traces, and
a lady, with a commanding air and figure had got out, and stood with
clasped hands, raising the handkerchief that was in them every now and
then to her eyes. Through the carriage door was now lifted a young
lady, who appeared to be lifeless. My dear old father was already beside
the elder lady, with his hat in his hand, evidently tendering his aid and
the resources of his schloss. The lady did not appear to hear him, or to
have eyes for anything but the slender girl who was being placed against
the slope of the bank.

I approached; the young lady was apparently stunned, but she was
certainly not dead. My father, who piqued himself on being something
of a physician, had just had his fingers to her wrist and assured the lady,
who declared herself her mother, that her pulse, though faint and irregular, was undoubtedly still distinguishable. The lady clasped her hands
and looked upward, as if in a momentary transport of gratitude; but
immediately she broke out again in that theatrical way which is, I
believe, natural to some people.

She was what is called a fine-looking woman for her time of life,
and must have been handsome; she was tall, but not thin, and dressed in
black velvet, and looked rather pale, but with a proud and commanding
countenance, though now agitated strangely.

"Was ever being so born to calamity?" I heard her say, with
clasped hands, as I came up. "Here am I, on a journey of life and death,
in prosecuting which to lose an hour is possibly to lose all. My child will
not have recovered sufficiently to resume her route for who can say how
long. I must leave her; I cannot, dare not, delay. How far on, sir, can
you tell, is the nearest village? I must leave her there; and shall not see
my darling, or even hear of her till my return, three months hence."

I plucked my father by the coat, and whispered earnestly in his ear,

"Oh! papa; pray ask her to let her stay with us—it would be so delightful. Do, pray."

"If Madame will entrust her child to the care of my daughter, and of her good gouvernante, Madame Perrodon, and permit her to remain as our guest, under my charge, until her return, it will confer a distinction and an obligation upon us, and we shall treat her with all the care and devotion which so sacred a trust deserves."

"I cannot do that, sir, it would be to task your kindness and chivalry too cruelly," said the lady, distractedly.

"It would, on the contrary, be to confer on us a very great kindness at the moment when we most need it. My daughter has just been disappointed by a cruel misfortune, in a visit from which she had long anticipated a great deal of happiness. If you confide this young lady to our care it will be her best consolation. The nearest village on your route is distant, and affords no such inn as you could think of placing your daughter at; you cannot allow her to continue her journey for any considerable distance without danger. If, as you say, you cannot suspend your journey, you must part with her to-night, and nowhere could you do so with more honest assurances of care and tenderness than here."

There was something in this lady's air and appearance so distinguished, and even imposing, and in her manner so engaging, as to impress one, quite apart from the dignity of her equipage, with a conviction that she was a person of consequence.

By this time the carriage was replaced in its upright position, and the horses, quite tractable, in the traces again.

The lady threw on her daughter a glance which I fancied was not quite so affectionate as one might have anticipated from the beginning of the scene; then she beckoned slightly to my father, and withdrew two or three steps with him out of hearing; and talked to him with a fixed and stern countenance, not at all like that with which she had hitherto spoken.

I was filled with wonder that my father did not seem to perceive the change, and also unspeakably curious to learn what it could be that she was speaking, almost in his ear, with so much earnestness and rapidity.

Two or three minutes at most, I think, she remained thus employed, then she turned, and a few steps brought her to where her daughter lay, supported by Madame Perrodon. She kneeled beside her for a moment and whispered, as Madame supposed, a little benediction

in her ear; then hastily kissing her, she stepped into her carriage, the
door was closed, the footmen in stately liveries jumped up behind, the
outriders spurred on, the postilions cracked their whips, the horses
plunged and broke suddenly into a furious canter that threatened soon
again to become a gallop, and the carriage whirled away, followed at
the same rapid pace by the two horsemen in the rear.

CHAPTER III

We Compare Notes

We followed the *cortège* with our eyes until it was swiftly lost to sight in
the misty wood; and the very sound of the hoofs and wheels died away
in the silent night air.

Nothing remained to assure us that the adventure had not been an
illusion of a moment but the young lady, who just at that moment
opened her eyes. I could not see, for her face was turned from me, but
she raised her head, evidently looking about her, and I heard a very
sweet voice ask complainingly, "Where is mamma?"

Our good Madame Perrodon answered tenderly, and added some
comfortable assurances.

I then heard her ask:

"Where am I? What is this place?" and after that she said, "I don't
see the carriage; and Matska, where is she?"

Madame answered all her questions in so far as she understood
them; and gradually the young lady remembered how the misadventure
came about, and was glad to hear that no one in, or in attendance on,
the carriage was hurt; and on learning that her mamma had left her
here, till her return in about three months, she wept.

I was going to add my consolations to those of Madame Perrodon
when Mademoiselle De Lafontaine placed her hand upon my arm, saying:

"Don't approach, one at a time is as much as she can at present
converse with; a very little excitement would possibly overpower her
now."

As soon as she is comfortably in bed, I thought, I will run up to her
room and see her.

My father in the meantime had sent a servant on horseback for the physician, who lived about two leagues away; and a bedroom was being prepared for the young lady's reception.

The stranger now rose, and leaning on Madame's arm, walked slowly over the drawbridge and into the castle gate.

In the hall, servants waited to receive her, and she was conducted forthwith to her room.

The room we usually sat in as our drawing-room is long, having four windows, that looked over the moat and drawbridge, upon the forest scene I have just described.

It is furnished in old carved oak, with large carved cabinets, and the chairs are cushioned with crimson Utrecht velvet. The walls are covered with tapestry, and surrounded with great gold frames, the figures being as large as life, in ancient and very curious costume, and the subjects represented are hunting, hawking, and generally festive. It is not too stately to be extremely comfortable; and here we had our tea, for with his usual patriotic leanings he insisted that the national beverage should make its appearance regularly with our coffee and chocolate.

We sat here this night, and with candles lighted, were talking over the adventure of the evening.

Madame Perrodon and Mademoiselle De Lafontaine were both of our party. The young stranger had hardly lain down in her bed when she sank into a deep sleep; and those ladies had left her in the care of a servant.

"How do you like our guest?" I asked, as soon as Madame entered. "Tell me all about her?"

"I like her extremely," answered Madame, "she is, I almost think, the prettiest creature I ever saw; about your age, and so gentle and nice."

"She is absolutely beautiful," threw in Mademoiselle, who had peeped for a moment into the stranger's room.

"And such a sweet voice!" added Madame Perrodon.

"Did you remark a woman in the carriage, after it was set up again, who did not get out," inquired Mademoiselle, "but only looked from the window?"

No, we had not seen her.

Then she described a hideous black woman, with a sort of coloured turban on her head, who was gazing all the time from the carriage window, nodding and grinning derisively towards the ladies, with gleaming eyes and large white eye-balls, and her teeth set as if in fury.

"Did you remark what an ill-looking pack of men the servants were?" asked Madame.

"Yes," said my father, who had just come in, "ugly, hang-dog looking fellows, as ever I beheld in my life. I hope they mayn't rob the poor lady in the forest. They are clever rogues, however; they got everything to rights in a minute."

"I dare say they are worn out with too long travelling," said Madame. "Besides looking wicked, their faces were so strangely lean, and dark, and sullen. I am very curious, I own; but I dare say the young lady will tell us all about it to-morrow, if she is sufficiently recovered."

"I don't think she will," said my father, with a mysterious smile, and a little nod of his head, as if he knew more about it than he cared to tell us.

This made me all the more inquisitive as to what had passed between him and the lady in the black velvet, in the brief but earnest interview that had immediately preceded her departure.

We were scarcely alone, when I entreated him to tell me. He did not need much pressing.

"There is no particular reason why I should not tell you. She expressed a reluctance to trouble us with the care of her daughter, saying she was in delicate health, and nervous, but not subject to any kind of seizure—she volunteered that—nor to any illusion; being, in fact, perfectly sane."

"How very odd to say all that!" I interpolated. "It was so unnecessary."

"At all events it *was* said," he laughed, "and as you wish to know all that passed, which was indeed very little, I tell you. She then said, 'I am making a long journey of *vital* importance'—she emphasized the word—'rapid and secret; I shall return for my child in three months; in the meantime, she will be silent as to who we are, whence we come, and whither we are travelling.' That is all she said. She spoke very pure French. When she said the word 'secret,' she paused for a few seconds, looking sternly, her eyes fixed on mine. I fancy she makes a great point of that. You saw how quickly she was gone. I hope I have not done a very foolish thing, in taking charge of the young lady."

For my part, I was delighted. I was longing to see and talk to her; and only waiting till the doctor should give me leave. You, who live in towns, can have no idea how great an event the introduction of a new friend is, in such a solitude as surrounded us.

The doctor did not arrive till nearly one o'clock; but I could no more have gone to my bed and slept, than I could have overtaken, on foot, the carriage in which the princess in black velvet had driven away.

When the physician came down to the drawing-room, it was to report very favourably upon his patient. She was now sitting up, her pulse quite regular, apparently perfectly well. She had sustained no injury, and the little shock to her nerves had passed away quite harmlessly. There could be no harm certainly in my seeing her, if we both wished it; and with this permission, I sent, forthwith, to know whether she would allow me to visit her for a few minutes in her room.

The servant returned immediately to say that she desired nothing more.

You may be sure I was not long in availing myself of this permission.

Our visitor lay in one of the handsomest rooms in the schloss. It was, perhaps, a little stately. There was a sombre piece of tapestry opposite the foot of the bed, representing Cleopatra with the asps to her bosom; and other solemn classic scenes were displayed, a little faded, upon the other walls. But there was gold carving, and rich and varied colour enough in the other decorations of the room, to more than redeem the gloom of the old tapestry.

There were candles at the bed side. She was sitting up; her slender pretty figure enveloped in the soft silk dressing-gown, embroidered with flowers, and lined with thick quilted silk, which her mother had thrown over her feet as she lay upon the ground.

What was it that, as I reached the bed side and had just begun my little greeting, struck me dumb in a moment, and made me recoil a step or two from before her? I will tell you.

I saw the very face which had visited me in my childhood at night, which remained so fixed in my memory, and on which I had for so many years so often ruminated with horror, when no one suspected of what I was thinking.

It was pretty, even beautiful; and when I first beheld it, wore the same melancholy expression.

But this almost instantly lighted into a strange fixed smile of recognition.

There was a silence of fully a minute, and then at length *she* spoke; *I* could not.

"How wonderful!" she exclaimed. "Twelve years ago, I saw your face in a dream, and it has haunted me ever since."

"Wonderful indeed!" I repeated, overcoming with an effort the horror that had for a time suspended my utterances. "Twelve years ago, in vision or reality, *I* certainly saw you. I could not forget your face. It has remained before my eyes ever since."

Her smile had softened. Whatever I had fancied strange in it, was gone, and it and her dimpling cheeks were now delightfully pretty and intelligent.

I felt reassured, and continued more in the vein which hospitality indicated, to bid her welcome, and to tell her how much pleasure her accidental arrival had given us all, and especially what a happiness it was to me.

I took her hand as I spoke. I was a little shy, as lonely people are, but the situation made me eloquent, and even bold. She pressed my hand, she laid hers upon it, and her eyes glowed, as, looking hastily into mine, she smiled again, and blushed.

She answered my welcome very prettily. I sat down beside her, still wondering; and she said:

"I must tell you my vision about you; it is so very strange that you and I should have had, each of the other, so vivid a dream, that each should have seen, I you and you me, looking as we do now, when of course we both were mere children. I was a child, about six years old, and I awoke from a confused and troubled dream, and found myself in a room, unlike my nursery, wainscoted clumsily in some dark wood, and with cupboards and bedsteads, and chairs and benches placed about it. The beds were, I thought, all empty, and the room itself without any one but myself in it; and I, after looking about me for some time, and admiring especially an iron candlestick, with two branches, which I should certainly know again, crept under one of the beds to reach the window; but as I got from under the bed, I heard some one crying; and looking up, while I was still upon my knees, I saw *you*— most assuredly you—as I see you now; a beautiful young lady, with golden hair and large blue eyes, and lips—your lips—you, as you are here. Your looks won me; I climbed on the bed and put my arms about you, and I think we both fell asleep. I was aroused by a scream; you were sitting up screaming. I was frightened, and slipped down upon the ground, and, it seemed to me, lost consciousness for a moment; and when I came to myself, I was again in my nursery at home. Your face I have never forgotten since. I could not be misled by mere resemblance. You *are* the lady whom I then saw."

It was now my turn to relate my corresponding vision, which I did, to the undisguised wonder of my new acquaintance.

"I don't know which should be most afraid of the other," she said, again smiling. "If you were less pretty I think I should be very much afraid of you, but being as you are, and you and I both so young, I feel only that I have made your acquaintance twelve years ago, and have already a right to your intimacy; at all events, it does seem as if we were destined, from our earliest childhood, to be friends. I wonder whether you feel as strangely drawn towards me as I do to you; I have never had a friend—shall I find one now?" She sighed, and her fine dark eyes gazed passionately on me.

Now the truth is, I felt rather unaccountably towards the beautiful stranger. I did feel, as she said, "drawn towards her," but there was also something of repulsion. In this ambiguous feeling, however, the sense of attraction immensely prevailed. She interested and won me; she was so beautiful and so indescribably engaging.

I perceived now something of languor and exhaustion stealing over her, and hastened to bid her good night.

"The doctor thinks," I added, "that you ought to have a maid to sit up with you to-night; one of ours is waiting, and you will find her a very useful and quiet creature."

"How kind of you, but I could not sleep, I never could with an attendant in the room. I shan't require any assistance—and, shall I confess my weakness, I am haunted with a terror of robbers. Our house was robbed once, and two servants murdered, so I always lock my door. It has become a habit—and you look so kind I know you will forgive me. I see there is a key in the lock."

She held me close in her pretty arms for a moment and whispered in my ear, "Good-night, darling, it is very hard to part with you, but good-night; to-morrow, but not early, I shall see you again."

She sank back on the pillow with a sigh, and her fine eyes followed me with a fond and melancholy gaze, and she murmured again, "Good-night, dear friend."

Young people like, and even love, on impulse. I was flattered by the evident, though as yet undeserved, fondness she showed me. I liked the confidence with which she at once received me. She was determined that we should be very dear friends.

Next day came and we met again. I was delighted with my companion; that is to say, in many respects.

Her looks lost nothing in daylight—she was certainly the most beautiful creature I had ever seen, and the unpleasant remembrance of the face presented in my early dream, had lost the effect of the first unexpected recognition.

She confessed that she had experienced a similar shock on seeing me, and precisely the same faint antipathy that had mingled with my admiration of her. We now laughed together over our momentary horrors.

CHAPTER IV

Her Habits—A Saunter

I told you that I was charmed with her in most particulars.

There were some that did not please me so well.

She was above the middle height of women. I shall begin by describing her. She was slender, and wonderfully graceful. Except that her movements were languid—*very* languid—indeed, there was nothing in her appearance to indicate an invalid. Her complexion was rich and brilliant; her features were small and beautifully formed; her eyes large, dark, and lustrous; her hair was quite wonderful, I never saw hair so magnificently thick and long when it was down about her shoulders; I have often placed my hands under it, and laughed with wonder at its weight. It was exquisitely fine and soft, and in colour a rich very dark brown, with something of gold. I loved to let it down, tumbling with its own weight, as, in her room, she lay back in her chair talking in her sweet low voice, I used to fold and braid it, and spread it out and play with it. Heavens! If I had but known all!

I said there were particulars which did not please me. I have told you that her confidence won me the first night I saw her; but I found that she exercised with respect to herself, her mother, her history, everything in fact connected with her life, plans, and people, an ever-wakeful reserve. I dare say I was unreasonable, perhaps I was wrong; I dare say I ought to have respected the solemn injunction laid upon my father by the stately lady in black velvet. But curiosity is a restless and unscrupulous passion, and no one girl can endure, with patience, that hers should be baffled by another. What harm could it do anyone to tell me what I so ardently desired to know? Had she no trust in my good sense or honour? Why would she not believe me when I assured her, so solemnly, that I would not divulge one syllable of what she told me to any mortal breathing?

There was a coldness, it seemed to me, beyond her years, in her smiling melancholy persistent refusal to afford me the least ray of light.

I cannot say we quarrelled upon this point, for she would not quarrel upon any. It was, of course, very unfair of me to press her, very ill-bred, but I really could not help it; and I might just as well have let it alone.

What she did tell me amounted, in my unconscionable estimation —to nothing.

It was all summed up in three very vague disclosures:

First.—Her name was Carmilla.

Second.—Her family was very ancient and noble.

Third.—Her home lay in the direction of the west.

She would not tell me the name of her family, nor their armorial bearings, nor the name of their estate, nor even that of the country they lived in.

You are not to suppose that I worried her incessantly on these subjects. I watched opportunity, and rather insinuated than urged my inquiries. Once or twice, indeed, I did attack her more directly. But no matter what my tactics, utter failure was invariably the result. Reproaches and caresses were all lost upon her. But I must add this, that her evasion was conducted with so pretty a melancholy and deprecation, with so many, and even passionate declarations of her liking for me, and trust in my honour, and with so many promises that I should at last know all, that I could not find it in my heart long to be offended with her.

She used to place her pretty arms about my neck, draw me to her, and laying her cheek to mine, murmur with her lips near my ear, "Dearest, your little heart is wounded; think me not cruel because I obey the irresistible law of my strength and weakness; if your dear heart is wounded, my wild heart bleeds with yours. In the rapture of my enormous humiliation I live in your warm life, and you shall die—die, sweetly die—into mine. I cannot help it; as I draw near to you, you, in your turn, will draw near to others, and learn the rapture of that cruelty, which yet is love; so, for a while, seek to know no more of me and mine, but trust me with all your loving spirit."

And when she had spoken such a rhapsody, she would press me more closely in her trembling embrace, and her lips in soft kisses gently glow upon my cheek.

Her agitations and her language were unintelligible to me.

From these foolish embraces, which were not of very frequent occurrence, I must allow, I used to wish to extricate myself; but my energies seemed to fail me. Her murmured words sounded like a lullaby in my ear, and soothed my resistance into a trance, from which I only seemed to recover myself when she withdrew her arms.

In these mysterious moods I did not like her. I experienced a strange tumultuous excitement that was pleasurable, ever and anon, mingled with a vague sense of fear and disgust. I had no distinct thoughts about her while such scenes lasted, but I was conscious of a love growing into adoration, and also of abhorrence. This I know is paradox, but I can make no other attempt to explain the feeling.

I now write, after an interval of more than ten years, with a trembling hand, with a confused and horrible recollection of certain occurrences and situations, in the ordeal through which I was unconsciously passing; though with a vivid and very sharp remembrance of the main current of my story. But, I suspect, in all lives there are certain emotional scenes, those in which our passions have been most wildly and terribly roused, that are of all others the most vaguely and dimly remembered.

Sometimes after an hour of apathy, my strange and beautiful companion would take my hand and hold it with a fond pressure, renewed again and again; blushing softly, gazing in my face with languid and burning eyes, and breathing so fast that her dress rose and fell with the tumultuous respiration. It was like the ardour of a lover; it embarrassed me; it was hateful and yet overpowering; and with gloating eyes she drew me to her, and her hot lips travelled along my cheek in kisses; and she would whisper, almost in sobs, "You are mine, you *shall* be mine, and you and I are one for ever." Then she has thrown herself back in her chair, with her small hands over her eyes, leaving me trembling.

"Are we related," I used to ask; "what can you mean by all this? I remind you perhaps of some one whom you love; but you must not, I hate it; I don't know you—I don't know myself when you look so and talk so."

She used to sigh at my vehemence, then turn away and drop my hand.

Respecting these very extraordinary manifestations I strove in vain to form any satisfactory theory—I could not refer them to affectation or trick. It was unmistakably the momentary breaking out of suppressed instinct and emotion. Was she, notwithstanding her mother's volunteered denial, subject to brief visitations of insanity; or was there here a disguise and a romance? I had read in old story books of such things.

What if a boyish lover had found his way into the house, and sought to prosecute his suit in masquerade, with the assistance of a clever old adventuress? But there were many things against this hypothesis, highly interesting as it was to my vanity.

I could boast of no little attentions such as masculine gallantry delights to offer. Between these passionate moments there were long intervals of common-place, of gaiety, of brooding melancholy, during which, except that I detected her eyes so full of melancholy fire, following me, at times I might have been as nothing to her. Except in these brief periods of mysterious excitement her ways were girlish; and there was always a languor about her, quite incompatible with a masculine system in a state of health.

In some respects her habits were odd. Perhaps not so singular in the opinion of a town lady like you, as they appeared to us rustic people. She used to come down very late, generally not till one o'clock, she would then take a cup of chocolate, but eat nothing; we then went out for a walk, which was a mere saunter, and she seemed, almost immediately, exhausted, and either returned to the schloss or sat on one of the benches that were placed, here and there, among the trees. This was a bodily languor in which her mind did not sympathise. She was always an animated talker, and very intelligent.

She sometimes alluded for a moment to her own home, or mentioned an adventure or situation, or an early recollection, which indicated a people of strange manners, and described customs of which we knew nothing. I gathered from these chance hints that her native country was much more remote than I had at first fancied.

As we sat thus one afternoon under the trees a funeral passed us by. It was that of a pretty young girl, whom I had often seen, the daughter of one of the rangers of the forest. The poor man was walking behind the coffin of his darling; she was his only child, and he looked quite heartbroken. Peasants walking two-and-two came behind, they were singing a funeral hymn.

I rose to mark my respect as they passed, and joined in the hymn they were very sweetly singing.

My companion shook me a little roughly, and I turned surprised. She said brusquely, "Don't you perceive how discordant that is?"

"I think it very sweet, on the contrary," I answered, vexed at the interruption, and very uncomfortable, lest the people who composed the little procession should observe and resent what was passing.

I resumed, therefore, instantly, and was again interrupted. "You pierce my ears," said Carmilla, almost angrily, and stopping her ears with her tiny fingers. "Besides, how can you tell that your religion and mine are the same; your forms wound me, and I hate funerals. What a fuss! Why, *you* must die—*everyone* must die; and all are happier when they do. Come home."

"My father has gone on with the clergyman to the churchyard. I thought you knew she was to be buried to-day."

"*She?* I don't trouble my head about peasants. I don't know who she is," answered Carmilla, with a flash from her fine eyes.

"She is the poor girl who fancied she saw a ghost a fortnight ago, and has been dying ever since, till yesterday, when she expired."

"Tell me nothing about ghosts. I shan't sleep to-night if you do."

"I hope there is no plague or fever coming; all this looks very like it," I continued. "The swineherd's young wife died only a week ago, and she thought something seized her by the throat as she lay in her bed, and nearly strangled her. Papa says such horrible fancies do accompany some forms of fever. She was quite well the day before. She sank afterwards, and died before a week."

"Well, *her* funeral is over, I hope, and *her* hymn sung; and our ears shan't be tortured with that discord and jargon. It has made me nervous. Sit down here, beside me; sit close; hold my hand; press it hard—hard—harder."

We had moved a little back, and had come to another seat.

She sat down. Her face underwent a change that alarmed and even terrified me for a moment. It darkened, and became horribly livid; her teeth and hands were clenched, and she frowned and compressed her lips, while she stared down upon the ground at her feet, and trembled all over with a continued shudder as irrepressible as ague. All her energies seemed strained to suppress a fit, with which she was then breathlessly tugging; and at length a low convulsive cry of suffering broke from her, and gradually the hysteria subsided. "There! That comes of strangling people with hymns!" she said at last. "Hold me, hold me still. It is passing away."

And so gradually it did; and perhaps to dissipate the sombre impression which the spectacle had left upon me, she became unusually animated and chatty; and so we got home.

This was the first time I had seen her exhibit any definable symptoms of that delicacy of health which her mother had spoken of. It was the first time, also, I had seen her exhibit anything like temper.

Both passed away like a summer cloud; and never but once afterwards did I witness on her part a momentary sign of anger. I will tell you how it happened.

She and I were looking out of one of the long drawing-room windows, when there entered the court-yard, over the drawbridge, a figure of a wanderer whom I knew very well. He used to visit the schloss generally twice a year.

It was the figure of a hunchback, with the sharp lean features that generally accompany deformity. He wore a pointed black beard, and he was smiling from ear to ear, showing his white fangs. He was dressed in buff, black, and scarlet, and crossed with more straps and belts than I could count, from which hung all manner of things. Behind, he carried a magic-lantern, and two boxes, which I well knew, in one of which was a salamander, and in the other a mandrake. These monsters used to make my father laugh. They were compounded of parts of monkeys, parrots, squirrels, fish, and hedgehogs, dried and stitched together with great neatness and startling effect. He had a fiddle, a box of conjuring apparatus, a pair of foils and masks attached to his belt, several other mysterious cases dangling about him, and a black staff with copper ferrules in his hand. His companion was a rough spare dog, that followed at his heels, but stopped short, suspiciously at the drawbridge, and in a little while began to howl dismally.

In the meantime, the mountebank, standing in the midst of the court-yard, raised his grotesque hat, and made us a very ceremonious bow, paying his compliments very volubly in execrable French, and German not much better. Then, disengaging his fiddle, he began to scrape a lively air, to which he sang with a merry discord, dancing with ludicrous airs and activity, that made me laugh, in spite of the dog's howling.

Then he advanced to the window with many smiles and salutations, and his hat in his left hand, his fiddle under his arm, and with a fluency that never took breath, he gabbled a long advertisement of all his accomplishments, and the resources of the various arts which he placed at our service, and the curiosities and entertainments which it was in his power, at our bidding to display.

"Will your ladyships be pleased to buy an amulet against the oupire, which is going like the wolf, I hear, through these woods," he said, dropping his hat on the pavement. "They are dying of it right and left, and here is a charm that never fails; only pinned to the pillow, and you may laugh in his face."

These charms consisted of oblong slips of vellum, with cabalistic ciphers and diagrams upon them.

Carmilla instantly purchased one, and so did I.

He was looking up, and we were smiling down upon him, amused; at least, I could answer for myself. His piercing black eye, as he looked up in our faces, seemed to detect something that fixed for a moment his curiosity.

In an instant he unrolled a leather case, full of all manner of odd little steel instruments.

"See here, my lady," he said, displaying it, and addressing me, "I profess, among other things less useful, the art of dentistry. Plague take the dog!" he interpolated. "Silence, beast! He howls so that your ladyships can scarcely hear a word. Your noble friend, the young lady at your right, has the sharpest tooth—long, thin, pointed, like an awl, like a needle; ha, ha! With my sharp and long sight, as I look up, I have seen it distinctly; now if it happens to hurt the young lady, and I think it must, here am I, here are my file, my punch, my nippers; I will make it round and blunt, if her ladyship pleases; no longer the tooth of a fish, but of a beautiful young lady as she is. Hey? Is the young lady displeased? Have I been too bold? Have I offended her?"

The young lady, indeed, looked very angry as she drew back from the window.

"How dares that mountebank insult us so? Where is your father? I shall demand redress from him. My father would have had the wretch tied up to the pump, and flogged with a cart-whip, and burnt to the bones with the castle brand!"

She retired from the window a step or two, and sat down, and had hardly lost sight of the offender, when her wrath subsided as suddenly as it had risen, and she gradually recovered her usual tone, and seemed to forget the little hunchback and his follies.

My father was out of spirits that evening. On coming in he told us that there had been another case very similar to the two fatal ones which had lately occurred. The sister of a young peasant on his estate, only a mile away, was very ill, had been, as she described it, attacked very nearly in the same way, and was now slowly but steadily sinking.

"All this," said my father, "is strictly referable to natural causes. These poor people infect one another with their superstitions, and so repeat in imagination the images of terror that have infested their neighbours."

"But that very circumstance frightens one horribly," said Carmilla.

"How so?" inquired my father.

"I am so afraid of fancying I see such things; I think it would be as bad as reality."

"We are in God's hands; nothing can happen without His permission, and all will end well for those who love Him. He is our faithful creator; He has made us all, and will take care of us."

"Creator! *Nature!*" said the young lady in answer to my gentle father. "And this disease that invades the country is natural. Nature. All things proceed from Nature—don't they? All things in the heaven, in the earth, and under the earth, act and live as Nature ordains? I think so."

"The doctor said he would come here to-day," said my father, after a silence. "I want to know what he thinks about it, and what he thinks we had better do."

"Doctors never did me any good," said Carmilla.

"Then you have been ill?" I asked.

"More ill than ever you were," she answered.

"Long ago?"

"Yes, a long time. I suffered from this very illness; but I forget all but my pain and weakness, and they were not so bad as are suffered in other diseases."

"You were very young then?"

"I dare say; let us talk no more of it. You would not wound a friend?" She looked languidly in my eyes, and passed her arm round my waist lovingly, and led me out of the room. My father was busy over some papers near the window.

"Why does your papa like to frighten us?" said the pretty girl, with a sigh and a little shudder.

"He doesn't, dear Carmilla, it is the very furthest thing from his mind."

"Are you afraid, dearest?"

"I should be very much if I fancied there was any real danger of my being attacked as those poor people were."

"You are afraid to die?"

"Yes, everyone is."

"But to die as lovers may—to die together, so that they may live together. Girls are caterpillars while they live in the world, to be finally butterflies when the summer comes; but in the meantime there are grubs and larvae, don't you see—each with their peculiar propensities, necessities and structure. So says Monsieur Buffon, in his big book, in the next room."

Later in the day the doctor came, and was closeted with papa for some time. He was a skilful man, of sixty and upwards, he wore powder, and shaved his pale face smooth as a pumpkin. He and papa emerged from the room together, and I heard papa laugh, and say as they came out:

"Well, I do wonder at a wise man like you. What do you say to hippogriffs and dragons?"

The doctor was smiling, and made answer, shaking his head—

"Nevertheless, life and death are mysterious states, and we know little of the resources of either."

And so they walked on, and I heard no more. I did not then know what the doctor had been broaching, but I think I guess it now.

CHAPTER V

A Wonderful Likeness

This evening there arrived from Gratz the grave, dark-faced son of the picture-cleaner, with a horse and cart laden with two large packing-cases, having many pictures in each. It was a journey of ten leagues, and whenever a messenger arrived at the schloss from our little capital of Gratz, we used to crowd about him in the hall, to hear the news.

This arrival created in our secluded quarters quite a sensation. The cases remained in the hall, and the messenger was taken charge of by the servants till he had eaten his supper. Then with assistants, and armed with hammer, ripping chisel, and turnscrew, he met us in the hall, where we had assembled to witness the unpacking of the cases.

Carmilla sat looking listlessly on, while one after the other the old pictures, nearly all portraits, which had undergone the process of renovation, were brought to light. My mother was of an old Hungarian family, and most of these pictures, which were about to be restored to their places, had come to us through her.

My father had a list in his hand, from which he read, as the artist rummaged out the corresponding numbers. I don't know that the pictures were very good, but they were, undoubtedly, very old, and some of them very curious also. They had, for the most part, the merit of being now seen by me, I may say, for the first time; for the smoke and dust of time had all but obliterated them.

"There is a picture that I have not seen yet," said my father. "In one corner, at the top of it, is the name, as well as I could read, 'Marcia Karnstein,' and the date '1698;' and I am curious to see how it has turned out."

I remembered it; it was a small picture, about a foot and a half high, and nearly square, without a frame; but it was so blackened by age that I could not make it out.

The artist now produced it, with evident pride. It was quite beautiful; it was startling; it seemed to live. It was the effigy of Carmilla!

"Carmilla, dear, here is an absolute miracle. Here you are, living, smiling, ready to speak, in this picture. Isn't it beautiful, papa? And see, even the mole on her throat."

My father laughed, and said, "Certainly it is a wonderful likeness," but he looked away, and to my surprise seemed but little struck by it, and went on talking to the picture-cleaner, who was also something of an artist, and discoursed with intelligence about the portraits or other works, which his art had just brought into light and colour, while *I* was more and more lost in wonder the more I looked at the picture.

"Will you let me hang this picture in my room, papa?" I asked.

"Certainly, dear," said he, smiling, "I'm very glad you think it so like. It must be prettier even than I thought it, if it is."

The young lady did not acknowledge this pretty speech, did not seem to hear it. She was leaning back in her seat, her fine eyes under their long lashes gazing on me in contemplation, and she smiled in a kind of rapture.

"And now you can read quite plainly the name that is written in the corner. It is not Marcia; it looks as if it was done in gold. The name is Mircalla, Countess Karnstein, and this is a little coronet over it, and underneath A. D. 1698. I am descended from the Karnsteins; that is, mamma was."

"Ah!" said the lady, languidly, "so am I, I think, a very long descent, very ancient. Are there any Karnsteins living now?"

"None who bear the name, I believe. The family were ruined, I believe, in some civil wars, long ago but the ruins of the castle are only about three miles away."

"How interesting!" she said, languidly. "But see what beautiful moonlight!" She glanced through the hall door, which stood a little open. "Suppose you take a little ramble round the court, and look down at the road and river."

"It is so like the night you came to us," I said.

She sighed, smiling.

She rose, and each with her arm about the other's waist, we walked out upon the pavement.

In silence, slowly we walked down to the drawbridge, where the beautiful landscape opened before us.

"And so you were thinking of the night I came here?" she almost whispered. "Are you glad I came?"

"Delighted, dear Carmilla," I answered.

"And you ask for a picture you think like me, to hang in your room," she murmured with a sigh, as she drew her arm closer about my waist, and let her pretty head sink upon my shoulder.

"How romantic you are, Carmilla," I said. "Whenever you tell me your story, it will be made up chiefly of some one great romance."

She kissed me silently.

"I am sure, Carmilla, you have been in love; that there is, at this moment, an affair of the heart going on."

"I have been in love with no one, and never shall," she whispered, "unless it should be you."

How beautiful she looked in the moonlight!

Shy and strange was the look with which she quickly hid her face in my neck and hair, with tumultuous sighs, that seemed almost to sob, and pressed in mine a hand that trembled.

Her soft cheek was glowing against mine. "Darling, darling," she murmured, "I live in you; and you would die for me, I love you so."

I started from her.

She was gazing on me with eyes from which all fire, all meaning had flown, and a face colourless and apathetic.

"Is there a chill in the air, dear?" she said drowsily. "I almost shiver; have I been dreaming? Let us come in. Come, come; come in."

"You look ill, Carmilla; a little faint. You certainly must take some wine," I said.

"Yes, I will. I'm better now. I shall be quite well in a few minutes. Yes, do give me a little wine," answered Carmilla, as we approached the door. "Let us look again for a moment; it is the last time, perhaps, I shall see the moonlight with you."

"How do you feel now, dear Carmilla? Are you really better?" I asked.

I was beginning to take alarm, lest she should have been stricken with the strange epidemic that they said had invaded the country about us.

"Papa would be grieved beyond measure," I added, "if he thought you were ever so little ill, without immediately letting us know. We have a very skilful doctor near this, the physician who was with papa to-day."

"I'm sure he is. I know how kind you all are: but, dear child, I am quite well again. There is nothing ever wrong with me, but a little weakness. People say I am languid; I am incapable of exertion; I can scarcely walk as far as a child of three years old; and every now and then the little strength I have falters, and I become as you have just seen me. But after all I am very easily set up again; in a moment I am perfectly myself. See how I have recovered."

So, indeed, she had; and she and I talked a great deal, and very animated she was; and the remainder of that evening passed without any recurrence of what I called her infatuations. I mean her crazy talk and looks, which embarrassed, and even frightened me.

But there occurred that night an event which gave my thoughts quite a new turn, and seemed to startle even Carmilla's languid nature into momentary energy.

CHAPTER VI
A Very Strange Agony

When we got into the drawing-room, and had sat down to our coffee and chocolate, although Carmilla did not take any, she seemed quite herself again, and Madame, and Mademoiselle De Lafontaine, joined us, and made a little card party, in the course of which papa came in for what he called his "dish of tea."

When the game was over he sat down beside Carmilla on the sofa, and asked her, a little anxiously, whether she had heard from her mother since her arrival.

She answered "No."

He then asked her whether she knew where a letter would reach her at present.

"I cannot tell," she answered, ambiguously, "but I have been thinking of leaving you; you have been already too hospitable and too kind to me. I have given you an infinity of trouble, and I should wish to take a carriage to-morrow, and post in pursuit of her; I know where I shall ultimately find her, although I dare not yet tell you."

"But you must not dream of such a thing," exclaimed my father, to my great relief. "We can't afford to lose you so, and I won't consent to your leaving us, except under the care of your mother, who was so good as to consent to your remaining with us till she should herself return. I should be quite happy if I knew that you heard from her; but this evening the accounts of the progress of the mysterious disease that has invaded our neighbourhood, grow even more alarming; and my beautiful guest, I do feel the responsibility, unaided by advice from your mother, very much. But I shall do my best; and one thing is certain, that you must not think of leaving us without her distinct direction to that effect. We should suffer too much in parting from you to consent to it easily."

"Thank you, sir, a thousand times for your hospitality," she answered, smiling bashfully. "You have all been too kind to me; I have seldom been so happy in all my life before, as in your beautiful château, under your care, and in the society of your dear daughter."

So he gallantly, in his old-fashioned way, kissed her hand, smiling, and pleased at her little speech.

I accompanied Carmilla as usual to her room, and sat and chatted with her while she was preparing for bed.

"Do you think," I said, at length, "that you will ever confide fully in me?"

She turned around smiling, but made no answer, only continued to smile on me.

"You won't answer that?" I said. "You can't answer pleasantly; I ought not to have asked you."

"You were quite right to ask me that, or anything. You do not know how dear you are to me, or you could not think any confidence too great to look for. But I am under vows, no nun half so awfully, and I dare not tell my story yet, even to you. The time is very near when you shall know everything. You will think me cruel, very selfish, but love is always selfish; the more ardent the more selfish. How jealous I am you cannot know. You must come with me, loving me, to death; or else hate me, and still come with me, and *hating* me through death and after. There is no such word as indifference in my apathetic nature."

"Now, Carmilla, you are going to talk your wild nonsense again," I said hastily.

"Not I, silly little fool as I am, and full of whims and fancies; for your sake I'll talk like a sage. Were you ever at a ball?"

"No; how you do run on. What is it like? How charming it must be."

"I almost forget, it is years ago."

I laughed.

"You are not so old. Your first ball can hardly be forgotten yet."

"I remember everything about it—with an effort. I see it all, as divers see what is going on above them, through a medium, dense, rippling, but transparent. There occurred that night what has confused the picture, and made its colours faint. I was all but assassinated in my bed, wounded *here,*" she touched her breast, "and never was the same since."

"Were you near dying?"

"Yes, a very—cruel love—strange love, that would have taken my life. Love will have its sacrifices. No sacrifice without blood. Let us go to sleep now; I feel lazy. How can I get up just now and lock my door?"

She was lying with her tiny hands buried in her rich wavy hair, under her cheek, her little head upon the pillow, and her glittering eyes followed me wherever I moved, with a kind of shy smile that I could not decipher.

I bid her good-night, and crept from the room with an uncomfortable sensation.

I often wondered whether our pretty guest ever said her prayers. *I* certainly had never seen her upon her knees. In the morning she never came down until long after our family prayers were over, and at night she never left the drawing room to attend our brief evening prayers in the hall.

If it had not been that it had casually come out in one of our careless talks that she had been baptised, I should have doubted her being a Christian. Religion was a subject on which I had never heard her speak a word. If I had known of the world better, this particular neglect or antipathy would not have so much surprised me.

The precautions of nervous people are infectious, and persons of a like temperament are pretty sure, after a time, to imitate them. I had adopted Carmilla's habit of locking her bed-room door, having taken into my head all her whimsical alarms about midnight invaders, and prowling assassins. I had also adopted her precaution of making a brief search through her room, to satisfy herself that no lurking assassin or robber was "ensconced."

These wise measures taken, I got into my bed and fell asleep. A light was burning in my room. This was an old habit, of very early date, and which nothing could have tempted me to dispense with.

Thus fortified I might take my rest in peace. But dreams come through stone walls, light up dark rooms, or darken light ones, and their persons make their exits and their entrances as they please, and laugh at locksmiths.

I had a dream that night that was the beginning of a very strange agony.

I cannot call it a nightmare, for I was quite conscious of being asleep. But I was equally conscious of being in my room, and lying in bed, precisely as I actually was. I saw, or fancied I saw, the room and its furniture just as I had seen it last, except that it was very dark, and I saw something moving round the foot of the bed, which at first I could not accurately distinguish. But I soon saw that it was a sooty-black animal that resembled a monstrous cat. It appeared to me about four or five feet long, for it measured fully the length of the hearth-rug as it passed over it; and it continued to-ing and fro-ing with the lithe sinister restlessness of a beast in a cage. I could not cry out, although as you may suppose, I was terrified. Its pace was growing faster, and the room rapidly darker and darker, and at length so dark that I could no longer see anything of it but its eyes. I felt it spring lightly on the bed. The two broad eyes approached my face, and suddenly I felt a stinging pain as if two large needles darted, an inch or two apart, deep into my breast. I waked with a scream. The room was lighted by the candle that burnt there all through the night, and I saw a female figure standing at the foot of the bed, a little at the right side. It was in a dark loose dress, and its hair was down and covered its shoulders. A block of stone could not have been more still. There was not the slightest stir of respiration. As I stared at it, the figure appeared to have changed its place, and was now nearer the door; then, close to it, the door opened, and it passed out.

I was now relieved, and able to breathe and move. My first thought was that Carmilla had been playing me a trick, and that I had forgotten to secure my door. I hastened to it, and found it locked as usual on the inside. I was afraid to open it—I was horrified. I sprang into my bed and covered my head up in the bedclothes, and lay there more dead than alive till morning.

CHAPTER VII

Descending

It would be vain my attempting to tell you the horror with which, even now, I recall the occurrence of that night. It was no such transitory terror as a dream leaves behind it. It seemed to deepen by time, and communicated itself to the room and the very furniture that had encompassed the apparition.

I could not bear the next day to be alone for a moment. I should have told papa, but for two opposite reasons. At one time I thought he would laugh at my story, and I could not bear its being treated as a jest; and at another, I thought he might fancy that I had been attacked by the mysterious complaint which had invaded our neighbourhood. I had myself no misgivings of the kind, and as he had been rather an invalid for some time, I was afraid of alarming him.

I was comfortable enough with my good-natured companions, Madame Perrodon, and the vivacious Mademoiselle Lafontaine. They both perceived that I was out of spirits and nervous, and at length I told them what lay so heavy at my heart.

Mademoiselle laughed, but I fancied that Madame Perrodon looked anxious.

"By-the-by," said Mademoiselle, laughing, "the long lime tree walk, behind Carmilla's bedroom window, is haunted!"

"Nonsense!" exclaimed Madame, who probably thought the theme rather inopportune, "and who tells that story, my dear?"

"Martin says that he came up twice, when the old yard-gate was being repaired before sunrise, and twice saw the same female figure walking down the lime tree avenue."

"So he well might, as long as they have cows to milk in the river fields," said Madame.

"I daresay; but Martin chooses to be frightened, and never did I see fool *more* frightened."

"You must not say a word about it to Carmilla, because she can see down that walk from her room window," I interposed, "and she is, if possible, a greater coward than I."

Carmilla came down rather later than usual that day.

"I was so frightened last night," she said, so soon as we were together, "and I am sure I should have seen something dreadful if it had not been for that charm I bought from the poor little hunchback whom I called such hard names. I had a dream of something black coming round my bed, and I awoke in a perfect horror, and I really thought, for some seconds, I saw a dark figure near the chimney piece, but I felt under my pillow for my charm, and the moment my fingers touched it, the figure disappeared, and I felt quite certain, only that I had it by me, that something frightful would have made its appearance, and, perhaps, throttled me, as it did those poor people we heard of."

"Well, listen to me," I began, and recounted my adventure, at the recital of which she appeared horrified.

"And had you the charm near you?" she asked, earnestly.

"No, I had dropped it into a china vase in the drawing-room, but I shall certainly take it with me to-night, as you have so much faith in it."

At this distance of time I cannot tell you, or even understand, how I overcame my horror so effectually as to lie alone in my room that night. I remember distinctly that I pinned the charm to my pillow. I fell asleep almost immediately, and slept even more soundly than usual all night.

Next night I passed as well. My sleep was delightfully deep and dreamless. But I wakened with a sense of lassitude and melancholy, which, however, did not exceed a degree that was almost luxurious.

"Well, I told you so," said Carmilla, when I described my quiet sleep, "I had such delightful sleep myself last night; I pinned the charm to the breast of my nightdress. It was too far away the night before. I am quite sure it was all fancy, except the dreams. I used to think that evil spirits made dreams, but our doctor told me it is no such thing. Only a fever passing by, or some other malady, as they often do, he said, knocks at the door, and not being able to get in, passes on, with that alarm."

"And what do you think the charm is?" said I.

"It has been fumigated or immersed in some drug, and is an antidote against the malaria," she answered.

"Then it acts only on the body?"

"Certainly; you don't suppose that evil spirits are frightened by bits of ribbon, or the perfumes of a druggist's shop? No, these complaints, wandering in the air, begin by trying the nerves, and so infect the brain; but before they can seize upon you, the antidote repels them. That I am sure is what the charm has done for us. It is nothing magical, it is simply natural."

I should have been happier if I could quite have agreed with Carmilla, but I did my best, and the impression was a little losing its force.

For some nights I slept profoundly; but still every morning I felt the same lassitude, and a languor weighed upon me all day. I felt myself a changed girl. A strange melancholy was stealing over me, a melancholy that I would not have interrupted. Dim thoughts of death began to open, and an idea that I was slowly sinking took gentle, and, somehow, not unwelcome possession of me. If it was sad, the tone of mind which this induced was also sweet. Whatever it might be, my soul acquiesced in it.

I would not admit that I was ill, I would not consent to tell my papa, or to have the doctor sent for.

Carmilla became more devoted to me than ever, and her strange paroxysms of languid adoration more frequent. She used to gloat on me with increasing ardour the more my strength and spirits waned. This always shocked me like a momentary glare of insanity.

Without knowing it, I was now in a pretty advanced stage of the strangest illness under which mortal ever suffered. There was an unaccountable fascination in its earlier symptoms that more than reconciled me to the incapacitating effect of that stage of the malady. This fascination increased for a time, until it reached a certain point, when gradually a sense of the horrible mingled itself with it, deepening, as you shall hear, until it discoloured and perverted the whole state of my life.

The first change I experienced was rather agreeable. It was very near the turning point from which began the descent of Avernus.

Certain vague and strange sensations visited me in my sleep. The prevailing one was of that pleasant, peculiar cold thrill which we feel in bathing, when we move against the current of a river. This was soon accompanied by dreams that seemed interminable, and were so vague that I could never recollect their scenery and persons, or any one connected portion of their action. But they left an awful impression, and a sense of exhaustion, as if I had passed through a long period of great mental exertion and danger. After all these dreams there remained on waking a remembrance of having been in a place very nearly dark, and of having spoken to people whom I could not see; and especially of one clear voice, of a female's, very deep, that spoke as if at a distance, slowly, and producing always the same sensation of indescribable solemnity and fear. Sometimes there came a sensation as if a hand was drawn softly along my cheek and neck. Sometimes it was as if warm lips kissed me, and longer and more lovingly as they reached my throat, but there the caress fixed itself. My heart beat faster, my breathing rose and fell rapidly and full drawn; a sobbing, that rose into a sense of strangulation, supervened, and turned into a dreadful convulsion, in which my senses left me, and I became unconscious.

It was now three weeks since the commencement of this unaccountable state. My sufferings had, during the last week, told upon my appearance. I had grown pale, my eyes were dilated and darkened underneath, and the languor which I had long felt began to display itself in my countenance.

My father asked me often whether I was ill; but, with an obstinacy which now seems to me unaccountable, I persisted in assuring him that I was quite well.

In a sense this was true. I had no pain, I could complain of no bodily derangement. My complaint seemed to be one of the imagination, or the nerves, and, horrible as my sufferings were, I kept them, with a morbid reserve, very nearly to myself.

It could not be that terrible complaint which the peasants call the oupire, for I had now been suffering for three weeks, and they were seldom ill for much more than three days, when death put an end to their miseries.

Carmilla complained of dreams and feverish sensations, but by no means of so alarming a kind as mine. I say that mine were extremely alarming. Had I been capable of comprehending my condition, I would have invoked aid and advice on my knees. The narcotic of an unsuspected influence was acting upon me, and my perceptions were benumbed.

I am going to tell you now of a dream that led immediately to an odd discovery.

One night, instead of the voice I was accustomed to hear in the dark, I heard one, sweet and tender, and at the same time terrible, which said, "Your mother warns you to beware of the assassin." At the same time a light unexpectedly sprang up, and I saw Carmilla, standing, near the foot of my bed, in her white nightdress, bathed, from her chin to her feet, in one great stain of blood.

I wakened with a shriek, possessed with the one idea that Carmilla was being murdered. I remember springing from my bed, and my next recollection is that of standing on the lobby, crying for help.

Madame and Mademoiselle came scurrying out of their rooms in alarm; a lamp burned always on the lobby, and seeing me, they soon learned the cause of my terror.

I insisted on our knocking at Carmilla's door. Our knocking was unanswered. It soon became a pounding and an uproar. We shrieked her name, but all was vain.

We all grew frightened, for the door was locked. We hurried back, in panic, to my room. There we rang the bell long and furiously. If my father's room had been at that side of the house, we would have called him up at once to our aid. But, alas! he was quite out of hearing, and to reach him involved an excursion for which we none of us had courage.

Servants, however, soon came running up the stairs; I had got on my dressing-gown and slippers meanwhile, and my companions were already similarly furnished. Recognizing the voices of the servants on the lobby, we sallied out together; and having renewed, as fruitlessly, our summons at Carmilla's door, I ordered the men to force the lock. They did so, and we stood, holding our lights aloft, in the doorway, and so stared into the room.

We called her by name; but there was still no reply. We looked round the room. Everything was undisturbed. It was exactly in the state in which I left it on bidding her good night. But Carmilla was gone.

CHAPTER VIII

Search

At sight of the room, perfectly undisturbed except for our violent entrance, we began to cool a little, and soon recovered our senses sufficiently to dismiss the men. It had struck Mademoiselle that possibly Carmilla had been wakened by the uproar at her door, and in her first panic had jumped from her bed, and hid herself in a press, or behind a curtain, from which she could not, of course, emerge until the majordomo and his myrmidons had withdrawn. We now recommenced our search, and began to call her by name again.

It was all to no purpose. Our perplexity and agitation increased. We examined the windows, but they were secured. I implored of Carmilla, if she had concealed herself, to play this cruel trick no longer —to come out, and to end our anxieties. It was all useless. I was by this time convinced that she was not in the room, nor in the dressing-room, the door of which was still locked on this side. She could not have passed it. I was utterly puzzled. Had Carmilla discovered one of those secret passages which the old housekeeper said were known to exist in the schloss, although the tradition of their exact situation had been lost? A little time would, no doubt, explain all—utterly perplexed as, for the present, we were.

It was past four o'clock, and I preferred passing the remaining hours of darkness in Madame's room. Daylight brought no solution of the difficulty.

The whole household, with my father at its head, was in a state of agitation next morning. Every part of the château was searched. The grounds were explored. Not a trace of the missing lady could be discovered. The stream was about to be dragged; my father was in distraction; what a tale to have to tell the poor girl's mother on her return. I, too, was almost beside myself, though my grief was quite of a different kind.

The morning was passed in alarm and excitement. It was now one o'clock, and still no tidings. I ran up to Carmilla's room, and found her standing at her dressing-table. I was astounded. I could not believe my eyes. She beckoned me to her with her pretty finger, in silence. Her face expressed extreme fear.

I ran to her in an ecstasy of joy; I kissed and embraced her again and again. I ran to the bell and rang it vehemently, to bring others to the spot, who might at once relieve my father's anxiety.

"Dear Carmilla, what has become of you all this time? We have been in agonies of anxiety about you," I exclaimed. "Where have you been? How did you come back?"

"Last night has been a night of wonders," she said.

"For mercy's sake, explain all you can."

"It was past two last night," she said, "when I went to sleep as usual in my bed, with my doors locked, that of the dressing-room, and that opening upon the gallery. My sleep was uninterrupted, and, so far as I know, dreamless; but I awoke just now on the sofa in the dressing-room there, and I found the door between the rooms open, and the other door forced. How could all this have happened without my being wakened? It must have been accompanied with a great deal of noise, and I am particularly easily wakened; and how could I have been carried out of my bed without my sleep having been interrupted, I whom the slightest stir startles?"

By this time, Madame, Mademoiselle, my father, and a number of the servants were in the room. Carmilla, was, of course, overwhelmed with inquiries, congratulations, and welcomes. She had but one story to tell, and seemed the least able of all the party to suggest any way of accounting for what had happened.

My father took a turn up and down the room, thinking. I saw Carmilla's eye follow him for a moment with a sly, dark glance.

When my father had sent the servants away, Mademoiselle having gone in search of a little bottle of valerian and sal-volatile, and there being no one in the room with Carmilla except my father, Madame, and myself, he came to her thoughtfully, took her hand very kindly, led her to the sofa, and sat down beside her.

"Will you forgive me, my dear, if I risk a conjecture, and ask a question?"

"Who can have a better right?" she said. "Ask what you please, and I will tell you everything. But my story is simply one of bewilderment and darkness. I know absolutely nothing. Put any question you please. But you know, of course, the limitations mamma has placed me under."

"Perfectly, my dear child. I need not approach the topics on which she desires our silence. Now, the marvel of last night consists in your having been removed from your bed and your room without being wakened, and this removal having occurred apparently while the windows were still secured, and the two doors locked upon the inside. I will tell you my theory, and first ask you a question."

Carmilla was leaning on her hand dejectedly; Madame and I were listening breathlessly.

"Now, my question is this. Have you ever been suspected of walking in your sleep?"

"Never since I was very young indeed."

"But you did walk in your sleep when you were very young?"

"Yes; I know I did. I have been told so often by my old nurse."

My father smiled and nodded.

"Well, what has happened is this. You got up in your sleep, unlocked the door, not leaving the key, as usual, in the lock, but taking it out and locking it on the outside; you again took the key out, and carried it away with you to some one of the five-and-twenty rooms on this floor, or perhaps upstairs or downstairs. There are so many rooms and closets, so much heavy furniture, and such accumulations of lumber, that it would require a week to search this old house thoroughly. Do you see, now, what I mean?"

"I do, but not all," she answered.

"And how, papa, do you account for her finding herself on the sofa in the dressing-room, which we had searched so carefully?"

"She came there after you had searched it, still in her sleep, and at last awoke spontaneously, and was as much surprised to find herself where she was as any one else. I wish all mysteries were as easily and innocently explained as yours, Carmilla," he said, laughing. "And so we may congratulate ourselves on the certainty that the most natural explanation of the occurrence is one that involves no drugging, no tampering with locks, no burglars, or poisoners, or witches—nothing that need alarm Carmilla, or any one else, for our safety."

Carmilla was looking charmingly. Nothing could be more beautiful than her tints. Her beauty was, I think, enhanced by that graceful languor that was peculiar to her. I think my father was silently contrasting her looks with mine, for he said:—

"I wish my poor Laura was looking more like herself;" and he sighed.

So our alarms were happily ended, and Carmilla restored to her friends.

CHAPTER IX

The Doctor

As Carmilla would not hear of an attendant sleeping in her room, my father arranged that a servant should sleep outside her door, so that she could not attempt to make another such excursion without being arrested at her own door.

That night passed quickly; and next morning early, the doctor, whom my father had sent for without telling me a word about it, arrived to see me.

Madame accompanied me to the library; and there the grave little doctor, with white hair and spectacles, whom I mentioned before, was waiting to receive me.

I told him my story, and as I proceeded he grew graver and graver.

We were standing, he and I, in the recess of one of the windows, facing one another. When my statement was over, he leaned with his shoulders against the wall, and with his eyes fixed on me earnestly, with an interest in which was a dash of horror.

After a minute's reflection, he asked Madame if he could see my father.

He was sent for accordingly, and as he entered, smiling, he said:

"I dare say, doctor, you are going to tell me that I am an old fool for having brought you here; I hope I am."

But his smile faded into shadow as the doctor, with a very grave face, beckoned him to him.

He and the doctor talked for some time in the same recess where I had just conferred with the physician. It seemed an earnest and argumentative conversation. The room is very large, and I and Madame stood together, burning with curiosity, at the further end. Not a word could we hear, however, for they spoke in a very low tone, and the deep recess of the window quite concealed the doctor from view, and very nearly my father, whose foot, arm, and shoulder only could we see: and the voices were, I suppose, all the less audible for the sort of closet which the thick wall and window formed.

After a time my father's face looked into the room; it was pale, thoughtful, and, I fancied, agitated.

"Laura, dear, come here for a moment. Madame, we shan't trouble you, the doctor says, at present."

Accordingly I approached, for the first time a little alarmed; for, although I felt very weak, I did not feel ill; and strength, one always fancies, is a thing that may be picked up when we please.

My father held out his hand to me as I drew near, but he was looking at the doctor, and he said:

"It certainly *is* very odd; I don't understand it quite. Laura, come here, dear; now attend to Doctor Spielsberg, and recollect yourself."

"You mentioned a sensation like that of two needles piercing the skin, somewhere about your neck, on the night when you experienced your first horrible dream. Is there still any soreness?"

"None at all," I answered.

"Can you indicate with your finger about the point at which you think this occurred?"

"Very little below my throat—*here,*" I answered.

I wore a morning dress, which covered the place I pointed to.

"Now you can satisfy yourself," said the doctor. "You won't mind your papa's lowering your dress a very little. It is necessary, to detect a symptom of the complaint under which you have been suffering."

I acquiesced. It was only an inch or two below the edge of my collar.

"God bless me!—so it is," exclaimed my father, growing pale.

"You see it now with your own eyes," said the doctor, with a gloomy triumph.

"What is it?" I exclaimed, beginning to be frightened.

"Nothing, my dear young lady, but a small blue spot, about the size of the tip of your little finger; and now," he continued, turning to papa, "the question is what is the best to be done?"

"Is there any danger?" I urged, in great trepidation.

"I trust not, my dear," answered the doctor. "I don't see why you should not recover. I don't see why you should not begin *immediately* to get better. That is the point at which the sense of strangulation begins?"

"Yes," I answered.

"And—recollect as well as you can—the same point was a kind of centre of that thrill which you described just now like the current of a cold stream running against you?"

"It may have been; I think it was."

"Ay, you see?" he added, turning to my father. "Shall I say a word to Madame?"

"Certainly," said my father.

He called Madame to him, and said:

"I find my young friend here far from well. It won't be of any great consequence, I hope; but it will be necessary that some steps be taken, which I will explain by-and-by; but in the meantime, Madame, you will be so good as not to let Miss Laura be alone for one moment. That is the only direction I need give for the present. It is indispensable."

"We may rely upon your kindness, Madame, I know," added my father.

Madame satisfied him eagerly.

"And you, dear Laura, I know you will observe the doctor's direction."

"I shall have to ask your opinion upon another patient, whose symptoms slightly resemble those of my daughter, that have just been detailed to you—very much milder in degree, but I believe quite of the same sort. She is a young lady—our guest; but as you say you will be passing this way again this evening, you can't do better than take your supper here, and you can then see her. She does not come down till the afternoon."

"I thank you," said the doctor. "I shall be with you, then, at about seven this evening."

And then they repeated their directions to me and to Madame, and with this parting charge my father left us, and walked out with the doctor; and I saw them pacing together up and down between the road and the moat, on the grassy platform in front of the castle, evidently absorbed in earnest conversation.

The doctor did not return. I saw him mount his horse there, take his leave, and ride away eastward through the forest. Nearly at the same time I saw the man arrive from Dranfeld with the letters, and dismount and hand the bag to my father.

In the meantime, Madame and I were both busy, lost in conjecture as to the reasons of the singular and earnest direction which the doctor and my father had concurred in imposing. Madame, as she afterwards told me, was afraid the doctor apprehended a sudden seizure, and that, without prompt assistance, I might either lose my life in a fit, or at least be seriously hurt.

This interpretation did not strike me; and I fancied, perhaps luckily for my nerves, that the arrangement was prescribed simply to secure a companion, who would prevent my taking too much exercise, or eating unripe fruit, or doing any of the fifty foolish things to which young people are supposed to be prone.

About half-an-hour after my father came in—he had a letter in his hand—and said:

"This letter has been delayed; it is from General Spielsdorf. He might have been here yesterday, he may not come till to-morrow, or he may be here to-day."

He put the open letter into my hand; but he did not look pleased, as he used to when a guest, especially one so much loved as the General, was coming. On the contrary, he looked as if he wished him at the bottom of the Red Sea. There was plainly something on his mind which he did not choose to divulge.

"Papa, darling, will you tell me this?" said I, suddenly laying my hand on his arm, and looking, I am sure, imploringly in his face.

"Perhaps," he answered, smoothing my hair caressingly over my eyes.

"Does the doctor think me very ill?"

"No, dear; he thinks, if right steps are taken, you will be quite well again, at least on the high road to a complete recovery, in a day or two," he answered, a little drily. "I wish our good friend, the General, had chosen any other time; that is, I wish you had been perfectly well to receive him."

"But do tell me papa," I insisted, *"what* does he think is the matter with me?"

"Nothing; you must not plague me with questions," he answered, with more irritation than I ever remember him to have displayed before; and seeing that I looked wounded, I suppose, he kissed me, and added, "You shall know all about it in a day or two; that is, all that *I* know. In the meantime, you are not to trouble your head about it."

He turned and left the room, but came back before I had done wondering and puzzling over the oddity of all this; it was merely to say that he was going to Karnstein, and had ordered the carriage to be ready at twelve, and that I and Madame should accompany him; he was going to see the priest who lived near those picturesque grounds, upon business, and as Carmilla had never seen them, she could follow, when she came down, with Mademoiselle, who would bring materials for what you call a pic-nic, which might be laid for us in the ruined castle.

At twelve o'clock, accordingly, I was ready, and not long after, my father, Madame and I set out upon our projected drive. Passing the drawbridge we turn to the right, and follow the road over the steep Gothic bridge, westward, to reach the deserted village and ruined castle of Karnstein.

No sylvan drive can be fancied prettier. The ground breaks into gentle hills and hollows, all clothed with beautiful wood, totally destitute of the comparative formality which artificial planting and early culture and pruning impart.

The irregularities of the ground often lead the road out of its course, and cause it to wind beautifully round the sides of broken hollows and the steeper sides of the hills, among varieties of ground almost inexhaustible.

Turning one of these points, we suddenly encountered our old friend, the General, riding towards us, attended by a mounted servant. His portmanteaus were following in a hired waggon, such as we term a cart.

The General dismounted as we pulled up, and, after the usual greetings, was easily persuaded to accept the vacant seat in the carriage, and send his horse on with his servant to the schloss.

CHAPTER X
Bereaved

It was about ten months since we had last seen him; but that time had sufficed to make an alteration of years in his appearance. He had grown thinner; something of gloom and anxiety had taken the place of that cordial serenity which used to characterise his features. His dark blue eyes, always penetrating, now gleamed with a sterner light from under his shaggy grey eyebrows. It was not such a change as grief alone usually induces, and angrier passions seemed to have had their share in bringing it about.

We had not long resumed our drive, when the General began to talk, with his usual soldierly directness, of the bereavement, as he termed it, which he had sustained in the death of his beloved niece and ward; and he then broke out in a tone of intense bitterness and fury, inveighing against the "hellish arts" to which she had fallen a victim, and expressing with more exasperation than piety, his wonder that Heaven should tolerate so monstrous an indulgence of the lusts and malignity of hell.

My father, who saw at once that something very extraordinary had befallen, asked him, if not too painful to him, to detail the circumstances which he thought justified the strong terms in which he expressed himself.

"I should tell you all with pleasure," said the General, "but you would not believe me."

"Why should I not?" he asked.

"Because," he answered testily, "you believe in nothing but what consists with your own prejudices and illusions. I remember when I was like you, but I have learned better."

"Try me," said my father; "I am not such a dogmatist as you suppose. Besides which, I very well know that you generally require proof for what you believe and am, therefore, very strongly predisposed to respect your conclusions."

"You are right in supposing that I have not been led lightly into a belief in the marvellous—for what I have experienced *is* marvellous— and I have been forced by extraordinary evidence to credit that which ran counter, diametrically, to all my theories. I have been made the dupe of a preternatural conspiracy."

Notwithstanding his profession of confidence in the General's penetration, I saw my father, at this point, glance at the General, with, as I thought, a marked suspicion of his sanity.

The General did not see it, luckily. He was looking gloomily and curiously into the glades and vistas of the woods that were opening before us.

"You are going to the Ruins of Karnstein?" he said. "Yes, it is a lucky coincidence; do you know I was going to ask you to bring me there to inspect them. I have a special object in exploring. There is a ruined chapel, ain't there, with a great many tombs of that extinct family?"

"So there are—highly interesting," said my father, "I hope you are thinking of claiming the title and estates?"

My father said this gaily, but the General did not recollect the laugh, or even smile, which courtesy exacts for a friend's joke; on the contrary, he looked grave and even fierce, ruminating on a matter that stirred his anger and horror.

"Something very different," he said, gruffly. "I mean to unearth some of those fine people. I hope by God's blessing, to accomplish a pious sacrilege here, which will relieve our earth of certain monsters, and enable honest people to sleep in their beds without being assailed by murderers. I have strange things to tell you, my dear friend, such as I myself would have scouted as incredible a few months since."

My father looked at him again, but this time not with a glance of suspicion—with an eye, rather, of keen intelligence and alarm.

"The house of Karnstein," he said, "has been long extinct: a hundred years at least. My dear wife was maternally descended from the Karnsteins. But the name and title have long ceased to exist. The castle is a ruin; the very village is deserted; it is fifty years since the smoke of a chimney was seen there; not a roof left."

"Quite true. I have heard a great deal about that since I last saw you; a great deal that will astonish you. But I had better relate everything in the order in which it occurred," said the General. "You saw my dear ward—my child, I may call her. No creature could have been more beautiful, and only three months ago none more blooming."

"Yes, poor thing! when I saw her last she certainly was quite lovely," said my father. "I was grieved and shocked more than I can tell you, my dear friend; I knew what a blow it was to you."

He took the General's hand, and they exchanged a kind pressure. Tears gathered in the old soldier's eyes. He did not seek to conceal them. He said:

"We have been very old friends; I knew you would feel for me, childless as I am. She had become an object of very dear interest to me, and repaid my care by an affection that cheered my home and made my life happy. That is all gone. The years that remain to me on earth may not be very long; but by God's mercy I hope to accomplish a service to mankind before I die, and to subserve the vengeance of Heaven upon the fiends who have murdered my poor child in the spring of her hopes and beauty!"

"You said, just now, that you intended relating everything as it occurred," said my father. "Pray do; I assure you that it is not mere curiosity that prompts me."

By this time we had reached the point at which the Drunstall road, by which the General had come, diverges from the road which we were travelling to Karnstein.

"How far is it to the ruins?" inquired the General, looking anxiously forward.

"About half a league," answered my father. "Pray let us hear the story you were so good as to promise."

CHAPTER XI

The Story

"With all my heart," said the General, with an effort; and after a pause in which to arrange his subject, he commenced one of the strangest narratives I ever heard.

"My dear child was looking forward with great pleasure to the visit you had been so good as to arrange for her to your charming daughter." Here he made me a gallant but melancholy bow. "In the meantime we had an invitation to my old friend the Count Carlsfeld, whose schloss is about six leagues to the other side of Karnstein. It was to attend the series of fêtes which, you remember, were given by him in honor of his illustrious visitor, the Grand Duke Charles."

"Yes; and very splendid, I believe, they were," said my father.

"Princely! But then his hospitalities are quite regal. He has Aladdin's lamp. The night from which my sorrow dates was devoted to a

magnificent masquerade. The grounds were thrown open, the trees
hung with coloured lamps. There was such a display of fireworks as
Paris itself had never witnessed. And such music—music, you know, is
my weakness—such ravishing music! The finest instrumental band, perhaps, in the world, and the finest singers who could be collected from all
the great operas in Europe. As you wandered through those fantasti-
cally illuminated grounds, the moon-lighted château throwing a rosy
light from its long rows of windows, you would suddenly hear these
ravishing voices stealing from the silence of some grove, or rising from
boats upon the lake. I felt myself, as I looked and listened, carried back
into the romance and poetry of my early youth.

"When the fireworks were ended, and the ball beginning, we returned to the noble suite of rooms that were thrown open to the dancers. A masked ball, you know, is a beautiful sight; but so brilliant a
spectacle of the kind I never saw before.

"It was a very aristocratic assembly. I saw myself almost the only
'nobody' present.

"My dear child was looking quite beautiful. She wore no mask.
Her excitement and delight added an unspeakable charm to her features, always lovely. I remarked a young lady, dressed magnificently,
but wearing a mask, who appeared to me to be observing my ward with
extraordinary interest. I had seen her, earlier in the evening, in the great
hall, and again, for a few minutes, walking near us, on the terrace under
the castle windows, similarly employed. A lady, also masked, richly and
gravely dressed, and with stately air, like a person of rank, accompanied
her as a chaperon. Had the young lady not worn a mask, I could of
course, have been much more certain upon the question whether she
was really watching my poor darling. I am now well assured that she
was.

"We were in one of the *salons*. My poor dear child had been dancing, and was resting a little in one of the chairs near the door; I was
standing near. The two ladies I have mentioned had approached, and
the younger took the chair next my ward; while her companion stood
beside me, and for a little time addressed herself, in a low tone, to her
charge.

"Availing herself of the privilege of her mask, she turned to me,
and in the tone of an old friend, and calling me by my name, opened a
conversation with me, which piqued my curiosity a good deal. She
referred to many scenes where she had met me—at Court, and at distinguished houses. She alluded to little incidents which I had long ceased

to think of, but which, I found, had only lain in abeyance in my memory, for they instantly started into life at her touch.

"I became more and more curious to ascertain who she was, every moment. She parried my attempts to discover very adroitly and pleasantly. The knowledge she showed of many passages in my life seemed to me all but unaccountable; and she appeared to take a not unnatural pleasure in foiling my curiosity, and in seeing me flounder, in my eager perplexity, from one conjecture to another.

"In the meantime the young lady, whom her mother called by the odd name of Millarca, when she once or twice addressed her, had, with the same ease and grace, got into conversation with my ward.

"She introduced herself by saying that her mother was a very old acquaintance of mine. She spoke of the agreeable audacity which a mask rendered practicable; she talked like a friend; she admired her dress, and insinuated very prettily her admiration of her beauty. She amused her with laughing criticisms upon the people who crowded the ballroom, and laughed at my poor child's fun. She was very witty and lively when she pleased, and after a time they had grown very good friends, and the young stranger lowered her mask, displaying a remarkably beautiful face. I had never seen it before, neither had my dear child. But though it was new to us, the features were so engaging, as well as lovely, that it was impossible not to feel the attraction powerfully. My poor girl did so. I never saw anyone more taken with another at first sight, unless, indeed, it was the stranger herself, who seemed quite to have lost her heart to her.

"In the meantime, availing myself of the licence of a masquerade, I put not a few questions to the elder lady.

" 'You have puzzled me utterly,' I said, laughing. 'Is that not enough? won't you, now, consent to stand on equal terms, and do me the kindness to remove your mask?'

" 'Can any request be more unreasonable?' she replied. 'Ask a lady to yield an advantage! Beside, how do you know you should recognize me? Years make changes.'

" 'As you see,' I said, with a bow, and, I suppose, a rather melancholy little laugh.

" 'As philosophers tell us,' she said; 'and how do you know that a sight of my face would help you?'

" 'I should take chance for that,' I answered. 'It is vain trying to make yourself out an old woman; your figure betrays you.'

" 'Years, nevertheless, have passed since I saw you, rather since you saw me, for that is what I am considering. Millarca, there, is my daughter; I cannot then be young, even in the opinion of people whom time has taught to be indulgent, and I may not like to be compared with what you remember me. You have no mask to remove. You can offer me nothing in exchange.'

" 'My petition is to your pity, to remove it.'

" 'And mine to yours, to let it stay where it is,' she replied.

" 'Well, then, at least you will tell me whether you are French or German; you speak both languages so perfectly.'

" 'I don't think I shall tell you that, General; you intend a surprise, and are meditating the particular point of attack.'

" 'At all events, you won't deny this,' I said, 'that being honoured by your permission to converse, I ought to know how to address you. Shall I say Madame la Comtesse?'

"She laughed, and she would, no doubt, have met me with another evasion—if, indeed, I can treat any occurrence in an interview every circumstance of which was pre-arranged, as I now believe, with the profoundest cunning, as liable to be modified by accident.

" 'As to that,' she began; but she was interrupted, almost as she opened her lips, by a gentleman, dressed in black, who looked particularly elegant and distinguished, with this drawback, that his face was the most deadly pale I ever saw, except in death. He was in no masquerade—in the plain evening dress of a gentleman; and he said, without a smile, but with a courtly and unusually low bow:—

" 'Will Madame la Comtesse permit me to say a very few words which may interest her?'

"The lady turned quickly to him, and touched her lip in token of silence; she then said to me, 'Keep my place for me, General; I shall return when I have said a few words.'

"And with this injunction, playfully given, she walked a little aside with the gentleman in black, and talked for some minutes, apparently very earnestly. They then walked away slowly together in the crowd, and I lost them for some minutes.

"I spent the interval in cudgelling my brains for conjecture as to the identity of the lady who seemed to remember me so kindly, and I was thinking of turning about and joining in the conversation between my pretty ward and the Countess's daughter, and trying whether, by the time she returned, I might not have a surprise in store for her, by having her name, title, château, and estates at my fingers' ends. But at this moment she returned, accompanied by the pale man in black, who said:

"'I shall return and inform Madame la Comtesse when her carriage is at the door.'

"He withdrew with a bow.

CHAPTER XII

A Petition

"'Then we are to lose Madame la Comtesse, but I hope only for a few hours,' I said, with a low bow.

"'It may be that only, or it may be a few weeks. It was very unlucky his speaking to me just now as he did. Do you now know me?'

"I assured her I did not.

"'You shall know me,' she said, 'but not at present. We are older and better friends than, perhaps, you suspect. I cannot yet declare myself. I shall in three weeks pass your beautiful schloss about which I have been making enquiries. I shall then look in upon you for an hour or two, and renew a friendship which I never think of without a thousand pleasant recollections. This moment a piece of news has reached me like a thunderbolt. I must set out now, and travel by a devious route, nearly a hundred miles, with all the dispatch I can possibly make. My perplexities multiply. I am only deterred by the compulsory reserve I practise as to my name from making a very singular request of you. My poor child has not quite recovered her strength. Her horse fell with her, at a hunt which she had ridden out to witness, her nerves have not yet recovered the shock, and our physician says that she must on no account exert herself for some time to come. We came here, in consequence, by very easy stages—hardly six leagues a day. I must now travel day and night, on a mission of life and death—a mission the critical and momentous nature of which I shall be able to explain to you when we meet, as I hope we shall, in a few weeks, without the necessity of any concealment.'

"She went on to make her petition, and it was in the tone of a person from whom such a request amounted to conferring, rather than seeking a favour. This was only in manner, and, as it seemed, quite unconsciously. Then the terms in which it was expressed, nothing could be more deprecatory. It was simply that I would consent to take charge of her daughter during her absence.

"This was, all things considered, a strange, not to say, an audacious request. She in some sort disarmed me, by stating and admitting everything that could be urged against it, and throwing herself entirely upon my chivalry. At the same moment, by a fatality that seems to have predetermined all that happened, my poor child came to my side, and, in an undertone, besought me to invite her new friend, Millarca, to pay us a visit. She had just been sounding her, and thought, if her mamma would allow her, she would like it extremely.

"At another time I should have told her to wait a little, until, at least, we knew who they were. But I had not a moment to think in. The two ladies assailed me together; and I must confess the refined and beautiful face of the young lady, about which there was something extremely engaging, as well as the elegance and fire of high birth, determined me; and quite overpowered, I submitted, and undertook, too easily, the care of the young lady, whom her mother called Millarca.

"The Countess beckoned to her daughter, who listened with grave attention while she told her, in general terms, how suddenly and peremptorily she had been summoned, and also of the arrangement she had made for her under my care, adding that I was one of her earliest and most valued friends.

"I made, of course, such speeches as the case seemed to call for, and found myself, on reflection, in a position which I did not half like.

"The gentleman in black returned, and very ceremoniously conducted the lady from the room.

"The demeanour of this gentleman was such as to impress me with the conviction that the Countess was a lady of very much more importance than her modest title alone might have led me to assume.

"Her last charge to me was that no attempt was to be made to learn more about her than I might have already guessed, until her return. Our distinguished host, whose guest she was, knew her reasons.

"'But here,' she said, 'neither I nor my daughter could safely remain more than a day. I removed my mask imprudently for a moment, about an hour ago, and, too late, I fancied you saw me. So I have resolved to seek an opportunity of talking a little to you. Had I found that you *had* seen me, I should have thrown myself on your high sense of honour to keep my secret for some weeks. As it is, I am satisfied that you did not see me; but if you now *suspect*, or, on reflection, *should* suspect, who I am, I commit myself, in like manner, entirely to your honour. My daughter will observe the same secresy, and I well know that you will, from time to time, remind her, lest she should thoughtlessly disclose it.'

"She whispered a few words to her daughter, kissed her hurriedly twice, and went away, accompanied by the pale gentleman in black, and disappeared in the crowd.

" 'In the next room,' said Millarca, 'there is a window that looks upon the hall door. I should like to see the last of mamma, and to kiss my hand to her.'

"We assented, of course, and accompanied her to the window. We looked out, and saw a handsome old-fashioned carriage, with a troop of couriers and footmen. We saw the slim figure of the pale gentleman in black, as he held a thick velvet cloak, and placed it about her shoulders and threw the hood over her head. She nodded to him, and just touched his hand with hers. He bowed low repeatedly as the door closed, and the carriage began to move.

" 'She is gone,' said Millarca with a sigh.

" 'She is gone,' I repeated to myself, for the first time—in the hurried moments that had elapsed since my consent—reflecting upon the folly of my act.

" 'She did not look up,' said the young lady, plaintively.

" 'The Countess had taken off her mask, perhaps, and did not care to show her face,' I said; 'and she could not know that you were in the window.'

"She sighed and looked in my face. She was so beautiful that I relented. I was sorry I had for a moment repented of my hospitality, and I determined to make her amends for the unavowed churlishness of my reception.

"The young lady, replacing her mask, joined my ward in persuading me to return to the grounds, where the concert was soon to be renewed. We did so, and walked up and down the terrace that lies under the castle windows. Millarca became very intimate with us, and amused us with lively descriptions and stories of most of the great people whom we saw upon the terrace. I liked her more and more every minute. Her gossip, without being ill-natured, was extremely diverting to me, who had been so long out of the great world. I thought what life she would give to our sometimes lonely evenings at home.

"This ball was not over until the morning sun had almost reached the horizon. It pleased the Grand Duke to dance till then, so loyal people could not go away, or think of bed.

"We had just got through a crowded saloon, when my ward asked me what had become of Millarca. I thought she had been by her side, and she fancied she was by mine. The fact was, we had lost her.

"All my efforts to find her were in vain. I feared that she had mistaken, in the confusion of the momentary separation from us, other people for her new friends, and had, possibly, pursued and lost them in the extensive grounds which were thrown open to us.

"Now, in its full force, I recognized a new folly in my having undertaken the charge of a young lady without so much as knowing her name; and fettered as I was by promises, of the reasons for imposing which I knew nothing, I could not even point my inquiries by saying that the missing young lady was the daughter of the Countess who had taken her departure a few hours before.

"Morning broke. It was clear daylight before I gave up my search. It was not till near two o'clock next day that we heard anything of my missing charge.

"At about that time a servant knocked at my niece's door, to say that he had been earnestly requested by a young lady, who appeared to be in great distress, to make out where she could find the General Baron Spielsdorf and the young lady, his daughter, in whose charge she had been left by her mother.

"There could be no doubt, notwithstanding the slight inaccuracy, that our young friend had turned up; and so she had. Would to Heaven we had lost her!

"She told my poor child a story to account for her having failed to recover us for so long. Very late, she said, she had got into the house-keeper's bedroom in despair of finding us, and had then fallen into a deep sleep which, long as it was, had hardly sufficed to recruit her strength after the fatigues of the ball.

"That day Millarca came home with us. I was only too happy, after all, to have secured so charming a companion for my dear girl.

CHAPTER XIII

The Wood-Man

"There soon, however, appeared some drawbacks. In the first place, Millarca complained of extreme languor—the weakness that remained after her late illness—and she never emerged from her room till the afternoon was pretty far advanced. In the next place, it was accidentally discovered, although she always locked her door on the inside, and never disturbed the key from its place, till she admitted the maid to assist at her toilet, that she was undoubtedly sometimes absent from her room in the very early morning, and at various times later in the day, before she wished it to be understood that she was stirring. She was repeatedly seen from the windows of the schloss, in the first faint grey of the morning, walking through the trees, in an easterly direction, and looking like a person in a trance. This convinced me that she walked in her sleep. But this hypothesis did not solve the puzzle. How did she pass out from her room, leaving the door locked on the inside. How did she escape from the house without unbarring door or window?

"In the midst of my perplexities, an anxiety of far more urgent kind presented itself.

"My dear child began to lose her looks and health, and that in a manner so mysterious, and even horrible, that I became thoroughly frightened.

"She was at first visited by appalling dreams; then, as she fancied, by a spectre, somtimes resembling Millarca, sometimes in the shape of a beast, indistinctly seen, walking round the foot of her bed, from side to side. Lastly came sensations. One, not unpleasant, but very peculiar, she said, resembled the flow of an icy stream against her breast. At a later time, she felt something like a pair of large needles pierce her, a little below the throat, with a very sharp pain. A few nights after, followed a gradual and convulsive sense of strangulation; then came unconsciousness."

I could hear distinctly every word the kind old General was saying, because by this time we were driving upon the short grass that spreads on either side of the road as you approach the roofless village which had not shown the smoke of a chimney for more than half a century.

You may guess how strangely I felt as I heard my own symptoms so exactly described in those which had been experienced by the poor girl who, but for the catastrophe which followed, would have been at that moment a visitor at my father's château. You may suppose, also, how I felt as I heard him detail habits and mysterious peculiarities which were, in fact, those of our beautiful guest, Carmilla!

A vista opened in the forest; we were on a sudden under the chimneys and gables of the ruined village, and the towers and battlements of the dismantled castle, round which gigantic trees are grouped, overhung us from a slight eminence.

In a frightened dream I got down from the carriage, and in silence, for we had each abundant matter for thinking; we soon mounted the ascent, and were among the spacious chambers, winding stairs, and dark corridors of the castle.

"And this was once the palatial residence of the Karnsteins!" said the old General at length, as from a great window he looked out across the village, and saw the wide, undulating expanse of forest. "It was a bad family, and here its blood-stained annals were written," he continued. "It is hard that they should, after death, continue to plague the human race with their atrocious lusts. That is the chapel of the Karnsteins, down there."

He pointed down to the grey walls of the Gothic building, partly visible through the foliage, a little way down the steep. "And I hear the axe of a woodman," he added, "busy among the trees that surround it; he possibly may give us the information of which I am in search, and point out the grave of Mircalla, Countess of Karnstein. These rustics preserve the local traditions of great families, whose stories die out among the rich and titled so soon as the families themselves become extinct."

"We have a portrait, at home, of Mircalla, the Countess Karnstein; should you like to see it?" asked my father.

"Time enough," dear friend, replied the General. "I believe that I have seen the original; and one motive which has led me to you earlier than I at first intended, was to explore the chapel which we are now approaching."

"What! see the Countess Mircalla," exclaimed my father; "why, she has been dead more than a century!"

"Not so dead as you fancy, I am told," answered the General.

"I confess, General, you puzzle me utterly," replied my father, looking at him, I fancied, for a moment with a return of the suspicion I detected before. But although there was anger and detestation, at times, in the old General's manner, there was nothing flighty.

"There remains to me," he said, as we passed under the heavy arch of the Gothic church—for its dimensions would have justified its being so styled—"but one object which can interest me during the few years that remain to me on earth, and that is to wreak on her the vengeance which, I thank God, may still be accomplished by a mortal arm."

"What vengeance can you mean?" asked my father, in increasing amazement.

"I mean, to decapitate the monster," he answered, with a fierce flush, and a stamp that echoed mournfully through the hollow ruin, and his clenched hand was at the same moment raised, as if it grasped the handle of an axe, while he shook it ferociously in the air.

"What!" exclaimed my father, more than ever bewildered.

"To strike her head off."

"Cut her head off!"

"Aye, with a hatchet, with a spade, or with anything that can cleave through her murderous throat. You shall hear," he answered, trembling with rage. And hurrying forward he said:

"That beam will answer for a seat; your dear child is fatigued; let her be seated, and I will, in a few sentences, close my dreadful story."

The squared block of wood, which lay on the grass-grown pavement of the chapel, formed a bench on which I was very glad to seat myself, and in the meantime the General called to the woodman, who had been removing some boughs which leaned upon the old walls; and, axe in hand, the hardy old fellow stood before us.

He could not tell us anything of these monuments; but there was an old man, he said, a ranger of this forest, at present sojourning in the house of the priest, about two miles away, who could point out every monument of the old Karnstein family; and, for a trifle, he undertook to bring back with him, if we would lend him one of our horses, in little more than half-an-hour.

"Have you been long employed about this forest?" asked my father of the old man.

"I have been a woodman here," he answered in his *patois,* "under the forester, all my days; so has my father before me, and so on, as many generations as I can count up. I could show you the very house in the village here, in which my ancestors lived."

"How came the village to be deserted?" asked the General.

"It was troubled by *revenants,* sir; several were tracked to their graves, there detected by the usual tests, and extinguished in the usual way, by decapitation, by the stake, and by burning; but not until many of the villagers were killed.

"But after all these proceedings according to law," he continued— "so many graves opened, and so many vampires deprived of their horrible animation—the village was not relieved. But a Moravian nobleman, who happened to be travelling this way, heard how matters were, and being skilled—as many people are in his country—in such affairs, he offered to deliver the village from its tormentor. He did so thus: There being a bright moon that night, he ascended, shortly after sunset, the tower of the chapel here, from whence he could distinctly see the churchyard beneath him; you can see it from that window. From this point he watched until he saw the vampire come out of his grave, and place near it the linen clothes in which he had been folded, and glide away towards the village to plague its inhabitants.

"The stranger, having seen all this, came down from the steeple, took the linen wrappings of the vampire, and carried them up to the top of the tower, which he again mounted. When the vampire returned from his prowlings and missed his clothes, he cried furiously to the Moravian, whom he saw at the summit of the tower, and who, in reply, beckoned him to ascend and take them. Whereupon the vampire, accepting his invitation, began to climb the steeple, and so soon as he had reached the battlements, the Moravian, with a stroke of his sword, clove his skull in twain, hurling him down to the churchyard, whither, descending by the winding stairs, the stranger followed and cut his head off, and next day delivered it and the body to the villagers, who duly impaled and burnt them.

"This Moravian nobleman had the authority from the then head of the family to remove the tomb of Mircalla, Countess Karnstein, which he did effectually, so that in a little while its site was quite forgotten."

"Can you point out where it stood?" asked the General, eagerly.

The forester shook his head and smiled.

"Not a living soul could tell you that now," he said; "besides, they say her body was removed; but no one is sure of that either."

Having thus spoken, as time pressed, he dropped his axe and departed, leaving us to hear the remainder of the General's strange story.

CHAPTER XIV

The Meeting

"My beloved child," he resumed, "was now growing rapidly worse. The physician who attended her had failed to produce the slightest impression upon her disease, for such I then supposed it to be. He saw my alarm, and suggested a consultation. I called in an abler physician, from Gratz. Several days elapsed before he arrived. He was a good and pious, as well as a learned man. Having seen my poor ward together, they withdrew to my library to confer and discuss. I, from the adjoining room, where I awaited their summons, heard these two gentlemen's voices raised in something sharper than a strictly philosophical discussion. I knocked at the door and entered. I found the old physician from Gratz maintaining his theory. His rival was combating it with undisguised ridicule, accompanied with bursts of laughter. This unseemly manifestation subsided and the altercation ended on my entrance.

" 'Sir,' said my first physician, 'my learned brother seems to think that you want a conjuror, and not a doctor.'

" 'Pardon me,' said the old physician from Gratz, looking displeased, 'I shall state my own view of the case in my own way another time. I grieve, Monsieur le Général, that by my skill and science I can be of no use. Before I go I shall do myself the honour to suggest something to you.'

"He seemed thoughtful, and sat down at a table, and began to write. Profoundly disappointed, I made my bow, and as I turned to go, the other doctor pointed over his shoulder to his companion who was writing, and then, with a shrug, significantly touched his forehead.

"This consultation, then, left me precisely where I was. I walked out into the grounds, all but distracted. The doctor from Gratz, in ten or fifteen minutes, overtook me. He apologised for having followed me, but said that he could not conscientiously take his leave without a few words more. He told me that he could not be mistaken; no natural disease exhibited the same symptoms; and that death was already very near. There remained, however, a day, or possibly two, of life. If the fatal seizure were at once arrested, with great care and skill her strength might possibly return. But all hung now upon the confines of the irrevocable. One more assault might extinguish the last spark of vitality which is, every moment, ready to die.

" 'And what is the nature of the seizure you speak of?' I entreated.

" 'I have stated all fully in this note, which I place in your hands, upon the distinct condition that you send for the nearest clergyman, and open my letter in his presence, and on no account read it till he is with you; you would despise it else, and it is a matter of life and death. Should the priest fail you, then, indeed, you may read it.'

"He asked me, before taking his leave finally, whether I would wish to see a man curiously learned upon the very subject, which, after I had read his letter, would probably interest me above all others, and he urged me earnestly to invite him to visit him there; and so took his leave.

"The ecclesiastic was absent, and I read the letter by myself. At another time, or in another case, it might have excited my ridicule. But into what quackeries will not people rush for a last chance, where all accustomed means have failed, and the life of a beloved object is at stake?

"Nothing, you will say, could be more absurd than the learned man's letter. It was monstrous enough to have consigned him to a madhouse. He said that the patient was suffering from the visits of a vampire! The punctures which she described as having occurred near the throat, were, he insisted, the insertion of those two long, thin, and sharp teeth which, it is well known, are peculiar to vampires; and there could be no doubt, he added, as to the well defined presence of the small livid mark which all concurred in describing as that induced by the demon's lips, and every symptom described by the sufferer was in exact conformity with those recorded in every case of a similar visitation.

"Being myself wholly sceptical as to the existence of any such portent as the vampire, the supernatural theory of the good doctor furnished, in my opinion, but another instance of learning and intelligence oddly associated with some one hallucination. I was so miserable, however, that, rather than try nothing, I acted upon the instructions of the letter.

"I concealed myself in the dark dressing-room, that opened upon the poor patient's room, in which a candle was burning, and watched there until she was fast asleep. I stood at the door, peeping through the small crevice, my sword laid on the table beside me, as my directions prescribed, until, a little after one, I saw a large black object, very ill-defined, crawl, as it seemed to me, over the foot of the bed, and swiftly spread itself up to the poor girl's throat, where it swelled, in a moment, into a great, palpitating mass.

"For a few moments I had stood petrified. I now sprang forward, with my sword in my hand. The black creature suddenly contracted toward the foot of the bed, glided over it, and, standing on the floor about a yard below the foot of the bed, with a glare of skulking ferocity and horror fixed on me, I saw Millarca. Speculating I know not what, I struck at her instantly with my sword; but I saw her standing near the door, unscathed. Horrified, I pursued, and struck again. She was gone! and my sword flew to shivers against the door.

"I can't describe to you all that passed on that horrible night. The whole house was up and stirring. The spectre Millarca was gone. But her victim was sinking fast, and before the morning dawned, she died."

The old General was agitated. We did not speak to him. My father walked to some little distance, and began reading the inscriptions on the tombstones; and thus occupied, he strolled into the door of a side chapel to prosecute his researches. The General leaned against the wall, dried his eyes, and sighed heavily. I was relieved on hearing the voices of Carmilla and Madame, who were at that moment approaching. The voices died away.

In this solitude, having just listened to so strange a story, connected, as it was, with the great and titled dead, whose monuments were moulding among the dust and ivy round us, and every incident of which bore so awfully upon my own mysterious case—in this haunted spot, darkened by the towering foliage that rose on every side, dense and high above its noiseless walls—a horror began to steal over me, and my heart sank as I thought that my friends were, after all, now about to enter and disturb this triste and ominous scene.

The old General's eyes were fixed on the ground, as he leaned with his hand upon the basement of a shattered monument.

Under a narrow, arched doorway, surmounted by one of those demoniacal grotesques in which the cynical and ghastly fancy of old Gothic carving delights, I saw very gladly the beautiful face and figure of Carmilla enter the shadowy chapel.

I was just about to rise and speak, and nodded smiling, in answer to her peculiarly engaging smile; when with a cry, the old man by my side caught up the woodman's hatchet, and started forward. On seeing him a brutalised change came over her features. It was an instantaneous and horrible transformation, as she made a crouching step backwards. Before I could utter a scream, he struck at her with all his force, but she dived under his blow, and unscathed, caught him in her tiny grasp by the wrist. He struggled for a moment to release his arm, but his hand opened, the axe fell to the ground, and the girl was gone.

He staggered against the wall. His grey hair stood upon his head, and a moisture shone over his face, as if he were at the point of death.

The frightful scene had passed in a moment. The first thing I recollect after, is Madame standing before me, and impatiently repeating again and again, the question, "Where is Mademoiselle Carmilla?"

I answered at length, "I don't know—I can't tell—she went there," and I pointed to the door through which Madame had just entered; "only a minute or two since."

"But I have been standing there, in the passage, ever since Mademoiselle Carmilla entered; and she did not return."

She then began to call "Carmilla" through every door and passage and from the windows, but no answer came.

"She called herself Carmilla?" asked the General, still agitated.

"Carmilla, yes," I answered.

"Aye," he said, "that is Millarca. That is the same person who long ago was called Mircalla, Countess Karnstein. Depart from this accursed ground, my poor child, as quickly as you can. Drive to the clergyman's house, and stay there till we come. Begone! May you never behold Carmilla more; you will not find her here."

CHAPTER XV
Ordeal and Execution

As he spoke one of the strangest-looking men I ever beheld, entered the chapel at the door through which Carmilla had made her entrance and her exit. He was tall, narrow-chested, stooping, with high shoulders, and dressed in black. His face was brown and dried in with deep furrows; he wore an oddly-shaped hat with a broad leaf. His hair, long and grizzled, hung on his shoulders. He wore a pair of gold spectacles, and walked slowly, with an odd shambling gait, with his face sometimes turned up to the sky, and sometimes bowed down toward the ground, seemed to wear a perpetual smile; his long thin arms were swinging, and his lank hands, in old black gloves ever so much too wide for them, waving and gesticulating in utter abstraction.

"The very man!" exclaimed the General, advancing with manifest delight. "My dear Baron, how happy I am to see you, I had no hope of meeting you so soon." He signed to my father, who had by this time returned, and leading the fantastic old gentleman, whom he called the Baron, to meet him. He introduced him formally, and they at once entered into earnest conversation. The stranger took a roll of paper from his pocket, and spread it on the worn surface of a tomb that stood by. He had a pencil case in his fingers, with which he traced imaginary lines from point to point on the paper, which from their often glancing from it, together, at certain points of the building, I concluded to be a plan of the chapel. He accompanied, what I may term his lecture, with occasional readings from a dirty little book, whose yellow leaves were closely written over.

They sauntered together down the side aisle, opposite to the spot where I was standing, conversing as they went; then they begun measuring distances by paces, and finally they all stood together, facing a piece of the side-wall, which they began to examine with great minuteness; pulling off the ivy that clung over it, and rapping the plaster with the ends of their sticks, scraping here, and knocking there. At length they ascertained the existence of a broad marble tablet, with letters carved in relief upon it.

With the assistance of the woodman, who soon returned, a monumental inscription, and carved escutcheon, were disclosed. They proved to be of those of the long lost monument of Mircalla, Countess Karnstein.

The old General, though not I fear given to the praying mood, raised his hands and eyes to heaven, in mute thanksgiving for some moments.

"To-morrow," I heard him say; "the commissioner will be here, and the Inquisition will be held according to law."

Then turning to the old man with the gold spectacles, whom I have described, he shook him warmly by both hands and said:

"Baron, how can I thank you? How can we all thank you? You will have delivered this region from a plague that has scourged its inhabitants for more than a century. The horrible enemy, thank God, is at last tracked."

My father led the stranger aside, and the General followed. I knew that he had led them out of hearing, that he might relate my case, and I saw them glance often quickly at me, as the discussion proceeded.

My father came to me, kissed me again and again, and leading me from the chapel said:

"It is time to return, but before we go home, we must add to our party the good priest, who lives but a little way from this; and persuade him to accompany us to the schloss."

In this quest we were successful: and I was glad, being unspeakably fatigued when we reached home. But my satisfaction was changed to dismay, on discovering that there were no tidings of Carmilla. Of the scene that had occurred in the ruined chapel, no explanation was offered to me, and it was clear that it was a secret which my father for the present determined to keep from me.

The sinister absence of Carmilla made the remembrance of the scene more horrible to me. The arrangements for that night were singular. Two servants and Madame were to sit up in my room that night; and the ecclesiastic with my father kept watch in the adjoining dressing-room.

The priest had performed certain solemn rites that night, the pur-

port of which I did not understand any more than I comprehended the
reason of this extraordinary precaution taken for my safety during
sleep.

I saw all clearly a few days later.

The disappearance of Carmilla was followed by the discontinuance
of my nightly sufferings.

You have heard, no doubt, of the appalling superstition that
prevails in Upper and Lower Styria, in Moravia, Silesia, in Turkish
Servia, in Poland, even in Russia; the superstition, so we must call it, of
the vampire.

If human testimony, taken with every care and solemnity, judi-
cially, before commissions innumerable, each consisting of many members, all chosen for integrity and intelligence, and constituting reports
more voluminous perhaps that exist upon any one other class of cases,
is worth anything, it is difficult to deny, or even to doubt the existence
of such a phenomenon as the vampire.

For my part I have heard no theory by which to explain what I
myself have witnessed and experienced, other than that supplied by the
ancient and well-attested belief of the country.

The next day the formal proceedings took place in the Chapel of
Karnstein. The grave of the Countess Mircalla was opened; and the
General and my father recognized each his perfidious and beautiful
guest, in the face now disclosed to view. The features, though a hundred
and fifty years had passed since her funeral, were tinted with the
warmth of life. Her eyes were open; no cadaverous smell exhaled from
the coffin. The two medical men, one officially present, the other on the
part of the promoter of the inquiry, attested the marvellous fact, that
there was a faint, but appreciable respiration, and a corresponding action of the heart. The limbs were perfectly flexible, the flesh elastic; and
the leaden coffin floated with blood, in which to a depth of seven inches,
the body lay immersed. Here then, were all the admitted signs and
proofs of vampirism. The body, therefore, in accordance with the ancient practice, was raised, and a sharp stake driven through the heart of
the vampire, who uttered a piercing shriek at the moment, in all respects such as might escape from a living person in the last agony. Then
the head was struck off, and a torrent of blood flowed from the severed
neck. The body and head were next placed on a pile of wood, and
reduced to ashes, which were thrown upon the river and borne away,
and that territory has never since been plagued by the visits of a vampire.

My father has a copy of the report of the Imperial Commission, with the signatures of all who were present at these proceedings, attached in verification of the statement. It is from this official paper that I have summarized my account of this last shocking scene.

CHAPTER XVI

Conclusion

I write all this you suppose with composure. But far from it; I cannot think of it without agitation. Nothing but your earnest desire so repeatedly expressed, could have induced me to sit down to a task that has unstrung my nerves for months to come, and reinduced a shadow of the unspeakable horror which years after my deliverance continued to make my days and nights dreadful, and solitude insupportably terrific.

Let me add a word or two about that quaint Baron Vordenburg, to whose curious lore we were indebted for the discovery of the Countess Mircalla's grave.

He had taken up his abode in Gratz, where, living upon a mere pittance, which was all that remained to him of the once princely estates of his family, in Upper Styria, he devoted himself to the minute and laborious investigation of the marvellously authenticated tradition of vampirism. He had at his fingers' ends all the great and little works upon the subject. "Magia Posthuma," "Phlegon de Mirabilibus," "Augustinus de curâ pro Mortuis," "Philosophicae et Christianae Cogitationes de Vampiris," by John Christofer Harenberg; and a thousand others, among which I remember only a few of those which he lent to my father. He had a voluminous digest of all the judicial cases, from which he had extracted a system of principles that appear to govern— some always, and others occasionally only—the condition of the vampire. I may mention, in passing, that the deadly pallor attributed to that sort of *revenants,* is a mere melodramatic fiction. They present, in the grave, and when they show themselves in human society, the appearance of healthy life. When disclosed to light in their coffins, they exhibit all the symptoms that are enumerated as those which proved the vampire life of the long-dead Countess Karnstein.

How they escape from their graves and return to them for certain hours every day, without displacing the clay or leaving any trace of disturbance in the state of the coffin or the cerements, has always been admitted to be utterly inexplicable. The amphibious existence of the vampire is sustained by daily renewed slumber in the grave. Its horrible lust for living blood supplies the vigour of its waking existence. The vampire is prone to be fascinated with an engrossing vehemence, resembling the passion of love, by particular persons. In pursuit of these it will exercise inexhaustible patience and stratagem, for access to a particular object may be obstructed in a hundred ways. It will never desist until it has satiated its passion, and drained the very life of its coveted victim. But it will, in these cases, husband and protract its murderous enjoyment with the refinement of an epicure, and heighten it by the gradual approaches of an artful courtship. In these cases it seems to yearn for something like sympathy and consent. In ordinary ones it goes direct to its object, overpowers with violence, and strangles and exhausts often at a single feast.

The vampire is, apparently, subject, in certain situations, to special conditions. In the particular instance of which I have given you a relation, Mircalla seemed to be limited to a name which, if not her real one, should at least reproduce, without the omission or addition of a single letter, those, as we say, anagrammatically, which compose it. *Carmilla* did this; so did *Millarca*.

My father related to the Baron Vordenburg, who remained with us for two or three weeks after the expulsion of Carmilla, the story about the Moravian nobleman and the vampire at Karnstein churchyard, and then he asked the Baron how he had discovered the exact position of the long-concealed tomb of the Countess Millarca? The Baron's grotesque features puckered up into a mysterious smile; he looked down, still smiling, on his worn spectacle-case and fumbled with it. Then looking up, he said:

"I have many journals, and other papers, written by that remarkable man; the most curious among them is one treating of the visit of which you speak, to Karnstein. The tradition, of course, discolours and distorts a little. He might have been termed a Moravian nobleman, for he had changed his abode to that territory, and was, beside, a noble. But he was, in truth, a native of Upper Styria. It is enough to say that in very early youth he had been a passionate and favoured lover of the beautiful Mircalla, Countess Karnstein. Her early death plunged him into inconsolable grief. It is the nature of vampires to increase and multiply, but according to an ascertained and ghostly law.

"Assume, at starting, a territory perfectly free from that pest. How does it begin, and how does it multiply itself? I will tell you. A person, more or less wicked, puts an end to himself. A suicide, under certain circumstances, becomes a vampire. That spectre visits living people in their slumbers; *they* die, and almost invariably, in the grave, develope into vampires. This happened in the case of the beautiful Mircalla, who was haunted by one of those demons. My ancestor, Vordenburg, whose title I still bear, soon discovered this, and in the course of the studies to which he devoted himself, learned a great deal more.

"Among other things, he concluded that suspicion of vampirism would probably fall, sooner or later, upon the dead Countess, who in life had been his idol. He conceived a horror, be she what she might, of her remains being profaned by the outrage of a posthumous execution. He has left a curious paper to prove that the vampire, on its expulsion from its amphibious existence, is projected into a far more horrible life; and he resolved to save his once beloved Mircalla from this.

"He adopted the stratagem of a journey here, a pretended removal of her remains, and a real obliteration of her monument. When age had stolen upon him, and from the vale of years he looked back on the scenes he was leaving, he considered, in a different spirit, what he had done; and a horror took possession of him. He made the tracings and notes which have guided me to the very spot, and drew up a confession of the deception that he had practised. If he had intended any further action in this matter, death prevented him; and the hand of a remote descendant has, too late for many, directed the pursuit to the lair of the beast."

We talked a little more, and among other things he said was this:

"One sign of the vampire is the power of the hand. The slender hand of Mircalla closed like a vice of steel on the General's wrist when he raised the hatchet to strike. But its power is not confined to its grasp; it leaves a numbness in the limb it seizes, which is slowly, if ever, recovered from."

The following Spring my father took me a tour through Italy. We remained away for more than a year. It was long before the terror of recent events subsided; and to this hour the image of Carmilla returns to memory with ambiguous alternations—sometimes the playful, languid, beautiful girl; sometimes the writhing fiend I saw in the ruined church; and often from a reverie I have started, fancying I heard the light step of Carmilla at the drawing-room door.

MARY ELIZABETH BRADDON *(1835–1915), who wrote under a variety of names, was one of the most prolific authors of the Victorian era. Her single most popular work was the novel* Lady Audley's Secret *(1861–62), which was often presented on the stage during the nineteenth century. Besides her novels and short fiction, Braddon also found time to edit* Belgravia, *a fashionable magazine for ladies.*

"If I could plot like Miss Braddon," wrote William Makepeace Thackeray, author of Vanity Fair, *"I would be the greatest writer in the English language."*

Like most Victorian authors, Braddon did not hesitate to produce melodramatic and thrilling "sensation" stories when they were in demand, and "Good Lady Ducayne," first published in The Strand Magazine *for February 1896, is one of her best.*

Good Lady Ducayne (1896)

BY MARY ELIZABETH BRADDON

I

Bella Rolleston had made up her mind that her only chance of earning her bread and helping her mother to an occasional crust was by going out into the great unknown world as companion to a lady. She was willing to go to any lady rich enough to pay her a salary and so eccentric as to wish for a hired companion. Five shillings told off reluctantly from one of those sovereigns which were so rare with the mother and daughter, and which melted away so quickly, five solid shillings, had been handed to a smartly-dressed lady in an office in Harbeck Street, London, W., in the hope that this very Superior Person would find a situation and a salary for Miss Rolleston. The Superior Person glanced at the two half-crowns as they lay on the table where Bella's hand had placed them, to make sure they were neither of them florins, before she wrote a description of Bella's qualifications and requirements in a formidable-looking ledger.

"Age?" she asked, curtly.

"Eighteen, last July."

"Any accomplishments?"

"No; I am not at all accomplished. If I were I should want to be a governess—a companion seems the lowest stage."

"We have some highly accomplished ladies on our books as companions, or chaperon companions."

"Oh, I know!" babbled Bella, loquacious in her youthful candor. "But that is quite a different thing. Mother hasn't been able to afford a piano since I was twelve years old, so I'm afraid I've forgotten how to play. And I have had to help mother with her needlework, so there hasn't been much time to study."

"Please don't waste time upon explaining what you can't do, but kindly tell me anything you can do," said the Superior Person, crushingly, with her pen poised between delicate fingers waiting to write. "Can you read aloud for two or three hours at a stretch? Are you active and handy, an early riser, a good walker, sweet tempered, and obliging?"

"I can say yes to all those questions except about the sweetness. I think I have a pretty good temper, and I should be anxious to oblige anybody who paid for my services. I should want them to feel that I was really earning my salary."

"The kind of ladies who come to me would not care for a talkative companion," said the Person, severely, having finished writing in her book. "My connection lies chiefly among the aristocracy, and in that class considerable deference is expected."

"Oh, of course," said Bella; "but it's quite different when I'm talking to you. I want to tell you all about myself once and forever."

"I am glad it is to be only once!" said the Person, with the edges of her lips.

The Person was of uncertain age, tightly laced in a black silk gown. She had a powdery complexion and a handsome clump of somebody else's hair on the top of her head. It may be that Bella's girlish freshness and vivacity had an irritating effect upon nerves weakened by an eight-hour day in that overheated second floor in Harbeck Street. To Bella the official apartment, with its Brussels carpet, velvet curtains and velvet chairs, and French clock, ticking loud on the marble chimney-piece, suggested the luxury of a palace, as compared with another second floor in Walworth where Mrs. Rolleston and her daughter had managed to exist for the last six years.

"Do you think you have anything on your books that would suit me?" faltered Bella, after a pause.

"Oh, dear, no; I have nothing in view at present," answered the

Person, who had swept Bella's half-crowns into a drawer, absent-mindedly, with the tips of her fingers. "You see, you are so very un-formed—so much too young to be companion to a lady of position. It is a pity you have not enough education for a nursery governess; that would be more in your line."

"And do you think it will be very long before you can get me a situation?" asked Bella, doubtfully.

"I really cannot say. Have you any particular reason for being so impatient—not a love affair, I hope?"

"A love affair!" cried Bella, with flaming cheeks. "What utter non-sense. I want a situation because mother is poor, and I hate being a burden to her. I want a salary that I can share with her."

"There won't be much margin for sharing in the salary you are likely to get at your age—and with your—very—unformed manners," said the Person, who found Bella's peony cheeks, bright eyes, and un-bridled vivacity more and more oppressive.

"Perhaps if you'd be kind enough to give me back the fee I could take it to an agency where the connection isn't quite so aristocratic," said Bella, who—as she told her mother in her recital of the interview—was determined not to be sat upon.

"You will find no agency that can do more for you than mine," replied the Person, whose harpy fingers never relinquished coin. "You will have to wait for your opportunity. Yours is an exceptional case: but I will bear you in mind, and if anything suitable offers I will write to you. I cannot say more than that."

The half-contemptuous bend of the stately head, weighted with borrowed hair, indicated the end of the interview. Bella went back to Walworth—tramped sturdily every inch of the way in the September afternoon—and "took off" the Superior Person for the amusement of her mother and the landlady, who lingered in the shabby little sitting-room after bringing in the tea-tray, to applaud Miss Rolleston's "taking off."

"Dear, dear, what a mimic she is!" said the landlady. "You ought to have let her go on the stage, mum. She might have made her fortune as an actress."

II

Bella waited and hoped, and listened for the postman's knocks which brought such store of letters for the parlors and the first floor, and so few for that humble second floor, where mother and daughter sat sewing with hand and with wheel and treadle, for the greater part of the day. Mrs. Rolleston was a lady by birth and education; but it had been her bad fortune to marry a scoundrel; for the last half-dozen years she had been that worst of widows, a wife whose husband had deserted her. Happily, she was courageous, industrious, and a clever needlewoman; and she had been able just to earn a living for herself and her only child, by making mantles and cloaks for a West-end house. It was not a luxurious living. Cheap lodgings in a shabby street off the Walworth Road, scanty dinners, homely food, well-worn raiment, had been the portion of mother and daughter; but they loved each other so dearly, and Nature had made them both so light-hearted, that they had contrived somehow to be happy.

But now this idea of going out into the world as companion to some fine lady had rooted itself into Bella's mind, and although she idolized her mother, and although the parting of mother and daughter must needs tear two loving hearts into shreds, the girl longed for enterprise and change and excitement, as the pages of old longed to be knights, and to start for the Holy Land to break a lance with the infidel.

She grew tired of racing downstairs every time the postman knocked, only to be told "nothing for you, miss," by the smudgy-faced drudge who picked up the letters from the passage floor. "Nothing for you, miss," grinned the lodging-house drudge, till at last Bella took heart of grace and walked up to Harbeck Street, and asked the Superior Person how it was that no situation had been found for her.

"You are too young," said the Person, "and you want a salary."

"Of course I do," answered Bella; "don't other people want salaries?"

"Young ladies of your age generally want a comfortable home."

"I don't," snapped Bella: "I want to help mother."

"You can call again this day week," said the Person; "or, if I hear of anything in the meantime, I will write to you."

No letter came from the Person, and in exactly a week Bella put on her neatest hat, the one that had been seldomest caught in the rain, and trudged off to Harbeck Street.

It was a dull October afternoon, and there was a greyness in the air which might turn to fog before night. The Walworth Road shops gleamed brightly through that grey atmosphere, and though to a young lady reared in Mayfair or Belgravia such shop-windows would have been unworthy of a glance, they were a snare and temptation for Bella. There were so many things that she longed for, and would never be able to buy.

Harbeck Street is apt to be empty at this dead season of the year, a long, long street, an endless perspective of eminently respectable houses. The Person's office was at the further end, and Bella looked down that long, grey vista almost despairingly, more tired than usual with the trudge from Walworth. As she looked, a carriage passed her, an old-fashioned, yellow chariot, on cee springs, drawn by a pair of high grey horses, with the stateliest of coachmen driving them, and a tall footman sitting by his side.

"It looks like the fairy godmother's coach," thought Bella. "I shouldn't wonder if it began by being a pumpkin."

It was a surprise when she reached the Person's door to find the yellow chariot standing before it, and the tall footman waiting near the doorstep. She was almost afraid to go in and meet the owner of that splendid carriage. She had caught only a glimpse of its occupant as the chariot rolled by, a plumed bonnet, a patch of ermine.

The Person's smart page ushered her upstairs and knocked at the official door. "Miss Rolleston," he announced, apologetically, while Bella waited outside.

"Show her in," said the Person, quickly; and then Bella heard her murmuring something in a low voice to her client.

Bella went in fresh, blooming, a living image of youth and hope, and before she looked at the Person her gaze was riveted by the owner of the chariot.

Never had she seen anyone as old as the old lady sitting by the Person's fire: a little old figure, wrapped from chin to feet in an ermine mantle; a withered, old face under a plumed bonnet—a face so wasted by age that it seemed only a pair of eyes and a peaked chin. The nose was peaked, too, but between the sharply pointed chin and the great, shining eyes, the small, aquiline nose was hardly visible.

"This is Miss Rolleston, Lady Ducayne."

Claw-like fingers, flashing with jewels, lifted a double eyeglass to

Lady Ducayne's shining black eyes, and through the glasses Bella saw those unnaturally bright eyes magnified to a gigantic size, and glaring at her awfully.

"Miss Torpinter has told me all about you," said the old voice that belonged to the eyes. "Have you good health? Are you strong and active, able to eat well, sleep well, walk well, able to enjoy all that there is good in life?"

"I have never known what it is to be ill, or idle," answered Bella.

"Then I think you will do for me."

"Of course, in the event of references being perfectly satisfactory," put in the Person.

"I don't want references. The young woman looks frank and innocent. I'll take her on trust."

"So like you, dear Lady Ducayne," murmured Miss Torpinter.

"I want a strong young woman whose health will give me no trouble."

"You have been so unfortunate in that respect," cooed the Person, whose voice and manner were subdued to a melting sweetness by the old woman's presence.

"Yes, I've been rather unlucky," grunted Lady Ducayne.

"But I am sure Miss Rolleston will not disappoint you, though certainly after your unpleasant experience with Miss Tomson, who looked the picture of health—and Miss Blandy, who said she had never seen a doctor since she was vaccinated—"

"Lies, no doubt," muttered Lady Ducayne, and then turning to Bella, she asked, curtly, "You don't mind spending the winter in Italy, I suppose?"

In Italy! The very word was magical. Bella's fair young face flushed crimson.

"It has been the dream of my life to see Italy," she gasped.

From Walworth to Italy! How far, how impossible such a journey had seemed to that romantic dreamer.

"Well, your dream will be realized. Get yourself ready to leave Charing Cross by the train deluxe this day week at eleven. Be sure you are at the station a quarter before the hour. My people will look after you and your luggage."

Lady Ducayne rose from her chair, assisted by her crutch-stick, and Miss Torpinter escorted her to the door.

"And with regard to salary?" questioned the Person on the way.

"Salary, oh, the same as usual—and if the young woman wants a

quarter's pay in advance you can write to me for a check," Lady Ducayne answered, carelessly.

Miss Torpinter went all the way downstairs with her client, and
waited to see her seated in the yellow chariot. When she came upstairs
again she was slightly out of breath, and she had resumed that superior
manner which Bella had found so crushing.

"You may think yourself uncommonly lucky, Miss Rolleston," she
said. "I have dozens of young ladies on my books whom I might have
recommended for this situation—but I remembered having told you to
call this afternoon—and I thought I would give you a chance. Old Lady
Ducayne is one of the best people on my books. She gives her companion a hundred a year, and pays all travelling expenses. You will live in
the lap of luxury."

"A hundred a year! How too lovely! Shall I have to dress very
grandly? Does Lady Ducayne keep much company?"

"At her age! No, she lives in seclusion—in her own apartments—
her French maid, her footman, her medical attendant, her courier."

"Why did those other companions leave her?" asked Bella.

"Their health broke down!"

"Poor things, and so they had to leave?"

"Yes, they had to leave. I suppose you would like a quarter's salary
in advance?"

"Oh, yes, please. I shall have things to buy."

"Very well, I will write for Lady Ducayne's check, and I will send
you the balance—after deducting my commission for the year."

"To be sure, I had forgotten the commission."

"You don't suppose I keep this office for pleasure."

"Of course not," murmured Bella, remembering the five shillings
entrance fee; but nobody could expect a hundred a year and a winter in
Italy for five shillings.

III

"From Miss Rolleston, at Cap Ferrino, to Mrs. Rolleston, in Beresford
Street, Walworth, London.

"*How I wish you could see this place, dearest; the blue sky, the
olive woods, the orange and lemon orchards between the cliffs and
the sea—sheltering in the hollow of the great hills—and with sum-*

mer waves dancing up to the narrow ridge of pebbles and weeds which is the Italian idea of a beach! Oh, how I wish you could see it all, mother dear, and bask in this sunshine, that makes it so difficult to believe the date at the head of this paper. November! The air is like an English June—the sun is so hot that I can't walk a few yards without an umbrella. And to think of you at Walworth while I am here! I could cry at the thought that perhaps you will never see this lovely coast, this wonderful sea, these summer flowers that bloom in winter. There is a hedge of pink geraniums under my window, mother—a thick, rank hedge, as if the flowers grew wild—and there are Dijon roses climbing over arches and palisades all along the terrace—a rose garden full of bloom in November! Just picture it all! You could never imagine the luxury of this hotel. It is nearly new, and has been built and decorated regardless of expense. Our rooms are upholstered in pale blue satin, which shows up Lady Ducayne's parchment complexion; but as she sits all day in a corner of the balcony basking in the sun, except when she is in her carriage, and all the evening in her armchair close to the fire, and never sees anyone but her own people, her complexion matters very little.

"She has the handsomest suite of rooms in the hotel. My bedroom is inside hers, the sweetest room—all blue satin and white lace— white enamelled furniture, looking-glasses on every wall, till I know my pert little profile as I never knew it before. The room was really meant for Lady Ducayne's dressing-room, but she ordered one of the blue satin couches to be arranged as a bed for me—the prettiest little bed, which I can wheel near the window on sunny mornings, as it is on castors and easily moved about. I feel as if Lady Ducayne were a funny old grandmother, who had suddenly appeared in my life, very, very rich, and very, very kind.

"She is not at all exacting. I read aloud to her a good deal, and she dozes and nods while I read. Sometimes I hear her moaning in her sleep—as if she had troublesome dreams. When she is tired of my reading she orders Francine, her maid, to read a French novel to her, and I hear her chuckle and groan now and then, as if she were more interested in those books than in Dickens or Scott. My French is not good enough to follow Francine, who reads very quickly. I have a great deal of liberty, for Lady Ducayne often tells me to run away and amuse myself; I roam about the hills for hours. Everything is so lovely. I lose myself in olive woods, always climbing up and up towards the pine woods above—and above the pines there are the *snow mountains that just show their white peaks above the dark hills. Oh, you poor dear, how can I ever make you understand what this place is like—you, whose poor, tired eyes have only the opposite side of Beresford Street? Sometimes I go no farther than the terrace in front of the hotel, which is a favorite lounging-place with everybody. The gardens lie below, and the tennis courts where I sometimes play with a very nice girl, the only person in the hotel with whom I have made friends. She is a year older than I, and has come to Cap Ferrino with her brother, a doctor—or a medical student, who is going to be a doctor. He passed his M.B. exam. at Edinburgh just before they left home, Lotta told me. He came to Italy entirely on his sister's account. She had a troublesome chest attack last summer and was ordered to winter abroad. They are orphans, quite alone in the world, and so fond of each other. It is very nice for me to have such a friend as Lotta. She is so thoroughly respectable. I can't help using that word, for some of the girls in this hotel go on in a way that I know you would shudder at. Lotta was brought up by an aunt, deep down in the country, and knows hardly anything about life. Her brother won't allow her to read a novel, French or English, that he has not read and approved.*

" 'He treats me like a child,' she told me, 'but I don't mind, for it's nice to know somebody loves me, and cares about what I do, and even about my thoughts.'

"Perhaps this is what makes some girls so eager to marry—the want of someone strong and brave and honest and true to care for them and order them about. I want no one, mother darling, for I have you, and you are all the world to me. No husband could ever come between us two. If I ever were to marry he would have only the second place in my heart. But I don't suppose I ever shall marry, or even know what it is like to have an offer of marriage. No young man can afford to marry a penniless girl nowadays. Life is too expensive.

"Mr. Stafford, Lotta's brother, is very clever, and very kind. He thinks it is rather hard for me to have to live with such an old woman as Lady Ducayne, but then he does not know how poor we are—you and I—and what a wonderful life this seems to me in this lovely place. I feel a selfish wretch for enjoying all my luxuries, while you, who want them so much more than I, have none of them— hardly know what they are like—do you, dearest?—for my scamp of

a father began to go to the dogs soon after you were married, and
since then life has been all trouble and care and struggle for you."

This letter was written when Bella had been less than a month at
Cap Ferrino, before the novelty had worn off the landscape, and before
the pleasure of luxurious surroundings had begun to cloy. She wrote to
her mother every week, such long letters as girls who have lived in
closest companionship with a mother alone can write; letters that are
like a diary of heart and mind. She wrote gaily always; but when the
new year began Mrs. Rolleston thought she detected a note of melancholy under all those lively details about the place and the people.

"My poor girl is getting homesick," she thought. "Her heart is in
Beresford Street."

It might be that she missed her new friend and companion, Lotta
Stafford, who had gone with her brother for a little tour to Genoa and
Spezia, and as far as Pisa. They were to return before February; but in
the meantime Bella might naturally feel very solitary among all those
strangers, whose manners and doings she described so well.

The mother's instinct had been true. Bella was not so happy as she
had been in that first flush of wonder and delight which followed the
change from Walworth to the Riviera. Somehow, she knew not how,
lassitude had crept upon her. She no longer loved to climb the hills, no
longer flourished her orange stick in sheer gladness of heart as her light
feet skipped over the rough ground and the coarse grass on the mountain side. The odor of rosemary and thyme, the fresh breath of the sea,
no longer filled her with rapture. She thought of Beresford Street and
her mother's face with a sick longing. They were so far—so far away!
And then she thought of Lady Ducayne, sitting by the heaped-up olive
logs in the overheated salon—thought of that wizened-nutcracker profile, and those gleaming eyes, with an invincible horror.

Visitors at the hotel had told her that the air of Cap Ferrino was
relaxing—better suited to age than to youth, to sickness than to health.
No doubt it was so. She was not so well as she had been at Walworth;
but she told herself that she was suffering only from the pain of separation from the dear companion of her girlhood, the mother who had
been nurse, sister, friend, flatterer, all things in this world to her. She
had shed many tears over that parting, had spent many a melancholy
hour on the marble terrace with yearning eyes looking westward, and
with her heart's desire a thousand miles away.

She was sitting in her favorite spot, an angle at the eastern end of the terrace, a quiet little nook sheltered by orange trees, when she heard a couple of Riviera habitués talking in the garden below. They were sitting on a bench against the terrace wall.

She had no idea of listening to their talk, till the sound of Lady Ducayne's name attracted her, and then she listened without any thought of wrong-doing. They were talking no secrets—just casually discussing a hotel acquaintance.

They were two elderly people whom Bella only knew by sight. An English clergyman who had wintered abroad for half his lifetime; a stout, comfortable, well-to-do spinster, whose chronic bronchitis obliged her to migrate annually.

"I have met her about Italy for the last ten years," said the lady; "but have never found out her real age."

"I put her down at a hundred—not a year less," replied the parson. "Her reminiscences all go back to the Regency. She was evidently then in her zenith; and I have heard her say things that showed she was in Parisian society when the First Empire was at its best—before Josephine was divorced."

"She doesn't talk much now."

"No; there's not much life left in her. She is wise in keeping herself secluded. I only wonder that wicked old quack, her Italian doctor, didn't finish her off years ago."

"I should think it must be the other way, and that he keeps her alive."

"My dear Miss Manders, do you think foreign quackery ever kept anybody alive?"

"Well, there she is—and she never goes anywhere without him. He certainly has an unpleasant countenance."

"Unpleasant," echoed the parson, "I don't believe the foul fiend himself can beat him in ugliness. I pity that poor young woman who has to live between old Lady Ducayne and Dr. Parravicini."

"But the old lady is very good to her companions."

"No doubt. She is very free with her cash; the servants call her good Lady Ducayne. She is a withered old female Croesus, and knows she'll never be able to get through her money, and doesn't relish the idea of other people enjoying it when she's in her coffin. People who live to be as old as she is become slavishly attached to life. I daresay she's generous to those poor girls—but she can't make them happy. They die in her service."

"Don't say they, Mr. Carton; I know that one poor girl died at Mentone last spring."

"Yes, and another poor girl died in Rome three years ago. I was there at the time. Good Lady Ducayne left her there in an English family. The girl had every comfort. The old woman was very liberal to her—but she died. I tell you, Miss Manders, it is not good for any young woman to live with two such horrors as Lady Ducayne and Parravicini."

They talked of other things—but Bella hardly heard them. She sat motionless, and a cold wind seemed to come down upon her from the mountains and to creep up to her from the sea, till she shivered as she sat there in the sunshine, in the shelter of the orange trees in the midst of all that beauty and brightness.

Yes, they were uncanny, certainly, the pair of them—she so like an aristocratic witch in her withered old age; he of no particular age, with a face that was more like a waxen mask than any human countenance Bella had ever seen. What did it matter? Old age is venerable, and worthy of all reverence; and Lady Ducayne had been very kind to her. Dr. Parravicini was a harmless, inoffensive student, who seldom looked up from the book he was reading. He had his private sitting-room, where he made experiments in chemistry and natural science—perhaps in alchemy. What could it matter to Bella? He had always been polite to her, in his far-off way. She could not be more happily placed than she was—in his palatial hotel, with this rich old lady.

No doubt she missed the young English girl who had been so friendly, and it might be that she missed the girl's brother, for Mr. Stafford had talked to her a good deal—had interested himself in the books she was reading, and her manner of amusing herself when she was not on duty.

"You must come to our little salon when you are 'off,' as the hospital nurses call it, and we can have some music. No doubt you play and sing?" Upon which Bella had to own with a blush of shame that she had forgotten how to play the piano ages ago.

"Mother and I used to sing duets sometimes between the lights, without accompaniment," she said, and the tears came into her eyes as she thought of the humble room, the half-hour's respite from work, the sewing machine standing where a piano ought to have been, and her mother's plaintive voice, so sweet, so true, so dear.

Sometimes she found herself wondering whether she would ever see that beloved mother again. Strange forebodings came into her mind. She was angry with herself for giving way to melancholy thoughts.

One day she questioned Lady Ducayne's French maid about those two companions who had died within three years.

"They were poor, feeble creatures," Francine told her. "They looked fresh and bright enough when they came to Miladi; but they ate too much, and they were lazy. They died of luxury and idleness. Miladi was too kind to them. They had nothing to do; and so they took to fancying things; fancying the air didn't suit them, that they couldn't sleep."

"I sleep well enough, but I have had a strange dream several times since I have been in Italy."

"Ah, you had better not begin to think about dreams, or you will be like those other girls. They were dreamers—and they dreamt themselves into the cemetery."

The dream troubled her a little, not because it was a ghastly or frightening dream, but on account of sensations which she had never felt before in sleep—a whirring of wheels that went round in her brain, a great noise like a whirlwind, but rhythmical like the ticking of a gigantic clock: and then in the midst of this uproar as of winds and waves she seemed to sink into a gulf of unconsciousness, out of sleep into far deeper sleep—total extinction. And then, after that black interval, there had come the sound of voices, and then again the whirr of wheels, louder and louder—and again the black—and then she awoke, feeling languid and oppressed.

She told Dr. Parravicini of her dream one day, on the only occasion when she wanted his professional advice. She had suffered rather severely from the mosquitoes before Christmas—and had been almost frightened at finding a wound upon her arm which she could only attribute to the venomous sting of one of these torturers. Parravicini put on his glasses, and scrutinized the angry mark on the round, white arm, as Bella stood before him and Lady Ducayne with her sleeve rolled up above her elbow.

"Yes, that's rather more than a joke," he said; "he has caught you on the top of a vein. What a vampire! But there's no harm done, signorina, nothing that a little dressing of mine won't heal. You must always show me any bite of this nature. It might be dangerous if neglected. These creatures feed on poison and disseminate it."

"And to think that such tiny creatures can bite like this," said Bella; "my arm looks as if it had been cut by a knife."

"If I were to show you a mosquito's sting under my microscope you wouldn't be surprised at that," replied Parravicini.

Bella had to put up with the mosquito bites, even when they came on the top of a vein, and produced that ugly wound. The wound recurred now and then at longish intervals, and Bella found Dr. Parravicini's dressing a speedy cure. If he were the quack his enemies called him, he had at least a light hand and a delicate touch in performing this small operation.

"Bella Rolleston to Mrs. Rolleston—April 14th.

"EVER DEAREST,

Behold the check for my second quarter's salary—five and twenty pounds. There is no one to pinch off a whole tenner for a year's commission as there was last time, so it is all for you, mother, dear. I have plenty of pocket-money in hand from the cash I brought away with me, when you insisted on my keeping more than I wanted. It isn't possible to spend money here—except on occasional tips to servants, or sous to beggars and children—unless one had lots to spend, for everything one would like to buy—tortoise-shell, coral, lace—is so ridiculously dear that only a millionaire ought to look at it. Italy is a dream of beauty: but for shopping, give me Newington Causeway.

"You ask me so earnestly if I am quite well that I fear my letters must have been very dull lately. Yes, dear, I am well—but I am not quite so strong as I was when I used to trudge to the West-end to buy half a pound of tea—just for a constitutional walk—or to Dulwich to look at the pictures. Italy is relaxing; and I feel what the people here call 'slack.' But I fancy I can see your dear face looking worried as you read this. Indeed, and indeed, I am not ill. I am only a little tired of this lovely scene—as I suppose one might get tired of looking at one of Turner's pictures if it hung on a wall that was always opposite one. I think of you every hour in every day—think of you and our homely little room—our dear little shabby parlor, with the armchairs from the wreck of your old home, and Dick singing in his cage over the sewing machine. Dear, shrill, maddening Dick, who, we flattered ourselves, was so passionately fond of us. Do tell me in your next letter that he is well.

"My friend Lotta and her brother never came back after all. They went from Pisa to Rome. Happy mortals! And they are to be on the

Italian lakes in May; which lake was not decided when Lotta last wrote to me. She has been a charming correspondent, and has confided all her little flirtations to me. We are all to go to Bellaggio next week—by Genoa and Milan. Isn't that lovely? Lady Ducayne travels by the easiest stages—except when she is bottled up in the train deluxe. We shall stop two days at Genoa and one at Milan. What a bore I shall be to you with my talk about Italy when I come home.

"Love and love—and ever more love from your adoring, BELLA."

IV

Herbert Stafford and his sister had often talked of the pretty English girl with her fresh complexion, which made such a pleasant touch of rosy color among all those sallow faces at the Grand Hotel. The young doctor thought of her with a compassionate tenderness—her utter loneliness in that great hotel where there were so many people, her bondage to that old, old woman, where everybody else was free to think of nothing but enjoying life. It was a hard fate; and the poor child was evidently devoted to her mother, and felt the pain of separation—"only two of them, and very poor, and all the world to each other," he thought.

Lotta told him one morning that they were to meet again at Bellaggio. "The old thing and her court are to be there before we are," she said. "I shall be charmed to have Bella again. She is so bright and gay—in spite of an occasional touch of homesickness. I never took to a girl on a short acquaintance as I did to her."

"I like her best when she is homesick," said Herbert; "for then I am sure she has a heart."

"What have you to do with hearts, except for dissection? Don't forget that Bella is an absolute pauper. She told me in confidence that her mother makes mantles for a West-end shop. You can hardly have a lower depth than that."

"I shouldn't think any less of her if her mother made matchboxes."

"Not in the abstract—of course not. Matchboxes are honest labor. But you couldn't marry a girl whose mother makes mantles."

"We haven't come to the consideration of that question yet," answered Herbert, who liked to provoke his sister.

In two years' hospital practice he had seen too much of the grim realities of life to retain any prejudices about rank. Cancer, phthisis, gangrene, leave a man with little respect for the humanity. The kernel is always the same—fearfully and wonderfully made—a subject for pity and terror.

Mr. Stafford and his sister arrived at Bellaggio in a fair May evening. The sun was going down as the steamer approached the pier; and all that glory of purple bloom which curtains every wall at this season of the year flushed and deepened in the glowing light. A group of ladies were standing on the pier watching the arrivals, and among them Herbert saw a pale face that startled him out of his wonted composure.

"There she is," murmured Lotta, at his elbow, "but how dreadfully changed. She looks a wreck."

They were shaking hands with her a few minutes later, and a flush had lighted up her poor pinched face in the pleasure of meeting.

"I thought you might come this evening," she said. "We have been here a week."

She did not add that she had been there every evening to watch the boat in, and a good many times during the day. The Grand Bretagne was close by, and it had been easy for her to creep to the pier when the boat bell rang. She felt a joy in meeting these people again; a sense of being with friends; a confidence which Lady Ducayne's goodness had never inspired in her.

"Oh, you poor darling, how awfully ill you must have been," exclaimed Lotta, as the two girls embraced.

Bella tried to answer, but her voice was choked with tears.

"What has been the matter, dear? That horrid influenza, I suppose?"

"No, no, I have not been ill—I have only felt a little weaker than I used to be. I don't think the air of Cap Ferrino quite agreed with me."

"It must have disagreed with you abominably. I never saw such a change in anyone. Do let Herbert doctor you. He is fully qualified, you know. He prescribed for ever so many influenza patients at the Londres. They were glad to get advice from an English doctor in a friendly way."

"I am sure he must be very clever!" faltered Bella, "but there is really nothing the matter. I am not ill, and if I were ill, Lady Ducayne's physician—"

"That dreadful man with the yellow face? I would as soon one of the Borgias prescribed for me. I hope you haven't been taking any of his medicines."

"No, dear, I have taken nothing. I have never complained of being ill."

This was said while they were all three walking to the hotel. The Staffords' rooms had been secured in advance, pretty ground-floor rooms, opening into the garden. Lady Ducayne's statelier apartments were on the floor above.

"I believe these rooms are just under ours," said Bella.

"Then it will be all the easier for you to run down to us," replied Lotta, which was not really the case, as the grand staircase was in the center of the hotel.

"Oh, I shall find it easy enough," said Bella. "I'm afraid you'll have too much of my society. Lady Ducayne sleeps away half the day in this warm weather, so I have a good deal of idle time; and I get awfully moped thinking of mother and home."

Her voice broke upon the last word. She could not have thought of that poor lodging which went by the name of home more tenderly had it been the most beautiful that art and wealth ever created. She moped and pined in this lovely garden, with the sunlit lake and the romantic hills spreading out their beauty before her. She was homesick and she had dreams; or, rather, an occasional recurrence of that one bad dream with all its strange sensations—it was more like a hallucination than dreaming—the whirring of wheels, the sinking into an abyss, the struggling back to consciousness. She had the dream shortly before she left Cap Ferrino, but not since she had come to Bellaggio, and she began to hope the air in this lake district suited her better, and that those strange sensations would never return.

Mr. Stafford wrote a prescription and had it made up at the chemist's near the hotel. It was a powerful tonic, and after two bottles, and a row or two on the lake, and some rambling over the hills and in the meadows where the spring flowers made earth seem paradise, Bella's spirits and looks improved as if by magic.

"It is a wonderful tonic," she said, but perhaps in her heart of hearts she knew that the doctor's kind voice, and the friendly hand that helped her in and out of the boat, and the lake, had something to do with her cure.

"I hope you don't forget that her mother makes mantles," Lotta said warningly.

"Or matchboxes; it is just the same thing, so far as I am concerned."

"You mean that in no circumstances could you think of marrying her?"

"I mean that if ever I love a woman well enough to think of marrying her, riches or rank will count for nothing with me. But I fear—I fear your poor friend may not live to be any man's wife."

"Do you think her so very ill?"

He sighed, and left the question unanswered.

One day, while they were gathering wild hyacinths in an upland meadow, Bella told Mr. Stafford about her bad dream.

"It is curious only because it is hardly like a dream," she said. "I daresay you could find some commonsense reason for it. The position of my head on my pillow, or the atmosphere, or something."

And then she described her sensations; how in the midst of sleep there came a sudden sense of suffocation; and then those whirring wheels, so loud, so terrible; and then a blank, and then a coming back to waking consciousness.

"Have you ever had chloroform given you—by a dentist, for instance?"

"Never—Dr. Parravicini asked me that question one day."

"Lately?"

"No, long ago, when we were in the train deluxe."

"Has Dr. Parravicini prescribed for you since you began to feel weak and ill?"

"Oh, he has given me a tonic from time to time, but I hate medicine, and took very little of the stuff. And then I am not ill, only weaker than I used to be. I was ridiculously strong and well when I lived at Walworth, and used to take long walks every day. Mother made me take those tramps to Dulwich or Norwood, for fear I should suffer from too much sewing machine; sometimes—but very seldom—she went with me. She was generally toiling at home while I was enjoying fresh air and exercise. And she was very careful about our food—that, however plain it was, it should be always nourishing and ample. I owe it to her care that I grew up such a great, strong creature."

"You don't look great or strong now, you poor dear," said Lotta.

"I'm afraid Italy doesn't agree with me."

"Perhaps it is not Italy, but being cooped up with Lady Ducayne that has made you ill."

"But I am never cooped up. Lady Ducayne is absurdly kind, and lets me roam about or sit in the balcony all day if I like. I have read more novels since I have been with her than in all the rest of my life."

"Then she is very different from the average old lady, who is usually a slave driver," said Stafford. "I wonder why she carries a companion about with her if she has so little need of society."

"Oh, I am only part of her state. She is inordinately rich—and the salary she gives me doesn't count. Apropos of Dr. Parravicini, I know he is a clever doctor, for he cures my horrid mosquito bites."

"A little ammonia would do that, in the early stage of the mischief. But there are no mosquitoes to trouble you now."

"Oh, yes, there are; I had a bite just before we left Cap Ferrino." She pushed up her loose lawn sleeve, and exhibited a scar, which he scrutinized intently, with a surprised and puzzled look.

"This is no mosquito bite," he said.

"Oh, yes it is—unless there are snakes or adders at Cap Ferrino."

"It is not a bite at all. You are trifling with me. Miss Rolleston—you have allowed that wretched Italian quack to bleed you. They killed the greatest man in modern Europe that way, remember. How very foolish of you."

"I was never bled in my life, Mr. Stafford."

"Nonsense! Let me look at your other arm. Are there any more mosquito bites?"

"Yes; Dr. Parravicini says I have a bad skin for healing, and that the poison acts more virulently with me than with most people."

Stafford examined both her arms in the broad sunlight, scars new and old.

"You have been very badly bitten, Miss Rolleston," he said, "and if ever I find the mosquito I shall make him smart. But, now tell me, my dear girl, on your word of honor, tell me as you would tell a friend who is sincerely anxious for your health and happiness—as you would tell your mother if she were here to question you—have you no knowledge of any cause for these scars except mosquito bites—no suspicion even?"

"No, indeed! No, upon my honor! I have never seen a mosquito biting my arm. One never does see the horrid little fiends. But I have heard them trumpeting under the curtains and I know that I have often had one of the pestilent wretches buzzing about me."

Later in the day Bella and her friends were sitting at tea in the garden, while Lady Ducayne took her afternoon drive with her doctor.

"How long do you mean to stop with Lady Ducayne, Miss Rolleston?" Herbert Stafford asked, after a thoughtful silence, breaking suddenly upon the trivial talk of the two girls.

"As long as she will go on paying me twenty-five pounds a quarter."

"Even if you feel your health breaking down in her service?"

"It is not the service that has injured my health. You can see that I have really nothing to do—to read aloud for an hour or so once or twice a week; to write a letter once in a while to a London tradesman. I shall never have such an easy time with anybody. And nobody else would give me a hundred a year."

"Then you mean to go on till you break down; to die at your post?"

"Like the other two companions? No! If ever I feel seriously ill— really ill—I shall put myself in a train and go back to Walworth without stopping."

"What about the other two companions?"

"They both died. It was very unlucky for Lady Ducayne. That's why she engaged me; she chose me because I was ruddy and robust. She must feel rather disgusted at my having grown white and weak. By-the-bye, when I told her about the good your tonic had done me, she said she would like to see you and have a little talk with you about her own case."

"And I should like to see Lady Ducayne. When did she say this?"

"The day before yesterday."

"Will you ask her if she will see me this evening?"

"With pleasure! I wonder what you will think of her? She looks rather terrible to a stranger; but Dr. Parravicini says she was once a famous beauty."

It was nearly ten o'clock when Mr. Stafford was summoned by message from Lady Ducayne, whose courier came to conduct him to her ladyship's salon. Bella was reading aloud when the visitor was admitted; and he noticed the languor in the low, sweet tones, the evident effort.

"Shut up the book," said the querulous old voice. "You are beginning to drawl like Miss Blandy."

Stafford saw a small, bent figure crouching over the piled up olive logs; a shrunken old figure in a gorgeous garment of black and crimson brocade, a skinny throat emerging from a mass of old Venetian lace, clasped with diamonds that flashed like fireflies as the trembling old head turned towards him.

The eyes that looked at him out of the face were almost as bright as the diamonds—the only living feature in that narrow parchment mask. He had seen terrible faces in the hospital—faces on which disease had set dreadful marks—but he had never seen a face that impressed him so painfully as this withered countenance, with its indescribable horror of death outlived, a face that should have been hidden under a coffin-lid years and years ago.

The Italian physician was standing on the other side of the fire-place, smoking a cigarette, and looking down at the little old woman brooding over the hearth as if he were proud of her.

"Good evening, Mr. Stafford; you can go to your room, Bella, and write your everlasting letter to your mother at Walworth," said Lady Ducayne. "I believe she writes a page about every wild flower she discovers in the woods and meadows. I don't know what else she can find to write about," she added, as Bella quietly withdrew to the pretty little bedroom opening out of Lady Ducayne's spacious apartment. Here, as at Cap Ferrino, she slept in a room adjoining the old lady's.

"You are a medical man, I understand, Mr. Stafford."

"I am a qualified practitioner, but I have not begun to practice."

"You have begun upon my companion, she tells me."

"I have prescribed for her, certainly, and I am happy to find my prescription has done her good; but I look upon that improvement as temporary. Her case will require more drastic treatment."

"Never mind her case. There is nothing the matter with the girl—absolutely nothing—except girlish nonsense; too much liberty and not enough work."

"I understand that two of your ladyship's previous companions died of the same disease," said Stafford, looking first at Lady Ducayne, who gave her tremulous old head an impatient jerk, and then at Parravicini, whose yellow complexion had paled a little under Stafford's scrutiny.

"Don't bother me about my companions, sir," said Lady Ducayne. "I sent for you to consult you about myself—not about a parcel of anemic girls. You are young, and medicine is a progressive science, the newspapers tell me. Where have you studied?"

"In Edinburgh—and in Paris."

"Two good schools. And know all the new-fangled theories, the modern discoveries—that remind one of the medieval witchcraft, of Albertus Magnus, and George Ripley; you have studied hypnotism—electricity?"

"And the transfusion of blood," said Stafford, very slowly, looking at Parravicini.

"Have you made any discovery that teaches you to prolong human life—any elixir—any mode of treatment? I want my life prolonged, young man. That man there has been my physician for thirty years. He does all he can to keep me alive—after his lights. He studies all the new theories of all the scientists—but he is old; he gets older every day—his brain-power is going—he is bigoted—prejudiced—can't receive new ideas—can't grapple with new systems. He will let me die if I am not on my guard against him."

"You are of an unbelievable ingratitude, Ecclenza," said Parravicini.

"Oh, you needn't complain. I have paid you thousands to keep me alive. Every year of my life has swollen your hoards; you know there is nothing to come to you when I am gone. My whole fortune is left to endow a home for indigent women of quality who have reached their ninetieth year. Come, Mr. Stafford, I am a rich woman. Give me a few years more in the sunshine, a few years more above ground, and I will give you the price of a fashionable London practice—I will set you up at the West-end."

"How old are you, Lady Ducayne?"

"I was born the day Louis XVI was guillotined."

"Then I think you have had your share of the sunshine and the pleasures of the earth, and that you should spend your few remaining days in repenting your sins and trying to make atonement for the young lives that have been sacrificed to your love of life."

"What do you mean by that, sir?"

"Oh, Lady Ducayne, need I put your wickedness and your physician's still greater wickedness in plain words? The poor girl who is now in your employment has been reduced from robust health to a condition of absolute danger by Dr. Parravicini's experimental surgery; and I have no doubt those other two young women who broke down in your service were treated by him in the same manner. I could take upon myself to demonstrate—by most convincing evidence, to a jury of medical men—that Dr. Parravicini has been bleeding Miss Rolleston after putting her under chloroform, at intervals, ever since she has been in your service. The deterioration in the girl's health speaks for itself; the lancet marks upon the girl's arms are unmistakable; and her description of a series of sensations, which she calls a dream, points unmistakably to the administration of chloroform while she was sleeping. A practice so nefarious, so murderous, must, if exposed, result in a sentence only less severe than the punishment of murder."

"I laugh," said Parravicini, with an airy motion of his skinny fingers; "I laugh at once at your theories and at your threats. I, Parravicini Leopold, have no fear that the law can question anything I have done."

"Take the girl away, and let me hear no more of her," cried Lady Ducayne, in the thin, old voice, which so poorly matched the energy and fire of the wicked old brain that guided its utterances. "Let her go back to her mother—I want no more girls to die in my service. There are girls enough and to spare in the world, God knows."

"If you ever engage another companion—or take another English girl into your service, Lady Ducayne, I will make all England ring with the story of your wickedness."

"I want no more girls. I don't believe in his experiments. They have been full of danger for me as well as for the girl—an air bubble, and I should be gone. I'll have no more of his dangerous quackery. I'll find some new man—a better man than you, sir, a discoverer like Pasteur, or Virchow, a genius—to keep me alive. Take your girl away, young man. Marry her if you like. I'll write a check for a thousand pounds, and let her go and live on beef and beer, and get strong and plump again. I'll have no more such experiments. Do you hear, Parravicini?" she screamed, vindictively, the yellow, wrinkled face distorted with fury, the eyes glaring at him.

The Staffords carried Bella Rolleston off to Varese next day, she very loath to leave Lady Ducayne, whose liberal salary afforded such help for the dear mother. Herbert Stafford insisted, however, treating Bella as coolly as if he had been the family physician, and she had been given over wholly to his care.

"Do you suppose your mother would let you stop here to die?" he asked. "If Mrs. Rolleston knew how ill you are, she would come post haste to fetch you."

"I shall never be well again till I get back to Walworth," answered Bella, who was low-spirited and inclined to tears this morning, a reaction after her good spirits of yesterday.

"We'll try a week or two at Varese first," said Stafford. "When you can walk halfway up Monte Generoso without palpitation of the heart, you shall go back to Walworth."

"Poor mother, how glad she will be to see me, and how sorry that I've lost such a good place."

This conversation took place on the boat when they were leaving Bellaggio. Lotta had gone to her friend's room at seven o'clock that morning, long before Lady Ducayne's withered eyelids had opened to the daylight, before even Francine, the French maid, was astir, and had helped to pack a Gladstone bag with essentials, and hustled Bella downstairs and out of doors before she could make any strenuous resistance.

"It's all right," Lotta assured her. "Herbert had a good talk with

Lady Ducayne last night, and it was settled for you to leave this morning. She doesn't like invalids, you see."

"No," sighed Bella, "she doesn't like invalids. It was very unlucky that I should break down, just like Miss Tomson and Miss Blandy."

"At any rate, you are not dead, like them," answered Lotta, "and my brother says you are not going to die."

It seemed rather a dreadful thing to be dismissed in that offhand way, without a word of farewell from her employer.

"I wonder what Miss Torpinter will say when I go to her for another situation," Bella speculated, ruefully, while she and her friends were breakfasting on board the steamer.

"Perhaps you may never want another situation," said Stafford.

"You mean that I may never be well enough to be useful to anybody?"

"No, I don't mean anything of the kind."

It was after dinner at Varese, when Bella had been induced to take a whole glass of Chianti, and quite sparkled after that unaccustomed stimulant, that Mr. Stafford produced a letter from his pocket.

"I forgot to give you Lady Ducayne's letter of adieu!" he said.

"What, did she write to me? I am so glad—I hated to leave her in such a cool way; for after all she was very kind to me, and if I didn't like her it was only because she was too dreadfully old."

She tore open the envelope. The letter was short and to the point:—

"Goodbye, child. Go and marry your doctor. I enclose a farewell gift for your trousseau.

—ADELINE DUCAYNE

"A hundred pounds, a whole year's salary—no—why, it's for a— A check for a thousand!" cried Bella. "What a generous old soul! She really is the dearest old thing."

"She just missed being very dear to you, Bella," said Stafford.

He had dropped into the use of her Christian name while they were on board the boat. It seemed natural now that she was to be in his charge till they all three went back to England.

"I shall take upon myself the privileges of an elder brother till we land at Dover," he said; "after that—well, it must be as you please."

The question of their future relations must have been satisfactorily settled before they crossed the Channel, for Bella's next letter to her mother communicated three startling facts.

First, that the inclosed check for £1,000 was to be invested in debenture stock in Mrs. Rolleston's name, and was to be her very own, income and principal, for the rest of her life.

Next, that Bella was going home to Walworth immediately.

And last, that she was going to be married to Mr. Herbert Stafford in the following autumn.

"And I am sure you will adore him, mother, as much as I do," wrote Bella.

"It is all good Lady Ducayne's doing. I never could have married if I had not secured that little nest-egg for you. Herbert says we shall be able to add to it as the years go by, and that wherever we live there shall be always a room in our house for you. The word 'mother-in-law' has no terrors for him."

ABRAHAM [BRAM] STOKER *was born in Dublin in 1847 and died in London in 1912. Although employed as a civil servant, his first love was the theater, and in 1877 he became manager for the famed theatrical actor-producer Henry Irving in London.*

Stoker's first stories appeared in the Irish press in the 1870s, but it was in the next decade, while he continued to work for Irving, that he truly found his voice as a writer. Through the 1890s, he wrote some of his best and most terrifying stories and also became interested in the Rumanian myths of the nosferatu, *"the undead." His extensive researches into that material resulted in his masterpiece, the novel* Dracula, *in 1897.*

Although it was much indebted to earlier tales, including Polidori's "The Vampyre" (1819), Rymer's Varney the Vampyre *(1845), and Le Fanu's "Carmilla" (1872),* Dracula *stands alone as the high point of vampire literature. Part of its success is due to the believably human situation of its characters, and of course to the sheer monstrosity and evil of Dracula himself. Much of the novel's immediate success was due to Stoker's innovative use of a contemporary setting; twentieth-century writers of horror fiction have learned that evil is more terrifying when it is met in a recognizable world, rather than in a remote locale in the distant past. And, too, Stoker's techniques for building suspense and concern in the reader are masterful. But beyond all this, Stoker succeeded in creating an archetype of evil that remains—and is likely to remain—supremely terrifying and yet disturbingly attractive.*

"Dracula's Guest" is not actually a short story but a self-contained chapter originally written as part of Stoker's manuscript of Dracula. *It was omitted from the published book only for technical reasons of length and was first published in 1914. In 1936 it was used as the basis for the film* Dracula's Daughter.

Dracula's Guest (1897)

BY BRAM STOKER

When we started for our drive the sun was shining brightly on Munich and the air was full of the joyousness of early summer. Just as we were about to depart, Herr Delbrück (the *maître d'hôtel* of the Quatre Saisons, where I was staying) came down, bareheaded, to the carriage and, after wishing me a pleasant drive, said to the coachman, still holding his hand on the handle of the carriage door: "Remember you are back by nightfall. The sky looks bright but there is a shiver in the north wind that says there may be a sudden storm. But I am sure you will not be late." Here he smiled and added, "for you know what night it is."

Johann answered with an emphatic, *"Ja, mein Herr,"* and, touching his hat, drove off quickly. When we had cleared the town, I said, after signalling to him to stop: "Tell me, Johann, what is tonight?"

He crossed himself as he answered laconically: "Walpurgisnacht." Then he took out his watch, a great, old-fashioned German silver thing as big as a turnip, and looked at it, with his eyebrows gathered together and a little impatient shrug of his shoulders. I realized that this was his way of respectfully protesting against the unnecessary delay and sank back in the carriage, merely motioning him to proceed. He started off rapidly, as if to make up for lost time. Every now and then the horses seemed to throw up their heads and sniffed the air suspiciously. On such occasions I often looked round in alarm. The road was pretty bleak, for we were traversing a sort of high, wind-swept plateau. As we drove, I saw a road that looked but little used and which seemed to dip through a little, winding valley. It looked so inviting that, even at the risk of offending him, I called Johann to stop—and when he had pulled up I told him I would like to drive down that road. He made all sorts of excuses and frequently crossed himself as he spoke. This somewhat piqued my curiosity so I asked him various questions. He answered fencingly and repeatedly looked at his watch in protest. Finally I said: "Well, Johann, I want to go down this road. I shall not ask you to come unless you like; but tell me why you do not like to go, that is all I ask." For answer he seemed to throw himself off the box, so quickly did he reach the ground. Then he stretched out his hands appealingly to me and implored me not to go. There was just enough of English mixed with the German for me to understand the drift of his talk. He seemed always just about to tell me something—the very idea of which evidently frightened him, but each time he pulled himself up, saying, as he crossed himself: "Walpurgisnacht!"

I tried to argue with him, but it was difficult to argue with a man when I did not know his language. The advantage certainly rested with him, for although he began to speak in English, of a very crude and broken kind, he always got excited and broke into his native tongue—and every time he did so he looked at his watch. Then the horses became restless and sniffed the air. At this he grew very pale and, looking around in a frightened way, he suddenly jumped forward, took them by the bridles and led them on some twenty feet. I followed and asked why he had done this. For answer he crossed himself, pointed to the spot we had left and drew his carriage in the direction of the other road, indicating a cross, and said, first in German, then in English: "Buried him—him what killed themselves."

I remembered the old custom of burying suicides at cross-roads: "Ah! I see, a suicide. How interesting!" But for the life of me I could not make out why the horses were frightened.

Whilst we were talking we heard a sort of sound between a yelp and a bark. It was far away, but the horses got very restless and it took Johann all his time to quiet them. He was pale and said, "It sounds like a wolf—but yet there are no wolves here now."

"No?" I said, questioning him; "isn't it long since the wolves were so near the city?"

"Long, long," he answered, "in the spring and summer, but with the snow the wolves have been here not so long."

Whilst he was petting the horses and trying to quiet them, dark clouds drifted rapidly across the sky. The sunshine passed away and a breath of cold wind seemed to drift past us. It was only a breath, however, and more in the nature of a warning than a fact, for the sun came out brightly again. Johann looked under his lifted hand at the horizon and said: "The storm of snow, he comes before long time." Then he looked at his watch again and, straightway, holding his reins firmly—for the horses were still pawing the ground restlessly and shaking their heads—he climbed to his box as though the time had come for proceeding on our journey.

I felt a little obstinate and did not at once get into the carriage.

"Tell me," I said, "about this place where the road leads," and I pointed down.

Again he crossed himself and mumbled a prayer before he answered, "It is unholy."

"What is unholy?" I enquired.

"The village."

"Then there is a village?"

"No, no. No one lives there hundreds of years." My curiosity was piqued, "But you said there was a village."

"There was."

"Where is it now?"

Whereupon he burst out into a long story in German and English, so mixed up that I could not quite understand exactly what he said, but roughly I gathered that long ago, hundreds of years, men had died there and been buried in their graves; and sounds were heard under the clay and when the graves were opened, men and women were found rosy with life, and their mouths red with blood. And so, in haste to save their lives (aye, and their souls!—and here he crossed himself) those who were left fled away to other places, where the living lived and the dead were dead and not—not something. He was evidently afraid to speak the last words. As he proceeded with his narration he grew more and more excited. It seemed as if his imagination had got hold of him and he ended in a perfect paroxysm of fear—white-faced, perspiring, trembling and looking round him, as if expecting that some dreadful presence would manifest itself there in the bright sunshine on the open plain. Finally, in an agony of desperation, he cried: "Walpurgisnacht!" and pointed to the carriage for me to get in. All my English blood rose at this and, standing back, I said: "You are afraid, Johann—you are afraid. Go home, I shall return alone; the walk will do me good." The carriage door was open. I took from the seat my oak walking-stick—which I always carry on my holiday excursions—and closed the door, pointing back to Munich, and said, "Go home, Johann—Walpurgisnacht doesn't concern Englishmen."

The horses were now more restive than ever and Johann was trying to hold them in, while excitedly imploring me not to do anything so foolish. I pitied the poor fellow, he was deeply in earnest, but all the same I could not help laughing. His English was quite gone now. In his anxiety he had forgotten that his only means of making me understand was to talk my language, so he jabbered away in his native German. It began to be a little tedious. After giving the direction, "Home!" I turned to go down the cross-road into the valley.

With a despairing gesture, Johann turned his horses towards Munich. I leaned on my stick and looked after him. He went slowly along the road for a while: then there came over the crest of the hill a man tall and thin. I could see so much in the distance. When he drew near the horses, they began to jump and kick about, then to scream with terror. Johann could not hold them in; they bolted down the road, running away madly. I watched them out of sight, then looked for the stranger, but I found that he, too, was gone.

With a light heart I turned down the side road through the deepening valley to which Johann had objected. There was not the slightest reason, that I could see, for his objection, and I daresay I tramped for a couple of hours without thinking of time or distance, and certainly without seeing a person or a house. So far as the place was concerned it was desolation itself. But I did not notice this particularly till, on turning a bend in the road, I came upon a scattered fringe of wood; then I recognized that I had been impressed unconsciously by the desolation of the region through which I had passed.

I sat down to rest myself and began to look around. It struck me that it was considerably colder than it had been at the commencement of my walk—a sort of sighing sound seemed to be around me, with, now and then, high overhead, a sort of muffled roar. Looking upwards I noticed that great thick clouds were drifting rapidly across the sky from north to south at a great height. There were signs of coming storm in some lofty stratum of the air. I was a little chilly and, thinking that it was the sitting still after the exercise of walking, I resumed my journey.

The ground I passed over was now much more picturesque. There were no striking objects that the eye might single out, but in all there was a charm of beauty. I took little heed of time and it was only when the deepening twilight forced itself upon me that I began to think of how I should find my way home. The brightness of the day had gone. The air was cold and the drifting of clouds high overhead was more marked. They were accompanied by a sort of far-away rushing sound, through which seemed to come at intervals that mysterious cry which the driver had said came from a wolf. For a while I hesitated. I had said I would see the deserted village, so on I went and presently came on a wide stretch of open country, shut in by hills all around. Their sides were covered with trees which spread down to the plain, dotting, in clumps, the gentler slopes and hollows which showed here and there. I followed with my eye the winding of the road and saw that it curved close to one of the densest of these clumps and was lost behind it.

As I looked there came a cold shiver in the air and the snow began to fall. I thought of the miles and miles of bleak country I had passed and then hurried on to seek the shelter of the wood in front. Darker and darker grew the sky and faster and heavier fell the snow, till the earth before and around me was a glistening white carpet, the farther edge of which was lost in misty vagueness. The road was here but crude and when on the level its boundaries were not so marked, as when it passed through the cuttings; and in a little while I found that I must have strayed from it, for I missed underfoot the hard surface and my feet sank deeper in the grass and moss. Then the wind grew strong and blew with ever increasing force, till I was fain to run before it. The air became icy cold and in spite of my exercise I began to suffer. The snow was now falling so thickly and whirling around me in such rapid eddies that I could hardly keep my eyes open. Every now and then the heavens were torn asunder by vivid lightning, and in the flashes I could see ahead of me a great mass of trees, chiefly yew and cypress, all heavily coated with snow.

I was soon amongst the shelter of the trees, and there, in comparative silence, I could hear the rush of the wind high overhead. Presently the blackness of the storm had become merged in the darkness of the night. By and by the storm seemed to be passing away: it now only came in fierce puffs or blasts. At such moments the weird sound of the wolf appeared to be echoed by many similar sounds around me.

Now and again, through the black mass of drifting cloud, came a straggling ray of moonlight, which lit up the expanse and showed me that I was at the edge of a dense mass of cypress and yew trees. As the snow had ceased to fall, I walked out from the shelter and began to investigate more closely. It appeared to me that, amongst so many old foundations as I had passed, there might be still standing a house in which, though in ruins, I could find some sort of shelter for a while. As I skirted the edge of the copse I found that a low wall encircled it, and following this I presently found an opening. Here the cypresses formed an alley leading up to a square mass of some kind of building. Just as I caught sight of this, however, the drifting clouds obscured the moon and I passed up the path in darkness. The wind must have grown colder, for I felt myself shiver as I walked; but there was hope of shelter and I groped my way blindly on.

I stopped, for there was a sudden stillness. The storm had passed and, perhaps in sympathy with nature's silence, my heart seemed to cease to beat. But this was only momentarily, for suddenly the moonlight broke through the clouds, showing me that I was in a graveyard and that the square object before me was a great massive tomb of marble, as white as the snow that lay on and all around it. With the moonlight there came a fierce sigh of the storm, which appeared to resume its course with a long, low howl, as of many dogs or wolves. I was awed and shocked and felt the cold perceptibly grow upon me till it seemed to grip me by the heart. Then, while the flood of moonlight still fell on the marble tomb, the storm gave further evidence of renewing, as though it was returning on its track. Impelled by some sort of fascination I approached the sepulchre to see what it was and why such a thing stood alone in such a place. I walked around it and read, over the Doric door, in German:

COUNTESS DOLINGEN OF GRATZ
IN STYRIA
SOUGHT AND FOUND DEATH
1801

On the top of the tomb, seemingly driven through the solid marble —for the structure was composed of a few vast blocks of stone—was a great iron spike or stake. On going to the back I saw, graven in great Russian letters:

THE DEAD TRAVEL FAST.

There was something so weird and uncanny about the whole thing that it gave me a turn and made me feel quite faint. I began to wish, for the first time, that I had taken Johann's advice. Here a thought struck me, which came under almost mysterious circumstances and with a terrible shock. This was Walpurgis Night!

Walpurgis Night, when, according to the belief of millions of people, the devil was abroad—when the graves were opened and the dead came forth and walked. When evil things of earth and air and water held revel. This very place the driver had specially shunned. This was the depopulated village of centuries ago. This was where the suicide lay; and this was the place where I was alone—unmanned, shivering with cold in a shroud of snow with a wild storm gathering again upon me! It took all my philosophy, all the religion I had been taught, all my courage, not to collapse in a paroxysm of fright.

And now a perfect tornado burst upon me. The ground shook as though thousands of horses thundered across it, and this time the storm bore on its icy wings, not snow, but great hailstones which drove with such violence that they might have come from the thongs of Balearic slingers—hailstones that beat down leaf and branch and made the shelter of the cypresses of no more avail than though their stems were standing corn. At the first I had rushed to the nearest tree, but I was soon fain to leave it and seek the only spot that seemed to afford refuge, the deep Doric doorway of the marble tomb. There, crouching against the massive bronze door, I gained a certain amount of protection from the beating of the hailstones, for now they only drove against me as they ricocheted from the ground and the side of the marble.

As I leaned against the door it moved slightly and opened inwards. The shelter of even a tomb was welcome in that pitiless tempest and I was about to enter it when there came a flash of forked lightning that lit up the whole expanse of the heavens. In the instant, as I am a living man, I saw, as my eyes were turned into the darkness of the tomb, a beautiful woman with rounded cheeks and red lips, seemingly sleeping on a bier. As the thunder broke overhead I was grasped as by the hand of a giant and hurled out into the storm. The whole thing was so sudden that, before I could realize the shock, moral as well as physical, I found the hailstones beating me down. At the same time I had a strange, dominating feeling that I was not alone. I looked towards the tomb. Just then there came another blinding flash, which seemed to strike the iron stake that surmounted the tomb and to pour through to the earth, blasting and crumbling the marble, as in a burst of flame. The dead woman rose for a moment of agony, while she was lapped in the flame, and her bitter scream of pain was drowned in the thundercrash. The last thing I heard was this mingling of dreadful sound, as again I was seized in the giant-grasp and dragged away, while the hailstones beat on me, and the air around seemed reverberant with the howling of wolves. The last sight that I remembered was a vague, white, moving mass, as if all the graves around me had sent out the phantoms of their sheeted-dead, and that they were closing in on me through the white cloudiness of the driving hail.

Gradually there came a sort of vague beginning of consciousness, then a sense of weariness that was dreadful. For a time I remembered nothing, but slowly my senses returned. My feet seemed positively racked with pain, yet I could not move them. They seemed to be numbed. There was an icy feeling at the back of my neck and all down my spine, and my ears, like my feet, were dead, yet in torment; but there was in my breast a sense of warmth which was, by comparison, delicious. It was as a nightmare—a physical nightmare, if one may use such an expression—for some heavy weight on my chest made it difficult for me to breathe.

This period of semi-lethargy seemed to remain a long time, and as it faded away I must have slept or swooned. Then came a sort of loathing, like the first stage of sea-sickness, and a wild desire to be free from something—I knew not what. A vast stillness enveloped me, as though all the world were asleep or dead—only broken by the low panting as of some animal close to me. I felt a warm rasping at my throat, then came a consciousness of the awful truth, which chilled me to the heart and sent the blood surging up through my brain. Some great animal was lying on me and now licking my throat. I feared to stir, for some instinct of prudence bade me lie still, but the brute seemed to realize that there was now some change in me, for it raised its head. Through my eyelashes I saw above me the two great flaming eyes of a gigantic wolf. Its sharp white teeth gleamed in the gaping red mouth and I could feel its hot breath fierce and acrid upon me.

For another spell of time I remembered no more. Then I became conscious of a low growl, followed by a yelp, renewed again and again. Then, seemingly very far away, I heard a "Holloa! holloa!" as of many voices calling in unison. Cautiously I raised my head and looked in the direction whence the sound came, but the cemetery blocked my view. The wolf still continued to yelp in a strange way and a red glare began to move round the grove of cypresses, as though following the sound. As the voices drew closer, the wolf yelped faster and louder. I feared to make either sound or motion. Nearer came the red glow, over the white pall which stretched into the darkness around me. Then all at once from beyond the trees there came at a trot a troop of horsemen bearing torches. The wolf rose from my breast and made for the cemetery. I saw one of the horsemen (soldiers, by their caps and their long military cloaks) raise his carbine and take aim. A companion knocked up his arm, and I heard the ball whizz over my head. He had evidently taken my body for that of the wolf. Another sighted the animal as it slunk away and a shot followed. Then, at a gallop, the troop rode forward—some towards me, others following the wolf as it disappeared amongst the snow-clad cypresses.

As they drew nearer I tried to move, but was powerless, although I could see and hear all that went on around me. Two or three of the soldiers jumped from their horses and knelt beside me. One of them raised my head and placed his hand over my heart.

"Good news, comrades!" he cried. "His heart still beats!"

Then some brandy was poured down my throat; it put vigour into me and I was able to open my eyes fully and look around. Lights and shadows were moving among the trees and I heard men call to one another. They drew together, uttering frightened exclamations, and the lights flashed as the others came pouring out of the cemetery pell-mell, like men possessed. When the farther ones came close to us, those who were around me asked them eagerly: "Well, have you found him?"

The reply rang out hurriedly: "No! no! Come away quick—quick! This is no place to stay, and on this of all nights!"

"What was it?" was the question, asked in all manner of keys. The answer came variously and all indefinitely as though the men were moved by some common impulse to speak, yet were restrained by some common fear from giving their thoughts.

"It—it—indeed!" gibbered one, whose wits had plainly given out for the moment.

"A wolf—and yet not a wolf!" another put in shudderingly.

"No use trying for him without the sacred bullet," a third remarked in a more ordinary manner.

"Serve us right for coming out on this night! Truly we have earned our thousand marks!" were the ejaculations of a fourth.

"There was blood on the broken marble," another said after a pause—"the lightning never brought that there. And for him—is he safe? Look at his throat! See, comrades, the wolf has been lying on him and keeping his blood warm."

The officer looked at my throat and replied: "He is all right, the skin is not pierced. What does it all mean? We should never have found him but for the yelping of the wolf."

"What became of it?" asked the man who was holding up my head and who seemed the least panic stricken of the party, for his hands were steady and without tremor. On his sleeve was the chevron of a petty officer.

"It went to its home," answered the man, whose long face was pallid and who actually shook with terror as he glanced around him fearfully. "There are graves enough there in which it may lie. Come, comrades—come quickly! Let us leave this cursed spot."

The officer raised me to a sitting posture, as he uttered a word of command, then several men placed me upon a horse. He sprang to the saddle behind me, took me in his arms, gave the word to advance and, turning our faces away from the cypresses, we rode away in swift, military order.

As yet my tongue refused its office and I was perforce silent. I must have fallen asleep, for the next thing I remembered was finding myself standing up, supported by a soldier on each side of me. It was almost broad daylight and to the north a red streak of sunlight was reflected, like a path of blood, over the waste of snow. The officer was telling the men to say nothing of what they had seen, except that they found an English stranger, guarded by a large dog.

"Dog! that was no dog," cut in the man who had exhibited such fear. "I think I know a wolf when I see one."

The young officer answered calmly: "I said a dog."

"Dog!" reiterated the other ironically. It was evident that his courage was rising with the sun and, pointing to me, he said, "Look at his throat. Is that the work of a dog, master?"

Instinctively I raised my hand to my throat, and as I touched it I cried out in pain. The men crowded round to look, some stooping down from their saddles, and again there came the calm voice of the young officer: "A dog, as I said. If aught else were said we should only be laughed at."

I was then mounted behind a trooper and we rode on into the suburbs of Munich. Here we came across a stray carriage, into which I was lifted, and it was driven off to the Quatre Saisons—the young officer accompanying me, whilst a trooper followed with his horse and the others rode off to their barracks.

When we arrived, Herr Delbrück rushed so quickly down the steps to meet me that it was apparent he had been watching within. Taking me by both hands he solicitously led me in. The officer saluted me and was turning to withdraw when I recognized his purpose, and insisted that he should come to my rooms. Over a glass of wine I warmly thanked him and his brave comrades for saving me. He replied simply that he was more than glad and that Herr Delbrück had at the first taken steps to make all the searching party pleased; at which ambiguous utterance the *maître d'hôtel* smiled, while the officer pleaded duty and withdrew.

"But Herr Delbrück," I enquired, "how and why was it that the soldiers searched for me?"

He shrugged his shoulders, as if in depreciation of his own deed, as he replied: "I was so fortunate as to obtain leave from the commander of the regiment in which I served, to ask for volunteers."

"But how did you know I was lost?" I asked.

"The driver came hither with the remains of his carriage, which had been upset when the horses ran away."

"But surely you would not send a search-party of soldiers merely on this account?"

"Oh, no!" he answered, "but even before the coachman arrived I had this telegram from the Boyar whose guest you are," and he took from his pocket a telegram which he handed to me, and I read:

Bistritz

Be careful of my guest—his safety is most precious to me. Should aught happen to him, or if he be missed, spare nothing to find him and ensure his safety. He is English and therefore adventurous. There are often dangers from snow and wolves and night. Lose not a moment if you suspect harm to him. I answer your zeal with my fortune—*Dracula*.

As I held the telegram in my hand the room seemed to whirl around me, and if the attentive *maître d'hôtel* had not caught me I think I should have fallen. There was something so strange in all this, something so weird and impossible to imagine, that there grew on me a sense of my being in some way the sport of opposite forces—the mere vague idea of which seemed in a way to paralyze me. I was certainly under some form of mysterious protection. From a distant country had come, in the very nick of time, a message that took me out of the danger of the snow-sleep and the jaws of the wolf.

Luella Miller
(1903)
BY MARY E. WILKINS-FREEMAN

Close to the village street stood the one-story house in which Luella Miller, who had an evil name in the village, had dwelt. She had been dead for years, yet there were those in the village who, in spite of the clearer light which comes on a vantage-point from a long-past danger, half believed in the tale which they had heard from their childhood. In their hearts, although they scarcely would have owned it, was a survival of the wild horror and frenzied fear of their ancestors who had dwelt in the same age with Luella Miller. Young people even would stare with a shudder at the old house as they passed, and children never played around it as was their wont around an untenanted building. Not a window in the old Miller house was broken: the panes reflected the morning sunlight in patches of emerald and blue, and the latch of the sagging front door was never lifted, although no bolt secured it. Since Luella Miller had been carried out of it, the house had had no tenant except one friendless old soul who had no choice between that and the far-off shelter of the open sky. This old woman, who had survived her kindred and friends, lived in the house one week, then one morning no smoke came out of the chimney, and a body of neighbours, a score strong, entered and found her dead in her bed. There were dark whispers as to the cause of her death, and there were those who testified to an expression of fear so exalted that it showed forth the state of the departing soul upon the dead face. The old woman had been hale and hearty when she entered the house, and in seven days she was dead; it seemed that she had fallen a victim to some uncanny power. The minister talked in the pulpit with covert severity against the sin of superstition; still the belief prevailed. Not a soul in the village but would have chosen the almshouse rather than that dwelling. No vagrant, if he heard the tale, would seek shelter beneath that old roof, unhallowed by nearly half a century of superstitious fear.

There was only one person in the village who had actually known Luella Miller. That person was a woman well over eighty, but a marvel of vitality and unextinct youth. Straight as an arrow, with the spring of one recently let loose from the bow of life, she moved about the streets, and she always went to church, rain or shine. She had never married, and had lived alone for years in a house across the road from Luella Miller's.

This woman had none of the garrulousness of age, but never in all her life had she ever held her tongue for any will save her own, and she never spared the truth when she essayed to present it. She it was who bore testimony to the life, evil, though possibly wittingly or designedly so, of Luella Miller, and to her personal appearance. When this old woman spoke—and she had the gift of description, although her thoughts were clothed in the rude vernacular of her native village—one could seem to see Luella Miller as she had really looked. According to this woman, Lydia Anderson by name, Luella Miller had been a beauty of a type rather unusual in New England. She had been a slight, pliant sort of creature, as ready with a strong yielding to fate and as unbreakable as a willow. She had glimmering lengths of straight, fair hair, which she wore softly looped round a long, lovely face. She had blue eyes full of soft pleading, little slender, clinging hands, and a wonderful grace of motion and attitude.

"Luella Miller used to sit in a way nobody else could if they sat up and studied a week of Sundays," said Lydia Anderson, "and it was a sight to see her walk. If one of them willows over there on the edge of the brook could start up and get its roots free of the ground, and move off, it would go just the way Luella Miller used to. She had a green shot silk she used to wear, too, and a hat with green ribbon streamers, and a lace veil blowing across her face and out sideways, and a green ribbon flyin' from her waist. That was what she came out bride in when she married Erastus Miller. Her name before she was married was Hill. There was always a sight of "l's" in her name, married or single. Erastus Miller was good lookin', too, better lookin' than Luella. Sometimes I used to think that Luella wa'n't so handsome after all. Erastus just about worshiped her. I used to know him pretty well. He lived next door to me, and we went to school together. Folks used to say he was waitin' on me, but he wa'n't. I never thought he was except once or twice when he said things that some girls might have suspected meant somethin'. That was before Luella came here to teach the district school. It was funny how she came to get it, for folks said she hadn't any education, and that one of the big girls, Lottie Henderson, used to do all the teachin' for her, while she sat back and did embroidery work on a cambric pocket-handkerchief. Lottie Henderson was a real smart girl, a splendid scholar, and she just set her eyes by Luella, as all the girls did. Lottie would have made a real smart woman, but she died when Luella had been here about a year—just faded away and died: nobody knew what ailed her. She dragged herself to that schoolhouse and helped Luella teach till the very last minute. The committee all knew how Luella didn't do much of the work herself, but they winked at it. It wa'n't long after Lottie died that Erastus married her. I always thought he hurried it up because she wa'n't fit to teach. One of the big boys used to help her after Lottie died, but he hadn't much government, and the school didn't do very well, and Luella might have had to give it up, for the committee couldn't have shut their eyes to things much longer. The boy that helped her was a real honest, innocent sort of fellow, and he was a good scholar, too. Folks said he overstudied, and that was the reason he was took crazy the year after Luella married, but I don't know. And I don't know what made Erastus Miller go into consumption of the blood the year after he was married: consumption wa'n't in his family. He just grew weaker and weaker, and went almost bent double when he tried to wait on Luella, and he spoke feeble, like an old man. He worked terrible hard till the last trying to save up a little to leave Luella. I've seen him out in the worst storms on a wood-sled—he used to cut and sell wood—and he was hunched up on top lookin' more dead than alive. Once I couldn't stand it: I went over and helped him pitch some wood on the cart—I was always strong in my arms. I wouldn't stop for all he told me to, and I guess he was glad enough for the help. That was only a week before he died. He fell on the kitchen floor while he was gettin' breakfast. He always got the breakfast and let Luella lay abed. He did all the sweepin' and the washin' and the ironin'

and most of the cookin'. He couldn't bear to have Luella lift her finger,
and she let him do for her. She lived like a queen for all the work she
did. She didn't even do her sewin'. She said it made her shoulder ache
to sew, and poor Erastus's sister Lily used to do all her sewin'. She
wa'n't able to, either; she was never strong in her back, but she did it
beautifully. She had to, to suit Luella, she was so dreadful particular. I
never saw anythin' like the fagottin' and hemstitchin' that Lily Miller
did for Luella. She made all Luella's weddin' outfit, and that green silk
dress, after Maria Babbit cut it. Maria she cut it for nothin', and she did
a lot more cuttin' and fittin' for nothin' for Luella, too. Lily Miller went
to live with Luella after Erastus died. She gave up her home, though she
was real attached to it and wa'n't a mite afraid to stay alone. She rented
it and she went to live with Luella right away after the funeral."

Then this old woman, Lydia Anderson, who remembered Luella
Miller, would go on to relate the story of Lily Miller. It seemed that on
the removal of Lily Miller to the house of her dead brother, to live with
his widow, the village people first began to talk. This Lily Miller had
been hardly past her first youth, and a most robust and blooming
woman, rosy-cheeked, with curls of strong, black hair overshadowing
round, candid temples and bright dark eyes. It was not six months after
she had taken up her residence with her sister-in-law that her rosy
colour faded and her pretty curves become wan hollows. White shadows began to show in the black rings of her hair, and the light died out
of her eyes, her features sharpened, and there were pathetic lines at her
mouth, which yet wore always an expression of utter sweetness and
even happiness. She was devoted to her sister; there was no doubt that
she loved her with her whole heart, and was perfectly content in her
service. It was her sole anxiety lest she should die and leave her alone.

"The way Lily Miller used to talk about Luella was enough to
make you mad and enough to make you cry," said Lydia Anderson.
"I've been in there sometimes toward the last when she was too feeble
to cook and carried her some blanc-mange or custard—somethin' I
thought she might relish, and she'd thank me, and when I asked her
how she was, say she felt better than she did yesterday, and asked me if
I didn't think she looked better, dreadful pitiful, and say poor Luella
had an awful time takin' care of her and doin' the work—she wa'n't
strong enough to do anythin'—when all the time Luella wa'n't liftin'
her finger and poor Lily didn't get any care except what the neighbours
gave her, and Luella eat up everythin' that was carried in for Lily. I had
it real straight that she did. Luella used to just sit and cry and do

nothin'. She did act real fond of Lily, and she pined away considerable, too. There was those that thought she'd go into a decline herself. But after Lily died, her Aunt Abby Mixter came, and then Luella picked up and grew as fat and rosy as ever. But poor Aunt Abby begun to droop just the way Lily had, and I guess somebody wrote to her married daughter, Mrs. Sam Abbot, who lived in Barre, for she wrote her mother that she must leave right away and come and make her a visit, but Aunt Abby wouldn't go. I can see her now. She was a real good-lookin' woman, tall and large, with a big, square face and a high fore-head that looked of itself kind of benevolent and good. She just tended out on Luella as if she had been a baby, and when her married daughter sent for her she wouldn't stir one inch. She'd always thought a lot of her daughter, too, but she said Luella needed her and her married daughter didn't. Her daughter kept writin' and writin', but it didn't do any good. Finally she came, and when she saw how bad her mother looked, she broke down and cried and all but went on her knees to have her come away. She spoke her mind out to Luella, too. She told her that she'd killed her husband and everybody that had anythin' to do with her, and she'd thank her to leave her mother alone. Luella went into hysterics, and Aunt Abby was so frightened that she called me after her daughter went. Mrs. Sam Abbot she went away fairly cryin' out loud in the buggy, the neighbours heard her, and well she might, for she never saw her mother again alive. I went in that night when Aunt Abby called for me, standin' in the door with her little green-checked shawl over her head. I can see her now. 'Do come over here, Miss Anderson,' she sung out, kind of gasping for breath. I didn't stop for anythin'. I put over as fast as I could, and when I got there, there was Luella laughin' and cryin' all together, and Aunt Abby trying to hush her, and all the time she herself was white as a sheet and shakin' so she could hardly stand. 'For the land sakes, Mrs. Mixter,' says I, 'you look worse than she does. You ain't fit to be up out of your bed.'

" 'Oh, there ain't anythin' the matter with me,' says she. Then she went on talkin' to Luella. 'There, there, don't, don't, poor little lamb,' says she. 'Aunt Abby is here. She ain't goin' away and leave you. Don't, poor little lamb.'

" 'Do leave her with me, Mrs. Mixter, and you get back to bed,' says I, for Aunt Abby had been layin' down considerable lately, though somehow she contrived to do the work.

" 'I'm well enough,' says she. 'Don't you think she had better have the doctor, Miss Anderson?'

" 'The doctor,' says I, 'I think *you* had better have the doctor. I think you need him much worse than some folks I could mention.' And I looked right straight at Luella Miller laughin' and cryin' and goin' on as if she was the centre of all creation. All the time she was actin' so—seemed as if she was too sick to sense anythin'—she was keepin' a sharp lookout as to how we took it out of the corner of one eye. I see her. You could never cheat me about Luella Miller. Finally I got real mad and I run home and I got a bottle of valerian I had, and I poured some boilin' hot water on a handful of catnip, and I mixed up that catnip tea with most half a wineglass of valerian, and I went with it over to Luella's. I marched right up to Luella, a-holdin' out of that cup, all smokin'. 'Now,' says I, 'Luella Miller, *you swaller this!'*

" 'What is—what is it, oh, what is it?' she sort of screeches out. Then she goes off a-laughin' enough to kill.

" 'Poor lamb, poor little lamb,' says Aunt Abby, standin' over her, all kind of tottery, and tryin' to bathe her head with camphor.

" *'You swaller this right down,'* says I. And I didn't waste any ceremony. I just took hold of Luella Miller's chin and I tipped her head back, and I caught her mouth open with laughin', and I clapped that cup to her lips and I fairly hollered at her: 'Swaller, swaller, swaller!' and she gulped it right down. She had to, and I guess it did her good. Anyhow, she stopped cryin' and laughin' and let me put her to bed, and she went to sleep like a baby inside of half an hour. That was more than poor Aunt Abby did. She lay awake all that night and I stayed with her, though she tried not to have me; said she wa'n't sick enough for watchers. But I stayed, and I made some good cornmeal gruel and I fed her a teaspoon every little while all night long. It seemed to me as if she was jest dyin' from bein' all wore out. In the mornin' as soon as it was light I run over to the Bisbees and sent Johnny Bisbee for the doctor. I told him to tell the doctor to hurry, and he come pretty quick. Poor Aunt Abby didn't seem to know much of anythin' when he got there. You couldn't hardly tell she breathed, she was so used up. When the doctor had gone, Luella came into the room lookin' like a baby in her ruffled nightgown. I can see her now. Her eyes were as blue and her face all pink and white like a blossom, and she looked at Aunt Abby in the bed sort of innocent and surprised. 'Why,' says she, 'Aunt Abby ain't got up yet?'

" 'No, she ain't,' says I, pretty short.

" 'I thought I didn't smell the coffee,' says Luella.

" 'Coffee,' says I. 'I guess if you have coffee this mornin' you'll make it yourself.'

" 'I never made the coffee in all my life,' says she, dreadful astonished. 'Erastus always made the coffee as long as he lived, and then Lily she made it, and then Aunt Abby made it. I don't believe I *can* make the coffee, Miss Anderson.'

" 'You can make it or go without, jest as you please,' says I.

" 'Ain't Aunt Abby goin' to get up?' says she.

" 'I guess she won't get up,' says I, 'sick as she is.' I was gettin' madder and madder. There was somethin' about that little pink-and-white thing standin' there and talkin' about coffee, when she had killed so many better folks than she was, and had jest killed another, that made me feel 'most as if I wished somebody would up and kill her before she had a chance to do any more harm.

" 'Is Aunt Abby sick?' says Luella, as if she was sort of aggrieved and injured.

" 'Yes,' says I, 'she's sick, and she's goin' to die, and then you'll be left alone, and you'll have to do for yourself and wait on yourself, or do without things.' I don't know but I was sort of hard, but it was the truth, and if I was any harder than Luella Miller had been I'll give up. I ain't never been sorry that I said it. Well, Luella, she up and had hysterics again at that, and I jest let her have 'em. All I did was to bundle her into the room on the other side of the entry where Aunt Abby couldn't hear her, if she wa'n't past it—I don't know but she was—and set her down hard in a chair and told her not to come back into the other room, and she minded. She had her hysterics in there till she got tired. When she found out that nobody was comin' to coddle her and do for her she stopped. At least I suppose she did. I had all I could do with poor Aunt Abby tryin' to keep the breath of life in her. The doctor had told me that she was dreadful low, and give me some very strong medicine to give to her in drops real often, and told me real particular about the nourishment. Well, I did as he told me real faithful till she wa'n't able to swaller any longer. Then I had her daughter sent for. I had begun to realize that she wouldn't last any time at all. I hadn't realized it before, though I spoke to Luella the way I did. The doctor he came, and Mrs. Sam Abbot, but when she got there it was too late; her mother was dead. Aunt Abby's daughter just give one look at her mother layin' there, then she turned sort of sharp and sudden and looked at me.

" 'Where is she?' says she, and I knew she meant Luella.

" 'She's out in the kitchen,' says I. 'She's too nervous to see folks die. She's afraid it will make her sick.'

"The Doctor he speaks up then. He was a young man. Old Doctor Park had died the year before, and this was a young fellow just out of college. 'Mrs. Miller is not strong,' says he, kind of severe, 'and she is quite right in not agitating herself.'

" 'You are another, young man; she's got her pretty claw on you,' thinks I, but I didn't say anythin' to him. I just said over to Mrs. Sam Abbot that Luella was in the kitchen, and Mrs. Sam Abbot she went out there, and I went, too, and I never heard anythin' like the way she talked to Luella Miller. I felt pretty hard to Luella myself, but this was more than I ever would have dared to say. Luella she was too scared to go into hysterics. She jest flopped. She seemed to jest shrink away to nothin' in that kitchen chair, with Mrs. Sam Abbot standin' over her and talkin' and tellin' her the truth. I guess the truth was most too much for her and no mistake, because Luella presently actually did faint away, and there wa'n't any sham about it, the way I always suspected there was about them hysterics. She fainted dead away and we had to lay her flat on the floor, and the Doctor he came runnin' out and he said somethin' about a weak heart dreadful fierce to Mrs. Sam Abbot, but she wa'n't a mite scared. She faced him jest as white as even Luella was layin' there lookin' like death and the Doctor feelin' of her pulse.

" 'Weak heart,' says she, 'weak heart; weak fiddlesticks! There ain't nothin' weak about that woman. She's got strength enough to hang onto other folks till she kills 'em. Weak? It was my poor mother that was weak: this woman killed her as sure as if she had taken a knife to her.'

"But the Doctor he didn't pay much attention. He was bendin' over Luella layin' there with her yellow hair all streamin' and her pretty pink-and-white face all pale, and her blue eyes like stars gone out, and he was holdin' onto her hand and smoothin' her forehead, and tellin' me to get the brandy in Aunt Abby's room, and I was sure as I wanted to be that Luella had got somebody else to hang onto, now Aunt Abby was gone, and I thought of poor Erastus Miller, and I sort of pitied the poor young Doctor, led away by a pretty face, and I made up my mind I'd see what I could do.

"I waited till Aunt Abby had been dead and buried about a month, and the Doctor was goin' to see Luella steady and folks were beginnin' to talk; then one evenin', when I knew the Doctor had been called out of town and wouldn't be round, I went over to Luella's. I found her all dressed up in a blue muslin with white polka dots on it, and her hair curled jest as pretty, and there wa'n't a young girl in the place could compare with her. There was somethin' about Luella Miller seemed to draw the heart right out of you, but she didn't draw it out of *me*. She was settin' rocking in the chair by her sittin'-room window, and Maria Brown had gone home. Maria Brown had been in to help her, or rather to do the work, for Luella wa'n't helped when she didn't do anythin'. Maria Brown was real capable and she didn't have any ties; she wa'n't married, and lived alone, so she'd offered. I couldn't see why she should do the work any more than Luella; she wa'n't any too strong; but she seemed to think she could and Luella seemed to think so, too, so she went over and did all the work—washed, and ironed, and baked, while Luella sat and rocked. Maria didn't live long afterward. She began to fade away just the same fashion the others had. Well, she was warned, but she acted real mad when folks said anythin': said Luella was a poor, abused woman, too delicate to help herself, and they'd ought to be ashamed, and if she died helpin' them that couldn't help themselves she would—and she did.

" 'I s'pose Maria has gone home,' says I to Luella, when I had gone in and sat down opposite her.

" 'Yes, Maria went half an hour ago, after she had got supper and washed the dishes,' says Luella, in her pretty way.

" 'I suppose she has got a lot of work to do in her own house to-night,' says I, kind of bitter, but that was all thrown away on Luella Miller. It seemed to her right that other folks that wa'n't any better able than she was herself should wait on her, and she couldn't get it through her head that anybody should think it *wa'n't* right.

" 'Yes,' says Luella, real sweet and pretty, 'yes, she said she had to do her washin' to-night. She has let it go for a fortnight along of comin' over here.'

" 'Why don't she stay home and do her washin' instead of comin' over here and doin' *your* work, when you are just as well able, and enough sight more so, than she is to do it?' says I.

"Then Luella she looked at me like a baby who has a rattle shook at it. She sort of laughed as innocent as you please. 'Oh, I can't do the work myself, Miss Anderson,' says she. 'I never did. Maria *has* to do it.'

"Then I spoke out: 'Has to do it!' says I. 'Has to do it! She don't have to do it, either. Maria Brown has her own home and enough to live

on. She ain't beholden to you to come over here and slave for you and
kill herself.'

"Luella she jest set and stared at me for all the world like a doll-
baby that was so abused that it was comin' to life.

" 'Yes,' says I, 'she's killin' herself. She's goin' to die just the way
Erastus did, and Lily, and your Aunt Abby. You're killin' her jest as
you did them. I don't know what there is about you, but you seem to
bring a curse,' says I. 'You kill everybody that is fool enough to care
anythin' about you and do for you.'

"She stared at me and she was pretty pale.

" 'And Maria ain't the only one you're goin' to kill,' says I. 'You're
goin' to kill Doctor Malcom before you're done with him.'

"Then a red colour came flamin' all over her face. 'I ain't goin' to
kill him, either,' says she, and she begun to cry.

" 'Yes, you *be!*' says I. Then I spoke as I had never spoke before.
You see, I felt it on account of Erastus. I told her that she hadn't any
business to think of another man after she'd been married to one that
had died for her: that she was a dreadful woman; and she was, that's
true enough, but sometimes I have wondered lately if she knew it—if
she wa'n't like a baby with scissors in its hand cuttin' everybody without knowin' what it was doin'.

"Luella she kept gettin' paler and paler, and she never took her
eyes off my face. There was somethin' awful about the way she looked
at me and never spoke one word. After awhile I quit talkin' and I went
home. I watched that night, but her lamp went out before nine o'clock,
and when Doctor Malcom came drivin' past and sort of slowed up he
see there wa'n't any light and he drove along. I saw her sort of shy out
of meetin' the next Sunday, too, so he shouldn't go home with her, and
I begun to think mebbe she did have some conscience after all. It was
only a week after that that Maria Brown died—sort of sudden at the
last, though everybody had seen it was comin'. Well, then there was a
good deal of feelin' and pretty dark whispers. Folks said the days of
witchcraft had come again, and they were pretty shy of Luella. She
acted sort of offish to the Doctor and he didn't go there, and there
wa'n't anybody to do anythin' for her. I don't know how she *did* get
along. I wouldn't go in there and offer to help her—not because I was
afraid of dyin' like the rest but I thought she was just as well able to do
her own work as I was to do it for her, and I thought it was about time
that she did it and stopped killin' other folks. But it wa'n't very long
before folks began to say that Luella herself was goin' into a decline jes

the way her husband, and Lily, and Aunt Abby and the others had, and I saw myself that she looked pretty bad. I used to see her goin' past from the store with a bundle as if she could hardly crawl, but I remembered how Erastus used to wait and 'tend when he couldn't hardly put one foot before the other, and I didn't go out to help her.

"But at last one afternoon I saw the Doctor come drivin' up like mad with his medicine chest, and Mrs. Babbit came in after supper and said that Luella was real sick.

" 'I'd offer to go in and nurse her,' says she, 'but I've got my children to consider, and mebbe it ain't true what they say, but it's queer how many folks that have done for her have died.'

"I didn't say anythin', but I considered how she had been Erastus's wife and how he had set his eyes by her, and I made up my mind to go in the next mornin', unless she was better, and see what I could do; but the next mornin' I see her at the window, and pretty soon she came steppin' out as spry as you please, and a little while afterward Mrs. Babbit came in and told me that the Doctor had got a girl from out of town, a Sarah Jones, to come there, and she said she was pretty sure that the Doctor was goin' to marry Luella.

"I saw him kiss her in the door that night myself, and I knew it was true. The woman came that afternoon, and the way she flew around was a caution. I don't believe Luella had swept since Maria died. She swept and dusted, and washed and ironed; wet clothes and dusters and carpets were flyin' over there all day, and every time Luella set her foot out when the Doctor wa'n't there there was that Sarah Jones helpin' of her up and down the steps, as if she hadn't learned to walk.

"Well, everybody knew that Luella and the Doctor were goin' to be married, but it wa'n't long before they began to talk about his lookin' so poorly, jest as they had about the others; and they talked about Sarah Jones, too.

"Well, the Doctor did die, and he wanted to be married first, so as to leave what little he had to Luella, but he died before the minister could get there, and Sarah Jones died a week afterward.

"Well, that wound up everything for Luella Miller. Not another soul in the whole town would lift a finger for her. There got to be a sort of panic. Then she began to droop in good earnest. She used to have to go to the store herself, for Mrs. Babbit was afraid to let Tommy go for her, and I've seen her goin' past and stoppin' every two or three steps to rest. Well, I stood it as long as I could, but one day I see her comin' with her arms full and stoppin' to lean against the Babbit fence, and I run out and took her bundles and carried them to her house. Then I went home and never spoke one word to her though she called after me dreadful kind of pitiful. Well, that night I was taken sick with a chill, and I was sick as I wanted to be for two weeks. Mrs. Babbit had seen me run out to help Luella and she came in and told me I was goin' to die on account of it. I didn't know whether I was or not, but I considered I had done right by Erastus's wife.

"That last two weeks Luella she had a dreadful hard time, I guess. She was pretty sick, and as near as I could make out nobody dared go near her. I don't know as she was really needin' anythin' very much, for there was enough to eat in her house and it was warm weather, and she made out to cook a little flour gruel every day, I know, but I guess she had a hard time, she that had been so petted and done for all her life.

"When I got so I could go out, I went over there one morning. Mrs. Babbit had just come in to say she hadn't seen any smoke and she didn't know but what it was somebody's duty to go in, but she couldn't help thinkin' of her children, and I got right up, though I hadn't been out of the house for two weeks, and I went in there, and Luella she was layin' on the bed, and she was dyin'.

"She lasted all that day and into the night. But I sat there after the new doctor had gone away. Nobody else dared to go there. It was about midnight that I left her for a minute to run home and get some medicine I had been takin', for I begun to feel rather bad.

"It was a full moon that night, and just as I started out of my door to cross the street back to Luella's, I stopped short, for I saw something."

Lydia Anderson at this juncture always said with a certain defiance that she did not expect to be believed, and then proceeded in a hushed voice:

"I saw what I saw, and I know I saw it, and I will swear on my death bed that I saw it. I saw Luella Miller and Erastus Miller, and Lily, and Aunt Abby, and Maria, and the Doctor, and Sarah, all goin' out of her door, and all but Luella shone white in the moonlight, and they were all helpin' her along till she seemed to fairly fly in the midst of them. Then it all disappeared. I stood a minute with my heart poundin', then I went over there. I thought of goin' for Mrs. Babbit, but I thought she'd be afraid. So I went alone, though I knew what had happened. Luella was layin' real peaceful, dead on her bed."

This was the story that the old woman, Lydia Anderson, told, but the sequel was told by the people who survived her, and this is the tale which has become folklore in the village.

Lydia Anderson died when she was eighty-seven. She had continued wonderfully hale and hearty for one of her years until about two weeks before her death.

One bright moonlight evening she was sitting beside a window in her parlour when she made a sudden exclamation, and was out of the house and across the street before the neighbour who was taking care of her could stop her. She followed as fast as possible and found Lydia Anderson stretched on the ground before the door of Luella Miller's deserted house, and she was quite dead.

The next night there was a red gleam of fire athwart the moonlight and the old house of Luella Miller was burned to the ground. Nothing is now left of it except a few old cellar stones and a lilac bush, and in summer a helpless trail of morning glories among the weeds, which might be considered emblematic of Luella herself.

FRANCIS MARION CRAWFORD *(1854–1909) is famed as the author of "For the Blood Is the Life" and "The Upper Berth," universally acknowledged as two of the most terrifying short stories ever written.*

Crawford, an American, was born in Italy but educated in America. A Sanskrit scholar, he lived for some years in India, where he edited a newspaper, then returned to Italy, where he died in Sorrento in 1909.

Some of Crawford's many novels deal with such themes as resurrection and hypnotism, but his fame as an author of horror fiction rests on a single collection of seven stories, Wandering Ghosts, *published posthumously in 1911.*

"For the Blood Is the Life," one of the most memorable vampire tales ever written, will keep Crawford's name alive for many years to come.

For the Blood Is the Life
(1911)
BY F. MARION CRAWFORD

We had dined at sunset on the broad roof of the old tower, because it was cooler there during the great heat of summer. Besides, the little kitchen was built at one corner of the great square platform, which made it more convenient than if the dishes had to be carried down the steep stone steps, broken in places and everywhere worn with age. The tower was one of those built all down the west coast of Calabria by the Emperor Charles V early in the sixteenth century, to keep off the Barbary pirates, when the unbelievers were allied with Francis I against the Emperor and the Church. They have gone to ruin, a few still stand intact, and mine is one of the largest. How it came into my possession ten years ago, and why I spend a part of each year in it, are matters which do not concern this tale. The tower stands in one of the loneliest spots in southern Italy, at the extremity of a curving rocky promontory, which forms a small but safe natural harbor at the southern extremity of the Gulf of Policastro, and just north of Cape Scalea, the birthplace of Judas Iscariot, according to the old local legend. The tower stands alone on this hooked spur of the rock, and there is not a house to be seen within three miles of it. When I go there I take a couple of sailors, one of whom is a fair cook, and when I am away it is in charge of a gnomelike little being who was once a miner and who attached himself to me long ago.

My friend, who sometimes visits me in my summer solitude, is an artist by profession, a Scandinavian by birth, and a cosmopolitan by force of circumstances. We had dined at sunset; the sunset glow had reddened and faded again, and the evening purple steeped the vast chain of the mountains that embrace the deep gulf to eastward and rear themselves higher and higher toward the south. It was hot, and we sat at the landward corner of the platform, waiting for the night breeze to come down from the lower hills. The color sank out of the air, there was a little interval of deep-gray twilight, and a lamp sent a yellow streak from the open door of the kitchen, where the men were getting their supper.

Then the moon rose suddenly above the crest of the promontory, flooding the platform and lighting up every little spur of rock and knoll of grass below us, down to the edge of the motionless water. My friend lighted his pipe and sat looking at a spot on the hillside. I knew that he was looking at it, and for a long time past I had wondered whether he would ever see anything there that would fix his attention. I knew that spot well. It was clear that he was interested at last, though it was a long time before he spoke. Like most painters, he trusts to his own eyesight, as a lion trusts his strength and a stag his speed, and he is always disturbed when he cannot reconcile what he sees with what he believes that he ought to see.

"It's strange," he said. "Do you see that little mound just on this side of the boulder?"

"Yes," I said, and I guessed what was coming.

"It looks like a grave," observed Holger.

"Very true. It does look like a grave."

"Yes," continued my friend, his eyes still fixed on the spot. "But the strange thing is that I see the body lying on the top of it. Of course," continued Holger, turning his head on one side as artists do, "it must be an effect of light. In the first place, it is not a grave at all. Secondly, if it were, the body would be inside and not outside. Therefore, it's an effect of the moonlight. Don't you see it?"

"Perfectly; I always see it on moonlight nights."

"It doesn't seem to interest you much," said Holger.

"On the contrary, it does interest me, though I am used to it. You're not so far wrong, either. The mound is really a grave."

"Nonsense!" cried Holger, incredulously. "I suppose you'll tell me what I see lying on it is really a corpse!"

"No," I answered, "it's not. I know, because I have taken the trouble to go down and see."

"Then what is it?" asked Holger.

"It's nothing."

"You mean that it's an effect of light, I suppose?"

"Perhaps it is. But the inexplicable part of the matter is that it makes no difference whether the moon is rising or setting, or waxing or waning. If there's any moonlight at all, from east or west or overhead, so long as it shines on the grave you can see the outline of the body on top."

Holger stirred up his pipe with the point of his knife, and then used his finger for a stopper. When the tobacco burned well he rose from his chair.

"If you don't mind," he said, "I'll go down and take a look at it."

He left me, crossed the roof, and disappeared down the dark steps. I did not move, but sat looking down until he came out of the tower below. I heard him humming an old Danish song as he crossed the open space in the bright moonlight, going straight to the mysterious mound. When he was ten paces from it, Holger stopped short, made two steps forward, and then three or four backward, and then stopped again. I knew what that meant. He had reached the spot where the Thing ceased to be visible—where, as he would have said, the effect of light changed.

Then he went on till he reached the mound and stood upon it. I could see the Thing still, but it was no longer lying down; it was on its knees now, winding its white arms round Holger's body and looking up into his face. A cool breeze stirred my hair at that moment, as the night wind began to come down from the hills, but it felt like a breath from another world.

The Thing seemed to be trying to climb to its feet, helping itself up by Holger's body while he stood upright, quite unconscious of it and apparently looking toward the tower, which is very picturesque when the moonlight falls upon it on that side.

"Come along!" I shouted. "Don't stay there all night!"

It seemed to me that he moved reluctantly as he stepped from the mound, or else with difficulty. That was it. The Thing's arms were still round his waist, but its feet could not leave the grave. As he came slowly forward it was drawn and lengthened like a wreath of mist, thin and white, till I saw distinctly that Holger shook himself, as a man does who feels a chill. At the same instant a little wail of pain came to me on the breeze—it might have been the cry of the small owl that lives among the rocks—and the misty presence floated swiftly back from Holger's advancing figure and lay once more at its length upon the mound.

Again I felt the cool breeze in my hair, and this time an icy thrill of dread ran down my spine. I remembered very well that I had once gone down there alone in the moonlight; that presently, being near, I had seen nothing; that, like Holger, I had gone and had stood upon the mound; and I remembered how, when I came back, sure that there was nothing there, I had felt the sudden conviction that there was something after all if I would only look behind me. I remembered the strong temptation to look back, a temptation I had resisted as unworthy of a man of sense, until, to get rid of it, I had shaken myself just as Holger did.

And now I knew that those white, misty arms had been round me too; I knew it in a flash, and I shuddered as I remembered that I had heard the night owl then too. But it had not been the night owl. It was the cry of the Thing.

I refilled my pipe and poured out a cup of strong southern wine; in less than a minute Holger was seated beside me again.

"Of course there's nothing there," he said, "but it's creepy, all the same. Do you know, when I was coming back I was so sure that there was something behind me that I wanted to turn round and look? It was an effort not to."

He laughed a little, knocked the ashes out of his pipe, and poured himself out some wine. For a while neither of us spoke, and the moon rose higher, and we both looked at the Thing that lay on the mound.

"You might make a story about that," said Holger after a long time.

"There is one," I answered. "If you're not sleepy, I'll tell it to you."

"Go ahead," said Holger, who likes stories.

Old Alario was dying up there in the village behind the hill. You remember him, I have no doubt. They say that he made his money by selling sham jewelry in South America, and escaped with his gains when he was found out. Like all those fellows, if they bring anything back with them, he at once set to work to enlarge his house; and, as there are no masons here, he sent all the way to Paola for two workmen. They were a rough-looking pair of scoundrels—a Neapolitan who had lost one eye and a Sicilian with an old scar half an inch deep across his left cheek. I often saw them, for on Sundays they used to come down here and fish off the rocks. When Alario caught the fever that killed him the masons were still at work. As he had agreed that part of their pay should be their board and lodging, he made them sleep in the house. His wife was dead, and he had an only son called Angelo, who was a much better sort than himself. Angelo was to marry the daughter of the richest man in the village, and, strange to say, though the marriage was arranged by their parents, the young people were said to be in love with each other.

For that matter, the whole village was in love with Angelo, and among the rest a wild, good-looking creature called Cristina, who was more like a gipsy than any girl I ever saw about here. She had very red lips and very black eyes, she was built like a greyhound, and had the tongue of the devil. But Angelo did not care a straw for her. He was rather a simple-minded fellow, quite different from his old scoundrel of a father, and under what I should call normal circumstances I really believe that he would never have looked at any girl except the nice plump little creature, with a fat dowry, whom his father meant him to marry. But things turned up which were neither normal nor natural.

On the other hand, a very handsome young shepherd from the hills above Maratea was in love with Cristina, who seems to have been quite indifferent to him. Cristina had no regular means of subsistence, but she was a good girl and willing to do any work or go on errands to any distance for the sake of a loaf of bread or a mess of beans, and permission to sleep under cover. She was especially glad when she could get something to do about the house of Angelo's father. There is no doctor in the village, and when the neighbors saw that old Alario was dying they sent Cristina to Scalea to fetch one. That was late in the afternoon, and if they had waited so long, it was because the dying miser refused to allow any such extravagance while he was able to speak. But while Cristina was gone, matters grew rapidly worse, the priest was brought to the bedside, and when he had done what he could he gave it as his opinion to the bystanders that the old man was dead, and left the house.

You know these people. They have a physical horror of death. Until the priest spoke, the room had been full of people. The words were hardly out of his mouth before it was empty. It was night now. They hurried down the dark steps and out into the street.

Angelo was away, Cristina had not come back—the simple woman servant who had nursed the sick man fled with the rest, and the body was left alone in the flickering light of the earthen oil lamp.

Five minutes later two men looked in cautiously and crept forward toward the bed. They were the one-eyed Neapolitan mason and his Sicilian companion. They knew what they wanted. In a moment they had dragged from under the bed a small but heavy iron-bound box, and long before any one thought of coming back to the dead man they had left the house and the village under cover of the darkness. It was easy enough, for Alario's house is the last toward the gorge which leads down here, and the thieves merely went out by the back door, got over the stone wall, and had nothing to risk after that except the possibility of meeting some belated countryman, which was very small indeed, since few of the people use that path. They had a mattock and shovel, and they made their way here without accident.

I am telling you this story as it must have happened, for, of course, there were no witnesses to this part of it. The men brought the box down by the gorge, intending to bury it until they should be able to come back and take it away in a boat. They must have been clever enough to guess that some of the money would be in paper notes, for they would otherwise have buried it on the beach in the wet sand, where it would have been much safer. But the paper would have rotted if they had been obliged to leave it there long, so they dug their hole down there, close to that boulder. Yes, just where the mound is now.

Cristina did not find the doctor in Scalea, for he had been sent for from a place up the valley, halfway to San Domenico. If she had found him, he would have come on his mule by the upper road, which is smoother but much longer. But Cristina took the short cut by the rocks, which passes about fifty feet above the mound, and goes round that corner. The men were digging when she passed, and she heard them at work. It would not have been like her to go by without finding out what the noise was, for she was never afraid of anything in her life, and, besides, the fishermen sometimes came ashore here at night to get a stone for an anchor or to gather sticks to make a little fire. The night was dark, and Cristina probably came close to the two men before she could see what they were doing. She knew them, of course, and they knew her, and understood instantly that they were in her power. There was only one thing to be done for their safety, and they did it. They knocked her on the head, they dug the hole deep, and they buried her quickly with the iron-bound chest. They must have understood that their only chance of escaping suspicion lay in getting back to the village before their absence was noticed, for they returned immediately, and were found half an hour later gossiping quietly with the man who was making Alario's coffin. He was a crony of theirs, and had been working at the repairs in the old man's house. So far as I have been able to make out, the only persons who were supposed to know where Alario kept his treasure were Angelo and the one woman servant I have mentioned. Angelo was away; it was the woman who discovered the theft.

It is easy enough to understand why no one else knew where the money was. The old man kept his door locked and the key in his pocket when he was out, and did not let the woman enter to clean the place unless he was there himself. The whole village knew that he had money somewhere, however, and the masons had probably discovered the whereabouts of the chest by climbing in at the window in his absence. If the old man had not been delirious until he lost consciousness, he would have been in frightful agony of mind for his riches. The faithful woman servant forgot their existence only for a few moments when she fled with the rest, overcome by the horror of death. Twenty minutes had not passed before she returned with the two hideous old hags who are always called in to prepare the dead for burial. Even then she had not at first the courage to go near the bed with them, but she made a pretense of dropping something, went down on her knees as if to find it, and looked under the bedstead. The walls of the room were newly white-washed down to the floor, and she saw at a glance that the chest was gone. It had been there in the afternoon, it had therefore been stolen in the short interval since she had left the room.

There are no carabineers stationed in the village; there is not so much as a municipal watchman, for there is no municipality. There never was such a place, I believe. Scalea is supposed to look after it in some mysterious way, and it takes a couple of hours to get anybody from there. As the old woman had lived in the village all her life, it did not even occur to her to apply to any civil authority for help. She simply set up a howl and ran through the village in the dark, screaming out that her dead master's house had been robbed. Many of the people looked out, but at first no one seemed inclined to help her. Most of them, judging her by themselves, whispered to each other that she had probably stolen the money herself. The first man to move was the father of the girl whom Angelo was to marry; having collected his household, all of whom felt a personal interest in the wealth which was to have come into the family, he declared it to be his opinion that the chest had been stolen by the two journeyman masons who lodged in the house. He headed a search for them, which naturally began in Alario's house and ended in the carpenter's workshop, where the thieves were found discussing a measure of wine with the carpenter over the half-finished coffin, by the light of one earthen lamp filled with oil and tallow. The search party at once accused the delinquents of the crime, and threatened to lock them up in the cellar till the carabineers could be fetched from Scalea. The two men looked at each other for one moment, and then without the slightest hesitation they put out the single light, seized the unfinished coffin between them, and using it as a sort of battering ram, dashed upon their assailants in the dark. In a few moments they were beyond pursuit.

That is the end of the first part of the story. The treasure had disappeared, and as no trace of it could be found the people naturally supposed that the thieves had succeeded in carrying it off. The old man was buried, and when Angelo came back at last he had to borrow money to pay for the miserable funeral, and had some difficulty in doing so. He hardly needed to be told that in losing his inheritance he had lost his bride. In this part of the world marriages are made on strictly business principles, and if the promised cash is not forthcoming on the appointed day the bride or the bridegroom whose parents have failed to produce it may as well take themselves off, for there will be no wedding. Poor Angelo knew that well enough. His father had been possessed of hardly any land, and now that the hard cash which he had brought from South America was gone, there was nothing left but debts for the building materials that were to have been used for enlarging and improving the old house. Angelo was beggared, and the nice plump little creature who was to have been his turned up her nose at him in the most approved fashion. As for Cristina, it was several days before she was missed, for no one remembered that she had been sent to Scalea for the doctor, who had never come. She often disappeared in the same way for days together, when she could find a little work here and there at the distant farms among the hills. But when she did not come back at all, people began to wonder, and at last made up their minds that she had connived with the masons and had escaped with them.

I paused and emptied my glass.

"That sort of thing could not happen anywhere else," observed Holger, filling his everlasting pipe again. "It is wonderful what a natural charm there is about murder and sudden death in a romantic country like this. Deeds that would be simply brutal and disgusting anywhere else become dramatic and mysterious because this is Italy and we are living in a genuine tower of Charles V built against genuine Barbary pirates."

"There's something in that," I admitted. Holger is the most romantic man in the world inside of himself, but he always thinks it necessary to explain why he feels anything.

"I suppose they found the poor girl's body with the box," he said presently.

"As it seems to interest you," I answered, "I'll tell you the rest of the story."

The moon had risen high by this time; the outline of the Thing on the mound was clearer to our eyes than before.

The village very soon settled down to its small, dull life. No one missed old Alario, who had been away so much on his voyages to South America that he had never been a familiar figure in his native place. Angelo lived in the half-finished house, and because he had no money to pay the old woman servant she would not stay with him, but once in a long time she would come and wash a shirt for him for old acquaintance' sake. Besides the house, he had inherited a small patch of ground at some distance from the village; he tried to cultivate it, but he had no heart in the work, for he knew he could never pay the taxes on it and on the house, which would certainly be confiscated by the Government, or seized for the debt of the building material, which the man who had supplied it refused to take back.

Angelo was very unhappy. So long as his father had been alive and rich, every girl in the village had been in love with him; but that was all changed now. It had been pleasant to be admired and courted, and invited to drink wine by fathers who had girls to marry. It was hard to be stared at coldly, and sometimes laughed at because he had been robbed of his inheritance. He cooked his miserable meals for himself, and from being sad became melancholy and morose.

At twilight, when the day's work was done, instead of hanging about in the open space before the church with young fellows of his own age, he took to wandering in lonely places on the outskirts of the village till it was quite dark. Then he slunk home and went to bed to save the expense of a light. But in those lonely twilight hours he began to have strange waking dreams. He was not always alone, for often when he sat on the stump of a tree, where the narrow path turns down the gorge, he was sure that a woman came up noiselessly over the rough stones, as if her feet were bare; and she stood under a clump of chestnut trees only half a dozen yards down the path, and beckoned to him without speaking. Though she was in the shadow he knew that her lips were red, and that when they parted a little and smiled at him she showed two small sharp teeth. He knew this at first rather than saw it, and he knew that it was Cristina, and that she was dead. Yet he was not afraid; he only wondered whether it was a dream, for he thought that if he had been awake he should have been frightened.

Besides, the dead woman had red lips, and that could only happen in a dream. Whenever he went near the gorge after sunset she was already there waiting for him, or else she very soon appeared, and he began to be sure that she came a little nearer to him every day. At first he had only been sure of her blood-red mouth, but now each feature grew distinct, and the pale face looked at him with deep and hungry eyes.

It was the eyes that grew dim. Little by little he came to know that some day the dream would not end when he turned away to go home, but would lead him down the gorge out of which the vision rose. She was nearer now when she beckoned to him. Her cheeks were not livid like those of the dead, but pale with starvation, with the furious and unappeased physical hunger of her eyes that devoured him. They feasted on his soul and cast a spell over him, and at last they were close to his own and held them. He could not tell whether her breath was as hot as fire or as cold as ice; he could not tell whether her red lips burned his or froze them, or whether her five fingers on his wrists seared scorching scars or bit his flesh like frost; he could not tell whether he was awake or asleep, whether she was alive or dead, but he knew that she loved him, she alone of all creatures, earthly or unearthly, and her spell had power over him.

When the moon rose high that night the shadow of that Thing was not alone down there upon the mound.

Angelo awoke in the cool dawn, drenched with dew and chilled through flesh, and blood, and bone. He opened his eyes to the faint gray light, and saw the stars still shining overhead. He was very weak, and his heart was beating so slowly that he was almost like a man fainting. Slowly he turned his head on the mound, as on a pillow, but the other face was not there. Fear seized him suddenly, a fear unspeakable and unknown; he sprang to his feet and fled up the gorge, and he never looked behind him until he reached the door of the house on the outskirts of the village. Drearily he went to his work that day, and wearily the hours dragged themselves after the sun, till at last he touched the sea and sank, and the great sharp hills above Maratea turned purple against the dove-colored eastern sky.

Angelo shouldered his heavy hoe and left the field. He felt less tired now than in the morning when he had begun to work, but he promised himself that he would go home without lingering by the gorge, and eat the best supper he could get himself, and sleep all night in his bed like a Christian man. Not again would he be tempted down the narrow way by a shadow with red lips and icy breath; not again would he dream that dream of terror and delight. He was near the village now; it was half an hour since the sun had set, and the cracked church bell sent little discordant echoes across the rocks and ravines to tell all good people that the day was done. Angelo stood still a moment where the path forked, where it led toward the village on the left, and down to the gorge on the right, where a clump of chestnut trees overhung the narrow way. He stood still a minute, lifting his battered hat from his head and gazing at the fast-fading sea westward, and his lips moved as he silently repeated the familiar evening prayer. His lips moved, but the words that followed them in his brain lost their meaning and turned into others, and ended in a name that he spoke aloud— Cristina! With the name, the tension of his will relaxed suddenly, reality went out and the dream took him again and bore him on swiftly and surely like a man walking in his sleep, down, down, by the steep path in the gathering darkness. And as she glided beside him, Cristina whispered strange sweet things in his ear, which somehow, if he had been awake, he knew that he could not quite have understood; but now they were the most wonderful words he had ever heard in his life. And she kissed him also, but not upon his mouth. He felt her sharp kisses upon his white throat, and he knew that her lips were red. So the wild dream sped on through twilight and darkness and moonrise, and all the glory of the summer's night. But in the chilly dawn he lay as one half dead upon the mound down there, recalling and not recalling, drained of his blood, yet strangely longing to give those red lips more. Then came the fear, the awful nameless panic, the mortal horror that guards the confines of the world we see not, neither know of as we know of other things, but which we feel when its icy chill freezes our bones and stirs our hair with the touch of a ghostly hand. Once more Angelo sprang from the mound and fled up the gorge in the breaking day, but his step was less sure this time, and he panted for breath as he ran; and when he came to the bright spring of water that rises halfway up the hillside, he dropped upon his knees and hands and plunged his whole face in and drank as he had never drunk before—for it was the thirst of the wounded man who has lain bleeding all night long upon the battlefield.

She had him fast now, and he could not escape her, but would come to her every evening at dusk until she had drained him of his last drop of blood. It was in vain that when the day was done he tried to take another turning and to go home by a path that did not lead near the gorge. It was in vain that he made promises to himself each morning at dawn when he climbed the lonely way up from the shore to the village. It was all in vain, for when the sun sank burning into the sea, and the coolness of the evening stole out as from a hiding-place to delight the weary world, his feet turned toward the old way, and she was waiting for him in the shadow under the chestnut trees; and then all happened as before, and she fell to kissing his white throat even as she flitted lightly down the way, winding one arm about him. And as his blood failed, she grew more hungry and more thirsty every day, and every day when he awoke in the early dawn it was harder to rouse himself to the effort of climbing the steep path to the village; and when he went to his work his feet dragged painfully, and there was hardly strength in his arms to wield the heavy hoe. He scarcely spoke to any one now, but the people said he was "consuming himself" for love of the girl he was to have married when he lost his inheritance; and they laughed heartily at the thought, for this is not a very romantic country. At this time, Antonio, the man who stays here to look after the tower, returned from a visit to his people, who live near Salerno. He had been away all the time since before Alario's death and knew nothing of what had happened. He has told me that he came back late in the afternoon and shut himself up in the tower to eat and sleep, for he was very tired. It was past midnight when he awoke, and when he looked out the waning moon was rising over the shoulder of the hill. He looked out toward the mound, and he saw something, and he did not sleep again that night. When he went out again in the morning it was broad daylight, and there was nothing to be seen on the mound but loose stones and driven sand. Yet he did not go very near it; he went straight up the path to the village and directly to the house of the old priest.

"I have seen an evil thing this night," he said; "I have seen how the dead drink the blood of the living. And the blood is the life."

"Tell me what you have seen," said the priest in reply.

Antonio told him everything he had seen.

"You must bring your book and your holy water tonight," he

added. "I will be here before sunset to go down with you, and if it pleases your reverence to sup with me while we wait, I will make ready."

"I will come," the priest answered, "for I have read in old books of these strange beings which are neither quick nor dead, and which lie ever fresh in their graves, stealing out in the dusk to taste life and blood."

Antonio cannot read, but he was glad to see that the priest understood the business; for, of course, the books must have instructed him as to the best means of quieting the half-living Thing forever.

So Antonio went away to his work, which consists largely in sitting on the shady side of the tower, when he is not perched upon a rock with a fishing line catching nothing. But on that day he went twice to look at the mound in the bright sunlight, and he searched round and round it for some hole through which the being might get in and out; but he found none. When the sun began to sink and the air was cooler in the shadows, he went up to fetch the old priest, carrying a little wicker basket with him; and in this they placed a bottle of holy water, and the basin, and sprinkler, and the stole which the priest would need; and they came down and waited in the door of the tower till it should be dark. But while the light still lingered very gray and faint, they saw something moving, just there, two figures, a man's that walked, and a woman's that flitted beside him, and while her head lay on his shoulder she kissed his throat. The priest has told me that, too, and that his teeth chattered and he grasped Antonio's arm. The vision passed and disappeared into the shadow. Then Antonio got the leathern flask of strong liquor, which he kept for great occasions, and poured such a draught as made the old man feel almost young again; and he got the lantern, and his pick and shovel, and gave the priest his stole to put on and the holy water to carry, and they went out together toward the spot where the work was to be done. Antonio says that in spite of the rum his own knees shook together, and the priest stumbled over his Latin. For when they were yet a few yards from the mound the flickering light of the lantern fell upon Angelo's white face, unconscious as if in sleep, and on his upturned throat, over which a very thin red line of blood trickled down into his collar; and the flickering light of the lantern played upon another face that looked up from the feast—upon two deep, dead eyes that saw in spite of death—upon parted lips redder than life itself— upon two gleaming teeth on which glistened a rosy drop. Then the priest, good old man, shut his eyes tight and showered holy water be-

fore him, and his cracked voice rose almost to a scream; and then
Antonio, who is no coward after all, raised his pick in one hand and the
lantern in the other, as he sprang forward, not knowing what the end
should be; and then he swears that he heard a woman's cry, and the
Thing was gone, and Angelo lay alone on the mound unconscious, with
the red line on his throat and the beads of deathly sweat on his cold
forehead. They lifted him, half-dead as he was, and laid him on the
ground close by! then Antonio went to work, and the priest helped him,
though he was old and could not do much; and they dug deep, and at
last Antonio, standing in the grave, stooped down with his lantern to
see what he might see.

His hair used to be dark brown, with grizzled streaks about the
temples; in less than a month from that day he was as gray as a badger.
He was a miner when he was young, and most of these fellows have
seen ugly sights now and then, when accidents have happened, but he
had never seen what he saw that night—that Thing which is neither
alive nor dead, that Thing that will abide neither above ground nor in
the grave. Antonio had brought something with him which the priest
had not noticed. He had made it that afternoon—a sharp stake shaped
from a piece of tough old driftwood. He had it with him now, and he
had his heavy pick, and he had taken the lantern down into the grave. I
don't think any power on earth could make him speak of what happened then, and the old priest was too frightened to look in. He says he
heard Antonio breathing like a wild beast, and moving as if he were
fighting with something almost as strong as himself; and he heard an
evil sound also, with blows, as of something violently driven through
flesh and bone; and then the most awful sound of all—a woman's
shriek, the unearthly scream of a woman neither dead nor alive, but
buried deep for many days. And he, the poor old priest, could only rock
himself as he knelt there in the sand, crying aloud his prayers and
exorcisms to drown these dreadful sounds. Then suddenly a small iron-
bound chest was thrown up and rolled over against the old man's knee,
and in a moment more Antonio was beside him, his face as white as
tallow in the flickering light of the lantern, shoveling the sand and
pebbles into the grave with furious haste, and looking over the edge till
the pit was half full; and the priest had said that there was much fresh
blood on Antonio's hands and on his clothes.

I had come to the end of my story. Holger finished his wine and
leaned back in his chair.

"So Angelo got his own again," he said. "Did he marry the prim and plump young person to whom he had been betrothed?"

"No; he had been badly frightened. He went to South America, and has not been heard of since."

"And that poor thing's body is there still, I suppose," said Holger. "Is it quite dead yet, I wonder?"

I wonder, too. But whether it is dead or alive, I should hardly care to see it, even in broad daylight.

Antonio is as gray as a badger, and he has never been quite the same man since that night.

The Transfer
(1912)

BY ALGERNON BLACKWOOD

The child began to cry in the early afternoon—about three o'clock, to
be exact. I remember the hour, because I had been listening with secret
relief to the sound of the departing carriage. Those wheels fading into
the distance down the gravel drive with Mrs. Frene, and her daughter
Gladys to whom I was governess, meant for me some hours' welcome
rest, and the June day was oppressively hot. Moreover, there was this
excitement in the little country household that had told upon us all, but
especially upon myself. This excitement, running delicately behind all
the events of the morning, was due to some mystery, and the mystery
was of course kept concealed from the governess. I had exhausted myself with guessing and keeping on the watch. For some deep and unexplained anxiety possessed me, so that I kept thinking of my sister's
dictum that I was really much too sensitive to make a good governess,
and that I should have done far better as a professional clairvoyante.

Mr. Frene, senior, "Uncle Frank," was expected for an unusual
visit from town about tea-time. That I knew. I also knew that his visit
was concerned somehow with the future welfare of little Jamie, Gladys'
seven-year-old brother. More than this, indeed, I never knew, and this
missing link makes my story in a fashion incoherent—an important bit

of the strange puzzle left out. I only gathered that the visit of Uncle Frank was of a condescending nature, that Jamie was told he must be upon his very best behavior to make a good impression, and that Jamie, who had never seen his uncle, dreaded him horribly already in advance. Then, trailing thinly through the dying crunch of the carriage wheels this sultry afternoon, I heard the curious little wail of the child's crying, with the effect, wholly unaccountable, that every nerve in my body shot its bolt electrically, bringing me to my feet with a tingling of unequivocal alarm. Positively, the water ran into my eyes. I recalled his white distress that morning when told that Uncle Frank was motoring down for tea and that he was to be "very nice indeed" to him. It had gone into me like a knife. All through the day, indeed, had run this nightmare quality of terror and vision.

"The man with the 'normous face?" he had asked in a little voice of awe, and then gone speechless from the room in tears that no amount of soothing management could calm. That was all I saw; and what he meant by "the 'normous face" gave me only a sense of vague presentiment. But it came as anticlimax somehow—a sudden revelation of the mystery and excitement that pulsed beneath the quiet of the stifling summer day. I feared for him. For of all that commonplace household I loved Jamie best, though professionally I had nothing to do with him. He was a high-strung, ultra-sensitive child, and it seemed to me that no one understood him, least of all his honest, tender-hearted parents; so that his little wailing voice brought me from my bed to the window in a moment like a call for help.

The haze of June lay over that big garden like a blanket; the wonderful flowers, which were Mr. Frene's delight, hung motionless; the lawns, so soft and thick, cushioned all other sounds; only the limes and huge clumps of guelder roses hummed with bees. Through this muted atmosphere of heat and haze the sound of the child's crying floated faintly to my ears—from a distance. Indeed, I wonder now that I heard it at all, for the next moment I saw him down beyond the garden, standing in his white sailor suit alone, two hundred yards away. He was down by the ugly patch where nothing grew—the Forbidden Corner. A faintness then came over me at once, a faintness as of death, when I saw him *there* of all places—where he never was allowed to go, and where, moreover, he was usually too terrified to go. To see him standing solitary in that singular spot, above all to hear him crying there, bereft me momentarily of the power to act. Then, before I could recover my composure sufficiently to call him in, Mr. Frene came round the corner from the Lower Farm with the dogs, and, seeing his son, performed that office for me. In his loud, good-natured, hearty voice he called him, and Jamie turned and ran as though some spell had broken just in time—ran into the open arms of his fond but uncomprehending father, who carried him indoors on his shoulder, while asking "what all this hubbub was about?" And, at their heels, the tailless sheep-dogs followed, barking loudly, and performing what Jamie called their "Gravel Dance," because they ploughed up the moist, rolled gravel with their feet.

I stepped back swiftly from the window lest I should be seen. Had I witnessed the saving of the child from fire or drowning the relief could hardly have been greater. Only Mr. Frene, I felt sure, would not say and do the right thing quite. He would protect the boy from his own vain imaginings, yet not with the explanation that could really heal. They disappeared behind the rose trees, making for the house. I saw no more till later, when Mr. Frene, senior, arrived.

To describe the ugly patch as "singular" is hard to justify, perhaps, yet some such word is what the entire family sought, though never—oh, never!—used. To Jamie and myself, though equally we never mentioned it, that treeless, flowerless spot was more than singular. It stood at the far end of the magnificent rose garden, a bald, sore place, where the black earth showed uglily in winter, almost like a piece of dangerous bog, and in summer baked and cracked with fissures where green lizards shot their fire in passing. In contrast to the rich luxuriance of death amid life, a center of disease that cried for healing lest it spread. But it never did spread. Behind it stood the thick wood of silver birches and, glimmering beyond, the orchard meadow, where the lambs played.

The gardeners had a very simple explanation of its barrenness—that the water all drained off it owing to the lie of the slopes immediately about it, holding no remnant to keep the soil alive. I cannot say. It was Jamie—Jamie who felt its spell and haunted it, who spent whole hours there, even while afraid, and for whom it was finally labelled "strictly out of bounds" because it stimulated his already big imagination, not wisely but too darkly—it was Jamie who buried ogres there and heard it crying in an earthy voice, swore that it shook its surface sometimes while he watched it, and secretly gave it food in the form of birds or mice or rabbits he found dead upon his wonderings. And it was Jamie who put so extraordinarily into words the *feeling* that the horrid spot had given me from the moment I first saw it.

"It's bad, Miss Gould," he told me.

"But, Jamie, nothing in Nature is bad—exactly; only different from the rest sometimes."

"Miss Gould, if you please, then it's empty. It's not fed. It's dying because it can't get the food it wants."

And when I stared into the little pale face where the eyes shone so dark and wonderful, seeking within myself for the right thing to say to him, he added, with an emphasis and conviction that made me suddenly turn cold: "Miss Gould"—he always used my name like this in all his sentences—"it's hungry, don't you see? But *I* know what would make it feel all right."

Only the conviction of an earnest child, perhaps, could have made so outrageous a suggestion worth listening to for an instant; but for me, who felt that things an imaginative child believed were important, it came with a vast disquieting shock of reality. Jamie, in this exaggerated way, had caught at the edge of a shocking fact—a hint of dark, undiscovered truth had leaped into that sensitive imagination. Why there lay horror in the words I cannot say, but I think some power of darkness trooped across the suggestion of that sentence at the end, "I know what would make it feel all right." I remember that I shrank from asking explanation. Small groups of other words, veiled fortunately by his silence, gave life to an unspeakable possibility that hitherto had lain at the back of my own consciousness. The way it sprang to life proves, I think, that my mind already contained it. The blood rushed from my heart as I listened. I remember that my knees shook. Jamie's idea was—had been all along—my own as well.

And now, as I lay down on my bed and thought about it all, I understood why the coming of his uncle involved somehow an experience that wrapped terror at its heart. With a sense of nightmare certainty that left me too weak to resist the preposterous idea, too shocked, indeed, to argue or reason it away, this certainty came with its full, black blast of conviction; and the only way I can put it into words, since nightmare horror really is not properly tellable at all, seems this: that there *was* something missing in that dying patch of garden; something lacking that it ever searched for; something, once found and taken, that would turn it rich and living as the rest; more—that there *was* some living person who could do this for it. Mr. Frene, senior, in a word, "Uncle Frank," was this person who out of his abundant life could supply the lack—unwittingly.

For this connection between the dying, empty patch and the person of this vigorous, wealthy, and successful man had already lodged itself in my subconsciousness before I was aware of it. Clearly it must have lain there all along, though hidden. Jamie's words, his sudden pallor, his vibrating emotion of fearful anticipation had developed the plate, but it was his weeping alone there in the Forbidden Corner that had printed it. The photograph shone framed before me in the air. I hid my eyes. But for the redness—the charm of my face goes to pieces unless my eyes are clear—I could have cried. Jamie's words that morning about the " 'normous face" came back upon me like a battering-ram.

Mr. Frene, senior, had been so frequently the subject of conversation in the family since I came, I had so often heard him discussed, and had then read so much about him in the papers—his energy, his philanthropy, his success with everything he laid his hand to—that a picture of the man had grown complete within me. I knew him as he was—within; or, as my sister would have said—clairvoyantly. And the only time I saw him (when I took Gladys to a meeting where he was chairman, and later *felt* his atmosphere and presence while for a moment he patronizingly spoke with her) had justified the portrait I had drawn. The rest, you may say, was a woman's wild imagining; but I think rather it was that kind of divining intuition which women share with children. If souls could be made visible, I would stake my life upon the truth and accuracy of my portrait.

For this Mr. Frene was a man who drooped alone, but grew vital in a crowd—because he used their vitality. He was a supreme, unconscious artist in the science of taking the fruits of others' work and living—for his own advantage. He vampired, unknowingly no doubt, every one with whom he came in contact; left them exhausted, tired, listless. Others fed him, so that while in a full room he shone, alone by himself and with no life to draw upon he languished and declined. In the man's immediate neighborhood you felt his presence draining you; he took your ideas, your strength, your very words, and later used them for his own benefit and aggrandizement. Not evilly, of course; the man was good enough; but you felt that he was dangerous owing to the facile way he absorbed into himself all loose vitality that was to be had. His eyes and voice and presence devitalized you. Life, it seemed, not highly organized enough to resist, must shrink from his too near approach and hide away for fear of being appropriated, for fear, that is, of—death.

Jamie, unknowingly, put in the finishing touch to my unconscious portrait. The man carried about with him some silent, compelling trick of drawing out all your reserves—then swiftly pocketing them. At first you would be conscious of taut resistance; this would slowly shade off into weariness; the will would become flaccid; then you either moved away or yielded—agreed to all he said with a sense of weakness pressing ever closer upon the edges of collapse. With a male antagonist it might be different, but even then the effort of resistance would generate force that *he* absorbed and not the other. He never gave out. Some instinct taught him how to protect himself from that. To human beings, I mean, he never gave out. This time it was a very different matter. He had no more chance than a fly before the wheels of a huge—what Jamie used to call—"attraction" engine.

So this was how I saw him—a great human sponge, crammed and soaked with the life, or proceeds of life, absorbed from others—stolen. My idea of a human vampire was satisfied. He went about carrying these accumulations of the life of others. In this sense his "life" was not really his own. For the same reason, I think, it was not so fully under his control as he imagined.

And in another hour this man would be here. I went to the window. My eye wandered to the empty patch, dull black there amid the rich luxuriance of the garden flowers. It struck me as a hideous bit of emptiness yawning to be filled and nourished. The idea of Jamie playing round its bare edge was loathsome. I watched the big summer clouds above, the stillness of the afternoon, the haze. The silence of the over-heated garden was oppressive. I had never felt a day so stifling, motion-less. It lay there waiting. The household, too, was waiting—waiting for the coming of Mr. Frene from London in his big motor-car.

And I shall never forget the sensation of icy shrinking and distress with which I heard the rumble of the car. He had arrived. Tea was all ready on the lawn beneath the lime trees, and Mrs. Frene and Gladys, back from their drive, were sitting in wicker chairs. Mr. Frene, junior, was in the hall to meet his brother, but Jamie, as I learned afterwards, had shown such hysterical alarm, offered such bold resistance, that it had been deemed wiser to keep him in his room. Perhaps, after all, his presence might not be necessary. The visit clearly had to do with some-thing on the uglier side of life—money, settlements, or what not; I never knew exactly; only that his parents were anxious, and that Uncle Frank had to be propitiated. It does not matter. That has nothing to do with the affair. What has to do with it—or I should not be telling the story—is that Mrs. Frene sent for me to come down "in my nice white dress, if I didn't mind," and that I was terrified, yet pleased, because it meant that a pretty face would be considered a welcome addition to the visi-tor's landscape. Also, most odd it was, I felt my presence was somehow inevitable, that in some way it was intended that I should witness what I did witness. And the instant I came upon the lawn—I hesitate to set it down, it sounds so foolish, disconnected—I could have sworn, as my eyes met his, that a kind of sudden darkness came, taking the summer brilliance out of everything, and that it was caused by troops of small black horses that raced about us from his person—to attack.

After a first momentary approving glance he took no further notice of me. The tea and talk went smoothly; I helped to pass the plates and cups, filling in pauses with little undertalk to Gladys. Jamie was never mentioned. Outwardly all seemed well, but inwardly everything was awful—skirting the edge of things unspeakable, and so charged with danger that I could not keep my voice from trembling when I spoke.

I watched his hard, bleak face; I noticed how thin he was, and the curious, oily brightness of his steady eyes. They did not glitter, but they drew you with a sort of soft, creamy shine like Eastern eyes. And everything he said or did announced what I may dare to call the *suction* of his presence. His nature achieved this result automatically. He dominated us all, yet so gently that until it was accomplished no one noticed it.

Before five minutes had passed, however, I was aware of one thing only. My mind focussed exclusively upon it, and so vividly that I marvelled the others did not scream, or run, or do something violent to prevent it. And it was this; that, separated merely by some dozen yards or so, this man, vibrating with the acquired vitality of others, stood within easy reach of that spot of yawning emptiness, waiting and eager to be filled. Earth scented her prey.

These two active "centers" were within fighting distance; he so thin, so hard, so keen, yet really spreading large with the loose "surround" of others' life he had appropriated, so practiced and triumphant; that other so patient, deep, with so mighty a draw of the whole earth behind it, and—ugh!—so obviously aware that its opportunity at last had come.

I saw it all as plainly as though I watched two great animals prepare for battle, both unconsciously; yet in some inexplicable way I saw it, of course, within me, and not externally. The conflict would be hideously unequal. Each side had already sent out emissaries, how long before I could not tell, for the first evidence *he* gave that something was going wrong with him was when his voice grew suddenly confused, he missed his words, and his lips trembled a moment and turned flabby. The next second his face betrayed that singular and horrid change, growing somehow loose about the bones of the cheek, and larger, so that I remembered Jamie's miserable phrase. The emissaries of the two kingdoms, the human and the vegetable, had met, I make it out, in that very second. For the first time in his long career of battening on others, Mr. Frene found himself pitted against a vaster kingdom than he knew and, so finding, shook inwardly in that little part that was his definite actual self. He felt the huge disaster coming.

"Yes, John," he was saying, in his drawling, self-congratulating voice, "Sir George gave me that car—gave it to me as a present. Wasn't it char—?" and then broke off abruptly, stammered, drew breath, stood up, and looked uneasily about him. For a second there was a gaping pause. It was like the click which starts some huge machinery moving— that instant's pause before it actually starts. The whole thing, indeed, then went with the rapidity of machinery running down and beyond control. I thought of a giant dynamo working silently and invisible.

"What's that?" he cried, in a soft voice charged with alarm. "What's that horrid place? And someone's crying there—who is it?"

He pointed to the empty patch. Then, before anyone could answer, he started across the lawn towards it, going every minute faster. Before anyone could move he stood upon the edge. He leaned over—peering down into it.

It seemed a few hours passed, but really they were seconds, for time is measured by the quality and not the quantity of sensations it contains. I saw it all with merciless, photographic detail, sharply etched amid the general confusion. Each side was intensely active, but only one side, the human, exerted *all* its force—in resistance. The other merely stretched out a feeler, as it were, from its vast, potential strength; no more was necessary. It was such a soft and easy victory. Oh, it was rather pitiful! There was no bluster or great effort, on one side at least. Close by his side I witnessed it, for I, it seemed, alone had moved and followed him. No one else stirred, though Mrs. Frene clattered noisily with the cups, making some sudden impulsive gesture with her hands, and Gladys, I remember, gave a cry—it was like a little scream—"Oh, mother, it's the heat, isn't it?" Mr. Frene, her father, was speechless, pale as ashes.

But the instant I reached his side, it became clear what had drawn me there thus instinctively. Upon the other side, among the silver birches, stood little Jamie. He was watching. I experienced—for him— one of those moments that shake the heart; a liquid fear ran all over me, the more effective because unintelligible really. Yet I felt that if I could know all, and what lay actually behind, my fear would be more than justified; that the thing *was* awful, full of awe.

And then it happened—a truly wicked sight—like watching a universe in action, yet all contained within a small square foot of space. I think he understood vaguely that if someone could only take his place he might be saved, and that was why, discerning instinctively the easiest substitute within reach, he saw the child and called aloud to him across the empty patch, "James, my boy, come here!"

His voice was like a thin report, but somehow flat and lifeless, as when a rifle misses fire, sharp, yet weak; it had no "crack" in it. It was really supplication. And, with amazement, I heard my own ring out imperious and strong, though I was not conscious of saying it, "Jamie, don't move. Stay where you are!" But Jamie, the little child, obeyed neither of us. Moving up nearer to the edge, he stood there—laughing! I heard that laughter, but could have sworn it did not come from him. The empty, yawning patch gave out that sound.

Mr. Frene turned sideways, throwing up his arms. I saw his hard, bleak face grow somehow wider, spread through the air, and downwards. A similar thing, I saw, was happening at the same time to his entire person, for it drew out into the atmosphere in a stream of movement. The face for a second made me think of those toys of green india rubber that children pull. It grew enormous. But this was an external impression only. What actually happened, I clearly understood, was that all this vitality and life he had transferred from others to himself for years was now in turn being taken from him and transferred—elsewhere.

One moment on the edge he wobbled horribly, then with that queer sideways motion, rapid yet ungainly, he stepped forward into the middle of the patch and fell heavily upon his face. His eyes, as he dropped, faded shockingly, and across the countenance was written plainly what I can only call an expression of destruction. He looked utterly destroyed. I caught a sound—from Jamie?—but this time not of laughter. It was like a gulp; it was deep and muffled and it dipped away into the earth. Again I thought of a troop of small black horses galloping away down a subterranean passage beneath my feet—plunging into the depths—their tramping growing fainter and fainter into buried distance. In my nostrils was a pungent smell of earth.

And then—all passed. I came back into myself. Mr. Frene, junior, was lifting his brother's head from the lawn where he had fallen from the heat, close beside the tea-table. He had never really moved from there. And Jamie, I learned afterwards, had been the whole time asleep upon his bed upstairs, worn out with his crying and unreasoning alarm. Gladys came running out with cold water, sponge and towel, brandy too—all kinds of things. "Mother, it *was* the heat, wasn't it?" I heard her whisper, but I did not catch Mrs. Frene's reply. From her face it struck me that she was bordering on collapse herself. Then the butler followed, and they just picked him up and carried him into the house. He recovered even before the doctor came.

But the queer thing to me is that I was convinced the others all had seen what I saw, only that no one said a word about it; and to this day no one *has* said a word. And that was, perhaps, the most horrid part of all.

From that day to this I have scarcely heard a mention of Mr. Frene, senior. It seemed as if he dropped suddenly out of life. The papers never mentioned him. His activities ceased, as it were. His after-life, at any rate, became singularly ineffective. Certainly he achieved nothing worth public mention. But it may be only that, having left the employ of Mrs. Frene, there was no particular occasion for me to hear anything.

The after-life of that empty patch of garden, however, was quite otherwise. Nothing, so far as I know, was done to it by gardeners, or in the way of draining it or bringing in new earth, but even before I left in the following summer it had changed. It lay untouched, full of great, luscious, driving weeds and creepers, very strong, full-fed, and bursting thick with life.

E. F. BENSON *(1867–1940) won a new audience in the 1980s as the author of the Lucia novels, which formed the basis for the short PBS television series "Mapp & Lucia." But those charming comedies, with their sophisticated social commentary, do not prepare one for the strength of Benson's supernatural stories.*

His first supernatural work was the novel The Judgement Books *(1895), but although he wrote other similar novels, his major efforts in the field were devoted to short stories. They are collected in* The Room in the Tower *(1912),* Visible and Invisible *(1923),* Spook Stories *(1928), and* More Spook Stories *(1934).*

Besides "The Room in the Tower," Benson's best-known stories include two other vampire tales, "Mrs. Amworth" and " 'And No Bird Sings.' "

The Room in the Tower (1912)

BY E. F. BENSON

It is probable that everybody who is at all a constant dreamer has had at least one experience of an event or a sequence of circumstances which have come to his mind in sleep being subsequently realized in the material world. But, in my opinion, so far from this being a strange thing, it would be far odder if this fulfillment did not occasionally happen, since our dreams are, as a rule, concerned with people whom we know and places with which we are familiar, such as might very naturally occur in the awake and day-lit world. True, these dreams are often broken into by some absurd and fantastic incident, which puts them out of court in regard to their subsequent fulfillment, but on the mere calculation of chances, it does not appear in the least unlikely that a dream imagined by anyone who dreams constantly should occasionally come true. Not long ago, for instance, I experienced such a fulfillment of a dream which seems to me in no way remarkable and to have no kind of psychical significance. The manner of it was as follows.

A certain friend of mine, living abroad, is amiable enough to write to me about once in a fortnight. Thus, when fourteen days or thereabout have elapsed since I last heard from him, my mind, probably either consciously or subconsciously, is expectant of a letter from him. One night last week I dreamed that as I was going upstairs to dress for dinner I heard, as I often hear, the sound of the postman's knock on my front door, and diverted my direction downstairs instead. There, among other correspondence, was a letter from him. Thereafter the fantastic entered, for on opening it I found inside the ace of diamonds, and scribbled across it in his well-known handwriting, "I am sending you this for safe custody, as you know it is running an unreasonable risk to keep aces in Italy." The next evening I was just preparing to go upstairs to dress when I heard the postman's knock, and did precisely as I had done in my dream. There, among other letters, was one from my friend. Only it did not contain the ace of diamonds. Had it done so, I should have attached more weight to the matter, which, as it stands, seems to me a perfectly ordinary coincidence. No doubt I consciously or subconsciously expected a letter from him, and this suggested to me my dream. Similarly, the fact that my friend had not written to me for a fortnight suggested to him that he should do so. But occasionally it is not so easy to find such an explanation, and for the following story I can find no explanation at all. It came out of the dark and out of the dark it has gone again.

All my life I have been a habitual dreamer: the nights are few, that is to say, when I do not find on awaking in the morning that some mental experience has been mine, and sometimes, all night long, apparently, a series of the most dazzling adventures befall me. Almost without exception these adventures are pleasant, though often merely trivial. It is of an exception that I am going to speak.

It was when I was about sixteen that a certain dream first came to me, and this is how it befell. It opened with my being set down at the door of a big red brick house, where, I understood, I was going to stay. The servant who opened the door told me that tea was going on in the garden, and led me through a low dark-panelled hall, with a large open fireplace, on to a cheerful green lawn set round with flower beds. There were grouped about the tea table a small party of people, but they were all strangers to me except one, who was a schoolfellow called Jack Stone, clearly the son of the house, and he introduced me to his mother and father and a couple of sisters. I was, I remember, somewhat astonished to find myself there, for the boy in question was scarcely known to me, and I rather disliked what I knew of him: moreover, he had left school nearly a year before. The afternoon was very hot, and an intolerable oppression reigned. On the far side of the lawn ran a red brick wall, with an iron gate in its center, outside which stood a walnut tree. We sat in the shadow of the house opposite a row of long windows, inside which I could see a table with cloth laid, glimmering with glass and silver. The garden front of the house was very long, and at one end of it stood a tower of three storys, which looked to me much older than the rest of the building.

Before long, Mrs. Stone, who, like the rest of the party, had sat in absolute silence, said to me, "Jack will show you your room: I have given you the room in the tower."

Quite inexplicably my heart sank at her words. I felt as if I had known that I should have the room in the tower, and that it contained something dreadful and significant. Jack instantly got up, and I understood that I had to follow him. In silence we passed through the hall, and mounted a great oak staircase with many corners, and arrived at a small landing with two doors set in it. He pushed one of these open for me to enter, and without coming himself, closed it behind me. Then I knew that my conjecture had been right: there was something awful in the room, and with the terror of nightmare growing swiftly and enveloping me, I awoke in a spasm of terror.

Now that dream or variations on it occurred to me intermittently for fifteen years. Most often it came in exactly this form, the arrival, the tea laid out on the lawn, the deadly silence succeeded by that one deadly sentence, the mounting with Jack Stone up to the room in the tower where horror dwelt, and it always came to a close in the nightmare of terror at that which was in the room, though I never saw what it was. At other times I experienced variations on this same theme. Occasionally, for instance, we would be sitting at dinner in the dining room, into the windows of which I had looked on the first night when the dream of this house had visited me, but wherever we were, there was the same silence, the same sense of dreadful oppression and foreboding. And the silence I knew would always be broken by Mrs. Stone saying to me, "Jack will show you your room: I have given you the room in the tower." Upon which (this was invariable) I had to follow him up the oak staircase with many corners, and enter the place that I dreaded more and more each time that I visited it in sleep. Or, again, I would find myself playing cards still in silence in a drawing room lit with immense chandeliers, that gave a blinding illumination. What the game was I have no idea; what I remember, with a sense of miserable anticipation, was that soon Mrs. Stone would get up and say to me, "Jack will show you your room: I have given you the room in the tower." This room where we played cards was next to the dining room, and, as I have said, was always brilliantly illuminated, whereas the rest of the house was full of dusk and shadows. And yet, how often, in spite of those bouquets of lights, have I not pored over the cards that were dealt to me, scarcely able for some reason to see them. Their designs, too, were strange: there were no red suits, but all were black, and among them there were certain cards which were black all over. I hated and dreaded those.

As this dream continued to occur, I got to know the greater part of the house. There was a smoking room beyond the drawing room, at the end of a passage with a green baize door. It was always very dark there, and as often as I went there I passed somebody whom I could not see in the doorway coming out. Curious developments, too, took place in the characters that peopled the dream, as might happen to living persons. Mrs. Stone, for instance, who, when I first saw her, had been black-haired, became gray, and instead of rising briskly, as she had done at first when she said, "Jack will show you your room: I have given you the room in the tower," got up feebly, as if the strength was leaving her limbs. Jack also grew up, and became a rather ill-looking young man, with a brown mustache, while one of the sisters ceased to appear, and I understood she was married.

Then it so happened that I was not visited by this dream for six months or more, and I began to hope, in such inexplicable dread did I hold it, that it had passed away for good. But one night after this interval I again found myself being shown out on the lawn for tea, and Mrs. Stone was not there, while the others were all dressed in black. At once I guessed the reason, and my heart leaped at the thought that perhaps this time I should not have to sleep in the room in the tower, and though we usually all sat in silence, on this occasion the sense of relief made me talk and laugh as I had never yet done. But even then matters were not altogether comfortable, for no one else spoke, but they all looked secretly at each other. And soon the foolish stream of my talk ran dry, and gradually an apprehension worse than anything I had previously known gained on me as the light slowly faded.

Suddenly a voice which I knew well broke the stillness, the voice of Mrs. Stone, saying, "Jack will show you your room: I have given you the room in the tower." It seemed to come from near the gate in the red brick wall that bounded the lawn, and looking up, I saw that the grass outside was sown thick with gravestones. A curious grayish light shone from them, and I could read the lettering on the grave nearest me, and it was, "In evil memory of Julia Stone." And as usual Jack got up, and again I found myself following him through the hall and up the staircase with many corners. On this occasion it was darker than usual, and when I passed into the room in the tower I could only just see the furniture, the position of which was already familiar to me. Also there was a dreadful odor of decay in the room, and I woke screaming.

The dream, with such variations and developments as I have mentioned, went on at intervals for fifteen years. Sometimes I would dream it two or three nights in succession; once, as I have said, there was an intermission of six months, but taking a reasonable average, I should say that I dreamed it quite as often as once in a month. It had, as is plain, something of nightmare about it, since it always ended in the same appalling terror, which, so far from getting less, seemed to me to gather fresh fear every time that I experienced it. There was, too, a strange and dreadful consistency about it. The characters in it, as I have mentioned, got regularly older, death and marriage visited this silent family, and I never in the dream, after Mrs. Stone died, set eyes on her again. But it was always her voice that told me that the room in the tower was prepared for me, and whether we had tea out on the lawn, or the scene was laid in one of the rooms overlooking it, I could always see her gravestone standing just outside the iron gate. It was the same, too, with the married daughter; usually she was not present, but once or twice she returned again, in company with a man, whom I took to be her husband. He, too, like the rest of them, was always silent. But, owing to the constant repetition of the dream, I ceased to attach, in my waking hours, any significance to it. I never met Jack Stone again in all those years, nor did I ever see a house that resembled this dark house of my dream. And then something happened.

I had been in London in this year, up till the end of July, and during the first week in August went down to stay with a friend in a house he had taken for the summer months, in the Ashdown Forest district of Sussex. I left London early, for John Clinton was to meet me at Forest Row Station, and we were going to spend the day golfing, and go to his house in the evening. He had his motor with him, and we set off, about five in the afternoon, after a thoroughly delightful day, for the drive, the distance being some ten miles. As it was still so early we did not have tea at the clubhouse, but waited till we should get home. As we drove, the weather, which up till then had been, though hot, deliciously fresh, seemed to me to alter in quality, and become very stagnant and oppressive, and I felt that indefinable sense of ominous apprehension that I am accustomed to before thunder. John, however, did not share my views, attributing my loss of lightness to the fact that I had lost both my matches. Events proved, however, that I was right, though I do not think that the thunderstorm that broke that night was the sole cause of my depression.

Our way lay through deep high-banked lanes, and before we had gone very far I fell asleep, and was only awakened by the stopping of the motor. And with a sudden thrill, partly of fear but chiefly of curiosity, I found myself standing in the doorway of my house of dream. We went, I half wondering whether or not I was dreaming still, through a low oak-panelled hall, and out on to the lawn, where tea was laid in the shadow of the house. It was set in flower beds; a red brick wall, with a gate in it, bounded one side; and out beyond that was a space of rough grass with a walnut tree. The facade of the house was very long, and at one end stood a three-storied tower, markedly older than the rest.

Here for the moment all resemblance to the repeated dream ceased. There was no silent and somehow terrible family, but a large assemblage of exceedingly cheerful persons, all of whom were known to me. And in spite of the horror with which the dream itself had always filled me, I felt nothing of it now that the scene of it was thus reproduced before me. But I felt the intensest curiosity as to what was going to happen.

Tea pursued its cheerful course, and before long, Mrs. Clinton got up. And at the moment I think I knew what she was going to say. She spoke to me, and what she said was:

"Jack will show you your room; I have given you the room in the tower."

At that, for half a second, the horror of the dream took hold of me again. But it quickly passed, and again I felt nothing more than the most intense curiosity. It was not very long before it was amply satisfied.

John turned to me.

"Right up at the top of the house," he said, "but I think you'll be comfortable. We're absolutely full up. Would you like to go and see it now? By Jove, I believe you are right, and that we are going to have a thunderstorm. How dark it has become."

I got up and followed him. We passed through the hall, and up the perfectly familiar staircase. Then he opened the door, and I went in. And at that moment sheer unreasoning terror again possessed me. I did not know for certain what I feared: I simply feared. Then like a sudden recollection, when one remembers a name which has long escaped the memory, I knew what I feared. I feared Mrs. Stone, whose grave with the sinister inscription, "In evil memory—" I had so often seen in my dream, just beyond the lawn which lay below my window. And then once more the fear passed so completely that I wondered what there was to fear, and I found myself, sober and quiet and sane, in the room in the tower, the name of which I had so often heard in my dream, and the scene of which was so familiar.

I looked round it with a certain sense of proprietorship, and found that nothing had been changed from the dreaming nights in which I knew it so well. Just to the left of the door was the bed, lengthways along the wall, with the head of it in the angle. In a line with it was the fireplace and a small bookcase; opposite the door the outer wall was pierced by two lattice-paned windows, between which stood the dressing table, while ranged along the fourth wall was the washing stand and a big cupboard. My luggage had already been unpacked, for the furniture of dressing and undressing lay orderly on the washstand and toilet table, while my dinner clothes were spread out on the coverlet of the bed. And then with a sudden start of unexplained dismay, I saw that there were two rather conspicuous objects which I had not seen before in my dreams: one a life-sized oil painting of Mrs. Stone, the other a black-and-white sketch of Jack Stone, representing him as he had appeared to me only a week before in the last of the series of these repeated dreams, a rather secret and evil-looking man of about thirty. His picture hung between the windows, looking straight across the room to the other portrait, which hung at the side of the bed. At that I looked next, and as I looked I felt once more the horror of nightmare seize me.

It represented Mrs. Stone as I had seen her last in my dreams: old and withered and white haired. But in spite of the evident feebleness of body, a dreadful exuberance and vitality shone through the envelope of flesh, an exuberance wholly malign, a vitality that foamed and frothed with unimaginable evil. Evil beamed from the narrow, leering eyes: it laughed in the demonlike mouth. The whole face was instinct with some secret and appalling mirth; the hands, clasped together on the knee, seemed shaking with suppressed and nameless glee. Then I saw also that it was signed in the left-hand corner, and wondering who the artist could be, I looked more closely, and read the inscription, "Julia Stone by Julia Stone."

There came a tap at the door, and John Clinton entered.

"Got everything you want?" he asked.

"Rather more than I want," I said, pointing to the picture.

He laughed.

"Hard-featured old lady," he said. "By herself, too, I remember. Anyhow she can't have flattered herself much."

"But don't you see?" said I. "It's scarcely a human face at all. It's the face of some witch, some devil."

He looked at it more closely.

"Yes; it isn't very pleasant," he agreed. "Scarcely a bedside manner, eh? Yes; I can imagine getting the nightmare, if I went to sleep with that close by my bed. I'll have it taken down if you like."

"I really wish you would," I said.

He rang the bell, and with the help of a servant we detached the picture and carried it out on to the landing, and put it with its face to the wall.

"By Jove, the old lady is a weight," said John, mopping his forehead. "I wonder if she had something on her mind."

The extraordinary weight of the picture had struck me too. I was about to reply, when I caught sight of my own hand. There was blood on it, in considerable quantities, covering the whole palm.

"I've cut myself somehow," I said.

John gave a little startled exclamation.

"Why, I have too," he said.

Simultaneously the footman took out his handkerchief and wiped his hand with it. I saw that there was blood also on his handkerchief.

John and I went back into the tower room and washed the blood off; but neither on his hand nor on mine was there the slightest trace of a scratch or cut. It seemed to me that, having ascertained this, we both, by a sort of tacit consent, did not allude to it again. Something in my case had dimly occurred to me that I did not wish to think about. It was but a conjecture, but I fancied that I knew the same thing had occurred to him.

The heat and oppression of the air, for the storm we had expected, was still undischarged, increased very much after dinner, and for some time most of the party, among whom were John Clinton and myself, sat outside on the path bounding the lawn, where we had had tea. The night was absolutely dark, and no twinkle of star or moon ray could penetrate the pall of cloud that overset the sky. By degrees our assembly thinned, the women went up to bed, the men dispersed to the smoking or billiard room, and by eleven o'clock my host and I were the only two left. All the evening I thought that he had something on his mind, and as soon as we were alone he spoke.

"The man who helped us with the picture had blood on his hand, too, did you notice?" he said. "I asked him just now if he had cut himself and he said that he supposed he must have, but that he could find no mark of it. Now where did that blood come from?"

By dint of telling myself that I was not going to think about it, I had succeeded in not doing so, and I did not want, especially just at bedtime, to be reminded of it.

"I don't know," said I, "and I don't really care so long as the picture of Mrs. Julia Stone is not by my bed."

He got up.

"But it's odd," he said. "Ha! Now you'll see another odd thing."

A dog of his, an Irish terrier by breed, had come out of the house as we talked. The door behind us into the hall was open, and a bright oblong of light shone across the lawn to the iron gate which led on to the rough grass outside, where the walnut tree stood. I saw that the dog had all his hackles up, bristling with rage and fright; his lips were curled back from his teeth, as if he were ready to spring at something, and he was growling to himself. He took not the slightest notice of his master or me, but stiffly and tensely walked across the grass to the iron gate. There he stood for a moment, looking through the bars and still growling. Then of a sudden his courage seemed to desert him: he gave one long howl, and scuttled back to the house with a curious crouching sort of movement.

"He does that half a dozen times a day," said John. "He sees something which he both hates and fears."

I walked to the gate and looked over it. Something was moving on the grass outside, and soon a sound which I could not instantly identify came to my ears. Then I remembered what it was: It was the purring of a cat. I lit a match, and saw the purrer, a big blue Persian, walking round and round in a little circle just outside the gate, stepping high and ecstatically, with tail carried aloft like a banner. Its eyes were bright and shining, and every now and then it puts its head down and sniffed at the grass.

I laughed.

"The end of that mystery, I am afraid," I said. "Here's a large cat having Walpurgis night all alone."

"Yes, that's Darius," said John. "He spends half the day and all night there. But that's not the end of the dog mystery, for Toby and he are the best of friends, but the beginning of the cat mystery. What's the cat doing there? And why is Darius pleased, while Toby is terror stricken?"

At that moment I remembered the rather horrible details of my dreams when I saw through the gate, just where the cat was now, the white tombstone with the sinister inscription. But before I could answer the rain began, as suddenly and heavily as if a tap had been turned on, and simultaneously the big cat squeezed through the bars of the gate, and came leaping across the lawn to the house for shelter. Then it sat in the doorway, looking out eagerly into the dark. It spat and struck at John with its paw, as he pushed it in, in order to close the door.

Somehow, with the portrait of Julia Stone in the passage outside, the room in the tower had absolutely no alarm for me, and as I went to bed, feeling very sleepy and heavy, I had nothing more than interest for the curious incident about our bleeding hands, and the conduct of the dog and cat. The last thing I looked at before I put out my light was the square empty space by my bed where the portrait had been. Here the paper was of its original full tint of dark red: over the rest of the walls it had faded. Then I blew out my candle and instantly fell asleep.

My awakening was equally instantaneous, and I sat bolt upright in bed under the impression that some bright light had been flashed in my face, though it was now absolutely pitch dark. I knew exactly where I was, in the room which I had dreaded in dreams, but no horror that I ever felt when asleep approached the fear that now invaded and froze my brain. Immediately after a peal of thunder crackled just above the house, but the probability that it was only a flash of lightning that awoke me gave no reassurance to my galloping heart. Something I knew was in the room with me, and instinctively I put out my right hand, which was nearest the wall, to keep it away. And my hand touched the edge of a picture-frame hanging close to me.

I sprang out of bed, upsetting the small table that stood by it, and I heard my watch, candle, and matches clatter on to the floor. But for the moment there was no need of light, for a blinding flash leaped out of the clouds, and showed me that by my bed again hung the picture of Mrs. Stone. And instantly the room went into a blackness again. But in that flash I saw another thing also, namely a figure that leaned over the end of my bed, watching me. It was dressed in some close-clinging white garment, spotted and stained with mould, and the face was that of the portrait.

Overhead the thunder cracked and roared, and when it ceased and the deathly stillness succeeded, I heard the rustle of movement coming nearer me, and, more horrible yet, perceived an odour of corruption and decay. And then a hand was laid on the side of my neck, and close beside my ear I heard quick-taken, eager breathing. Yet I knew that this thing, though it could be perceived by touch, by smell, by eye and by ear, was still not of this earth, but something that had passed out of the body and had power to make itself manifest. Then a voice, already familiar to me, spoke.

"I knew you would come to the room in the tower," it said. "I have been long waiting for you. At last you have come. Tonight I shall feast; before long we will feast together."

And the quick breathing came closer to me; I could feel it on my neck.

At that the terror, which I think had paralyzed me for the moment, gave way to the wild instinct of self-preservation. I hit wildly with both arms, kicking out at the same moment, and heard a little animal-squeal, and something soft dropped with a thud beside me. I took a couple of steps forward, nearly tripping up over whatever it was that lay there, and by the merest good luck found the handle of the door. In another second I ran out on the landing, and had banged the door behind me. Almost at the same moment I heard a door open somewhere below, and John Clinton, candle in hand, came running upstairs.

"What is it?" he asked. "I sleep just below you, and heard a noise as if—Good heavens, there's blood on your shoulder."

I stood there, so he told me afterwards, swaying from side to side, white as a sheet, with the mark on my shoulder as if a hand covered with blood had been laid there.

"It's in there," I said, pointing. "She, you know. The portrait is in there, too, hanging up on the place we took it from."

At that he laughed.

"My dear fellow, this is mere nightmare," he said.

He pushed by me, and opened the door, I standing there simply inert with terror, unable to stop him, unable to move.

"Phew! What an awful smell," he said.

Then there was silence; he had passed out of my sight behind the open door. Next moment he came out again, as white as myself, and instantly shut it.

"Yes, the portrait's there," he said, "and on the floor is a thing—a thing spotted with earth, like what they bury people in. Come away quick, come away."

How I got downstairs I hardly know. An awful shuddering and nausea of the spirit rather than of the flesh had seized me, and more than once he had to place my feet upon the steps, while every now and then he cast glances of terror and apprehension up the stairs. But in time we came to his dressing room on the floor below, and there I told him what I have described.

The sequel can be made short; indeed, some of my readers have perhaps already guessed what it was, if they remember that inexplicable affair of the churchyard at West Fawley, some eight years ago, when an attempt was made three times to bury the body of a certain woman who had committed suicide. On each occasion the coffin was found in the course of a few days again protruding from the ground. After the third attempt, in order that the thing should not be talked about, the body was buried elsewhere in unconsecrated ground. Where it was buried was just outside the iron gate of the garden belonging to the house where this woman had lived. She had committed suicide in a room at the top of the tower in that house. Her name was Julia Stone.

Subsequently the body was again secretly dug up, and the coffin was found to be full of blood.

MONTAGUE RHODES JAMES *(1862–1936) is without doubt the finest writer of English ghost stories in the twentieth century, although he wrote only about three dozen stories in all. An academic all his life, James became a fellow of King's College, Cambridge, in 1887 and provost in 1905. In 1918 he became provost of Eton, where he happily remained until his death.*

In 1894, following an old English tradition, James wrote his first ghost story, "Canon Alberic's Scrap-book," to entertain his friends at Christmas. His first collection, Ghost Stories of an Antiquary, *appeared in 1905, followed by* More Ghost Stories of an Antiquary *(1911), A* Thin Ghost *(1919), and A* Warning to the Curious *(1925). The Collected Ghost Stories (which is not actually complete) has been in print since its first publication in 1931.*

An admirer of J. Sheridan Le Fanu and a skilled antiquarian, James rescued many of Le Fanu's stories from oblivion and published an important collection of them, Madame Crowl's Ghost *in 1923.*

One of James's stories, "The Haunted Doll's House," was written especially to fill one of the tiny books included in the library of Queen Mary's famous doll's house, built in 1924. Whether Her Majesty ever read it—or anything as unnerving as "An Episode of Cathedral History" —is not recorded.

An Episode of Cathedral History
(1919)

BY M. R. JAMES

There was once a learned gentleman who was deputed to examine and report upon the archives of the Cathedral of Southminster. The examination of these records demanded a very considerable expenditure of time: hence it became advisable for him to engage lodgings in the city: for though the Cathedral body were profuse in their offers of hospitality, Mr. Lake felt that he would prefer to be master of his day. This was recognised as reasonable. The Dean eventually wrote advising Mr. Lake, if he were not already suited, to communicate with Mr. Worby, the principal Verger, who occupied a house convenient to the church and was prepared to take in a quiet lodger for three or four weeks. Such an arrangement was precisely what Mr. Lake desired. Terms were easily agreed upon, and early in December, like another Mr. Datchery (as he remarked to himself), the investigator found himself in the occupation of a very comfortable room in an ancient and "cathedraly" house.

One so familiar with the customs of Cathedral churches, and treated with such obvious consideration by the Dean and Chapter of this Cathedral in particular, could not fail to command the respect of the Head Verger. Mr. Worby even acquiesced in certain modifications of statements he had been accustomed to offer for years to parties of visitors. Mr. Lake, on his part, found the Verger a very cheery companion, and took advantage of any occasion that presented itself for enjoying his conversation when the day's work was over.

One evening, about nine o'clock, Mr. Worby knocked at his lodger's door. "I've occasion," he said, "to go across to the Cathedral, Mr. Lake, and I think I made you a promise when I did so next I would give you the opportunity to see what it looked like at night time. It's quite fine and dry outside, if you care to come."

"To be sure I will; very much obliged to you, Mr. Worby, for thinking of it, but let me get my coat."

"Here it is, sir, and I've another lantern here that you'll find advisable for the steps, as there's no moon."

"Anyone might think we were Jasper and Durdles, over again, mightn't they?" said Lake, as they crossed the close, for he had ascertained that the Verger had read *Edwin Drood*.

"Well, so they might," said Mr. Worby, with a short laugh, "though I don't know whether we ought to take it as a compliment. Odd ways, I often think, they had at that Cathedral, don't it seem so to you, sir? Full choral matins at seven o'clock in the morning all the year round. Wouldn't suit our boys' voices nowadays, and I think there's one or two of the men would be applying for a rise if the Chapter was to bring it in—particular the alltoes."

They were now at the south-west door. As Mr. Worby was unlocking it, Lake said, "Did you ever find anybody locked in here by accident?"

"Twice I did. One was a drunk sailor; however he got in I don't know. I s'pose he went to sleep in the service, but by the time I got to him he was praying fit to bring the roof in. Lor'! what a noise that man did make! said it was the first time he'd been inside a church for ten years, and blest if ever he'd try it again. The other was an old sheep: them boys it was, up to their games. That was the last time they tried it

on, though. There, sir, now you see what we look like; our late Dean
used now and again to bring parties in, but he preferred a moonlight
night, and there was a piece of verse he'd say to 'em, relating to a
Scotch cathedral, I understand; but I don't know; I almost think the
effect's better when it's all dark-like. Seems to add to the size and
height. Now if you won't mind stopping somewhere in the nave while I
go up into the choir where my business lays, you'll see what I mean."

Accordingly Lake waited, leaning against a pillar, and watched the
light wavering along the length of the church, and up the steps into the
choir, until it was intercepted by some screen or other furniture, which
only allowed the reflection to be seen on the piers and roof. Not many
minutes had passed before Worby reappeared at the door of the choir
and by waving his lantern signalled to Lake to rejoin him.

"I suppose it *is* Worby, and not a substitute," thought Lake to
himself, as he walked up the nave. There was, in fact, nothing unto-
ward. Worby showed him the papers which he had come to fetch out of
the Dean's stall, and asked him what he thought of the spectacle: Lake
agreed that it was well worth seeing. "I suppose," he said, as they
walked towards the altar-steps together, "that you're too much used to
going about here at night to feel nervous—but you must get a start
every now and then, don't you, when a book falls down or a door
swings to?"

"No, Mr. Lake, I can't say I think much about noises, not nowadays: I'm much more afraid of finding an escape of gas or a burst in the
stove pipes than anything else. Still there have been times, years ago.
Did you notice that plain altar-tomb there—fifteenth century we say it
is, I don't know if you agree to that? Well, if you didn't look at it, just
come back and give it a glance, if you'd be so good." It was on the north
side of the choir, and rather awkwardly placed: only about three feet
from the enclosing stone screen. Quite plain, as the Verger had said, but
for some ordinary stone panelling. A metal cross of some size on the
northern side (that next to the screen) was the solitary feature of any
interest.

Lake agreed that it was not earlier than the Perpendicular period:
"But," he said, "unless it's the tomb of some remarkable person, you'll
forgive me for saying that I don't think it's particularly noteworthy."

"Well, I can't say as it is the tomb of anybody noted in 'istory,"
said Worby, who had a dry smile on his face, "for we don't own any
record whatsoever of who it was put up to. For all that, if you've half an
hour to spare, sir, when we get back to the house, Mr. Lake, I could tell

you a tale about that tomb. I won't begin on it now; it strikes cold here, and we don't want to be dawdling about all night."

"Of course I should like to hear it immensely."

"Very well, sir, you shall. Now if I might put a question to you," he went on, as they passed down the choir aisle, "in our little local guide— and not only there, but in the little book on our Cathedral in the series —you'll find it stated that this portion of the building was erected previous to the twelfth century. Now of course I should be glad enough to take that view, but—mind the step, sir—but, I put it to you—does the lay of the stone 'ere in this portion of the wall"—which he tapped with his key—"does it to your eye carry the flavour of what you might call Saxon masonry? No, I thought not; no more it does to me: now, if you'll believe me, I've said as much to those men—one's the librarian of our Free Library here, and the other came down from London on purpose —fifty times, if I have once, but I might just as well have talked to that bit of stonework. But there it is, I suppose everyone's got their opinions."

The discussion of this peculiar trait of human nature occupied Mr. Worby almost up to the moment when he and Lake re-entered the former's house. The condition of the fire in Lake's sitting-room led to a suggestion from Mr. Worby that they should finish the evening in his own parlour. We find them accordingly settled there some short time afterwards.

Mr. Worby made his story a long one, and I will not undertake to tell it wholly in his own words, or in his own order. Lake committed the substance of it to paper immediately after hearing it, together with some few passages of the narrative which had fixed themselves *verbatim* in his mind; I shall probably find it expedient to condense Lake's record to some extent.

Mr. Worby was born, it appeared, about the year 1828. His father before him had been connected with the Cathedral, and likewise his grandfather. One or both had been choristers, and in later life both had done work as mason and carpenter respectively about the fabric. Worby himself, though possessed, as he frankly acknowledged, of an indifferent voice, had been drafted into the choir at about ten years of age.

It was in 1840 that the wave of the Gothic revival smote the Cathedral of Southminster. "There was a lot of lovely stuff went then, sir," said Worby, with a sigh. "My father couldn't hardly believe it when he got his orders to clear out the choir. There was a new dean just come in —Dean Burscough it was—and my father had been 'prenticed to a good firm of joiners in the city, and knew what good work was when he saw it. Crool it was, he used to say: all that beautiful wainscot oak, as good as the day it was put up, and garlands-like of foliage and fruit, and lovely old gilding work on the coats of arms and the organ pipes. All went to the timber yard—every bit except some little pieces worked up in the Lady Chapel, and 'ere in this overmantel. Well—I may be mistook, but I say our choir never looked as well since. Still there was a lot found out about the history of the church, and no doubt but what it did stand in need of repair. There was very few winters passed but what we'd lose a pinnacle." Mr. Lake expressed his concurrence with Worby's views of restoration, but owns to a fear about this point lest the story proper should never be reached. Possibly this was perceptible in his manner.

Worby hastened to reassure him, "Not but what I could carry on about that topic for hours at a time, and do so when I see my opportunity. But Dean Burscough he was very set on the Gothic period, and nothing would serve him but everything must be made agreeable to that. And one morning after service he appointed for my father to meet him in the choir, and he came back after he'd taken off his robes in the vestry, and he'd got a roll of paper with him, and the verger that was then brought in a table, and they begun spreading it out on the table with prayer books to keep it down, and my father helped 'em, and he saw it was a picture of the inside of a choir in a Cathedral; and the Dean —he was a quick-spoken gentleman—he says, 'Well, Worby, what do you think of that?' 'Why,' says my father, 'I don't think I 'ave the pleasure of knowing that view. Would that be Hereford Cathedral, Mr. Dean?' 'No, Worby,' says the Dean, 'that's Southminster Cathedral as we hope to see it before many years.' 'Indeed, sir,' says my father, and that was all he did say—leastways to the Dean—but he used to tell me he felt really faint in himself when he looked round our choir as I can remember it, all comfortable and furnished-like, and then see this nasty little dry picter, as he called it, drawn out by some London architect. Well, there I am again. But you'll see what I mean if you look at this old view."

Worby reached down a framed print from the wall. "Well, the long and the short of it was that the Dean he handed over to my father a copy of an order of the Chapter that he was to clear out every bit of the choir—make a clean sweep—ready for the new work that was being designed up in town, and he was to put it in hand as soon as ever he could get the breakers together. Now then, sir, if you look at that view, you'll see where the pulpit used to stand: that's what I want you to notice, if you please." It was, indeed, easily seen; an unusually large structure of timber with a domed sounding-board, standing at the east end of the stalls on the north side of the choir, facing the bishop's throne. Worby proceeded to explain that during the alterations, services were held in the nave, the members of the choir being thereby disappointed of an anticipated holiday, and the organist in particular incurring the suspicion of having wilfully damaged the mechanism of the temporary organ that was hired at considerable expense from London.

The work of demolition began with the choir screens and organ loft, and proceeded gradually eastwards, disclosing, as Worby said, many interesting features of older work. While this was going on, the members of the Chapter were, naturally, in and about the choir a great deal, and it soon became apparent to the elder Worby—who could not help overhearing some of their talk—that, on the part of the senior Canons especially, there must have been a good deal of disagreement before the policy now being carried out had been adopted. Some were of opinion that they should catch their deaths of cold in the return-stalls, unprotected by a screen from the draughts in the nave: others objected to being exposed to the view of persons in the choir aisles, especially, they said, during the sermons, when they found it helpful to listen in a posture which was liable to misconstruction. The strongest opposition, however, came from the oldest of the body, who up to the last moment objected to the removal of the pulpit. "You ought not to touch it, Mr. Dean," he said with great emphasis one morning, when the two were standing before it: "you don't know what mischief you may do." "Mischief? it's not a work of any particular merit, Canon." "Don't call me Canon," said the old man with great asperity, "that is, for thirty years I've been known as Dr. Ayloff, and I shall be obliged, Mr. Dean, if you would kindly humour me in that matter. And as to the pulpit (which I've preached from for thirty years, though I don't insist on that), all I'll say is, I *know* you're doing wrong in moving it." "But what sense could there be, my dear Doctor, in leaving it where it is, when we're fitting up the rest of the choir in a totally different *style?* What reason could be given—apart from the look of the thing?" "Reason! reason!" said old Dr. Ayloff; "if you young men—if I may say so without any disrespect, Mr. Dean—if you'd only listen to reason a little, and not be always asking for it, we should get on better. But there, I've said my say." The old gentleman hobbled off, and as it proved, never entered the Cathedral again. The season—it was a hot summer—turned sickly on a sudden. Dr. Ayloff was one of the first to go, with some affection of the muscles of the thorax, which took him painfully at night. And at many services the number of choirmen and boys was very thin.

Meanwhile the pulpit had been done away with. In fact, the sounding-board (part of which still exists as a table in a summerhouse in the palace garden) was taken down within an hour or two of Dr. Ayloff's protest. The removal of the base—not effected without considerable trouble—disclosed to view, greatly to the exultation of the restoring party, an altar-tomb—the tomb, of course, to which Worby had attracted Lake's attention that same evening. Much fruitless research was expended in attempts to identify the occupant; from that day to this he has never had a name put to him. The structure had been most carefully boxed in under the pulpit-base, so that such slight ornament as it possessed was not defaced; only on the north side of it there was what looked like an injury; a gap between two of the slabs composing the side. It might be two or three inches across. Palmer, the mason, was directed to fill it up in a week's time, when he came to do some other small jobs near that part of the choir.

The season was undoubtedly a very trying one. Whether the church was built on a site that had once been a marsh, as was suggested, or for whatever reason, the residents in its immediate neighbourhood had, many of them, but little enjoyment of the exquisite sunny days and the calm nights of August and September. To several of the older people —Dr. Ayloff, among others, as we have seen—the summer proved downright fatal, but even among the younger, few escaped either a sojourn in bed for a matter of weeks, or at the least, a brooding sense of oppression, accompanied by hateful nightmares. Gradually there formulated itself a suspicion—which grew into a conviction—that the alterations in the Cathedral had something to say in the matter. The widow of a former old verger, a pensioner of the Chapter of Southminster, was visited by dreams, which she retailed to her friends, of a shape that slipped out of the little door of the south transept as the dark fell in, and flitted—taking a fresh direction every night—about the Close, disappearing for a while in house after house, and finally emerging again when the night sky was paling. She could see nothing of it, she said, but that it was a moving form: only she had an impression that when it returned to the church, as it seemed to do in the end of the dream, it turned its head: and then, she could not tell why, but she thought it had red eyes. Worby remembered hearing the old lady tell this dream at a tea-party in the house of the chapter clerk. Its recurrence might, perhaps, he said, be taken as a symptom of approaching illness; at any rate before the end of September the old lady was in her grave.

The interest excited by the restoration of this great church was not confined to its own county. One day that summer an F.S.A., of some celebrity, visited the place. His business was to write an account of the discoveries that had been made, for the Society of Antiquaries, and his wife, who accompanied him, was to make a series of illustrative drawings for his report. In the morning she employed herself in making a general sketch of the choir; in the afternoon she devoted herself to details. She first drew the newly-exposed altar-tomb, and when that was finished, she called her husband's attention to a beautiful piece of diaper-ornament on the screen just behind it, which had, like the tomb itself, been completely concealed by the pulpit. Of course, he said, an illustration of that must be made; so she seated herself on the tomb and began a careful drawing which occupied her till dusk.

Her husband had by this time finished his work of measuring and description, and they agreed that it was time to be getting back to their hotel. "You may as well brush my skirt, Frank," said the lady, "it must have got covered with dust, I'm sure." He obeyed dutifully; but, after a moment, he said, "I don't know whether you value this dress particularly, my dear, but I'm inclined to think it's seen its best days. There's a great bit of it gone." "Gone? Where?" said she. "I don't know where it's gone, but it's off at the bottom edge behind here." She pulled it hastily into sight, and was horrified to find a jagged tear extending some way into the substance of the stuff; very much, she said, as if a dog had rent it away. The dress was, in any case, hopelessly spoilt, to her great vexation, and though they looked everywhere, the missing piece could not be found. There were many ways, they concluded, in which the injury might have come about, for the choir was full of old bits of woodwork with nails sticking out of them. Finally, they could only suppose that one of these had caused the mischief, and that the workmen, who had been about all day, had carried off that particular piece with the fragment of dress still attached to it.

It was about this time, Worby thought, that his little dog began to wear an anxious expression when the hour for it to be put into the shed in the back yard approached. (For his mother had ordained that it must not sleep in the house.) One evening, he said, when he was just going to pick it up and carry it out, it looked at him "like a Christian, and waved its 'and, and, I was going to say—well, you know 'ow they do carry on sometimes, and the end of it was I put it under my coat, and 'uddled it upstairs—and I'm afraid I as good as deceived my poor mother on the subject. After that the dog acted very artful with 'iding itself under the bed for half an hour or more before bedtime came, and we worked it so as my mother never found out what we'd done." Of course Worby was glad of its company anyhow, but more particularly when the nuisance that is still remembered in Southminster as "the crying" set in.

"Night after night," said Worby, "that dog seemed to know it was coming; he'd creep out, he would, and snuggle into the bed and cuddle right up to me shivering, and when the crying come he'd be like a wild thing, shoving his head under my arm, and I was fully near as bad. Six or seven times we'd hear it, not more, and when he'd dror out his 'ed again I'd know it was over for that night. What was it like, sir? Well, I never heard but one thing that seemed to hit it off. I happened to be playing about in the Close, and there was two of the Canons met and said 'Good morning' one to another. 'Sleep well last night?' says one—it was Mr. Henslow that one, and Mr. Lyall was the other. 'Can't say I did,' says Mr. Lyall, 'rather too much of Isaiah xxxiv.14 for me.' 'xxxiv.14,' says Mr. Henslow, 'what's that?' 'You call yourself a Bible reader!' says Mr. Lyall. (Mr. Henslow, you must know, he was one of what used to be termed Simeon's lot—pretty much what we should call the Evangelical party.) 'You go and look it up.' I wanted to know what he was getting at myself, and so off I ran home and got out my own Bible, and there it was: 'the satyr shall cry to his fellow.' Well, I thought, is that what we've been listening to these past nights? and I tell you it made me look over my shoulder a time or two. Of course I'd asked my father and mother about what it could be before that, but they both said it was most likely cats: but they spoke very short, and I could see they was troubled. My word! that was a noise—'ungry-like, as if it was calling after someone that wouldn't come. If ever you felt you wanted company, it would be when you was waiting for it to begin again. I believe two or three nights there was men put on to watch in different parts of the Close; but they all used to get together in one corner, the nearest they could to the High Street, and nothing came of it.

"Well, the next thing was this. Me and another of the boys—he's in business in the city now as a grocer, like his father before him—we'd gone up in the choir after morning service was over, and we heard old Palmer the mason bellowing to some of his men. So we went up nearer, because we knew he was a rusty old chap and there might be some fun going. It appears Palmer 'd told this man to stop up the chink in that old tomb. Well, there was this man keeping on saying he'd done it the best he could, and there was Palmer carrying on like all possessed about it. 'Call that making a job of it?' he says. 'If you had your rights you'd get the sack for this. What do you suppose I pay you your wages for? What do you suppose I'm going to say to the Dean and Chapter when they come round, as come they may do any time, and see where you've been bungling about covering the 'ole place with mess and plaster and Lord knows what?' 'Well, master, I done the best I could,' says the man; 'I don't know no more than what you do 'ow it come to fall out this way. I tamped it right in the 'ole,' he says, 'and now it's fell out,' he says, 'I never see.'

" 'Fell out!' says old Palmer, 'why it's nowhere near the place. Blowed out, you mean'; and he picked up a bit of plaster, and so did I, that was laying up against the screen, three or four feet off, and not dry yet; and old Palmer he looked at it curious-like, and then he turned round on me and he says, 'Now then, you boys, have you been up to some of your games here?' 'No,' I says, 'I haven't, Mr. Palmer; there's none of us been about here till just this minute'; and while I was talking the other boy, Evans, he got looking in through the chink, and I heard him draw in his breath, and he came away sharp and up to us, and says he, 'I believe there's something in there. I saw something shiny.' 'What! I dare say!' says old Palmer; 'well, I ain't got time to stop about there. You, William, you go off and get some more stuff and make a job of it this time; if not, there'll be trouble in my yard,' he says.

"So the man he went off, and Palmer too, and us boys stopped behind, and I says to Evans, 'Did you really see anything in there?' 'Yes,' he says, 'I did indeed.' So then I says, 'Let's shove something in and stir it up.' And we tried several of the bits of wood that was laying about, but they were all too big. Then Evans he had a sheet of music he'd brought with him, an anthem or a service, I forget which it is now, and he rolled it up small and shoved it in the chink; two or three times he did it, and nothing happened. 'Give it to me, boy,' I said, and I had a try. No, nothing happened. Then, I don't know why I thought of it, I'm sure, but I stooped down just opposite the chink and put my two fingers in my mouth and whistled—you know the way—and at that I seemed to think I heard something stirring, and I says to Evans, 'Come away,' I says; 'I don't like this.' 'Oh, rot,' he says, 'give me that roll,' and he took it and shoved it in. And I don't think ever I see anyone go so pale as he did. 'I say, Worby,' he says, 'it's caught, or else someone's got hold of it.' 'Pull it out or leave it,' I says. 'Come and let's get off.' So he gave a good pull, and it came away. Leastways most of it did, but the end was gone. Torn off it was, and Evans looked at it for a second and then he gave a sort of a croak and let it drop, and we both made off out of there as quick as ever we could. When we got outside Evans says to me, 'Did you see the end of that paper?' 'No,' I says, 'only it was torn.' 'Yes, it was,' he says, 'but it was wet too, and black!' Well, partly because of the fright we had, and partly because that music was wanted in a day or two, and we knew there'd be a set-out about it with the organist, we didn't say nothing to anyone else, and I suppose the workmen they swept up the bit that was left along with the rest of the rubbish. But Evans, if you were to ask him this very day about it, he'd stick to it he saw that paper wet and black at the end where it was torn."

After that the boys gave the choir a wide berth, so that Worby was not sure what was the result of the mason's renewed mending of the tomb. Only he made out from fragments of conversation dropped by the workmen passing through the choir that some difficulty had been met with, and that the governor—Mr. Palmer to wit—had tried his own hand at the job. A little later, he happened to see Mr. Palmer himself knocking at the door of the Deanery and being admitted by the butler. A day or so after that, he gathered from a remark his father let fall at breakfast, that something a little out of the common was to be done in the Cathedral after morning service on the morrow. "And I'd just as soon it was today," his father added; "I don't see the use of running risks." " 'Father,' I says, 'what are you going to do in the Cathedral tomorrow?' And he turned on me as savage as I ever see him—he was a wonderful good-tempered man as a general thing, my poor father was. 'My lad,' he says, 'I'll trouble you not to go picking up your elders' and betters' talk: it's not manners and it's not straight. What I'm going to do or not going to do in the Cathedral tomorrow is none of your business: and if I catch sight of you hanging about the place tomorrow after your work's done, I'll send you home with a flea in your ear. Now you mind that.' Of course I said I was very sorry and that, and equally of course I went off and laid my plans with Evans. We knew there was a stair up in the corner of the transept which you can get up to the triforium, and in them days the door to it was pretty well always open, and even if it wasn't we knew the key usually laid under a bit of matting hard by. So we made up our minds we'd be putting away music and that, next morning while the rest of the boys was clearing off, and then slip up the stairs and watch from the triforium if there was any signs of work going on.

"Well, that same night I dropped off asleep as sound as a boy does, and all of a sudden the dog woke me up, coming into the bed, and thought I, now we're going to get it sharp, for he seemed more frightened than usual. After about five minutes sure enough came this cry. I can't give you no idea what it was like; and so near too—nearer than I'd heard it yet—and a funny thing, Mr. Lake, you know what a place this Close is for an echo, and particular if you stand this side of it. Well, this crying never made no sign of an echo at all. But, as I said, it was dreadful near this night; and on the top of the start I got with hearing it, I got another fright; for I heard something rustling outside in the passage. Now to be sure I thought I was done; but I noticed the dog seemed to perk up a bit, and next there was someone whispered outside the door, and I very near laughed out loud, for I knew it was my father and mother that had got out of bed with the noise. 'Whatever is it?' says my mother. 'Hush! I don't know,' says my father, excited-like, 'don't disturb the boy. I hope he didn't hear nothing.'

"So, me knowing they were just outside, it made me bolder, and I slipped out of bed across to my little window—giving on the Close—but the dog he bored right down to the bottom of the bed—and I looked out. First go off I couldn't see anything. Then right down in the shadow under a buttress I made out what I shall always say was two spots of red—a dull red it was—nothing like a lamp or a fire, but just so as you could pick 'em out of the black shadow. I hadn't but just sighted 'em when it seemed we wasn't the only people that had been disturbed, because I see a window in a house on the left-hand side become lighted up, and the light moving. I just turned my head to make sure of it, and then looked back into the shadow for those two red things, and they were gone, and for all I peered about and stared, there was not a sign more of them. Then come my last fright that night—something come against my bare leg—but that was all right: that was my little dog had come out of bed, and prancing about making a great to-do, only holding his tongue, and me seeing he was quite in spirits again, I took him back to bed and we slept the night out!

"Next morning I made out to tell my mother I'd had the dog in my room, and I was surprised, after all she'd said about it before, how quiet she took it. 'Did you?' she says. 'Well, by good rights you ought to go without your breakfast for doing such a thing behind my back: but I don't know as there's any great harm done, only another time you ask my permission, do you hear?' A bit after that I said something to my father about having heard cats again. *'Cats'* he says; and he looked over at my poor mother, and she coughed and he says, 'Oh! ah! yes, cats. I believe I heard 'em myself.'

"That was a funny morning altogether: nothing seemed to go right. The organist he stopped in bed, and the minor Canon he forgot it was the 19th day and waited for the *Venite;* and after a bit the deputy he set off playing the chant for evensong, which was a minor; and then the Decani boys were laughing so much they couldn't sing, and when it came to the anthem the solo boy he got took with the giggles, and made out his nose was bleeding, and shoved the book at me what hadn't practised the verse and wasn't much of a singer if I had known it. Well, things was rougher, you see, fifty years ago, and I got a nip from the counter-tenor behind me that I remembered.

"So we got through somehow, and neither the men nor the boys weren't by way of waiting to see whether the Canon in residence—Mr. Henslow it was—would come to the vestries and fine 'em, but I don't believe he did: for one thing I fancy he'd read the wrong lesson for the first time in his life, and knew it. Anyhow, Evans and me didn't find no difficulty in slipping up the stairs as I told you, and when we got up we laid ourselves down flat on our stomachs where we could just stretch our heads out over the old tomb, and we hadn't but just done so when we heard the verger that was then, first shutting the iron porch-gates and locking the south-west door, and then the transept door, so we knew there was something up, and they meant to keep the public out for a bit.

"Next thing was, the Dean and the Canon come in by their door on the north, and then I see my father, and old Palmer, and a couple of their best men, and Palmer stood a talking for a bit with the Dean in the middle of the choir. He had a coil of rope and the men had crows. All of 'em looked a bit nervous. So there they stood talking, and at last I heard the Dean say, 'Well, I've no time to waste, Palmer. If you think this'll satisfy Southminster people, I'll permit it to be done; but I must say this, that never in the whole course of my life have I heard such arrant nonsense from a practical man as I have from you. Don't you agree with me, Henslow?' As far as I could hear Mr. Henslow said something like 'Oh well! we're told, aren't we, Mr. Dean, not to judge others?' And the Dean he gave a kind of sniff, and walked straight up to the tomb, and took his stand behind it with his back to the screen, and the others they come edging up rather gingerly. Henslow, he stopped on the south side and scratched on his chin, he did. Then the Dean spoke up: 'Palmer,' he says, 'which can you do easiest, get the slab off the top, or shift one of the side slabs?'

"Old Palmer and his men they pottered about a bit looking round the edge of the top slab and sounding the sides on the south and east and west and everywhere but the north. Henslow said something about it being better to have a try at the south side, because there was more light and more room to move about in. Then my father, who'd been 'awatching of them, went round to the north side, and knelt down and felt the slab by the chink, and he got up and dusted his knees and says to the Dean: 'Beg pardon, Mr. Dean, but I think if Mr. Palmer'll try this here slab he'll find it'll come out easy enough. Seems to me one of the men could prise it out with his crow by means of this chink.' 'Ah! thank you, Worby,' says the Dean; 'that's a good suggestion. Palmer, let one of your men do that, will you?'

"So the man come round, and put his bar in and bore on it, and just that minute when they were all bending over, and we boys got our heads well over the edge of the triforium, there came a most fearful crash down at the west end of the choir, as if a whole stack of big timber had fallen down a flight of stairs. Well, you can't expect me to tell you everything that happened all in a minute. Of course there was a terrible commotion. I heard the slab fall out, and the crowbar on the floor, and I heard the Dean say, 'Good God!'

"When I looked down again I saw the Dean tumbled over on the floor, the men was making off down the choir, Henslow was just going to help the Dean up, Palmer was going to stop the men (as he said afterwards) and my father was sitting on the altar step with his face in his hands. The Dean he was very cross. 'I wish to goodness you'd look where you're coming to, Henslow,' he says. 'Why you should all take to your heels when a stick of wood tumbles down I cannot imagine'; and all Henslow could do, explaining he was right away on the other side of the tomb, would not satisfy him.

"Then Palmer came back and reported there was nothing to account for this noise and nothing seemingly fallen down, and when the Dean finished feeling of himself they gathered round—except my father, he sat where he was—and someone lighted up a bit of candle and they looked into the tomb. 'Nothing there,' says the Dean, 'what did I tell you? Stay! here's something. What's this? a bit of music paper, and a piece of torn stuff—part of a dress it looks like. Both quite modern—no interest whatever. Another time perhaps you'll take the advice of an educated man'—or something like that, and off he went, limping a bit, and out through the north door, only as he went he called back angry to Palmer for leaving the door standing open. Palmer called out 'Very sorry, sir,' but he shrugged his shoulders, and Henslow says, 'I fancy Mr. Dean's mistaken. I closed the door behind me, but he's a little upset.' Then Palmer says, 'Why, where's Worby?' and they saw him sitting on the step and went up to him. He was recovering himself, it seemed, and wiping his forehead, and Palmer helped him up on to his legs, as I was glad to see.

"They were too far off for me to hear what they said, but my father pointed to the north door in the aisle, and Palmer and Henslow both of them looked very surprised and scared. After a bit, my father and Henslow went out of the church, and the others made what haste they could to put the slab back and plaster it in. And about as the clock struck twelve the Cathedral was opened again and us boys made the best of our way home.

"I was in a great taking to know what it was had given my poor father such a turn, and when I got in and found him sitting in his chair taking a glass of spirits, and my mother standing looking anxious at him, I couldn't keep from bursting out and making confession where I'd been. But he didn't seem to take on, not in the way of losing his temper. 'You was there, was you? Well, did you see it?' 'I saw everything, father,' I said, 'except when the noise came.' 'Did you see what it was knocked the Dean over?' he says, 'that what come out of the monument? You didn't? Well, that's a mercy.' 'Why, what was it, father?' I said. 'Come, you must have seen it,' he says. '*Didn't* you see? A thing like a man, all over hair, and two great eyes to it?'

"Well, that was all I could get out of him that time, and later on he seemed as if he was ashamed of being so frightened, and he used to put me off when I asked him about it. But years after when I was got to be a grown man, we had more talk now and again on the matter, and he always said the same thing. 'Black it was,' he'd say, 'and a mass of hair, and two legs, and the light caught on its eyes.'

"Well, that's the tale of that tomb, Mr. Lake; it's one we don't tell to our visitors, and I should be obliged to you not to make any use of it till I'm out of the way. I doubt Mr. Evans'll feel the same as I do, if you ask him."

This proved to be the case. But over twenty years have passed by, and the grass is growing over both Worby and Evans; so Mr. Lake felt no difficulty about communicating his notes—taken in 1890—to me. He accompanied them with a sketch of the tomb and a copy of the short inscription on the metal cross which was affixed at the expense of Dr. Lyall to the centre of the northern side. It was from the Vulgate of Isaiah xxiv., and consisted merely of the three words—

IBI CUBAVIT LAMIA.

CLARK ASHTON SMITH *(1893–1961) was one of the most important writers, with H. P. Lovecraft and Robert E. Howard, in the early days of* Weird Tales *magazine. After contributing some verse and translating some of Baudelaire's poetry for its pages in the 1920s, Smith published a large number of stories there and in other pulp magazines between 1930 and 1936. After that time, he virtually stopped writing fiction, although he continued writing poetry and developing his interest in sculpture until his death.*

When he was still a teenager, Smith's first book of poetry, The Star-Treader and Other Poems *(1912), brought him extravagant praise from fellow writers, including Ambrose Bierce, and from the literary press of his native California, where he was hailed as "the Keats of the Pacific coast."*

But it is as a writer of prose fantasy that Smith's reputation will endure. The complexity of his inventions, coupled with a richly poetic style, can be seen nowhere better than in "A Rendezvous in Averoigne."

A Rendezvous in Averoigne (1931)
BY CLARK ASHTON SMITH

Gerard de l'Automne was meditating the rimes of a new ballade in honor of Fleurette, as he followed the leaf-arrased pathway toward Vyones through the woodland of Averoigne. Since he was on his way to meet Fleurette, who had promised to keep a rendezvous among the oaks and beeches like any peasant girl, Gerard himself made better progress than the ballade. His love was at that stage which, even for a professional troubadour, is more productive of distraction than inspiration; and he was recurrently absorbed in a meditation upon other than merely verbal felicities.

The grass and trees had assumed the fresh enamel of a mediaeval May; the turf was figured with little blossoms of azure and white and yellow, like an ornate broidery; and there was a pebbly stream that murmured beside the way, as if the voices of undines were parleying deliciously beneath its waters. The sun-lulled air was laden with a wafture of youth and romance; and the longing that welled from the heart of Gerard seemed to mingle mystically with the balsams of the wood.

Gerard was a *trouvère* whose scant years and many wanderings had brought him a certain renown. After the fashion of his kind he had roamed from court to court, from chateau to chateau; and he was now the guest of the Comte de la Frênaie, whose high castle held dominion over half the surrounding forest. Visiting one day that quaint cathedral town, Vyones, which lies so near to the ancient wood of Averoigne, Gerard had seen Fleurette, the daughter of a well-to-do mercer named Guillaume Cochin; and had become more sincerely enamored of her blond piquancy than was to be expected from one who had been so frequently susceptible in such matters. He had managed to make his feelings known to her; and, after a month of *billets-doux,* ballads and stolen interviews contrived by the help of a complaisant waiting-woman, she had made this woodland tryst with him in the absence of her father from Vyones. Accompanied by her maid and a man-servant, she was to leave the town early that afternoon and meet Gerard under a certain beech-tree of enormous age and size. The servants would then withdraw discreetly; and the lovers, to all intents and purposes, would be alone. It was not likely that they would be seen or interrupted; for the gnarled and immemorial wood possessed an ill-repute among the peasantry. Somewhere in this wood there was the ruinous and haunted Chateau des Faussesflammes; and, also, there was a double tomb, within which the Sieur Hugh du Malinbois and his chatelaine, who were notorious for sorcery in their time, had lain unconsecrated for more than two hundred years. Of these, and their phantoms, there were grisly tales; and there were stories of *loup-garous* and goblins, of fays and devils and vampires that infested Averoigne. But to these tales Gerard had given little heed, considering it improbable that such creatures would fare abroad in open daylight. The madcap Fleurette had professed herself unafraid also; but it had been necessary to promise the servants a substantial *pourboire,* since they shared fully the local superstitions.

Gerard had wholly forgotten the legendry of Averoigne, as he hastened along the sun-flecked path. He was nearing the appointed beech-tree, which a turn of the path would soon reveal; and his pulses quickened and became tremulous, as he wondered if Fleurette had already reached the trysting-place. He abandoned all effort to continue his ballade, which, in the three miles he had walked from La Frênaie, had not progressed beyond the middle of a tentative first stanza.

His thoughts were such as would befit an ardent and impatient lover. They were now interrupted by a shrill scream that rose to an unendurable pitch of fear and horror, issuing from the green stillness of the pines beside the way. Startled, he peered at the thick branches; and as the scream fell back to silence, he heard the sound of dull and hurrying footfalls, and a scuffling as of several bodies. Again the scream arose. It was plainly the voice of a woman in some distressful peril. Loosening his dagger in its sheath, and clutching more firmly a long hornbeam staff which he had brought with him as a protection against the vipers which were said to lurk in Averoigne, he plunged without hesitation or premeditation among the low-hanging boughs from which the voice had seemed to emerge.

In a small open space beyond the trees, he saw a woman who was struggling with three ruffians of exceptionally brutal and evil aspect. Even in the haste and vehemence of the moment, Gerard realized that he had never before seen such men or such a woman. The woman was clad in a gown of emerald green that matched her eyes; in her face was the pallor of dead things, together with a faery beauty; and her lips were dyed as with the scarlet of newly flowing blood. The men were dark as Moors, and their eyes were red slits of flame beneath oblique brows with animal-like bristles. There was something very peculiar in the shape of their feet; but Gerard did not realize the exact nature of the peculiarity till long afterward. Then he remembered that all of them were seemingly club-footed, though they were able to move with surpassing agility. Somehow, he could never recall what sort of clothing they had worn.

The woman turned a beseeching gaze upon Gerard as he sprang forth from amid the boughs. The men, however, did not seem to heed his coming; though one of them caught in a hairy clutch the hands which the woman sought to reach toward her rescuer.

Lifting his staff, Gerard rushed upon the ruffians. He struck a tremendous blow at the head of the nearest one—a blow that should have leveled the fellow to earth. But the staff came down on unresisting air, and Gerard staggered and almost fell headlong in trying to recover his equilibrium. Dazed and uncomprehending, he saw the knot of struggling figures had vanished utterly. At least, the three men had vanished; but from the middle branches of a tall pine beyond the open space, the death-white features of the woman smiled upon him for a moment with faint, inscrutable guile ere they melted among the needles.

Gerard understood now; and he shivered as he crossed himself. He had been deluded by phantoms or demons, doubtless for no good purpose; he had been the gull of a questionable enchantment. Plainly there was something after all in the legends he had heard, in the ill-renown of the forest of Averoigne.

He retraced his way toward the path he had been following. But when he thought to reach again the spot from which he had heard that shrill unearthly scream, he saw that there was no longer a path; nor, indeed, any feature of the forest which he could remember or recognize. The foliage about him no longer displayed a brilliant verdure; it was sad and funereal, and the trees themselves were either cypress-like, or were already sere with autumn or decay. In lieu of the purling brook there lay before him a tarn of waters that were dark and dull as clotting blood, and which gave back no reflection of the brown autumnal sedges that trailed therein like the hair of suicides, and the skeletons of rotting osiers that writhed above them.

Now, beyond all question, Gerard knew that he was the victim of an evil enchantment. In answering that beguileful cry for succor, he had exposed himself to the spell, had been lured within the circle of its power. He could not know what forces of wizardry or demonry had willed to draw him thus; but he knew that his situation was fraught with supernatural menace. He gripped the hornbeam staff more tightly in his hand, and prayed to all the saints he could remember, as he peered about for some tangible bodily presence of ill.

The scene was utterly desolate and lifeless, like a place where cadavers might keep their tryst with demons. Nothing stirred, not even a dead leaf; and there was no whisper of dry grass or foliage, no song of birds nor murmuring of bees, no sigh nor chuckle of water. The corpse-gray heavens above seemed never to have held a sun; and the chill, unchanging light was without source or destination, without beams or shadows.

Gerard surveyed his environment with a cautious eye; and the more he looked the less he liked it: for some new and disagreeable detail was manifest at every glance. There were moving lights in the wood that vanished if he eyed them intently; there were drowned faces in the tarn that came and went like livid bubbles before he could discern their features. And, peering across the lake, he wondered why he had not seen the many-turreted castle of hoary stone whose nearer walls were based in the dead waters. It was so gray and still and vasty, that it seemed to have stood for incomputable ages between the stagnant tarn and the equally stagnant heavens. It was ancienter than the world, it was older than the light: it was coeval with fear and darkness; and a horror dwelt upon it and crept unseen but palpable along its bastions.

There was no sign of life about the castle; and no banners flew above its turrets or its donjon. But Gerard knew, as surely as if a voice had spoken aloud to warn him, that here was the fountainhead of the sorcery by which he had been beguiled. A growing panic whispered in his brain, he seemed to hear the rustle of malignant plumes, the mutter of demonian threats and plottings. He turned, and fled among the funereal trees.

Amid his dismay and bewilderment, even as he fled, he thought of Fleurette and wondered if she were awaiting him at their place of rendezvous, or if she and her companions had also been enticed and led astray in a realm of damnable unrealities. He renewed his prayers, and implored the saints for her safety as well as his own.

The forest through which he ran was a maze of bafflement and eeriness. There were no landmarks, there were no tracks of animals or men; and the swart cypresses and sere autumnal trees grew thicker and thicker as if some malevolent will were marshalling them against his progress. The boughs were like implacable arms that stroke to retard him; he could have sworn that he felt them twine about him with the strength and suppleness of living things. He fought them, insanely, desperately, and seemed to hear a crackling of infernal laughter in their twigs as he fought. At last, with a sob of relief, he broke through into a sort of trail. Along this trail, in the mad hope of eventual escape, he ran like one whom a fiend pursues; and after a short interval he came again to the shores of the tarn, above whose motionless waters the high and hoary turrets of that time-forgotten castle were still dominant. Again he turned and fled; and once more, after similar wanderings and like struggles, he came back to the inevitable tarn.

With a leaden sinking of his heart, as into some ultimate slough of despair and terror, he resigned himself and made no further effort to escape. His very will was benumbed, was crushed down as by the incumbence of a superior volition that would no longer permit his puny recalcitrance. He was unable to resist when a strong and hateful compulsion drew his footsteps along the margent of the tarn toward the looming castle.

When he came nearer, he saw that the edifice was surrounded by a moat whose waters were stagnant as those of the lake, and were mantled with the iridescent scum of corruption. The drawbridge was down and the gates were open, as if to receive an expected guest. But still there was no sign of human occupancy; and the walls of the great gray building were silent as those of a sepulcher. And more tomb-like even than the rest was the square and overtowering bulk of the mighty donjon.

Impelled by the same power that had drawn him along the lakeshore, Gerard crossed the drawbridge and passed beneath the frowning barbican into a vacant courtyard. Barred windows looked blankly down; and at the opposite end of the court a door stood mysteriously open, revealing a dark hall. As he approached the doorway, he saw that a man was standing on the threshold; though a moment previous he could have sworn that it was untenanted by any visible form.

Gerard had retained his hornbeam staff; and though his reason told him that such a weapon was futile against any supernatural foe, some obscure instinct prompted him to clasp it valiantly as he neared the waiting figure on the sill.

The man was inordinately tall and cadaverous, and was dressed in black garments of a superannuate mode. His lips were strangely red amid his bluish beard and the mortuary whiteness of his face. They were like the lips of the woman who, with her assailants, had disappeared in a manner so dubious when Gerard had approached them. His eyes were pale and luminous as marsh-lights; and Gerard shuddered at his gaze and at the cold, ironic smile of his scarlet lips that seemed to reserve a world of secrets all too dreadful and hideous to be disclosed.

"I am the Sieur du Malinbois," the man announced. His tones were both unctuous and hollow, and served to increase the repugnance felt by the young troubadour. And when his lips parted, Gerard had a glimpse of teeth that were unnaturally small and were pointed like the fangs of some fierce animal.

"Fortune has willed that you should become my guest," the man went on. "The hospitality which I can proffer you is rough and inadequate, and it may be that you will find my abode a trifle dismal. But at least I can assure you of a welcome no less ready than sincere."

"I thank you for your kind offer," said Gerard. "But I have an appointment with a friend; and I seem in some unaccountable manner to have lost my way. I should be profoundly grateful if you would direct me toward Vyones. There should be a path not far from here; and I have been so stupid as to stray from it."

The words rang empty and hopeless in his own ears even as he uttered them; and the name that his strange host had given—the Sieur du Malinbois—was haunting his mind like the funereal accents of a knell; though he could not recall at that moment the macabre and spectral ideas which the name tended to evoke.

"Unfortunately, there are no paths from my chateau to Vyones," the stranger replied. "As for your rendezvous, it will be kept in another manner, at another place, than the one appointed. I must therefore insist that you accept my hospitality. Enter, I pray; but leave your hornbeam staff at the door. You will have no need of it any longer."

Gerard thought that he made a moue of distaste and aversion with his over-red lips as he spoke the last sentences; and that his eyes lingered on the staff with an obscure apprehensiveness. And the strange emphasis of his words and demeanor served to awaken other fantasmal and macabre thoughts in Gerard's brain; though he could not formulate them fully till afterward. And somehow he was prompted to retain the weapon, no matter how useless it might be against an enemy of spectral or diabolic nature. So he said:

"I must crave your indulgence if I retain the staff. I have made a vow to carry it with me, in my right hand or never beyond arm's reach, till I have slain two vipers."

"That is a queer vow," rejoined his host. "However, bring it with you if you like. It is of no matter to me if you choose to encumber yourself with a wooden stick."

He turned abruptly, motioning Gerard to follow him. The troubadour obeyed unwillingly, with one rearward glance at the vacant heavens and the empty courtyard. He saw with no great surprise that a sudden and furtive darkness had closed in upon the chateau without moon or star, as if it had been merely waiting for him to enter before it descended. It was thick as the folds of a cerecloth, it was airless and stifling like the gloom of a sepulcher that has been sealed for ages; and Gerard was aware of a veritable oppression, a corporeal and psychic difficulty in breathing, as he crossed the threshold.

He saw that cressets were now burning in the dim hall to which his host had admitted him; though he had not perceived the time and agency of their lighting. The illumination they afforded was singularly vague and indistinct, and the thronging shadows of the hall were unexplainably numerous, and moved with a mysterious disquiet; though the flames themselves were still as tapers that burn for the dead in a windless vault.

At the end of the passage, the Sieur du Malinbois flung open a heavy door of dark and somber wood. Beyond, in what was plainly the eating-room of the chateau, several people were seated about a long table by the light of cressets no less dreary and dismal than those in the hall. In the strange, uncertain glow, their faces were touched with a gloomy dubiety, with a lurid distortion; and it seemed to Gerard that shadows hardly distinguishable from the figures were gathered around the board. But nevertheless he recognized the woman in the emerald green who had vanished in so doubtful a fashion amid the pines when Gerard answered her call for succor. At one side, looking very pale and forlorn and frightened, was Fleurette Cochin. At the lower end reserved for retainers and inferiors, there sat the maid and the man-servant who had accompanied Fleurette to her rendezvous with Gerard.

The Sieur du Malinbois turned to the troubadour with a smile of sardonic amusement.

"I believe you have already met everyone assembled," he observed. "But you have not yet been formally presented to my wife, Agathe, who is presiding over the board. Agathe, I bring to you Gerard d l'Automne, a young troubadour of much note and merit."

The woman nodded slightly, without speaking, and pointed to a chair opposite Fleurette. Gerard seated himself, and the Sieur du Malinbois assumed according to feudal custom a place at the head of the table beside his wife.

Now, for the first time, Gerard noticed that there were servitors who came and went in the room, setting upon the table various wines and viands. The servitors were preternaturally swift and noiseless, and somehow it was very difficult to be sure of their precise features or their costumes. They seemed to walk in an adumbration of sinister insoluble twilight. But the troubadour was disturbed by a feeling that they resembled the swart demoniac ruffians who had disappeared together with the woman in green when he approached them.

The meal that ensued was a weird and funereal affair. A sense of insuperable constraint, of smothering horror and hideous oppression, was upon Gerard; and though he wanted to ask Fleurette a hundred questions, and also demand an explanation of sundry matters from his host and hostess, he was totally unable to frame the words or to utter them. He could only look at Fleurette, and read in her eyes a duplication of his own helpless bewilderment and nightmare thralldom. Nothing was said by the Sieur du Malinbois and his lady, who were exchanging glances of a secret and baleful intelligence all through the meal; and Fleurette's maid and man-servant were obviously paralyzed by terror, like birds beneath the hypnotic gaze of deadly serpents.

The foods were rich and of strange savor; and the wines were fabulously old, and seemed to retain in their topaz or violet depths the unextinguished fire of buried centuries. But Gerard and Fleurette could barely touch them; and they saw that the Sieur du Malinbois and his lady did not eat or drink at all. The gloom of the chamber deepened; the servitors became more furtive and spectral in their movements; the stifling air was laden with unformulable menace, was constrained by the spell of a black and lethal necromancy. Above the aromas of the rare foods, the bouquets of the antique wines, there crept forth the choking mustiness of hidden vaults and embalmed centurial corruption, together with the ghostly spice of a strange perfume that seemed to emanate from the person of the chatelaine. And now Gerard was remembering many tales from the legendry of Averoigne, which he had heard and disregarded; was recalling the story of a Sieur du Malinbois and his lady, the last of the name and the most evil, who had been buried somewhere in this forest hundreds of years ago; and whose tomb was shunned by the peasantry since they were said to continue their sorceries even in death. He wondered what influence had bedrugged his memory, that he had not recalled it wholly when he had first heard the name. And he was remembering other things and other stories, all of which confirmed his instinctive belief regarding the nature of the people into whose hands he had fallen. Also, he recalled a folklore superstition concerning the use to which a wooden stake can be put; and realized why the Sieur du Malinbois had shown a peculiar interest in the hornbeam staff. Gerard had laid the staff beside his chair when he sat down; and he was reassured to find that it had not vanished. Very quietly and unobtrusively, he placed his foot upon it.

The uncanny meal came to an end; and the host and his chatelaine arose.

"I shall now conduct you to your rooms," said the Sieur du Malinbois, including all of his guests in a dark, inscrutable glance. "Each of you can have a separate chamber, if you so desire; or Fleurette Cochin and her maid Angelique can remain together; and the manservant Raoul can sleep in the same room with Messire Gerard."

A preference for the latter procedure was voiced by Fleurette and the troubadour. The thought of uncompanioned solitude in that castle of timeless midnight and nameless mystery was abhorrent to an insupportable degree.

The four were now led to their respective chambers, on opposite sides of a hall whose length was but indeterminately revealed by the dismal lights. Fleurette and Gerard bade each other a dismayed and reluctant good-night beneath the constraining eye of their host. Their rendezvous was hardly the one which they had thought to keep; and both were overwhelmed by the supernatural situation amid whose dubious horrors and ineluctable sorceries they had somehow become involved. And no sooner had Gerard left Fleurette than he began to curse himself for a poltroon because he had not refused to part from her side; and he marvelled at the spell of drug-like involition that had bedrowsed all his faculties. It seemed that his will was not his own, but had been thrust down and throttled by an alien power.

The room assigned to Gerard and Raoul was furnished with a couch, and a great bed whose curtains were of antique fashion and fabric. It was lighted with tapers that had a funereal suggestion in their form, and which burned dully in an air that was stagnant with the mustiness of dead years.

"May you sleep soundly," said the Sieur du Malinbois. The smile that accompanied and followed the words was no less unpleasant than the oily and sepulchral tone in which they were uttered. The troubadour and the servant were conscious of profound relief when he went out and closed the leaden-clanging door. And their relief was hardly diminished even when they heard the click of a key in the lock.

Gerard was now inspecting the room; and he went to the one window, through whose small and deep-set panes he could see only the pressing darkness of a night that was veritably solid, as if the whole place were buried beneath the earth and were closed in by clinging mold. Then, with an excess of unsmothered rage at his separation from Fleurette, he ran to the door and hurled himself against it, he beat upon it with his clenched fists, but in vain. Realizing his folly, and desisting at last, he turned to Raoul.

"Well, Raoul," he said, "what do you think of all this?"

Raoul crossed himself before he answered; and his face had assumed the vizard of a mortal fear.

"I think, Messire," he finally replied, "that we have all been decoyed by a malefic sorcery; and that you, myself, the demoiselle Fleurette, and the maid Angelique, are all in deadly peril of both soul and body."

"That, also, is my thought," said Gerard. "And I believe it would be well that you and I should sleep only by turns; and that he who keeps vigil should retain in his hands my hornbeam staff, whose end I shall now sharpen with my dagger. I am sure that you know the manner in which it should be employed if there are any intruders; for if such should come, there would be no doubt as to their character and their intentions. We are in a castle which has no legitimate existence, as the guests of people who have been dead, or supposedly dead, for more than two hundred years. And such people, when they stir abroad, are prone to habits which I need not specify."

"Yes, Messire." Raoul shuddered; but he watched the sharpening of the staff with considerable interest. Gerard whittled the hard wood to a lance-like point, and hid the shavings carefully. He even carved the outline of a little cross near the middle of the staff, thinking that this might increase its efficacy or save it from molestation. Then, with the staff in his hand, he sat down upon the bed, where he could survey the little room from between the curtains.

"You can sleep first, Raoul." He indicated the couch, which was near the door.

The two conversed in a fitful manner for some minutes. After hearing Raoul's tale of how Fleurette, Angelique and himself had been led astray by the sobbing of a woman amid the pines, and had been unable to retrace their way, the troubadour changed the theme. And henceforth he spoke idly and of matters remote from his real preoccupations, to fight down his torturing concern for the safety of Fleurette. Suddenly he became aware that Raoul had ceased to reply; and saw that the servant had fallen asleep on the couch. At the same time an irresistible drowsiness surged upon Gerard himself in spite of all his volition, in spite of the eldritch terrors and forebodings that still murmured in his brain. He heard through his growing hebetude a whisper as of shadowy wings in the castle halls; he caught the sibilation of ominous voices, like those of familiars that respond to the summoning of wizards; and he seemed to hear, even in the vaults and towers and remote chambers, the tread of feet that were hurrying on malign and secret errands. But oblivion was around him like the meshes of a sable net; and it closed in relentlessly upon his troubled mind, and drowned the alarms of his agitated senses.

When Gerard awoke at length, the tapers had burned to their sockets; and a sad and sunless daylight was filtering through the window. The staff was still in his hand; and though his senses were still dull with the strange slumber that had drugged them, he felt that he was unharmed. But peering between the curtains, he saw that Raoul was lying mortally pale and lifeless on the couch, with the air and look of an exhausted moribund.

He crossed the room, and stooped above the servant. There was a small red wound on Raoul's neck; and his pulses were slow and feeble, like those of one who has lost a great amount of blood. His very appearance was withered and vein-drawn. And a phantom spice arose from the couch—a lingering wraith of the perfume worn by the chatelaine Agathe.

Gerard succeeded at last in arousing the man; but Raoul was very weak and drowsy. He could remember nothing of what had happened during the night; and his horror was pitiful to behold when he realized the truth.

"It will be your turn next, Messire," he cried. "These vampires mean to hold us here amid their unhallowed necromancies till they have drained us of our last drop of blood. Their spells are like mandragora or the sleepy sirups of Cathay; and no man can keep awake in their despite."

Gerard was trying the door; and somewhat to his surprise he found it unlocked. The departing vampire had been careless, in the lethargy of her repletion. The castle was very still; and it seemed to Gerard that the animating spirit of evil was now quiescent; that the shadowy wings of horror and malignity, the feet that had sped on baleful errands, the summoning sorcerers, the responding familiars, were all lulled in a temporary slumber.

He opened the door, he tiptoed along the deserted hall, and knocked at the portal of the chamber allotted to Fleurette and her maid. Fleurette, fully dressed, answered his knock immediately; and he caught her in his arms without a word, searching her wan face with a tender anxiety. Over her shoulder he could see the maid Angelique, who was sitting listlessly on the bed with a mark on her white neck similar to the wound that had been suffered by Raoul. He knew, even before Fleurette began to speak, that the nocturnal experiences of the demoiselle and her maid had been identical with those of himself and the man-servant.

While he tried to comfort Fleurette and reassure her, his thoughts were now busy with a rather curious problem. No one was abroad in the castle; and it was more than probable that the Sieur du Malinbois and his lady were both asleep after the nocturnal feast which they had undoubtedly enjoyed. Gerard pictured to himself the place and the fashion of their slumber; and he grew even more reflective as certain possibilities occurred to him.

"Be of good cheer, sweetheart," he said to Fleurette. "It is in my mind that we may soon escape from this abominable mesh of enchantments. But I must leave you for a little and speak again with Raoul, whose help I shall require in a certain matter."

He went back to his own chamber. The man-servant was sitting on the couch and was crossing himself feebly and muttering prayers with a faint, hollow voice.

"Raoul," said the troubadour a little sternly, "you must gather all your strength and come with me. Amid the gloomy walls that surround us, the somber ancient halls, the high towers and the heavy bastions, there is but one thing that veritably exists; and all the rest is a fabric of illusion. We must find the reality whereof I speak, and deal with it like true and valiant Christians. Come, we will now search the castle ere the lord and chatelaine shall awaken from their vampire lethargy."

He led the way along the devious corridors with a swiftness that betokened much forethought. He had reconstructed in his mind the hoary pile of battlements and turrets as he had seen them on the previous day; and he felt that the great donjon, being the center and stronghold of the edifice, might well be the place which he sought. With the sharpened staff in his hand, with Raoul lagging bloodlessly at his heels, he passed the doors of many secret rooms, the many windows that gave on the blindness of an inner court, and came at last to the lower storey of the donjon-keep.

It was a large, bare room, entirely built of stone, and illumined only by narrow slits high up in the wall, that had been designed for the use of archers. The place was very dim; but Gerard could see the glimmering outlines of an object not ordinarily to be looked for in such a situation, that arose from the middle of the floor. It was a tomb of marble; and stepping nearer, he saw that it was strangely weatherworn and was blotched by lichens of gray and yellow, such as flourish only within access of the sun. The slab that covered it was doubly broad and massive, and would require the full strength of two men to lift.

Raoul was staring stupidly at the tomb. "What now, Messire?" he queried.

"You and I, Raoul, are about to intrude upon the bedchamber of our host and hostess."

At his direction, Raoul seized one end of the slab; and he himself took the other. With a mighty effort that strained their bones and sinews to the cracking-point, they sought to remove it; but the slab hardly stirred. At length, by grasping the same end in unison, they were able to tilt the slab; and it slid away and dropped to the floor with a thunderous crash. Within, there were two open coffins, one of which contained the Sieur Hugh du Malinbois and the other his lady Agathe. Both of them appeared to be slumbering peacefully as infants; a look of tranquil evil, of pacified malignity, was imprinted upon their features; and their lips were dyed with a fresher scarlet than before.

Without hesitation or delay, Gerard plunged the lancelike end of his staff into the bosom of the Sieur du Malinbois. The body crumbled as if it were wrought of ashes kneaded and painted to human semblance; and a slight odor as of age-old corruption arose to the nostrils of Gerard. Then the troubadour pierced in like manner the bosom of the chatelaine. And simultaneously with her dissolution, the walls and floor of the donjon seemed to dissolve like a sullen vapor, they rolled away on every side with a shock as of unheard thunder. With a sense of weird vertigo and confusion Gerard and Raoul saw that the whole chateau had vanished like the towers and battlements of a bygone storm; that the dead lake and its rotting shores no longer offered their malefic illusions to the eye. They were standing in a forest glade, in the full unshadowed light of the afternoon sun; and all that remained of the dismal castle was the lichen-mantled tomb that stood open beside them. Fleurette and her maid were a little distance away; and Gerard ran to the mercer's daughter and took her in his arms. She was dazed with wonderment, like one who emerges from the nightlong labyrinth of an evil dream, and finds that all is well.

"I think, sweetheart," said Gerard, "that our next rendezvous will not be interrupted by the Sieur du Malinbois and his chatelaine."

But Fleurette was still bemused with wonder, and could only respond to his words with a kiss.

CATHERINE L. MOORE *(born 1911) won instant fame in the fantasy field with the publication of her first story, "Shambleau," in 1933 in* Weird Tales. *Throughout the 1930s, she produced a steady stream of science fiction stories that remain classics today. After her marriage to science fiction writer Henry Kuttner in 1940, they collaborated on many stories. Following his death in 1958, Moore devoted her efforts to film work in Hollywood, writing scripts for many television series, including "77 Sunset Strip" and "Maverick."*

"Shambleau" was one of the first science fiction stories to deal with sexual themes and was instrumental in the genre's maturing process. Its highly charged language and Freudian implications, combined with a tense and compelling narrative, still weave their spell.

Shambleau
(1933)
BY C. L. MOORE

Man has conquered space before. You may be sure of that. Somewhere beyond the Egyptians, in that dimness out of which come echoes of half-mythical names—Atlantis, Mu—somewhere back of history's first beginnings there must have been an age when mankind, like us today, built cities of steel to house its star-roving ships and knew the names of the planets in their own native tongues—heard Venus' people call their wet world "Sha-ardol" in that soft, sweet, slurring speech and mimicked Mars' guttural "Lakkdiz" from the harsh tongues of Mars' dryland dwellers. You may be sure of it. Man has conquered Space before, and out of that conquest faint, faint echoes run still through a world that has forgotten the very fact of a civilization which must have been as mighty as our own. There have been too many myths and legends for us to doubt it. The myth of the Medusa, for instance, can never have had its roots in the soil of Earth. That tale of the snake-haired Gorgon whose gaze turned the gazer to stone never originated about any creature that Earth nourished. And those ancient Greeks who told the story must have remembered, dimly and half believing, a tale of antiquity about some strange being from one of the outlying planets their remotest ancestors once trod.

"Shambleau! Ha . . . Shambleau!" The wild hysteria of the mob rocketed from wall to wall of Lakkdarol's narrow streets and the storming of heavy boots over the slag-red pavement made an ominous undernote to that swelling bay, "Shambleau! Shambleau!"

Northwest Smith heard it coming and stepped into the nearest doorway, laying a wary hand on his heat-gun's grip, and his colorless eyes narrowed. Strange sounds were common enough in the streets of Earth's latest colony on Mars—a raw, red little town where anything might happen, and very often did. But Northwest Smith, whose name is known and respected in every dive and wild outpost on a dozen wild planets, was a cautious man, despite his reputation. He set his back against the wall and gripped his pistol, and heard the rising shout come nearer and nearer.

Then into his range of vision flashed a red running figure, dodging like a hunted hare from shelter to shelter in the narrow street. It was a girl—a berry-brown girl in a single tattered garment whose scarlet burnt the eyes with its brilliance. She ran wearily, and he could hear her gasping breath from where he stood. As she came into view he saw her hesitate and lean one hand against the wall for support, and glance wildly around for shelter. She must not have seen him in the depths of the doorway, for as the bay of the mob grew louder and the pounding of feet sounded almost at the corner she gave a despairing little moan and dodged into the recess at his very side.

When she saw him standing there, tall and leather-brown, hand on his heat-gun, she sobbed once, inarticulately, and collapsed at his feet, a huddle of burning scarlet and bare, brown limbs.

Smith had not seen her face, but she was a girl, and sweetly made and in danger; and though he had not the reputation of a chivalrous man, something in her hopeless huddle at his feet touched that chord of sympathy for the underdog that stirs in every Earthman, and he pushed her gently into the corner behind him and jerked out his gun, just as the first of the running mob rounded the corner.

It was a motley crowd, Earthmen and Martians and a sprinkling of Venusian swampmen and strange, nameless denizens of unnamed planets—a typical Lakkdarol mob. When the first of them turned the corner and saw the empty street before them there was a faltering in the rush and the foremost spread out and began to search the doorways on both sides of the street.

"Looking for something?" Smith's sardonic call sounded clear above the clamor of the mob.

They turned. The shouting died for a moment as they took in the scene before them—tall Earthman in the space-explorer's leathern garb,

all one color from the burning of savage suns save for the sinister pallor
of his no-colored eyes in a scarred and resolute face, gun in his steady
hand and the scarlet girl crouched behind him, panting.

The foremost of the crowd—a burly Earthman in tattered leather
from which the Patrol insignia had been ripped away—stared for a
moment with a strange expression of incredulity on his face over-
spreading the savage exultation of the chase. Then he let loose a deep-
throated bellow, "Shambleau!" and lunged forward. Behind him the
mob took up the cry again, "Shambleau! Shambleau! Shambleau!" and
surged after.

Smith, lounging negligently against the wall, arms folded and gun-
hand draped over his left forearm, looked incapable of swift motion, but
at the leader's first forward step the pistol swept in a practiced half-
circle and the dazzle of blue-white heat leaping from its muzzle seared
an arc in the slag pavement at his feet. It was an old gesture, and not a
man in the crowd but understood it. The foremost recoiled swiftly
against the surge of those in the rear, and for a moment there was
confusion as the two tides met and struggled. Smith's mouth curled into
a grim curve as he watched. The man in the mutilated Patrol uniform
lifted a threatening fist and stepped to the very edge of the deadline,
while the crowd rocked to and fro behind him.

"Are you crossing that line?" queried Smith in an ominously gentle
voice.

"We want that girl!"

"Come and get her!" Recklessly Smith grinned into his face. He
saw danger there, but his defiance was not the foolhardy gesture it
seemed. An expert psychologist of mobs from long experience, he
sensed no murder here. Not a gun had appeared in any hand in the
crowd. They desired the girl with an inexplicable bloodthirstiness he
was at a loss to understand, but toward himself he sensed no such fury.
A mauling he might expect, but his life was in no danger. Guns would
have appeared before now if they were coming out at all. So he grinned
in the man's angry face and leaned lazily against the wall.

Behind their self-appointed leader the crowd milled impatiently,
and threatening voices began to rise again. Smith heard the girl moan at
his feet.

"What do you want with her?" he demanded.

"She's Shambleau! Shambleau, you fool! Kick her out of there—
we'll take care of her!"

"I'm taking care of her," drawled Smith.

"She's Shambleau, I tell you! Damn your hide, man, we never let those things live! Kick her out here!"

The repeated name had no meaning to him, but Smith's innate stubbornness rose defiantly as the crowd surged forward to the very edge of the arc, their clamor growing louder. "Shambleau! Kick her out here! Give us Shambleau! Shambleau!"

Smith dropped his indolent pose like a cloak and planted both feet wide, swinging up his gun threateningly. "Keep back!" he yelled. "She's mine! Keep back!"

He had no intention of using that heat-beam. He knew by now that they would not kill him unless he started the gunplay himself, and he did not mean to give up his life for any girl alive. But a severe mauling he expected, and he braced himself instinctively as the mob heaved within itself.

To his astonishment a thing happened then that he had never known to happen before. At his shouted defiance the foremost of the mob—those who had heard him clearly—drew back a little, not in alarm but evidently surprised. The ex-Patrolman said, "Yours! She's *yours?*" in a voice from which puzzlement crowded out the anger.

Smith spread his booted legs wide before the crouching figure and flourished his gun.

"Yes," he said. "And I'm keeping her! Stand back there!"

The man stared at him wordlessly, and horror, disgust and incredulity mingled on his weather-beaten face. The incredulity triumphed for a moment and he said again,

"Yours!"

Smith nodded defiance.

The man stepped back suddenly, unutterable contempt in his very pose. He waved an arm to the crowd and said loudly, "It's—his!" and the press melted away, gone silent, too, and the look of contempt spread from face to face.

The ex-Patrolman spat on the slag-paved street and turned his back indifferently. "Keep her, then," he advised briefly over one shoulder. "But don't let her out again in this town!"

Smith stared in perplexity almost open-mouthed as the suddenly scornful mob began to break up. His mind was in a whirl. That such bloodthirsty animosity should vanish in a breath he could not believe. And the curious mingling of contempt and disgust on the faces he saw baffled him even more. Lakkdarol was anything but a puritan town—it did not enter his head for a moment that his claiming the brown girl as his own had caused that strangely shocked revulsion to spread through the crowd. No, it was something more deeply-rooted than that. Instinctive, instant disgust had been in the faces he saw—they would have looked less so if he had admitted cannibalism or *Pharol*-worship.

And they were leaving his vicinity as swiftly as if whatever unknowing sin he had committed were contagious. The street was emptying as rapidly as it had filled. He saw a sleek Venusian glance back over his shoulder as he turned the corner and sneer, "Shambleau!" and the word awoke a new line of speculation in Smith's mind. Shambleau! Vaguely of French origin, it must be. And strange enough to hear it from the lips of Venusians and Martian drylanders, but it was their use of it that puzzled him more. "We never let those things live," the ex-Patrolman had said. It reminded him dimly of something . . . an ancient line from some writing in his own tongue . . . "Thou shalt not suffer a witch to live." He smiled to himself at the similarity, and simultaneously was aware of the girl at his elbow.

She had risen soundlessly. He turned to face her, sheathing his gun, and stared at first with curiosity and then in the entirely frank openness with which men regard that which is not wholly human. For she was not. He knew it at a glance, though the brown, sweet body was shaped like a woman's and she wore the garment of scarlet—he saw it was leather—with an ease that few unhuman beings achieve toward clothing. He knew it from the moment he looked into her eyes, and a shiver of unrest went over him as he met them. They were frankly green as young grass, with slit-like, feline pupils that pulsed unceasingly, and there was a look of dark, animal wisdom in their depths—that look of the beast which sees more than man.

There was no hair upon her face—neither brows nor lashes, and he would have sworn that the tight scarlet turban bound around her head covered baldness. She had three fingers and a thumb, and her feet had four digits apiece too, and all sixteen of them were tipped with round claws that sheathed back into the flesh like a cat's. She ran her tongue over her lips—a thin, pink, flat tongue as feline as her eyes—and spoke with difficulty. He felt that that throat and tongue had never been shaped for human speech.

"Not—afraid now," she said softly, and her little teeth were white and pointed as a kitten's.

"What did they want you for?" he asked her curiously. "What had you done? Shambleau . . . is that your name?"

"I—not talk your—speech," she demurred hesitantly.

"Well, try to—I want to know. Why were they chasing you? Will you be safe on the street now, or hadn't you better get indoors somewhere? They looked dangerous."

"I—go with you." She brought it out with difficulty.

"Say you!" Smith grinned. "What are you, anyhow? You look like a kitten to me."

"Shambleau." She said it somberly.

"Where d'you live? Are you a Martian?"

"I come from—from far—from long ago—far country———"

"Wait!" laughed Smith. "You're getting your wires crossed. You're not a Martian?"

She drew herself up very straight beside him, lifting the turbaned head, and there was something queenly in the poise of her.

"Martian?" she said scornfully. "My people—are—are—you have no word. Your speech—hard for me."

"What's yours? I might know it—try me."

She lifted her head and met his eyes squarely, and there was in hers a subtle amusement—he could have sworn it.

"Some day I—speak to you in—my own language," she promised, and the pink tongue flicked out over her lips, swiftly, hungrily.

Approaching footsteps on the red pavement interrupted Smith's reply. A dryland Martian came past, reeling a little and exuding an aroma of *segir*-whisky, the Venusian brand. When he caught the red flash of the girl's tatters he turned his head sharply, and as his *segir*-steeped brain took in the fact of her presence he lurched toward the recess unsteadily, bawling, "Shambleau, by *Pharol!* Shambleau!" and reached out a clutching hand.

Smith struck it aside contemptuously.

"On your way, drylander," he advised.

The man drew back and stared, blear-eyed.

"Yours, eh?" he croaked. "*Zut!* You're welcome to it!" And like the ex-Patrolman before him he spat on the pavement and turned away, muttering harshly in the blasphemous tongue of the drylands.

Smith watched him shuffle off, and there was a crease between his colorless eyes, a nameless unease rising within him.

"Come on," he said abruptly to the girl. "If this sort of thing is going to happen we'd better get indoors. Where shall I take you?"

"With—you," she murmured.

He stared down into the flat green eyes. Those ceaselessly pulsing pupils disturbed him, but it seemed to him, vaguely, that behind the animal shallows of her gaze was a shutter—a closed barrier that might at any moment open to reveal the very deeps of that dark knowledge he sensed there.

Roughly he said again, "Come on, then," and stepped down into the street.

She pattered along a pace or two behind him, making no effort to keep up with his long strides, and though Smith—as men know from Venus to Jupiter's moons—walks as softly as a cat, even in spacemen's boots, the girl at his heels slid like a shadow over the rough pavement, making so little sound that even the lightness of his footsteps was loud in the empty street.

Smith chose the less frequented ways of Lakkdarol, and somewhat shamefacedly thanked his nameless gods that his lodgings were not far away, for the few pedestrians he met turned and stared after the two with that by now familiar mingling of horror and contempt which he was as far as ever from understanding.

The room he had engaged was a single cubicle in a lodging-house on the edge of the city. Lakkdarol, raw camp-town that it was in those days, could have furnished little better anywhere within its limits, and Smith's errand there was not one he wished to advertise. He had slept in worse places than this before, and knew that he would do so again.

There was no one in sight when he entered, and the girl slipped up the stairs at his heels and vanished through the door, shadowy, unseen by anyone in the house. Smith closed the door and leaned his broad shoulders against the panels, regarding her speculatively.

She took in what little the room had to offer in a glance—frowsy bed, rickety table, mirror hanging unevenly and cracked against the wall, unpainted chairs—a typical camp-town room in an Earth settlement abroad. She accepted its poverty in that single glance, dismissed it, then crossed to the window and leaned out for a moment, gazing across the low roof-tops toward the barren countryside beyond, red slag under the late afternoon sun.

"You can stay here," said Smith abruptly, "until I leave town. I'm waiting here for a friend to come in from Venus. Have you eaten?"

"Yes," said the girl quickly. "I shall—need no—food for—a while."

"Well—" Smith glanced around the room. "I'll be in sometime

tonight. You can go or stay just as you please. Better lock the door behind me."

With no more formality than that he left her. The door closed and he heard the key turn, and smiled to himself. He did not expect, then, ever to see her again.

He went down the steps and out into the late-slanting sunlight with a mind so full of other matters that the brown girl receded very quickly into the background. Smith's errand in Lakkdarol, like most of his errands, is better not spoken of. Man lives as he must, and Smith's living was a perilous affair outside the law and ruled by the ray-gun only. It is enough to say that the shipping-port and its cargoes out-bound interested him deeply just now, and that the friend he awaited was Yarol the Venusian, in that swift little Edsel ship the *Maid* that can flash from world to world with a derisive speed that laughs at Patrol boats and leaves pursuers floundering in the ether far behind. Smith and Yarol and the *Maid* were a trinity that had caused the Patrol leaders much worry and many gray hairs in the past, and the future looked very bright to Smith himself that evening as he left his lodging-house.

Lakkdarol roars by night, as Earthmen's camp-towns have a way of doing on every planet where Earth's outposts are, and it was beginning lustily as Smith went down among the awakening lights toward the center of town. His business there does not concern us. He mingled with the crowds where the lights were brightest, and there was the click of ivory counters and the jingle of silver, and red *segir* gurgled invitingly from black Venusian bottles, and much later Smith strolled homeward under the moving moons of Mars, and if the street wavered a little under his feet now and then—why, that is only understandable. Not even Smith could drink red *segir* at every bar from the *Martian Lamb* to the *New Chicago* and remain entirely steady on his feet. But he found his way back with very little difficulty—considering—and spent a good five minutes hunting for his key before he remembered he had left it in the inner lock for the girl.

He knocked then, and there was no sound of footsteps from within, but in a few moments the latch clicked and the door swung open. She retreated soundlessly before him as he entered, and took up her favorite place against the window, leaning back on the sill and outlined against the starry sky beyond. The room was in darkness.

Smith flipped the switch by the door and then leaned back against the panels, steadying himself. The cool night air had sobered him a little, and his head was clear enough—liquor went to Smith's feet, not his head, or he would never have come this far along the lawless way he had chosen. He lounged against the door now and regarded the girl in the sudden glare of the bulbs, blinded a little as much at the scarlet of her clothing as at the light.

"So you stayed," he said.

"I—waited," she answered softly, leaning farther back against the sill and clasping the rough wood with slim, three-fingered hands, pale brown against the darkness.

"Why?"

She did not answer that, but her mouth curved into a slow smile. On a woman it would have been reply enough—provocative, daring. On Shambleau there was something pitiful and horrible in it—so human on the face of one half-animal. And yet . . . that sweet brown body curving so softly from the tatters of scarlet leather—the velvety texture of that brownness—the white-flashing smile. . . . Smith was aware of a stirring excitement within him. After all—time would be hanging heavy now until Yarol came. . . . Speculatively he allowed the steel-pale eyes to wander over her, with a slow regard that missed nothing. And when he spoke he was aware that his voice had deepened a little. . . .

"Come here," he said.

She came forward slowly, on bare clawed feet that made no sound on the floor, and stood before him with downcast eyes and mouth trembling in that pitifully human smile. He took her by the shoulders— velvety soft shoulders, of a creamy smoothness that was not the texture of human flesh. A little tremor went over her, perceptibly, at the contact of his hands. Northwest Smith caught his breath suddenly and dragged her to him . . . sweet yielding brownness in the circle of his arms . . . heard her own breath catch and quicken as her velvety arms closed about his neck. And then he was looking down into her face, very near, and the green animal eyes met his with the pulsing pupils and the flicker of—something—deep behind their shallows—and through the rising clamor of his blood, even as he stooped his lips to hers, Smith felt something deep within him shudder away—inexplicable, instinctive, revolted. What it might be he had no words to tell, but the very touch of her was suddenly loathsome—so soft and velvet and unhuman—and it might have been an animal's face that lifted itself to his mouth—the dark knowledge looked hungrily from the darkness of those slit pupils —and for a mad instant he knew that same wild, feverish revulsion he had seen in the faces of the mob. . . .

"God!" he gasped, a far more ancient invocation against evil than he realized, then or ever, and he ripped her arms from his neck, swung her away with such a force that she reeled half across the room. Smith fell back against the door, breathing heavily, and stared at her while the wild revolt died slowly within him.

She had fallen to the floor beneath the window, and as she lay there against the wall with bent head he saw, curiously, that her turban had slipped—the turban that he had been so sure covered baldness—and a lock of scarlet hair fell below the binding leather, hair as scarlet as her garment, as unhumanly red as her eyes were unhumanly green. He stared, and shook his head dizzily and stared again, for it seemed to him that the thick lock of crimson had moved, *squirmed* of itself against her cheek.

At the contact of it her hands flew up and she tucked it away with a very human gesture and then dropped her head again into her hands. And from the deep shadow of her fingers he thought she was staring up at him covertly.

Smith drew a deep breath and passed a hand across his forehead. The inexplicable moment had gone as quickly as it came—too swiftly for him to understand or analyze it. "Got to lay off the *segir,*" he told himself unsteadily. Had he imagined that scarlet hair? After all, she was no more than a pretty brown girl-creature from one of the many half-human races peopling the planets. No more than that, after all. A pretty little thing, but animal. . . . He laughed a little shakily.

"No more of that," he said. "God knows I'm no angel, but there's got to be a limit somewhere. Here." He crossed to the bed and sorted out a pair of blankets from the untidy heap, tossing them to the far corner of the room. "You can sleep there."

Wordlessly she rose from the floor and began to rearrange the blankets, the uncomprehending resignation of the animal eloquent in every line of her.

Smith had a strange dream that night. He thought he had awakened to a room full of darkness and moonlight and moving shadows, for the nearer moon of Mars was racing through the sky and everything on the planet below her was endued with a restless life in the dark. And something . . . some nameless, unthinkable *thing* . . . was coiled about his throat . . . something like a soft snake, wet and warm. It lay loose and light about his neck . . . and it was moving gently, very gently, with a soft, caressive pressure that sent little thrills of delight through every nerve and fiber of him, a perilous delight—beyond physical pleasure, deeper than joy of the mind. That warm softness was caressing the very roots of his soul with a terrible intimacy. The ecstasy of it left him weak, and yet he knew—in a flash of knowledge born of this impossible dream—that the soul should not be handled. . . . And with that knowledge a horror broke upon him, turning the pleasure into a rapture of revulsion, hateful, horrible—but still most foully sweet. He tried to lift his hands and tear the dream-monstrosity from his throat— tried but half-heartedly; for though his soul was revolted to its very deeps, yet the delight of his body was so great that his hands all but refused the attempt. But when at last he tried to lift his arms a cold shock went over him and he found that he could not stir . . . his body lay stony as marble beneath the blankets, a living marble that shuddered with a dreadful delight through every rigid vein.

The revulsion grew strong upon him as he struggled against the paralyzing dream—a struggle of soul against sluggish body—titanically, until the moving dark was streaked with blankness that clouded and closed about him at last and he sank back into the oblivion from which he had awakened.

Next morning, when the bright sunlight shining through Mars' clear thin air awakened him, Smith lay for a while trying to remember. The dream had been more vivid than reality, but he could not now quite recall . . . only that it had been more sweet and horrible than anything else in life. He lay puzzling for a while, until a soft sound from the corner aroused him from his thoughts and he sat up to see the girl lying in a catlike coil on her blankets, watching him with round, grave eyes. He regarded her somewhat ruefully.

"Morning," he said. "I've just had the devil of a dream. . . . Well, hungry?"

She shook her head silently, and he could have sworn there was a covert gleam of strange amusement in her eyes.

He stretched and yawned, dismissing the nightmare temporarily from his mind.

"What am I going to do with you?" he inquired, turning to more immediate matters. "I'm leaving here in a day or two and I can't take you along, you know. Where'd you come from in the first place?"

Again she shook her head.

"Not telling? Well, it's your own business. You can stay here until I give up the room. From then on you'll have to do your own worrying."

He swung his feet to the floor and reached for his clothes.

Ten minutes later, slipping the heat-gun into its holster at his thigh, Smith turned to the girl. "There's food-concentrate in that box on the table. It ought to hold you until I get back. And you'd better lock the door again after I've gone."

Her wide, unwavering stare was his only answer, and he was not sure she had understood, but at any rate the lock clicked after him as before, and he went down the steps with a faint grin on his lips.

The memory of last night's extraordinary dream was slipping from him, as such memories do, and by the time he had reached the street the girl and the dream and all of yesterday's happenings were blotted out by the sharp necessities of the present.

Again the intricate business that had brought him here claimed his attention. He went about it to the exclusion of all else, and there was a good reason behind everything he did from the moment he stepped out into the street until the time when he turned back again at evening; though had one chosen to follow him during the day his apparently aimless rambling through Lakkdarol would have seemed very pointless.

He must have spent two hours at the least idling by the space-port, watching with sleepy, colorless eyes the ships that came and went, the passengers, the vessels lying at wait, the cargoes—particularly the cargoes. He made the rounds of the town's saloons once more, consuming many glasses of varied liquors in the course of the day and engaging in idle conversation with men of all races and worlds, usually in their own languages, for Smith was a linguist of repute among his contemporaries. He heard the gossip of the spaceways, news from a dozen planets of a thousand different events. He heard the latest joke about the Venusian Emperor and the latest report on the Chino-Aryan war and the latest song hot from the lips of Rose Robertson, whom every man on the civilized planets adored as "the Georgia Rose." He passed the day quite profitably, for his own purposes, which do not concern us now, and it was not until late evening, when he turned homeward again, that the thought of the brown girl in his room took definite shape in his mind, though it had been lurking there, formless and submerged, all day.

He had no idea what comprised her usual diet, but he bought a can of New York roast beef and one of Venusian frog-broth and a dozen fresh canal-apples and two pounds of that Earth lettuce that grows so vigorously in the fertile canal-soil of Mars. He felt that she must surely find something to her liking in this broad variety of edibles, and—for his day had been very satisfactory—he hummed *The Green Hills of Earth* to himself in a surprisingly good baritone as he climbed the stairs.

The door was locked, as before, and he was reduced to kicking the lower panels gently with his boot, for his arms were full. She opened the door with that softness that was characteristic of her and stood regarding him in the semi-darkness as he stumbled to the table with his load. The room was unlit again.

"Why don't you turn on the lights?" he demanded irritably after he had barked his shin on the chair by the table in an effort to deposit his burden there.

"Light and—dark—they are alike—to me," she murmured.

"Cat eyes, eh? Well, you look the part. Here, I've brought you some dinner. Take your choice. Fond of roast beef? Or how about a little frog-broth?"

She shook her head and backed away a step.

"No," she said. "I can not—eat your food."

Smith's brows wrinkled. "Didn't you have any of the food tablets?"

Again the red turban shook negatively.

"Then you haven't had anything for—why, more than twenty-four hours! You must be starved."

"Not hungry," she denied.

"What can I find for you to eat, then? There's time yet if I hurry. You've got to eat, child."

"I shall—eat," she said softly. "Before long—I shall—feed. Have no—worry."

She turned away then and stood at the window, looking out over the moonlit landscape as if to end the conversation. Smith cast her a puzzled glance as he opened the can of roast beef. There had been an odd undernote in that assurance that, undefinably, he did not like. And the girl had teeth and tongue and presumably a fairly human digestive system, to judge from her human form. It was nonsense for her to pretend that he could find nothing that she could eat. She must have had some of the food concentrate after all, he decided, prying up the thermos lid of the inner container to release the long-sealed savor of the hot meal inside.

"Well, if you won't eat you won't," he observed philosophically as he poured hot broth and diced beef into the dishlike lid of the thermos can and extracted the spoon from its hiding-place between the inner and outer receptacles. She turned a little to watch him as he pulled up a rickety chair and sat down to the food, and after a while the realization that her green gaze was fixed so unwinkingly upon him made the man nervous, and he said between bites of creamy canal-apple, "Why don't you try a little of this? It's good."

"The food—I eat is—better," her soft voice told him in its hesitant murmur, and again he felt rather than heard a faint undernote of unpleasantness in the words. A sudden suspicion struck him as he pondered on that last remark—some vague memory of horror-tales told about campfires in the past—and he swung round in the chair to look at her, a tiny, creeping fear unaccountably arising. There had been that in her words—in her unspoken words, that menaced. . . .

She stood up beneath his gaze demurely, wide green eyes with their pulsing pupils meeting his without a falter. But her mouth was scarlet and her teeth were sharp. . . .

"What food do you eat?" he demanded. And then, after a pause, very softly, "Blood?"

She stared at him for a moment, uncomprehending; then something like amusement curled her lips and she said scornfully, "You think me—vampire, eh? No—I am Shambleau!"

Unmistakably there were scorn and amusement in her voice at the suggestion, but as unmistakably she knew what he meant—accepted it as a logical suspicion—vampires! Fairy tales—but fairy tales this unhuman, outland creature was most familiar with. Smith was not a credulous man, nor a superstitious one, but he had seen too many strange things himself to doubt that the wildest legend might have a basis of fact. And there was something namelessly strange about her. . . .

He puzzled over it for a while between deep bites of the canal-apple. And though he wanted to question her about a great many things, he did not, for he knew how futile it would be.

He said nothing more until the meat was finished and another canal-apple had followed the first, and he had cleared away the meal by the simple expedient of tossing the empty can out of the window. Then he lay back in the chair and surveyed her from half-closed eyes, colorless in a face tanned like saddle-leather. And again he was conscious of the brown, soft curves of her, velvety—subtle arcs and planes of smooth flesh under the tatters of scarlet leather. Vampire she might be, unhuman she certainly was, but desirable beyond words as she sat submissive beneath his low regard, her red-turbaned head bent, her clawed fingers lying in her lap. They sat very still for a while, and the silence throbbed between them.

She was so like a woman—an Earth woman—sweet and submissive and demure, and softer than soft fur, if he could forget the three-fingered claws and the pulsing eyes—and that deeper strangeness beyond words. . . . (Had he dreamed that red lock of hair that moved? Had it been *segir* that woke the wild revulsion he knew when he held her in his arms? Why had the mob so thirsted for her?) He sat and stared, and despite the mystery of her and the half-suspicions that thronged his mind—for she was so beautifully soft and curved under those revealing tatters—he slowly realized that his pulses were mounting, became aware of a kindling within . . . brown girl-creature with downcast eyes . . . and then the lids lifted and the green flatness of a cat's gaze met his, and last night's revulsion woke swiftly again, like a warning bell that clanged as their eyes met—animal, after all, too sleek and soft for humanity, and that inner strangeness. . . .

Smith shrugged and sat up. His failings were legion, but the weakness of the flesh was not among the major ones. He motioned the girl to her pallet of blankets in the corner and turned to his own bed.

From deeps of sound sleep he awoke much later. He awoke suddenly and completely, and with that inner excitement that presages something momentous. He awoke to brilliant moonlight, turning the room so bright that he could see the scarlet of the girl's rags as she sat up on her pallet. She was awake, she was sitting with her shoulder half turned to him and her head bent, and some warning instinct crawled coldly up his spine as he watched what she was doing. And yet it was a very ordinary thing for a girl to do—any girl, anywhere. She was unbinding her turban. . . .

He watched, not breathing, a presentiment of something horrible stirring in his brain, inexplicably. . . . The red folds loosened, and—he knew then that he had not dreamed—again a scarlet lock swung down against her cheek . . . a hair, was it? a lock of hair? . . . thick as a thick worm it fell, plumply, against that smooth cheek . . . more scarlet than blood and thick as a crawling worm . . . and like a worm it crawled.

Smith rose on an elbow, not realizing the motion, and fixed an unwinking stare, with a sort of sick, fascinated incredulity, on that—that lock of hair. He had not dreamed. Until now he had taken it for granted that it was the *segir* which had made it seem to move on that evening before. But now . . . it was lengthening, stretching, moving of itself. It must be hair, but it *crawled;* with a sickening life of its own it squirmed down against her cheek, caressingly, revoltingly, impossibly. . . . Wet, it was, and round and thick and shining. . . .

She unfastened the last fold and whipped the turban off. From what he saw then Smith would have turned his eyes away—and he had looked on dreadful things before, without flinching—but he could not stir. He could only lie there on his elbow staring at the mass of scarlet, squirming—worms, hairs, what?—that writhed over her head in a dreadful mockery of ringlets. And it was lengthening, falling, somehow growing before his eyes, down over her shoulders in a spilling cascade, a mass that even at the beginning could never have been hidden under the skull-tight turban she had worn. He was beyond wondering, but he realized that. And still it squirmed and lengthened and fell, and she shook it out in a horrible travesty of a woman shaking out her unbound hair—until the unspeakable tangle of it—twisting, writhing, obscenely scarlet—hung to her waist and beyond, and still lengthened, an endless mass of crawling horror that until now, somehow, impossibly, had been hidden under the tight-bound turban. It was like a nest of blind, restless red worms . . . it was—it was like naked entrails endowed with an unnatural aliveness, terrible beyond words.

Smith lay in the shadows, frozen without and within in a sick numbness that came of utter shock and revulsion.

She shook out the obscene, unspeakable tangle over her shoulders, and somehow he knew that she was going to turn in a moment and that he must meet her eyes. The thought of that meeting stopped his heart with dread, more awfully than anything else in this nightmare horror; for nightmare it must be, surely. But he knew without trying that he could not wrench his eyes away—the sickened fascination of that sight held him motionless, and somehow there was a certain beauty. . . .

Her head was turning. The crawling awfulnesses rippled and squirmed at the motion, writhing thick and wet and shining over the soft brown shoulders about which they fell now in obscene cascades that all but hid her body. Her head was turning. Smith lay numb. And very slowly he saw the round of her cheek foreshorten and her profile come into view, all the scarlet horrors twisting ominously, and the profile shortened in turn and her full face came slowly round toward the bed—moonlight shining brilliantly as day on the pretty girl-face, demure and sweet, framed in tangled obscenity that crawled. . . .

The green eyes met his. He felt a perceptible shock, and a shudder rippled down his paralyzed spine, leaving an icy numbness in its wake. He felt the goose-flesh rising. But that numbness and cold horror he scarcely realized, for the green eyes were locked with his in a long, long look that somehow presaged nameless things—not altogether unpleas-

ant things—the voiceless voice of her mind assailing him with little
murmurous promises. . . .

For a moment he went down into a blind abyss of submission; and
then somehow the very sight of that obscenity in eyes that did not then
realize they saw it, was dreadful enough to draw him out of the seductive darkness . . . the sight of her crawling and alive with unnamable
horror.

She rose, and down about her in a cascade fell the squirming scarlet of—of what grew upon her head. It fell in a long, alive cloak to her
bare feet on the floor, hiding her in a wave of dreadful, wet, writhing
life. She put up her hands and like a swimmer she parted the waterfall
of it, tossing the masses back over her shoulders to reveal her own
brown body, sweetly curved. She smiled exquisitely, and in starting
waves back from her forehead and down about her in a hideous background writhed the snaky wetness of her living tresses. And Smith
knew that he looked upon Medusa.

The knowledge of that—the realization of vast backgrounds reaching into misted history—shook him out of his frozen horror for a moment, and in that moment he met her eyes again, smiling, green as glass
in the moonlight, half hooded under drooping lids. Through the twisting scarlet she held out her arms. And there was something soul-shak-
ingly desirable about her, so that all the blood surged to his head suddenly and he stumbled to his feet like a sleeper in a dream as she swayed
toward him, infinitely graceful, infinitely sweet in her cloak of living
horror.

And somehow there was beauty in it, the wet scarlet writhings
with moonlight sliding and shining along the thick, worm-round tresses
and losing itself in the masses only to glint again and move silvery along
writhing tendrils—an awful, shuddering beauty more dreadful than any
ugliness could be.

But all this, again, he but half realized, for the insidious murmur
was coiling again through his brain, promising, caressing, alluring,
sweeter than honey; and the green eyes that held his were clear and
burning like the depths of a jewel, and behind the pulsing slits of darkness he was staring into a greater dark that held all things. . . . He
had known—dimly he had known when he first gazed into those flat
animal shallows that behind them lay this—all beauty and terror, all
horror and delight, in the infinite darkness upon which her eyes opened
like windows, paned with emerald glass.

Her lips moved, and in a murmur that blended indistinguishably with the silence and the sway of her body and the dreadful sway of her —her hair—she whispered—very softly, very passionately, "I shall—speak to you now—in my own tongue—oh, beloved!"

And in her living cloak she swayed to him, the murmur swelling seductive and caressing in his innermost brain—promising, compelling, sweeter than sweet. His flesh crawled to the horror of her, but it was a perverted revulsion that clasped what it loathed. His arms slid round her under the sliding cloak, wet, wet and warm and hideously alive—and the sweet velvet body was clinging to his, her arms locked about his neck—and with a whisper and a rush the unspeakable horror closed about them both.

In nightmares until he died he remembered that moment when the living tresses of Shambleau first folded him in their embrace. A nauseous, smothering odor as the wetness shut around him—thick, pulsing worms clasping every inch of his body, sliding, writhing, their wetness and warmth striking through his garments as if he stood naked to their embrace.

All this in a graven instant—and after that a tangled flash of conflicting sensation before oblivion closed over him. For he remembered the dream—and knew it for nightmare reality now, and the sliding, gently moving caresses of those wet, warm worms upon his flesh was an ecstasy above words—that deeper ecstasy that strikes beyond the body and beyond the mind and tickles the very roots of the soul with unnatural delight. So he stood, rigid as marble, as helplessly stony as any of Medusa's victims in ancient legends were, while the terrible pleasure of Shambleau thrilled and shuddered through every fiber of him; through every atom of his body and the intangible atoms of what men call the soul, through all that was Smith the dreadful pleasure ran. And it was truly dreadful. Dimly he knew it, even as his body answered to the root-deep ecstasy, a foul and dreadful wooing from which his very soul shuddered away—and yet in the innermost depths of that soul some grinning traitor shivered with delight. But deeply, behind all this, he knew horror and revulsion and despair beyond telling, while the intimate caresses crawled obscenely in the secret places of his soul—knew that the soul should not be handled—and shook with the perilous pleasure through it all.

And this conflict and knowledge, this mingling of rapture and revulsion all took place in the flashing of a moment while the scarlet worms coiled and crawled upon him, sending deep, obscene tremors of that infinite pleasure into every atom that made up Smith. And he could

not stir in that slimy, ecstatic embrace—and a weakness was flooding
that grew deeper after each succeeding wave of intense delight, and the
traitor in his soul strengthened and drowned out the revulsion—and
something within him ceased to struggle as he sank wholly into a blaz-
ing darkness that was oblivion to all else but that devouring rapture. . . .

The young Venusian climbing the stairs to his friend's lodging-
room pulled out his key absent-mindedly, a pucker forming between his
fine brows. He was slim, as all Venusians are, as fair and sleek as any of
them, and as with most of his countrymen the look of cherubic innocence on his face was wholly deceptive. He had the face of a fallen
angel, without Lucifer's majesty to redeem it; for a black devil grinned
in his eyes and there were faint lines of ruthlessness and dissipation
about his mouth to tell of the long years behind him that had run the
gamut of experiences and made his name, next to Smith's, the most
hated and the most respected in the records of the Patrol.

He mounted the stairs now with a puzzled frown between his eyes.
He had come into Lakkdarol on the noon liner—the *Maid* in her hold
very skillfully disguised with paint and otherwise—to find in lamentable
disorder the affairs he had expected to be settled. And cautious inquiry
elicited the information that Smith had not been seen for three days.
That was not like his friend—he had never failed before, and the two
stood to lose not only a large sum of money but also their personal
safety by the inexplicable lapse on the part of Smith. Yarol could think
of one solution only: fate had at last caught up with his friend. Nothing
but physical disability could explain it.

Still puzzling, he fitted his key in the lock and swung the door
open.

In that first moment, as the door opened, he sensed something very
wrong. . . . The room was darkened, and for a while he could see
nothing, but at the first breath he scented a strange, unnamable odor,
half sickening, half sweet. And deep stirrings of ancestral memory
awoke within him—ancient swamp-born memories from Venusian ancestors far away and long ago. . . .

Yarol laid his hand on his gun, lightly, and opened the door wider.
In the dimness all he could see at first was a curious mound in the far
corner. . . . Then his eyes grew accustomed to the dark, and he saw it
more clearly, a mound that somehow heaved and stirred within itself.
. . . A mound of—he caught his breath sharply—a mound like a mass

of entrails, living, moving, writhing with an unspeakable aliveness. Then a hot Venusian oath broke from his lips and he cleared the door-sill in a swift stride, slammed the door and set his back against it, gun ready in his hand, although his flesh crawled—for he *knew*. . . .

"Smith!" he said softly, in a voice thick with horror. "Northwest!"

The moving mass stirred—shuddered—sank back into crawling quiescence again.

"Smith! Smith!" The Venusian's voice was gentle and insistent, and it quivered a little with terror.

An impatient ripple went over the whole mass of aliveness in the corner. It stirred again, reluctantly, and then tendril by writhing tendril it began to part itself and fall aside, and very slowly the brown of a spaceman's leather appeared beneath it, all slimed and shining.

"Smith! Northwest!" Yarol's persistent whisper came again, ur-gently, and with a dreamlike slowness the leather garments moved . . . a man sat up in the midst of the writhing worms, a man who once, long ago, might have been Northwest Smith. From head to foot he was slimy from the embrace of the crawling horror about him. His face was that of some creature beyond humanity—dead-alive, fixed in a gray stare, and the look of terrible ecstasy that overspread it seemed to come from somewhere far within, a faint reflection from immeasurable distances beyond the flesh. And as there is mystery and magic in the moonlight which is after all but a reflection of the everyday sun, so in that gray face turned to the door was a terror unnamable and sweet, a reflection of ecstasy beyond the understanding of any who have known only earthly ecstasy themselves. And as he sat there turning a blank, eyeless face to Yarol the red worms writhed ceaselessly about him, very gently, with a soft, caressive motion that never slacked.

"Smith . . . come here! Smith . . . get up . . . Smith, Smith!" Yarol's whisper hissed in the silence, commanding, urgent—but he made no move to leave the door.

And with a dreadful slowness, like a dead man rising, Smith stood up in the nest of slimy scarlet. He swayed drunkenly on his feet, and two or three crimson tendrils came writhing up his legs to the knees and wound themselves there, supportingly, moving with a ceaseless caress that seemed to give him some hidden strength, for he said then, without inflection,

"Go away. Go away. Leave me alone." And the dead ecstatic face never changed.

"Smith!" Yarol's voice was desperate. "Smith, listen! Smith, can't you hear me?"

"Go away," the monotonous voice said. "Go away. Go away. Go—"

"Not unless you come too. Can't you hear? Smith! Smith! I'll—"

He hushed in mid-phrase, and once more the ancestral prickle of race-memory shivered down his back, for the scarlet mass was moving again, violently, rising. . . .

Yarol pressed back against the door and gripped his gun, and the name of a god he had forgotten years ago rose to his lips unbidden. For he knew what was coming next, and the knowledge was more dreadful than any ignorance could have been.

The red, writhing mass rose higher, and the tendrils parted and a human face looked out—no, half human, with green cat-eyes that shone in that dimness like lighted jewels, compellingly. . . .

Yarol breathed "Shar!" again, and flung up an arm across his face, and the tingle of meeting that green gaze for even an instant went thrilling through him perilously.

"Smith!" he called in despair. "Smith, can't you hear me?"

"Go away," said that voice that was not Smith's. "Go away."

And somehow, although he dared not look, Yarol knew that the—the other—had parted those worm-thick tresses and stood there in all the human sweetness of the brown, curved woman's body, cloaked in living horror. And he felt the eyes upon him, and something was crying insistently in his brain to lower that shielding arm. . . . He was lost—he knew it, and the knowledge gave him that courage which comes from despair. The voice in his brain was growing, swelling, deafening him with a roaring command that all but swept him before it—command to lower that arm—to meet the eyes that opened upon darkness—to submit—and a promise, murmurous and sweet and evil beyond words, of pleasure to come. . . .

But somehow he kept his head—somehow, dizzily, he was gripping his gun in his upflung hand—somehow, incredibly, crossing the narrow room with averted face, groping for Smith's shoulder. There was a moment of blind fumbling in emptiness, and then he found it, and gripped the leather that was slimy and dreadful and wet—and simultaneously he felt something loop gently about his ankle and a shock of repulsive pleasure went through him, and then another coil, and another, wound about his feet. . . .

Yarol set his teeth and gripped the shoulder hard, and his hand shuddered of itself, for the feel of that leather was slimy as the worms about his ankles, and a faint tingle of obscene delight went through him from the contact.

That caressive pressure on his legs was all he could feel, and the voice in his brain drowned out all other sounds, and his body obeyed him reluctantly—but somehow he gave one heave of tremendous effort and swung Smith, stumbling, out of that nest of horror. The twining tendrils ripped loose with a little sucking sound, and the whole mass quivered and reached after, and then Yarol forgot his friend utterly and turned his whole being to the hopeless task of freeing himself. For only a part of him was fighting, now—only a part of him struggled against the twining obscenities, and in his innermost brain the sweet, seductive murmur sounded, and his body clamored to surrender. . . .

"*Shar! Shar y'danis . . . Shar mor'la-rol—*" prayed Yarol, gasping and half unconscious that he spoke, boy's prayers that he had forgotten years ago, and with his back half turned to the central mass he kicked desperately with his heavy boots at the red, writhing worms about him. They gave back before him, quivering and curling themselves out of reach, and though he knew that more were reaching for his throat from behind, at least he could go on struggling until he was forced to meet those eyes. . . .

He stamped and kicked and stamped again, and for one instant he was free of the slimy grip as the bruised worms curled back from his heavy feet, and he lurched away dizzily, sick with revulsion and despair as he fought off the coils, and then he lifted his eyes and saw the cracked mirror on the wall. Dimly in its reflection he could see the writhing scarlet horror behind him, cat face peering out with its demure girl-smile, dreadfully human, and all the red tendrils reaching after him. And remembrance of something he had read long ago swept incongruously over him, and the gasp of relief and hope that he gave shook for a moment the grip of the command in his brain.

Without pausing for a breath he swung the gun over his shoulder, the reflected barrel in line with the reflected horror in the mirror, and flicked the catch.

In the mirror he saw its blue flame leap in a dazzling spate across the dimness, full into the midst of that squirming, reaching mass behind him. There was a hiss and a blaze and a high, thin scream of inhuman malice and despair—the flame cut a wide arc and went out as the gun fell from his hand, and Yarol pitched forward to the floor.

Northwest Smith opened his eyes to Martian sunlight streaming thinly through the dingy window. Something wet and cold was slapping his face, and the familiar fiery sting of *segir*-whisky burnt his throat.

"Smith!" Yarol's voice was saying from far away. "N. W.! Wake up, damn you! Wake up!"

"I'm—awake," Smith managed to articulate thickly. "Wha's matter?"

Then a cup-rim was thrust against his teeth and Yarol said irritably, "Drink it, you fool!"

Smith swallowed obediently and more of the fire-hot *segir* flowed down his grateful throat. It spread a warmth through his body that awakened him from the numbness that had gripped him until now, and helped a little toward driving out the all-devouring weakness he was becoming aware of slowly. He lay still for a few minutes while the warmth of the whisky went through him, and memory sluggishly began to permeate his brain with the spread of the *segir*. Nightmare memories . . . sweet and terrible . . . memories of—

"God!" gasped Smith suddenly, and tried to sit up. Weakness smote him like a blow, and for an instant the room wheeled as he fell back against something firm and warm—Yarol's shoulder. The Venusian's arm supported him while the room steadied, and after a while he twisted a little and stared into the other's black gaze.

Yarol was holding him with one arm and finishing the mug of *segir* himself, and the black eyes met his over the rim and crinkled into sudden laughter, half hysterical after that terror that was passed.

"By *Pharol!*" gasped Yarol, choking into his mug. "By *Pharol*, N. W.! I'm never gonna let you forget this! Next time you have to drag me out of a mess I'll say—"

"Let it go," said Smith. "What's been going on? How—"

"Shambleau." Yarol's laughter died. "Shambleau! What were you doing with a thing like that?"

"What was it?" Smith asked soberly.

"Mean to say you didn't know? But where'd you find it? How—"

"Suppose you tell me first what you know," said Smith firmly. "And another swig of that *segir*, too, please. I need it."

"Can you hold the mug now? Feel better?"

"Yeah—some. I can hold it—thanks. Now go on."

"Well—I don't know just where to start. They call them Shambleau—"

"Good God, is there more than one?"

"It's a—a sort of race, I think, one of the very oldest. Where they come from nobody knows. The name sounds a little French, doesn't it? But it goes back beyond the start of history. There have always been Shambleau."

"I never heard of 'em."

"Not many people have. And those who know don't care to talk about it much."

"Well, half this town knows. I hadn't any idea what they were talking about, then. And I still don't understand, but—"

"Yes, it happens like this, sometimes. They'll appear, and the news will spread and the town will get together and hunt them down, and after that—well, the story doesn't get around very far. It's too—too unbelievable."

"But—my God, Yarol!—what was it? Where'd it come from? How—"

"Nobody knows just where they come from. Another planet— maybe some undiscovered one. Some say Venus—I know there are some rather awful legends of them handed down in our family—that's how I've heard about it. And the minute I opened that door, awhile back—I —I think I knew that smell. . . ."

"But—what *are* they?"

"God knows. Not human, though they have the human form. Or that may be only an illusion . . . or maybe I'm crazy. I don't know. They're a species of the vampire—or maybe the vampire is a species of —of them. Their normal form must be that—that mass, and in that form they draw nourishment from the—I suppose the life-forces of men. And they take some form—usually a woman form, I think, and key you up to the highest pitch of emotion before they—begin. That's to work the life-force up to intensity so it'll be easier. . . . And they give, always, that horrible, foul pleasure as they—feed. There are some men who, if they survive the first experience, take to it like a drug—can't give it up—keep the thing with them all their lives—which isn't long— feeding it for that ghastly satisfaction. Worse than smoking *ming* or—or 'praying to *Pharol.*' "

"Yes," said Smith. "I'm beginning to understand why that crowd was so surprised and—and disgusted when I said—well, never mind. Go on."

"Did you get to talk to—to it?" asked Yarol.

"I tried to. It couldn't speak very well. I asked it where it came from and it said—'from far away and long ago'—something like that."

"I wonder. Possibly some unknown planet—but I think not. You know there are so many wild stories with some basis of fact to start from, that I've sometimes wondered—mightn't there be a lot more of even worse and wilder superstitions we've never even heard of? Things like this, blasphemous and foul, that those who know have to keep still about? Awful, fantastic things running around loose that we never hear rumors of at all!

"These things—they've been in existence for countless ages. No one knows when or where they first appeared. Those who've seen them, as we saw this one, don't talk about it. It's just one of those vague, misty rumors you find half hinted at in old books sometimes. . . . I believe they are an older race than man, spawned from ancient seed in times before ours, perhaps on planets that have gone to dust, and so horrible to man that when they are discovered the discoverers keep still about it —forget them again as quickly as they can.

"And they go back to time immemorial. I suppose you recognized the legend of Medusa? There isn't any question that the ancient Greeks knew of them. Does it mean that there have been civilizations before yours that set out from Earth and explored other planets? Or did one of the Shambleau somehow make its way into Greece three thousand years ago? If you think about it long enough you'll go off your head! I wonder how many other legends are based on things like this—things we don't suspect, things we'll never know.

"The Gorgon, Medusa, a beautiful woman with—with snakes for hair, and a gaze that turned men to stone, and Perseus finally killed her —I remembered this just by accident, N. W., and it saved your life and mine—Perseus killed her by using a mirror as he fought to reflect what he dared not look at directly. I wonder what the old Greek who first started that legend would have thought if he'd known that three thousand years later his story would save the lives of two men on another planet. I wonder what that Greek's own story was, and how he met the thing, and what happened. . . .

"Well, there's a lot we'll never know. Wouldn't the records of that race of—of *things*, whatever they are, be worth reading! Records of other planets and other ages and all the beginnings of mankind! But I don't suppose they've kept any records. I don't suppose they've even any place to keep them—from what little I know, or anyone knows about it, they're like the Wandering Jew, just bobbing up here and there

at long intervals, and where they stay in the meantime I'd give my eyes
to know! But I don't believe that terribly hypnotic power they have
indicates any superhuman intelligence. It's their means of getting food
—just like a frog's long tongue or a carnivorous flower's odor. Those
are physical because the frog and the flower eat physical food. The
Shambleau uses a—a mental reach to get mental food. I don't quite
know how to put it. And just as a beast that eats the bodies of other
animals acquires with each meal greater power over the bodies of the
rest, so the Shambleau, stoking itself up with the life-forces of men,
increases its power over the minds and the souls of other men. But I'm
talking about things I can't define—things I'm not sure exist.

"I only know that when I felt—when those tentacles closed around
my legs—I didn't want to pull loose, I felt sensations that—that—oh,
I'm fouled and filthy to the very deepest part of me by that—pleasure—
and yet—"

"I know," said Smith slowly. The effect of the *segir* was beginning
to wear off, and weakness was washing back over him in waves, and
when he spoke he was half meditating in a low voice, scarcely realizing
that Yarol listened. "I know it—much better than you do—and there's
something so indescribably awful that the thing emanates, something so
utterly at odds with everything human—there aren't any words to say
it. For a while I was a part of it, literally, sharing its thoughts and
memories and emotions and hungers, and—well, it's over now and I
don't remember very clearly, but the only part left free was that part of
me that was but insane from the—the obscenity of the thing. And yet it
was a pleasure so sweet—I think there must be some nucleus of utter
evil in me—in everyone—that needs only the proper stimulus to get
complete control; because even while I was sick all through from the
touch of those—things—there was something in me that was—was simply gibbering with delight. . . . Because of that I saw things—and
knew things—horrible, wild things I can't quite remember—visited unbelievable places, looked backward through the memory of that—creature—I was one with, and saw—God, I wish I could remember!"

"You ought to thank your God you can't," said Yarol soberly.

His voice roused Smith from the half-trance he had fallen into, and
he rose on his elbow, swaying a little from weakness. The room was
wavering before him, and he closed his eyes, not to see it, but he asked,
"You say they—they don't turn up again? No way of finding—another?"

Yarol did not answer for a moment. He laid his hands on the other man's shoulders and pressed him back, and then sat staring down into the dark, ravaged face with a new, strange, undefinable look upon it that he had never seen there before—whose meaning he knew, too well.

"Smith," he said finally, and his black eyes for once were steady and serious, and the little grinning devil had vanished from behind them, "Smith, I've never asked your word on anything before, but I've —I've earned the right to do it now, and I'm asking you to promise me one thing."

Smith's colorless eyes met the black gaze unsteadily. Irresolution was in them, and a little fear of what that promise might be. And for just a moment Yarol was looking, not into his friend's familiar eyes, but into a wide gray blankness that held all horror and delight—a pale sea with unspeakable pleasures sunk beneath it. Then the wide stare focused again and Smith's eyes met his squarely and Smith's voice said, "Go ahead. I'll promise."

"That if you ever should meet a Shambleau again—ever, anywhere —you'll draw your gun and burn it to hell the instant you realize what it is. Will you promise me that?"

There was a long silence. Yarol's somber black eyes bored relentlessly into the colorless ones of Smith, not wavering. And the veins stood out on Smith's tanned forehead. He never broke his word—he had given it perhaps half a dozen times in his life, but once he had given it, he was incapable of breaking it. And once more the gray seas flooded in a dim tide of memories, sweet and horrible beyond dreams. Once more Yarol was staring into blankness that hid nameless things. The room was very still.

The gray tide ebbed. Smith's eyes, pale and resolute as steel, met Yarol's levelly.

"I'll—try," he said. And his voice wavered.

CARL JACOBI *(born 1908) made his professional debut in* Weird Tales *magazine in 1932 with a short story that had previously won a University of Minnesota literary contest. Thereafter, he became a frequent contributor to* Weird Tales, Thrilling Mystery, *and other pulp magazines and anthologies. After pursuing a career as a journalist for part of his life, Jacobi continues writing "weird" fiction after more than half a century. His latest collection of stories,* Disclosures in Scarlet, *was published in 1972.*

"Revelations in Black," his best-known story, appeared in Weird Tales *in April 1933.*

Revelations in Black (1933)

BY CARL JACOBI

It was a dreary, forlorn establishment way down on Harbor Street. An old sign announced the legend: "Giovanni Larla—Antiques," and a dingy window revealed a display half masked in dust.

Even as I crossed the threshold that cheerless September afternoon, driven from the sidewalk by a gust of rain and perhaps a fascination for all antiques, the gloominess fell upon me like a material pall. Inside was half darkness, piled boxes and a monstrous tapestry, frayed with the warp showing in worn places. An Italian Renaissance wine cabinet shrank despondently in its corner and seemed to frown at me as I passed.

"Good afternoon, *Signor*. There is something you wish to buy? A picture, a ring, a vase perhaps?"

I peered at the squat bulk of the Italian proprietor there in the shadows and hesitated.

"Just looking around," I said, turning to the jumble about me. "Nothing in particular. . . ."

The man's oily face moved in smile as though he had heard the remark a thousand times before. He sighed, stood there in thought a moment, the rain drumming and swishing against the outer pane. Then very deliberately he stepped to the shelves and glanced up and down them considering. At length he drew forth an object which I perceived to be a painted chalice.

"An authentic Sixteenth Century Tandart," he murmured. "A work of art, *Signor.*"

I shook my head. "No pottery," I said. "Books perhaps, but no pottery."

He frowned slowly. "I have books too," he replied, "rare books which nobody sells but me, Giovanni Larla. But you must look at my other treasures too."

There was, I found, no hurrying the man. A quarter of an hour passed during which I had to see a Glycon cameo brooch, a carved chair of some indeterminate style and period, and a muddle of yellowed statuettes, small oils and one or two dreary Portland vases. Several times I glanced at my watch impatiently, wondering how I might break away from this Italian and his gloomy shop. Already the fascination of its dust and shadows had begun to wear off, and I was anxious to reach the street.

But when he had conducted me well toward the rear of the shop, something caught my fancy. I drew then from the shelf the first book of horror. If I had but known the events that were to follow, if I could only have had a foresight into the future that September day, I swear I would have avoided the book like a leprous thing, would have shunned that wretched antique store and the very street it stood on like places accursed. A thousand times I have wished my eyes had never rested on that cover in black. What writhings of the soul, what terrors, what unrest, what madness would have been spared me!

But never dreaming the secret of its pages I fondled it casually and remarked:

"An unusual book. What is it?"

Larla glanced up and scowled.

"That is not for sale," he said quietly. "I don't know how it got on these shelves. It was my poor brother's."

The volume in my hand was indeed unusual in appearance. Measuring but four inches across and five inches in length and bound in black velvet with each outside corner protected with a triangle of ivory, it was the most beautiful piece of book-binding I had ever seen. In the center of the cover was mounted a tiny piece of ivory intricately cut in the shape of a skull. But it was the title of the book that excited my interest. Embroidered in gold braid, the title read:

"Five Unicorns and a Pearl."

I looked at Larla. "How much?" I asked and reached for my wallet.

He shook his head. "No, it is not for sale. It is . . . it is the last work of my brother. He wrote it just before he died in the institution."

"The institution?"

Larla made no reply but stood staring at the book, his mind obviously drifting away in deep thought. A moment of silence dragged by. There was a strange gleam in his eyes when finally he spoke. And I thought I saw his fingers tremble slightly.

"My brother, Alessandro, was a fine man before he wrote that book," he said slowly. "He wrote beautifully, *Signor,* and he was strong and healthy. For hours I could sit while he read to me his poems. He was a dreamer, Alessandro; he loved everything beautiful, and the two of us were very happy.

"All . . . until that terrible night. Then he . . . but no . . . a year has passed now. It is best to forget." He passed his hand before his eyes and drew in his breath sharply.

"What happened?" I asked.

"Happened, *Signor?* I do not really know. It was all so confusing. He became suddenly ill, ill without reason. The flush of sunny Italy, which was always on his cheek, faded, and he grew white and drawn. His strength left him day by day. Doctors prescribed, gave medicines, but nothing helped. He grew steadily weaker until . . . until that night."

I looked at him curiously, impressed by his perturbation.

"And then—?"

Hands opening and closing, Larla seemed to sway unsteadily; his liquid eyes opened wide to the brows.

"And then . . . oh, if I could but forget! It was horrible. Poor Alessandro came home screaming, sobbing. He was . . . he was stark, raving mad!

"They took him to the institution for the insane and said he needed a complete rest, that he had suffered from some terrific mental shock. He . . . died three weeks later with the crucifix on his lips."

For a moment I stood there in silence, staring out at the falling rain. Then I said:

"He wrote this book while confined to the institution?"

Larla nodded absently.

"Three books," he replied. "Two others exactly like the one you have in your hand. The bindings he made, of course, when he was quite well. It was his original intention, I believe, to pen in them by hand the verses of Marini. He was very clever at such work. But the wanderings of his mind which filled the pages now, I have never read. Nor do I intend to. I want to keep with me the memory of him when he was happy. This book has come on these shelves by mistake. I shall put it with his other possessions."

My desire to read the few pages bound in velvet increased a thousand-fold when I found they were unobtainable. I have always had an interest in abnormal psychology and have gone through a number of books on the subject. Here was the work of a man confined in the asylum for the insane. Here was the unexpurgated writing of an educated brain gone mad. And unless my intuition failed me, here was a suggestion of some deep mystery. My mind was made up. I must have it.

I turned to Larla and chose my words carefully.

"I can well appreciate your wish to keep the book," I said, "and since you refuse to sell, may I ask if you would consider lending it to me for just one night? If I promised to return it in the morning? . . ."

The Italian hesitated. He toyed undecidedly with a heavy gold watch chain.

"No, I am sorry . . ."

"Ten dollars and back tomorrow unharmed."

Larla studied his shoe.

"Very well, *Signor,* I will trust you. But please, I ask you, please be sure and return it."

That night in the quiet of my apartment I opened the book. Immediately my attention was drawn to three lines scrawled in a feminine hand across the inside of the front cover, lines written in a faded red solution that looked more like blood than ink. They read:

"Revelations meant to destroy but only binding without the stake. Read, fool, and enter my field, for we are chained to the spot. Oh wo unto Larla."

I mused over these undecipherable sentences for some time without solving their meaning. At last, I turned to the first page and began the last work of Alessandro Larla, the strangest story I had ever in my years of browsing through old books, come upon.

"On the evening of the fifteenth of October I turned my steps into the cold and walked until I was tired. The roar of the present was in the distance when I came to twenty-six bluejays silently contemplating the ruins. Passing in the midst of them I wandered by the skeleton trees and seated myself where I could watch the leering fish. A child worshipped.

Glass threw the moon at me. Grass sang a litany at my feet. And the pointed shadow moved slowly to the left.

"I walked along the silver gravel until I came to five unicorns galloping beside water of the past. Here I found a pearl, a magnificent pearl, a pearl beautiful but black. Like a flower it carried a rich perfume, and once I thought the odor was but a mask, but why should such a perfect creation need a mask?

"I sat between the leering fish and the five galloping unicorns, and I fell madly in love with the pearl. The past lost itself in drabness and—"

I laid the book down and sat watching the smoke-curls from my pipe eddy ceilingward. There was much more, but I could make no sense of any of it. All was in that strange style and completely incomprehensible. And yet it seemed the story was more than the mere wanderings of a madman. Behind it all seemed to lie a narrative cloaked in symbolism.

Something about the few sentences had cast an immediate spell of depression over me. The vague lines weighed upon my mind, and I felt myself slowly seized by a deep feeling of uneasiness.

The air of the room grew heavy and close. The open casement and the out-of-doors seemed to beckon to me. I walked to the window, thrust the curtain aside, stood there, smoking furiously. Let me say that regular habits have long been a part of my make-up. I am not addicted to nocturnal strolls or late meanderings before seeking my bed; yet now, curiously enough, with the pages of the book still in my mind I suddenly experienced an indefinable urge to leave my apartment and walk the darkened streets.

I paced the room nervously. The clock on the mantel pushed its ticks slowly through the quiet. And at length I threw my pipe to the table, reached for my hat and coat and made for the door.

Ridiculous as it may sound, upon reaching the street I found that urge had increased to a distinct attraction. I felt that under no circumstances must I turn any direction but northward, and although this way led into a district quite unknown to me, I was in a moment pacing forward, choosing streets deliberately and heading without knowing why toward the outskirts of the city. It was a brilliant moonlight night in September. Summer had passed and already there was the smell of frosted vegetation in the air. The great chimes in Capitol tower were sounding midnight, and the buildings and shops and later the private houses were dark and silent as I passed.

Try as I would to erase from my memory the queer book which I had just read, the mystery of its pages hammered at me, arousing my curiosity. "Five Unicorns and a Pearl!" What did it all mean?

More and more I realized as I went on that a power other than my own will was leading my steps. Yet once when I did momentarily come to a halt that attraction swept upon me as inexorably as the desire for a narcotic.

It was far out on Easterly Street that I came upon a high stone wall flanking the sidewalk. Over its ornamented top I could see the shadows of a dark building set well back in the grounds. A wrought-iron gate in the wall opened upon a view of wild desertion and neglect. Swathed in the light of the moon, an old courtyard strewn with fountains, stone benches and statues lay tangled in rank weeds and undergrowth. The windows of the building, which evidently had once been a private dwelling, were boarded up, all except those on a little tower or cupola rising to a point in front. And here the glass caught the blue-gray light and refracted it into the shadows.

Before that gate my feet stopped like dead things. The psychic power which had been leading me had now become a reality. Directly from the courtyard it emanated, drawing me toward it with an intensity that smothered all reluctance.

Strangely enough, the gate was unlocked; and feeling like a man in a trance I swung the creaking hinges and entered, making my way along a grass-grown path to one of the benches. It seemed that once inside the court the distant sounds of the city died away, leaving a hollow silence broken only by the wind rustling through the tall dead weeds. Rearing up before me, the building with its dark wings, cupola and facade oddly resembled a colossal hound, crouched and ready to spring.

There were several fountains, weather-beaten and ornamented with curious figures, to which at the time I paid only casual attention. Farther on, half hidden by the underbrush, was the life-size statue of a little child kneeling in position of prayer. Erosion on the soft stone had disfigured the face, and in the half-light the carved features presented an expression strangely grotesque and repelling.

How long I sat there in the quiet, I don't know. The surroundings under the moonlight blended harmoniously with my mood. But more than that I seemed physically unable to rouse myself and pass on.

It was with a suddenness that brought me electrified to my feet that I became aware of the significance of the objects about me. Held motionless, I stood there running my eyes wildly from place to place, refusing to believe. Surely I must be dreaming. In the name of all that was unusual this . . . this absolutely couldn't be. And yet—

It was the fountain at my side that had caught my attention first. Across the top of the water basin were *five stone unicorns,* all identically carved, each seeming to follow the other in galloping procession. Looking farther, prompted now by a madly rising recollection, I saw that the cupola, towering high above the house, eclipsed the rays of the moon and threw *a long pointed shadow* across the ground *at my left.* The other fountain some distance away was ornamented with the figure of a stone fish, *a fish* whose empty eye-sockets *were leering* straight in my direction. And the climax of it all—the wall! At intervals of every three feet on the top of the street expanse were mounted crude carven stone shapes of birds. And counting them I saw that *those birds were twenty-six bluejays.*

Unquestionably—startling and impossible as it seemed—I was in the same setting as described in Larla's book! It was a staggering revelation, and my mind reeled at the thought of it. How strange, how odd that I should be drawn to a portion of the city I had never before frequented and thrown into the midst of a narrative written almost a year before!

I saw now that Alessandro Larla, writing as a patient in the institution for the insane, had seized isolated details but neglected to explain them. Here was a problem for the psychologist, the mad, the symbolic, the incredible story of the dead Italian. I was bewildered and I pondered for an answer.

As if to soothe my perturbation there stole into the court then a faint odor of perfume. Pleasantly it touched my nostrils, seemed to blend with the moonlight. I breathed it in deeply as I stood there by the fountain. But slowly that odor became more noticeable, grew stronger, a sickish sweet smell that began to creep down my lungs like smoke. Heliotrope! The honeyed aroma blanketed the garden, thickened the air.

And then came my second surprise of the evening. Looking about to discover the source of the fragrance I saw opposite me, seated on another stone bench, a woman. She was dressed entirely in black, and her face was hidden by a veil. She seemed unaware of my presence. Her head was slightly bowed, and her whole position suggested a person in deep contemplation.

I noticed also the thing that crouched by her side. It was a dog, a tremendous brute with a head strangely out of proportion and eyes as

large as the ends of big spoons. For several moments I stood staring at
the two of them. Although the air was quite chilly, the woman wore no
over-jacket, only the black dress relieved solely by the whiteness of her
throat.

With a sigh of regret at having my pleasant solitude thus disturbed
I moved across the court until I stood at her side. Still she showed no
recognition of my presence, and clearing my throat I said hesitatingly:

"I suppose you are the owner here. I . . . I really didn't know the
place was occupied, and the gate . . . well, the gate was unlocked. I'm
sorry I trespassed."

She made no reply to that, and the dog merely gazed at me in
dumb silence. No graceful words of polite departure came to my lips,
and I moved hesitatingly toward the gate.

"Please don't go," she said suddenly, looking up. "I'm lonely. Oh,
if you but knew how lonely I am!" She moved to one side on the bench
and motioned that I sit beside her. The dog continued to examine me
with its big eyes.

Whether it was the nearness of that odor of heliotrope, the suddenness of it all, or perhaps the moonlight, I did not know, but at her
words a thrill of pleasure ran through me, and I accepted the proffered
seat.

There followed an interval of silence, during which I puzzled for a
means to start conversation. But abruptly she turned to the beast and
said in German:

"Fort mit dir, Johann!"

The dog rose obediently to its feet and stole slowly off into the
shadows. I watched it for a moment until it disappeared in the direction
of the house. Then the woman said to me in English which was slightly
stilted and marked with an accent:

"It has been ages since I have spoken to anyone . . . We are
strangers. I do not know you, and you do not know me. Yet . . .
strangers sometimes find in each other a bond of interest. Supposing
. . . supposing we forget customs and formality of introduction? Shall
we?"

For some reason I felt my pulse quicken as she said that. "Please
do," I replied. "A spot like this is enough introduction in itself. Tell me,
do you live here?"

She made no answer for a moment, and I began to fear I had taken
her suggestion too quickly. Then she began slowly:

"My name is Perle von Mauren, and I am really a stranger to your country, though I have been here now more than a year. My home is in Austria near what is now the Czechoslovakian frontier. You see, it was to find my only brother that I came to the United States. During the war he was a lieutenant under General Mackensen, but in 1916, in April I believe it was, he . . . he was reported missing.

"War is a cruel thing. It took our money; it took our castle on the Danube, and then—my brother., Those following years were horrible. We lived always in doubt, hoping against hope that he was still living.

"Then after the Armistice a fellow officer claimed to have served next to him on grave-digging detail at a French prison camp near Monpré. And later came a thin rumor that he was in the United States. I gathered together as much money as I could and came here in search of him."

Her voice dwindled off, and she sat in silence staring at the brown weeds. When she resumed, her voice was low and wavering.

"I . . . found him . . . but would to God I hadn't! He . . . he was no longer living."

I stared at her. "Dead?" I asked.

The veil trembled as though moved by a shudder, as though her thoughts had exhumed some terrible event of the past. Unconscious of my interruption she went on:

"Tonight I came here—I don't know why—merely because the gate was unlocked, and there was a place of quiet within. Now have I bored you with my confidences and personal history?"

"Not at all," I replied. "I came here by chance myself. Probably the beauty of the place attracted me. I dabble in amateur photography occasionally and react strongly to unusual scenes. Tonight I went for a midnight stroll to relieve my mind from the bad effect of a book I was reading."

She made a strange reply to that, a reply away from our line of thought and which seemed an interjection that escaped her involuntarily.

"Books," she said, "are powerful things. They can fetter one more than the walls of a prison."

She caught my puzzled stare at the remark and added hastily: "It is odd that we should meet here."

For a moment I didn't answer. I was thinking of her heliotrope perfume, which for a woman of her apparent culture was applied in far too great a quantity to show good taste. The impression stole upon me that the perfume cloaked some secret, that if it were removed I should find . . . but what?

The hours passed, and still we sat there talking, enjoying each other's companionship. She did not remove her veil, and though I was burning with desire to see her features, I had not dared to ask her to. A strange nervousness had slowly seized me. The woman was a charming conversationalist, but there was about her an indefinable something which produced in me a distinct feeling of unease.

It was, I should judge, but a few moments before the first streaks of a dawn when it happened. As I look back now, even with mundane objects and thoughts on every side, it is not difficult to realize the significance of that vision. But at the time my brain was too much in a whirl to understand.

A thin shadow moving across the garden attracted my gaze once again into the night about me. I looked up over the spire of the deserted house and started as if struck by a blow. For a moment I thought I had seen a curious cloud formation racing low directly above me, a cloud black and impenetrable with two wing-like ends strangely in the shape of a monstrous flying bat.

I blinked my eyes hard and looked again.

"That cloud!" I exclaimed, "that strange cloud! . . . Did you see—"

I stopped and stared dumbly.

The bench at my side was empty. The woman had disappeared.

During the next day I went about my professional duties in the law office with only half interest, and my business partner looked at me queerly several times when he came upon me mumbling to myself. The incidents of the evening before were rushing through my mind. Questions unanswerable hammered at me. That I should have come upon the very details described by mad Larla in his strange book: the leering fish, the praying child, the twenty-six bluejays, the pointed shadow of the cupola—it was unexplainable; it was weird.

"Five Unicorns and a Pearl." The unicorns were the stone statues ornamenting the old fountain, yes—but the pearl? With a start I suddenly recalled the name of the woman in black: *Perle* von Mauren. What did it all mean?

Dinner had little attraction for me that evening. Earlier I had gone to the antique-dealer and begged him to loan me the sequel, the second volume of his brother Alessandro. When he had refused, objected because I had not yet returned the first book, my nerves had suddenly jumped on edge. I felt like a narcotic fiend faced with the realization that he could not procure the desired drug. In desperation, yet hardly knowing why, I offered the man more money, until at length I had come away, my powers of persuasion and my pocketbook successful.

The second volume was identical in outward respects to its predecessor except that it bore no title. But if I was expecting more disclosures in symbolism I was doomed to disappointment. Vague as "Five Unicorns and a Pearl" had been, the text of the sequel was even more wandering and was obviously only the ramblings of a mad brain. By watching the sentences closely I did gather that Alessandro Larla had made a second trip to his court of the twenty-six bluejays and met there again his "pearl."

There was the paragraph toward the end that puzzled me. It read: *"Can it possibly be? I pray that it is not. And yet I have seen it and heard it snarl. Oh, the loathsome creature! I will not, I will not believe it."*

I closed the book and tried to divert my attention elsewhere by polishing the lens of my newest portable camera. But again, as before, that same urge stole upon me, that same desire to visit the garden. I confess that I had watched the intervening hours until I would meet the woman in black again; for strangely enough, in spite of her abrupt exit before, I never doubted that she would be there waiting for me. I wanted her to lift the veil. I wanted to talk with her. I wanted to throw myself once again into the narrative of Larla's book.

Yet the whole thing seemed preposterous, and I fought the sensation with every ounce of will-power I could call to mind. Then it suddenly occurred to me what a remarkable picture she would make, sitting there on the stone bench, clothed in black, with the classic background of the old courtyard. If I could but catch the scene on a photographic plate. . . .

I halted my polishing and mused a moment. With a new electric flash-lamp, that handy invention which has supplanted the old mussy flash-powder, I could illuminate the garden and snap the picture with ease. And if the result were satisfactory it would make a worthy contribution to the International Camera Contest at Geneva next month.

The idea appealed to me, and gathering together the necessary equipment I drew on an ulster (for it was a wet, chilly night) and slipped out of my rooms and headed northward. Mad, unseeing fool that I was! If only I had stopped then and there, returned the book to the antique-dealer and closed the incident! But the strange magnetic attraction had gripped me in earnest, and I rushed headlong into the horror.

A fall rain was drumming the pavement, and the streets were deserted. Off to the east, however, the heavy blanket of clouds glowed with a soft radiance where the moon was trying to break through, and a strong wind from the south gave promise of clearing the skies before long. With my coat collar turned well up at the throat I passed once again into the older section of the town and down forgotten Easterly Street. I found the gate to the grounds unlocked as before, and the garden a dripping place masked in shadow.

The woman was not there. Still the hour was early, and I did not for a moment doubt that she would appear later. Gripped now with the enthusiasm of my plan, I set the camera carefully on the stone fountain, training the lens as well as I could on the bench where we had sat the previous evening. The flash-lamp with its battery handle I laid within easy reach.

Scarcely had I finished my arrangements when the crunch of gravel on the path caused me to turn. She was approaching the stone bench, heavily veiled as before and with the same sweeping black dress.

"You have come again," she said as I took my place beside her.

"Yes," I replied. "I could not stay away."

Our conversation that night gradually centered about her dead brother, although I thought several times that the woman tried to avoid the subject. He had been, it seemed, the black sheep of the family, had led more or less of a dissolute life and had been expelled from the University of Vienna not only because of his lack of respect for the pedagogues of the various sciences but also because of his queer unorthodox papers on philosophy. His sufferings in the war prison camp must have been intense. With a kind of grim delight she dwelt on his horrible experiences in the grave-digging detail which had been related to her by the fellow officer. But of the manner in which he had met his death she would say absolutely nothing.

Stronger than on the night before was the sweet smell of heliotrope. And again as the fumes crept nauseatingly down my lungs there came that same sense of nervousness, that same feeling that the perfume was hiding something I should know. The desire to see beneath the veil had become maddening by this time, but still I lacked the boldness to ask her to lift it.

Toward midnight the heavens cleared and the moon in splendid contrast shone high in the sky. The time had come for my picture.

"Sit where you are," I said. "I'll be back in a moment."

Stepping to the fountain I grasped the flash-lamp, held it aloft for an instant and placed my finger on the shutter lever of the camera. The woman remained motionless on the bench, evidently puzzled as to the meaning of my movements. The range was perfect. A click, and a dazzling white light enveloped the courtyard about us. For a brief second she was outlined there against the old wall. Then the blue moonlight returned, and I was smiling in satisfaction.

"It ought to make a beautiful picture," I said.

She leaped to her feet.

"Fool!" she cried hoarsely. "Blundering fool! What have you done?"

Even though the veil was there to hide her face I got the instant impression that her eyes were glaring at me, smouldering with hatred. I gazed at her curiously as she stood erect, head thrown back, body apparently taut as wire, and a slow shudder crept down my spine. Then without warning she gathered up her dress and ran down the path toward the deserted house. A moment later she had disappeared somewhere in the shadows of the giant bushes.

I stood there by the fountain, staring after her in a daze. Suddenly, off in the umbra of the house's facade there rose a low animal snarl.

And then before I could move, a huge gray shape came hurtling through the long weeds, bounding in great leaps straight toward me. It was the woman's dog, which I had seen with her the night before. But no longer was it a beast passive and silent. Its face was contorted in diabolic fury, and its jaws were dripping slaver. Even in that moment of terror as I stood frozen before it, the sight of those white nostrils and those black hyalescent eyes emblazoned itself on my mind, never to be forgotten.

Then with a lunge it was upon me. I had only time to thrust the flashlamp upward in half protection and throw my weight to the side. My arm jumped in recoil. The bulb exploded, and I could feel those teeth clamp down hard on the handle. Backward I fell, a scream gurgling to my lips, a terrific heaviness surging upon my body.

I struck out frantically, beat my fists into that growling face. My fingers groped blindly for its throat, sank deep into the hairy flesh. I could feel its very breath mingling with my own now, but desperately I hung on.

The pressure of my hands told. The dog coughed and fell back. And seizing that instant I struggled to my feet, jumped forward and planted a terrific kick straight into the brute's middle.

"*Fort mit dir, Johann!*" I cried, remembering the woman's German command.

It leaped back and, fangs bared, glared at me motionless for a moment. Then abruptly it turned and slunk off through the weeds.

Weak and trembling, I drew myself together, picked up my camera and passed through the gate toward home.

Three days passed. Those endless hours I spent confined to my apartment suffering the tortures of the damned.

On the day following the night of my terrible experience with the dog I realized I was in no condition to go to work. I drank two cups of strong black coffee and then forced myself to sit quietly in a chair, hoping to soothe my nerves. But the sight of the camera there on the table excited me to action. Five minutes later I was in the dark room arranged as my studio, developing the picture I had taken the night before. I worked feverishly, urged on by the thought of what an unusual contribution it would make for the amateur contest next month at Geneva, should the result be successful.

An exclamation burst from my lips as I stared at the still-wet print. There was the old garden clear and sharp with the bushes, the statue of the child, the fountain and the wall in the background, but the bench— the stone bench was empty. There was no sign, not even a blur of the woman in black.

I rushed the negative through a saturated solution of mercuric chloride in water, then treated it with ferrous oxalate. But even after this intensifying process the second print was like the first, focused in every detail, the bench standing in the foreground in sharp relief, but no trace of the woman.

She had been in plain view when I snapped the shutter. Of that I was positive. And my camera was in perfect condition. What then was wrong? Not until I had looked at the print hard in the daylight would I believe my eyes. No explanation offered itself, none at all; and at length, confused, I returned to my bed and fell into a heavy sleep.

Straight through the day I slept. Hours later I seemed to wake from a vague nightmare, and had not strength to rise from my pillow. A great physical faintness had overwhelmed me. My arms, my legs, lay like dead things. My heart was fluttering weakly. All was quiet, so still that the clock on my bureau ticked distinctly each passing second. The curtain billowed in the night breeze, though I was positive I had closed the casement when I entered the room.

And then suddenly I threw back my head and screamed! For slowly, slowly creeping down my lungs was that detestable odor of heliotrope!

Morning, and I found all was not a dream. My head was ringing, my hands trembling, and I was so weak I could hardly stand. The doctor I called in looked grave as he felt my pulse.

"You are on the verge of a complete collapse," he said. "If you do not allow yourself a rest it may permanently affect your mind. Take things easy for a while. And if you don't mind, I'll cauterize those two little cuts on your neck. They're rather raw wounds. What caused them?"

I moved my fingers to my throat and drew them away again tipped with blood.

"I . . . I don't know," I faltered.

He busied himself with his medicines, and a few minutes later reached for his hat.

"I advise that you don't leave your bed for a week at least," he said. "I'll give you a thorough examination then and see if there are any signs of anemia." But as he went out the door I thought I saw a puzzled look on his face.

Those subsequent hours allowed my thoughts to run wild once more. I vowed I would forget it all, go back to my work and never look upon the books again. But I knew I could not. The woman in black persisted in my mind, and each minute away from her became a torture. But more than that, if there had been a decided urge to continue my reading in the second book, the desire to see the third book, the last of the trilogy, was slowly increasing to an obsession.

At length I could stand it no longer, and on the morning of the third day I took a cab to the antique store and tried to persuade Larla to give me the third volume of his brother. But the Italian was firm. I had already taken two books, neither of which I had returned. Until I brought them back he would not listen. Vainly I tried to explain that one was of no value without the sequel and that I wanted to read the entire narrative as a unit. He merely shrugged his shoulders.

Cold perspiration broke out on my forehead as I heard my desire disregarded. I argued. I pleaded. But to no avail.

At length when Larla had turned the other way I seized the third book as I saw it lying on the shelf, slid it into my pocket and walked guiltily out. I made no apologies for my action. In the light of what developed later it may be considered a temptation inspired, for my will at the time was a conquered thing blanketed by that strange lure.

Back in my apartment I dropped into a chair and hastened to open the velvet cover. Here was the last chronicling of that strange series of events which had so completely become a part of my life during the past five days. Larla's volume three. Would all be explained in its pages? If so, what secret would be revealed?

With the light from a reading-lamp glaring full over my shoulder I opened the book, thumbed through it slowly, marveling again at the exquisite hand-printing. It seemed then as I sat there that an almost palpable cloud of quiet settled over me, muffling the distant sounds of the street. Something indefinable seemed to forbid me to read farther. Curiosity, that queer urge told me to go on. Slowly, I began to turn the pages, one at a time, from back to front.

Symbolism again. Vague wanderings with no sane meaning.

But suddenly my fingers stopped! My eyes had caught sight of the last paragraph on the last page, the final pennings of Alessandro Larla. I read, re-read, and read again those blasphemous words. I traced each word in the lamplight, slowly, carefully, letter for letter. Then the horror of it burst within me.

In blood-red ink the lines read:

"What shall I do? She has drained my blood and rotted my soul. My pearl is black as all evil. The curse be upon her brother, for it is he who made her thus. I pray the truth in these pages will destroy them for ever.

"Heaven help me, Perle von Mauren and her brother, Johann, are vampires!"

I leaped to my feet.

"Vampires!"

I clutched at the edge of the table and stood there swaying. Vampires! Those horrible creatures with a lust for human blood, taking the shape of men, of bats, of dogs.

The events of the past days rose before me in all their horror now, and I could see the black significance of every detail.

The brother, Johann—some time since the war he had become a vampire. When the woman sought him out years later he had forced this terrible existence upon her too.

With the garden as their lair the two of them had entangled poor Alessandro Larla in their serpentine coils a year before. He had loved the woman, had worshipped her. And then he had found the awful truth that had sent him stumbling home, raving mad.

Mad, yes, but not mad enough to keep him from writing the fact in his three velvet-bound books. He had hoped the disclosures would dispatch the woman and her brother for ever. But it was not enough.

I whipped the first book from the table and opened the cover. There again I saw those scrawled lines which had meant nothing to me before.

"Revelations meant to destroy but only binding without the stake. Read, fool, and enter my field, for we are chained to the spot. Oh, wo unto Larla!"

Perle von Mauren had written that. The books had not put an end to the evil life of her and her brother. No, only one thing could do that. Yet the exposures had not been written in vain. They were recorded for mortal posterity to see.

Those books bound the two vampires, Perle von Mauren, Johann, to the old garden, kept them from roaming the night streets in search of victims. Only him who had once passed through the gate could they pursue and attack.

It was the old metaphysical law: evil shrinking in the face of truth.

Yet if the books had found their power in chains they had also opened a new avenue for their attacks. Once immersed in the pages of the trilogy, the reader fell helplessly into their clutches. Those printed lines had become the outer reaches of their web. They were an entrapping net within which the power of the vampires always crouched.

That was why my life had blended so strangely with the story of Larla. The moment I had cast my eyes on the opening paragraph I had fallen into their coils to do with as they had done with Larla a year before. I had been drawn relentlessly into the tentacles of the woman in black. Once I was past the garden gate the binding spell of the books was gone, and they were free to pursue me and to—

A giddy sensation rose within me. Now I saw why the doctor had been puzzled. Now I saw the reason for my physical weakness. She had been—feasting on my blood! But if Larla had been ignorant of the one way to dispose of such a creature, I was not. I had not vacationed in south Europe without learning something of these ancient evils.

Frantically I looked about the room. A chair, a table, one of my cameras with its long tripod. I seized one of the wooden legs of the tripod in my hands, snapped it across my knee. Then, grasping the two broken pieces, both now with sharp splintered ends, I rushed hatless out of the door to the street.

A moment later I was racing northward in a cab bound for Easterly Street.

"Hurry!" I cried to the driver as I glanced at the westering sun. "Faster, do you hear?"

We shot along the cross-streets, into the old suburbs and toward the outskirts of town. Every traffic halt found me fuming at the delay. But at length we drew up before the wall of the garden.

I swung the wrought-iron gate open and with the wooden pieces of the tripod still under my arm, rushed in. The courtyard was a place of reality in the daylight, but the moldering masonry and tangled weeds were steeped in silence as before.

Straight for the house I made, climbing the rotten steps to the front entrance. The door was boarded up and locked. I retraced my steps and began to circle the south wall of the building. It was this direction I had seen the woman take when she had fled after I had tried to snap her picture. Well toward the rear of the building I reached a small half-open door leading to the cellar. Inside, cloaked in gloom, a narrow corridor stretched before me. The floor was littered with rubble and fallen masonry, the ceiling interlaced with a thousand cobwebs.

I stumbled forward, my eyes quickly accustoming themselves to the half-light from the almost opaque windows.

At the end of the corridor a second door barred my passage. I thrust it open—and stood swaying there on the sill staring inward.

Beyond was a small room, barely ten feet square, with a low-raftered ceiling. And by the light of the open door I saw side by side in the center of the floor—two white wood coffins.

How long I stood there leaning weakly against the stone wall I don't know. There was an odor drifting from out of that chamber. Heliotrope! But heliotrope defiled by the rotting smell of an ancient grave.

Then suddenly I leaped to the nearest coffin, seized its cover and ripped it open.

Would to heaven I could forget that sight that met my eyes. There lay the woman in black—unveiled.

That face—it was divinely beautiful, the hair black as sable, the cheeks a classic white. But the lips—! I grew suddenly sick as I looked upon them. They were scarlet . . . and sticky with human blood.

I reached for one of the tripod stakes, seized a flagstone from the floor and with the pointed end of the wood resting directly over the woman's heart, struck a crashing blow. The stake jumped downward. A violent contortion shook the coffin. Up to my face rushed a warm, nauseating breath of decay.

I wheeled and hurled open the lid of her brother's coffin. With only a glance at the young masculine Teutonic face I raised the other stake high in the air and brought it stabbing down with all the strength in my right arm.

In the coffins now, staring up at me from eyeless sockets, were two gray and moldering skeletons.

The rest is but a vague dream. I remember rushing outside, along the path to the gate and down Easterly, away from that accursed garden of the jays.

At length, utterly exhausted, I reached my apartment. Those mundane surroundings that confronted me were like balm to my eyes. But there centered into my gaze three objects lying where I had left them, the three volumes of Larla.

I turned to the grate on the other side of the room and flung the three of them onto the still glowing coals.

There was an instant hiss, and yellow flame streaked upward and began eating into the velvet. The fire grew higher . . . higher . . . and diminished slowly.

And as the last glowing spark died into a blackened ash there swept over me a mighty feeling of quiet and relief.

MANLY WADE WELLMAN *(1903–1986) was born in Portuguese West Africa, where his father was a medical officer. In the United States, Wellman was working as a reporter when he sold his first story to* Weird Tales *magazine in 1927. For several decades he was a frequent contributor to a wide range of pulp magazines. In addition, he wrote several works of history and biography, utilizing his extensive knowledge of American folklore.*

Wellman's well-beloved fantasy stories of John the Minstrel, he of the silver-stringed guitar, were first collected in Who Fears the Devil? *in 1963. Other stories are collected in two large volumes,* Worse Things Waiting *(1973) and* Lonely Vigils *(1981).*

"School for the Unspeakable" was first published in Weird Tales *in 1937.*

School for the Unspeakable (1937)

BY MANLY WADE WELLMAN

Bart Setwick dropped off the train at Carrington and stood for a moment on the station platform, an honest-faced, well-knit lad in tweeds. This little town and its famous school would be his home for the next eight months; but which way to the school? The sun had set, and he could barely see the shop signs across Carrington's modest main street. He hesitated, and a soft voice spoke at his very elbow:

"Are you for the school?"

Startled, Bart Setwick wheeled. In the gray twilight stood another youth, smiling thinly and waiting as if for an answer. The stranger was all of nineteen years old——that meant maturity to young Setwick, who was fifteen——and his pale face had shrewd lines to it. His tall, shambling body was clad in high-necked jersey and unfashionably tight trousers. Bart Setwick skimmed him with the quick, appraising eye of young America.

"I just got here," he replied. "My name's Setwick."

"Mine's Hoag." Out came a slender hand. Setwick took it and found it froggy-cold, with a suggestion of steel-wire muscles. "Glad to meet you. I came down on the chance someone would drop off the train. Let me give you a lift to the school."

Hoag turned away, felinely light for all his ungainliness, and led his new acquaintance around the corner of the little wooden railway station. Behind the structure, half hidden in its shadow, stood a shabby buggy with a lean bay horse in the shafts.

"Get in," invited Hoag, but Bart Setwick paused for a moment. His generation was not used to such vehicles. Hoag chuckled and said, "Oh, this is only a school wrinkle. We run to funny customs. Get in."

Setwick obeyed. "How about my trunk?"

"Leave it." The taller youth swung himself in beside Setwick and took the reins. "You'll not need it tonight."

He snapped his tongue and the bay horse stirred, drew them around and off down a bush-lined side road. Its hoofbeats were oddly muffled.

They turned a corner, another, and came into open country. The lights of Carrington, newly kindled against the night, hung behind like a constellation settled down to Earth. Setwick felt a hint of chill that did not seem to fit the September evening.

"How far is the school from town?" he asked.

"Four or five miles," Hoag replied in his hushed voice. "That was deliberate on the part of the founders—they wanted to make it hard for the students to get to town for larks. It forced us to dig up our own amusements." The pale face creased in a faint smile, as if this were a pleasantry. "There's just a few of the right sort on hand tonight. By the way, what did you get sent out for?"

Setwick frowned his mystification. "Why, to go to school. Dad sent me."

"But what for? Don't you know that this is a high-class prison prep? Half of us are lunkheads that need poking along, the other half are fellows who got in scandals somewhere else. Like me." Again Hoag smiled.

Setwick began to dislike his companion. They rolled a mile or so in silence before Hoag again asked a question:

"Do you go to church, Setwick?"

The new boy was afraid to appear priggish, and made a careless show with, "Not very often."

"Can you recite anything from the Bible?" Hoag's soft voice took on an anxious tinge.

"Not that I know of."

"Good," was the almost hearty response. "As I was saying, there's only a few of us at the school tonight—only three, to be exact. And we don't like Bible-quoters."

Setwick laughed, trying to appear sage and cynical. "Isn't Satan
reputed to quote the Bible to his own . . ."

"What do you know about Satan?" interrupted Hoag. He turned
full on Setwick, studying him with intent, dark eyes. Then, as if answering his own question: "Little enough, I'll bet. Would you like to know
about him?"

"Sure I would," replied Setwick, wondering what the joke would
be.

"I'll teach you after a while," Hoag promised cryptically, and silence fell again.

Half a moon was well up as they came in sight of a dark jumble of
buildings.

"Here we are," announced Hoag, and then, throwing back his
head, he emitted a wild, wordless howl that made Setwick almost jump
out of the buggy. "That's to let the others know we're coming," he
explained. "Listen!"

Back came a seeming echo of the howl, shrill, faint and eery. The
horse wavered in its muffled trot, and Hoag clucked it back into step.
They turned in at a driveway well grown up in weeds, and two minutes
more brought them up to the rear of the closest building. It was dim
gray in the wash of moonbeams, with blank inky rectangles for windows. Nowhere was there a light, but as the buggy came to a halt
Setwick saw a young head pop out of a window on the lower floor.

"Here already, Hoag?" came a high, ready voice.

"Yes," answered the youth at the reins, "and I've brought a new
man with me."

Thrilling a bit to hear himself called a man, Setwick alighted.

"His name's Setwick," went on Hoag. "Meet Andoff, Setwick. A
great friend of mine."

Andoff flourished a hand in greeting and scrambled out over the
windowsill. He was chubby and squat and even paler than Hoag, with a
low forehead beneath lank, wet-looking hair, and black eyes set wide
apart in a fat, stupid-looking face. His shabby jacket was too tight for
him, and beneath worn knickers his legs and feet were bare. He might
have been an overgrown thirteen or an undeveloped eighteen.

"Felcher ought to be along in half a second," he volunteered.

"Entertain Setwick while I put up the buggy," Hoag directed him.

Andoff nodded, and Hoag gathered the lines in his hands, but
paused for a final word.

"No funny business yet, Andoff," he cautioned seriously. "Setwick, don't let this lard-bladder rag you or tell you wild stories until I come back."

Andoff laughed shrilly. "No, no wild stories," he promised. "You'll do the talking, Hoag."

The buggy trundled away, and Andoff swung his fat, grinning face to the new arrival.

"Here comes Felcher," he announced. "Felcher, meet Setwick."

Another boy had bobbed up, it seemed, from nowhere. Setwick had not seen him come around the corner of the building, or slip out of a door or window. He was probably as old as Hoag, or older, but so small as to be almost a dwarf, and frail to boot. His most notable characteristic was his hairiness. A great mop covered his head, bushed over his neck and ears, and hung unkemptly to his bright, deep-set eyes. His lips and cheeks were spread with a rank down, and a curly thatch peeped through the unbuttoned collar of his soiled white shirt. The hand he offered Setwick was almost simian in its shagginess and in the hardness of its palm. Too, it was cold and damp. Setwick remembered the same thing of Hoag's handclasp.

"We're the only ones here so far," Felcher remarked. His voice, surprisingly deep and strong for so small a creature, rang like a great bell.

"Isn't even the headmaster here?" inquired Setwick, and at that the other two began to laugh uproariously, Andoff's fife-squeal rendering an obligato to Felcher's bell-boom. Hoag, returning, asked what the fun was.

"Setwick asks," groaned Felcher, "why the headmaster isn't here to welcome him."

More fife-laughter and bell-laughter.

"I doubt if Setwick would think the answer was funny," Hoag commented, and then chuckled softly himself.

Setwick, who had been well brought up, began to grow nettled.

"Tell me about it," he urged, in what he hoped was a bleak tone, "and I'll join your chorus of mirth."

Felcher and Andoff gazed at him with eyes strangely eager and yearning. Then they faced Hoag.

"Let's tell him" they both said at once, but Hoag shook his head.

"Not yet. One thing at a time. Let's have the song first."

They began to sing. The first verse of their offering was obscene, with no pretense of humor to redeem it. Setwick had never been squeamish, but he found himself definitely repelled. The second verse seemed less objectionable, but it hardly made sense:

All they tried to teach here
Now goes untaught.
Ready, steady, each here,
Knowledge we sought.
What they called disaster
Killed us not, O master!
Rule us, we beseech here,
Eye, hand, and thought.

It was something like a hymn, Setwick decided; but before what altar would such hymns be sung? Hoag must have read that question in his mind.

"You mentioned Satan in the buggy on the way out," he recalled, his knowing face hanging like a mask in the half dimness close to Setwick. "Well, that was a Satanist song."

"It was? Who made it?"

"I did," Hoag informed him. "How do you like it?"

Setwick made no answer. He tried to sense mockery in Hoag's voice, but could not find it. "What," he asked finally, "does all this Satanist singing have to do with the headmaster?"

"A lot," came back Felcher deeply, and "A lot," squealed Andoff.

Hoag gazed from one of his friends to the other, and for the first time he smiled broadly. It gave him a toothy look.

"I believe," he ventured quietly but weightily, "that we might as well let Setwick in on the secret of our little circle."

Here it would begin, the new boy decided—the school hazing of which he had heard and read so much. He had anticipated such things with excitement, even eagerness, but now he wanted none of them. He did not like his three companions, and he did not like the way they approached whatever it was they intended to do. He moved backward a pace or two, as if to retreat.

Swift as darting birds, Hoag and Andoff closed in at either elbow. Their chill hands clutched him and suddenly he felt lightheaded and sick. Things that had been clear in the moonlight went hazy and distorted.

"Come on and sit down, Setwick," invited Hoag, as though from a great distance. His voice did not grow loud or harsh, but it embodied real menace. "Sit on that windowsill. Or would you like us to carry you?"

At the moment Setwick wanted only to be free of their touch, and so he walked unresistingly to the sill and scrambled up on it. Behind him was the blackness of an unknown chamber, and at his knees gathered the three who seemed so eager to tell him their private joke.

"The headmaster was a proper churchgoer," began Hoag, as though he were the spokesman for the group. "He didn't have any use for devils or devil-worship. Went on record against them when he addressed us in chapel. That was what started us."

"Right," nodded Andoff, turning up his fat, larval face. "Anything he outlawed, we wanted to do. Isn't that logic?"

"Logic and reason," wound up Felcher. His hairy right hand twiddled on the sill near Setwick's thigh. In the moonlight it looked like a big, nervous spider.

Hoag resumed. "I don't know of any prohibition of his it was easier or more fun to break."

Setwick found that his mouth had gone dry. His tongue could barely moisten his lips. "You mean," he said, "that you began to worship devils?"

Hoag nodded happily, like a teacher at an apt pupil. "One vacation I got a book on the cult. The three of us studied it, then began ceremonies. We learned the charms and spells, forward and backward . . ."

"They're twice as good backward," put in Felcher, and Andoff giggled.

"Have you any idea, Setwick," Hoag almost cooed, "what it was that appeared in our study the first time we burned wine and sulfur, with the proper words spoken over them?"

Setwick did not want to know. He clenched his teeth. "If you're trying to scare me," he managed to growl out, "it certainly isn't going to work."

All three laughed once more, and began to chatter out their protestations of good faith.

"I swear that we're telling the truth, Setwick," Hoag assured him. "Do you want to hear it, or don't you?"

Setwick had very little choice in the matter, and he realized it. "Oh, go ahead," he capitulated, wondering how it would do to crawl backward from the sill into the darkness of the room.

Hoag leaned toward him, with the air as of one confiding. "The headmaster caught us. Caught us red-handed."

"Book open, fire burning," chanted Felcher.

"He had something very fine to say about the vengeance of heaven," Hoag went on. "We got to laughing at him. He worked up a frenzy. Finally he tried to take heaven's vengeance into his own hands —tried to visit it on us, in a very primitive way. But it didn't work."

Andoff was laughing immoderately, his fat arms across his bent belly.

"He thought it worked," he supplemented between high gurgles, "but it didn't."

"Nobody could kill us," Felcher added. "Not after the oaths we'd taken, and the promises that had been made us."

"What promises?" demanded Setwick, who was struggling hard not to believe. "Who made you any promises?"

"Those we worshiped," Felcher told him. If he were simulating earnestness, it was a supreme bit of acting. Setwick, realizing this, was more daunted than he cared to show.

"When did all these things happen?" was his next question.

"When?" echoed Hoag. "Oh, years and years ago."

"Years and years ago," repeated Andoff.

"Long before you were born," Felcher assured him.

They were standing close together, their backs to the moon that shone in Setwick's face. He could not see their expressions clearly. But their three voices—Hoag's soft, Felcher's deep and vibrant, Andoff's high and squeaky—were absolutely serious.

"I know what you're arguing within yourself," Hoag announced somewhat smugly. "How can we, who talk about those many past years, seem so young? That calls for an explanation, I'll admit." He paused, as if choosing words. "Time—for us—stands still. It came to a halt on that very night, Setwick; the night our headmaster tried to put an end to our worship."

"And to us," smirked the gross-bodied Andoff, with his usual air of self-congratulation at capping one of Hoag's statements.

"The worship goes on," pronounced Felcher, in the same chanting manner that he had affected once before. "The worship goes on, and we go on, too."

"Which brings us to the point," Hoag came in briskly. "Do you want to throw in with us, Setwick?—make the fourth of this lively little party?"

"No, I don't," snapped Setwick vehemently.

They fell silent, and gave back a little—a trio of bizarre silhouettes against the pale moonglow. Setwick could see the flash of their staring eyes among the shadows of their faces. He knew that he was afraid, but hid his fear. Pluckily he dropped from the sill to the ground. Dew from the grass spattered his sock-clad ankles between oxfords and trouser cuffs.

"I guess it's my turn to talk," he told them levelly. "I'll make it short. I don't like you, nor anything you've said. And I'm getting out of here."

"We won't let you," said Hoag, hushed but emphatic.

"We won't let you," murmured Andoff and Felcher together, as though they had rehearsed it a thousand times.

Setwick clenched his fists. His father had taught him to box. He took a quick, smooth stride toward Hoag and hit him hard in the face. Next moment all three had flung themselves upon him. They did not seem to strike or grapple or tug, but he went down under their assault. The shoulders of his tweed coat wallowed in sand, and he smelled crushed weeds. Hoag, on top of him, pinioned his arms with a knee on each bicep. Felcher and Andoff were stooping close.

Glaring up in helpless rage, Setwick knew once and for all that this was no schoolboy prank. Never did practical jokers gather around their victim with such staring, green-gleaming eyes, such drawn jowls, such quivering lips.

Hoag bared white fangs. His pointed tongue quested once over them.

"Knife!" he muttered, and Felcher fumbled in a pocket, then passed him something that sparkled in the moonlight.

Hoag's lean hand reached for it, then whipped back. Hoag had lifted his eyes to something beyond the huddle. He choked and whimpered inarticulately, sprang up from Setwick's laboring chest, and fell back in awkward haste. The others followed his shocked stare, then as suddenly cowered and retreated in turn.

"It's the master!" wailed Andoff.

"Yes," roared a gruff new voice. "Your old headmaster—and I've come back to master you!"

Rising upon one elbow, the prostrate Setwick saw what they had seen—a tall, thick-bodied figure in a long dark coat, topped with a square, distorted face and a tousle of white locks. Its eyes glittered with their own pale, hard light. As it advanced slowly and heavily it emitted a snigger of murderous joy. Even at first glance Setwick was aware that it cast no shadow.

"I am in time," mouthed the newcomer. "You were going to kill this poor boy."

Hoag had recovered and made a stand. "Kill him?" he quavered, seeming to fawn before the threatening presence. "No. We'd have given him life—"

"You call it life?" trumpeted the long-coated one. "You'd have sucked out his blood to teem your own dead veins, damned him to your filthy condition. But I'm here to prevent you!"

A finger pointed, huge and knuckly, and then came a torrent of language. To the nerve-stunned Setwick it sounded like a bit from the New Testament, or perhaps from the Book of Common Prayer. All at once he remembered Hoag's avowed dislike for such quotations.

His three erstwhile assailants reeled as if before a high wind that chilled or scorched. "No, no! Don't!" they begged wretchedly.

The square old face gaped open and spewed merciless laughter. The knuckly finger traced a cross in the air, and the trio wailed in chorus as though the sign had been drawn upon their flesh with a tongue of flame.

Hoag dropped to his knees. "Don't!" he sobbed.

"I have power," mocked their tormenter. "During years shut up I won it, and now I'll use it." Again a triumphant burst of mirth. "I know you're damned and can't be killed, but you can be tortured! I'll make you crawl like worms before I'm done with you!"

Setwick gained his shaky feet. The long coat and the blocky head leaned toward him.

"Run, you!" dinned a rough roar in his ears. "Get out of here—and thank God for the chance!"

Setwick ran, staggering. He blundered through the weeds of the driveway, gained the road beyond. In the distance gleamed the lights of Carrington. As he turned his face toward them and quickened his pace he began to weep, chokingly, hysterically, exhaustingly.

He did not stop running until he reached the platform in front of the station. A clock across the street struck ten, in a deep voice not unlike Felcher's. Setwick breathed deeply, fished out his handkerchief and mopped his face. His hand was quivering like a grass stalk in a breeze.

"Beg pardon!" came a cheery hail. "You must be Setwick."

As once before on this same platform, he whirled around with startled speed. Within touch of him stood a broad-shouldered man of thirty or so, with horn-rimmed spectacles. He wore a neat Norfolk jacket and flannels. A short briar pipe was clamped in a good-humored mouth.

"I'm Collins, one of the masters at the school," he introduced himself. "If you're Setwick, you've had us worried. We expected you on that seven o'clock train, you know. I dropped down to see if I couldn't trace you."

Setwick found a little of his lost wind. "But I've—been to the school," he mumbled protestingly. His hand, still trembling, gestured vaguely along the way he had come.

Collins threw back his head and laughed, then apologized.

"Sorry," he said. "It's no joke if you really had all that walk for nothing. Why, that old place is deserted—used to be a catch-all for incorrigible rich boys. They closed it about fifty years ago, when the headmaster went mad and killed three of his pupils. As a matter of coincidence, the master himself died just this afternoon, in the state hospital for the insane."

AUGUST W. DERLETH, *who made a major contribution to the development of American genre fiction, was born in 1909 in Sauk City, Wisconsin, where he died in 1971. Although in many eyes his major work was a series of regional novels about Wisconsin's Sac Prairie, he also wrote a large number of detective stories and horror tales.*

A hugely prolific and energetic man, Derleth contributed more than a hundred stories to Weird Tales *magazine, edited many anthologies of short fiction, encouraged many young authors who would later achieve great fame, brought to the attention of the public the work of horror master H. P. Lovecraft, and in 1939 founded Arkham House, a publishing firm specializing in fantasy fiction.*

Many of Derleth's stories in Weird Tales *were published under the pseudonym Stephen Grendon. One of the best of them is "The Drifting Snow," a unique and subtle variant on the vampire theme.*

The Drifting Snow
(1939)
BY AUGUST DERLETH

Aunt Mary's advancing footsteps halted suddenly, short of the table, and Clodetta turned to see what was keeping her. She was standing very rigidly, her eyes fixed upon the French windows just opposite the door through which she had entered, her cane held stiffly before her.

Clodetta shot a quick glance across the table toward her husband, whose attention had also been drawn to his aunt; his face vouchsafed her nothing. She turned again to find that the old lady had transferred her gaze to her, regarding her stonily and in silence. Clodetta felt uncomfortable.

"Who withdrew the curtains from the west windows?"

Clodetta flushed, remembering. "I did, Aunt. I'm sorry. I forgot about your not wanting them drawn away."

The old lady made an odd, grunting sound, shifting her gaze once again to the French windows. She made a barely perceptible movement, and Lisa ran forward from the shadow of the hall, where she had been regarding the two at table with stern disapproval. The servant went directly to the west windows and drew the curtains.

Aunt Mary came slowly to the table and took her place at its head. She put her cane against the side of her chair, pulled at the chain about her neck so that her lorgnette lay in her lap, and looked from Clodetta to her nephew, Ernest.

Then she fixed her gaze on the empty chair at the foot of the table, and spoke without seeming to see the two beside her.

"I told both of you that none of the curtains over the west windows was to be withdrawn after sundown, and you must have noticed that none of those windows has been for one instant uncovered at night. I took especial care to put you in rooms facing east, and the sitting-room is also in the east."

"I'm sure Clodetta didn't mean to go against your wishes, Aunt Mary," said Ernest abruptly.

"No, of course not, Aunt."

The old lady raised her eyebrows, and went on impassively. "I didn't think it wise to explain why I made such a request. I'm not going to explain. But I do want to say that there is a very definite danger in drawing away the curtains. Ernest has heard that before, but you, Clodetta, have not."

Clodetta shot a startled glance at her husband. The old lady caught it, and said, "It's all very well to believe that my mind's wandering or that I'm getting eccentric, but I shouldn't advise you to be satisfied with that."

A young man came suddenly into the room and made for the seat at the foot of the table, into which he flung himself with an almost inaudible greeting to the other three.

"Late again, Henry," said the old lady.

Henry mumbled something and began hurriedly to eat. The old lady sighed, and began presently to eat also, whereupon Clodetta and Ernest did likewise. The old servant, who had continued to linger behind Aunt Mary's chair, now withdrew, not without a scornful glance at Henry.

Clodetta looked up after a while and ventured to speak, "You aren't as isolated as I thought you might be up here, Aunt Mary."

"We aren't, my dear, what with telephones and cars and all. But only twenty years ago it was quite a different thing, I can tell you." She smiled reminiscently and looked at Ernest. "Your grandfather was living then, and many's the time he was snowbound with no way to let anybody know."

"Down in Chicago when they speak of 'up north' or the 'Wisconsin woods' it seems very far away," said Clodetta.

"Well, it *is* far away," put in Henry, abruptly. "And, Aunt, I hope you've made some provision in case we're locked in here for a day or two. It looks like snow outside, and the radio says a blizzard's coming."

The old lady grunted and looked at him. "Ha, Henry—you're overly concerned, it seems to me. I'm afraid you've been regretting this trip ever since you set foot in my house. If you're worrying about a snowstorm, I can have Sam drive you down to Wausau, and you can be in Chicago tomorrow."

"Of course not."

Silence fell, and presently the old lady called gently, "Lisa," and the servant came into the room to help her from her chair, though, as Clodetta had previously said to her husband, "She didn't need help."

From the doorway, Aunt Mary bade them all good-night, looking impressively formidable with her cane in one hand and her unopened lorgnette in the other, and vanished into the dusk of the hall, from which her receding footsteps sounded together with those of the servant, who was seldom seen away from her. These two were alone in the house most of the time, and only very brief periods when the old lady had up her nephew Ernest, "dear John's boy," or Henry, of whose father the old lady never spoke, helped to relieve the pleasant somnolence of their quiet lives. Sam, who usually slept in the garage, did not count.

Clodetta looked nervously at her husband, but it was Henry who said what was uppermost in their thoughts.

"I think she's losing her mind," he declared matter-of-factly. Cutting off Clodetta's protest on her lips, he got up and went into the sitting-room, from which came presently the strains of music from the radio.

Clodetta fingered her spoon idly and finally said, "I do think she is a little queer, Ernest."

Ernest smiled tolerantly. "No, I don't think so. I've an idea why she keeps the west windows covered. My grandfather died out there— he was overcome by the cold one night, and froze on the slope of the hill. I don't rightly know how it happened—I was away at the time. I suppose she doesn't like to be reminded of it."

"But where's the danger she spoke of, then?"

He shrugged. "Perhaps it lies in her—she might be affected and affect us in turn." He paused for an instant, and finally added, "I suppose she *does* seem a little strange to you—but she was like that as long as I can remember; next time you come, you'll be used to it."

Clodetta looked at her husband for a moment before replying. At last she said, "I don't think I like the house, Ernest."

"Oh, nonsense, darling." He started to get up, but Clodetta stopped him.

"Listen Ernest. I remembered perfectly well Aunt Mary's not wanting those curtains drawn away—but I just felt I had to do it. I didn't want to, but—*something made me do it.*" Her voice was unsteady.

"Why, Clodetta," he said, faintly alarmed. "Why didn't you tell me before?"

She shrugged. "Aunt Mary might have thought I'd gone woolgathering."

"Well, it's nothing serious, but you've let it bother you a little and that isn't good for you. Forget it; think of something else. Come and listen to the radio."

They rose and moved toward the sitting-room together. At the door Henry met them. He stepped aside a little, saying, "I might have known we'd be marooned up here," and adding, as Clodetta began to protest, "We're going to be all right. There's a wind coming up and it's beginning to snow, and I know what that means." He passed them and went into the deserted dining-room, where he stood a moment looking at the too long table. Then he turned aside and went over to the French windows, from which he drew away the curtains and stood there peering out into the darkness. Ernest saw him standing at the window, and protested from the sitting-room.

"Aunt Mary doesn't like those windows uncovered, Henry."

Henry half turned and replied, "Well, *she* may think it's dangerous, but I can risk it."

Clodetta, who had been staring beyond Henry into the night through the French windows, said suddenly, "Why, there's someone out there!"

Henry looked quickly through the glass and replied, "No, that's the snow; it's coming down heavily, and the wind's drifting it this way and that." He dropped the curtains and came away from the windows.

Clodetta said uncertainly, "Why, I could have sworn I saw someone out there, walking past the window."

"I suppose it does look that way from here," offered Henry, who had come back into the sitting-room. "But personally, I think you've let Aunt Mary's eccentricities impress you too much."

Ernest made an impatient gesture at this, and Clodetta did not answer. Henry sat down before the radio and began to move the dial slowly. Ernest had found himself a book, and was becoming interested, but Clodetta continued to sit with her eyes fixed upon the still slowly moving curtains cutting off the French windows. Presently she got up and left the room, going down the long hall into the east wing, where she tapped gently upon Aunt Mary's door.

"Come in," called the old lady.

Clodetta opened the door and stepped into the room where Aunt Mary sat in her dressing-robe, her dignity, in the shape of her lorgnette and cane, resting respectively on her bureau and in the corner. She looked surprisingly benign, as Clodetta at once confessed.

"Ha, thought I was an ogre in disguise, did you?" said the old lady, smiling in spite of herself. "I'm really not, you see, but I am a sort of bogy about the west windows, as you have seen."

"I wanted to tell you something about those windows, Aunt Mary," said Clodetta. She stopped suddenly. The expression on the old lady's face had given way to a curiously dismaying one. It was not anger, not distaste—it was a lurking suspense. Why, the old lady was afraid!

"What?" she asked Clodetta shortly.

"I was looking out—just for a moment or so—and I thought I saw someone out there."

"Of course, you didn't, Clodetta. Your imagination, perhaps, or the drifting snow."

"My imagination? Maybe. But there was no wind to drift the snow, though one has come up since."

"I've often been fooled that way, my dear. Sometimes I've gone out in the morning to look for footprints—there weren't any, ever. We're pretty far away from civilization in a snowstorm, despite our telephones and radios. Our nearest neighbor is at the foot of the long, sloping rise —over three miles away—and all wooded land between. There's no highway nearer than that."

"It was so clear, I could have sworn to it."

"Do you want to go out in the morning and look?" asked the old lady shortly.

"Of course not."

"Then you didn't see anything?"

It was half question, half demand. Clodetta said, "Oh, Aunt Mary, you're making an issue of it now."

"Did you or didn't you in your own mind see anything, Clodetta?"

"I guess I didn't, Aunt Mary."

"Very well. And now do you think we might talk about something more pleasant?"

"Why, I'm sure—I'm sorry, Aunt. I didn't know that Ernest's grandfather had died out there."

"Ha, he's told you that, has he? Well?"

"Yes, he said that was why you didn't like the slope after sunset— that you didn't like to be reminded of his death."

The old lady looked at Clodetta impassively. "Perhaps he'll never know how near right he was."

"What do you mean, Aunt Mary?"

"Nothing for you to know, my dear." She smiled again, her sternness dropping from her. "And now I think you'd better go, Clodetta; I'm tired."

Clodetta rose obediently and made for the door, where the old lady stopped her. "How's the weather?"

"It's snowing—hard, Henry says—and blowing."

The old lady's face showed her distaste at the news. "I don't like to hear that, not at all. Suppose someone should look down that slope tonight?" She was speaking to herself, having forgotten Clodetta at the door. Seeing her again abruptly, she said, "But you don't know, Clodetta. Goodnight."

Clodetta stood with her back against the closed door, wondering what the old lady could have meant. *But you don't know, Clodetta.* That was curious. For a moment or two the old lady had completely forgotten her.

She moved away from the door, and came upon Ernest just turning into the east wing.

"Oh, there you are," he said. "I wondered where you had gone."

"I was talking a bit with Aunt Mary."

"Henry's been at the west windows again—and now *he* thinks there's someone out there."

Clodetta stopped short. "Does he really think so?"

Ernest nodded gravely. "But the snow's drifting frightfully, and I can imagine how that suggestion of yours worked on his mind."

Clodetta turned and went back along the hall. "I'm going to tell Aunt Mary."

He started to protest, but to no avail, for she was already tapping on the old lady's door, and indeed opening the door and entering the room before he could frame an adequate protest.

"Aunt Mary," she said, "I didn't want to disturb you again, but Henry's been at the French windows in the dining-room, and he says he's seen someone out there."

The effect on the old lady was magical. "He's seen them!" she exclaimed. Then she was on her feet, coming rapidly over to Clodetta. "How long ago?" she demanded, seizing her almost roughly by the arms. "Tell me, quickly. How long ago did he see them?"

Clodetta's amazement kept her silent for a moment, but at last she spoke, feeling the old lady's keen eyes staring at her. "It was some time ago, Aunt Mary, after supper."

The old lady's hands relaxed, and with it her tension. "Oh," she said, and turned and went back slowly to her chair, taking her cane from the corner where she had put it for the night.

"Then there *is* someone out there?" challenged Clodetta, when the old lady had reached her chair.

For a long time, it seemed to Clodetta, there was no answer. Then presently the old lady began to nod gently, and a barely audible "Yes" escaped her lips.

"Then we had better take them in, Aunt Mary."

The old lady looked at Clodetta earnestly for a moment; then she replied, her voice firm and low, her eyes fixed upon the wall beyond. "We can't take them in, Clodetta—because they're not alive."

At once Henry's words came flashing into Clodetta's memory— "She's losing her mind"—and her involuntary start betrayed her thought.

"I'm afraid I'm not mad, my dear—I hoped at first I might be, but I wasn't. I'm not, now. There was only one of them out there at first— the girl; Father is the other. Quite long ago, when I was young, my father did something which he regretted all his days. He had a too strong temper, and it maddened him. One night he found out that one of my brothers—Henry's father—had been very familiar with one of the servants, a very pretty girl, older than I was. He thought she was to blame, though she wasn't, and he didn't find it out until too late. He drove her from the house, then and there. Winter had not yet set in, but it was quite cold, and she had some five miles to go to her home. We begged Father not to send her away—though we didn't know what was wrong then—but he paid no attention to us. The girl had to go.

"Not long after she had gone, a biting wind came up, and close upon it a fierce storm. Father had already repented his hasty action, and sent some of the men to look for the girl. They didn't find her, but in the morning she was found frozen to death on the long slope of the hill to the west."

The old lady sighed, paused a moment, and went on. "Years later —she came back. She came in a snowstorm, as she went; but she had become a vampire. We all saw her. We were at supper table, and Father saw her first. The boys had already gone upstairs, and Father and the two of us girls, my sister and I, did not recognize her. She was just a dim shape floundering about in the drifting snow beyond the French windows. Father ran out to her, calling to us to send the boys after him. We never saw him alive again. In the morning we found him in the same spot where years before the girl had been found. He, too, had died of exposure.

"Then, a few years after—she returned with the snow, and she brought him along; he, too, had become a vampire. They stayed until the last snow, always trying to lure someone out there. After that, I knew, and had the windows covered during the winter nights, from sunset to dawn, because they never went beyond the west slope.

"Now you know, Clodetta."

Whatever Clodetta was going to say was cut short by running footsteps in the hall, a hasty rap, and Ernest's head appearing suddenly in the open doorway.

"Come on, you two," he said, almost gayly, "there *are* people out on the west slope—a girl and an old man—and Henry's gone out to fetch them in!"

Then, triumphant, he was off. Clodetta came to her feet, but the old lady was before her, passing her and almost running down the hall, calling loudly for Lisa, who presently appeared in nightcap and gown from her room.

"Call Sam, Lisa," said the old lady, "and send him to me in the dining-room."

She ran on into the dining-room, Clodetta close on her heels. The French windows were open, and Ernest stood on the snow-covered terrace beyond, calling his cousin. The old lady went directly over to him, even striding into the snow to his side, though the wind drove the snow against her with great force. The wooded western slope was lost in a snow-fog; the nearest trees were barely discernible.

"Where could they have gone?" Ernest said, turning to the old lady, whom he had thought to be Clodetta. Then, seeing that it was the old lady, he said, "Why, Aunt Mary—and so little on, too! You'll catch your death of cold."

"Never mind, Ernest," said the old lady. "I'm all right. I've had Sam get up to help you look for Henry—but I'm afraid you won't find him."

"He can't be far; he just now went out."

"He went before you saw where; he's far enough gone."

Sam came running into the blowing snow from the dining-room, muffled in a greatcoat. He was considerably older than Ernest, almost the old lady's age. He shot a questioning glance at her and asked, "Have they come again?"

Aunt Mary nodded. "You'll have to look for Henry. Ernest will help you. And remember, don't separate. And don't go far from the house."

Clodetta came with Ernest's overcoat, and together the two women stood there, watching them until they were swallowed up in the wall of driven snow. Then they turned slowly and went back into the house.

The old lady sank into a chair facing the windows. She was pale and drawn, and looked, as Clodetta said afterward, "as if she'd fallen together." For a long time she said nothing. Then, with a gentle little sigh, she turned to Clodetta and spoke.

"Now there'll be three of them out there."

Then, so suddenly that no one knew how it happened, Ernest and Sam appeared beyond the windows, and between them they dragged Henry. The old lady flew to open the windows, and the three of them, cloaked in snow, came into the room.

"We found him—but the cold's hit him pretty hard, I'm afraid," said Ernest.

The old lady sent Lisa for cold water, and Ernest ran to get himself other clothes. Clodetta went with him, and in their rooms told him what the old lady had related to her.

Ernest laughed. "I think you believed that, didn't you, Clodetta? Sam and Lisa do, I know, because Sam told me the story long ago. I think the shock of Grandfather's death was too much for all three of them."

"But the story of the girl, and then——"

"That part's true, I'm afraid. A nasty story, but it did happen."

"But those people Henry and I saw!" protested Clodetta weakly.

Ernest stood without movement. "That's so," he said, "I saw them, too. Then they're out there yet, and we'll have to find them!" He took up his overcoat again, and went from the room, Clodetta protesting in a shrill unnatural voice. The old lady met him at the door of the dining-room, having overheard Clodetta pleading with him.

"No, Ernest—you can't go out there again," she said. "There's no one there."

He pushed gently into the room and called to Sam, "Coming Sam? There're still two of them out there—we almost forgot them."

Sam looked at him strangely. "What do you mean?" he demanded roughly. He looked challengingly at the old lady, who shook her head.

"The girl and the old man, Sam. We've got to get them, too."

"Oh, *them,*" said Sam. "They're dead!"

"Then I'll go out alone," said Ernest.

Henry came to his feet suddenly, looking dazed. He walked forward a few steps, his eyes traveling from one to the other of them, yet apparently not seeing them. He began to speak abruptly, in an unnatural child-like voice.

"*The snow,*" he murmured, "*the snow—the beautiful hands, so little, so lovely—her beautiful hands—and the snow, the beautiful, lovely snow, drifting and falling about her. . . .*"

He turned slowly and looked toward the French windows, the others following his gaze. Beyond was a wall of white, where the snow was drifting against the house. For a moment Henry stood quietly watching; then suddenly a white figure came forward from the snow—a young girl, cloaked in long snow-whips, her glistening eyes strangely fascinating.

The old lady flung herself forward, her arms outstretched to cling to Henry, but she was too late. Henry had run toward the windows, had opened them, and even as Clodetta cried out, had vanished into the wall of snow beyond.

Then Ernest ran forward, but the old lady threw her arms around him and held him tightly, murmuring, "You shall not go! Henry is gone beyond our help!"

Clodetta came to help her, and Sam stood menacingly at the French windows, now closed against the wind and the sinister snow. So they held him, and would not let him go.

"And tomorrow," said the old lady in a harsh whisper, "we must go to their graves and stake them down. We should have gone before."

In the morning they found Henry's body crouched against the bole of an ancient oak, where two others had been found years before. There were almost obliterated marks of where something had dragged him, a long, uneven swath in the snow, and yet no footprints, only strange, hollowed places along the way, as if the wind had whirled the snow away, and only the wind.

But on his skin were signs of the snow vampire—the delicate small prints of a young girl's hands.

PETER SCHUYLER MILLER *(1912–1974) was trained as a chemist and worked most of his life as a technical writer. In the 1930s he contributed fiction to the pulp magazines, and in 1945 he began reviewing science fiction for the leading magazine in the field,* Astounding Science Fiction. *His reviews appeared there for nearly thirty years until his death in 1974. In 1963 Miller received a Hugo Award for his reviews, and it is safe to say that Miller's insightful criticism was helpful in the modern development of science fiction as a genre.*

And when he turned to horror fiction, he produced "Over the River."

Over the River (1941)

BY P. SCHUYLER MILLER

The shape of his body showed in the frozen mud, where he had lain facedown under the fallen tree. His footprints were sharp in the melting snow, and his feet had left dark, wet blotches where he had climbed the rock. He had lain there for a long time. Long enough it was for time to have lost its meaning.

The moon was coming up over the nearer mountain, full and white, etched across with the pattern of naked branches. Its light fell on his upturned face, on his sunken, brilliant eyes and the puffy blue of jowls on which the beard had started to grow, then stopped. It shone down on the world of trees and rocks of which he was a part, and gave it life.

The night was warm. In the valley the snow had long been gone. Flowers were pushing up through the moist earth; frogs were Pan-piping in every low spot; great trout stirred in the deep pools of the river. It was May, but on the mountain, under the north-facing ledges where the sun never came, the snow was still banked deep with an edge of blue ice, and needles of frost glistened in the black mud of the forest floor.

It was May. All through the warm night, squadrons of birds were passing across the face of the moon. All night long their voices drifted down out of the dark like gossip from another world. But to a listener in the night another voice was clearer, louder, more insistent—now like the striking of crystal cymbals, now like an elfin chuckling, always a breathless, never-ending whisper—the voice of running water.

He heard none of these things. He stood where he had first come into the full moonlight, his face turned up to receive it, drinking in its brightness. It tingled in him like a draft from the things he had forgotten, in another world. It dissolved the dull ache of cold that was in his body and mind, that stiffened his swollen limbs, and lay like an icy nugget behind his eyes. It soaked into him, and into the world about him, so that every corner shone with its own pale light, white and vaporous, as far as he could see.

It was a strange world. What that other world had been like, before, he did not remember, but this was different. The moonlight flooded it with a pearly mist through which the columns of the trees rose like shadowy stalagmites. The light-mist was not from the moon alone; it was a part of this new world and of the things that were in it. The gray lichens under his feet were outlined with widening ripples of light. Light pulsed through the rough bark of the tree trunks and burned like tiny corpse-candles at the tip of every growing twig. The spruces and balsams were furred with silvery needles of light. A swirling mist of light hung ankle-deep over the forest floor, broken by black islands of rock. Light was in everything in this new world he was in, save only for the rock, and for himself.

He drank in the moonlight through every pore, and it burned gloriously in him and flowed down through every vein and bone of his body, driving out the dank cold that was in his flesh. But the light that soaked into him did not shine out again as it did from the budding trees, and the moss, and the lichens. He looked down at his swollen hands and flexed their puffed blue fingers; he moved his toes in their sodden boots, and felt the clammy touch of the wet rags that clung to his body. Under them, out of the moonlight, he was still cold with that pervading chill that was like the frozen breath of winter in him. He squatted in the pool of light that lay over the ledge and stripped them from him, clumsily and painfully, then lay back on the stone and stared up into the smiling visage of the moon.

Time passed, but whether it was minutes or hours, or whether there were still such things as minutes and hours, he could not have said. Time had no meaning for him in this new, strange world. Time passed, because the moon was higher and its light stronger and warmer on his naked flesh, but he did not sense its passage. Every part of the forest pulsed with its own inner light in response. As the feeling of warmth grew in him it brought another feeling, a dull hunger gnawing at his vitals, making him restless. He moved close to a great beech whose limbs reached high above the tops of the other trees around it, and felt the quick chill as its shadow fell across him. Then he had clasped it in both arms, his whole body pressing eagerly against its glowing trunk, and the light that welled out of it was thrilling through him like a flame, stirring every atom of him. He tweaked a long, pointed bud from a twig. It lay in his palm like a jewel of pale fire before he raised it to his mouth and felt its warmth spread into him.

He ate buds as long as he could find them, stripping them from the twigs with clumsy fingers, grubbing hungrily in the moss for the ones that fell. He crushed them between his teeth and swallowed them, and the fire that glowed in them spread into his chilled flesh and warmed it a little. He tore patches of lichen from the rock, but they were tough and woody and he could not swallow them. He broke off spruce twigs, needled with the life-light, but the resin in them burned his lips and tongue and choked him.

He sat, hunched against a rock, staring blindly into the growing depths of the forest. The things he had swallowed had helped a little to alleviate the cold that was in his bones, but they did not dull the gnawing hunger or the thirst that was torturing him. They had life, and the warmth that was life, but not the thing he needed—the thing he must somehow have.

At the edge of his field of vision something moved. It drifted noiselessly through the burning treetops, like a puff of luminous cloud. It settled on a branch above his head, and he twisted his neck back and stared up at it with hollow, burning eyes. The white light-mist was very bright about it. He could feel its warmth, even at this distance. And there was something more. The hunger gripped him, fiercer than ever, and thirst shriveled his gullet.

The owl had seen him and decided that he was another rotting stump. It sat hunched against the trunk of the great spruce, looking and listening for its prey. Presently it was rewarded by some small sound or a wafted scent, and spread its silent wings to float like a phantom into the night. It did not see the misshapen thing, it had thought a stump, struggle to its feet and follow.

A porcupine, high in a birch, saw the owl pass and ignored it, as it well could. A roosting crow woke suddenly and froze on its perch, petrified with terror. But the great bird swept past, intent on other prey.

There were clearings in the forest, even this high, where trees had been cut off and brambles had followed. All manner of small creatures followed the brambles, and here was rich hunting for the owl and its kind.

He came to the edge of the clearing in time to see the owl strike and hear the scream of the hurt rabbit. To his eyes it was as though a bolt of shining fire had plunged through the night to strike a second ball of fire on the ground. Shambling forward, careless of the briars, he hurled himself on the two animals before the owl could free itself or take the air again.

The huge bird slashed at him savagely with beak and talons, laying open the puffy flesh of his face in great, curving gashes, but he bit deep into its breast, through feathers and skin, tearing at its flesh with his teeth and letting the hot, burning blood gush into his parched throat and spill over his cracked lips. His fingers kneaded and tore at its body, breaking it into bits that he could stuff into his mouth. Feathers and bone he spat out, and the rabbit's fur when the owl was gone, but the hollow in his belly was filled, and the thirst gone, and the aching cold in his numbed bones had been washed away. It seemed to him that his fingers were shining a little with the same wan light that emanated from the other things of the forest.

He hunted all that night, through the clearing and the nearby forest, and found and ate two wood mice and a handful of grubs and other insects. He found that the tightly coiled fiddleheads of growing ferns were full of life and more palatable than buds or lichens. As the deadening cold left him he could move more freely, think more keenly, but the thirst was growing on him again.

Out of the lost memories of that world he had left, the murmur of running water came to him. Water should quench thirst. He could hear it below him on the mountainside, through the mist, splashing over bare stones, gurgling through tunnels in the roots and moss. He heard it in the distance, far below in the valley, roaring against the boulders and leaping over ledges in foaming abandon. As he listened, a chill crept over him, as though a shadow were passing, but the feeling left him. Slowly and painfully he began to pick his way down the mountainside.

The water burst out at the base of a rock wall, lay for a little in a deep, clear pool under the cliff and then slipped away through the moss, twisting and turning, sliding over flat stones and diving into crevices, welling up in tiny, sparkling fountains and vanishing again under tangles of matted roots and fallen tree trunks, growing and running ever faster until it leaped over the last cliff and fell in a spatter of flashing drops into the valley. He saw it, and stopped.

Black vapor lay close over it like a carpet. It made a pathway of black, winding through the luminous mist that hung over the forest floor. Where the rill lay quiet in a pool it was thin, and the moonlight struck through and sparkled on the clear water, but where the little stream hurried over roots and stones, the black fog lay dense and impenetrable, dull and lifeless.

He licked his lips uneasily with his swollen tongue and moved cautiously forward. The chill had come on him again, numbing his nerves, dulling his laboring brain. Water quenched thirst; he still remembered that somehow, and this singing, shining stuff was water. At the base of the cliff, where the water welled up under the rock, the black fog was thinnest. He knelt and dipped his cupped hands into the water.

As the black mist closed over them, all feeling went out of his hands. Cold—terrible, numbing cold—ate its way like acid into his flesh and bones. The mist was draining the warmth—the life—out of him, through his hands and arms—sucking him dry of the life-stuff he had drunk with the owl's blood and soaked in from the moon's white rays. He swayed to his feet, then collapsed in a heap beside the stream.

He lay there helpless for a long time. Little by little the moonlight revived him. Little by little the numbness went out of his muscles, and he could move his legs and grip things with his fingers. He pulled his legs under him and got to his feet, leaning against the cliff for support. He stared with burning eyes at the water, and felt the first clutching at his gullet and the hunger gnawing in his vitals. Water was death to him. The black fog that lay close over running water was deadly, draining the life-force out of whatever touched it. It was death! But blood—fresh, burning, glowing blood was life!

Something rattled in the shadow of the cliff. His eyes found it—a lolloping bundle of fiery spines, humping along a worn path that led over the rocks to the little pool, a porcupine come to drink. He sensed the life in it, and hunger twisted his belly, but the black barrier of running water was between him and it.

It shambled down to the pool's edge and drank, the glow of its bristling body shining through the black fog over the water. It crossed the little rill where it was narrowest, below the pool, and came rattling up the path toward him, unafraid.

He killed it. His face and body were studded with quills before it was dead, but he tore open its body with his two numb hands and let its hot blood swill down his throat and give him back the warmth and life that the black mist had drained out of him. Blood was all he needed—

he had learned that—and he left the porcupine's limp carcass by the path and turned back into the forest.

Water was everywhere, here on the lower slopes of the mountain. Its black runways ribbed the glowing floor of the forest on every side. It made a wall of cold about the place where he was, so that he had to climb back to the summit of the ridge and go around its sources.

The sun rose, bringing a scathing golden light that shriveled his pallid flesh, and brought the thirst up unbearably in his throat, driving him to the shelter of a cave. Blood would quench that awful, growing thirst, and drive out the cold that crept relentlessly over him, but it was hard to find blood. Other things would kill the cold—buds and growing things—but they could not quench the thirst or appease the savage hunger in him.

There was another night, at last, and he stood in the bright light of the shrinking moon high on a bare spur overlooking the valley. All the world lay before him, washed in silver and lined with black. He could see mountain after mountain, furred with the light of growing trees, blanketed in the glowing mist, their bald black crowns outlined against the moonlit clouds. He could see the mountain torrents streaking down their flanks, like inky ribbons, joining, broadening, flowing down to join the river that roared sullenly under its black shroud in the valley at his feet.

The valley was full of life. It was alive with growing things, and the white mist that rose from them and clothed them filled it in the brim with a broth of light through which the river and its tributaries cut sharp black lines of cold. There were other lights—yellow constellations of lamplight scattered over the silver meadows. Many of them clustered at the mouth of the valley, where the mountains drew apart, but they grew fewer and fewer as they followed the black barrier of the river, and at the head of the valley below him one glowing spark burned alone.

He stood with the moonlight washing his naked, dead-white body, staring at that speck of golden light. There was something he should know about it—something that was hidden in that other world he had been in. There was something that drew him to it—an invisible thread, stretched across space through the white night, binding him to it.

The next day he lay buried under a rotting log, halfway down the mountain. The following night, soon after moonrise, he came on a doe, its back broken, pinned under a fallen tree. He tore its throat out and drank the fuming blood that poured heat and life through his body, waking him, filling him with vigor. The cold was gone, and he was sure now that his fingers were glowing with a light of their own. Now he was really alive!

He followed a ridge, and before sunrise he came to the river's edge. The blackness was an impenetrable wall, hiding the other shore. Through it he could hear the rush of running water over gravel, the gurgle of eddies and the mutter of rapids. The sound tormented him and brought the thirst back into his throat, but he drew back into the forest, for the sky was already brightening in the east.

When the moon rose on the fourth night he had found nothing to eat. Its light brought him down out of the forest again, to the river's edge, where it broadened into a quiet millpond. The black fog was thin over the glassy surface of the water, and through it he saw the yellow lamplight of the house that had drawn him down from the mountain.

He stood waist-deep in the weeds that bordered the pond, watching those two yellow rectangles. Back in the icy blankness of his mind a memory was struggling to be known. But it belonged to the other world, the world he had left behind, and it faded.

The reflection of the lights lay in the still water of the pond. So still was it that the mist was but a black gauze drawn across the lamplight, dulling it. The water lay like a sheet of black glass, hard and polished, with the phantoms of the pines on its other bank growing upside-down in its quiet depths. The stars were reflected there in little winking spots, and the dwindling circle of the moon.

He did not hear the door slam, there among the pines. A new feeling was growing in him. It was strange. It was not thirst—not hunger. It submerged them in its all-powerful compulsion. It gripped his muscles and took them out of his control, forcing him step by step through the cattails to the river's edge. There was something he must do. Something—

She came out of the shadows and stood in the moonlight on the other bank, looking up at the moon. The lamplight was behind her and the silver torrent of the moon, poured over her slim, white body, over her shining black hair, caressing every line and curve of her long, slim figure. Her own light clung to her like a silver aura, soft and warm, welling out of her white skin and clinging lovingly about her, cloaking her beauty with light. That beauty drew him—out of the shadows, out of the forest, into the moonlight.

She did not see him at first. The night was warm and there was the first perfume of spring in the air. She stood on a rock at the water's edge, her arms lifted, her hands clasping her flood of night-black hair behind her head. All her young body was taut, stretching, welcoming the moonlight and the touch of the night breeze that sent little cat paws shivering over the glassy water. The moon seemed to be floating in the water, there just beyond her reach. She knotted her hair in a bun behind her head and stepped down quickly into the water. She stood with it just above her knees, watching the ripples widen and break the mirror surface of the pond. She followed their spread across that glassy disc.

She saw him.

He stood there, his face half in shadow, hunched and naked. His arms were skeleton's arms and his ribs showed under skin that hung in flabby white folds from his shoulders. His eyes were black pits and a stubble of black beard was smeared across his sagging cheeks. The mark of the owl's claws was across his face and it was pocked with purple blotches where he had pulled out the porcupine quills. Some of them were still in his side, where the beast's tail had lashed him. His flesh was livid white in the moonlight, blotched and smeared with the dark stain of death.

She saw him and knew him. Her hand went to the little cross that glowed like a coal of hidden fire in the hollow of her throat. Her voice rose and choked back:

"Joe! *Joe!*"

He saw her and remembered her. The thread he had felt on the mountain had been her presence, pulling him to her, stronger than thirst or hunger, stronger than death, stronger even than the black fog over the river. It was between them now, tightening, dragging him step by step into the silent water. Ripples broke against his legs and he felt the black mist rising from them, felt the numbness creeping into his feet, into his legs, up into his body. It was a day since he had killed the deer and had blood to warm him. He could not go on. He stood knee-deep, staring at her across the little space that separated them. He tried to speak, to call her name, but he had forgotten words.

Then she screamed and ran, a stream of white fire through the shadows, and he heard the house door slam after her and saw the shades come down, one after the other, over the yellow lamplight. He stood there, staring after her, until the cold crept up and began to choke him, and he turned and stumbled painfully ashore.

The moon found him high on the mountain, climbing from ledge to ledge, above the sources of the rushing torrents that walled him in, making his way towards the saddle that closed the valley's end. He could not cross running water, but he could go around it. He killed a rabbit and its blood helped him to go on, with the cold seeping up through his bones and hunger and thirst tearing at him like wild things. The new hunger, the yearning that drew him to the girl in the valley, was stronger than they. It was all that mattered now.

The moon was still in the sky when he stood under the pines before the closed door of the house. Half the night was gone, and clouds were gathering, filling up the sky and strewing long streamers across the moon's shrunken face. In the east thunder muttered, rolling among the mountains until it died away beneath the sound of the river.

The tie that was between them was like a rope of iron, pulling him across the narrow clearing to the doorstep of the house. The door was closed and the shades drawn over the windows on either side of it, but yellow lamplight streamed out through cracks in its weathered panels. He raised a hand to touch it and drew back as he saw the pattern of crossed planks that barred him and his kind.

He whimpered low in his throat, like the doe he had killed. The cross wove a steel net across the doorway that he could not break. He stepped back, off the doorstep. Then the door opened. She stood there.

Her back was to the light and he could see only the slim silhouette of her body, with the cross of golden fire at her throat and the aura of silvery mist clinging about her, so warm and bright that he was sure it must drown out the moonlight. Even through the dress she wore the fire of her young vitality shone out. He stood bathing in it, yearning for it, as the hunger and thirst and aching longing welled up in him through the bitter cold.

It was a minute perhaps, or five minutes, or only seconds until she spoke. Her voice was faint.

"Joe," she said. "Joe dear. You're hurt. Come inside."

The pattern of the cross on the door could not bar him after her welcome. He felt the barrier dissolve as he stepped through. The clouds had drawn away and the moon made a bright spot through the open door. He stood in it, watching her, seeing the familiar room with its scrubbed board floor, its plastered walls, its neat, black stove—seeing them as if for the first time. They stirred no memory in him. But the girl drew him.

He saw her dark eyes blacken with horror and the blood drain out of her cheeks and lips as she saw him for the first time in the lamplight. He looked down at his hands—the flesh cheese-white and sloughing—at his naked, discolored body, smeared with mud and stained with spilled blood. He whimpered, down in his throat, and took a stumbling step toward her, but her hand went up to the little crucifix at her throat and she slipped quickly around the table, placing it between them.

He stared at the cross. The golden fire that burned in it separated them as surely as the cold black fog of running water had done. Across the table he could feel its pure radiance, hot as sunlight. It would shrivel him to a cinder. He whined again, in agony, like a whipped dog. The longing for her was sheer torment now, drowning out all else, but it could not force him nearer.

The girl followed his gaze. The crucifix had been his gift—before—in that other world. She knew that, though he did not. Slowly she unfastened the ribbon that held it and dropped it into his outstretched hand.

The cross burned into his flesh like a hot coal. He snatched back his hand but the burning metal clung. He felt the heat of it coursing up his arm, and hurled it savagely across the room. He seized the table with both hands and flung it out of his way. Then she was before him, her back against the wall, her face a mask of horror. He heard her scream.

In him the terrible yearning that had drawn him down from the mountain had submerged the hunger and thirst and cold that had been his only driving forces before he knew her. Now, as they stood face to face, the older, stronger forces surged up in him and took possession of his numbed mind. With her scream a dam in him seemed to burst. He felt her warm, slim body twisting and jerking under his tightening fingers. He sensed the fragrance that rose from her. He saw her eyes, mad with fear, staring into his.

When it was over the hunger was gone, and the thirst. The cold had gone out of his bones. His muscles were no longer cramped and leaden. The yearning was gone, too. He looked down incuriously at the heap of shredded rags on the floor and turned to go.

At that moment the storm broke. The door was still open, and as he turned it seemed to be closed by a curtain of falling water. The black fog swirled among the raindrops, blotting out the world. He thrust out an exploring hand, marked with the charred brand of the cross, and snatched it back as he felt the chill of the mist.

He heard their voices only a moment before they stood there—three men, dripping, crowded together in the doorway, staring at the thing on the floor—and at him. For a flicker he remembered: Louis—her brother—and Jean and old Paul. The dogs were with them, but they slunk back, whining, afraid.

Louis knew him, as his sister had—as the others did. His whisper had hate in it as much as fear. It was on all their faces. They knew the curse that was on the unshriven of Joe Labatie's blood. They had known what it meant when he did not come down from the mountain on the night of the first storm. But only Louis, of them all, had seen the tree topple and pin him down. Louis it was who had made the mark of the cross in the snow that drifted over him and left him there. Louis Larue, who would not see the Labatie curse fall on his sister or her children after her.

It was old Paul whose gun bellowed. They saw the buckshot tear through that death-white body—saw the dark fluid that dripped from the awful wound—saw the dead thing that was Joe Labatie, his skull's eyes burning, as he surged toward them. They ran.

Louis held his ground, but the thing that rushed upon him was like a charging bear. It struck him and hurled him to the floor. Its slippery fingers bit into his shoulders; its hideous face hung close to his. But the crucifix at his throat saved him, as it might have saved her, and the thing recoiled and plunged out into the storm.

The rain was like ice on his naked body as he fled, rinsing the strength out of him as it might dissolve salt. The black mist filled the forest, blotting out the silver light of its living things. It closed over his body and sank into it, sucking out the unnatural life he had drunk in blood, draining it of warmth. He felt the great cold growing in him again. The moon was gone, and he was blind—cold and numb and blind. He crashed into a tree, and then another, and then his weakening legs buckled under him and he fell facedown at the river's edge.

He lay in the running water, shrouded in the black fog, feeling them approach. He heard their footsteps on the gravel, and felt their hands on him, dragging him out of the water, turning him over. He saw them—three pillars of white light, the yellow fire of their crucifixes at their throats, the black mist billowing around their bodies as they stood staring down at him. He felt Louis' boot as it swung brutally into his side and felt the bones snap and the flesh tear, but there was no pain—only the cold, the bitter, freezing cold that was always in him.

He knew that they were busy at something, but the cold was creeping up into his brain, behind his eyes, as the rain wrapped him in its deadly mist. Perhaps when the moon rose again its light would revive him. Perhaps he would kill again and feel the hot blood in his throat, and be free of the cold. He could barely see now, though his eyes were open and staring. He could see that old Paul had a long stake of wood in his hands, sharpened to a point. He saw Louis take it and raise it in both hands above his head. He saw Louis' teeth shine white in a savage grin.

He saw the stake sweep down—

FRITZ LEIBER, JR., *the son of a noted Shakespearean actor, was born in Chicago in 1910. He had a short career on the stage himself, and later appeared in several films. In 1939 he began publishing stories that have long since secured his reputation as one of the true masters of modern horror fiction, a position acknowledged with a Life Achievement Award presented to him in 1976 at the Second World Fantasy Convention.*

Leiber's work has spanned science fiction, fantasy, and sword-and-sorcery, but it is as a writer of horror fiction that he is likely to be remembered. Among his novels are such modern classics as Conjure Wife *(1943, filmed in 1944 as* Weird Woman *and in 1962 as* Burn, Witch, Burn), Gather, Darkness! *(1943), and* Our Lady of Darkness *(1977).*

Among his most memorable stories—many of which deal with the terrors of modern urban life, often as Leiber witnesses them from his own San Francisco apartment—are "Smoke Ghost" (1941), "Gonna Roll the Bones" (1967), and, especially, "The Girl with the Hungry Eyes."

The Girl with the Hungry Eyes (1949)

BY FRITZ LEIBER

All right, I'll tell you why the Girl gives me the creeps. Why I can't stand to go downtown and see the mob slavering up at her on the tower, with that pop bottle or pack of cigarettes or whatever it is beside her. Why I hate to look at magazines any more because I know she'll turn up somewhere in a brassière or a bubble bath. Why I don't like to think of millions of Americans drinking in that poisonous half-smile. It's quite a story—more story than you're expecting.

No, I haven't suddenly developed any long-haired indignation at the evils of advertising and the national glamor-girl complex. That'd be a laugh for a man in my racket, wouldn't it? Though I think you'll agree there's something a little perverted about trying to capitalize on sex that way. But it's okay with me. And I know we've had the Face and the Body and the Look and what not else, so why shouldn't someone come along who sums it all up so completely, that we have to call her the Girl and blazon her on all the billboards from Times Square to Telegraph Hill?

But the Girl isn't like any of the others. She's unnatural. She's morbid. She's unholy.

Oh, these are modern times, you say, and the sort of thing I'm hinting at went out with witchcraft. But you see I'm not altogether sure myself what I'm hinting at, beyond a certain point. There are vampires and vampires, and not all of them suck blood.

And there were the murders, if they were murders. Besides, let me ask you this. Why, when America is obsessed with the Girl, don't we find out more about her? Why doesn't she rate a *Time* cover with a droll biography inside? Why hasn't there been a feature in *Life* or the *Post?* A profile in *The New Yorker?* Why hasn't *Charm* or *Mademoiselle* done her career saga? Not ready for it? Nuts!

Why haven't the movies snapped her up? Why hasn't she been on "Information, Please"? Why don't we see her kissing candidates at political rallies? Why isn't she chosen queen of some sort of junk or other at a convention?

Why don't we read about her tastes and hobbies, her views of the Russian situation? Why haven't the columnists interviewed her in a kimono on the top floor of the tallest hotel in Manhattan and told us who her boyfriends are?

Finally—and this is the real killer—why hasn't she ever been drawn or painted?

Oh no she hasn't. If you knew anything about commercial art, you'd know that. Every blessed one of those pictures was worked up from a photograph. Expertly? Of course. They've got the top artists on it. But that's how it's done.

And now I'll tell you the why of all that. It's because from the top to the bottom of the whole world of advertising, news, and business, there isn't a solitary soul who knows where the Girl came from, where she lives, what she does, who she is, even what her name is.

You heard me. What's more, not a single solitary soul ever sees her —except one poor damned photographer, who's making more money off her than he ever hoped to in his life and who's scared and miserable as hell every minute of the day.

No, I haven't the faintest idea who he is or where he has his studio. But I know there has to be such a man and I'm morally certain he feels just like I said.

Yes, I might be able to find her, if I tried. I'm not sure though—by now she probably has other safeguards. Besides, I don't want to.

Oh, I'm off my rocker, am I? That sort of thing can't happen in the

Era of the Atom? People can't keep out of sight that way, not even Garbo?

Well, I happen to know they can, because last year I was that poor damned photographer I was telling you about. Yes, last year, when the Girl made her first poisonous splash right here in this big little city of ours.

Yes, I know you weren't here last year and you don't know about it. Even the Girl had to start small. But if you hunted through the files of the local newspapers, you'd find some ads, and I might be able to locate you some of the old displays—I think Lovelybelt is still using one of them. I used to have a mountain of photos myself, until I burned them.

Yes, I made my cut off her. Nothing like what that other photographer must be making, but enough so it still bought this whiskey. She was funny about money. I'll tell you about that.

But first picture me then. I had a fourth-floor studio in that rathole the Hauser Building, not far from Ardleigh Park.

I'd been working at the Marsh-Mason studios until I'd gotten my bellyful of it and decided to start in for myself. The Hauser Building was awful—I'll never forget how the stairs creaked—but it was cheap and there was a skylight.

Business was lousy. I kept making the rounds of all the advertisers and agencies, and some of them didn't object to me too much personally, but my stuff never clicked. I was pretty near broke. I was behind on my rent. Hell, I didn't even have enough money to have a girl.

It was one of those dark gray afternoons. The building was very quiet—I'd just finished developing some pix I was doing on speculation for Lovelybelt Girdles and Budford's Pool and Playground. My model had left. A Miss Leon. She was a civics teacher at one of the high schools and modeled for me on the side, just lately on speculation, too. After one look at the prints, I decided that Miss Leon probably wasn't just what Lovelybelt was looking for—or my photography either. I was about to call it a day.

And then the street door slammed four storys down and there were steps on the stairs and she came in.

She was wearing a cheap, shiny black dress. Black pumps. No stockings. And except that she had a gray cloth coat over one of them, those skinny arms of hers were bare. Her arms are pretty skinny, you know, or can't you see things like that any more?

And then the thin neck, the slightly gaunt, almost prim face, the tumbling mass of dark hair, and looking out from under it the hungriest eyes in the world.

That's the real reason she's plastered all over the country today, you know—those eyes. Nothing vulgar, but just the same they're looking at you with a hunger that's all sex and something more than sex. That's what everybody's been looking for since the Year One—something a little more than sex.

Well, boys, there I was, alone with the Girl, in an office that was getting shadowy, in a nearly empty building. A situation that a million male Americans have undoubtedly pictured to themselves with various lush details. How was I feeling? Scared.

I know sex can be frightening. That cold heart-thumping when you're alone with a girl and feel you're going to touch her. But if it was sex this time, it was overlaid with something else.

At least I wasn't thinking about sex.

I remember that I took a backward step and that my hand jerked so that the photos I was looking at sailed to the floor.

There was the faintest dizzy feeling like something was being drawn out of me. Just a little bit.

That was all. Then she opened her mouth and everything was back to normal for a while.

"I see you're a photographer, mister," she said. "Could you use a model?"

Her voice wasn't very cultivated.

"I doubt it," I told her, picking up the pix. You see, I wasn't impressed. The commercial possibilities of her eyes hadn't registered on me yet, by a long shot. "What have you done?"

Well, she gave me a vague sort of story and I began to check her knowledge of model agencies and studios and rates and what not and pretty soon I said to her, "Look here, you never modeled for a photographer in your life. You just walked in here cold."

Well, she admitted that was more or less so.

All along through our talk I got the idea she was feeling her way, like someone in a strange place. Not that she was uncertain of herself, or of me, but just of the general situation.

"And you think anyone can model?" I asked her pityingly.

"Sure," she said.

"Look," I said, "a photographer can waste a dozen negatives trying to get one halfway human photo of an average woman. How many do you think he'd have to waste before he got a real catchy, glamorous photo of her?"

"I think I could do it," she said.

Well, I should have kicked her out right then. Maybe I admired the cool way she stuck to her dumb little guns. Maybe I was touched by her underfed look. More likely I was feeling mean on account of the way my pictures had been snubbed by everybody and I wanted to take it out on her by showing her up.

"Okay, I'm going to put you on the spot," I told her. "I'm going to try a couple of shots of you. Understand it's strictly on spec. If somebody should ever want to use a photo of you, which is about one chance in two million, I'll pay you regular rates for your time. Not otherwise."

She gave me a smile. The first. "That's swell by me," she said.

Well, I took three or four shots, close-ups of her face since I didn't fancy her cheap dress, and at least she stood up to my sarcasm. Then I remembered I still had the Lovelybelt stuff and I guess the meanness was still working in me because I handed her a girdle and told her to go behind the screen and get into it and she did, without getting flustered as I'd expected, and since we'd gone that far, I figured we might as well shoot the beach scene to round it out, and that was that.

All this time I wasn't feeling anything particular one way or the other, except every once in a while I'd get one of those faint dizzy flashes and wonder if there was something wrong with my stomach or if I could have been a bit careless with my chemicals.

Still, you know, I think the uneasiness was in me all the while.

I tossed her a card and pencil. "Write your name and address and phone," I told her and made for the darkroom.

A little later she walked out. I didn't call any good-byes. I was irked because she hadn't fussed around or seemed anxious about her poses, or even thanked me, except for that one smile.

I finished developing the negatives, made some prints, glanced at them, decided they weren't a great deal worse than Miss Leon. On an impulse I slipped them in with the pictures I was going to take on the rounds next morning.

By now I'd worked long enough, so I was a bit fagged and nervous, but I didn't dare waste enough money on liquor to help that. I wasn't very hungry. I think I went to a cheap movie.

I didn't think of the Girl at all, except maybe to wonder faintly why in my present womanless state I hadn't made a pass at her. She had seemed to belong to a—well, distinctly more approachable social strata than Miss Leon. But then, of course, there were all sorts of arguable reasons for my not doing that.

Next morning I made the rounds. My first step was Munsch's Brewery. They were looking for a "Munsch Girl." Papa Munsch had a sort of affection for me, though he razzed my photography. He had a good natural judgment about that, too. Fifty years ago he might have been one of the shoestring boys who made Hollywood.

Right now he was out in the plant, pursuing his favorite occupation. He put down the beaded schooner, smacked his lips, gabbled something technical to someone about hops, wiped his fat hands on the big apron he was wearing, and grabbed my thin stack of pictures.

He was about halfway through, making noises with his tongue and teeth, when he came to her. I kicked myself for even having stuck her in.

"That's her," he said. "The photography's not so hot, but that's the girl."

It was all decided. I wonder now why Papa Munsch sensed what the Girl had right away, while I didn't. I think it was because I saw her first in the flesh, if that's the right word.

At the time I just felt faint.

"Who is she?" he asked.

"One of my new models." I tried to make it casual.

"Bring her out tomorrow morning," he told me. "And your stuff. We'll photograph her here.

"Here, don't look so sick," he added. "Have some beer."

Well, I went away telling myself it was just a fluke, so that she'd probably blow it tomorrow with her inexperience, and so on.

Just the same, when I reverently laid my next stack of pictures on Mr. Fitch, of Lovelybelt's, rose-colored blotter, I had hers on top.

Mr. Fitch went through the motions of being an art critic. He leaned over backward, squinted his eyes, waved his long fingers, and said, "Hmm. What do you think, Miss Willow? Here, in this light, of course, the photograph doesn't show the bias cut. And perhaps we should use the Lovelybelt Imp instead of the Angel. Still, the girl. . . . Come over here, Binns." More finger-waving. "I want a married man's reaction."

He couldn't hide the fact that he was hooked.

Exactly the same thing happened at Budford's Pool and Playground, except that Da Costa didn't need a married man's say-so.

"Hot stuff," he said, sucking his lips. "Oh boy, you photographers!"

I hotfooted it back to the office and grabbed up the card I'd given her to put down her name and address.

It was blank.

I don't mind telling you that the next five days were about the worst I ever went through, in an ordinary way. When next morning rolled around and I still hadn't got hold of her, I had to start stalling.

"She's sick," I told Papa Munsch over the phone.

"She at a hospital?" he asked me.

"Nothing that serious," I told him.

"Get her out here then. What's a little headache?"

"Sorry, I can't."

Papa Munsch got suspicious. "You really got this girl?"

"Of course I have."

"Well, I don't know. I'd think it was some New York model, except I recognized your lousy photography."

I laughed.

"Well, look, you get her here tomorrow morning, you hear?"

"I'll try."

"Try nothing. You get her out here."

He didn't know half of what I tried. I went around to all the model and employment agencies. I did some slick detective work at the photographic and art studios. I used up some of my last dimes putting advertisements in all three papers. I looked at high school yearbooks and at employee photos in local house organs. I went to restaurants and drugstores, looking at waitresses, and to dime stores and department stores, looking at clerks. I watched the crowds coming out of movie theaters. I roamed the streets.

Evenings, I spent quite a bit of time along Pickup Row. Somehow that seemed the right place.

The fifth afternoon I knew I was licked. Papa Munsch's deadline—he'd given me several, but this was it—was due to run out at six o'clock. Mr. Fitch had already canceled.

I was at the studio window, looking out at Ardleigh Park.

She walked in.

I'd gone over this moment so often in my mind that I had no trouble putting on my act. Even the faint dizzy feeling didn't throw me off.

"Hello," I said, hardly looking at her.

"Hello," she said.

"Not discouraged yet?"

"No." It didn't sound uneasy or defiant. It was just a statement.

I snapped a look at my watch, got up and said curtly, "Look here, I'm going to give you a chance. There's a client of mine looking for a girl your general type. If you do a real good job you might break into the modeling business.

"We can see him this afternoon if we hurry," I said. I picked up my stuff. "Come on. And next time if you expect favors, don't forget to leave your phone number."

"Uh-uh," she said, not moving.

"What do you mean?" I said.

"I'm not going out to see any client of yours."

"The hell you aren't," I said. "You little nut, I'm giving you a break."

She shook her head slowly. "You're not fooling me, baby. You're not fooling me at all. They want me." And she gave me the second smile.

At the time I thought she must have seen my newspaper ad. Now I'm not so sure.

"And now I'll tell you how we're going to work," she went on. "You aren't going to have my name or address or phone number. Nobody is. And we're going to do all the pictures right here. Just you and me."

You can imagine the roar I raised at that. I was everything—angry, sarcastic, patiently explanatory, off my nut, threatening, pleading.

I would have slapped her face off, except it was photographic capital.

In the end all I could do was phone Papa Munsch and tell him her conditions. I knew I didn't have a chance, but I had to take it.

He gave me a really angry bawling out, said "no" several times and hung up.

It didn't worry her. "We'll start shooting at ten o'clock tomorrow," she said.

It was just like her, using that corny line from the movie magazines.

About midnight Papa Munsch called me up.

"I don't know what insane asylum you're renting this girl from," he said, "but I'll take her. Come around tomorrow morning and I'll try to get it through your head just how I want the pictures. And I'm glad I got you out of bed!"

After that it was a breeze. Even Mr. Fitch reconsidered and, after taking two days to tell me it was quite impossible, he accepted the conditions too.

Of course you're all under the spell of the Girl, so you can't understand how much self-sacrifice it represented on Mr. Fitch's part when he agreed to forego supervising the photography of my model in the Lovelybelt Imp or Vixen or whatever it was we finally used.

Next morning she turned up on time according to her schedule, and we went to work. I'll say one thing for her, she never got tired and she never kicked at the way I fussed over shots. I got along okay, except I still had that feeling of something being shoved away gently. Maybe you've felt it just a little, looking at her picture.

When we finished I found out there were still more rules. It was about the middle of the afternoon. I started with her to get a sandwich and coffee.

"Uh-uh," she said, "I'm going down alone. And look, baby, if you ever try to follow me, if you ever so much as stick your head out of that window when I go, you can hire yourself another model."

You can imagine how all this crazy stuff strained my temper—and my imagination. I remember opening the window after she was gone—I waited a few minutes first—and standing there getting some fresh air and trying to figure out what could be behind it, whether she was hiding from the police, or was somebody's ruined daughter, or maybe had got the idea it was smart to be temperamental, or more likely Papa Munsch was right and she was partly nuts.

But I had my pictures to finish up.

Looking back, it's amazing to think how fast her magic began to take hold of the city after that. Remembering what came after, I'm frightened of what's happening to the whole country—and maybe the world. Yesterday I read something in *Time* about the Girl's picture turning up on billboards in Egypt.

The rest of my story will help show you why I'm frightened in that big, general way. But I have a theory, too, that helps explain, though it's one of those things that's beyond that "certain point." It's about the Girl. I'll give it to you in a few words.

You know how modern advertising gets everybody's mind set in the same direction, wanting the same things, imagining the same things.

And you know the psychologists aren't so skeptical of telepathy as they used to be.

Add up the two ideas. Suppose the identical desires of millions of people focussed on one telepathic person. Say a girl. Shaped her in their image.

Imagine her knowing the hiddenmost hungers of millions of men. Imagine her seeing deeper into those hungers than the people that had them, seeing the hatred and the wish for death behind the lust. Imagine her shaping herself in that complete image, keeping herself as aloof as marble. Yet imagine the hunger she might feel in answer to their hunger.

But that's getting a long way from the facts of my story. And some of those facts are darn solid. Like money. We made money.

That was the funny thing I was going to tell you. I was afraid the Girl was going to hold me up. She really had me over a barrel, you know.

But she didn't ask for anything but the regular rates. Later on I insisted on pushing more money at her, a whole lot. But she always took it with that same contemptuous look, as if she were going to toss it down the first drain when she got outside.

Maybe she did.

At any rate, I had money. For the first time in months I had money enough to get drunk, buy new clothes, take taxicabs. I could make a play for any girl I wanted to. I only had to pick.

And so of course I had to go and pick . . .

But first let me tell you about Papa Munsch.

Papa Munsch wasn't the first of the boys to try to meet my model but I think he was the first to really go soft on her. I could watch the change in his eyes as he looked at her pictures. They began to get sentimental, reverent. Mama Munsch had been dead for two years.

He was smart about the way he planned it. He got me to drop some information which told him when she came to work, and then one morning he came pounding up the stairs a few minutes before.

"I've got to see her, Dave," he told me.

I argued with him, I kidded him, I explained he didn't know just how serious she was about her crazy ideas. I even pointed out he was cutting both our throats. I even amazed myself by bawling him out.

He didn't take any of it in his usual way. He just kept repeating, "But, Dave, I've got to see her."

The street door slammed.

"That's her," I said, lowering my voice. "You've got to get out."

He wouldn't, so I shoved him in the darkroom, "And keep quiet," I whispered. "I'll tell her I can't work today."

I knew he'd try to look at her and probably come busting in, but there wasn't anything else I could do.

The footsteps came to the fourth floor. But she never showed at the door. I got uneasy.

"Get that bum out of there!" she yelled suddenly from beyond the door. Not very loud, but in her commonest voice.

"I'm going up to the next landing," she said. "And if that fat-bellied bum doesn't march straight down to the street, he'll never get another picture of me except spitting in his lousy beer."

Papa Munsch came out of the darkroom. He was white. He didn't look at me as he went out. He never looked at her pictures in front of me again.

That was Papa Munsch. Now it's me I'm telling about. I talked around the subject with her, I hinted, eventually I made my pass.

She lifted my hand off her as if it were a damp rag.

"No, baby," she said. "This is working time."

"But afterward . . ." I pressed.

"The rules still hold." And I got what I think was the fifth smile.

It's hard to believe, but she never budged an inch from that crazy line. I mustn't make a pass at her in the office, because our work was very important and she loved it and there mustn't be any distractions. And I couldn't see her anywhere else, because if I tried to, I'd never snap another picture of her—and all this with more money coming in all the time and me never so stupid as to think my photography had anything to do with it.

Of course I wouldn't have been human if I hadn't made more passes. But they always got the wet-rag treatment and there weren't any more smiles.

I changed. I went sort of crazy and light-headed—only sometimes I felt my head was going to burst. And I started to talk to her all the time. About myself.

It was like being in a constant delirium that never interfered with business. I didn't pay any attention to the dizzy feeling. It seemed natural.

I'd walk around and for a moment the reflector would look like a sheet of white-hot steel, or the shadows would seem like armies of moths, or the camera would be a big black coal car. But the next instant they'd come all right again.

I think sometimes I was scared to death of her. She'd seem the strangest, most horrible person in the world. But other times. . . .

And I talked. It didn't matter what I was doing—lighting her, posing her, fussing with props, snapping my pictures—or where she was —on the platform, behind the screen, relaxing with a magazine—I kept up a steady gab.

I told her everything I knew about myself. I told her about my first girl. I told her about my brother Bob's bicycle. I told her about running away on a freight, and the licking Pa gave me when I came home. I told her about shipping to South America and the blue sky at night. I told her about Betty. I told her about my mother dying of cancer. I told her about being beaten up in a fight in an alley behind a bar. I told her about Mildred. I told her about the first picture I ever sold. I told her how Chicago looked from a sailboat. I told her about the longest drunk I was ever on. I told her about Marsh-Mason. I told her about Gwen. I told her about how I met Papa Munsch. I told her about hunting her. I told her about how I felt now.

She never paid the slightest attention to what I said. I couldn't even tell if she heard me.

It was when we were getting our first nibble from national advertisers that I decided to follow her when she went home.

Wait, I can place it better than that. Something you'll remember from the out-of-town papers—those maybe murders I mentioned. I think there were six.

I say "maybe" because the police could never be sure they weren't heart attacks. But there's bound to be suspicion when attacks happen to people whose hearts have been okay, and always at night when they're alone and away from home and there's a question of what they were doing.

The six deaths created one of those "mystery poisoner" scares. And afterward there was a feeling that they hadn't really stopped, but were being continued in a less suspicious way.

That's one of the things that scares me now.

But at that time my only feeling was relief that I'd decided to follow her.

I made her work until dark one afternoon. I didn't need any excuses, we were snowed under with orders. I waited until the street door slammed, then I ran down. I was wearing rubber-soled shoes. I'd slipped on a dark coat she'd never seen me in, and a dark hat.

I stood in the doorway until I spotted her. She was walking by Ardleigh Park toward the heart of town. It was one of those warm fall nights. I followed her on the other side of the street. My idea for tonight was just to find out where she lived. That would give me a hold on her.

She stopped in front of a display window of Everley's department store, standing back from the flow. She stood there looking in.

I remembered we'd done a big photograph of her for Everley's, to make a flat model for a lingerie display. That was what she was looking at.

At the time it seemed all right to me that she should adore herself, if that was what she was doing.

When people passed she'd turn away a little or drift back farther into the shadows.

Then a man came by alone. I couldn't see his face very well, but he looked middle-aged. He stopped and stood looking in the window.

She came out of the shadows and stepped up beside him.

How would you boys feel if you were looking at a poster of the Girl and suddenly she was there beside you, her arm linked with yours?

This fellow's reaction showed plain as day. A crazy dream had come to life for him.

They talked for a moment. Then he waved a taxi to the curb. They got in and drove off.

I got drunk that night. It was almost as if she'd known I was following her and had picked that way to hurt me. Maybe she had. Maybe this was the finish.

But the next morning she turned up at the usual time and I was back in the delirium, only now with some new angles added.

That night when I followed her she picked a spot under a streetlight, opposite one of the Munsch Girl billboards.

Now it frightens me to think of her lurking that way.

After about twenty minutes a convertible slowed down going past her, backed up, swung into the curb.

I was closer this time. I got a good look at the fellow's face. He was a little younger, about my age.

Next morning the same face looked up at me from the front page of the paper. The convertible had been found parked on a side street. He had been in it. As in the other maybe-murders, the cause of death was uncertain.

All kinds of thoughts were spinning in my head that day, but there were only two things I knew for sure. That I'd got the first real offer from a national advertiser, and that I was going to take the Girl's arm and walk down the stairs with her when we quit work.

She didn't seem surprised. "You know what you're doing?" she said.

"I know."

She smiled. "I was wondering when you'd get around to it."

I began to feel good. I was kissing everything good-bye, but I had my arm around hers.

It was another of those warm fall evenings. We cut across into Ardleigh Park. It was dark there, but all around the sky was a sallow pink from the advertising signs.

We walked for a long time in the park. She didn't say anything and she didn't look at me, but I could see her lips twitching and after a while her hand tightened on my arm.

We stopped. We'd been walking across the grass. She dropped down and pulled me after her. She put her hands on my shoulders. I was looking down at her face. It was the faintest sallow pink from the glow in the sky. The hungry eyes were dark smudges.

I was fumbling with her blouse. She took my hand away, not like she had in the studio. "I don't want that," she said.

First I'll tell you what I did afterward. Then I'll tell you why I did it. Then I'll tell you what she said.

What I did was run away. I don't remember all of that because I was dizzy, and the pink sky was swinging against the dark trees. But after a while I staggered into the lights of the street. The next day I closed up the studio. The telephone was ringing when I locked the door and there were unopened letters on the floor. I never saw the Girl again in the flesh, if that's the right word.

I did it because I didn't want to die. I didn't want the life drawn out of me. There are vampires and vampires, and the ones that suck blood aren't the worst. If it hadn't been for the warning of those dizzy flashes, and Papa Munsch and the face in the morning paper, I'd have gone the way the others did. But I realized what I was up against while there was still time to tear myself away. I realized that wherever she came from, whatever shaped her, she's the quintessence of the horror behind the bright billboard. She's the smile that tricks you into throwing away your money and your life. She's the eyes that lead you on and on, and then show you death. She's the creature you give everything for and never really get. She's the being that takes everything you've got and gives nothing in return. When you yearn toward her face on the billboards, remember that. She's the lure. She's the bait. She's the Girl.

And this is what she said, "I want you. I want your high spots. I want everything that's made you happy and everything that's hurt you bad. I want your first girl. I want that shiny bicycle. I want that licking. I want that pinhole camera. I want Betty's legs. I want the blue sky filled with stars. I want your mother's death. I want your blood on the cobblestones. I want Mildred's mouth. I want the first picture you sold. I want the lights of Chicago. I want the gin. I want Gwen's hands. I want your wanting me. I want your life. Feed me, baby, feed me."

CYRIL M. KORNBLUTH *(1923–1958) possessed one of the most inventive and individual minds ever to work in the field of science fiction. From the time his stories first appeared in the 1940s, they won attention for the quality of their writing, for their social and political content, and for the moral questions they often raised.*

Many of his works are regarded as classics. They include his collaborative novel with Frederik Pohl The Space Merchants *(1952); his own novel* The Syndic *(1953); and his short stories "The Little Black Bag" (1950) and "The Marching Morons" (1951).*

All of Kornbluth's stories are intense, richly imagined, and emotionally powerful, and especially so in an outright horror story such as "The Mindworm." Characteristically, Kornbluth's treatment of the vampire theme is a highly original one.

The Mindworm
(1950)
BY C. M. KORNBLUTH

The handsome j. g. and the pretty nurse held out against it as long as they reasonably could, but blue Pacific water, languid tropical nights, the low atoll dreaming on the horizon—and the complete absence of any other nice young people for company on the small, uncomfortable parts boat—did their work. On June 30th they watched through dark glasses as the dazzling thing burst over the fleet and the atoll. Her manicured hand gripped his arm in excitement and terror. Unfelt radiation sleeted through their loins.

A storekeeper-third-class named Bielaski watched the young cou-·ple with more interest than he showed in Test Able. After all, he had twenty-five dollars riding on the nurse. That night he lost it to a chief bosun's mate who had backed the j. g.

In the course of time, the careless nurse was discharged under conditions other than honorable. The j. g., who didn't like to put things in writing, phoned her all the way from Manila to say it was a damned shame. When her gratitude gave way to specific inquiry, their overseas connection went bad and he had to hang up.

She had a child, a boy, turned it over to a foundling home, and vanished from his life into a series of good jobs and finally marriage.

The boy grew up stupid, puny and stubborn, greedy and miserable. To the home's hilarious young athletics director he suddenly said: "You hate me. You think I make the rest of the boys look bad."

The athletics director blustered and laughed, and later told the doctor over coffee: "I watch myself around the kids. They're sharp—they catch a look or a gesture and it's like a blow in the face to them, I know that, so I watch myself. So how did he know?"

The doctor told the boy: "Three pounds more this month isn't bad, but how about you pitch in and clean up your plate *every* day? Can't live on meat and water; those vegetables make you big and strong."

The boy said: "What's 'neurasthenic' mean?"

The doctor later said to the director: "It made my flesh creep. I was looking at his little spindling body and dishing out the old pep talk about growing big and strong, and inside my head I was thinking 'we'd call him neurasthenic in the old days' and then out he popped with it. What should we do? Should we do anything? Maybe it'll go away. I don't know anything about these things. I don't know whether anybody does."

"Reads minds, does he?" asked the director. *Be damned if he's going to read my mind about Shultz Meat Market's ten percent.* "Doctor, I think I'm going to take my vacation a little early this year. Has anybody shown any interest in adopting the child?"

"Not him. He wasn't a baby doll when we got him, and at present he's an exceptionally unattractive-looking kid. You know how people don't give a damn about anything but their looks."

"Some couples would take anything, or so they tell me."

"Unapproved for foster-parenthood, you mean?"

"Red tape and arbitrary classifications sometimes limit us too severely in our adoptions."

"If you're going to wish him on some screwball couple that the courts turned down as unfit, I want no part of it."

"You don't have to have any part of it, doctor. By the way, which dorm does he sleep in?"

"West," grunted the doctor, leaving the office.

The director called a few friends—a judge, a couple the judge referred him to, a court clerk. Then he left by way of the east wing of the building.

The boy survived three months with the Berrymans. Hard-drinking Mimi alternately caressed and shrieked at him; Edward W. tried to be a good scout and just gradually lost interest, looking clean through

him. He hit the road in June and got by with it for a while. He wore a
Boy Scout uniform, and Boy Scouts can turn up anywhere, any time.
The money he had taken with him lasted a month. When the last penny
of the last dollar was three days spent, he was adrift on a Nebraska
prairie. He had walked out of the last small town because the constable
was beginning to wonder what on earth he was hanging around for and
who he belonged to. The town was miles behind on the two-lane highway; the infrequent cars did not stop.

One of Nebraska's "rivers," a dry bed at this time of year, lay
ahead, spanned by a railroad culvert. There were some men in its shade,
and he was hungry.

They were ugly, dirty men, and their thoughts were muddled and
stupid. They called him "Shorty" and gave him a little dirty bread and
some stinking sardines from a can. The thoughts of one of them became
less muddled and uglier. He talked to the rest out of the boy's hearing,
and they whooped with laughter. The boy got ready to run, but his legs
wouldn't hold him up.

He could read the thoughts of the men quite clearly as they headed
for him. Outrage, fear, and disgust blended in him and somehow turned
inside-out and one of the men was dead on the dry ground, grasshop-
pers vaulting onto his flannel shirt, the others backing away, frightened
now, not frightening.

He wasn't hungry any more; he felt quite comfortable and satisfied.
He got up and headed for the other men, who ran. The rearmost of
them was thinking *Jeez he folded up the evil eye we was only gonna—*

Again the boy let the thoughts flow into his head and again he
flipped his own thoughts around them; it was quite easy to do. It was
different—this man's terror from the other's lustful anticipation. But
both had their points . . .

At his leisure, he robbed the bodies of three dollars and twenty-
four cents.

Thereafter his fame preceded him like a death wind. Two years on
the road and he had his growth and his fill of the dull and stupid minds
he met there. He moved to northern cities, a year here, a year there,
quiet, unobtrusive, prudent, an epicure.

Sebastian Long woke suddenly, with something on his mind. As
night fog cleared away he remembered, happily. Today he started the
Demeter Bowl! At last there was time, at last there was money—six
hundred and twenty-three dollars in the bank. He had packed and

shipped the three dozen cocktail glasses last night, engraved with Mrs. Klausman's initials—his last commercial order for as many months as the Bowl would take.

He shifted from nightshirt to denims, gulped coffee, boiled an egg but was too excited to eat it. He went to the front of his shop-work-room-apartment, checked the lock, waved at neighbors' children on their way to school, and ceremoniously set a sign in the cluttered window.

It said: "NO COMMERCIAL ORDERS TAKEN UNTIL FUR-THER NOTICE."

From a closet he tenderly carried a shrouded object that made a double armful and laid it on his workbench. Unshrouded, it was a glass bowl—*what* a glass bowl! The clearest Swedish lead glass, the purest lines he had ever seen, his secret treasure since the crazy day he had bought it, long ago, for six months' earnings. His wife had given him hell for that until the day she died. From the closet he brought a portfolio filled with sketches and designs dating back to the day he had bought the bowl. He smiled over the first, excitedly scrawled—a florid, rococo conception, unsuited to the classicism of the lines and the serenity of the perfect glass.

Through many years and hundreds of sketches he had refined his conception to the point where it was, he humbly felt, not unsuited to the medium. A strongly-molded Demeter was to dominate the piece, a matron as serene as the glass, and all the fruits of the earth would flow from her gravely outstretched arms.

Suddenly and surely, he began to work. With a candle he thinly smoked an oval area on the outside of the bowl. Two steady fingers clipped the Demeter drawing against the carbon black; a hair-fine needle in his other hand traced her lines. When the transfer of the design was done, Sebastian Long readied his lathe. He fitted a small copper wheel, slightly worn as he liked them, into the chuck and with his fingers charged it with the finest rouge from Rouen. He took an ashtray cracked in delivery and held it against the spinning disk. It bit in smoothly, with the *wiping* feel to it that was exactly right.

Holding out his hands, seeing that the fingers did not tremble with excitement, he eased the great bowl to the lathe and was about to make the first tiny cut of the millions that would go into the masterpiece.

Somebody knocked on his door and rattled the doorknob.

Sebastian Long did not move or look toward the door. Soon the busybody would read the sign and go away. But the pounding and the rattling of the knob went on. He eased down the bowl and angrily went to the window, picked up the sign, and shook it at whoever it was—he couldn't make out the face very well. But the idiot wouldn't go away.

The engraver unlocked the door, opened it a bit, and snapped: "The shop is closed. I shall not be taking any orders for several months. Please don't bother me now."

"It's about the Demeter Bowl," said the intruder.

Sebastian Long stared at him. "What the devil do you know about my Demeter Bowl?" He saw the man was a stranger, undersized by a little, middle-aged . . .

"Just let me in please," urged the man. "It's important. Please!"

"I don't know what you're talking about," said the engraver. "But what do you know about my Demeter Bowl?" He hooked his thumbs pugnaciously over the waistband of his denims and glowered at the stranger. The stranger promptly took advantage of his hand being removed from the door and glided in.

Sebastian Long thought briefly that it might be a nightmare as the man darted quickly about his shop, picking up a graver and throwing it down, picking up a wire scratch-wheel and throwing it down. "Here, you!" he roared, as the stranger picked up a crescent wrench which he did not throw down.

As Long started for him, the stranger darted to the workbench and brought the crescent wrench down shatteringly on the bowl.

Sebastian Long's heart was bursting with sorrow and rage; such a storm of emotions as he never had known thundered through him. Paralyzed, he saw the stranger smile with anticipation.

The engraver's legs folded under him and he fell to the floor, drained and dead.

The Mindworm, locked in the bedroom of his brownstone front, smiled again, reminiscently.

Smiling, he checked the day on a wall calender.

"Dolores!" yelled her mother in Spanish. "Are you going to pass the whole day in there?"

She had been practicing low-lidded, sexy half-smiles like Lauren Bacall in the bathroom mirror. She stormed out and yelled in English: "I don't know how many times I tell you not to call me that Spick name no more!"

"Dolly!" sneered her mother. "Dah-lee! When was there a Saint Dah-lee that you call yourself after, eh?"

The girl snarled a Spanish obscenity at her mother and ran down the tenement stairs. Jeez, she was gonna be late for sure!

Held up by a stream of traffic between her and her streetcar, she danced with impatience. Then the miracle happened. Just like in the movies, a big convertible pulled up before her and its lounging driver said, opening the door: "You seem to be in a hurry. Could I drop you somewhere?"

Dazed at the sudden realization of a hundred daydreams, she did not fail to give the driver a low-lidded, sexy smile as she said: "Why, *thanks!*" and climbed in. He wasn't no Cary Grant, but he had all his hair . . . kind of small, but so was she . . . and jeez, the convertible had *leopard-skin seat covers!*

The car was in the stream of traffic, purring down the avenue. "It's a lovely day," she said. "Really too nice to work."

The driver smiled shyly, kind of like Jimmy Stewart but of course not so tall, and said: "I feel like playing hooky myself. How would you like a spin down Long Island?"

"Be wonderful!" The convertible cut left on an odd-numbered street.

"Play hooky, you said. What do you do?"

"Advertising."

"Advertising!" Dolly wanted to kick herself for ever having doubted, for ever having thought in low, self-loathing moments that it wouldn't work out, that she'd marry a grocer or a mechanic and live forever after in a smelly tenement and grow old and sick and stooped. She felt vaguely in her happy daze that it might have been cuter, she might have accidentally pushed him into a pond or something, but this was cute enough. An advertising man, leopard-skin seat covers . . . what more could a girl with a sexy smile and a nice little figure want?

Speeding down the South Shore she learned that his name was Michael Brent, exactly as it ought to be. She wished she could tell him she was Jennifer Brown or one of those real cute names they had nowadays, but was reassured when he told her he thought Dolly Gonzalez was a beautiful name. He didn't, and she noticed the omission, add: "It's the most beautiful name I ever heard!" That, she comfortably thought as she settled herself against the cushions, would come later.

They stopped at Medford for lunch, a wonderful lunch in a little restaurant where you went down some steps and there were candles on the table. She called him "Michael" and he called her "Dolly." She learned that he liked dark girls and thought the stories in *True Story* really were true, and that he thought she was just tall enough, and that Greer Garson was wonderful, but not the way she was, and that he thought her dress was just wonderful.

They drove slowly after Medford, and Michael Brent did most of the talking. He had traveled all over the world. He had been in the war and wounded—just a flesh wound. He was thirty-eight, and had been married once, but she died. There were no children. He was alone in the world. He had nobody to share his town house in the 50's, his country place in Westchester, his lodge in the Maine woods. Every word sent the girl floating higher and higher on a tide of happiness; the signs were unmistakable.

When they reached Montauk Point, the last sandy bit of the continent before blue water and Europe, it was sunset, with a great wrinkled sheet of purple and rose stretching half across the sky and the first stars appearing above the dark horizon of the water.

The two of them walked from the parked car out onto the sand, alone, bathed in glorious Technicolor. Her heart was nearly bursting with joy as she heard Michael Brent say, his arms tightening around her: "Darling, will you marry me?"

"Oh, *yes*, Michael!" she breathed, dying.

The Mindworm, drowsing, suddenly felt the sharp sting of danger. He cast out through the great city, dragging tentacles of thought:

". . . die if she don't let me . . ."

". . . six an' six is twelve an' carry one an' three is four . . ."

". . . gobblegobble madre de dios pero soy gobblegobble . . ."

". . . parlay Domino an' Missab and shoot the roll on Duchess Peg in the feature . . ."

". . . melt resin add the silver chloride and dissolve in oil of lavender stand and decant and fire to cone zero twelve give you shimmering streaks of luster down the walls . . ."

". . . moiderin' square-headed gobblegobble tried ta poke his eye out wassamatta witta ref . . ."

". . . O God I am most heartily sorry I have offended thee in . . ."

". . . talk like a commie . . ."

". . . gobblegobblegobble two dolla twenny-fi' sense gobble . . ."

". . . just a nip and fill it up with water and brush my teeth . . ."

". . . really know I'm God but fear to confess their sins . . ."

". . . dirty lousy rock-headed claw-handed paddle-footed goggle-eyed snot-nosed hunch-backed feeble-minded pot-bellied son of . . ."

". . . write on the wall alfie is a stunkur and then . . ."

". . . thinks I believe it's a television set but I know he's got a bomb in there but who can I tell who can help so alone . . ."

". . . gabble was ich weiss nicht gabble geh bei Broadvay gabble . . ."

". . . habt mein daughter Rosie such a fella gobblegobble . . ."

". . . wonder if that's one didn't look back . . ."

". . . seen with her in the Medford restaurant . . ."

The Mindworm struck into that thought.

". . . not a mark on her but the M. E.'s have been wrong before and heart failure don't mean a thing anyway try to talk to her old lady authorize an autopsy get Pancho little guy talks Spanish be best . . ."

The Mindworm knew he would have to be moving again—soon. He was sorry; some of the thoughts he had tapped indicated good . . . hunting?

Regretfully, he again dragged his net:

". . . with chartreuse drinks I mean drapes could use a drink come to think of it . . ."

". . . reep-beep-reep-beep reepiddy-beepiddy-beep bop man wadda beat . . ."

" $\sum_{r=l+1} \phi(\alpha_r, \alpha_r) - \sum_{s=1} \phi(\alpha_s, \alpha_s)$. *What the Hell was that?*"

The Mindworm withdrew, in frantic haste. The intelligence was massive, its overtones those of a vigorous adult. He had learned from certain dangerous children that there was peril of a leveling flow. Shaken and scared, he contemplated traveling. He would need more than that wretched girl had supplied, and it would not be epicurean. There would be no time to find individuals at a ripe emotional crisis, or goad them to one. It would be plain—munching. The Mindworm drank a glass of water, also necessary to his metabolism.

EIGHT FOUND DEAD
IN UPTOWN MOVIE;
"MOLESTER" SOUGHT

Eight persons, including three women, were found dead Wednesday night of unknown causes in widely separated seats in the balcony of the Odeon Theater at 117th St. and Broadway. Police are seeking a man described by the balcony usher, Michael Fenelly, 18, as "acting like a woman-molester."

Fenelly discovered the first of the fatalities after seeing the man "moving from one empty seat to another several times." He went to ask a woman in a seat next to one the man had just vacated whether he had annoyed her. She was dead.

Almost at once, a scream rang out. In another part of the balcony Mrs. Sadie Rabinowitz, 40, uttered the cry when another victim toppled from his seat next to her.

Theater manager I. J. Marcusohn stopped the show and turned on the house lights. He tried to instruct his staff to keep the audience from leaving before the police arrived. He failed to get word to them in time, however, and most of the audience was gone when a detail from the 24th Pct. and an ambulance from Harlem Hospital took over at the scene of the tragedy.

The Medical Examiner's office has not yet made a report as to the causes of death. A spokesman said the victims showed no signs of poisoning or violence. He added that it "was inconceivable that it could be a coincidence."

Lt. John Braidwood of the 24th Pct. said of the alleged molester: "We got a fair description of him and naturally we will try to bring him in for questioning."

Clickety-click, clickety-click, clickety-click sang the rails as the Mindworm drowsed in his coach seat.

Some people were walking forward from the diner. One was thinking: "Different-looking fellow. (a) he's aberrant. (b) he's nonaberrant and ill. Cancel (b)—respiration normal, skin smooth and healthy, no tremor of limbs, well-groomed. Is aberrant (1) trivially. (2) significantly. Cancel (1)—displayed no involuntary interest when . . . odd! *Running* for the washroom! Unexpected because (a) neat grooming indicates amour propre inconsistent with amusing others; (b) evident health inconsistent with . . ." It had taken one second, was fully detailed.

The Mindworm, locked in the toilet of the coach, wondered what the next stop was. He was getting off at it—not frightened, just careful. Dodge them, keep dodging them and everything would be all right. Send out no mental taps until the train was far away and everything would be all right.

He got off at a West Virginia coal and iron town surrounded by ruined mountains and filled with the offscourings of Eastern Europe. Serbs, Albanians, Croats, Hungarians, Slovenes, Bulgarians, and all possible combinations and permutations thereof. He walked slowly from the smoke-stained, brownstone passenger station. The train had roared on its way.

". . . ain' no gemmum that's fo sho', fi-cen' tip fo' a good shine lak ah give um . . ."

". . . dumb bassar don't know how to make out a billa lading yet he ain't never gonna know so fire him get it over with . . ."

". . . gabblegabblegabble . . ." Not a word he recognized in it.

". . . gobblegobble dat tam vooman I brek she nack . . ."

". . . gobble trink visky chin glassabeer gobblegobblegobble . . ."

". . . gabblegabblegabble . . ."

". . . makes me so gobblegobble mad little no-good tramp no she ain' but I don' like no standup from no dame . . ."

A blond, square-headed boy fuming under a street light.

". . . out wit' Casey Oswiak I could kill that dumb bohunk alla time trine ta paw her . . ."

It was a possibility. The Mindworm drew near.

". . . stand me up for that gobblegobble bohunk I oughtta slap her inna mush like my ole man says . . ."

"Hello," said the Mindworm.

"Waddaya wan'?"

"Casey Oswiak told me to tell you not to wait up for your girl. He's taking her out tonight."

The blond boy's rage boiled into his face and shot from his eyes. He was about to swing when the Mindworm began to feed. It was like pheasant after chicken, venison after beef. The coarseness of the environment, or the ancient strain? The Mindworm wondered as he strolled down the street. A girl passed him:

". . . oh but he's gonna be mad like last time wish I came right away so jealous kinda nice but he might bust me one some day be nice to him tonight there he is lam'post leaning on it looks kinda funny gawd I hope he ain't drunk looks kinda funny sleeping sick or bozhe moi gabblegabblegabble . . ."

Her thoughts trailed into a foreign language of which the Mindworm knew not a word. After hysteria had gone she recalled, in the foreign language, that she had passed him.

The Mindworm, stimulated by the unfamiliar quality of the last feeding, determined to stay for some days. He checked in at a Main Street hotel.

Musing, he dragged his net:

". . . gobblegobblewhompyeargobblecheskygobblegabblechy-esh . . ."

". . . take him down cellar beat the can off the damn chesky thief put the fear of god into him teach him can't bust into no boxcars in *mah* parta the caounty . . ."

". . . gabblegabble . . ."

". . . phone ole Mister Ryan in She-cawgo and he'll tell them three-card monte grifters who got the horse-room rights in this necka the woods by damn don't pay protection money for no protection . . ."

The Mindworm followed that one further; it sounded as though it could lead to some money if he wanted to stay in the town long enough.

The Eastern Europeans of the town, he mistakenly thought, were like the tramps and bums he had known and fed on during his years on the road—stupid and safe, safe and stupid, quite the same thing.

In the morning he found no mention of the square-headed boy's death in the town's paper and thought it had gone practically unnoticed. It had—by the paper, which was of, by, and for the coal and iron company and its native-American bosses and straw bosses. The other town, the one without a charter or police force, with only an imported weekly newspaper or two from the nearest city, noticed it. The other town had roots more than two thousand years deep, which are hard to pull up. But the Mindworm didn't know it was there.

He fed again that night, on a giddy young streetwalker in her room. He had astounded and delighted her with a fistful of ten-dollar bills before he began to gorge. Again the delightful difference from city-bred folk was there. . . .

Again in the morning he had been unnoticed, he thought. The chartered town, unwilling to admit that there were streetwalkers or that they were found dead, wiped the slate clean; its only member who really cared was the native-American cop on the beat who had collected weekly from the dead girl.

The other town, unknown to the Mindworm, buzzed with it. A delegation went to the other town's only public officer. Unfortunately he was young, American-trained, perhaps even ignorant about some important things. For what he told them was: "My children, that is foolish superstition. Go home."

The Mindworm, through the day, roiled the surface of the town proper by allowing himself to be roped into a poker game in a parlor of the hotel. He wasn't good at it, he didn't like it, and he quit with relief when he had cleaned six shifty-eyed, hard-drinking loafers out of about three hundred dollars. One of them went straight to the police station and accused the unknown of being a sharper. A humorous sergeant, the Mindworm was pleased to note, joshed the loafer out of his temper.

Nightfall again, hunger again . . .

He walked the streets of the town and found them empty. It was strange. The native-American citizens were out, tending bar, walking their beats, locking up their newspaper on the stones, collecting their rents, managing their movies—but where were the others? He cast his net:

". . . gobblegobblegobble whomp year gobble . . ."

". . . crazy old pollack mama of mine try to lock me in with Errol Flynn at the Majestic never know the difference if I sneak out the back . . ."

That was near. He crossed the street and it was nearer. He homed on the thought:

". . . jeez he's a hunka man like Stanley but he never looks at me that Vera Kowalik I'd like to kick her just once in the gobblegobblegobble crazy old mama won't be American so ashamed . . ."

It was half a block, no more, down a side street. Brick houses, two stories, with back yards on an alley. She was going out the back way.

How strangely quiet it was in the alley.

". . . ea-sy down them steps fix that damn board that's how she caught me last time what the hell are they all so scared of went to see Father Drugas won't talk bet somebody got it again that Vera Kowalik and her big . . ."

". . . gobble bozhe gobble whomp year gobble . . ."

She was closer; she was closer.

"All think I'm a kid show them who's a kid bet if Stanley caught me alone out here in the alley dark and all he wouldn't think I was a kid that damn Vera Kowalik her folks don't think she's a kid . . ."

For all her bravado she was stark terrified when he said: "Hello."

"Who—who—who—?" she stammered.

Quick, before she screamed. Her terror was delightful.

Not too replete to be alert, he cast about, questing.

". . . gobblegobblegobble whomp year."

The countless eyes of the other town, with more than two thousand years of experience in such things, had been following him. What he had sensed as a meaningless hash of noise was actually an impassioned outburst in a nearby darkened house.

"Fools! fools! Now he has taken a virgin! I said not to wait. What will we say to her mother?"

An old man with handlebar mustache and, in spite of the heat, his shirt sleeves decently rolled down and buttoned at the cuffs, evenly replied: "My heart in me died with hers, Casimir, but one must be sure. It would be a terrible thing to make a mistake in such an affair."

The weight of conservative elder opinion was with him. Other old men with mustaches, some perhaps remembering mistakes long ago, nodded and said: "A terrible thing. A terrible thing."

The Mindworm strolled back to his hotel and napped on the made bed briefly. A tingle of danger awakened him. Instantly he cast out:

". . . gobblegobble whompyear."

". . . whampyir."

"WAMPYIR!"

Close! Close and deadly!

The door of his room burst open, and mustached old men with their shirt sleeves rolled down and decently buttoned at the cuffs unhesitatingly marched in, their thoughts a turmoil of alien noises, foreign gibberish that he could not wrap his mind around, disconcerting, from every direction.

The sharpened stake was through his heart and the scythe blade through his throat before he could realize that he had not been the first of his kind; and that what clever people have not yet learned, some quite ordinary people have not yet entirely forgotten.

RICHARD MATHESON *(born 1926) has had a brilliant career as novelist, short story writer, and screenwriter since his memorable first story, "Born of Man and Woman," appeared in* The Magazine of Fantasy and Science Fiction *in 1950. His television work includes many scripts for the classic "Twilight Zone" (including the famous* Nightmare at 20,000 Feet *episode), as well as many detective and western series.*

His novels include one of the most famous vampire tales ever written, I Am Legend *(1954), about a world in which everyone, with a single exception, has become a vampire;* The Shrinking Man *(1956), adapted by Matheson himself for the 1957 film;* A Stir of Echoes *(1958); and* Hell House *(1971), filmed as* The Legend of Hell House *(1973). Perhaps his best, and best-known, novel is the fantasy/love story,* Bid Time Return *(1975), which won a World Fantasy Award as Best Novel of the Year at the Second World Fantasy Convention in 1976 and was later filmed as* Somewhere in Time.

Matheson's short stories have always been unique, even when he writes about familiar subject matter. Vampires have drawn his attention most notably in I Am Legend, *in "No Such Thing as a Vampire," and in the story included here, "Drink My Blood" (1951), which has also been published under the title "Blood Son."*

Drink My Blood
(1951)
BY RICHARD MATHESON

The people on the block decided definitely that Jules was crazy when they heard about his composition.

There had been suspicions for a long time.

He made people shiver with his blank stare. His coarse guttural tongue sounded unnatural in his frail body. The paleness of his skin upset many children. It seemed to hang loose around his flesh. He hated sunlight.

And his ideas were a little out of place for the people who lived on the block.

Jules wanted to be a vampire.

People declared it common knowledge that he was born on a night when winds uprooted trees. They said he was born with three teeth.

They said he'd used them to fasten himself on his mother's breast, drawing blood with the milk.

They said he used to cackle and bark in his crib after dark. They said he walked at two months and sat staring at the moon whenever it shone.

Those were things that people said.

His parents were always worried about him. An only child, they noticed his flaws quickly.

They thought he was blind until the doctor told them it was just a vacuous stare. He told them that Jules, with his large head, might be a genius or an idiot. It turned out he was an idiot.

He never spoke a word until he was five. Then one night coming up to supper, he sat down at the table and said, "Death."

His parents were torn between delight and disgust. They finally settled for a place in between the two feelings. They decided that Jules couldn't have realized what the word meant.

But Jules did.

From that night on, he built up such a large vocabulary that everyone who knew him was astonished. He not only acquired every word spoken to him, words from signs, magazines, books; he made up his own words.

Like nighttouch. Or killove. They were really several words that melted into each other. They said things Jules felt but couldn't explain with other words.

He used to sit on the porch while the other children played hopscotch, stickball and other games. He sat there and stared at the sidewalk and made up words.

Until he was twelve Jules kept pretty much out of trouble. Of course there was the time they found him undressing Olive Jones in an alley. And another time he was discovered dissecting a kitten on his bed.

But there were many years in between. Those scandals were forgotten.

In general he went through childhood merely disgusting people.

He went to school but never studied. He spent about two or three terms in each grade. The teachers all knew him by his first name. In some subjects, like reading and writing, he was almost brilliant.

In others he was hopeless.

One Saturday when he was twelve, Jules went to the movies. He saw *Dracula*.

When the show was over he walked, a throbbing nerve mass, through the little-girl and -boy ranks.

He went home and locked himself in the bathroom for two hours.

His parents pounded on the door and threatened but he wouldn't come out.

Finally he unlocked the door and sat down at the supper table. He had a bandage on his thumb and a satisfied look on his face.

The morning after he went to the library. It was Sunday. He sat on the steps all day, waiting for it to open. Finally he went home.

The next morning he came back instead of going to school.

He found *Dracula* on the shelves. He couldn't borrow it because he wasn't a member and to be a member he had to bring in one of his parents.

So he stuck the book down his pants and left the library and never brought it back.

He went to the park and sat down and read the book through. It was late evening before he finished.

He started at the beginning again, reading as he ran from street-light to streetlight, all the way home.

He didn't hear a word of the scolding he got for missing lunch and supper. He ate, went in his room and read the book to the finish. They asked him where he got the book. He said he found it.

As the days passed Jules read the story over and over. He never went to school.

Late at night, when he had fallen into an exhausted slumber, his mother used to take the book into the living room and show it to her husband.

One night they noticed that Jules had underlined certain sentences with dark shaky pencil lines.

Like: "The lips were crimson with fresh blood and the stream had trickled over her chin and stained the purity of her lawn death robe."

Or: "When the blood began to spurt out, he took my hands in one of his, holding them tight and, with the other seized my neck and pressed my mouth to the wound. . . ."

When his mother saw this, she threw the book down the garbage chute.

The next morning when Jules found the book missing he screamed and twisted his mother's arm until she told him where the book was.

Then he ran down to the cellar and dug in the piles of garbage until he found the book.

Coffee grounds and egg yolk on his hands and wrists, he went to the park and read it again.

For a month he read the book avidly. Then he knew it so well he threw it away and just thought about it.

Absence notes were coming from school. His mother yelled. Jules decided to go back for a while.

He wanted to write a composition.

One day he wrote it in class. When everyone was finished writing, the teacher asked if anyone wanted to read their compositions to the class.

Jules raised his hand.

The teacher was surprised. But she felt charity. She wanted to encourage him. She drew in her tiny jab of a chin and smiled.

"All right," she said, "pay attention, children. Jules is going to read us his composition."

Jules stood up. He was excited. The paper shook in his hands.

"My Ambition by . . ."

"Come to the front of the class, Jules, dear."

Jules went to the front of the class. The teacher smiled lovingly. Jules started again.

"My Ambition by Jules Dracula."

The smile sagged.

"When I grow up I want to be a vampire."

The teacher's smiling lips jerked down and out. Her eyes popped wide.

"I want to live forever and get even with everybody and make all the girls vampires. I want to smell of death."

"Jules!"

"I want to have a foul breath that stinks of dead earth and crypts and sweet coffins."

The teacher shuddered. Her hands twitched on her green blotter. She couldn't believe her ears. She looked at the children. They were gaping. Some of them were giggling. But not the girls.

"I want to be all cold and have rotten flesh with stolen blood in the veins."

"That will . . . hrrumph!"

The teacher cleared her throat mightily.

"That will be all, Jules," she said.

Jules talked louder and desperately.

"I want to sink my terrible white teeth in my victims' necks. I want them to . . ."

"Jules! Go to your seat this instant!"

"I want them to slide like razors in the flesh and into the veins," read Jules ferociously.

The teacher jolted to her feet. Children were shivering. None of them were giggling.

"Then I want to draw my teeth out and let the blood flow easy in my mouth and run hot in my throat and . . ."

The teacher grabbed his arm. Jules tore away and ran to a corner. Barricaded behind a stool he yelled:

"And drip off my tongue and run out of my lips down my victims' throats! I want to drink girls' blood!"

The teacher lunged for him. She dragged him out of the corner. He clawed at her and screamed all the way to the door and the principal's office.

"That is my ambition! That is my ambition! That is my ambition!"

It was grim.

Jules was locked in his room. The teacher and the principal sat with Jules' parents. They were talking in sepulchral voices.

They were recounting the scene.

All along the block parents were discussing it. Most of them didn't believe it at first. They thought their children made it up.

Then they thought what horrible children they'd raised if the children could make up such things.

So they believed it.

After that everyone watched Jules like a hawk. People avoided his touch and look. Parents pulled their children off the street when he approached. Everyone whispered tales of him.

There were more absence notes.

Jules told his mother he wasn't going to school any more. Nothing would change his mind. He never went again.

When a truant officer came to the apartment Jules would run over the roofs until he was far away from there.

A year wasted by.

Jules wandered the streets searching for something; he didn't know what. He looked in alleys. He looked in garbage cans. He looked in lots. He looked on the east side and the west side and in the middle.

He couldn't find what he wanted.

He rarely slept. He never spoke. He stared down all the time. He forgot his special words.

Then.

One day in the park, Jules strolled through the zoo.

An electric shock passed through him when he saw the vampire bat.

His eyes grew wide and his discolored teeth shone dully in a wide smile.

From that day on, Jules went daily to the zoo and looked at the bat. He spoke to it and called it the Count. He felt in his heart it was really a man who had changed.

A rebirth of culture struck him.

He stole another book from the library. It told all about wildlife.

He found the page on the vampire bat. He tore it out and threw the book away.

He learned the section by heart.

He knew how the bat made its wound. How it lapped up the blood like a kitten drinking cream. How it walked on folded wing stalks and hind legs like a black furry spider. Why it took no nourishment but blood.

Month after month Jules stared at the bat and talked to it. It became the one comfort in his life. The one symbol of dreams come true.

One day Jules noticed that the bottom of the wire covering the cage had come loose.

He looked around, his black eyes shifting. He didn't see anyone looking. It was a cloudy day. Not many people were there.

Jules tugged at the wire.

It moved a little.

Then he saw a man come out of the monkey house. So he pulled back his hand and strolled away, whistling a song he had just made up.

Late at night, when he was supposed to be asleep, he would walk barefoot past his parents' room. He would hear his father and mother snoring. He would hurry out, put on his shoes and run to the zoo.

Every time the watchman was not around, Jules would tug at the wiring.

He kept on pulling it loose.

When he had finished and had to run home, he pushed the wire in again. Then no one could tell.

All day Jules would stand in front of the cage and look at the Count and chuckle and tell him he'd soon be free again.

He told the Count all the things he knew. He told the Count he was going to practice climbing down walls headfirst.

He told the Count not to worry. He'd soon be out. Then, together, they could go all around and drink girls' blood.

One night Jules pulled the wire out and crawled under it into the cage.

It was very dark.

He crept on his knees to the little wooden house. He listened to see if he could hear the Count squeaking.

He stuck his arm in the black doorway. He kept whispering.

He jumped when he felt a needle jab in his finger.

With a look of great pleasure on his thin face, Jules drew the fluttering hairy bat to him.

He climbed down from the cage with it and ran out of the zoo; out of the park. He ran down the silent streets.

It was getting late in the morning. Light touched the dark skies with gray. He couldn't go home. He had to have a place.

He went down an alley and climbed over a fence. He held tight to the bat. It lapped at the dribble of blood from his finger.

He went across a yard and into a little deserted shack.

It was dark inside and damp. It was full of rubble and tin cans and soggy cardboard and excrement.

Jules made sure there was no way the bat could escape.

Then he pulled the door tight and put a stick through the metal loop.

He felt his heart beating hard and his limbs trembling.

He let go of the bat. It flew to a dark corner and hung on the wood.

Jules feverishly tore off his shirt. His lips shook. He smiled a crazy smile.

He reached down into his pants pocket and took out a little penknife he had stolen from his mother.

He opened it and ran a finger over the blade. It sliced through the flesh.

With shaking fingers he jabbed at his throat. He hacked. The blood ran through his fingers.

"Count! Count!" he cried in frenzied joy. "Drink my red blood! Drink me! Drink me!"

He stumbled over the tin cans and slipped and felt for the bat. It sprang from the wood and soared across the shack and fastened itself on the outer side.

Tears ran down Jules' cheeks.

He gritted his teeth. The blood ran across his shoulders and across his thin hairless chest.

His body shook in fever. He staggered back toward the other side. He tripped and felt his side torn open on the sharp edge of a tin can.

His hands went out. They clutched the bat. He placed it against his throat. He sank on his back on the cool wet earth. He sighed.

He started to moan and clutch at his chest. His stomach heaved. The black bat on his neck silently lapped his blood.

Jules felt his life seeping away.

He thought of all the years past. The waiting. His parents. School. Dracula. Dreams. For this. This sudden glory.

Jules' eyes flickered open.

The side of the reeking shack swam about him.

It was hard to breathe. He opened his mouth to gasp in the air. He sucked it in. It was foul. It made him cough. His skinny body lurched on the cold ground.

Mists crept away in his brain.

One by one like drawn veils.

Suddenly his mind was filled with terrible clarity.

He knew he was lying half-naked on garbage and letting a flying bat drink his blood.

With a strangled cry, he reached up and tore away the furry throbbing bat. He flung it away from him. It came back, fanning his face with its vibrating wings.

Jules staggered to his feet.

He felt for the door. He could hardly see. He tried to stop his throat from bleeding so.

He managed to get the door open.

Then, lurching into the dark yard, he fell on his face in the long grass blades.

He tried to call out for help.

But no sounds, save a bubbling mockery of words, came from his lips.

He heard the fluttering wings.

Then, suddenly, they were gone.

Strong fingers lifted him gently. Through dying eyes Jules saw the tall dark man whose eyes shone like rubies.

"My son," the man said.

CHARLES BEAUMONT *was the pseudonym of Charles Nutt (1929–1967), one of the finest writers who ever worked in the genre of dark fantasy.*

Beaumont sold his first story in 1951. When Playboy *magazine began publishing his highly polished tales in 1956, he achieved considerable notoriety, but his great ambition was to be a screenwriter. His first film was* Queen of Outer Space *(1958), but he went on to write* The Premature Burial *(1963) with Ray Russell;* Burn, Witch, Burn *(1964) with Richard Matheson;* The Seven Faces of Dr. Lao *(1964); and several films directed by Roger Corman based on stories by Edgar Allen Poe, including* The Masque of the Red Death.

Beaumont's letters, which remain unpublished, reveal a man intent on having a good time, driving fast cars, finding enough money to pay the bills, loving every minute of his life, allowing nothing to escape his critical eye and his sharp pen, and struggling every day to write better than the previous day. In light of all this, his personal tragedy is all the sadder. In 1964 Beaumont began suffering from a rare wasting disease from which he died just six weeks after his thirty-eighth birthday.

Beaumont's short stories are often cited by many writers today, myself included, as a strong factor in making them want to be writers themselves. His stories are often ironic, even bitter, and merciless in their depiction of human nature, while they are always flawlessly structured and beautifully written. They can be sampled in a 1982 paperback anthology called Best of Beaumont.

In the introduction to a 1962 anthology he edited, Beaumont wrote about "the most terrifying monster of them all. He's called The Mind." To emphasize the point, Beaumont called that book The Fiend in You.

Place of Meeting
(1953)
BY CHARLES BEAUMONT

It swept down from the mountains, a loose, crystal-smelling wind, an autumn chill of moving wetness. Down from the mountains and into the town, where it set the dead trees hissing and the signboards creaking. And it even went into the church, because the bell was ringing and there was no one to ring the bell.

The people in the yard stopped their talk and listened to the rusty music.

Big Jim Kroner listened too. Then he cleared his throat and clapped his hands—thick hands, calloused and work-dirtied.

"All right," he said loudly. "All right, let's us settle down now." He walked out from the group and turned. "Who's got the list?"

"Got it right here, Jim," a woman said, coming forward with a loose-leaf folder.

"All present?"

"Everybody except that there German, Mr. Grunin—Grunger—"

Kroner smiled; he made a megaphone of his hands. "Grüninger— Barthold Grüninger?"

A small man with a mustache called out excitedly, "Ja, ja! . . . s'war schwer den Friedhof zu finden."

"All right. That's all we wanted to know, whether you was here or not." Kroner studied the pages carefully. Then he reached into the back pocket of his overalls and withdrew a stub of pencil and put the tip to his mouth.

"Now, before we start off," he said to the group, "I want to know is there anybody here that's got a question or anything to ask?" He looked over the crowd of silent faces. "Anybody don't know who I am? No?"

It came another wind then, mountain-scattered and fast: it billowed dresses, set damp hair moving; it pushed over pewter vases, and smashed dead roses and hydrangeas to swirling dust against the gritty tombstones. Its clean rain smell was gone now, though, for it had passed over the fields with the odors of rotting life.

Kroner made a check mark in the notebook. "Anderson," he shouted. "Edward L."

A man in overalls like Kroner's stepped forward.

"Andy, you covered Skagit valley, Snohomish and King counties, as well as Seattle and the rest?"

"Yes, sir."

"What you got to report?"

"They're all dead," Anderson said.

"You looked everywhere? You was real careful?"

"Yes, sir. Ain't nobody alive in the whole state."

Kroner nodded and made another check mark. "That's all, Andy. Next: Avakian, Katina."

A woman in a wool skirt and gray blouse walked up from the back, waving her arms. She started to speak.

Kroner tapped his stick. "Listen here for a second, folks," he said.

"For those that don't know how to talk English, you know what this is all about—so when I ask my question, you just nod up-and-down for yes (like this) and sideways (like this) for no. Makes it a lot easier for those of us as don't remember too good. All right?"

There were murmurings and whispered consultations and for a little while the yard was full of noise. The woman called Avakian kept nodding.

"Fine," Kroner said. "Now, Miss Avakian. You covered what? . . . Iran, Iraq, Turkey, Syria. Did you—find—an-ybody a-live?"

The woman stopped nodding. "No," she said. "No, no."

Kroner checked the name. "Let's see here. Boleslavsky, Peter. You go on back, Miss Avakian."

A man in bright city clothes walked briskly to the tree clearing. "Yes, sir," he said.

"What have you got for us?"

The man shrugged. "Well, I tell you; I went over New York with a fine-tooth comb. Then I hit Brooklyn and Jersey. Nothin', man. Nothin' nowhere."

"He is right," a dark-faced woman said in a tremulous voice. "I was there too. Only the dead in the streets, all over, all over the city; in the cars I looked even, in the *offices.* Everywhere is people dead."

"Chavez, Pietro. Baja California."

"All dead, señor chief."

"Ciodo, Ruggiero. Capri."

The man from Capri shook his head violently.

"Denman, Charlotte. Southern United States."

"Dead as doornails . . ."

"Elgar, David S. . . .

"Ferrazio, Ignatz . . .

"Goldfarb, Bernard . . .

"Halpern . . .

"Ives . . . Kranek . . . O'Brian . . ."

The names exploded in the pale evening air like deep gunshots; there was much head-shaking, many people saying, "No. No."

At last Kroner stopped marking. He closed the notebook and spread his big workman's hands. He saw the round eyes, the trembling mouths, the young faces; he saw all the frightened people.

A girl began to cry. She sank to the damp ground, and covered her face and made these crying sounds. An elderly man put his hand on her head. The elderly man looked sad. But not afraid. Only the young ones seemed afraid.

"Settle down now," Kroner said firmly. "Settle on down. Now, listen to me. I'm going to ask you all the same question one more time, because we got to be sure." He waited for them to grow quiet. "All right. This here is all of us, every one. We've covered all the spots. Did anybody here find one single solitary sign of life?"

The people were silent. The wind had died again, so there was no sound at all. Across the corroded wire fence the gray meadows lay strewn with the carcasses of cows and horses and, in one of the fields, sheep. No flies buzzed near the dead animals; there were no maggots burrowing. No vultures; the sky was clean of birds. And in all the untended rolling hills of grass and weeds which had once sung and pulsed with a million voices, in all the land there was only this immense stillness now, still as years, still as the unheard motion of the stars.

Kroner watched the people. The young woman in the gay print dress; the tall African with his bright paint and cultivated scars; the fierce-looking Swede looking not so fierce now in this graying twilight. He watched all the tall and short and old and young people from all over the world, pressed together now, a vast silent polyglot in this country meeting place, this always lonely and long-deserted spot—deserted even before the gas bombs and the disease and the flying pestilences that had covered the earth in three days and three nights. Deserted. Forgotten.

"Talk to us, Jim," the woman who had handed him the notebook said. She was new.

Kroner put the list inside his big overalls pocket.

"Tell us," someone else said. "How shall we be nourished? What will we do?"

"The world's all dead," a child moaned. "Dead as dead, the whole world . . ."

"Todo el mund—"

"Monsieur Kroner, Monsieur Kroner, what will we do?"

Kroner smiled. "Do?" He looked up through the still-hanging poison cloud, the dun blanket, up to where the moon was now risen in full coldness. His voice was steady, but it lacked life. "What some of us have done before," he said. "We'll go back and wait. It ain't the first time. It ain't the last."

A little fat bald man with old eyes sighed and began to waver in the October dusk. The outline of his form wavered and disappeared in the shadows under the trees where the moonlight did not reach. Others followed him as Kroner talked.

"Same thing we'll do again and likely keep on doing. We'll go back and—sleep. And we'll wait. Then it'll start all over again and folks'll build their cities—new folks with new blood—and then we'll wake up. Maybe a long time yet. But it ain't so bad; it's quiet, and time passes." He lifted a small girl of fifteen or sixteen with pale cheeks and red lips. "Come on, now! Why, just think of the appetite you'll have all built up!"

The girl smiled. Kroner faced the crowd and waved his hands, large hands, rough from the stone of midnight pyramids and the feel of muskets, boil-speckled from night hours in packing plants and trucking lines; broken by the impact of a tomahawk and a machine-gun bullet; but white where the dirt was not caked, and bloodless. Old hands, old beyond years.

As he waved, the wind came limping back from the mountains. It blew the heavy iron bell high in the steepled white barn, and set the signboards creaking, and lifted ancient dusts and hissed again through the dead trees.

Kroner watched the air turn black. He listened to it fill with the flappings and the flutterings and the squeakings. He waited; then he stopped waving and sighed and began to walk.

He walked to a place of vines and heavy brush. Here he paused for a moment and looked out at the silent place of high dark grass, of hidden huddled tombs, of scrolls and stone-frozen children stained silver in the night's wet darkness; at the crosses he did not look. The people were gone; the place was empty.

Kroner kicked away the foliage. Then he got into the coffin and closed the lid.

Soon he was asleep.

The Living Dead
(1967)
BY ROBERT BLOCH

All day long he rested, while the guns thundered in the village below. Then, in the slanting shadows of the late afternoon, the rumbling echoes faded into the distance and he knew it was over. The American advance had crossed the river. They were gone at last, and it was safe once more.

Above the village, in the crumbling ruins of the great château atop the wooded hillside, Count Barsac emerged from the crypt.

The Count was tall and thin—cadaverously thin, in a manner most hideously appropriate. His face and hands had a waxen pallor; his hair was dark, but not as dark as his eyes and the hollows beneath them. His cloak was black, and the sole touch of color about his person was the vivid redness of his lips when they curled in a smile.

He was smiling now, in the twilight, for it was time to play the game.

The name of the game was Death, and the Count had played it many times.

He had played it in Paris on the stage of the Grand Guignol; his name had been plain Eric Karon then, but still he'd won a certain renown for his interpretation of bizarre roles. Then the war had come and, with it, his opportunity.

Long before the Germans took Paris, he'd joined their Underground, working long and well. As an actor he'd been invaluable.

And this, of course, was his ultimate reward—to play the supreme role, not on the stage, but in real life. To play without the artifice of spotlights, in true darkness; this was the actor's dream come true. He had even helped to fashion the plot.

"Simplicity itself," he told his German superiors. "Château Barsac has been deserted since the Revolution. None of the peasants from the village dare to venture near it, even in daylight, because of the legend. It is said, you see, that the last Count Barsac was a vampire."

And so it was arranged. The shortwave transmitter had been set up in the large crypt beneath the château, with three skilled operators in attendance, working in shifts. And he, "Count Barsac," in charge of the entire operation, as guardian angel. Rather, as guardian demon.

"There is a graveyard on the hillside below," he informed them. "A humble resting place for poor and ignorant people. It contains a single imposing crypt—the ancestral tomb of the Barsacs. We shall open that crypt, remove the remains of the last Count, and allow the villagers to discover that the coffin is empty. They will never dare come near the spot or the château again, because this will prove that the legend is true —Count Barsac is a vampire, and walks once more."

The question came then. "What if there are sceptics? What if someone does not believe?"

And he had his answer ready. "They will believe. For at night I shall walk—I, Count Barsac."

After they saw him in the makeup, wearing the black cloak, there were no more questions. The role was his.

The role was his, and he'd played it well. The Count nodded to himself as he climbed the stairs and entered the roofless foyer of the château, where only a configuration of cobwebs veiled the radiance of the rising moon.

Now, of course, the curtain must come down. If the American advance had swept past the village below, it was time to make one's bow and exit. And that too had been well arranged.

During the German withdrawal another advantageous use had been made of the tomb in the graveyard. A cache of Air Marshal Goering's art treasures now rested safely and undisturbed within the crypt. A truck had been placed in the château. Even now the three wireless operators would be playing new parts—driving the truck down the hillside to the tomb, placing the *objets d'art* in it.

By the time the Count arrived there, everything would be packed. They would then don the stolen American Army uniforms, carry the forged identifications and permits, drive through the lines across the river, and rejoin the German forces at a predesignated spot. Nothing had been left to chance. Someday, when he wrote his memoirs . . .

But there was not time to consider that now. The Count glanced up through the gaping aperture in the ruined roof. The moon was high. It was time to leave.

In a way he hated to go. Where others saw only dust and cobwebs he saw a stage—the setting of his finest performance. Playing a vampire's role had not addicted him to the taste of blood—but as an actor he enjoyed the taste of triumph. And he had triumphed here.

"Parting is such sweet sorrow." Shakespeare's line. Shakespeare, who had written of ghosts and witches, of bloody apparitions. Because Shakespeare knew that his audiences, the stupid masses, believed in such things—just as they still believed today. A great actor could always make them believe.

The Count moved into the shadowy darkness outside the entrance of the château. He started down the pathway toward the beckoning trees.

It was here, amid the trees, that he had come upon Raymond, one evening weeks ago. Raymond had been his most appreciative audience —a stern, dignified, white-haired elderly man, mayor of the village of Barsac. But there had been nothing dignified about the old fool when he'd caught sight of the Count looming up before him out of the night. He'd screamed like a woman and run.

Probably Raymond had been prowling around, intent on poaching, but all that had been forgotten after his encounter in the woods. The mayor was the one to thank for spreading the rumors that the Count was again abroad. He and Clodez, the oafish miller, had then led an armed band to the graveyard and entered the Barsac tomb. What a fright they got when they discovered the Count's coffin open and empty!

The coffin had contained only dust that had been scattered to the winds, but they could not know that. Nor could they know about what had happened to Suzanne.

The Count was passing the banks of the small stream now. Here, on another evening, he'd found the girl—Raymond's daughter, as luck would have it—in an embrace with young Antoine LeFevre, her lover.

Antoine's shattered leg had invalided him out of the army, but he ran like a deer when he glimpsed the cloaked and grinning Count. Suzanne had been left behind and that was unfortunate, because it was necessary to dispose of her. Her body had been buried in the woods, beneath great stones, and there was no question of discovery; still, it was a regrettable incident.

In the end, however, everything was for the best. Now silly super-stitious Raymond was doubly convinced that the vampire walked. He had seen the creature himself, had seen the empty tomb and the open coffin; his own daughter had disappeared. At his command none dared venture near the graveyard, the woods, or the château beyond.

Poor Raymond! He was not even a mayor any more—his village had been destroyed in the bombardment. Just an ignorant, broken old man, mumbling his idiotic nonsense about the "living dead."

The Count smiled and walked on, his cloak fluttering in the breeze, casting a batlike shadow on the pathway before him. He could see the graveyard now, the tilted tombstones rising from the earth like leprous fingers rotting in the moonlight. His smile faded; he did not like such thoughts. Perhaps the greatest tribute to his talent as an actor lay in his actual aversion to death, to darkness and what lurked in the night. He hated the sight of blood, had developed within himself an almost claus-trophobic dread of the confinement of the crypt.

Yes, it had been a great role, but he was thankful it was ending. It would be good to play the man once more, and cast off the creature he had created.

As he approached the crypt he saw the truck waiting in the shad-ows. The entrance to the tomb was open, but no sounds issued from it. That meant his colleagues had completed their task of loading and were ready to go. All that remained now was to change his clothing, remove the makeup and depart.

The Count moved to the darkened truck. And then . . .

Then they were upon him, and he felt the tines of the pitchfork bite into his back, and as the flash of lanterns dazzled his eyes he heard the stern command. "Don't move!"

He didn't move. He could only stare as they surrounded him—Antoine, Clodez, Raymond, and the others, a dozen peasants from the village. A dozen armed peasants, glaring at him in mingled rage and fear, holding him at bay.

But how could they dare?

The American corporal stepped forward. That was the answer, of

course—the American corporal and another man in uniform, armed
with a sniper's rifle. They were responsible. He didn't even have to see
the riddled corpses of the three shortwave operators piled in the back of
the truck to understand what had happened. They'd stumbled on his
men while they worked, shot them down, then summoned the villagers.

Now they were jabbering questions at him, in English, of course.
He understood English, but he knew better than to reply. "Who are
you? Were these men working under your orders? Where were you
going with this truck?"

The Count smiled and shook his head. After a while they stopped,
as he knew they would.

The corporal turned to his companion. "Okay," he said. "Let's
go." The other man nodded and climbed into the cab of the truck as the
motor coughed into life. The corporal moved to join him, then turned
to Raymond.

"We're taking this across the river," he said. "Hang on to our
friend here—they'll be sending a guard detail for him within an hour."

Raymond nodded.

The truck drove off into the darkness.

And as it was dark now—the moon had vanished behind a cloud.
The Count's smile vanished, too, as he glanced around at his captors. A
rabble of stupid clods, surly and ignorant. But armed. No chance of
escaping. And they kept staring at him, and mumbling.

"Take him into the tomb."

It was Raymond who spoke, and they obeyed, prodding their captive forward with pitchforks. That was when the Count recognized the
first faint ray of hope. For they prodded him most gingerly, no man
coming close, and when he glared at them their eyes dropped.

They were putting him in the crypt because they were afraid of
him. Now the Americans were gone, they feared him once more—
feared his presence and his power. After all, in their eyes he was a
vampire—he might turn into a bat and vanish entirely. So they wanted
him in the tomb for safekeeping.

The Count shrugged, smiled his most sinister smile, and bared his
teeth. They shrank back as he entered the doorway. He turned and, on
impulse, furled his cape. It was an instinctive final gesture, in keeping
with his role—and it provoked the appropriate response. They moaned,
and old Raymond crossed himself. It was better, in a way, than any
applause.

In the darkness of the crypt the Count permitted himself to relax a trifle. He was offstage now. A pity he'd not been able to make his exit the way he'd planned, but such were the fortunes of war. Soon he'd be taken to the American headquarters and interrogated. Undoubtedly there would be some unpleasant moments, but the worst that could befall him was a few months in a prison camp. And even the Americans must bow to him in appreciation when they heard the story of his masterful deception.

It was dark in the crypt, and musty. The Count moved about restlessly. His knee grazed the edge of the empty coffin set on a trestle in the tomb. He shuddered involuntarily, loosening his cape at the throat. It would be good to remove it, good to be out of here, good to shed the role of vampire forever. He'd played it well, but now he was anxious to be gone.

There was a mumbling audible from outside, mingled with another and less identifiable noise—a scraping sound. The Count moved to the closed door of the crypt and listened intently; but now there was only silence.

What were the fools doing out there? He wished the Americans would hurry back. It was too hot in here. And why the sudden silence?

Perhaps they'd gone.

Yes. That was it. The Americans had told them to wait and guard him, but they were afraid. They really believed he was a vampire—old Raymond had convinced them of that. So they'd run off. They'd run off, and he was free, he could escape now . . .

So the Count opened the door.

And he saw them then, saw them standing and waiting, old Raymond staring sternly for a moment before he moved forward. He was holding something in his hand, and the Count recognized it, remembering the scraping sound that he'd heard.

It was a long wooden stake with a sharp point.

Then he opened his mouth to scream, telling them it was only a trick, he was no vampire, they were a pack of superstitious fools . . .

But all the while they bore him back into the crypt, lifting him up and thrusting him into the open coffin, holding him there as the grim-faced Raymond raised the pointed stake above his heart.

It was only when the stake came down that he realized there's such a thing as playing a role too well.

The short stories of British author ROBERT AICKMAN *(1914–1981)* stand as a high point of horror–fantasy literature in the second half of the twentieth century. Many writers in the field, as well as readers, consider him the best of our time.

Trained as an architect, Aickman began publishing in Great Britain in 1951. Although his interests were broad—besides writing film and drama criticism, he also founded Great Britain's Inland Waterways Association—he confined his fiction to short forms and made himself a master of the short story's power to create chilling effects.

Collections of his stories, with some duplication of contents, include We Are for the Dark *(1951)*, Dark Entries *(1964)*, Powers of Darkness *(1966)*, Sub Rosa *(1968)*, Cold Hand in Mine *(1975)*, Tales of Love and Death *(1977)*, and Painted Devils *(1979)*.

Aickman's great power was in creating lifelike characters in a realistic setting, and then imbuing that world with a chilling touch of the supernatural. Nowhere is his ability to create an effect of subtle horror more evident than in "Pages from a Young Girl's Journal," which won the 1975 World Fantasy Award for best short fiction of the year.

Pages from a Young Girl's Journal (1975)

BY ROBERT AICKMAN

3 OCTOBER. Padua—Ferrara—Ravenna. We've reached Ravenna only four days after leaving that horrid Venice. And all in a hired carriage! I feel sore and badly bitten too. It was the same yesterday, and the day before, and the day before that. I wish I had someone to talk to. This evening, Mamma did not appear for dinner at all. Papa just sat there saying nothing and looking at least two hundred years old instead of only one hundred, as he usually does. I wonder how old he *really* is? But it's no good wondering. We shall never know, or at least I shan't. I often think Mamma *does* know, or very nearly. I wish Mamma were someone I could talk to, like Caroline's Mamma. I often used to think that Caroline and her Mamma were more like sisters together, though of course I could never say such a thing. But then Caroline is pretty and gay, whereas I am pale and quiet. When I came up here to my room

after dinner, I just sat in front of the long glass and stared and stared. I must have done it for half an hour or perhaps an hour. I only rose to my feet when it had become quite dark outside.

I don't like my room. It's much too big and there are only two wooden chairs, painted in greeny-blue with gold lines, or once painted like that. I hate having to lie on my bed when I should prefer to sit and everyone knows how bad it is for the back. Besides, this bed, though it's enormous, seems to be as hard as when the earth's dried up in summer. Not that the earth's like that here. Far from it. The rain has never stopped since we left Venice. Never once. Quite unlike what Miss Gisborne said before we set out from my dear, dear Derbyshire. This bed really is *huge*. It would take at least eight people my size. I don't like to think about it. I've just remembered: it's the third of the month so that we've been gone exactly half a year. What a lot of places I have been to in that time—or been through! Already I've quite forgotten some of them. I never properly saw them in any case. Papa has his own ideas and one thing I'm sure of is that they are quite unlike other people's ideas. To me the whole of Padua is just a man on a horse—stone or bronze, I suppose, but I don't even know which. The whole of Ferrara is a huge palace—castle—fortress that simply frightened me, so that I didn't *want* to look. It was as big as this bed—in its own way, of course. And those were two large, famous towns I have visited this very week. Let alone where I was perhaps two months ago! What a farce! as Caroline's Mamma always says. I wish she were here now and Caroline too. No one ever hugged and kissed me and made things happy as they do.

The contessa has at least provided me with no fewer than twelve candles. I found them in one of the drawers. I suppose there's nothing else to do but read—except perhaps to say one's prayers. Unfortunately, I finished all the books I brought with me long ago, and it's so difficult to buy any new ones, especially in English. However, I managed to purchase two very long ones by Mrs. Radcliffe before we left Venice. Unfortunately, though there are twelve candles, there are only two candlesticks, both broken, like everything else. Two candles *should* be enough, but all they seem to do is make the room look even larger and darker. Perhaps they are not-very-good foreign candles. I noticed that they seemed very dirty and discoloured in the drawer. In fact, one of them looked quite black. That one must have lain in the drawer a very long time. By the way, there is a framework hanging from the ceiling in the middle of the room. I cannot truthfully describe it as a chandelier: perhaps as the ghost of a chandelier. In any case, it is a long way from even the foot of the bed. They do have the most *enormous* rooms in these foreign houses where we stay. Just as if it were very warm the whole time, which it certainly is not. What a farce!

As a matter of fact, I'm feeling quite cold at this moment, even though I'm wearing my dark-green woollen dress that in Derbyshire saw me through the whole of last winter. I wonder if I should be any warmer *in* bed? It is something I can never make up my mind about. Miss Gisborne always calls me "such a chilly mortal". I see I have used the present tense. I wonder if that is appropriate in the case of Miss Gisborne? Shall I ever see Miss Gisborne again? I mean in *this* life, of course.

Now that six days have passed since I have made an entry in this journal, I find that I am putting down *everything*, as I always do once I make a start. It is almost as if nothing could happen to me as long as I keep on writing. That is simply silly, but I sometimes wonder whether the silliest things are not often the truest.

I write down words on the page, but what do I say? Before we started, everyone told me that, whatever else I did, I *must* keep a journal, a travel journal. I do not think this a travel journal at all. I find that when I am travelling with Papa and Mamma, I seem hardly to look at the outside world. Either we are lumbering along, with Papa and Mamma naturally in the places from which something can be seen, or at least from which things can be best seen; or I find that I am alone in some great vault of a bedroom for hours and hours and hours, usually quite unable to go to sleep, sometimes for the whole night. I should see so much more if I could sometimes walk about the different cities on my own—naturally, I do not mean at night. I wish that were possible. Sometimes I really hate being a girl. Even Papa cannot hate my being a girl more than I do sometimes.

And then when there *is* something to put down, it always seems to be the same thing! For example, here we are in still another of these households to which Papa always seems to have an entrée. Plainly it is very wicked of me, but I sometimes wonder *why* so many people should want to know Papa, who is usually so silent and disagreeable, and always so old! Perhaps the answer is simple enough: it is that they never meet him—or Mamma—or me. We drive up, Papa gives us all over to the major-domo or someone, and the family never sets eyes on us, because the family is never at home. These foreign families seem to have terribly many houses and always to be living in another of them. And when one of the family *does* appear, he or she usually seems to be almost as old as Papa and hardly able to speak a word of English. I think I have a pretty voice, though it's difficult to be quite sure, but I deeply wish I had worked harder at learning foreign languages. At least —the trouble is that Miss Gisborne is so bad at teaching them. I must say *that* in my own defence, but it doesn't help much now. I wonder how Miss Gisborne would be faring if she were in this room with me? Not much better than I am, if you ask me.

I have forgotten to say, though, that this is one of the times when we *are* supposed to be meeting the precious family; though, apparently, it consists only of two people, the contessa and her daughter. Sometimes I feel that I have already seen enough women without particularly wanting to meet any new ones, whatever their ages. There's something rather monotonous about women—unless, of course, they're like Caroline and her Mamma, which none of them are, or could be. So far the contessa and her daughter have not appeared. I don't know why not, though no doubt Papa knows. I am told that we are to meet them both tomorrow. I expect very little. I wonder if it will be warm enough for me to wear my green satin dress instead of my green woollen dress? Probably not.

And this is the town where the great, the immortal Lord Byron lives in sin and wildness! Even Mamma has spoken of it several times. Not that this melancholy house is actually *in* the town. It is a villa at some little distance away from it, though I do not know in which direction, and I am sure that Mamma neither knows nor cares. It seemed to me that after we passed through the town this afternoon, we travelled on for fifteen or twenty minutes. Still, to be even in the same *region* as Lord Byron must somewhat move even the hardest heart; and my heart, I am very sure, is not hard in the least.

I find that I have been scribbling away for nearly an hour. Miss Gisborne keeps on saying that I am too prone to the insertion of unnecessary hyphens, and that it is a weakness. If a weakness it is, I intend to cherish it.

I know that an hour has passed because there is a huge clock somewhere that sounds every quarter. It must be a *huge* clock because of the noise it makes, and because everything abroad *is* huge.

I am colder than ever and my arms are quite stiff. But I must drag off my clothes somehow, blow out the candles, and insinuate my tiny self into this enormous, frightening bed. I do hate the lumps you get all over your body when you travel abroad, and so much hope I don't get many more during the night. Also I hope I don't start feeling thirsty, as there's no water of any kind, let alone water safe to drink.

Ah, Lord Byron, living out there in riot and wickedness! It is impossible to forget him. I wonder what he would think of *me?* I do hope there are not too many biting things in this room.

4 OCTOBER. What a surprise! The contessa has said it will be quite in order for me to go for short walks in the town, provided I have my maid with me; and when Mamma at once pointed out that I had no maid, offered the services of her own! To think of this happening the very day after I wrote down in this very journal that it could never happen! I am now quite certain that it would have been perfectly correct for me to walk about the other towns too. I daresay that Papa and Mamma suggested otherwise only because of the difficulty about the maid. Of course I *should* have a maid, just as Mamma should have a maid too and Papa a man, and just as we should all have a proper carriage of our one, with our crest on the doors! If it was that we were too poor, it would be humiliating. As we are not too poor (I am sure we are not), it is farcical. In any case, Papa and Mamma went on making a fuss, but the contessa said we had now entered the States of the Church, and were, therefore, all living under the special beneficence of God. The contessa speaks English very well and even knows the English *idioms,* as Miss Gisborne calls them.

Papa screwed up his face when the contessa mentioned the States of the Church, as I knew he would. Papa remarked several times while we were on the way here that the Papal States, as he calls them, are the most misgoverned in Europe and that it was not only as a Protestant that he said so. I wonder. When Papa expresses opinions of that kind, they often seem to me to be just notions of his own, like his notions of the best way to travel. After the contessa had spoken as she did, I felt— very strongly—that it must be rather beautiful to be ruled directly by the Pope and his cardinals. Of course, the cardinals and even the Pope are subject to error, as are our own bishops and rectors, all being but men, as Mr. Biggs-Hartley continually emphasizes at home; but, all the same, they simply *must* be nearer to God than the sort of people who rule us in England. I do not think Papa can be depended upon to judge such a question.

I am determined to act upon the contessa's kind offer. Miss Gisborne says that though I am a pale little thing, I have very much a will of my own. Here will be an opportunity to prove it. There may be certain difficulties because the contessa's maid can only speak Italian; but when the two of us shall be alone together, it is I who shall be mistress and she who will be maid, and nothing can change that. I have seen the girl. She is a pretty creature, apart from the size of her nose.

Today it has been wet, as usual. This afternoon we drove round Ravenna in the contessa's carriage: a proper carriage for once, with arms on the doors and a footman as well as the coachman. Papa has paid off our hired coach. I suppose it has lumbered away back to Fusina, opposite to Venice. I expect I can count upon our remaining in Ravenna for a week. That seems to be Papa's usual sojourn in one of our major stopping places. It is not very long, but often it is quite long enough, the way we live.

This afternoon we saw Dante's Tomb, which is simply by the side of the street, and went into a big church with the Throne of Neptune in it, and then into the Tomb of Galla Placidia, which is blue inside, and very beautiful. I was on the alert for any hint of where Lord Byron might reside, but it was quite unnecessary to speculate, because the contessa almost shouted it out as we rumbled along one of the streets: "The Palazzo Guiccioli. See the netting acrosss the bottom of the door to prevent Lord Byron's animals from straying." "Indeed, indeed," said Papa, looking out more keenly than he had at Dante's Tomb. No more was said, because, though both Papa and Mamma had more than once alluded to Lord Byron's present way of life so that I should be able to understand things that might come up in conversation, yet neither the contessa nor Papa and Mamma knew how much I might really understand. Moreover, the little contessina was in the carriage, sitting upon a cushion on the floor at her Mamma's feet, making five of us in all, foreign carriages being as large as everything else foreign; and I daresay *she* knew nothing at all, sweet little innocent.

"Contessina" is only a kind of nickname or *sobriquet,* used by the family and the servants. The contessina is really a contessa: in foreign noble families, if one person is a duke, then all the other men seem to be dukes also, and all the women duchesses. It is very confusing and nothing like such a good arrangement as ours, where there is only one duke and one duchess to each family. I do not know the little contessina's age. Most foreign girls look far older than they really are, whereas most of our girls look younger. The contessa is *very* slender, a veritable sylph. She has an olive complexion, with no blemish of any kind. People often write about "olive complexions": the contessina really has one. She has absolutely enormous eyes, the shape of broad beans, and not far off that

in colour; but she never uses them to look at anyone. She speaks so little
and often has such an empty, lost expression that one might think her
more than slightly simple; but I do not think she is. Foreign girls are
raised quite differently from the way our girls are raised. Mamma frequently refers to this, pursing her lips. I must admit that I cannot see
myself finding in the contessina a friend, pretty though she is in her own
way, with feet about half the size of mine or Caroline's.

When foreign girls grow up to become women, they usually continue, poor things, to look older than they are. I am sure this applies to
the contessa. The contessa has been very kind to me—in the few hours
that I have so far known her—and even seems to be a little sorry for me
—as, indeed, I am for her. But I do not understand the contessa. Where
was she last night? Is the little contessina her only child? What has
become of her husband? Is it because he is dead that she seems—and
looks—so sad? Why does she want to live in such a big house—it is
called a villa, but one might think it a palazzo—when it is all falling to
bits, and much of it barely even furnished? I should like to ask Mamma
these questions, but I doubt whether she would have the right answers,
or perhaps any answers.

The contessa did appear for dinner this evening, and even the little
contessina. Mamma was there too: in that frock I dislike. It really is the
wrong kind of red—especially for Italy, where *dark* colours seem to be
so much worn. The evening was better than last evening; but then it
could hardly have been worse. (Mr. Biggs-Hartley says we should never
say that: things can *always* be worse.) It was not a *good* evening. The
contessa was trying to be quite gay, despite her own obvious trouble,
whatever that is; but neither Papa nor Mamma know how to respond
and I know all too well that I myself am better at thinking about things
than at casting a spell in company. What I like most is just a few friends
I know really well and whom I can truly trust and love. Alas, it is long
since I have had even one such to clasp by the hand. Even letters seem
mostly to lose themselves en route, and I can hardly wonder; supposing
people are still bothering to write them in the first place, needless to say,
which it is difficult to see why they should be after all this time. When
dinner was over, Papa and Mamma and the contessa played an Italian
game with both playing cards and dice. The servants had lighted a fire
in the salone and the contessina sat by it doing nothing and saying
nothing. If given a chance, Mamma would have remarked that "the
child should have been in bed long ago", and I am sure she should. The
contessa wanted to teach me the game, but Papa said at once that I was

too young, which is absolutely farcical. Later in the evening, the contessa, after playing a quite long time with Papa and Mamma, said that
tomorrow she would put her foot down (the contessa knows so many
such expressions that one would swear she must have *lived* in England)
and would *insist* on my learning. Papa screwed his face up and Mamma
pursed her lips in the usual way. I had been doing needlework, which I
shall never like nor see any point in when servants can always do it for
us; and I found that I was thinking many deep thoughts. And then I
noticed that a small tear was slowly falling down the contessa's face.
Without thinking, I sprang up; but then the contessa smiled, and I sat
down. One of my deep thoughts was that it is not so much particular
disasters that make people cry, but something always there in life itself,
something that a light falls on when we are trying to enjoy ourselves in
the company of others.

I must admit that the horrid lumps are going down. I certainly do
not seem to have acquired any more, which is an advantage when compared with what happened every night in Dijon, that smelly place. But I
wish I had a more cheerful room, with better furniture, though tonight
I have succeeded in bringing to bed one of our bottles of mineral water
and even a glass from which to drink it. It is only the Italian mineral
water, of course, which Mamma says may be very little safer than the
ordinary water; but as all the ordinary water seems to come from the
dirty wells one sees down the side streets, I think that Mamma exagger-
ates. I admit, however, that it is not like the bottled water one buys in
France. How farcical to have to buy water in a bottle, anyway! All the
same, there are some things that I have grown to *like* about foreign
countries; perhaps even to prefer. It would never do to let Papa and
Mamma hear me talk in such a way. I often wish I were not so sensitive,
so that the rooms I am given and things of that kind did not matter so
much. And yet Mamma is more sensitive about the water than I am! I
am sure it is not so *important*. It can't be. To me it is *obvious* that
Mamma is *less* sensitive than I am, where *important* things are concerned. My entire life is based on that obvious fact; my real life, that is.

I rather wish the contessina would invite me to share *her* room,
because I think she is sensitive in the same way that I am. But perhaps
the little girl sleeps in the contessa's room. I should not really mind
that. I do not *hate* or even dislike the little contessina. I expect she
already has troubles herself. But Papa and Mamma would never agree
to it anyway, and now I have written all there is to write about this

perfectly ordinary, but somehow rather odd, day. In this big cold room, I can hardly move with chilliness.

5 OCTOBER. When I went in to greet Mamma this morning, Mamma had the most singular news. She told me to sit down (Mamma and Papa have more chairs in their rooms than I have, and more of other things too), and then said that there was to be a party! Mamma spoke as though it would be a dreadful ordeal, which it was impossible for us to avoid; and she seemed to take it for granted that I should receive the announcement in the same way. I do not know what I really thought about it. It is true that I have never enjoyed a party yet (not that I have been present at many of them); but all day I have been aware of feeling different inside myself, lighter and swifter in some way, and by this evening I cannot but think it is owing to the knowledge that a party lies before me. After all, foreign parties may be different from parties at home, and probably are. I keep pointing that out to myself. This particular party will be given by the contessa, who, I feel sure, knows more about it than does Mamma. If she does, it will not be the only thing that the contessa knows more about than Mamma.

The party is to be the day after tomorrow. While we were drinking our coffee and eating our panini (always very flaky and powdery in Italy), Mamma asked the contessa whether she was sure there would be time enough for the preparations. But the contessa only smiled—in a very polite way, of course. It is probably easier to do things quickly in Italy (when one really wants to, that is), because everyone has so many servants. It is hard to believe that the contessa has much money, but she seems to keep more servants than we do, and, what is more, they behave more like slaves than like servants, quite unlike our Derbyshire keel-the-pots. Perhaps it is simply that everyone is so fond of the contessa. That I should entirely understand. Anyway, preparations for the party have been at a high pitch all day, with people hanging up banners, and funny smells from the kitchen quarters. Even the Bath House at the far end of the formal garden (it is said to have been built by the Byzantines) has had the spiders swept out and been populated with cooks, perpetrating I know not what. The transformation is quite bewildering. I wonder when Mamma first knew of what lay ahead? Surely it must at least have been before we went to bed last night?

I feel I should be vexed that a new dress is so impracticable. A train of seamstresses would have to work day and night for 48 hours, as in the fairy tales. I should like that (who would not?), but I am not at all sure that *I* should be provided with a new dress even if whole weeks were available in which to make it. Papa and Mamma would probably still agree that I had quite enough dresses already even if it were the Pope and his cardinals who were going to entertain me. All the same, I am not really vexed. I sometimes think that I am deficient in a proper interest in clothes, as Caroline's Mamma calls it. Anyway, I have learned from experience that new dresses are more often than not thoroughly disappointing. I keep reminding myself of that.

The other important thing today is that I have been out for my first walk in the town with the contessa's maid, Emilia. I just swept through what Papa had to say on the subject, as I had promised myself. Mamma was lying down at the time, and the contessa simply smiled her sweet smile and sent for Emilia to accompany me.

I must admit that the walk was not a *complete* success. I took with me our copy of Mr. Grubb's *Handbook to Ravenna and Its Antiquities* (Papa could hardly say No, lest I do something far worse), and began looking places up on the map with a view to visiting them. I felt that this was the best way to start, and that, once started, I could wait to see what life would lay before me. I am often quite resolute when there is some specific situation to be confronted. The first difficulty was the quite long walk into Ravenna itself. Though it was nothing at all to me, and though it was not raining, Emilia soon made it clear that she was unaccustomed to walking a step. This could only have been an affectation, or rather pretension, because everyone knows that girls of that kind come from peasant families, where I am quite sure they have to walk about all day, and much more than merely walk about. Therefore, I took no notice at all, which was made easier by my hardly understanding a word that Emilia actually said. I simply pushed and dragged her forward. Sure enough, she soon gave up all her pretences, and made the best of the situation. There were some rough carters on the road and large numbers of horrid children, but for the most part they stopped annoying us as soon as they saw who we were, and in any case it was as nothing to the roads into Derby, where they have lately taken to throwing stones at the passing carriages.

The next trouble was that Emilia was not in the least accustomed to what I had in mind when we reached Ravenna. Of course people do not go again and again to look at their own local antiquities, however old they may be; and least of all, I suspect, Italian people. When she was not accompanying her mistress, Emilia was used to going to town only for some precise purpose: to buy something, to sell something, or to deliver a letter. There was that in her attitude which made me think of the saucy girls in the old comedies: whose only work is to fetch and carry billets-doux, and sometimes to take the places of their mistresses, with their mistresses' knowledge or otherwise. I did succeed in visiting another of these Bath Houses, this one a public spectacle and called the Baptistry of the Orthodox, because it fell into Christian hands after the last days of the Romans, who built it. It was, of course, far larger than the Bath House in the contessa's garden, but in the interior rather dark and with a floor so uneven that it was difficult not to fall. There was also a horrible dead animal inside. Emilia began laughing, and it was quite plain what she was laughing at. She was striding about as if she were back on her mountains and the kind of thing she seemed to be suggesting was that if I proposed to walk all the way to the very heel or toe of Italy she was quite prepared to walk with me, and perhaps to walk ahead of me. As an English girl, I did not care for this, nor for the complete reversal of Emilia's original attitude, almost suggesting that she has a deliberate and impertinent policy of keeping the situation between us under her own control. So, as I have said, the walk was not a complete success. All the same, I have made a start. It is obvious that the world has more to offer than would be likely to come my way if I were to spend my whole life creeping about with Papa at one side of me and Mamma at the other. I shall think about how best to deal with Emilia now that I better understand her ways. I was not in the least tired when we had walked back to the villa. I despise girls who get tired, quite as much as Caroline despises them.

Believe it or not, Mamma was still lying down. When I went in, she said that she was resting in preparation for the party. But the party is not until the day after tomorrow. Poor dear Mamma might have done better not to have left England in the first place! I must take great care that I am not like that when I reach the same time of life and am married, as I suppose I shall be. Looking at Mamma in repose, it struck me that she would still be quite pretty if she did not always look so tired and worried. Of course she was once far prettier than I am now. I know that well. I, alas, am not really pretty at all. I have to cultivate other graces, as Miss Gisborne puts it.

I saw something unexpected when I was going upstairs to bed. The little contessina had left the salone before the rest of us and, as usual, without a word. Possibly it was only I who saw her slip out, she went so quietly. I noticed that she did not return and supposed that, at her age, she was quite worn out. Assuredly, Mamma would have said so. But then when I myself was going upstairs, holding my candle, I saw for myself what had really happened. At the landing, as we in England should call it, there is in one of the corners an odd little closet or cabinet, from which two doors lead off, both locked, as I know because I have cautiously turned the handles for myself. In this corner, by the light of my candle, I saw the contessina, and she was being hugged by a man. I think it could only have been one of the servants, though I was not really able to tell. Perhaps I am wrong about that, but I am not wrong about it being the contessina. They had been there in complete darkness, and, what is more, they never moved a muscle as I came up the stairs and walked calmly along the passage in the opposite direction. I suppose they hoped I should fail to see them in the dimness. They must have supposed that no one would be coming to bed just yet. Or perhaps they were lost to all sense of time, as Mrs. Radcliffe expresses it. I have very little notion of the contessina's age, but she often looks about twelve or even less. Of course I shall say nothing to anybody.

6 OCTOBER. I have been thinking on and off all day about the differences between the ways we are supposed to behave and the ways we actually do behave. And both are different from the ways in which God calls upon us to behave, and which we can never achieve whatever we do and however hard we apply ourselves, as Mr. Biggs-Hartley always emphasizes. We seem, every one of us, to be at least three different people. And that's just to start with.

I am disappointed by the results of my little excursion yesterday with Emilia. I had thought that there was so much of which I was deprived by being a girl and so being unable to go about on my own, but now I am not sure that I have been missing anything. It is almost as if the nearer one approaches to a thing, the less it proves to be there, to exist at all. Apart, of course, from the bad smells and bad words and horrid rough creatures from which and from whom we women are supposed to be "shielded". But I am waxing metaphysical; against which Mr. Biggs-Hartley regularly cautions us. I wish Caroline were with us. I believe I might feel quite differently about things if she were here to go about with me, just the two of us. Though, needless to say, it would make no difference to what the things truly were—or were not. It is curious that things should seem not to exist when visited with one person, and then to exist after all if visited with another person. Of course it is all just fancy, but what (I think at moments like this) is not?

I am so friendless and alone in this alien land. It occurs to me that

I must have great inner strength to bear up as I do and to fulfil my duties with so little complaint. The contessa has very kindly given me a book of Dante's verses, with the Italian on one side and an English translation on the page opposite. She remarked that it would aid me to learn more of her language. I am not sure that it will. I have dutifully read through several pages of the book, and there is nothing in this world that I like more than reading, but Dante's ideas are so gloomy and complicated that I suspect he is no writer for a woman, certainly not for an English woman. Also his face frightens me, so critical and severe. After looking at his portrait, beautifully engraved at the beginning of the book, I begin to fear that I shall see that face looking over my shoulder as I sit gazing into the looking glass. No wonder Beatrice would have nothing to do with him. I feel that he was quite deficient in the graces that appeal to our sex. Of course one must not even hint such a thing to an Italian, such as the contessa, for to all Italians Dante is as sacred as Shakespeare or Dr. Johnson is to us.

For once I am writing this during the afternoon. I suspect that I am suffering from ennui and, as that is a sin (even though only a minor one), I am occupying myself in order to drive it off. I know by now that I am much more prone to such lesser shortcomings as ennui and indolence than to such vulgarities as letting myself be embraced and kissed by a servant. And yet it is not that I feel myself wanting in either energy or passion. It is merely that I lack for anything or anyone worthy of such feelings, and refuse to spend them upon what is unworthy. But what a "merely" is that! How well I understand the universal ennui that possesses our neighbour, Lord Byron! I, a tiny slip of a girl, feel, at least in this particular, at one with the great poet! There might be consolation in the thought, were I capable of consolation. In any case, I am sure that there will be nothing more that is worth record before my eyes close tonight in slumber.

Later. I was wrong! After dinner tonight, it struck me simply to ask the contessa whether she had ever *met* Lord Byron. I suppose it might not be a thing she would proclaim unsolicited, either when Papa and Mamma were present, or, for reasons of delicacy, on one of the two rare occasions when she and I were alone; but I thought that I might now be sufficiently simpatica to venture a discreet enquiry.

I fear that I managed it very crudely. When Papa and Mamma had become involved in one of their arguments together, I walked across the room and sat down at the end of the sofa on which the contessa was reclining; and when she smiled at me and said something agreeable, I simply blurted out my question, quite directly. "Yes, *mia cara,*" she replied, "I have met him, but we cannot invite him to our party because he is too political, and many people do not agree with his politics. Indeed, they have already led to several deaths; which some are reluctant to accept at the hands of a *straniero,* however eminent." And of course it *was* the wonderful possibility of Lord Byron attending the contessa's party that *had been* at the back of my thoughts. Not for the first time, the contessa showed her fascinating insight into the minds of others—or assuredly into my mind.

7 OCTOBER. The day of the party! It is quite early in the morning and the sun is shining as I have not seen it shine for some time. Perhaps it regularly shines at this time of the day, when I am still asleep? "What you girls miss by not getting up!" as Caroline's Mamma always exclaims, though she is the most indulgent of parents. The trouble is that one *always* awakens early just when it is most desirable that one should slumber longest; as today, with the party before us. I am writing this now because I am *quite certain* that I shall be nothing but a tangle of nerves all day and, after everything is over, utterly spent and exhausted. So, for me, it always is with parties! I am glad that the day after tomorrow will be Sunday.

8 OCTOBER. I met a man at the party who, I must confess, interested me very much; and, beside that, what matters, as Mrs. Fremlinson enquires in *The Hopeful and the Despairing Heart, almost* my favourite of all books, as I truly declare?

Who could believe it? Just now, while I was still asleep, there was a knocking at my door, just loud enough to awaken me, but otherwise so soft and discreet, and there was the contessa *herself,* in the most beautiful negligée, half-rose-coloured and half-mauve, with a tray on which were things to eat and drink, a complete foreign breakfast, in fact! I must acknowledge that at that moment I could well have devoured a complete English breakfast, but what could have been kinder or more thoughtful on the part of the charming contessa? Her dark hair (but not so dark as with the majority of the Italians) had not yet been dressed, and hung about her beautiful, though sad, face, but I noticed that all her rings were on her fingers, flashing and sparkling in the sunshine. "Alas, *mia cara,*" she said, looking round the room, with its many deficiencies; "the times that were and the times that are." Then she actually bent over my face, rested her hand lightly on the top of my night-gown, and kissed me. "But how pale you look!" she continued. "You are white as a lily on the altar." I smiled. "I am English," I said, "and I lack strong colouring." But the contessa went on staring at me. Then she said: "The party has quite fatigued you?" She seemed to express it as a question, so I replied, with vigour: "Not in the least, I assure you, Contessa. It was the most beautiful evening of my life" (which was unquestionably the truth and no more than the truth). I sat up in the big bed and, so doing, saw myself in the glass. It was true that I *did* look pale, unusually pale. I was about to remark upon the earliness of the hour, when the contessa suddenly seemed to draw herself together with a gasp and turn remarkably pale herself, considering the native hue of her skin. She stretched out her hand and pointed. She seemed to be pointing at the pillow behind me. I looked round, disconcerted by her demeanour; and I saw an irregular red mark upon the pillow, not a very large mark, but undoubtedly a mark of blood. I raised my hands to my throat. *"Dio Illustrissimo!"* cried out the contessa. *"Ell' e stregata!"* I know enough Italian, from Dante and from elsewhere, to be informed of what that means: "She is bewitched." I leapt out of bed and threw my arms round the contessa before she could flee, as she seemed disposed to do. I besought her to say more, but I was all the time fairly sure that she would not. Italians, even educated ones, still take the idea of "witchcraft" with a seriousness that to us seems unbelievable; and regularly fear even to speak of it. Here I knew by instinct that Emilia and her mistress would be at one. Indeed, the contessa seemed most uneasy at my mere embrace, but she soon calmed herself, and left the room saying, quite pleasantly, that she must have a word with my parents about me. She even managed to wish me *"Buon appetito"* of my little breakfast.

I examined my face and throat in the looking-glass and there, sure enough, was a small scar on my neck which explained everything—except, indeed, how I had come by such a mark, but for that the novelties, the rigours, and the excitements of last night's party would *entirely* suffice. One cannot expect to enter the tournament of love and emerge unscratched: and it is into the tournament that, as I thrill to think, I verily have made my way. I fear it is perfectly typical of the Italian manner of seeing things that a perfectly natural, and very tiny, mishap should have such a disproportionate effect upon the contessa. For myself, an English girl, the mark upon my pillow does not even disturb me.

We must hope that it does not cast into screaming hysterics the girl whose duty it will be to change the linen.

If I look especially pale, it is partly because the very bright sunlight makes a contrast. I returned at once to bed and rapidly consumed every scrap and drop that the contessa had brought to me. I seemed quite weak from lack of sustenance, and indeed I have but the slenderest recollection of last night's fare, except that, naturally, I drank far more than on most previous days of my short life, probably more than on *any*.

And now I lie here in my pretty night-gown and nothing else, with my pen in my hand and the sun on my face, and think about *him!* I did not believe such people existed in the real world. I thought that such writers as Mrs. Fremlinson and Mrs. Radcliffe *improved* men, in order to reconcile their female readers to their lot, and to put their less numerous male readers in a good conceit of themselves. Caroline's Mamma and Miss Gisborne, in their quite different ways, have both indicated as much most clearly; and my own observation hitherto of the opposite sex has confirmed the opinion. But now I have actually met a man at whom even Mrs. Fremlinson's finest creation does but hint! He is an Adonis! an Apollo! assuredly a god! Where he treads, sprouts asphodel!

The first romantic thing was that he was not properly presented to me—indeed, he was not presented at all. I know this was very incorrect, but it cannot be denied that it was very exciting. Most of the guests were dancing an old-fashioned *minuetto,* but as I did not know the steps, I was sitting at the end of the room with Mamma, when Mamma was suddenly overcome in some way and had to leave. She emphasized that she would be back in only a minute or two, but almost as soon as she had gone, *he* was standing there, quite as if he had emerged from between the faded tapestries that covered the wall or even from the tapestries themselves, except that he looked very far from faded, though later, when more candles were brought in for supper, I saw that he was older than I had at first supposed, with such a wise and experienced look as I have never seen on any other face.

Of course he had not only to speak to me at once, or I should have risen and moved away, but to *compel* me, with his eyes and words, to remain. He said something pleasant about my being the only rosebud in a garden otherwise autumnal, but I am not such a goose as never to have heard speeches like that before, and it was what he said next that made me fatally hesitate. He said (and never, *never* shall I forget his words): "As we are both visitants from a world that is not this one, we should know one another". It was so exactly what I always feel about myself, as this journal (I fancy) makes clear, that I could not but yield a trifle to his apperceptiveness in finding words for my deepest conviction, extremely irregular and dangerous though I well knew my position to be. *And* he spoke in beautiful English; his accent (not, I think, an Italian one) only making his words the more choice-sounding and delightful!

I should remark here that it was not true that *all* the contessa's guests were "autumnal", even though most of them certainly were. Sweet creature that she is, she had invited several *cavalieri* from the local nobility *expressly* for my sake, and several of them had duly been presented to me, but with small conversation resulting, partly because there was so little available of a common tongue, but more because each single *cavaliero* seemed to me very much what in Derbyshire we call a peg-Jack. It was typical of the contessa's sympathetic nature that she perceived the unsuccess of these *rencontres,* and made no attempt to fan flames that were never so much as faint sparks. How unlike the matrons of Derbyshire, who, when they have set their minds to the task, will work the bellows in such cases not merely for a whole single evening, but for weeks, months, or, on occasion, years! But then it would be unthinkable to apply the word "matron" to the lovely contessa! As it was, the four *cavalieri* were left to make what they could of the young contessina and such other *bambine* as were on parade.

I pause for a moment seeking words in which to describe him. He is above the average tall, and, while slender and elegant, conveys a wondrous impression of force and strength. His skin is somewhat pallid, his nose aquiline and commanding (though with quivering, sensitive nostrils), his mouth scarlet and (I must apply the word) passionate. Just to look at his mouth made me think of great poetry and wide seas. His fingers are very long and fine, but powerful in their grip: as I learned for myself before the end of the evening. His hair I at first thought quite black, but I saw later that it was delicately laced with grey, perhaps even white. His brow is high, broad, and noble. Am I describing a god or a man? I find it hard to be sure.

As for his conversation I can only say that, indeed, it was not of this world. He proffered none of the empty chatter expected at social gatherings; which, in so far as it has any meaning at all, has a meaning quite different from that which the words of themselves convey—a meaning often odious to me. Everything he said (at least after that first conventional compliment) spoke to something deep within me, and everything I said in reply was what I really wanted to say. I have been able to talk in that way before with no man of any kind, from Papa downwards; and with very few women. And yet I find it difficult to recall what subjects we discussed. I think that may be a *consequence* of the feeling with which we spoke. The feeling I not merely recollect but feel still—all over and through me—deep and warm—transfiguring. The subjects, no. They were life, and beauty, and art, and nature, and myself: in fact, *everything.* Everything, that is, except the very different and very silly things that almost everyone else talks about all the time, chatter and chump without stopping this side of the churchyard. He did once observe that "Words are what prevail with women", and I could only smile, it was so true.

Fortunately, Mamma *never* re-appeared. As for the rest of them, I daresay they were more relieved than otherwise to find the gauche little English girl off their hands, so to speak, and apparently provided for. With Mamma indisposed, the obligation to watch over me would descend upon the contessa, but her I saw only in the distance. Perhaps she was resolved not to intrude where *I* should not wish it. If so, it would be what I should expect of her. I do not know.

Then came supper. Much to my surprise (and chagrin), my friend, if so I may call him, excused himself from participating. His explanation, lack of appetite, could hardly be accepted as sufficient or courteous, but the words he employed, succeeded (as always, I feel, with him) in purging the offence. He affirmed most earnestly that I must sustain myself even though he were unable to escort me, and that he would await my return. As he spoke, he gazed at me so movingly that I could but accept the situation, though I daresay I had as little appetite (for the coarse foods of this world) as he. I perceive that I have so far omitted to refer to the beauty and power of his eyes; which are so dark as to be almost black—at least by the light of candles. Glancing back at him, perhaps a little keenly, it occurred to me that he might be bashful about showing himself in his full years by the bright lights of the supper tables. It is a vanity *by no means* confined to my own sex. Indeed he seemed almost to be shrinking away from the augmented brightness even at this far end of the room. And this for all the impression of strength which was the most marked thing about him. Tactfully I made to move off. "You will return?" he asked, so anxiously and compellingly. I remained calm. I merely smiled.

And then Papa caught hold of me. He said that Mamma, having gone upstairs, had succumbed totally, as I might have known in advance she would do, and in fact *did* know; and that, when I had supped, I had "better come upstairs also". At that Papa elbowed me through to the tables and started trying to stuff me like a turkey, but, as I have said, I had little gusto for it, so little that I cannot now name a single thing that I ate, or that Papa ate either. Whatever it was, I "washed it down" (as we say in Derbyshire) with an unusual quantity (for me) of the local wine, which people, including Papa, always say is so "light", but which always seems to me no "lighter" than any other, but noticeably "heavier" than some I could name. What is more, I had already consumed a certain amount of it earlier in the evening when I was supposed to be flirting with the local peg-Jacks. One curious thing is that Papa, who never fails to demur at my doing almost anything else, seems to have no objection to my drinking wine quite heavily. I do not think I have ever known him even try to impose a limit. That is material, of course, only in the rare absence of Mamma, to whom this observation does not apply. But Mamma herself is frequently unwell after only two or three glasses. At supper last night, I was in a state of "trance": eating food was well-nigh impossible, but drinking wine almost fatally facile. Then Papa started trying to push me off to bed again —or perhaps to hold Mamma's head. After all that wine, and with my new friend patiently waiting for me, it was farcical. But I had to dispose of Papa somehow, so I promised him faithfully, and forgot my promise (whatever it was) immediately. Mercifully, I have not so far set eyes upon Papa since that moment.

Or, in reality, upon *anyone* until the contessa waked me this morning: on anyone but *one*.

There he was quietly awaiting me among the shadows cast by the slightly swaying tapestries and by the flapping bannerets ranged round the walls above us. This time he actually clutched my hand in his eagerness. It was only for a moment, of course, but I felt the firmness of his grip. He said he hoped he was not keeping me from the dance floor, but I replied No, oh No. In truth, I was barely even capable of dancing at that moment; and I fancy that the measures trod by the musty relics around us were, at the best of times, not for me. Then he said, with a slight smile, that once he had been a great dancer. Oh, I said idly and under the power of the wine; where was that? At Versailles, he replied; and in Petersburg. I must say that, wine or no wine, this surprised me; because surely, as everyone knows, Versailles was burned down by the incendiaries in 1789, a good thirty years ago? I must have glanced at him significantly, because he then said, smiling once more, though

faintly: "Yes, I am very, *very* old." He said it with such curious emphasis that he did not seem to demand some kind of denial, as such words
normally do. In fact, I could find nothing immediate to say at all. And
yet it was nonsense, and denial would have been sincere. I do not know
his age, and find even an approximation difficult, but "very, very old"
he most certainly is not, but in all important ways one of the truly
youngest people that can be imagined, and one of the most truly ardent.
He was wearing the most beautiful black clothes, with a tiny Order of
some kind, I am sure *most* distinguished, because so unobtrusive. Papa
has often remarked that the flashy display of Honours is no longer
correct.

In some ways the most romantic thing of all is that I do not even
know his name. As people were beginning to leave the party, not so very
late, I suppose, as most of the people were, after all, quite old, he took
my hand and this time held it, nor did I even affect to resist. "We shall
meet again," he said, "many times;" looking so deeply and steadily into
my eyes that I felt he had penetrated my inmost heart and soul. Indeed,
there was something so powerful and mysterious about my own feelings
at that moment that I could only murmur "Yes," in a voice so weak
that he could hardly have heard me, and then cover my eyes with my
hands, those eyes into which he had been gazing so piercingly. For a
moment (it cannot have been longer, or my discomposure would have
been observed by others), I sank down into a chair with all about me
black and swimming, and when I had recovered myself, he was no
longer there, and there was nothing to do but be kissed by the contessa,
who said "You're looking tired, child," and be hastened to my big bed,
immediately.

And though new emotions are said to deprive us of rest (as I have
myself been able to confirm on one or two occasions), I seem to have
slept immediately too, and very deeply, and for a very long time. I
know, too, that I dreamed remarkably, but I cannot at all recollect of
what. Perhaps I do not need the aid of memory, for surely I can
surmise?

On the first occasion since I have been in Italy, the sun is truly very
hot. I do not think I shall write any more today. I have already covered
pages in my small, clear handwriting, which owes so much to Miss
Gisborne's patience and severity, and to her high standards in all matters touching young girlhood. I am rather surprised that I have been left
alone for so long. Though Papa and Mamma do not seem to me to
accomplish very much in proportion to the effort they expend, yet they

are very inimical to "lying about and doing nothing", especially in my case, but in their own cases also, as I must acknowledge. I wonder how Mamma is faring after the excitement of last night? I am sure I should arise, dress, and ascertain; but instead I whisper to myself that once more I feel powerfully drawn towards the embrace of Morpheus.

9 OCTOBER. Yesterday morning I decided that I had already recorded enough for one single day (though for what wonderful events I had to try, however vainly, to find words!), but there are few private occupations in this world about which I care more than inscribing the thoughts and impressions of my heart in this small, secret journal, which no one else shall ever in this world see (I shall take good care of that), so that I am sure I should again have taken up my pen in the evening, had there been any occurrence sufficiently definite to write about. *That,* I fear, is what Miss Gisborne would call one of my overloaded sentences, but overloaded sentences can be the reflection, I am sure, of overloaded spirits, and even be their only relief and outlet! How well at this moment do I recall Miss Gisborne's moving counsel: Only find the right words for your troubles, and your troubles become half-joys. Alas, for me at this hour there can be no right words: in some strange way that I can by no means grasp hold of, I find myself fire and ice in equal parts. I have never before felt so greatly alive and yet I catch in myself an eerie conviction that my days are now closely numbered. It does not frighten me, as one would expect it to do. Indeed, it is very nearly a relief. I have never moved at my ease in this world, despite all the care that has been lavished on me; and if I had never known Caroline, I can only speculate what would have become of me. And now! What is Caroline, hitherto my dearest friend (and sometimes her Mamma too), by comparison with . . . Oh, there *are* no words. Also I have not completely recovered from the demands which last night made upon me. This is something I am rather ashamed of and shall admit to no one. But it is true. As well as being torn by emotion, I am worn to a silken thread.

The contessa, having appeared in my room yesterday morning, then disappeared and was not seen again all day, as on the day we arrived. All the same she seemed to have spoken to Mamma about me, as she had said she would be doing. This soon became clear.

It was already afternoon before I finally rose from my bed and ventured from my sunny room. I was feeling very hungry once more, and I felt that I really must find out whether Mamma was fully recovered. So I went first and knocked at the door of Mamma and Papa's rooms. As there was no answer, I went downstairs, and, though there was no one else around (when it is at all sunny, most Italians simply lie down in the shade), there was Mamma, in full and blooming health, on the terrace overlooking the garden. She had her workbox with her and was sitting in the full sun trying to do two jobs at once, perhaps three, in her usual manner. When Mamma is feeling quite well, she always fidgets terribly. I fear that she lacks what the gentleman we met in Lausanne called "the gift of repose". (I have never forgotten that expression.)

Mamma set about me at once. "Why didn't you dance with even one of those nice young men whom the contessa had gone to the trouble of inviting simply for your sake? The contessa is very upset about it. Besides, what have you been doing all the morning? This lovely, sunny day? And what is all this other rubbish the contessa has been trying to tell me about you? I cannot understand a word of it. Perhaps you can enlighten me? I suppose it is something I ought to know about. No doubt it is a consequence of your father and mother agreeing to your going into the town on your own?"

Needless to say, I know by this time how to reply to Mamma when she rants on in terms such as these.

"The contessa is very upset about it all," Mamma exclaimed again after I had spoken; as if a band of knaves had stolen all the spoons, and I had been privy to the crime. "She is plainly hinting at something which courtesy prevents her putting into words, and it is something to do with you. I should be obliged if you would tell me what it is. Tell me at once," Mamma commanded very fiercely.

Of course I was aware that something had taken place between the contessa and me that morning, and by now I knew very well what lay behind it: in one way or another the contessa had divined my *rencontre* of the evening before and had realized something (though how far from the whole!) of the effect it had made upon me. Even to me she had expressed herself in what English people would regard as an overwrought, Italianate way. It was clear that she had said something to Mamma on the subject, but of a veiled character, as she did not wish actually to betray me. She had, indeed, informed me that she was going to do this, and I now wished that I had attempted to dissuade her. The fact is that I had been so somnolent as to be half without my wits.

"Mamma," I said, with the dignity I have learned to display at these times, "if the contessa has anything to complain of in my conduct, I am sure she will complain only when I am present." And, indeed, I *was* sure of that; though doubtful whether the contessa would ever consider complaining about me at all. Her addressing herself to Mamma in the present matter was, I could be certain, an attempt to aid me in some way, even though possibly misdirected, as was almost inevitable with someone who did not know Mamma very well.

"You are defying me, child," Mamma almost screamed. "You are defying your own mother." She had so worked herself up (surely about nothing? Even less than usual?) that she managed to prick herself. Mamma is constantly pricking herself when she attempts needlework, mainly, I always think, because she *will* not concentrate upon any one particular task; and she keeps a wad of lint in her box against the next time it occurs. This time, however, the lint seemed to be missing, and she appeared to have inflicted quite a gash. Poor Mamma flapped about like a bird beneath a net, while the blood was beginning to flow quite freely. I bent forward and sucked it away with my tongue. It was really strange to have Mamma's blood in my mouth. The strangest part was that it tasted delightful; almost like an exceptionally delicious sweetmeat! I feel my own blood mantling to my cheek as I write the words now.

Mamma then managed to staunch the miniature wound with her pocket handkerchief: one of the pretty ones she had purchased in Besançon. She was looking at me in her usual critical way, but all she said was: "It is perhaps fortunate that we are leaving here on Monday."

Though it was our usual routine, nothing had been said on the present occasion, and I was aghast. (Here, I suppose, *was* something definite to record yesterday evening!)

"What!" I cried. "Leave the sweet contessa so soon! Leave, within only a week, the town where Dante walked and wrote!" I smile a little as I perceive how, without thinking, I am beginning to follow the flamboyant, Italian way of putting things. I am not really sure that Dante did *write* anything much in Ravenna, but to Italians such objections have little influence upon the choice of words. I realize that it is a habit I must guard against taking to an extreme.

"Where Dante walked may be not at all a suitable place for you to walk," rejoined Mamma, uncharitably, but with more sharpness of phrase and thought than is customary with her. She was fondling her injured thumb the while, and had nothing to mollify her acerbity towards me. The blood was beginning to redden the impromptu bandage, and I turned away with what writers call "very mixed feelings".

All the same, I did manage to see some more of the wide world before we left Ravenna; and on the very next day, this day, Sunday, and even though it is a Sunday. Apparently, there is no English church in Ravenna, so that all we could compass was for Papa to read a few prayers this morning and go through the Litany, with Mamma and me making the responses. The major-domo showed the three of us to a special room for the purpose. It had nothing in it but an old table with shaky legs and a line of wooden chairs: all dustier and more decrepit even than other things I have seen in the villa. Of course all this has happened in previous places when it was a Sunday, but never before under such dispiriting conditions—even, as I felt, *unhealthy* conditions. I was *most* disagreeably affected by the entire experience and *entirely* unable to imbibe the Word of God, as I should have done. I have never felt like that before even at the least uplifting of Family Prayers. Positively *irreverent* thoughts raced uncontrolledly through my little head: for example, I found myself wondering how efficacious God's Word could be for Salvation when droned and stumbled over by a mere un-canonized layman such as Papa—no, I mean, of course, *unordained*, but I have let the first word stand because it is so comic when applied to Papa, who is always denouncing "the Roman Saints" and all they represent, such as frequent days of public devotion in their honour. English people speak so unkindly of the Roman Catholic priests, but at least they have all, including the most unworthy of them, been touched by hands that go back and back and back to Saint Peter and so to the Spurting Fountain of Grace itself. You can hardly say the same for Papa, and I believe that even Mr. Biggs-Hartley's consecrationary position is a matter of dispute. I feel very strongly that the Blood of the Lamb cannot be mediated unless by the Elect or washed in by hands that are not strong and white.

Oh, how can he fulfil his promise that "We shall meet again", if Papa and Mamma drag me, protesting, from the place where we met first? Let alone meet "Many times"? These thoughts distract me, as I need not say; and yet I am quite sure that they distract me less than one might expect. For that the reason is simple enough: deep within me I *know* that some wondrous thing, some special election, has passed between him and me, and that meet again we shall in consequence, and no doubt "Many times". Distracted about it all though I am, I am simultaneously so sure as to be almost at peace: fire and ice, as I have said. I find I can still sometimes think about other things, which was by no means the case when I fancied, long, long ago, that I was "in love" (perish the thought!) with Mr. Franklin Stobart. Yes, yes, my wondrous friend has brought to my wild soul a measure of peace at last! I only wish I did not feel so tired. Doubtless it will pass when the events of the night before last are more distant (what sadness, though, when they are! What sadness, happen what may!), and, I suppose, this afternoon's tiring walk also. No, *not* "tiring". I refuse to admit the word, and that malapert Emilia returned home "fresh as a daisy", to use the expression her kind of person uses where I come from.

But what a walk it proved to be, none the less! We wandered through the *Pineta di Classe:* a perfectly enormous forest between Ravenna and the sea, with pine trees like very thick, dark, bushy umbrellas, and, so they say, either a brigand or a bear hiding behind each one of them! I have never seen such pine trees before; not in France or Switzerland or the Low Countries, let alone in England. They are more like trees in the *Thousand Nights and a Night* (not that I have read that work), dense enough at the top and stout-trunked enough for rocks to nest in! And such countless numbers of them, all so old! Left without a guide, I should easily have found myself lost within only a few minutes, so many and so vague are the different tracks among the huge conifers but I have to admit that Emilia, quite shed now of her *bien élevée* finicking, strode out almost like a boy, and showed a knowledge of the best routes that I could only wonder at and take advantage of. There is now almost an understanding between me and Emilia, and it is mainly from her that I am learning an amount of Italian that is beginning quite to surprise me. All the time I recall, however, that it is a very simple language: the great poet of *Paradise Lost* (not that I have read that work either) remarked that it was unnecessary to set aside special periods for instruction in Italian, because one could simply pick it up as one went along. So it is proving between me and Emilia.

The forest routes are truly best suited to gentlemen on horseback, and at one place two such emerged from one of the many tracks going off to our left. *"Guardi!"* cried out Emilia and clutched my arm as if she were my intimate. "Milord Byron and Signor Shelley!" (I do not attempt to indicate Emilia's funny approximation to the English names.) What a moment in my life—or in anyone's life! To see at the same time two persons both so great and famous and both so irrevocably doomed! There was not, of course, time enough for any degree of close observation, though Mr. Shelley seemed slightly to acknowledge with his crop our standing back a little to allow him and his friend free passage, but I fear that my main impression was of both *giaours* looking considerably older than I had expected and Lord Byron considerably more corpulent (as well as being quite grey-headed, though I believe only at the start of his life's fourth decade). Mr. Shelley was remarkably untidy in his dress and Lord Byron most comical: in that respect at least, the reality was in accord with the report. Both were without hats or caps. They cantered away down the track up which we had walked. They were talking in loud voices (Mr. Shelley's noticeably high in pitch), both together, above the thudding of their horses' hoofs. Neither of them really stopped talking even when slowing in order to wheel, so to speak, round the spot where we stood.

And so I have at length set eyes upon the fabled Lord Byron! A wondrous moment indeed; but how much more wondrous for me if it had occurred before that recent most wondrous of all possible moments! But it would be very wrong of me to complain because the red and risen moon has quite dimmed my universal nightlight! Lord Byron, that child of destiny, is for the whole world and, no doubt, for all time, or at least for a great deal of it! My fate is a different one and I draw it to my breast with a young girl's eager arms!

"Come gentili!" exclaimed Emilia, gazing after our two horsemen. It was not perhaps the most appropriate comment upon Lord Byron, or even upon Mr. Shelley, but there was nothing for me to reply (even if I could have found the Italian words), so on went our walk, with Emilia now venturing so far as to sing, in a quite pretty voice, and me lacking heart to chide her, until in the end the pine-trees parted and I got my first glimpse of the Adriatic Sea, and, within a few more paces, a whole wide prospect of it. (The Venetian Lagoon I refuse to take seriously.) The Adriatic Sea is linked with the Mediterranean Sea, indeed quite properly a part or portion of it, so that I can now say to myself that I have "seen the Mediterranean"; which good old Doctor Johnson defined as the true object of all travel. It was almost as if at long last my own eyes had seen the Holy Grail, with the Redemptive Blood streaming forth in golden splendour; and I stood for whole moments quite lost in my own deep thoughts. The world falls from me once more in a moment as I muse upon that luminous, rapturous flood.

But I can write no more. So unwontedly weary do I feel that the vividness of my vision notwithstanding is something to be marvelled at. It is as if my hand were guided as was Isabella's by the distant Traffio in Mrs. Fremlinson's wonderful book; so that Isabella was enabled to leave a record of the strange events that preceded her death—without which record, as it now occurs to me, the book, fiction though it be, could hardly with sense have been written at all. The old moon is drenching my sheets and my night-gown in brightest crimson. In Italy, the moon is always full and always so red.

Oh, when next shall I see my friend, my paragon, my genius!

10 OCTOBER. I have experienced so sweet and great a dream that I must write down the fact before it is forgotten, and even though I find that already there is almost nothing left that *can* be written. I have dreamed that he was with me; that he indued my neck and breast with kisses that were at once the softest and the sharpest in the world; that he filled my ears with thoughts so strange that they could have come only from a world afar.

And now the Italian dawn is breaking: all the sky is red and purple. The rains have gone, as if for ever. The crimson sun calls to me to take flight before it is once more autumn and then winter. Take flight! Today we are leaving for Rimini! Yes, it is but to Rimini that I am to repair. It is farcical.

And in my dawn-red room there is once again blood upon my person. But this time I know. It is at his embrace that my being springs forth, in joy and welcome; his embrace that is at once the softest and the sharpest in the world. How strange that I could ever have failed to recall such bliss!

I rose from my bed to look for water, there being, once more, none in my room. I found that I was so weak with happiness that I all but fainted. But after sinking for a moment upon my bed, I somewhat recovered myself and succeeded in gently opening the door. And what should I find there? Or, rather, whom? In the faintly lighted corridor, at some distance, stood silently none other than the little contessina, whom I cannot recollect having previously beheld since her Mamma's *soirée à danse*. She was dressed in some kind of loose dark wrapper, and I may only leave between her and her conscience what she can have been doing. No doubt for some good reason allied therewith, she seemed turned to stone by the sight of *me*. Of course I was in *déshabillé* even more complete than her own. I had omitted even to cover my night-gown. And upon that there was blood—as if I had suffered an injury. When I walked towards her reassuringly (after all, we are but two young girls and I am not her judge—nor anyone's), she gave a low croaking scream and fled from me as if I had been the Erl Queen herself, but still almost silently, no doubt for her same good reasons. It was foolish of the little contessina, because all I had in mind to do was to take her in my arms, and then to kiss her in token of our common humanity and the strangeness of our encounter at such an hour.

I was disconcerted by the contessina's childishness (these Italians manage to be shrinking *bambine* and hardened women of the world at one and the same time), and, again feeling faint, leaned against the passage wall. When I stood full on my feet once more, I saw by the crimson light coming through one of the dusty windows that I had reached out to stop myself falling and left a scarlet impression of my hand on the painted plaster. It is difficult to excuse and impossible to remove. How I weary of these *règles* and conventionalities by which I have hitherto been bound! How I long for the measureless liberty that has been promised me and of which I feel so complete a future assurance!

But I managed to find some water (the contessa's villa is no longer of the kind that has servitors alert—or supposedly alert—all night in the larger halls), and with this water I did what I could, at least in my own room. Unfortunately I had neither enough water nor enough strength to do all. Besides, I begin to grow reckless.

11 OCTOBER. No dear dream last night!

Considerable crafty unpleasantness, however, attended our departure yesterday from Ravenna. Mamma disclosed that the contessa was actually lending us her own carriage. "It's because she wants to see the last of us," said Mamma to me, looking at the cornice. "How can that be, Mamma?" I asked. "Surely, she's hardly seen us at all? She was invisible when we arrived, and now she's been almost invisible again for days." "There's no connection between those two things," Mamma replied. "At the time we arrived, the contessa was feeling unwell, as we mothers often do, you'll learn that for yourself soon. But for the last few days, she's been very upset by your behaviour, and now she wants us to go." As Mamma was still looking at the wall instead of at me, I put out the tip of my tongue, only the merest scrap of it, but *that* Mamma did manage to see, and had lifted her hand several inches before she recollected that I was now as good as an adult and so not to be corrected by a simple cuff.

And then when we were all about to enter the draggled old carriage, lo and behold the contessa did manage to haul herself into the light, and I caught her actually crossing herself behind my back, or what she no doubt thought was behind my back. I had to clench my hands to stop myself spitting at her. I have since begun to speculate whether she did not really *intend* me to see what she did. I was once so fond of the contessa, so drawn to her—I can still *remember* that quite well—but *all* is now changed. A week, I find, can sometimes surpass a lifetime; and so, for that matter, can one single indelible night. The contessa took great care to prevent her eyes once meeting mine, though, as soon as I perceived this, I never for a moment ceased glaring at her like a little basilisk. She apologised to Papa and Mamma for the absence of the contessina whom she described as being in bed with screaming megrims or the black cramp or some other malady (I truly cared not what! nor care now!) no doubt incident to girlish immaturity in Italy! And Papa and Mamma made response as if they really minded about the silly little child! Another way of expressing their disapproval of *me,* needless to observe. My considered opinion is that the contessina and her Mamma are simply two of a kind, but that the contessa has had time to become more skilled in concealment and duplicity. I am sure that all Italian females are alike, when one really knows them. The contessa had made me dig my finger-nails so far into my palms that my hands hurt all the rest of the day and still look as if I had caught a dagger in each of them, as in Sir Walter Scott's tale.

We had a coachman and a footman on the box, neither of them at all young, but more like two old wiseacres; and, when we reached Classe, we stopped in order that Papa, Mamma, and I could go inside the church, which is famous for its mosaics, going back, as usual to the Byzantines. The big doors at the western end were open in the quite hot sunshine and indeed the scene inside did look very pretty, all pale azure, the colour of Heaven, and shining gold; but I saw no more of it than that, because as I was about to cross the threshold, I was again overcome by my faintness, and sitting down on a bench, bade Papa and Mamma go in without me, which they immediately did, in the sensible English way, instead of trying to make an ado over me, in the silly Italian way. The bench was of marble, with arms in the shape of lions, and though the marble was worn, and cut, and pock-marked, it was a splendid, heavy object, carved, if I mistake not, by the Romans themselves. Seated on it, I soon felt better once more, but then I noticed the two fat old men on the coach doing something or other to the doors and windows. I supposed they were greasing them, which I am sure would have been very much in order, as would have been a considerable application of paint to the entire vehicle. But when Papa and Mamma at last came out of the church, and we all resumed our places, Mamma soon began to complain of a smell, which she said was, or at least resembled, that of the herb, garlic. Of course when one is abroad, the smell of garlic is *everywhere,* so that I quite understood when Papa merely told Mamma not to be fanciful; but then I found that I myself was more and more affected, so that we completed the journey in almost total silence, none of us, except Papa, having much appetite for the very crude meal set before us en route at Cesenatico. "You're looking white," said Papa to me, as we stepped from the coach. Then he added to Mamma, but hardly attempting to prevent my hearing, "I can see why the contessa spoke to you as she did". Mamma merely shrugged her shoulders: something she would never have thought of doing before we came abroad, but which now she does frequently. I nearly said something spiteful. At the end, the contessa, when she condescended to appear at all, was constantly disparaging my appearance, and indeed I am pale, paler than I once was, though always I have been pale enough, pale as a little phantom; but only I know the reason for the change in me, and no one else shall know it ever, because no one else ever can. It is not so much a "secret". Rather is it a revelation.

In Rimini we are but stopping at the inn; and we are almost the only persons to be doing so. I cannot wonder at this: the inn is a gaunt, forbidding place; the *padrona* has what in Derbyshire we call a "hare-lip"; and the attendance is of the worst. Indeed, no one has so far ventured to come near me. All the rooms, including mine, are very large; and all lead into one another, in the style of 200 years ago. The building resembles a palazzo that has fallen upon hard times, and perhaps that is what it is. At first I feared that my dear Papa and Mamma were to be ensconced in the apartment adjoining my own, which would have suited me not at all, but, for some reason, it has not happened, so that between my room and the staircase are two dark and empty chambers, which would once have caused me alarm, but which now I welcome. Everything is poor and dusty. Shall I ever repose abroad in such ease and *bien-être* as one takes for granted in Derbyshire? Why No, I shall not: and a chill runs down my back as I inscribe the words; but a chill more of excitement than of fear. Very soon now shall I be entirely elsewhere and entirely above such trivia.

I have opened a pair of the big windows, a grimy and, I fear, a noisy task. I flitted out in the moonlight on to the stone balcony, and gazed down into the *piazza.* Rimini seems now to be a very poor town, and there is nothing of the nocturnal uproar and riot which are such usual features of Italian existence. At this hour, all is completely silent

—even strangely so. It is still very warm, but there is a mist between the earth and the moon.

I have crept into another of these enormous Italian beds. He is winging towards me. There is no further need for words. I have but to slumber, and that will be simple, so exhausted I am.

12, 13, 14 OCTOBER. Nothing to relate but him, and of him nothing that can be related.

I am very tired, but it is tiredness that follows exaltation, not the vulgar tiredness of common life. I noticed today that I no longer have either shadow or reflection. Fortunately Mamma was quite destroyed (as the Irish simpletons express it) by the journey from Ravenna, and has not been seen since. How many, many hours one's elders pass in retirement! How glad I am never to have to experience such bondage! How I rejoice when I think about the new life which spreads before me into infinity, the new ocean which already laps at my feet, the new vessel with the purple sail and the red oars upon which I shall at any moment embark! When one is confronting so tremendous a transformation, how foolish seem words, but the habit of them lingers even when I have hardly strength to hold the pen! Soon, soon, new force will be mine, fire that is inconceivable; and the power to assume any night-shape that I may wish, or to fly through the darkness with none. What love is his! How chosen among all women am I; and I am just a little English girl! It is a miracle, and I shall enter the halls of Those Other Women with pride.

Papa is so beset by Mamma that he has failed to notice that I am eating nothing and drinking only water; that at our horrid, odious meals I am but feigning.

Believe it or not, yesterday we visited, Papa and I, the Tempio Malatestiano. Papa went as an English Visitor: I (at least by comparison with Papa) as a Pythoness. It is a beautiful edifice, among the most beautiful in the world, they say. But for me a special splendour lay in the noble and amorous dead it houses, and in the control over them which I feel increase within me. I was so rent and torn with new power that Papa had to help me back to the inn. Poor Papa, burdened, as he supposes, by *two* weak invalid women! I could almost pity him.

I wish I had reached the pretty little contessina and kissed her throat.

15 OCTOBER. Last night I opened my pair of windows (the other pair resists me, weak—in terms of this world—as I am), and, without quite venturing forth, stood there in nakedness and raised both my arms. Soon a soft wind began to rustle, where all had previously been still as death. The rustling steadily rose to roaring, and the faint chill of the night turned to heat as when an oven door is opened. A great crying out and weeping, a buzzing and screaming and scratching, swept in turmoil past the open window, as if invisible (or almost invisible) bodies were turning around and around in the air outside, always lamenting and accusing. My head was split apart by the sad sounds and my body as moist as if I were an Ottoman. Then, on an instant, all had passed by. *He* stood there before me in the dim embrasure of the window. "That," he said, "is Love as the elect of this world know it."

"The *elect?*" I besought him, in a voice so low that it was hardly a voice at all (but what matter?). "Why yes," he seemed to reaffirm. "Of this world, the elect."

16 OCTOBER. The weather in Italy changes constantly. Today once more it is cold and wet.

They have begun to suppose me ill. Mamma, back on her legs for a spell, is fussing like a blowfly round a dying lamb. They even called in a *medico*, after discussing at length in my presence whether an Italian physician could be regarded as of any utility. With what voice I have left, I joined in vigorously that he could not. All the same, a creature made his appearance: wearing fusty black, and, believe it or not, a grey *wig*—in all, a veritable Pantalone. What a farce! With my ever sharper fangs, I had him soon despatched, and yelling like the Old Comedy he belonged to. Then I spat forth his enfeebled, senile lymph, cleaning my lips of his skin and smell, and returned, hugging myself, to my couch.

Janua mortis vita, as Mr. Biggs-Hartley says in his funny dog latin. And to think that today is Sunday! I wonder why no one has troubled to pray over me?

17 OCTOBER. I have been left alone all day. Not that it matters.

Last night came the strangest and most beautiful event of my life, a seal laid upon my future.

I was lying here with my double window open, when I noticed that mist was coming in. I opened my arms to it, but my blood began to trickle down my bosom from the wound in my neck, which of course no longer heals—though I seem to have no particular trouble in concealing the mark from the entire human race, not forgetting learned men with certificates from the University of Sciozza.

Outside in the *piazza* was a sound of shuffling and nuzzling, as of sheep being folded on one of the farms at home. I climbed out of bed, walked across, and stepped on to the balcony.

The mist was filtering the moonlight into a silver-grey that I have never seen elsewhere.

The entire *piazza*, a very big one, was filled with huge, grizzled wolves, all perfectly silent, except for the small sounds I have mentioned, all with their tongues flopping and lolling, black in the silvery light, and all gazing up at my window.

Rimini is near to the Apennine Mountains, where wolves notoriously abound, and commonly devour babies and small children. I suppose that the coming cold is drawing them into the towns.

I smiled at the wolves. Then I crossed my hands on my little bosom and curtsied. They will be prominent among my new people. My blood will be theirs, and theirs mine.

I forgot to say that I have contrived to lock my door. Now, I am assisted in such affairs.

Somehow I have found my way back to bed. It has become exceedingly cold, almost icy. For some reason I think of all the empty rooms in this battered old palazzo (as I am sure it once was), so fallen from their former stateliness. I doubt if I shall write any more. I do not think I shall have any more to say.

RONALD CHETWYND-HAYES *(born 1919) began publishing in England in 1954 and has since produced a large number of horror stories and novels, and some science fiction tales as well. He has also been active as an editor, succeeding Robert Aickman as editor of the annual* Fontana Book of Great Ghost Stories *for some years, starting in 1973.*

The Monster Club (1975), containing five stories, is generally considered his best work. While each story is excellent in itself, they are linked together by material that is as funny and clever as it is horrific. It is in this book that Chetwynd-Hayes set forth his "Monsteral Table," a chart naming all the possible offspring of interbreeding among monsters.

Not surprisingly, The Monster Club, *in which "The Werewolf and the Vampire" first appeared, was made into a successful film starring Vincent Price, with John Carradine playing Chetwynd-Hayes himself.*

The Werewolf and the Vampire (1975)

BY R. CHETWYND-HAYES

George Hardcastle's downfall undoubtedly originated in his love for dogs. He could not pass one without stopping and patting its head. A flea-bitten mongrel had only to turn the corner of the street and he was whistling, calling out: "Come on, boy. Come on then," and behaving in the altogether outrageous fashion that is peculiar to the devoted animal lover.

Tragedy may still have been averted had he not decided to spend a day in the Greensand Hills. Here in the region of Clandon Down, where dwarf oaks, pale birches and dark firs spread up in a long sweep to the northern heights, was a vast hiding place where many forms of often invisible life lurked in the dense undergrowth. But George, like many before him, knew nothing about this, and tramped happily up the slope, aware only that the air was fresh, the silence absolute and he was young.

The howl of what he supposed to be a dog brought him to an immediate standstill and for a while he listened, trying to determine from which direction the sound came. Afterwards he had reason to remember that none of the conditions laid down by legend and superstition prevailed. It was midafternoon and in consequence there was not, so far as he was aware, a full moon. The sun was sending golden spears of light through the thick foliage and all around was a warm, almost overpowering atmosphere, tainted with the aroma of decaying under-growth. The setting was so commonplace and he was such an ordinary young man—not very bright perhaps, but gifted with good health and clean boyish good looks, the kind of Saxon comeliness that goes with a clear skin and blond hair.

The howl rang out again, a long, drawn-out cry of canine anguish, and now it was easily located. Way over to his left, somewhere in the midst of, or just beyond a curtain of, saplings and low, thick bushes. Without thought of danger, George turned off the beaten track and plunged into the dim twilight that held perpetual domain during the summer months under the interlocked higher branches. Imagination supplied a mental picture of a gin-trap and a tortured animal that was lost in a maze of pain. Pity lent speed to his feet and made him ignore the stinging offshoots that whipped at his face and hands, while bram-bles tore his trousers and coiled round his ankles. The howl came again, now a little to his right, but this time it was followed by a deep throated growl, and if George had not been the person he was, he might have paid heed to this warning note of danger.

For some fifteen minutes, he ran first in one direction, then an-other, finally coming to rest under a giant oak which stood in a small clearing. For the first time fear came to him in the surrounding gloom. It did not seem possible that one could get lost in an English wood, but here, in the semilight, he conceived the ridiculous notion that night left its guardians in the wood during the day, which would at any moment move in and smother him with shadows.

He moved away from the protection of the oak tree and began to walk in the direction he thought he had come, when the growl erupted from a few yards to his left. Pity fled like a leaf before a raging wind, and stark terror fired his brain with blind, unreasoning panic. He ran, fell, got up and ran again, and from behind came the sound of a heavy body crashing through undergrowth, the rasp of laboured breathing, the bestial growl of some enraged being. Reason had gone, coherent thought had been replaced by an animal instinct for survival; he knew that whatever ran behind him was closing the gap.

Soon, and he dare not turn his head, it was but a few feet away. There was snuffling, whining, terribly eager growling, and suddenly he shrieked as a fierce, burning pain seared his right thigh. Then he was down on the ground and the agony rose up to become a scarlet flame, until it was blotted out by a merciful darkness.

An hour passed, perhaps more, before George Hardcastle returned to consciousness. He lay quite still and tried to remember why he should be lying on the ground in a dense wood, while a dull ache held mastery over his right leg. Then memory sent its first cold tentacles shuddering across his brain and he dared to sit up and face reality.

The light had faded: night was slowly reinforcing its advance guard, but he was still able to see the dead man who lay but a few feet away. He shrank back with a little muffled cry and tried to dispel this vision of a purple face and bulging eyes, by the simple act of closing his own. But this was not a wise action for the image of that awful countenance was etched upon his brain, and the memory was even more macabre than the reality. He opened his eyes again, and there it was: a man in late middle life, with grey, close-cropped hair, a long moustache and yellow teeth, that were bared in a death grin. The purple face suggested he had died of a sudden heart attack.

The next hour was a dimly remembered nightmare. George dragged himself through the undergrowth and by sheer good fortune emerged out on to one of the main paths.

He was found next morning by a team of boy scouts.

Police and an army of enthusiastic volunteers scoured the woods, but no trace of a ferocious wild beast was found. But they did find the dead man, and he proved to be a farm worker who had a reputation locally of being a person of solitary habits. An autopsy revealed he had died of a heart attack, and it was assumed that this had been the result of his efforts in trying to assist the injured boy.

The entire episode assumed the proportions of a nine-day wonder, and then was forgotten.

Mrs. Hardcastle prided herself on being a mother who, while combating illness, did not pamper it. She had George back on his feet within three weeks and despatched him on prolonged walks. Being an obedient youth he followed these instructions to the letter, and so, on one overcast day, found himself at Hampton Court. As the first drops of rain were caressing his face, he decided to make a long-desired tour of the staterooms. He wandered from room to room, examined pictures, admired four-poster beds, then listened to a guide who was explaining the finer points to a crowd of tourists. By the time he had reached the Queen's Audience Room, he felt tired, so seated himself on one of the convenient window-seats. For some while he sat looking out at the rain-drenched gardens, then with a yawn, he turned and gave a quick glance along the long corridor that ran through a series of open doorways.

Suddenly his attention was captured by a figure approaching over the long carpet. It was that of a girl in a black dress; she was a beautiful study in black and white. Black hair, white face and hands, black dress. Not that there was anything sinister about her, for as she drew nearer he could see the look of indescribable sadness in the large, black eyes, and the almost timid way she looked round each room. Her appearance was outstanding, so vivid, like a black and white photograph that had come to life.

She entered the Queen's Audience Room and now he could hear the light tread of her feet, the whisper of her dress, and even those small sounds seemed unreal. She walked round the room, looking earnestly at the pictures, then as though arrested by a sudden sound, she stopped. Suddenly the lovely eyes came round and stared straight at George.

They held an expression of alarmed surprise, that gradually changed to one of dawning wonderment. For a moment George could only suppose she recognised him, although how he had come to forget her, was beyond his comprehension. She glided towards him, and as she came a small smile parted her lips. She sank down on the far end of the seat and watched him with those dark, wondering eyes.

She said: "Hullo. I'm Carola."

No girl had made such an obvious advance towards George before, and shyness, not to mention shock, robbed him of speech. Carola seemed to be reassured by his reticence, for her smile deepened and when she spoke her voice held a gentle bantering tone.

"What's the matter? Cat got your tongue?"

This impertinent probe succeeded in freeing him from the chains of shyness and he ventured to make a similar retort.

"I can speak when I want to."

"That's better. I recognised the link at once. We have certain family connections, really. Don't you think so?"

This question was enough to dry up his powers of communication for some time, but presently he was able to breathe one word. "Family!"

"Yes." She nodded and her hair trembled like black silk in sunlight. "We must be at least distantly related in the allegorical sense. But don't let's talk about that. I am so pleased to be able to walk about in daylight. It is so dreary at night, and besides, I'm not really myself then."

George came to the conclusion that this beautiful creature was at least slightly mad, and therefore made a mundane, but what he thought must be a safe remark.

"Isn't it awful weather?"

She frowned slightly and he got the impression he had committed a breach of good taste.

"Don't be so silly. You know it's lovely weather. Lots of beautiful cloud."

He decided this must be a joke. There could be no other interpretation. He capped it by another.

"Yes, and soon the awful sun will come out."

She flinched as though he had hit her, and there was the threat of tears in the lovely eyes.

"You beast. How could you say a dreadful thing like that? There won't be any sun, the weather forecast said so. I thought you were nice, but all you want to do is frighten me."

And she dabbed her eyes with a black lace handkerchief, while George tried to find his way out of a mental labyrinth where every word seemed to have a double meaning.

"I am sorry. But I didn't mean . . ."

She stifled a tiny sob. "How would you like it if I said—silver bullets?"

He scratched his head, wrinkled his brow and then made a wry grimace.

"I wouldn't know what you meant, but I wouldn't mind."

She replaced the lace handkerchief in a small handbag, then got up and walked quickly away. George watched her retreating figure until it disappeared round the corner in the direction of the long gallery. He muttered: "Potty. Stark raving potty."

On reflection he decided it was a great pity that her behaviour was so erratic, because he would have dearly liked to have known her better. In fact, when he remembered the black hair and white face, he was aware of a deep disappointment, a sense of loss, and he had to subdue an urge to run after her. He remained seated in the window bay and when he looked out on to the gardens, he saw the rain had ceased, but thick cloud banks were billowing across the sky. He smiled gently and murmured, "Lovely clouds—horrible sunshine."

George was half way across Anne Boleyn's courtyard when a light touch on his shoulder made him turn, and there was Carola of the white face and black hair, with a sad smile parting her lips.

"Look," she said, "I'm sorry I got into a huff back there, but I can't bear to be teased about—well, you know what. But you are one of us, and we mustn't quarrel. All forgiven?"

George said, "Yes, I'm sorry I offended you. But I didn't mean to." And at that moment he was so happy, so ridiculously elated, he was prepared to apologise for breathing.

"Good." She sighed and took hold of his arm as though it were the most natural action in the world. "We'll forget all about it. But, please, don't joke about such things again."

"No. Absolutely not." George had not the slightest idea what it was he must not joke about, but made a mental note to avoid mention of the weather and silver bullets.

"You must come and meet my parents," Carola insisted, "they'll be awfully pleased to see you. I bet they won't believe their noses."

This remark was in the nature of a setback, but George's newly found happiness enabled him to ignore it—pretend it must be a slip of the tongue.

"That's very kind of you, but won't it be a bit sudden? I mean, are you sure it will be convenient?"

She laughed, a lovely little silver sound and, if possible, his happiness increased.

"You are a funny boy. They'll be tickled pink, and so they should be. For the first time for years, we won't have to be careful of what we say in front of a visitor."

George had a little mental conference and came to the conclusion that this was meant to be a compliment. So he said cheerfully, "I don't mind what people say. I like them to be natural."

Carola thought that was a very funny remark and tightened her grip on his arm, while laughing in a most enchanting fashion.

"You have a most wonderful sense of humour. Wait until I tell Daddy that one. 'I like them to be natural . . .' "

And she collapsed into a fit of helpless laughter in which George joined, although he was rather at a loss to know what he had said that was so funny. Suddenly the laugh was cut short, was killed by a gasp of alarm, and Carola was staring at the western sky where the clouds had taken on a brighter hue. The words came out as a strangled whisper.

"The sun! O Lucifer, the sun is coming out."

"Is it?" George looked up and examined the sky with assumed interest. "I wouldn't be surprised if you're not right . . ." Then he stopped and looked down at his lovely companion with concern. "I'm sorry, you . . . you don't like the sun, do you?"

Her face was a mask of terror and she gave a terrible little cry of anguish. George's former suspicion of insanity returned, but she was still appealing—still a flawless pearl on black velvet. He put his arm round the slim shoulders, and she hid her eyes against his coat. The muffled, tremulous whisper came to him.

"Please take me home. Quickly."

He felt great joy in the fact that he was able to bring comfort.

"There's no sign of sunlight. Look, it was only a temporary break in the clouds."

Slowly the dark head was raised, and the eyes, so bright with unshed tears, again looked up at the western sky. Now, George was rewarded, for her lips parted, the skin round her eyes crinkled and her entire face was transformed by a wonderful, glorious smile.

"Oh, how beautiful! Lovely, lovely, *lovely* clouds. The wind is up there, you know. A big, fat wind-god, who blows out great bellows of mist, so that we may not be destroyed by demon-sun. And sometimes he shrieks his rage across the sky; at others he whispers soft comforting words and tells us to have faith. The bleak night of loneliness is not without end."

George was acutely embarrassed, not knowing what to make of this allegorical outburst. But the love and compassion he had so far extended to dogs, was now enlarged and channelled towards the lovely, if strange, young girl by his side.

"Come," he said, "let me take you home."

George pulled open a trellis iron gate and allowed Carola to precede him up a crazy-paved path, which led to a house that gleamed with new paint and well-cleaned windows. Such a house could have been found in any one of a thousand streets in the London suburbs, and brashly proclaimed that here lived a woman who took pride in the crisp whiteness of her curtains, and a man who was no novice in the art of wielding a paint brush. They had barely entered the tiny porch, where the red tiles shone like a pool at sunset, when the door was flung open and a plump, grey-haired woman clasped Carola in her arms.

"Ee, love, me and yer dad were that worried. We thought you'd got caught in a sun-storm."

Carola kissed her mother gently, on what George noted was another dead-white cheek, then turned and looked back at him with shining eyes.

"Mummy, this . . ." She giggled and shook her head. "It's silly, but I don't know your name."

"George. George Hardcastle."

To say Carola's mother looked alarmed is a gross understatement. For a moment she appeared to be terrified, and clutched her daughter as though they were both confronted by a man-eating tiger. Then Carola laughed softly and whispered into her mother's ear. George watched the elder woman's expression change to one of incredulity and dawning pleasure.

"You don't say so, love? Where on earth did you find him?"

"In the Palace," Carola announced proudly. "He was sitting in the Queen's Audience Room."

Mummy almost ran forward and, after clasping the startled George with both hands, kissed him soundly on either cheek. Then she stood back and examined him with obvious pleasure.

"I ought to have known," she said, nodding her head as though with sincere conviction. "Been out of touch for too long. But what will you think of me manners? Come in, love. Father will be that pleased. It's not much of a death for him, with just us two women around."

Again George was aware of a strange slip of the tongue, which he could only assume was a family failing. So he beamed with the affability that is expected from a stranger who is the recipient of sudden hospitality, and allowed himself to be pulled into a newly decorated hall, and relieved of his coat. Then Mummy opened a door and ordered in a shouted whisper: "Father, put yer tie on, we've got company." There was a startled snort, as though someone had been awakened from a fireside sleep, and Mummy turned a bright smile on George.

"Would you like to go upstairs and wash yer hands, like? Make yourself comfy, if you get my meaning."

"No, thank you. Very kind, I'm sure."

"Well then, you'd best come into parlour."

The "parlour" had a very nice paper on the walls, bright pink lamps, a well stuffed sofa and matching armchairs, a large television set, a low, imitation walnut table, a record player, some awful coloured prints, and an artificial log electric fire. A stout man with thinning grey hair struggled up from the sofa, while he completed the adjustment of a tie that was more eye-catching than tasteful.

"Father," Mummy looked quickly round the room as though to

seek reassurance that nothing was out of place, "this is George. A young man that Carola has brought home, like." Then she added in an undertone, "He's all right. No need to worry."

Father advanced with outstretched hand and announced in a loud, very hearty voice: "Ee, I'm pleased to meet ye, lad. I've always said it's about time the lass found 'erself a young spark. But the reet sort is 'ard to come by, and that's a fact."

Father's hand was unpleasantly cold and flabby, but he radiated such an air of goodwill, George was inclined to overlook it.

"Now, Father, you're embarrassing our Carola," Mummy said. And indeed the girl did appear to be somewhat disconcerted, only her cheeks instead of blushing, had assumed a greyish tinge. "Now, George, don't stand around, lad. Sit yerself down and make yerself at 'ome. We don't stand on ceremony here."

George found himself on the sofa next to Father, who would insist on winking, whenever their glances met. In the meanwhile Mummy expressed solicitous anxiety regarding his well-being.

"Have you supped lately? I know you young doggies don't 'ave to watch yer diet like we do, so just say what you fancy. I've a nice piece of 'am in t' fridge, and I can fry that with eggs, in no time at all."

George knew that somewhere in that kindly invitation there had been another slip of the tongue, but he resolutely did not think about it.

"That's very kind of you, but really . . ."

"Let 'er do a bit of cooking, lad," Father pleaded. "She don't get much opportunity, if I can speak without dotting me *i*'s and crossing me *t*'s."

"If you are sure it will be no trouble."

Mummy made a strange neighing sound. "Trouble! 'Ow you carry on. It's time for us to have a glass of something rich, anyway."

Mother and daughter departed for the kitchen and George was left alone with Father, who was watching him with an embarrassing interest.

"Been on 'olidays yet, lad?" he enquired.

"No, it's a bit late now . . ."

Father sighed with the satisfaction of a man who is recalling a pleasant memory. "We 'ad smashing time in Clacton. Ee, the weather was summat greet. Two weeks of thick fog—couldn't see 'and in front of face."

George said, "Oh, dear," then lasped into silence while he digested this piece of information. Presently he was aware of an elbow nudging his ribs.

"I know it's delicate question, lad, so don't answer if you'd rather not. But—'ow often do you change?"

George thought it was a very delicate question, and could only think of a very indelicate reason why it had been asked. But his conception of politeness demanded he answer.

"Well . . . every Friday actually. After I've had a bath."

Father gasped with astonishment. "As often as that! I'm surprised. The last lad I knew in your condition only changed when the moon was full."

George said, "Goodness gracious!" and then tried to ask a very pertinent question. "Why, do I . . ."

Father nodded. "There's a goodish pong. But don't let it worry you. We can smell it, because we've the reet kind of noses."

An extremely miserable, not to say self-conscious, young man was presently led across the hall and into the dining-room, where one place was set with knife, fork and spoon, and three with glass and drinking straw. He was too dejected to pay particular heed to this strange and unequal arrangement, and neither was he able to really enjoy the plate of fried eggs and ham that Mummy put down before him, with the remark: "Here you are, lad, get wrapped round that, and you'll not starve."

The family shared the contents of a glass jug between them, and as this was thick and red, George could only suppose it to be tomato juice. They all sucked through straws; Carola, as was to be expected, daintily, Mummy with some anxiety, and Father greedily. When he had emptied his glass, he presented it for a refill and said: "You know, Mother, that's as fine a jug of AB as you've ever served up."

Mummy sighed. "It's not so bad. Mind you, youngsters don't get what I call top-grade nourishment, these days. There's nothing like getting yer teeth stuck into the real thing. This stuff 'as lost the natural goodness."

Father belched and made a disgusting noise with his straw.

"We must be thankful, Mother. There's many who 'asn't a drop to wet their lips, and be pleased to sup from tin."

George could not subdue a natural curiosity and the question slipped out before he had time to really think about it.

"Excuse me, but don't you ever eat anything?"

The shocked silence which followed told him he had committed a well nigh unforgivable sin. Father dropped his glass and Carola said, "Oh, George," in a very reproachful voice, while Mummy creased her brow into a very deep frown.

"George, haven't you ever been taught manners?"

It was easy to see she spoke more in sorrow than anger, and although the exact nature of his transgression was not quite clear to George, he instantly apologised.

"I am very sorry, but . . ."

"I should think so, indeed." Mummy continued to speak gently but firmly. "I never expected to hear a question like that at my table. After all, you wouldn't like it if I were to ask who or what you chewed up on one of your moonlight strolls. Well, I've said me piece, and now we'll forget that certain words were ever said. Have some chocolate pudding."

Even while George smarted under this rebuke, he was aware that once again, not so much a slip of the tongue, as a sentence that demanded thought had been inserted between an admonishment and a pardon. There was also a growing feeling of resentment. It seemed that whatever he said to this remarkable family gave offence, and his supply of apologies was running low. He waited until Mummy had served him with a generous helping of chocolate pudding, and then replenished the three glasses from the jug, before he relieved his mind.

"I don't chew anyone."

Mummy gave Father an eloquent glance, and he cleared his throat.

"Listen, lad, there are some things you don't mention in front of ladies. What you do in change period is between you and black man. So let's change subject."

Like all peace-loving people George sometimes reached a point where war, or to be more precise, attack seemed to be the only course of action. Father's little tirade brought him to such a point. He flung down his knife and fork and voiced his complaints.

"Look here, I'm fed up. If I mention the weather, I'm ticked off. If I ask why you never eat, I'm in trouble. I've been asked when I change, told that I stink. Now, after being accused of chewing people, I'm told I mustn't mention it. Now, I'll tell you something. I think you're all round the bend."

Carola burst into tears and ran from the room: Father swore, or rather he said, "Satan's necktie," which was presumably the same thing, and Mummy looked very concerned.

"Just a minute, son." She raised a white, rather wrinkled forefinger. "You're trying to tell us you don't know the score?"

"I haven't the slightest idea what you're talking about," George retorted.

Mummy and Father looked at each other for some little while, then as though prompted by a single thought, they both spoke in unison.

"He's a just bittener."

"Someone should tell 'im," Mummy stated, after she had watched the, by now, very frightened George for an entire minute. "It should come from a man."

"If 'e 'ad gumption he were born with, 'e'd know," Father said, his face becoming quite grey with embarrassment. "Hell's bells, my dad didn't 'ave to tell me I were vampire."

"Yes, but you can see he's none too bright," Mummy pointed out. "We can't all 'ave your brains. No doubt the lad has 'eart, and I say 'eart is better than brains any day. Been bitten lately, lad?"

George could only nod and look longingly at the door.

"Big long thing, with a wet snout, I wouldn't be surprised. It's a werewolf you are, son. You can't deceive the noses of we vamps: yer glands are beginning to play up—give out a bit of smell, see? I should think . . . What's the state of the moon, Father?"

"Seven eights."

Mummy nodded with grim relish. "I should think you're due for a change round about Friday night. Got any open space round your way?"

"There's . . ." George took a deep breath. "There's Clapham Common."

"Well, I should go for a run round there. Make sure you cover your face up. Normal people go all funny like when they first lays eyes on a werewolf. Start yelling their 'eads off, mostly."

George was on his feet and edging his way towards the door. He was praying for the priceless gift of disbelief. Mummy was again displaying signs of annoyance.

"Now there's no need to carry on like that. You must 'ave known we were all vampires—what did you think we were drinking? Raspberry juice? And let me tell you this. We're the best friends you've got. No one else will want to know you, once full moon is peeping over barn door. So don't get all lawn tennis with us . . ."

But George was gone. Running across the hall, out of the front door, down the crazy-paving path, and finally along the pavement. People turned their heads as he shouted: "They're mad . . . mad . . . mad . . ."

There came to George—as the moon waxed full—a strange restlessness. It began with insomnia, which rocketed him out of a deep sleep into a strange, instant wakefulness. He became aware of an urge to go for long moonlit walks; and when he had surrendered to this temptation, an overwhelming need to run, leap, roll over and over down a grassy bank, anything that would enable him to break down the hated walls of human convention—and express. A great joy—greater than he had ever known—came to him when he leaped and danced on the common, and could only be released by a shrill, doglike howl that rose up from the sleeping suburbs and went out, swift as a beam of light, to the face of mother-moon.

This joy had to be paid for. When the sun sent its first enquiring rays in through George's window, sanity returned and demanded a reckoning. He examined his face and hands with fearful expectancy. So far as he was aware there had been no terrible change, as yet. But these were early days—or was it nights? Sometimes he would fling himself down on his bed and cry out his great desire for disbelief.

"It can't happen. Mad people are sending me mad."

The growing strangeness of his behaviour could not go undetected. He was becoming withdrawn, apt to start at every sound, and betrayed a certain distrust of strangers by an eerie widening of his eyes, and later, the baring of his teeth in a mirthless grin. His mother commented on these peculiarities in forcible language.

"I think you're going up the pole. Honest I do. The milkman told me yesterday, he saw you snarling at Mrs. Redfern's dog."

"It jumped out at me," George explained. "You might have done the same."

Mrs. Hardcastle shook her head. "No. I can honestly say I've never snarled at a dog in my life. You never inherited snarling from me."

"I'm all right." George pleaded for reassurance. "I'm not turning into—anything."

"Well, you should know." George could not help thinking that his mother was regarding him with academic interest, rather than concern. "Do you go out at nights after I'm asleep?"

He found it impossible to lie convincingly, so he countered one question with another. "Why should I do that?"

"Don't ask me. But some nut has been seen prancing round the common at three o'clock in the morning. I just wondered."

The physical change came gradually. One night he woke with a severe pain in his right hand and lay still for a while, not daring to examine it. Then he switched on the bedside lamp with his left hand and, after further hesitation, brought its right counterpart out from the sheets. A thick down had spread over the entire palm and he found the fingers would not straighten. They had curved and the nails were thicker and longer than he remembered. After a while the fear—the loathing—went away, and it seemed most natural for him to have claws for fingers and hair-covered hands. Next morning his right hand was as normal as his left, and at that period he was still able to dismiss, even if with little conviction, the episode as a bad dream.

But one night there was a dream—a nightmare of the blackest kind, where fantasy blended with fact and George was unable to distinguish one from the other. He was running over the common, bounding with long, graceful leaps, and there was a wonderful joy in his heart and a limitless freedom in his head. He was in a black and white world. Black grass, white-tinted trees, grey sky, white moon. But with all the joy, all the freedom, there was a subtle, ever-present knowledge, that this was an unnatural experience, that he should be utilising all his senses to dispel. Once his brain—that part which was still unoccupied territory—screamed: "Wake up," but he was awake, for did not the black grass crunch beneath his feet, and the night breeze ruffle his fur? A large cat was running in front, trying to escape—up trees—across the roofs—round bushes—he finally trapped it in a hole. Shrieks—scratching claws—warm blood—tearing teeth . . . It was good. He was fulfilled.

Next morning when he awoke in his own bed, it could have been dismissed as a mad dream, were it not for the scratches on his face and hands and the blood in his hair. He thought of psychiatrists, asylums, priests, religion, and at last came to the only possible conclusion. There was, so far as he knew, only one set of people on earth who could explain and understand.

Mummy let George in. Father shook him firmly by the hand. Carola kissed him gently and put an arm round his shoulders when he started to cry.

"We don't ask to be what we are," she whispered. "We keep more horror than we give away."

"We all 'ave our place in the great graveyard," Father said. "You hunt, we sup, ghouls tear, shaddies lick, mocks blow, and fortunately shadmocks can only whistle."

"Will I always be—what I am?" George asked.

They all nodded. Mummy grimly, Father knowingly, Carola sadly.

"Until the moon leaves the sky," they all chanted.

"Or you are struck in the heart by a silver bullet," Carola whispered, "fired by one who has only thought about sin. Or maybe when you are very, very old, the heart may give out after a transformation . . ."

"Don't be morbid," Mummy ordered. "Poor lad's got enough on plate without you adding to it. Make him a nice cup of tea. And you can mix us a jug of something rich while you're about it. Don't be too 'eavy-handed on the O group."

They sat round the artificial log fire, drinking tea, asborbing nourishment, three giving, one receiving advice, and there was a measure of cosiness.

"All 'M's' should keep away from churches, parsons and boy scouts," Father said.

"Run from a cross and fly from a prayer," intoned Mummy.

"Two can run better than one," Carola observed shyly.

Next day George told his mother he intended to leave home and set up house for himself. Mrs. Hardcastle did not argue as strongly as she might have had a few weeks earlier. What with one thing and another, there was a distinct feeling that the George, who was standing so grim and white-faced in the kitchen doorway, was not the one she had started out with. She said, "Right, then. I'd say it's about time," and helped him to pack.

Father, who knew someone in the building line, found George a four-roomed cottage that was situated on the edge of a churchyard, and this he furnished with a few odds and ends that the family were willing to part with. The end product was by no means as elegant or deceptive as the house at Hampton Court, but it was somewhere for George to come back to after his midnight run.

He found the old legends had been embellished, for he experienced no urge to rend or even bite. There was no reason why he should; the body was well fed and the animal kingdom only hunts when goaded by hunger. It was sufficient for him to run, leap, chase his tail by moonlight, and sometimes howl with the pure joy of living. And it is pleasant to record that his joy grew day by day.

For obvious reasons the wedding took place in a registry office, and it seemed that the dark gods smiled down upon the union, for there was a thick fog that lasted from dawn to sunset. The wedding-supper and the reception which followed were, of necessity, simple affairs. There was a wedding cake for those that could eat it: a beautiful, three-tier structure, covered with pink icing, and studded with what George hoped were glacé cherries. He of course had invited no guests, for there was much that might have alarmed or embarrassed the uninitiated. Three ghouls in starched, white shrouds, sat gnawing something that was best left undescribed. The bride and her family sipped a basic beverage from red goblets, and as the bridegroom was due for a turn, he snarled when asked to pass the salt. Then there was Uncle Deitmark, a vampire of the old school, who kept demanding a trussed-up victim, so that he could take his nourishment direct from the neck.

But finally the happy couple were allowed to depart, and Mummy and Father wept as they threw the traditional coffin nails after the departing hearse. "Ee, it were champion," Father exclaimed, wiping his eyes on the back of his hand. "Best blood-up I've seen for many a day. You did 'em proud, Mother."

"I believe in giving the young 'uns a good send-off," Mummy said. "Now they must open their own vein, as the saying goes."

Carola and George watched the moon come up over the church steeple, which was a little dangerous for it threw the cross into strong relief, but on that one night they would have defied the very Pope of Rome himself.

"We are no longer alone," Carola whispered. "We love and are loved, and that surely has transformed us from monsters into gods."

"If happiness can transform a tumbledown cottage into paradise," George said, running his as yet uncurved fingers through her hair, "then I guess we are gods."

But he forgot that every paradise must have its snake, and their particular serpent was disguised in the rotund shape of the Reverend John Cole. This worthy cleric had an allegorical nose for smelling out hypothetical evil, and it was not long before he was considering the inhabitants of the house by the churchyard with a speculative eye.

He called when George was out and invited Carola to join the young wives' altar dressing committee. She turned grey and begged to be excused. Mr. Cole then suggested she partake in a brief reading from holy scripture, and Carola shrank from the proffered Bible, even as a rabbit recoils from a hooded cobra. Then the Reverend John Cole accidentally dropped his crucifix on to her lap, and she screamed like one who is in great pain, before falling to the floor in a deathlike faint. And the holy minister departed with the great joy that comes to the sadist who knows he is only doing his duty.

Next day George met the Reverend Cole, who was hastening to the death bed of a sinful woman, and laid a not too gentle hand on the flabby arm.

"I understand you frightened my wife, when I was out yesterday."

The clergyman bared his teeth and, although George was now in the shape with which he had been born, they resembled two dogs preparing to fight.

"I'm wondering," the Reverend Cole said, "what kind of woman recoils from the good book and screams when the crucifix touches her."

"Well, it's like this," George tightened his grip on the black-clad arm, "we are both allergic to Bibles, crosses and nosy parsons. I am apt to burn one, break two, and pulverise three. Am I getting through?"

"And I have a duty before God and man," John Cole said, looking down at the retaining hand with marked distaste, "and that is to stamp out evil wherever it be found. And may I add, with whatever means that are at my disposal."

They parted in mutual hate, and George in his innocence decided to use fear as an offensive weapon, not realising that its wounds strengthen resistance more often than they weaken. One night, when the moon was full, turning the graveyard into a gothic wonderland, the Reverend John Cole met something that robbed him of speech for nigh on twelve hours. It walked on bent hindlegs, and had two very long arms which terminated in talons that seemed hungry for the ecclesiastical throat, and a nightmare face whose predominant feature was a long, slavering snout.

At the same time, Mrs. Cole, a very timid lady who had yet to learn of the protective virtues of two pieces of crossed wood, was trying so hard not to scream as a white-faced young woman advanced across the bedroom. The reaction of husband and wife was typical of their individual characters. The Reverend John Cole, after the initial cry, did not stop running until he was safely barricaded in the church with a processional cross jammed across the doorway. Mrs. Cole, being unable to scream, promptly fainted, and hence fared worse than her fleetfooted spouse. John Cole, after his run, was a little short of breath: Mary Cole, when she returned to consciousness, was a little short of blood.

Mr. Cole was an erratic man who often preached sermons guaranteed to raise the scalps of the most urbane congregation, if that is to say, they took the trouble to listen. The tirade which was poured out from the pulpit on the Sunday after Mrs. Cole's loss and Mr. Cole's fright, woke three slumbering worshippers, and caused a choirboy to swallow his chewing-gum.

"The devil has planted his emissaries in our midst," the vicar proclaimed. "Aye, do they dwell in the church precincts and do appear to the God-fearing in their bestial form."

The chewing-gum-bereft choirboy giggled, and Mr. Cole's wrath rose and erupted into admonishing words.

"Laugh not. I say to you of little faith, laugh not. For did I not come face to face—aye, but a few yards from where you now sit—with a fearsome beast that did drool and nuzzle, and I feared that my windpipe might soon lie upon my shirtfront. But, and this be the truth, which did turn my bowels to water, there was the certain knowledge that I was in the presence of a creature that is without precedence in Satan's hierarchy—the one—the only—the black angel of hell—the dreaded werewolf."

At least ten people in the congregation thought their vicar had at last turned the corner and become stark raving mad. Twenty more did not understand what he was talking about, and one old lady assumed she was listening to a brilliant interpretation of Revelation, chapter XIII, verses 1 to 3. The remainder of the congregation had not been listening, but noted the vicar was in fine fettle, roaring and pounding the pulpit with his customary gusto. His next disclosure suffered roughly the same reception.

"My dear wife—my helpmeet, who has walked by my side these past twenty years—was visited in her chamber by a female of the species . . ." Mr. Cole nodded bitterly. "A vampire, an unclean thing that has crept from its foul grave, and did take from my dear one, that which she could ill afford to lose . . ."

Ignorance, inattention, Mr. Cole's words fell on very stony ground and no one believed—save Willie Mitcham. Willie did believe in vampires, werewolves, and, in fact, also accepted the existence of banshees, demons, poltergeists, ghosts of every description, monsters of every shape and form, and the long wriggly thing, which as everyone knows, has yet to be named. As Willie was only twelve years of age, he naturally revelled in his belief, and moreover made himself an expert on demonology. To his father's secret delectation and his mother's openly expressed horror, he had an entire cupboard filled with literature that dwelt on every aspect of the subject. He knew, for example, that the only sure way of getting a banshee off your back is to spit three times into an open grave, bow three times to the moon, then chant in a loud voice.

> Go to the north, go to the south,
> Go to the devil, but shut your mouth.
> Scream not by day, or howl by night,
> But gibber alone by candlelight.

He also knew, for had not the facts been advertised by printed page, television set, and cinema screen, that the only sure way of killing a vampire is to drive a sharp pointed object through its heart between the hours of sunrise and sunset. He was also joyfully aware of the fatal consequences that attend the arrival of a silver bullet in a werewolf's hairy chest. So it was that Willie listened to the Reverend John Cole with ears that heard and understood, and he wanted so desperately to shout out the simple and time-honoured cures, the withal, the ways and means, the full, glorious, and gory details. But his mother nudged him in the ribs and told him to stop fidgeting, so he could only sit and seethe with well-nigh uncontrollable impatience.

One bright morning in early March the total population of the graveyard cottage was increased by one. The newly risen sun peeped in through the neatly curtained windows and gazed down upon, what it is to be hoped, was the first baby werevamp. It was like all newly born infants, small, wrinkled, extremely ugly, and favoured its mother in so far as it had been born with two prominent eye-teeth. Instead of crying, it made a harsh hissing sound, not unlike that of an infant king-cobra, and was apt to bite anything that moved.

"Isn't he sweet?" Carola sighed, then waved a finger at her offspring, who promptly curled back an upper lip and made a hissing snarl. "Yes he is . . . he's a sweet 'ickle diddums . . . he's Mummy's 'ickle diddums . . ."

"I think he's going to be awfully clever," George stated after a while. "What with that broad forehead and those dark eyes, one can see there is a great potential for intelligence. He's got your mouth, darling."

"Not yet he hasn't," Carola retorted, "but he soon will have, if I'm not careful. I suppose he's in his humvamp period now, but when the moon is full, he'll have sweet little hairy talons, and a dinky-winky little tail."

Events proved her to be absolutely correct.

The Reverend John Cole allowed several weeks to pass before he made an official call on the young parents. During this time he reinforced his courage, of which it must be confessed he had an abundance; sought advice from his superiors, who were not at all helpful; and tried to convince anyone who would listen of the danger in their midst. His congregation shrank, people crossed the road whenever he came into view, and he was constantly badgered by a wretched little boy, who poured out a torrent of nauseating information. But at last the vicar was as ready for the fatal encounter as he ever would be, and so, armed with a crucifix, faith and a small bottle of whisky, he went forth to do battle. From his bedroom window that overlooked the vicarage, Willie Mitcham watched the black figure as it trudged along the road. He flung the window open and shouted: "Yer daft coot. It's a full moon."

No one answered Mr. Cole's thunderous assault on the front door. This was not surprising, as Carola was paying Mrs. Cole another visit, and George was chasing a very disturbed sheep across a stretch of open moorland. Baby had not yet reached the age when answering doors would be numbered among his accomplishments. At last the reverend gentleman opened the door and, after crossing himself with great fervour, entered the cottage.

He found himself in the living-room, a cosy little den with whitewashed walls, two ancient chairs, a folding table, and some very nice rugs on the floor. There was also a banked-up fire, and a beautiful old ceiling oil-lamp that George had cleverly adapted for electricity. Mr. Cole called out: "Anyone there?" and, receiving no answer, sank down into one of the chairs to wait. Presently, the chair being comfortable, the room warm, the clergyman felt his caution dissolve into a hazy atmosphere of well-being. His head nodded, his eyelids flickered, his mouth fell open and, in no time at all, a series of gentle snores filled the room with their even cadence.

It is right to say Mr. Cole fell asleep reluctantly, and while he slept he displayed a certain amount of dignity. But he awoke with a shriek and began to thresh about in a most undignified manner. There was a searing pain in his right ankle, and when he moved something soft and rather heavy flopped over his right foot and at the same time made a strange hissing sound. The vicar screamed again and kicked out with all his strength, and that which clung to his ankle went hurling across the room and landed on a rug near the window. It hissed, yelped, then turning over, began to crawl back towards the near prostrate clergyman. He tried to close his eyes, but they insisted on remaining open and so permitted him to see something that a person with a depraved sense of humour might have called a baby. A tiny, little white—oh, so white —face, which had two microscopic fangs jutting out over the lower lip. But for the rest it was very hairy; had two wee claws, and a proudly erect, minute tail, that was, at this particular moment in time, lashing angrily from side to side. Its little hind legs acted as projectors and enabled the hair-covered torso to leap along at quite an amazing speed. There was also a smear of Mr. Cole's blood round the mouth; and the eyes held an expression that suggested the ecclesiastical fluid was appealing to the taste-buds, and their owner could hardly wait to get back to the fount of nourishment.

Mr. Cole released three long, drawn-out screams, then, remembering that legs have a decided and basic purpose, leaped for the door. It was truly an awe-inspiring sight to see a portly clergyman, who had more than reached the years of discretion, running between graves, leaping over tombstones, and sprinting along paths. Baby-werevamp squatted on his hind legs and looked as wistfully as his visage permitted after the swiftly retreating cleric. After a while baby set up a prolonged howl, and thumped the floor with clenched claws. His distress was understandable. He had just seen a well-filled feeding bottle go running out of the door.

Willie Mitcham had at last got through. One of the stupid, blind, not to mention thick-headed adults had been finally shocked into seeing the light. When Willie found the Reverend John Cole entangled in a hawthorn bush, he also stumbled on a man who was willing to listen to advice from any source. He had also retreated from the frontiers of sanity, and was therefore in a position to be driven, rather than to command.

"I saw 'im." Willie was possibly the happiest boy in the world at that moment. "I saw 'im with his 'orrible fangs and he went leaping towards the moors."

Mr. Cole said, "Ah!" and began to count his fingers.

"And I saw 'er," Willie went on. "She went to your house and drifted up to the main bedroom window. Just like in the film *Mark of the Vampire.*"

"Destroy all evil," the Reverend Cole shouted. "Root it out. Cut into . . ."

"Its 'eart," Willie breathed. "The way to kill a vampire is drive a stake through its 'eart. And a werewolf must be shot with a silver bullet fired by 'im who has only thought about sin."

"From what authority do you quote this information?" the vicar demanded.

"Me 'orror comics," Willie explained. "They give all the details, and if you go and see the *Vampire of 'Ackney Wick,* you'll see a 'oly father cut off the vampire's 'ead and put a sprig of garlic in its mouth."

"Where are these documents?" the clergyman enquired.

Mr. and Mrs. Mitcham were surprised and perhaps a little alarmed when their small son conducted the vicar through the kitchen and, after a perfunctory "It's all right, Mum, parson wants to see me 'orror comics," led the frozen-faced clergyman upstairs to the attic.

It was there that Mr. Cole's education was completed. Assisted by lurid pictures and sensational text, he learned of the conception, habits, hobbies and disposal procedures of vampires, werewolves and other breathing or non-breathing creatures that had attended the same school.

"Where do we get . . . ?" he began.

"A tent peg and Mum's coal 'ammer will do fine." Willie was quick to give expert advice.

"But a silver bullet." The vicar shook his head. "I cannot believe there is a great demand . . ."

"Two of Grandad's silver collar studs melted down with a soldering iron, and a cartridge from Dad's old .22 rifle. Mr. Cole, please say we can do it. I promise never to miss Sunday school again, if you'll say we can do it."

The Reverend John Cole did not consider the problem very long. A bite from a baby werevamp is a great decision maker.

"Yes," he nodded, "we have been chosen. Let us gird up our loins, gather the sinews of battle, and go forth to destroy the evil ones."

"Coo!" Willie nodded vigorously. "All that blood. Can I cut 'er 'ead off?"

If anyone had been taking the air at two o'clock next morning, they might have seen an interesting sight. A large clergyman, armed with a crucifix and a coal hammer, was creeping across the churchyard, followed by a small boy with a tent peg in one hand and a light hunting rifle in the other.

They came to the cottage and Mr. Cole first turned the handle, then pushed the door open with his crucifix. The room beyond was warm and cosy; firelight painted a dancing pattern on the ceiling, the brass lamp twinkled and glittered like a suspended star, and it was as though a brightly designed nest had been carved out of the surrounding darkness. John Cole strode into the room like a black marble angel of doom and, raising his crucifix, bellowed, "I have come to drive out the iniquity, burn out the sin. For, thus saith the Lord, cursed be you who hanker after darkness."

There was a sigh, a whimper—maybe a hissing whimper. Carola was crouched in one corner, her face whiter than a slab of snow in moonlight, her eyes dark pools of terror, her lips deep, deep red, as though they had been brought to life by a million, blood-tinted kisses, and her hands were pale ghost-moths, beating out their life against the invisible wall of intolerance. The vicar lowered his cross and the whimper grew up and became a cry of despair.

"Why?"

"Where is the foul babe that did bite my ankle?"

Carola's staring eyes never left the crucifix towering over her.

"I took him . . . took him . . . to his grandmother."

"There is more of your kind? Are you legion? Has the devil's spawn been hatched?"

"We are on the verge of extinction."

The soul of the Reverend John Cole rejoiced when he saw the deep terror in the lovely eyes, and he tasted the fruits of true happiness when she shrieked. He bunched the front of her dress up between trembling fingers and jerked her first upright, then down across the table. She made a little hissing sound; an instinctive token of defiance, and for a moment the delicate ivory fangs were bared and nipped the clergyman's hand, but that was all. There was no savage fight for existence, no calling on the dark gods; just a token resistance, the shedding of a tiny dribble of blood, then complete surrender. She lay back across the table, her long, black hair brushing the floor, as though this were the inevitable conclusion from which she had been too long withheld. The vicar placed the tip of the tent peg over her heart, and taking the coal hammer from the overjoyed Willie, shouted the traditional words.

"Get thee to hell. Burn for ever and a day. May thy foul carcase be food for jackals, and thy blood drink for pariah dogs."

The first blow sent the tent peg in three or four inches, and the sound of a snapping rib grated on the clergyman's ear, so that for a moment he turned his head aside in revulsion. Then, as though alarmed lest his resolve weaken, he struck again, and the blood rose up in a scarlet fountain; a cascade of dancing rubies, each one reflecting the room with its starlike lamp, and the dripping, drenched face of a man with a raised coal hammer. The hammer, like the mailed hand of fate, fell again, and the ruby fountain sank low, then collapsed into a weakly gushing pool. Carola released her life in one long, drawn-out sigh, then became a black and white study in still life.

"You gotta cut 'er 'ead off," Willie screamed. "Ain't no good, unless you cut 'er 'ead off and put a sprig of garlic in 'er mouth."

But Mr. Cole had, at least temporarily, had a surfeit of blood. It matted his hair, clogged his eyes, salted his mouth, drenched his clothes from neck to waist, and transformed his hands into scarlet claws.

Willie was fumbling in his jacket pocket.

"I've got me mum's bread knife here, somewhere. Should go through 'er neck a treat."

The reverend gentleman wiped a film of red from his eyes and then daintily shook his fingers.

"Truly is it said a little child shall lead them. Had I been more mindful of the Lord's business, I would have brought me a tenon saw."

He was not more than half way through his appointed task, when the door was flung back and George entered. He was on the turn. He was either about to "become," or return to "as was." His silhouette filled the moonlit doorway, and he became still; a black menace that was no less dangerous because it did not move. Then he glided across the room, round the table and the Reverend John Cole retreated before him.

George gathered up the mutilated remains of his beloved, then raised agony-filled eyes.

"We loved—she and I. Surely, that should have forgiven us much. Death we would have welcomed—for what is death, but a glorious reward for having to live. But this . . . ."

He pointed to the jutting tent peg, the half-severed head, then looked up questioningly at the clergyman. Then the Reverend John Cole took up his cross and, holding it before him, he called out in a voice that had been made harsh by the dust of centuries.

"I am Alpha and Omega, saith the Lord, and into the pit which is before the beginning and after the end shall ye be cast. For you and your kind are a stench and an abomination, and whatever evil is done unto you shall be deemed good in my sight."

The face of George Hardcastle became like an effigy carved from rock. Then it seemed to shimmer, the lines dissolved and ran one into the other; the hairline advanced, while the eyes retreated into deep sockets, and the jaw and nose merged and slithered into a long, pointed snout. The werewolf dropped the mangled remains of its mate and advanced upon her killer.

"Satanus Avaunt."

The Reverend Cole thrust his crucifix forward as though it were a weapon of offence, only to have it wrenched from his grasp and broken by a quick jerk of hair-covered wrists. The werewolf tossed the pieces to one side, then with a howl leaped forward and buried his long fangs into the vicar's shoulder.

The two locked figures—one representing good, the other evil—swayed back and forth in the lamplight, and there was no room in either hate-fear-filled brain for the image of one small boy, armed with a rifle. The sharp little cracking sound could barely be heard above the grunting, snarling battle that was being raged near the hanging brass lamp, but the result was soon apparent. The werewolf shrieked, before twisting round and staring at the exuberant Willie, as though in dumb reproach. Then it crashed to the floor. When the clergyman had recovered sufficiently to look down, he saw the dead face of George Hardcastle, and had he been a little to the right of the sanity frontier, there might well have been terrible doubts.

"Are you going to finish cutting off 'er head?" Willie enquired.

They put the Reverend John Cole in a quiet house surrounded by a beautiful garden. Willie Mitcham they placed in a home, as a juvenile court decided, in its wisdom, that he was in need of care and protection. The remains of George and Carola they buried in the churchyard and said some beautiful words over their graves.

It is a great pity they did not listen to Willie, who after all knew what he was talking about when it came to a certain subject.

One evening, when the moon was full, two gentlemen who were employed in the house surrounded by the beautiful garden, opened the door, behind which resided all that remained of the Reverend John Cole. They both entered the room and prepared to talk. They never did. One dropped dead from pure, cold terror, and the other achieved a state of insanity which had so far not been reached by one of his patients.

The Reverend John Cole had been bitten by a baby werevamp, nipped by a female vampire, and clawed and bitten by a full-blooded buck werewolf.

Only the good Lord above, and the bad one below, knew what he was.

CHARLES L. GRANT *(born 1942)* *is one of the foremost authors of dark fantasy in America today. A resident of New Jersey for most of his life, Grant concentrates on small-town America and the lives of fairly ordinary people, lives that become something other than ordinary when normality suddenly disappears.*

Grant's residence in Connecticut while he attended Trinity College resulted in a memorable series of novels, written in Grant's personal style of "quiet" horror, about the fictional New England town of Oxrun Station. His other novels include The Nestling *(1982),* Night Songs *(1984),* The Tea Party *(1985), and* The Pet *(1986).*

Grant won his earliest reputation with his short stories, of which he has published more than a hundred. Some of his best are collected in Tales from the Nightside *(1981).*

Vampires are the center of attention in The Soft Whisper of the Dead *(1982), a very traditional vampire tale told in the style of the nineteenth century. But Grant's usual method, especially in his short stories, is to employ the devices of dark fantasy to explore the inner recesses of the human mind. That is what he does in "Love-Starved," which was first published in* The Magazine of Fantasy and Science Fiction *in August 1979.*

Love-Starved (1979)

BY CHARLES L. GRANT

You really think I'm that different, do you?

Oh, I know you meant it as a compliment, don't worry. But seeing as how we've known each other for so long now, I'll give you your due, and a warning at the same time that you won't believe a word of it. And I won't mind if you laugh, or raise an eyebrow or two. As a matter of fact, I'll be disappointed if you don't. I'm a fair man, I think, and you really should know what you're getting yourself into.

No, of couse I'm not trying to break tomorrow's engagement.

But as I said: I'm a fair man.

Can't you see it in my eyes?

So. Where should I begin? With a woman, I suppose, though I hope you won't be jealous. It's all very pertinent. Believe me, it is.

What it comes down to, I think, is that I remember Alicia Chou, not because of the experience we shared, but because it was she who stopped me from even dreaming about marriage again. Or about love in the sense you would ordinarily consider it.

Unrequited passion? I hardly think so, though I've considered it, that's true. That sounds too much like a line from a grade B, 1940s film; though, if I were pressed, I would have to admit that in a grotesquely perverse way I may love her yet. Or part of me does, anyway. But that's the one thing I can't explain just now. I'm not even sure that I'll ever have the answer.

The attraction certainly wasn't her astonishing, almost exquisite beauty—I told you not to be jealous, be patient—though that too lingers, rather like an aftertaste uncommitted to being either sweet or sour. And if that sounds odd to say in this day and age, it's because she herself was a strange one, in a way only someone like myself can truly appreciate.

As of this moment, to be frank, I honestly cannot think of exactly what it was about her that affected me first, despite the apparent simplicity of the problem. But, then, perhaps I'm still too close to the situation after ten short years.

Tell you what. Let's turn this into a game of sorts. You order yourself another one of those pink things (none for me, thanks; perhaps later), and we'll pretend we're in one of those nineteenth-century country inns, whiling away the winter evenings scaring the hell out of each other with nonsensical ghost stories. I haven't much time, but I think I can give you a hint of what's happening—not that I expect that you'll take it. No one ever does. Which is odd, my dear, because it's not only happening to me.

If you'll remember, it was a remarkably short time before the photography studio I'd opened downtown was doing extremely well for its rather limited size. Over the first few months I'd been commissioned to shoot cover material for just about every men's and general circulation magazine going; there were even a few location trips to Europe thrown in to sweeten the lot. But when July came around, I felt myself going stale—my head was beginning to feel groggy in the same way you feel when you've just completed two or three final exams in a row. Every model was getting that same vapid, hurry-up-you-creep-these-lights-are-hot look. Every location was flat and uninviting. I dreaded going to work, dreaded even waking up in the morning. And naturally, all this eventually surfaced in the final product. I had obviously been pushing too hard, too fast, trying to make a few bucks and a name.

Finally, when the very thought of sticking my eye anywhere near a lens made me want to gag, I said the hell with it, and I left. Oh, a few clients squealed and wrung their hot little hands; a few editors growled at me over the phone; but when I told them all in the plainest, nonadvertising language what they could do with their precious campaigns and covers, all they did was purse their lips and shake their heads and tell me I needed a vacation.

So I took one. As simple as that.

I packed a bag and fled the city without looking back. It had been some time since I'd bothered driving with the top down, and the wind cresting over the windshield felt absolutely great. Just cool enough to take the sting out of the hot sun, and strong enough to make me feel glad I still had all my hair. Everything, then, and every miserable working day was blown so far away I had to think to remember what I did for a living. Knowing me as you do, you're not going to believe this, but I was even singing out loud at the top of my voice and thinking I should have practiced for the Met.

Whim chose my direction, and I paid little attention to the odometer, gladly patching a tire or two myself simply because there was no appointment I had to make by two o'clock or we'll cancel the contract and find someone else more reliable, thank you. God, but that was a magnificent feeling! On the second morning out, in fact, I'd stuffed my watch into the glove compartment and didn't put it on again for three days. It's almost supernatural, the freedom one feels when you don't turn your wrist every ten minutes to see that ten minutes have passed since the last time you looked. Incredible. And wonderful.

But then, by hook, crook, or some other heavy-handed and cliché-scarred beck of Fate's temptation, I found myself missing a few familiar comforts and ended up back in the Cape Cod I'd bought over there on Hawthorne Street, right on the river above the bend. I guess I had it in the back of my mind all along, in spite of the fact that my conscious plan was just to keep driving until I'd refueled, you should pardon the pun. I'd picked it up already furnished, but I'd never had a chance to really enjoy the overstuffed chairs and the dusty bookcases, the stereo, the TV, and God knew what else; I'd seldom stayed there more than just to sleep, and sometimes not that, if you know what I mean. But now . . . Lord, I could roam through the cool and quiet, let that old place soak out of my system everything the drive in the country hadn't banished. I turned myself into the absolute sloth, and I loved it, every minute, even fell in love with the shadows in the house.

And though I wasn't used to taking things easy, I had no problem at all falling into the slow, casual tempo of summer neighborhood life. Early evening walks really *seeing* the place where I'd chosen to live, scuffing leaves in the park and listening to bandstand music after a leisurely cooked dinner, once even stringing a hammock between two trees in the yard and humming in time to the river that marked the end of my lot.

It was . . . beautiful, because, for I don't know how many champagne days, I was actually seeing things through my own eyes instead of a camera's, and I was totally convinced I couldn't have been happier.

Then, one afternoon, I was baking in a sauce of suntan oil on a small section of riverbank set aside as a beach. I spent a lot of good time watching the kids splashing around, dunking each other and really getting frustrated learning to swim in the river's moderate currents. For a while there I really got involved rooting for one little guy who was experimenting holding his breath and trying not to drown at the same time. I was timing him by counting thousands and making bets with myself, when this indescribable pair of legs blocked my view.

Now I know that some men are devotees of the decolletage, and others are—as one of my girls once put it—admirers of ass; but I prefer those anatomical delights that carry the rest of the woman around. It has always been my solemn creed that bust or buttock, nose or navel, aren't anything at all without a fine pair of legs to support them. Not that this woman didn't have the appropriate accessories, mind you . . . but Lord, those legs! All the Troys in history would have gladly fallen for them, would have definitely been singed by the rest of her. Curiously, she was wearing a one-piece bathing suit that would have aroused attention on any beach simply because it was so out of place it was quaint. Black, too, her hair, curled inward slightly at the ends and cut to a point between her shoulders.

I lay there quietly, waiting for her to turn around, and paradoxically hoping that she would stay facing the water.

But she turned, abruptly, and looked straight into my eyes.

(As I do now, so I can see you're not jealous.)

Disconcerted though I was, her stare wasn't at all unfriendly. She was Eurasian: so temptingly French (perhaps), so tantalizingly Oriental (perhaps), that a dozen years' concentration couldn't have discovered where one began and the other left off.

When I sat up, she knelt directly in front of me and smiled, her deep tan looking darker in the shadow of her lips. I felt a bit fuzzy, as if I'd had too much sun and beer, but I managed a weak grin in return. Obviously, I wasn't at the top of my form.

"I'm sorry," I said, thinking all the while how brilliant that sounded and how stupidly seventeenish I was feeling.

"For what?" She laughed clear into eyes perfectly framed by black bangs.

"You got me. For staring at you, I guess. It's not exactly the most polite form of introduction."

She laughed again, tossing her head from side to side, and damned if I didn't feel shocked—at myself. Right at that moment I wanted to rape that animal—there's no other word—kneeling so primly not a hand's breadth from my feet. I know you know me well enough to understand that I'm not one to get upset over an occasional erotic impulse; but the sheer force of that woman had to be felt to be believed.

And while I was smothering in this sense-overload trance, she covered her mouth with silver-painted nails and swung around on her heels until she was resting on the grass beside me. Which is how we spent the rest of the afternoon. Seduction without words.

Except . . . most of the time I tried to stay just a few inches behind her. To avoid her eyes.

Alicia Chou. Eyes brown-black, with a single gold fleck in each, just off-center.

And when I finally introduced myself, she said, "Carroll is an odd name for a man, isn't it?" Her voice was less a purr than a growl lurking beneath thin velvet. "Your father must have been a very handsome man."

The touch of her hand on my knee, thigh, shoulder—the gentle way she brushed my back was colder than the lotion she rubbed absently into my skin.

Cobra and mouse.

Once, she kissed the back of my neck, and I nearly grabbed a mirror from a passing woman to see if I'd been branded.

Everyone smiled at us. The adults at me, the children at her. What a handsome couple, I knew they were thinking.

It was only natural, then, that I asked her to dinner.

She wouldn't tell me where she was staying—a wise precaution for a woman alone—but promised to meet me at my place at seven. We parted and I ran—you're laughing, but I did—I ran home and stood in front of the bedroom mirror, thinking that all that had happened was far too good to be even remotely true. I scowled at my reflection: too much hair for a smallish head, eyes too blue, nose too long and too sharp, ears too close to my head. No leading man, that was for certain, and thus no physical reason why Alicia should clasp me so suddenly to her not insubstantial bosom. I laughed aloud. By God, Carroll, I said to myself, you've been picked up! You've actually been picked up. By a raving nymphomaniac, a psychotic murderess . . . I couldn't have cared less. She was elegantly available and I was on vacation.

What I hadn't planned on, of course, was falling in love.

And that is the wrong place to laugh, my dear. It was marvelous, right out of Hollywood, magnificent . . . and terrifying.

If I'd listened to myself then, I wouldn't be telling you this now.

So she came, and we drove to a riverbank restaurant in a hotel in the next town. Dined and danced and stood on the balcony that faced the water. I kissed her cheek, felt giddy with the wine, kissed her lips . . . and when it was over I was drained, so drained that I had to lean against the marble railing to keep from collapsing.

For one second, hardly worth mentioning then, I hated her.

Then it was over and we headed back to my home. There had been no innuendo conversation. The slight turn of her mouth, the graceful flow of her hands spoke for her. She never asked about my job, family, income or tailor. I myself had been too stunned by what I'd thought was instant love to mumble even a hello and you look wonderful and why don't we dance.

I never felt the pain that lanced my will.

Neither do I remember the drive back to the house, the opening of the door, the walk upstairs. I couldn't help but feel as if the world had wound down to slow motion, so languid her movements, so careful the display of her smile and her charm.

She sat on the edge of the bed and gestured toward the chair I kept by the nightstand. "Drink?"

Why not, I thought. Get bombed, Carroll, and let's get on with whoever is raping who.

"Of course," I said, mixed what she asked and finally, at last, she let me sit down.

We toasted each other, and I loved her again.

Then her gaze narrowed over the top of the champagne glass, and I realized with a start how I had spent most of the afternoon avoiding those eyes, all the evening losing myself in them. But when, as an experiment in masculine control, I tried to break away, I couldn't. And my palms became unaccountably moist.

"Carroll is a strange name," she said.

"You've already said that once, Alicia," I said, grinning stupidly. "It was my dear departed mother's idea, not knowing what she would have at the time and not feeling like coming up with two sets for the sexes."

"I love you, strange name," she whispered. Not a word out of place, not a change in tone. Something broke briefly through the sparkling cloud I felt over me, but I couldn't put a name to it and so shrugged it away.

Instead, I emptied the glass and set it on the floor beside me. Cleared my throat and said, "This is going to sound . . . well, it's going to sound ridiculous, under the circumstances, Alicia—but, damnit, I think I love you, too." It was all so bloody serious, so intolerably solemn that I wanted to laugh. But I couldn't; I was too nervous. Not of breaking the spell that nights and champagne and mysterious women weave, but of her and those eyes with their single flecks of gold.

"For how long, strange name?"

"Shouldn't that be obvious? Forever. How else?"

It was she who laughed then. Deeply. In her throat. And as she did, I became inexplicably angry. Didn't she know, I demanded of myself, that in thirty-four goddamned years on this road I had said that only once before when I'd meant it—to a cheerleader in high school. Who had also laughed, but loudly and shrilly, with her head thrown back and her eyes rolled heavenward in total disbelief.

"Strange name, love me," Alicia said.

I hesitated. I stalled. Her request became a demand.

And I did, and am now regrettably forced to resort to the old purple-prose lines of jungle passions and animal ferocity. But that, I'm afraid, is exactly the way it was. Stripped, perspiring even before we began, stalking each other without benefit of cinematic loveplay, manual directions of foreplay and stimulation. Sheets and blankets were literally torn, glasses were shattered, bottles smashed . . . again and again and again . . . and again.

"Love me," she hissed.

And I did. Bleeding, drawing blood, bruised and bruising . . . again and again.

"More," she crooned.

I did. God, I did.

Dawn, and I did not see it. Dusk, and I could not see it. Crying, laughing—a haze of cigarette smoke, a waste basket gushing uneaten meals one of us made downstairs in the kitchen.

It must have been her. I couldn't have moved.

We stood by the window in caftan robes and watched the river pass a beautifully bright day beneath us, beneath the willows. It was peaceful and wonderful; I held her gently against my chest and told her so, whispering in her ear all the idiot lovephrases that men think original when the loving is done.

"Then love me," she whispered back.

The radio played Brahms and Vaughan Williams. Nothing louder for this room, on this day, at this time.

"Love me," she sang.

I told her how, when I was in college up there in Hartford, I had exhausted myself during one summer vacation visiting ten European cities in less than sixteen days. I must have been drunk when I said it, I don't remember now, but I suddenly turned mawkish and sentimental, muttering "Those were the good old days" over and over again and praising their lack of tears and responsibility and extolling my love for them in dreams and bursts of unbidden nostalgia. I told her about an Irish setter I once had, how he could never go with us on vacation because he always got carsick and had to stay at the vet's. About the cheerleader. About the models. About the slices of my soul that went into my work.

"Love me," she comforted.

Everything is relative, said the speeding turtle to the snail. There must have been Time someplace, but two days were gone before I first began to think that I was losing my mind.

Alicia was sleeping at my side, peacefully, evenly. My mouth was burlap, my head cement, and, God, dear God, how everything ached! For one nauseating moment I thought of a morning a couple years back when I'd eaten tainted food in a Boston fast-food joint and they used a fool stomach pump while I was semi-conscious. I groaned and pushed myself up on my elbows, looking for a mirror to see if in fact I was really turning into an airless balloon; but a pain I knew instantly was frighteningly abnormal flattened me like a hammer, and I had to gasp for a breath. Beyond that, however, I felt . . . nothing. I registered the room and what I could see through the window, but there was nothing left inside me to hang the pictures on.

That, I think, is when the terror began. As if I were suffering a malaria attack, I simultaneously grew cold and soaked the sheets with a bath of perspiration that made me tremble. And I grew still more terrified when I tried to cry out with that slow-growing pain, and my mind said there was no reason, and my mouth made no sound.

I fell asleep then, unwillingly, and I dreamt as I do now—in blacks and greys and splashes of sterile white. And once, in that dream, I heard someone mention food, and I heaved dryly for ten minutes before I could fall asleep again.

The last thing I recall seeing was a floating, broken camera.

I woke once more. I think it was daylight. I really don't know because Alicia was bending over me, her lips parted and smiling.

"Can you love me, strange name?" she asked, carelessly tracing a meaningless pattern from my chest to my stomach to my groin and back.

"My God, Alicia!"

"Can you love?" she insisted.

"My God, no!'

She pouted through a smile that told me she knew better.

"Alicia, please."

"You don't love me anymore."

A fleeting array of artfully shadowed images: of Alicia in her gown, the swimsuit, the robe, her nakedness atavistic in the arousal it produced, all made me smile lazily until I turned my head . . . and saw the look in her eyes.

And in that final moment before she smiled again, I knew at last what I'd been trying to avoid: Alicia was still hungry, and she kissed me, hard, before I finally passed out.

So then. Before you tell me what you think, my dear, let me tell you what I think you've already decided. Let's see: maybe I'm simply crazy, right? Ah, too easy. Perhaps then it's a fantasy, cleverly manipulated to hide a disastrous affaire. Or, better yet, perhaps I had become so drunk at dinner that I was physically incapable of playing the Don Juan in anything more than high-sounding words, thus striking myself low with assorted simple trauma.

I was right, wasn't I.

Well, it all sounds very intelligent, I admit; all very up-to-date and properly sophisticated. In fact, if I didn't have to hurry along right now, you might even have convinced me, given enough time.

But I really must run, as I warned you at the start. And, for heaven's sakes, stop worrying about my health. I'll promise you now, if you like, that I'll dine without fail later this evening.

Ah, my darling, you *are* jealous, aren't you?

But you know me, first things first; so please don't worry, I won't forget. You see, there's this wonderfully attractive brunette named Claire who's dying to see the river from my bedroom. Look, why don't you have another drink on me, and I'll see you tomorrow. I've worked up a marvelous appetite talking with you, and Claire is waiting for me right this moment.

I think you'd like her. She's a wonderful girl. A great girl. She thinks the gold in my eyes is sexy.

She loves me. She really does.

But just so you'll know that I will keep my promise, lean over here and I'll give you a kiss.

One kiss.

That's all.

One kiss.

I'm hungry.

CHELSEA QUINN YARBRO *(born 1942) began publishing in 1969 and has since written nearly three dozen books, including science fiction, fantasy, mysteries, horror, and nonfiction. But, interesting and varied as all her work is, nothing matches—in the quality of the writing itself, the intensity of the reading experience, or in sheer popularity—her series of five novels about the immortal vampire le Comte de Saint-Germain. Those novels are* Hotel Transylvania *(1978),* The Palace *(1978),* Blood Games *(1979),* Path of the Eclipse *(1981), and* Tempting Fate *(1982).*

Her portrayal of the Count is a sympathetic one, and Yarbro uses her extensive knowledge of history to set the evil behavior of humanity in contrast with the "dark" history of her vampire. He himself, depending on the circumstances around him, sometimes seems a hero, sometimes an anti-hero. In either case, Saint-Germain is one of the most memorable characters in nearly two centuries of vampire literature in the English language.

Despite requests for more, Yarbro has written only the five novels about Saint-Germain, and five related works of short fiction, including "Cabin 33."

Cabin 33
(1980)
BY CHELSEA QUINN YARBRO

In the winter there were the skiers, and in the summer the place was full of well-to-do families escaping to the mountains, but it was in the off-seasons, the spring and the fall, when Lost Saints Lodge was most beautiful.

Mrs. Emmons, who always came in September, sat at her table in the spacious dining room, one hand to her bluish-silver hair as she smiled up at the Lodge's manager. "I do so look forward to my stay here, Mr. Rogers," she said archly, and put one stubby, beringed hand on his.

"It's good of you to say so," Mr. Rogers responded in a voice that managed to be gracious without hinting the least encouragement to the widow.

"I hear that you have a new chef." She looked around the dining room again. "Not a very large crowd tonight."

Mr. Rogers followed her glance and gave a little, eloquent shrug.

"It's off-season, Mrs. Emmons. We're a fifth full, which is fine, since it gives us a breather before winter, and allows us a little time to keep the cabins up. We do the Lodge itself in the spring, but you're not here then."

"I'm not fond of crowds," Mrs. Emmons said, lifting her head in a haughty way it had taken her years to perfect.

Nor, thought Mr. Rogers, of the summer and winter prices. He gave her half a smile. "Certainly off-season is less hectic."

She took a nervous sip from the tall stem glass before her. Mrs. Emmons did not like margaritas, and secretly longed for a side-car, but she knew that such drinks were considered old-fashioned and she had reached that point in her life when she dreaded the reality of age. "Tell me," she said as she put the glass down, "is that nice Mr. Franciscus still with you?"

"Of course." Mr. Rogers had started away from the table, but he paused as he said this, a flicker of amusement in his impassive face.

"I've always liked to hear him play. He knows all the old songs." There was more of a sigh in her tone than she knew.

"He does indeed," Mr. Rogers agreed. "He'll be in the lounge after eight, as always."

"Oh, good," Mrs. Emmons said, a trifle too brightly before she turned her attention to the waiter who had appeared at her elbow.

Mr. Rogers was out of the dining room and halfway across the lobby when an inconspicuous door on the mezzanine opened and a familiar voice called his name. Mr. Rogers looked up swiftly, and turned toward the stairs that led to the mezzanine.

The door opened onto a small library comfortably furnished in dark-stained wood and substantial Victorian chairs upholstered in leather. There was one person in the room at the moment, and he smiled as Mr. Rogers closed the door. When he spoke, it was not in English.

"I just saw Mrs. Emmons in the dining room," Mr. Rogers said with a tinge of weariness. "She's looking forward to seeing that 'nice Mr. Franciscus.' "

"Oh, God," said Mr. Franciscus in mock horror. "I suppose that Mrs. Granger will be here soon, too?"

"She's due to arrive on Wednesday." Both men had been standing, Mr. Franciscus by the tall north-facing windows, Mr. Rogers by the door. "I've given them cabins A28 and A52, back to back over the creek."

"And if the water doesn't bother them, they'll have a fine time," Mr. Franciscus said. "I didn't have time to tune the harpsichord, so I'll have to use the piano tonight." He came away from the windows and sank into the nearest chair.

"I don't think anyone will mind." Mr. Rogers turned the chair by the writing table to a new angle as he sat.

"Perhaps not, but I should have done it." He propped his elbows on the arms of the chair and linked his fingers under his chin. His hands were beautifully shaped but surprisingly small for a pianist. "There's part of the ridge trail that's going to need reinforcement before winter or we'll have a big wash-out at the first thaw."

"I'll send Matt out to fix it. Is that where you were this afternoon? Out on the trails?" There was a mild interest but his questions were calmly asked and as calmly answered.

"Part of the time. That ranger . . . Jackson, Baxter, something like that, told me to remind you about the fire watch."

"Backus," Mr. Rogers said automatically. "Ever since that scare in Fox Hollow, he's been jittery about fire. He's the one who put up all the call stations on the major trails."

"It's good that someone is concerned. They lost sixteen cabins at Fox Hollow," Franciscus responded with a touch of severity. "If we had the same problem here, there's a great deal more to lose—and one hundred twenty-four cabins would be a major loss."

Mr. Rogers said nothing, watching Franciscus levelly.

"We're going to need some improvements on the stable. The roof is not in good repair and the tack room could stand some sprucing up. The hay-ride wagon should be repainted. If we can get this done before winter it would be helpful." He brushed his black jeans to rid them of dust. His boots were English, not Western, made to order in fine black leather. There was an elegance about him that had little to do with his black clothing. He stared at Mr. Rogers a moment. "Are there any disturbances that I should know about? You seem apprehensive."

"No," Mr. Rogers said slowly, after giving the matter his consideration. "It's just the usual off-season doldrums, I guess. We're a little fuller than we were last fall. There's a retired couple from Chillicothe, name of Barnes, in cabin 12, they're new; a couple from Lansing with a teen-aged daughter in cabin 19. I think the girl is recovering from some sort of disease, at least that's what her mother told me—their name is Harper. There's a jumpy MD in cabin 26, Dr. Muller. Amanda Farnsworth is back again. I've put her in cabin A65."

"It's been—what?—three years since she was here last?" Franciscus asked.

"Three years." Mr. Rogers nodded. "There's also a new fellow up in cabin 33."

"Cabin 33? Isn't that a little remote?" He glanced swiftly toward the window and the wooded slope beyond the badminton courts and swimming pool. A wide, well-marked path led up the hill on the far side of these facilities, winding in easy ascent into the trees. Cabin 33 was the last cabin on the farthest branch of the trail, more than a quarter mile from the lodge and dining room.

"He requested it," Mr. Rogers said with a slight shrug. "I told him he would find it cold and quite lonely. He said that was fine."

"If that's what he wants . . ." Franciscus dismissed the newcomer with a turn of his hand. "What about the regulars? Aside from Mrs. Emmons, God save us, and Mrs. Granger?"

"We'll have the Blakemores for two weeks, starting on the weekend. Myron Shire is coming to finish his new book, as usual. Sally and Elizabeth Jenkins arrive next Tuesday. Sally wrote to say that Elizabeth's been in the sanatorium again and we are not to serve her anything alcoholic. We'll have all four Lellands for ten days, and then they'll go on to the Coast. Harriet Goodman is coming for six weeks, and should arrive sometime today. Sam Potter is coming with his latest young man. The Davies. The Coltraines. The Wylers. The Pastores. Professor Harris. Jim Sutton will be here, but for five days only. His newspaper wants him to cover that murder trial in Denver, so he can't stay as long as usual. The Lindholms. He's looking poorly and Martha said that he has had heart trouble this year. Richard Bachmere and his cousin, whose name I can never remember . . ."

"Samuel," Franciscus supplied.

"That's the one. The Muramotos won't be here until Thanksgiving this year. He's attending a conference in Seattle. The Browns. The Matins. The Luis. Tim Halloran is booked in for the weekend only, but Cynthia is in Mexico and won't be here at all. And that's about it." Mr. Rogers folded his hands over his chest.

"Not bad for fall off-season. What's the average stay?" Franciscus inquired as he patted the dust from his pantleg, wrinkling his nose as the puffs rose.

"No, not bad for off-season. The average stay is just under two weeks, and if this year is like the last three years, we'll pick up an odd reservation or two between now and the skiers. We'll have a pretty steady flow from now until Thanksgiving. We're underbooked until just before Christmas, when we open the slopes. But those twelve cabins still have to be readied."

Franciscus nodded. "Before the skiers." He stared at his boot where his ankle was propped on his knee. "We'd better hire that band for the winter season, I think. I don't want to be stuck doing four sets a night again. Have you asked around Standing Rock for winter help?"

"Yes. We've got four women and three men on standby." He consulted his watch. "The restaurant linen truck should be here in a few minutes. I'd better get over to the kitchen. What time were you planning to start this evening?"

Franciscus shrugged. "Oh, eight-thirty sounds about right for this small crowd. I don't imagine they'll want music much after midnight. We can let Ross do a couple late sets with his guitar if there's enough of an audience. If not, then Frank can keep the bar open as long as he wants. How does that sound to you?"

"Good for the whole week. Saturday will be busier, and we'll have more guests by then. We'll make whatever arrangements are necessary." He rose. "Kathy's determined to serve chateaubriand in forcemeat on Saturday, and I'm afraid I'm going to have to talk her out of it. I know that the chef's special should live up to its name, but the price of beef today . . ." He rolled his eyes up as if in appeal to heaven.

"Why not indulge her? It's better she make chateaubriand in forcemeat for an off-season crowd than for the skiers. Let her have an occasional extravagance. She's a fine chef, isn't she?" Franciscus leaned back in his chair.

"So they tell me," said Mr. Rogers, switching back to English.

"Then why not?" He reached for his black hat with the silver band. "Just make sure she understands that you can't do this too often. She'll appreciate it." He got to his feet as well. "I want to take one more look through the stable before I get changed for tonight. We've got six guest stalls ready. The Browns always bring those pride-cut geldings they're so proud of. I'll get changed about the time you start serving dinner."

"Fine." Mr. Rogers held the door open and let Franciscus leave ahead of him. "I'll tell Mrs. Emmons."

Franciscus chuckled. "You've no pity, my friend. If she requests 'When the Moon Comes Over the Mountain,' I will expire, I promise you."

The two men were still smiling when they reached the lobby once more. A tall, tweedy woman in her early forties stood at the registration desk and looked around as Mr. Rogers and Franciscus reached the foot of the stairs. "Oh, there you are," she said to the men and gave them her pleasant, horsey grin.

Mr. Rogers said, "Good afternoon, Ms. Goodman" at the same time that Franciscus said, "Hello, Harriet."

"Mr. Rogers. Mr. Franciscus." She extended her hand to them, taking the manager's first. There were three leather bags by her feet and though she wore no makeup beyond lipstick, she now, as always, smelled faintly of *Joy.*

As he slipped behind the registration desk, Mr. Rogers found her reservation card at once and was filling in the two credit lines for her. "Six weeks this time, Ms. Goodman?"

"Yes. I'm giving myself some extra vacation. I'm getting tired. Six years on the lecture circuit is too wearing." She looked over the form. "Cabin 21. My favorite," she remarked as she scribbled her name at the bottom of the form. "Is Scott around to carry my bags?"

"I'm sorry. Scott's off at U.S.C. now," Mr. Rogers said as he took the form back.

"U.S.C.? He got the scholarship? Well, good for him. He's a very bright boy. I thought it was a shame that he might lose that opportunity." She held out her hand for the key.

"He got the scholarship," Mr. Rogers said with a quick glance at Franciscus.

"I'll be happy to carry your bags, Harriet," Franciscus volunteered. "I'm curious to know how your work's been going."

Her hazel eyes were expressive and for a moment they flickered with a pleasant alarm. Then it was gone and her social polish returned. "Thank you very much. I don't know the etiquette for tipping the musician-cum-wrangler, but . . ."

"No tip," Franciscus said rather sharply. "Call it a courtesy for a welcome friend." He had already picked up the smallest bag and was gathering up the other two.

"I must say, I envy the shape you're in. Lugging those things around wears me out. But look at you. And you must be at least my age." She had started toward the door and the broad, old-fashioned porch that led to the path to cabin 21.

Franciscus was a few steps behind her. "I'm probably older than you think," he said easily. He was walking briskly, his heels tapping smartly on the flagging.

They were almost to cabin 21 when a frail-looking teen-ager in an inappropriate shirtwaist dress stepped out onto the path. Franciscus recognized her from Mr. Rogers' description of the new guests in cabin 19.

"Excuse me," she said timorously, "but could you tell me where the nearest path to the lake is?"

Harriet Goodman gave the teen-ager a quick, discerning glance, and Franciscus answered her. "You'll have to go past the lodge and take the widest path. It runs right beside the badminton courts. You can't miss it. There's a sign. But I'm afraid there's no lifeguard, so if you want to swim, you should, perhaps, use the pool. We haven't got the canoes and boats out yet, either. Two more days and they'll be ready."

"It's all right," she said in a quick, shaky voice. "I just want to walk a bit." She clutched her hands nervously, then moved sideways along the path away from them.

"That's one jumpy filly," Harriet Goodman said when the girl was out of earshot. "Who is she?"

"She's new," Franciscus said, resuming the walk to Harriet's cabin. "Mr. Rogers said that she's apparently recovering from an illness of some sort." Having seen the girl, he doubted that was the real problem, but kept his opinion to himself.

Harriet had made a similar assessment. "Recovering from an illness, my ass."

There were five wooden steps down to the door of cabin 21, which was tucked away from the rest on the path, the last one of the twelve on this walk. Harriet Goodman opened the door. "Oh, thank goodness. You people always air out the cabins. I can't tell you how much I hate that musty smell." She tossed her purse on the couch and went to the bedroom beyond. "Everything's fine. Let me check the bathroom." She disappeared and came back. "New paint and fixtures. You're angels."

"The owner doesn't like his property to get run-down," Franciscus said, as he put the bags on the racks in the bedroom.

Harriet Goodman watched him, her hands on her hips. "You know, Franciscus, you puzzle me," she said with her usual directness.

"I do? Why?" He was faintly amused and his fine brows lifted to punctuate his inquiry.

"Because you're content to remain here, I guess." There was a puckering of her forehead.

"I like it here. I value my privacy."

"Privacy?" she echoed, not believing him. "In the middle of a resort."

"What better place?" He hesitated, then went on. "I do like privacy, but not isolation. I have time for myself, and though there are many people around me, almost all of them pass through my life like, well, shadows."

"Shadows."

He heard the melancholy in her voice. "I said *almost* all. You're not a candidate for shadow-dom, Harriet. And you know it."

Her laughter was gently self-deriding. "That will teach me to fish for compliments."

Franciscus looked at her kindly before he left the cabin. "You're being unkind to yourself. What am I but, as you call it, a musician-cum-wrangler?" He nodded to her and strolled to the door.

Her eyes narrowed as she stared at the door he had closed behind him. "Yes, Franciscus. What are you?"

He preferred playing the harpsichord to the piano, though the old instrument was cantankerous with age. He had his wrenches laid out on the elaborately painted bench and was busy with tuning forks when the teen-ager found him at work.

"Oh! I didn't mean . . ." She turned a curiously mottled pale pink. "You're busy. I heard music and I thought . . ."

"Hardly music," Franciscus said as he jangled a discordant arpeggio on the worn keys.

"I think it's pretty." Her eyes pleaded with him not to contradict her.

His curiosity was piqued. "That's kind of you to say, but it will sound a great deal better once I get it tuned."

"May I watch? I won't say anything. I promise." Her hands were knotting in the nervous way he had noticed before.

"If you wish. It's boring, so don't feel you have to stay." His penetrating dark eyes rested on her cornflower blue ones, then he gave his attention to the harpsichord again. He used his D tuning fork, struck it and placed it against the raised lid of the instrument for resonance. He worked quickly, twisting the metal tuning pegs quickly. Methodically he repeated the process with all the Ds on the keyboard.

"Is that hard, what you're doing?" she asked when he had worked his way up to F#.

"Hard? No, not when I've got my tuning forks. I can do it without them, but it takes longer because I have difficulty allowing for the resonances, the over and undertones, in my mind." He did not mind the interruption, though he did not stop his task. He selected the G fork and struck it expertly.

"You have perfect pitch?" She found the idea exciting. "I've never known anyone with perfect pitch."

"Yes." Franciscus placed the vibrating fork against the wood, and the note, eerily pure, hummed loudly in the room. "That's the resonant note of this instrument, which is why it's so much louder than the others."

The teen-aged girl looked awed. "That's amazing."

"No, it's physics," he corrected her wryly. What was wrong with that child? Franciscus asked himself. From her height and the shape of her body, she had to be at least sixteen, but she had the manner of a much younger person. Perhaps she had truly been ill. Or perhaps she was recovering from something more harmful than illness. "All instruments have one particular resonant note. In the ancient world, this was attributed to magic," he went on, watching her covertly.

"Did they? That's wonderful." She sounded so forlorn that he worried she might cry.

"Is something the matter, Miss . . ."

"Harper," she said, with an unaccountable blush. "Emillie Harper."

"Hello, Miss Harper. I'm R. G. Franciscus." He offered her his right hand gravely.

She was about to take it when a stranger came into the room. He was a tall, lean man dressed, like Franciscus, predominantly in black, but unlike Franciscus, he wore the color with an air of menace. There was a flamboyance, a theatricality about him: his dark hair was perfectly silvered at the temples and there was a Byronic grandeur in his demeanor. His ruddy mouth curved in a romantic sneer, and though he was certainly no older than Franciscus, he gave the impression of world-weariness that the other, shorter man conspicuously lacked.

"I didn't mean to interrupt," he announced for form's sake, in a fine deep voice that oozed ennui.

"Quite all right," Franciscus assured him. "I'm almost finished tuning, and Miss Harper and I were discussing resonance. Is there anything I can do for you? Dinner service began a quarter hour ago, if you're hungry."

The stranger gave a slight shudder. "Dinner. No. I'm looking for the manager. Have you seen Mr. Rogers?" His soulful brown eyes roved around the lounge as if he suspected the man he sought to be lurking in the shadows.

"He should be with the chef. He usually is at the start of dinner," Franciscus told him with unimpaired good humor. "Give him another ten minutes and he'll be out."

"I need to see Mr. Rogers at once," the stranger stated with great finality. "It's urgent."

Emillie Harper clenched her hands tightly and stared from one man to the other. Her blue eyes were distressed and she moved in quick, fluttery starts, as if attempting to flee invisible shackles.

"Miss Harper," Franciscus said calmly, "I'm going to the kitchen to get Mr. Rogers for this . . . gentleman. Would you like to come with me?" He took his black wool jacket from the bench and began to roll down his shirt sleeves. With a twitch he adjusted the black silk ascot at his neck before shrugging on the jacket.

The depth of gratitude in the girl's eyes was pathetic. "Oh, yes. I would. Please."

Franciscus regarded the tall interloper. "If you'll be good enough to wait at the registration desk, Mr. Rogers will join you shortly. It's the best I can do, Mr. . . ."

"Lorpicar," was the answer. "I'm in cabin 33."

"Are you." Franciscus had already led Emillie Harper to the door of the lounge. He sensed that Mr. Lorpicar wanted him to look back, and for that reason, he did not, although he felt a deep curiosity possess him as he led the frightened girl away.

Jim Sutton walked into the lounge shortly after ten the next evening, while Franciscus was doing his second set. The reporter was dressed with his usual finicky elegance in contrast to his face which held the comfortable appeal of a rumpled bed. He waved to Franciscus and took a seat at the bar, waiting for the buzzy and unobtrusive sounds of the harpsichord to cease.

"It's good to see you again, Mr. Sutton," the bartender said as he approached. "Cruzan with lime juice, isn't it?"

"Good to see you again, Frank. You're right about the drink." He had often been amused by the tales he had heard of reporters and bourbon: he had never liked the stuff. Rum was another matter. He put a ten dollar bill on the highly polished mahogany of the bar as Frank brought him one of the neat, square glasses used at Lost Saints Lodge with little ice and a fair amount of rum. "When eight of this is gone, you tell me."

"Sure thing, Mr. Sutton," said the bartender in his faded southern accent as he gave the reporter an indulgent smile before answering the imperious summons of Mrs. Emmons at the far end of the bar.

Jim Sutton was into his second drink when Franciscus slipped onto the stool beside him. "I liked what you were playing," he said by way of greeting.

Franciscus shrugged. "Haydn filtered through Duke Ellington."

"Keeps the peasants happy." He had braced his elbows on the bar and was looking over the lounge. It wasn't crowded but it was far from empty. "You're doing well this year. Rogers said that business was up again."

"It is." Franciscus took the ten dollar bill and stuffed it into Jim Sutton's vest pocket. "Frank, Mr. Sutton is my guest tonight. Present me with a tab at the end of the evening."

"Okay, Franciscus," came the answer from the other end of the bar.

"You don't use any nicknames?" Jim Sutton asked.

"I don't encourage them." He looked at the reporter and thought there was more tension in the sardonic, kindly eyes than he had seen before. "How's it going?"

"I wish I had more time off," Sutton muttered as he finished his drink and set the square glass back on the bar. "This last year . . . God! The mass murders in Detroit, and that cult killing in Houston, and the radiation victims in St. Louis, and now this trial in Denver. I thought I was through with that when I came back from Viet Nam. I tell you, it's getting to me."

Franciscus said nothing, but he hooked the rather high heels of his custom-made black shoes over the foot brace of the stool and prepared himself to listen.

It was more than five minutes later that Jim Sutton began to speak again. "I've heard all the crap about reporters being cold sons-of-bitches. It's true of a lot of them. It's easier if you can do it that way. What can you say, though, when you look at fourteen bodies, neatly eviscerated, after two weeks of decomposition in a muddy riverbank? What do you tell the public about the twenty-six victims of a radiation leak at a reactor? Do you know what those poor bastards looked like? And the paper's managers, who know nothing about journalism, talking about finding ways to attract more advertisers! Shit!" Frank had replaced the empty glass with another. Jim Sutton looked at it, and took it with a sigh. "I've been going to a shrink. I used to scoff at the guys who did, but I've had to join them. Lelland University has offered me a post on the faculty. Three years ago I would have laughed at them, but I'm thinking about it."

"Do you want to teach?" It was the first question that Franciscus had asked and it somewhat startled Jim Sutton.

"I don't know. I've never done it. I know that my professors were blithering incompetents, and much of what they told me wasn't worth wiping my ass with. Still, I tell myself that I could make a difference, that if I had had the kind of reporter I am now for a teacher, I would have saved myself a lot of grief. Or maybe I'm just running away, and in a year, I'll be slavering to be back on the job." He tasted the drink and set it aside.

"Why not try teaching for a year, just to find out if you want to do it, and then make up your mind? Your paper will give you leave, won't it?" His suggestion was nonchalant and he said it in such a way that he did not require a response.

Jim Sutton thought about it a moment. "I could do that. It gives me an out. Whether it works or it doesn't, there is a way for me to tell myself I made the right decision." He made a barking sound that was supposed to be a laugh.

"I've got another set coming up," Franciscus said as he got off the stool. "Any requests?"

"Sure." This had become a challenge with them in the last three years. "The ballet music from Tchaikovsky's *Maid of Orleans.*" He said it with a straight face, thinking that this was sufficiently obscure, as he himself had only heard it once, and that was a fluke.

Franciscus said, "The court scene dances? All of them?" He was unflustered and the confident, ironic smile returned. "Too easy, Jim; much too easy."

Jim Sutton shook his head. "I should have known. I'll stump you one day." He took another sip of the rum, and added, "Here's a bit of trivia for you—Tchaikovsky collected the music of the Count de Saint-Germain. Do you know who he was?"

"Oh, yes. I know." He had stepped back.

"Yeah, well . . ." Before he could go on, he was interrupted by Mrs. Emmons at the end of the bar who caroled out, "Oh, Mr. Franciscus, would you play 'When the Moon Comes Over the Mountain' for me?"

Emillie Harper was noticeably pale the next day as she sat by the pool in her tunic swimsuit with ruffled neck and hem. She gave a wan smile to Harriet Goodman as the older woman came through the gate onto the wide, mosaiced deck around the pool.

"Good morning," Harriet called as she saw the girl. "I thought I was the first one out."

"No," Emillie said hastily. "I haven't had much sun, so mother said I'd better do my swimming in the morning and evening."

"Good advice," Harriet concurred. "You won't be as likely to burn."

"I was hoping there might be swimming at night," she said wistfully. "I heard that Mr. Rogers has night swimming in the summer."

"Talk to him about it," Harriet suggested as she spread her towel over the depiction of a Roman bireme. She had often been struck with the very Roman feel of the swimming pool here at Lost Saints Lodge. For some reason it did not have that phony feel that so many others had. The mosaics were part of it, but that was not it entirely. Harriet Goodman had a nose for authenticity, and she could smell it here and wondered why. It was cool but she did not deceive herself that her frisson came from the touch of the wind.

"Pardon me," Emillie said a bit later, "but haven't I seen you before? I know that sounds stupid," she added, blushing.

Harriet had cultivated her considerable charm for many years, and she used it now on the distressed girl. "Why, not at all—it's very kind of you. I do occasional television appearances and I lecture all over the country. If I made enough of an impression for you to remember me, I'm flattered."

Emillie's face brightened a little, though on someone as apprehensive and colorless as the teen-ager was, enthusiasm was difficult to perceive. "I did see you. A while ago," she added guiltily.

"Well, I've been around for quite a time," Harriet said as she lay back on the towel. What was bothering the girl? she wondered.

"I'm sorry, but I don't remember what it was you talked about." Emillie was afraid she had insulted the older woman, and was trying to keep from withdrawing entirely.

"Child abuse. I'm a psychiatrist, Miss Harper. But at the moment, I am also on vacation." Her voice was expertly neutral, and she made no move that would suggest disapproval.

"A psychiatrist?" She repeated the word as if it were contaminated.

Harriet had experienced that reaction too many times to be disturbed by it. "Yes, more Jungian than Freudian. I got into child abuse by accident." She had a rich chuckle. "That does sound ominous, doesn't it? What I meant to say, though Freud would have it that my sloppy grammar was hidden truth, is that I became interested in studying child abuse unintentionally. Since I'm a woman, when I first went into practice I had few male patients. A great many men don't feel comfortable with a woman analyst. After a while, I discovered that a fair number of my women patients were either child abusers themselves or were married to men who were." She raised her head and glanced over at the demure girl several feet away. "Now it's you who should forgive me. Here I've told you I'm on vacation and the next thing, I'm starting shop talk."

"It's all right," Emillie said in a politely gelid tone.

They had been there quite the better part of half an hour when the gate opened again. Mrs. Emmons, in a lavish flowered purple bathing suit and outrageous rhinestoned sunglasses, sauntered up to the edge of the pool. "Oh, hello, girls," she called to the others. "Isn't it a beautiful morning?"

"Christ!" Harriet expostulated, and lay back in the sun.

A little bit later, Mrs. Granger arrived, wearing an enormous flowered hat and a beach robe of such voluminous cut that the shrunken body it covered seemed like illicit cargo. By that time Mrs. Emmons was splashing in the shallow end of the pool and hooting with delight.

Pink more with embarrassment than the sun, Emillie Harper gathered up her towel, mumbled a few words that might be construed as excuses, and fled. Harriet propped herself on her elbow and watched Emillie go, scowling, her senses on the alert.

There was a low rock at the tip of the point, and Jim Sutton sat on it, fishing rod at the ready, gazing out over the lake to the steep slope rising on the western bank. A discarded, half-eaten sandwich had already begun to attract ants to the side of the rock.

"Hello, Jim," Harriet said as she came up behind him.

"Hi," he answered, not turning. "There's a spurious rumor that this lake has been stocked with trout."

"But no luck," she inferred.

"No luck." He reeled in the line and cast again. "I got four eighteen-inchers last year."

"Maybe it's the wrong time of day." She had the good sense to stay back from the rock where he sat, though only part of her reason had to do with fishing. "I hear that you'll have to make your stay short this year. There's that trial in Denver . . ."

"There is indeed." He looked down and saw the remains of his sandwich, which he kicked away.

"Mustn't litter," Harriet admonished him lightly.

"Who's littering? I'm supporting the ecological chain by providing a feeding niche," he shot back. "I don't know why I bother. Nothing's going to bite today."

Harriet selected the least-rough part of a fallen log and sat on it, rather gingerly, and was pleased when it held. So much fallen wood was rotten, no matter how sound it appeared. "I'll buy you a drink if you'd like to come back to the Lodge with me."

"A very handsome offer. How can I refuse." He began to reel in his line. "You in cabin 21?"

"As usual. And you?"

"Cabin A42. As usual." He caught up his leader and held it carefully, inspecting his hook and bait before turning to her.

"Then we're almost neighbors." That was a polite fiction: a steep pathway connected the two wider trails on which their cabins were located, and the distance required a good ten minutes after dark.

"Perhaps you'd like to come by." She was careful not to sound too wistful.

"Sounds good." He faced her now, and came up beside her. "Don't worry about me, Harriet. I do take a reasonable amount of care of myself. We're neither of us children, anymore."

She put an arm across his back. "No, we're not children." They were much the same height, so their kiss was almost too easy. "I miss that."

"So do I." They started up the trail together, walking side by side. "Anyone new in your life?"

"No one important," she said with a shrug. "And you?"

"There was one woman, very sensual, but . . . I don't know. Like covering a disaster. Everything afterward is an anticlimax."

They had reached the first turning in the road and were startled to see the strange guest from cabin 33 coming toward them. Mr. Lorpicar

nodded to both Harriet and Sutton, but did not speak, continuing down
the path with an expression at once determined and abstracted.

"That's one strange duck," Harriet said as they resumed their
walk.

"He's the one in cabin 33, isn't he?" Jim Sutton asked, giving the
retreating figure a quick look over his shoulder.

"I think so." She dug her hands deep into the pockets of her hiking
slacks, watching Jim Sutton with covert concern.

"I saw him after lunch with that Harper girl. I've seen her before, I
know I have. I just can't place her . . ." They were at the crest of a
gentle rise and through the pines they could see the back of the Lodge.
"I hate it when I can't remember faces."

Harriet smiled gently. "You'll think of it. Probably it isn't this girl
at all, but another one, equally colorless. Both her parents look like
frightened hares." She thought about this as they approached the
Lodge. "You'd think one of them would be a tyrant to have the daughter turn out that way. I thought that one of them might be pious or
invalidish, but they're as painfully ordinary as the girl is."

"Such language for a psychiatrist," Jim Sutton admonished her,
and then they went up the steps into the Lodge, into the lounge, and
they did not talk about Emillie Harper or the peculiar Mr. Lorpicar
anymore.

Nick Wyler was a hale sort of man, whose body and gestures were
always a little too large for his surroundings. He enjoyed his own flamboyance, and was sincerely upset if others did not enjoy it, too. His wife,
Eleanore, was a stately woman, given to wearing long skirts and Guate-
malan peasant blouses. They had taken cabin A68, right on the lake,
one of the largest and most expensive cabins at Lost Saints Lodge.

"Rogers, you're outdoing yourself," Nick Wyler announced as he
came into the dining room. "I'm impressed, very impressed."

Mr. Rogers made a polite gesture which was very nearly a bow.
"It's good of you to say so."

"That mysterious owner of yours does things right. You may tell
him I said so." He gave a sweeping gesture that took in the entire dining
room and implied the rest of the building. "Really beautiful restoration.
None of the schlock that's turning up all over the place. I'd bet my eye
teeth that the lowboy in the foyer is genuine. English, eighteenth century." He beamed and waited for his expertise to be confirmed.

"Actually, it's Dutch," Mr. Rogers said at his most apologetic. "It was built at the Hague in 1761." Before Nick Wyler could take issue with this, or embark on another round of compliments, Mr. Rogers had turned away and was leading Mrs. Emmons and Mrs. Granger to their table by the window.

"The chef's special this evening, ladies, is stuffed pork chops. And in addition to the usual dessert menu, the chef has prepared a custard-filled tart. If you'll simply tell the waiter, he'll see that your selections are brought promptly."

"I like him," Mrs. Granger confided in a loud, gravelly voice. "He knows what service means."

Mr. Rogers had signaled for the waiter and was once again at the door of the dining room. All three Harpers were waiting for him, and smiled ingratiatingly, as if they were the inferiors. Mr. Harper was solicitous of his wife and daughter and respectful to Mr. Rogers.

"Our table there, Doris, Emillie. Mr. Rogers will lead the way." He was so eager to behave properly that he was infuriating.

As Mr. Rogers held the chair for Doris Harper, he saw, with real pleasure, Harriet Goodman and Jim Sutton come in from the lounge. He hastened back to them. "A table together, I assume?"

"Why make more work than's necessary?" Jim asked magnanimously. "Harriet's got the nicer table, anyway." His voice dropped and he stared once more at the Harpers. "I know I've seen that girl. I know it."

"It'll come to you," Harriet told him patiently as they followed Mr. Rogers. She was growing tired of hearing him speculate. They saw each other so rarely that she resented time lost in senseless preoccupation with others.

Franciscus appeared in the door to the lounge and motioned to Mr. Rogers, and when the manager reached him, he said, "Where's Lorpicar? I saw him out on the trails today. Has he come back?"

"I haven't seen him," Mr. Rogers said quietly. "Oh, dear."

"I'll go have a look for him if he hasn't turned up by the end of dinner." He was dressed for playing in the lounge, not for riding at night, but he did not appear to be put out. "I saw the Blakemores come in this afternoon. I think he might be willing to play a while, and he's a good enough pianist for it."

"Last year he did an entire evening for us," Mr. Rogers recalled, not precisely relieved. "I'll make a few inquiries here, in case one of the other guests has seen Lorpicar." He watched Franciscus return to the lounge, and then went to seat the Browns and the Lindholms, who waited for him.

Dinner was almost finished and Mr. Rogers had discovered nothing about the reclusive man in cabin 33. He was about to return with this unpleasant piece of information when he saw the stranger stride through the doors into the foyer.

"Mr. Lorpicar," Mr. Rogers said as he came forward. "You're almost too late for dinner."

The cold stare that Mr. Lorpicar gave the manager was enough to silence a lesser man, but Mr. Rogers gave his blandest smile. "We were concerned when you did not return."

"What I do is my own business," Mr. Lorpicar declared, and stepped hastily into the dining room and went directly to the Harpers' table.

At the approach of Mr. Lorpicar, Emillie looked up and turned even paler than usual. "Gracious," she murmured as the formidable man bore down on her.

"I wonder who this is supposed to impress?" Harriet said very softly to Jim.

"Shush!" was the answer, with a gesture for emphasis. The rest of the dining room buzzed with conversation, and then fell silent as many eyes turned toward the Harper table.

"You did not come," Mr. Lorpicar accused Emillie. "I waited for you and you did not come."

"I couldn't," she answered breathlessly.

Mr. Rogers, watching from the door, felt rather than saw Franciscus appear at his elbow.

"Trouble?" Franciscus asked in a low voice.

"Very likely," was the manager's reply.

"See here . . ." Emillie's father began, but the tall, dark-clad man cut him off.

"I am not speaking to you. I am speaking to Emillie and no one else." His burning gaze went back to the girl's face. "I want to see you tonight. I must see you tonight."

The diners were silent, their reactions ranging from shock to cynical amusement to disgust to envy. Jim Sutton watched closely, his face revealing nothing, his eyes narrowed.

"I don't know if I can," she faltered, pushing her fork through the remains of her meal.

"You will." He reached out and tilted her head upward. "You will."

Doris Harper gave a little shriek and stared at her water glass as her husband pressed pleats into his napkin.

"I don't know . . ." Emillie began, but got no further.

"Excuse me," Franciscus said with utmost urbanity. "If Miss Harper wishes to continue what is obviously a private conversation in the lounge, I'll be glad to offer you my company so that her parents need not be concerned. If she would prefer not to talk with you just at present, Mr. Lorpicar, it might be best if you take a seat for the meal or . . ."

Mr. Lorpicar failed to shove Franciscus out of his way, but he did brush past him with a softly spoken curse, followed by a declaration to the room at large. "I'll eat later," and added, in the same breath to Emillie Harper, "We haven't finished yet."

Franciscus left the dining room almost at once, but not before he had bent down to Emillie and said quietly, "If you would rather not be importuned by Mr. Lorpicar, you have only to tell me so." Then he made his way back to the lounge, and if he heard the sudden rush of conversation, there was no indication of it in his manner.

There were five people in the lounge now and Frank was smothering a yawn at the bar.

"I've been meaning to tell you all evening," Harriet said to Franciscus, "that was a masterful stroke you gave in the dining room."

Franciscus raised his fine brows in polite disbelief. "It seemed the best way to deal with a very awkward situation." He looked at Jim Sutton on the other side of the small table. "Do you remember where you've seen the girl yet?"

"No." The admission bothered him; he ground out his cigarette in the fine crystal ashtray.

"You know," Harriet went on with professional detachment, "it was most interesting to watch Emillie. Most of the people in the room were looking at Lorpicar, but I found Emillie the more interesting of the two. For all her protestations, she was absolutely rapt. She looked at that man as if he were her salvation, or he a god and she his chosen acolyte. Can you imagine feeling that way for a macho nerd like Lorpicar?"

"Is macho nerd a technical term?" Franciscus asked, favoring her with a delighted, sarcastic smile.

"Of course. All conscientious psychiatrists use it." She was quite unrufflable.

"Acolytes!" Jim Sutton burst out, slapping his hand on the table top and spilling his drink. "That's it!"

"What?" Harriet inquired in her best calming tones.

"That girl. Their last name isn't Harper, it's Matthisen. She was the one who caused all the furor when that religious fake in Nevada brought the suit against her for breach of contract. He makes all his followers sign contracts with him, as a way to stop the kind of prosecution that some of the other cults have run into. She, Emillie, was one of Reverend Masters' converts. She was kidnapped back by one of the professional deprogrammers. A man by the name of Eric Saul. He got himself declared persona non grata in Nevada for his work with Emillie. Reverend Masters brought suit against Emillie for breach of contract and against her parents and Eric Saul for conspiracy." His face was flushed. "I read most of the coverage of the trial. Loren Hapgood defended the Matthisens and Saul. Part of the defense was that not only was the girl under age—she was sixteen then—but that she was socially unsophisticated and particularly vulnerable to that sort of coercion." He took his glass and tossed off the rum with a tight, eager smile.

"Didn't Enid Hume serve as expert witness?" Harriet asked, thinking of her illustrious colleague. "She's been doing a lot of that in similar cases."

"Yes, she and that guy from L.A. I can't remember his name right off. It's something like Dick Smith. You know the one I mean. The psychologist who did the book a couple years back." He leaned toward Harriet, and both were so caught up in what Jim was saying that they were startled when Franciscus put in a question.

"Who won?" He sat back in his chair, hands folded around the uppermost crossed knee.

"The defense," Jim Sutton said promptly. "The argument was that she was under age and that the nature of the agreement had not been explained to her family. There was also a demonstration that she was more gullible to a con of that sort than a great many others might be."

Harriet pursed her lips. "Enid told me about this, or a similar case, and said that she was worried about kids like Emillie. They're always seeking someone stronger than they are, so that they don't have to deal with their own fears of weakness, but can identify with their master. Reverend Masters is fortunate in his name," she added wryly. "I've seen women who feel that way about domineering husbands, kids who feel that way about parents, occasionally, adults who feel that way about religious or industrial or political leaders. It's one of the attitudes that make tyranny possible." Harriet had a glass of port she had been nursing, but now she took a fair amount of the ripe liquid into her mouth.

"Reverend Masters." Jim Sutton repeated the name three or four times to himself. "You know, he's a tall man, like Lorpicar. Not the same type. A blond, fallen-angel face, one of those men who looks thirty-five until he's sixty. He's in Arizona or New Mexico now, I think. Some place where the locals aren't watching him too closely."

"And do you think he'll continue?" Franciscus inquired gently of the two.

"Yes," Harriet said promptly. "There are always people who need a person like Masters in their lives. They invent him if they have to. He's a magnet to them."

"That's damn cynical for a woman in your line of work," Jim Sutton chided her. "You make it sound so hopeless."

For a moment Harriet looked very tired and every one of her forty-two years. "There are times I think it is hopeless. It might be just because I deal with child abuse, but there are times I feel that it's not going to get any better, and all the work and caring and heartbreak will be for nothing. It will go on and on and on."

Jim Sutton regarded her with alarm, but Franciscus turned his dark, compassionate eyes on her. "I understand your feeling—far better than you think. Harriet, your caring, your love is never wasted. It may not be used, but it is never wasted."

She stared at Franciscus astonished.

"You know it is true, Harriet," Franciscus said kindly. "You know it or you wouldn't be doing the work you do. And now, if you'll excuse me . . ." he went on in his usual tones, and rose from the table. "I have a few chores I must finish before the bar closes up for the night." He was already moving across the dimly lit room, and stopped only once on his way to speak to the Wylers.

"Well, well, well, what do you know," Jim Sutton observed, a laconic smile curving his mouth. "I'm beginning to see why you have dreams about him. He's got a great line."

"That wasn't a line," Harriet said quietly.

Jim nodded, contrition in his face. "Yeah. I know." He stared into his glass. "Are the dreams like that?"

Her answer was wry but her expression was troubled. "Not exactly. I haven't had one yet this time. I kind of miss it."

"You've got the real thing instead. Your place or mine tonight?" He put his hand on her shoulder. "Look, I didn't mean that the way it sounded. Erotic dreams, who doesn't have them? Franciscus is a good guy."

"I only have the dreams when I'm here," Harriet said, as if to explain to herself. "I wish I knew why." Her laugh was sad. "I wouldn't mind having them elsewhere. Dreams like that . . ."

"It's probably the proximity," Jim Sutton said, and then, sensing her withdrawal, "I'm not jealous of the other men you sleep with, so I sure as hell am not going to be jealous of a dream." He finished his rum and cocked his head in the direction of the door. "Ready?"

"God, yes," she sighed, and followed him out of the lounge into the night.

For the last two days Emillie Harper had wandered about listlessly, oblivious to the stares and whispers that followed her. She had taken to wearing slacks and turtleneck sweaters, claiming she was cold. Her face was wan and her eyes were fever-bright.

"I'm worried about that child," Harriet said to Franciscus as they came back from the stable.

"Victim's syndrome, do you think?" Franciscus asked, his voice carefully neutral.

"More than that. I can't imagine that Lorpicar is a good lay. Men like that almost never are." She was sore from the ride, since she had not been on a horse in eight months, but she walked energetically, doing her best to ignore the protesting muscles, and reminding herself that if she walked normally now, she would be less stiff in the morning.

"Do you think they're sleeping together?" Franciscus asked. They were abreast of the enclosed swimming pool now and could hear Mrs. Emmons' familiar hoots of delight.

"What else? She drags around all day, hardly eats, and meets him somewhere at night. And I've yet to see him up before dusk." She nodded to Myron Shires, who had set a chair out on the lawn in front of the Lodge and had propped a portable typewriter on his knees and was tapping the keys with pianistic intensity. There was a two-beat pause as he waved an off-handed greeting.

"Why do you think that Lorpicar wants her?" Franciscus persisted.

"Because she's the youngest woman here, because she adores him," Harriet said distastefully. "She likes his foreign air, his domination. Poor kid."

"Foreign?" Franciscus asked, reserving his own judgment.

"He does cultivate one," Harriet allowed, glancing up as a large pickup with a two-horse trailer passed by. "Where would you say he comes from?"

Franciscus laughed. "Peoria."

"Do you say that because you're foreign yourself?" She made her inquiry casually, and added, "Your English is almost perfect, but there's something about the rhythm of it, or the word choice. You don't speak it natively, do you?"

"No, not natively." His answer, though terse, was not critical.

Harriet felt herself encouraged. "I've wondered just where you do come from . . ."

They had started up the wide steps of the porch, heading toward the engraved-glass doors that led into the foyer. There was a joyous shout from inside and the doors flew open.

Franciscus' face froze and then lit with a delight Harriet had never seen before. He stopped on the second step and opened his arms to the well-dressed young woman who raced toward him. They stood embraced for some little time; then he kissed her eyelids and murmured to her, "Ah, mon coeur, how good to see you again."

"And you." The young woman was perhaps twenty-two, though her face was a little young in appearance. Her dark hair fell around her shoulders, her violet eyes danced. She was sensibly dressed in a twill pantsuit with cotton shirt and high, serviceable boots. Harriet had seen enough tailor-made garments in her life to know that this young woman wore such clothes.

"You must forgive me," Franciscus said, recalling himself. "Harriet, this is Madelaine de Montalia, though the *de* is mere courtesy these days, of course." He had stepped back, but he held Madelaine's hand firmly in his.

"A pleasure," Harriet said. She had never before felt herself to be as much an intruder as she did standing there on the steps of the Lodge. The strength of the intimacy between Franciscus and Madelaine was so great that it was a force in the air. Harriet wanted to find a graceful way to excuse herself, but could think of none. She admitted to herself that she was curious about the young woman, and felt an indefinable sort of envy.

"You must not be shocked," Madelaine said to Harriet. "We are blood relatives, Sain . . . Franciscus and I. There are not so many of us left, and he and I have been very close."

You've been close in more ways than blood, Harriet thought to herself, but did not voice this observation. She felt a wistfulness, knowing that few of her old lovers would respond to her now as Franciscus did to Madelaine. "I'm not shocked," she managed to say.

"Harriet is a psychiatrist, my dear," Franciscus explained.

"Indeed?" Madelaine was genuinely pleased. "I am an archeologist."

"You seem fairly young to have . . ." She did not know how to express her feelings, and made a gesture in compensation.

"My face!" Madelaine clapped her free hand to her cheek. "It is very difficult, Harriet, to look so young. I assure you that I am academically qualified. I've done postdoctoral work in Europe and Asia. You mustn't assume I'm as young as I look." Her dismay was quite genuine and she turned to Franciscus. "You're worse than I am."

"It runs in the family," Harriet suggested, looking from Madelaine to Franciscus.

"Something like that," he agreed. "Harriet, will you forgive me if I leave you here?"

"Certainly. You probably want to catch up on everything." She still felt a twinge of regret, but rigorously overcame it. "I'll see you in the lounge tonight." As she started back down the stairs and along the wooded path toward her cabin, she heard Madelaine say, "I've brought one of my colleagues. I hope that's all right."

"I'm sure Mr. Rogers can work something out with the owner," Franciscus said, and was rewarded with mischievous laughter.

Harriet dug her hands into her pockets and told herself that the hurt she felt was from her unaccustomed riding, and not from loneliness.

The moon was three days past full and one edge was ragged, as if mice had been at it. Soft light illumed the path by the lake where Emillie Harper walked, her face pensive, her heart full of unspoken longing. No one, not even Reverend Masters, had made her feel so necessary as Mr. Lorpicar. A delicious shudder ran through her and she stopped to look at the faint reflection of her form in the water. She could not see the expression of her face—the image was too indistinct for that. Yet she could feel the smile and the lightness of her desires. She had never experienced any feeling before that was as irresistible as what Lorpicar summoned up in her.

A shadow crossed the moon, and she looked up, smiling her welcome and anticipation. In the next instant a change came over her, and her disappointment was almost ludicrous.

"Good evening, Miss Harper," Franciscus said kindly. He was astride his gray mare, saddle and bridle as English as his boots.

"Hello," she said listlessly.

He smiled at her as he dismounted. "I felt you might be here by the lake. Your parents are very worried about you."

"Them!" She had hoped to sound independent and confident, but even to her own ears the word was petulant.

"Yes, them. They asked me if I'd look for you, and I said that I would. I thought you'd prefer talking to me than to your father."

Emillie's chin rose. "I heard that you had a Frenchwoman come to visit you."

"And so I have," Franciscus said with prompt geniality. "She's a very old friend. We're related in a way."

"Oh, are you French?" she asked, interested in spite of herself.

"No, though I've lived there upon occasion." He was leading the gray now, walking beside Emillie with easy strides, not rushing the girl, but in a subtle way not permitting her to dawdle.

"I'd like to go to France. I'd like to go to Europe. I want to be someplace interesting." Her lower lip pouted and she folded her arms.

Franciscus shook his head. "My dear Emillie, interesting is often another word for dangerous. There is an old Chinese curse to that effect."

Emillie tossed her head and her pale brown hair shimmered in the moonlight. She hoped that Mr. Lorpicar was able to see her, for she knew that her pale hair, ordinarily mousy in the daylight, turned a wonderful shade of lunar gold in bright nights. She did not look at the man beside her. "You don't know what it is to be bored."

"I don't?" His chuckle was not quite kind. "I know more of boredom than you could imagine. But I have learned."

"Learned what?" she challenged, staring along the path with ill-concealed expectation.

He did not answer her question, but remarked, "I don't think that Mr. Lorpicar will be joining you tonight." He did not add that he had gone to cabin 33 earlier and made a thorough investigation of the aloof guest. "You know, Emillie, you're letting yourself . . ." He did not go on. When had such advice ever been heeded? he asked himself.

"Get carried away?" she finished for him with as much defiance as she could find within herself. "I want to be carried away. I want something exciting to happen to me before it's too late."

Franciscus stopped and felt his mare nudge his shoulder with her nose. "Too late? You aren't even twenty."

She glared at him, saying darkly, "You don't know what it's like. My father wanted me to marry Ray Gunnerman! Can you imagine?"

Though Franciscus knew nothing of this unfortunate young man, he said with perfect gravity, "You're hardly at an age to get married, are you?"

"Father thinks I am. He says that I need someone to take care of me, to protect me. He thinks that I can't manage on my own." Her voice had become shrill and she had gone ahead of him on the path.

Privately, Franciscus thought that Mr. Harper might be justified in his conviction, for Emillie Harper was certainly predisposed to harm herself through her desire to be controlled. "You know," he said reminiscently, "I knew a woman, oh, many years ago . . ."

"That Frenchwoman?" Emillie asked so sharply that Franciscus raised his fine brows.

"No, this woman was Italian. She was a very attractive widow, and she wanted new sensations in her life. There always had to be more, and eventually, she ran out of new experiences, which frightened her badly, and she turned to the most rigorous austerity, which was just another form of sensation for her. I'm telling you about her because I think you might want to examine your life now."

"You want me to settle for Ray Gunnerman?" she demanded, flushing in that unbecoming, mottled way.

"No. But you should realize that life is not something that is done to you, but a thing that you experience for yourself. If you always look outside yourself for your definitions, you may never discover what is genuinely your own—your self." He could tell from the set of her jaw that she did not believe him.

"What happened to that Italian woman?" she asked him when he fell silent.

"She died in a fire." Which was no more than the truth. "Come, Emillie. It's time you went back to your cabin. Mr. Lorpicar won't be coming now, I think."

"You just don't want me to see him. That's the second time you said he wasn't coming." She thought he would be impressed with her determination, and was shocked when he smiled gently.

"Of course I don't want you to see him—he's a very dangerous man, Emillie."

"He's not dangerous," she protested, though with little certainty. "He wants to see me."

"I am sure he does," Franciscus agreed dryly. "But you were with him last night and the night before. Surely you can forgo tonight, for your parents' peace of mind, if not your own protection."

"Well, I'll go up to see him tomorrow afternoon," Emillie declared, putting her hands on her hips, alarmed to discover that they were trembling.

"Tomorrow afternoon? That's up to you." There was a sad amusement in his dark eyes, but he did nothing to change her mind.

"I will." She looked across the curve of the lake to the hillside where cabin 33 was located. The path was a little less than a quarter mile around the shore, but from where she stood, the cabin was no more than a hundred fifty yards away. The still water was marked by a moon path that lay like a radiant silver bar between her and the far bank where Mr. Lorpicar waited for her in vain. "He has to see me," she insisted, but turned back on the path.

"That's a matter of opinion," Franciscus said and changed the subject. "Are you going to be at the picnic at the south end of the lake tomorrow? The chef is making Mexican food."

"Oh, picnics are silly," she said with the hauteur that only a woman as young as she could express.

"But Kathy is an excellent chef, isn't she?" he asked playfully, knowing that Lost Saints Lodge had a treasure in her.

"Yes," she allowed. "I liked that stuff she made with asparagus and walnuts. I didn't know it could be a salad."

"I understand her enchiladas and chihuahueños are superb." He was able to speak with complete sincerity.

"I might come for a little while," she said when she had given the matter her consideration. "But that's not a promise."

"Of course not," he agreed gravely as they walked past the bathing beach and pier and turned toward the break in the trees and the path that went from the beach to the badminton courts to the Lodge itself and to cabin 19 beyond, where the Harpers waited for their daughter.

Harriet Goodman was deep in conversation with Madelaine de Montalia, though most of the other guests gathered around the stone fireplace where a large, ruddy-cheeked woman held court while she put the finishing touches on the meal.

"And lots of garlic, comino, and garlic," the chef was instructing the others who stood around her, intoxicated by the smells that rose from the various cooking vessels. "Mexican or Chinese, there's no such thing as too much garlic." She paused. "Most of the time. Now, making Kung-Pao chicken . . ." and she was off on another description.

"I don't know how she does it," Harriet said loudly enough to include Franciscus in her remark.

"She's an artist," Franciscus said simply. He was stretched out under a young pine, his hands propped behind his head, his eyes all but closed.

Mrs. Emmons bustled around the wooden tables setting out the heavy square glasses that were part of the picnic utensils. "I must say, the owner must be quite a surprising man—real glass on a picnic," she enthused.

"He's something of a snob," Mr. Rogers said, raising his voice to call, "Mr. Franciscus, what's your opinion?"

Franciscus smiled. "Oh, I concur, Mr. Rogers."

"Are you going to spend the entire afternoon supine?" Madelaine asked him as Harriet rose to take her place in line for food.

"Probably." He did not look at her but there was a softening to his face that revealed more than any words or touching could.

"Madelaine!" Harriet called from her place in line. "Do you want some of this? Shall I bring you a plate?"

The dark-haired young woman looked up. "Thank you, Harriet, but no. I am still having jet lag, I think."

"Aren't you hungry?" Harriet asked, a solicitous note in her voice.

"Not at present." She paused and added, "My assistant will provide something for me later."

Harriet recalled the cherub-faced Egyptian student who had arrived with Madelaine. "Where's she?"

"Nadia is resting. She will be here later, perhaps." She leaned back against the tree trunk and sighed.

"Nadia is devoted to you, my heart?" Franciscus asked quietly.

"Very." She had picked up a piece of bark and was toying with it, turning it over in her hands, feeling the rough and the smooth of it.

"Good. Are you happy?" There was no anxiety in his question, but a little sadness.

Madelaine's answer was not direct. "You told me many years ago that your life is very lonely. I understand that, for I am lonely, but I would rather be lonely, having my life as it is, than to have succumbed at nineteen and never have known all that I know. When I am with you, I am happy. The rest of the time, I am content, and I am always learning."

"And the work hasn't disappointed you?" His voice was low and lazy, caressing her.

"Not yet. Every time I think that I have truly begun to understand a city or a people, something new comes to light, and I discover that I know almost nothing, and must begin again." She was pulling at the weeds that grew near the base of the tree.

"This doesn't disappoint you?"

"No. Once in a while, I become annoyed, and I suppose if my time were short, I might feel more urgency, but, as it is . . ." She shrugged as only a Frenchwoman can.

A shadow fell across them. "Excuse me," said Mr. Harper, "but have you seen my daughter, Emillie? She went out very early this morning, but I thought surely she'd be back by now." He gave Franciscus an ingratiating smile.

Franciscus opened his eyes. "You mean she isn't here?"

"No. My wife thought that she might have gone swimming, but her suit was in the bathroom, and it's quite chilly in the mornings . . ." He held a plate of enchiladas and chalupas, and he was wearing a plaid shirt and twill slacks that were supposed to make him look the outdoors sort, but only emphasized the slope of his shoulders and the pallor of his skin.

Alert now, Franciscus sat up. "When did you actually see your daughter last?"

"Well, she came in quite late, and Doris waited for her. They had a talk, and Doris left her about two, she says." His face puckered. "You don't think anything has happened to her, do you?"

"You must think so," Franciscus said with an odd combination of kindness and asperity.

"Well, yes," the middle-aged man said apologetically. "After everything the child has been through . . ." He stopped and looked at the food on his plate as if there might be revelations in the sauces.

Franciscus got to his feet. "If it will make you less apprehensive,

I'll check out the Lodge and the pool for her, and find out if any of the staff have seen her."

"Would you?" There was a weak, manipulative kind of gratitude in the man's pale eyes, and Franciscus began to understand why it was that Emillie Harper had become the victim of the Reverend Masters.

"I'll go now." He touched Madelaine's hair gently. "You'll forgive me, my heart?"

She smiled up at him, saying cryptically, "The Count to the rescue."

"You're incorrigible," he responded affectionately as he put his black hat on. "I'll be back in a while. Tell Mr. Rogers where I've gone, will you?"

"I'll be happy to." Madelaine patted his leg, then watched as he strode off.

"He seems reliable," Mr. Harper said to Madelaine, asking for reassurance.

"He is," she said shortly, leaned back against the tree and closed her eyes.

Mr. Harper looked at her, baffled, then wandered off toward the tables, looking for his wife.

Kathy had served most of the food and had launched into a highly technical discussion with Jim Sutton about the proper way to cook scallops.

Emillie Harper was not at the Lodge, in the recreation building, at the swimming pool, the badminton courts, or the beach area of the resort. Franciscus had checked all those places and had found no trace of the girl. Those few guests who had not gone on the picnic had not seen her, and the staff could not recall noticing her.

At first Franciscus had assumed that Emillie was giving a show of childish petulance—she clearly resented Franciscus' interference in her tryst the night before. As he walked along the shore trail past the small dock, he wondered if he had been hasty, and his steps faltered. He glanced north, across the bend of the lake toward the hillside where cabin 33 was, and involuntarily his face set in anger. Why, of all the resorts in the Rocky Mountains, did Mr. Milan Lorpicar have to choose Lost Saints Lodge for his stay?

A sound intruded on his thoughts, the persistent clacking of a typewriter. The door to cabin 8 stood ajar, and Franciscus could see Myron Shires hunched over on the couch, his typewriter on the coffee table, his fingers moving like a pair of dancing spiders over the keys. Beside the typewriter there was a neat stack of pages about two inches high. The sound stopped abruptly. "Franciscus," Myron Shires said, looking up quickly.

"Good afternoon, Mr. Shires. I thought you'd be at the picnic." He liked the big, slightly distracted man, and was pleased to let him intrude on his thoughts.

"Well, I'm planning to go," he said. "What time is it?"

"After one," Franciscus said, smiling now.

"After one?" Shires repeated, amazed. "How on earth . . ."

"There's plenty of food," Franciscus assured him, not quite smiling at Myron Shires' consternation.

Shires laughed and gave a self-deprecating shrug. "I ought to have a keeper. My ex-wife hated it when I forgot things like this, but I get so caught up in . . ." He broke off. "You weren't sent to fetch me, were you?"

"No," Franciscus said, leaning against the door. "As a matter of fact I was looking for the Harper girl. Her parents are worried because she hasn't shown up for lunch."

"The Harper girl?" Shires said. "Is that the skittish teen-ager who looks like a ghost most of the time?"

"That's her," Franciscus nodded. "Have you seen her?"

Shires was gathering his pages into a neat stack and did not answer at once. "Not today, no. I did see her last night, walking along the trail on the other side of the beach. She stopped under the light and I thought that she was really quite graceful."

Franciscus almost dismissed this, remembering his encounter with Emillie the night before, but his curiosity was slightly piqued: he wanted to know how long the girl had waited for Mr. Lorpicar. "When was that?" he asked.

"Oh, quite late. Three, three-thirty in the morning. You know me —I'm night people." He had put the pages into a box and was putting his typewriter into its case.

"Three?" Franciscus said, dismayed. "Are you sure?"

"Well, it might have been a little earlier," Shires allowed as he closed the lid of the case. "Not much earlier, though, because I had my radio on until two and it had been off for a time." He caught sight of Franciscus' face. "Is anything wrong?"

Franciscus sighed. "I hope not." He looked at the novelist. "Do you think you can find your way to the picnic without me?"

Myron Shires laughed. "I'm absentminded, but not *that* absent-minded," he said with real joviality. "Kathy's picnics are one of the best draws this place offers." He had put his typewriter aside and was pulling on a light jacket.

"Would you be kind enough to tell Mr. Rogers what you've told me?" Franciscus added as he went to the door.

"That I saw the Harper girl go out late? Certainly." He was plainly puzzled but too courteous to ask about the matter.

"I'll explain later, I hope. And, if you can, contrive that her parents don't hear what you say." He had the door open.

"I'm not a complete boor, Franciscus." He had picked up his key from the ashtray on the end table and turned to address a further remark to Franciscus, but the man was gone.

The path to cabin 33 was well kept. There were rails on the down-hill side of it, and neat white stones on the other, and at night the lanterns were turned on, making a pool of light every fifty feet. Franciscus knew the route well, and he walked it without reading any of the signs that pointed the way to the various clusters of cabins. He moved swiftly, though with such ease that his speed was not apparent. The trail turned and grew steeper, but his pace did not slacken.

Cabin 33 had been built eight years before, when all the cabins at the north end of the lake had been added. It was of medium size, with a front room, a bedroom, bath and kitchenette, with a screened porch which was open in the summer but now had its winter shutters in place.

Franciscus made a quick circle of the place, then waited to see if Mr. Milan Lorpicar would make an appearance. The cabin was silent. Coming back to the front of cabin 33, Franciscus rapped with his knuckles. "Mr. Lorpicar?" A glance at the red tab by the doorframe told him that the maid had not yet come to change the bed and vacuum the rugs, which was not surprising with the small staff that the Lodge kept during the off-season. The more remote cabins were serviced in the late afternoon.

A second knock, somewhat louder, brought no response, and Franciscus reached into his pocket, extracting his passkey. He pounded the door one more time, recalling with certain amusement the time he had burst in on a couple at the most awkward of moments, made even more so because the husband of the woman and wife of the man were waiting for their absent partners in the recreation hall. The tension in his neck told him that this occasion would be different.

The door opened slowly onto a perfectly orderly front room. Nothing there hinted that the cabin was occupied. There were no magazines, no papers, no cameras, no clothes, no fishing tackle, nothing except what Lost Saints Lodge provided.

Emillie was in the bedroom, stretched out with only the spread over her, drawn up to her chin. She was wan, her closed eyes like bruises in her face, her mouth slightly parted.

"Emillie?" Franciscus said quietly, not wanting to alarm her. She did not awaken, so he came nearer after taking a swift look around the room to be sure that they were alone. "Emillie Harper," he said more sharply.

The girl gave a soft moan, but her eyes did not open.

Franciscus lifted the spread and saw, as he suspected, that she was naked. He was startled to see how thin she was, ribs pressing against her skin, her hips rising like promontories at either side of her abdomen. There were dark blotches here and there on her body, and he nodded grimly as he recognized them.

"God, an amateur," he said under his breath, and dropped the spread over Emillie.

A quick search revealed the girl's clothes in a heap on the bathroom floor. There was no sign of Lorpicar there, either—no toothbrush, no razor. Franciscus nodded, picked up the clothes and went back to the bedroom. He pulled the spread aside once more, and then, with deft persistence, he began to dress the unconscious Emillie Harper.

"I don't know what's wrong," Doctor Eric Muller said as he stood back from the bed. He smoothed his graying hair nervously. "This isn't my field, you know. Most of my patients are referred to me. I'm not very good at off-the-cuff diagnoses like this, and without a lab and more tests, I really couldn't say . . ."

Franciscus recalled that Mister Rogers had warned him that the doctor was jumpy, and so he schooled his patience. "Of course. I understand. But you will admit that it isn't usual for a girl, or a young woman, if you prefer, to be in this condition."

"No, not usual," the doctor agreed, refusing to meet Franciscus' eyes. "Her parents ought to get her to an emergency room, somewhere."

"The nearest emergency facility," Franciscus said coolly, "is thirty miles away and is operated by the forest service. They're better suited to handling broken ankles, burns, and snake bites than cases like this."

Doctor Muller tightened his clasped hands. "Well, all I can recommend is that she be taken somewhere. I can't be of much help, I'm afraid."

"Why not?" Franciscus asked. He had hoped that the doctor would be able to tell the Harpers something reassuring when he left this room.

"There aren't lab facilities here, are there? No. And I'm not licensed in this state, and with the way malpractice cases are going, I can't take responsibility. There's obviously something very wrong with the girl, but I don't think it's too serious." Doctor Muller was already edging toward the door. "Do you think Mister Rogers would mind if I checked out early?"

"That's your business, Doctor," Franciscus said with a condemning lift of his fine brows.

"There'll have to be a refund. I paid in advance." There was a whine under the arrogance, and Franciscus resisted the urge to shout at him.

"I don't think Mister Rogers would stop you from going," he said with an elegant inclination of his head.

"Yes. Well." The door opened and closed like a trap being sprung.

Franciscus remained looking down at the girl on the bed. She was in cabin 19 now, in the smaller bedroom, and her parents hovered outside. Harriet Goodman was with them, and occasionally her steady, confident tones penetrated to the darkened room.

There was a knock, and Franciscus turned to see Mr. Harper standing uncertainly near the door. "The doctor said he didn't know what was wrong. He said there would have to be tests . . ."

"A very wise precaution," Franciscus agreed with a reassuring smile. "But it's probably nothing more than overdoing. She's been looking a little washed out the last few days, and all her activity probably caught up with her." It was plausible enough, he knew, and Mr. Harper was searching for an acceptable explanation. "You'll probably want to call the doctor in Fox Hollow. He makes calls. And he will be able to order the right transportation for her if there is anything more than fatigue the matter." He knew that Mr. Harper was wavering, so he added, "Also, it will save Emillie embarrassment if the condition is minor."

Mr. Harper wagged his head quickly. "Yes. Yes, that's important. Emillie hates . . . attention." He came nearer the bed. "Is there any change?"

"Not that I've noticed." It was the truth, he knew, but only a portion of it. "You might like Ms. Goodman or my friend Ms. Montalia to sit with Emillie until she wakes up."

"Oh, her mother and I will do that," Mr. Harper said at once.

Franciscus realized that he had pressed the matter too much. "Of course. But I'm sure that either lady would be pleased to help out while you take dinner, or speak with Dr. Fitzallen, when he comes." It was all Franciscus could do to hold back his sardonic smile. Mr. Harper was so transparently reassured by that very proper name, and would doubtless be horrified when the physician, a forty-two-year-old Kiowa, arrived. That was for later, he thought.

"Did you . . . anyone . . . give her first aid?" Mr. Harper asked in growing distress.

"I know some first aid," Franciscus said kindly. "I checked her pulse, and breathing, and did my best to determine that no bones were broken." It was a facile lie, and not in the strictest sense dishonest. "Mr. Harper," he went on in sterner tones, "your daughter is suffering from some sort of psychological problem, isn't she?" Though he could not force the frightened father to discuss his daughter's involvement with the Reverend Masters, he felt he had to dispel the illusion that all was well.

"Not exactly," he said, watching Franciscus uneasily.

"Because," Franciscus went on relentlessly, "if she is, this may be a form of shock, and in that case, the treatment might be adjusted to her needs." He waited, not moving, standing by Emillie as if guarding her.

"There has been a little difficulty," Mr. Harper said when he could not endure the silence.

"Be sure you tell Dr. Fitzallen all about it. Otherwise he may, inadvertently, do the wrong thing." With a nod, he left the bedside and went to the door to the sitting room. "Harriet," he said crisply as he started across the room, "get Jim and join me for a drink."

Harriet Goodman was wise enough to ask no questions of him, though there were many of them building up in her as she hastened after him.

"I was *horrified!*" Mrs. Emmons announced with delight as she told Mrs. Granger, who had been asleep with a headache, of the excitement she had missed. "The girl was white as a sheet—I can't tell you." She signaled Frank, the bartender, to send over another round of margaritas, though she still longed for a side-car.

At the other end of the lounge, Franciscus sat with Harriet Good-man and Jim Sutton. His face was turned away from the two old women who were now regaling Frank with a catalogue of their feelings on this occasion. "I can't insist, of course," he said to Jim Sutton.

"Let's hear it for the First Amendment," Jim said. "I don't like to sit on good stories, and this one is a beauty." He was drinking coffee and it had grown cold as they talked. Now he made a face as he tasted it, "Christ, this is awful."

Harriet Goodman regarded Franciscus gravely. "That child may be seriously ill."

"She is in danger, I'll concede that," Franciscus responded.

"It's more than that. I helped her mother undress her, and there were some very disturbing . . ." She could not find a word that satis-fied her.

"I saw them," Franciscus said calmly, but quietly so that this reve-lation would not attract the two women at the other end of the lounge.

"Saw them?" Harriet repeated, and Jim Sutton leaned forward.

"What were they like? Harriet hasn't told me anything about this."

Franciscus hesitated a moment. "There were a number of marks on her and . . . scratches."

Jim Sutton shook his head. "That guy Lorpicar must be one hell of a kink in bed."

"That's not funny, Jim," Harriet reprimanded him sharply.

"No, it's not," he agreed. "What . . . how did she get the marks? Was it Lorpicar?"

"Probably," Franciscus said. "She was in his cabin, on his bed, with just the spread over her." He let this information sink in, and then said, "With what Emillie has already been through with that Reverend Masters, she's in no shape for more notoriety. And if this gets a lot of press attention . . ."

"Which it might," Jim allowed.

Franciscus gestured his accord and went on, ". . . then she might not come out of it very well. The family has already changed its name, and that means there was a lot of pressure on them to begin with. If this is added . . ."

"Yes," Harriet said in her calm way. "You're right. Whatever is happening to that girl, it must be dealt with circumspectly. That means you, Jim."

"It means you, too. You can't go putting this in a casebook and getting a big publicity tour for it," Jim shot back, more caustically than he had intended.

"Both of you, stop it," Franciscus said with such assurance and resignation that the other two were silenced at once, like guilty children. "I'm asking that you each suspend your first inclinations and keep quiet about what is going on here. If it gets any worse, then you'll have to do whatever your professions demand. However, Harriet, with your training, I hope that you'll be willing to spend some time with Emillie once she regains consciousness."

"You seem fairly certain that she will regain consciousness," Harriet snapped.

"Oh, I'm certain. I've seen this condition before. Not here. I hadn't expected to encounter this . . . affliction here." He stared toward the window and the long, dense shadows that heralded night. There were patches of yellow sunlight at the ends of dusty bars of light, and the air was still.

"If you know what it is, why didn't you tell the Harpers?" Jim Sutton demanded, sensing a greater mystery.

"Because they wouldn't believe me. They want to talk to a doctor, not to me. Jorry Fitzallen is welcome to talk to me after he's seen Emillie."

Harriet tried to smile. "You're right about her parents. They do need to hear bad news from men with authority." She stood up. "I want to change before dinner, and I've got less than half an hour to do that. I'll look in on the girl on my way back to the cabin."

"Thank you," Franciscus said, then turned his attention to Jim Sutton. "Well? Are you willing to sit on this story for a little while?"

He shrugged. "I'm on vacation. There's a murder trial coming up in Denver that will keep my paper in advertisers for the next six months. I'll pretend that I haven't seen or heard a thing. Unless it gets bigger. That would make a difference." He raised his glass in a toast. "I must be running out of steam—two years ago, maybe even last year, I would have filed the story and be damned. It might be time to be a teacher, after all." He tossed off his drink and looked away.

The dining room was about to open when Franciscus came through the foyer beside the lobby calling out, "Mr. Rogers, may I see you a moment."

The manager looked up from his stand by the entrance to the dining room. "Why, certainly, Mr. Franciscus. In the library?"

"Fine." Franciscus was already climbing the stairs, and he held the door for Mr. Rogers as he came up.

"It's about Lorpicar?" Mr. Rogers said as the door closed.

"Yes. I've been up to his cabin and checked it out. Wherever he's staying, it's not there. No one is staying there. That means that there are almost a hundred other places he could be. I've asked the staff to check their unoccupied cabins for signs of entry, but I doubt he'd be that foolish, though God knows he's bungled enough so far . . ." He pounded the bookcase with his small fist, and the heavy oak sagged. "We don't even know that he's at the resort. He could be camping out beyond the cabins."

"What about Fox Hollow? Do you think he could have gone that far?" Mr. Rogers asked, and only the slightly higher pitch of his voice belied the calm of his demeanor.

"I doubt it. That ranger . . . Backus, he would have seen something if Lorpicar were commuting." He sat down. "The idiot doesn't know enough not to leave bruises!"

"And the girl?" Mr. Rogers said.

"I think we got her in time. If we can keep Lorpicar away from her for a couple of nights, she'll be all right. Certainly no worse than she was in the hands of Reverend Masters." He laughed once, mirthlessly.

"What are you going to do?" Mr. Rogers had not taken a seat, but watched as Franciscus paced the area between the bookcases and the overstuffed Victorian chairs.

"Find him. Before he makes a worse mistake." He halted, his hand to his forehead. "He could have chosen any resort in the Rockies!"

"And what would have happened to that girl if you had not found her?" He expected no answer and got none.

"Harriet thinks that giving Emillie a crucifix would not be a good idea, considering what she's been through. She's probably right, but it makes our job tougher. Because you can be completely confident that Lorpicar believes the myths." Franciscus looked out the window. "I'll see if Kathy can spare some garlic. That will help."

"I'll tell her that you want some," Mr. Rogers promised.

Suddenly Franciscus chuckled. "I'm being an Uncle . . . what? Not Tom, surely. An Uncle Vlad? Uncle Bela? But what else can I do? Either we stop this rash youngster or Madelaine, and you, and I will be exposed to needless risk." He gave Mr. Rogers a steady look and though Franciscus was quite short, he had a kind of majesty in his stance. "We've come through worse, old friend. I'm not blaming you, I'm miffed at myself for being caught napping."

Mr. Rogers allowed himself to smile. "Thank you for that." He took a step toward the door. "I'd better go down and start dinner seating. Oh." He turned in the open door. "There was a call from Fox Hollow. Jorry Fitzallen will be here by eight."

"Good. By then, I'll have a better idea where we stand."

Franciscus' confidence was destined to be short-lived. He had left the library and had not yet reached the glass doors opening onto the porch when he heard an anguished shout from the area of the lounge and Harriet Goodman started toward him.

"Franciscus!" she called in a steadier tone, though by that time, Mrs. Emmons had turned on her barstool and was watching with undisguised enthusiasm while Nick and Eleanore Wyler paused on the threshold of the dining room to listen to the latest. Eleanore Wyler was wearing a long Algerian caftan with elaborate piping embroidery with little mirrors worked into it, and she shimmered in the dusk.

Assuming a levity he did not feel, Franciscus put his small hands on his hips. "Ms. Goodman, if that frog is still living under your bathtub . . ." It had happened the year before and had become a harmless joke. The Wylers had been most amused by it, and Nick Wyler chortled and began in a loud voice to remind Eleanore of the various methods that were used to rout the offending frog.

Under the cover of this hearty basso, Harriet nodded gratefully. "Thanks. I realized as soon as I spoke that I should have remained quiet. You've got your wits about you, which is more than I do." She put her hand up to wipe her brow, saying very softly, "I'm sorry, but Emillie is missing."

"Missing?" Franciscus repeated, genuinely alarmed.

"I heard Mrs. Harper making a fuss, so I went up the path to their cabin and asked what was wrong. She said she'd been out of Emillie's bedroom for a few moments—I gather from her choice of euphemisms that she was in the john—and when she came back the bedroom door was open and Emillie was nowhere to be seen."

Franciscus rubbed his smooth-shaven face. "I see. Thank you. And if you'll excuse me now . . ." He had motioned to Mr. Rogers, but did not approach the manager. Instead he was out the glass doors in a few seconds, walking swiftly on the east-bound path past the parking lot to the trail leading to the Harpers' cabin 19. His thoughts, which had been in turmoil when Harriet had spoken to him, were now focused and untainted by anger. He had let the matter go on too long, he told himself, but without useless condemnation. He had not supposed that any vampire would be as obvious, as flamboyantly inept as Milan Lorpicar. He lengthened his stride and steeled himself to deal with Doris Harper.

Jorry Fitzallen had required little persuasion—he allowed himself to be put up in one of the best cabins and provided with one of Kathy's special late suppers. He was curious about the girl, he said, and would not be needed in Fox Hollow that night unless an emergency arose. He spent the evening listening to the descriptions of the missing girl from her parents, from Harriet Goodman, from all those who had seen Emillie, and all those who had an opinion. From Jim Sutton he got the background of Emillie's disputes with Reverend Masters, and shook his head with distress. He had treated a few of the good Reverend's followers and had some strong words about that cult leader. He was not able to talk to Dr. Eric Muller, for though the physician had examined Emillie Harper, he kept insisting that he was only a dermatologist and had never encountered anything like Emillie's wounds before and did not want to again. At last Jorry Fitzallen abandoned the questions for the pleasure of talking shop with Harriet Goodman.

There was no music in the lounge that night, for Mr. Franciscus was out with half the day staff, searching for Emillie Harper, and for the strange Mr. Lorpicar.

"I *knew* he was not to be trusted," Mrs. Emmons told the Jenkins sisters, Sally and Elizabeth, who had arrived that afternoon shortly before Emillie Harper was reported missing.

"But how could you? What was he like?" Sally asked, watching her sister stare longingly at Mrs. Emmons' margarita.

"Well, *you* know. Men like that—oh, very handsome in a *savage* way. Tall, dark, atrocious manners, and *so* domineering!" Her intended condemnation was wistful. "Anyone could see at once that there would be no discouraging such a man once he made up his mind about a woman."

The Wylers, at the next table, were indulging in more speculation. "If she had bruises all over her, maybe he simply beat her up. Girls like to be treated rough if they're inhibited, and if ever I saw someone who is . . ." Nick Wyler asserted loudly.

"I can't imagine what that poor child must have gone through,"

Eleanore agreed in a tone that implied she knew what she would want done to her, had Mr. Lorpicar—and everyone was certain that her assailant was Mr. Lorpicar—chosen her instead of Emillie Harper.

The Browns, Ted and Katherine, came in and were instantly seized upon for news. Since they had brought their own horses, they had been out on the trails with Franciscus and two others. Enjoying this moment of attention, they described their meeting with the ranger named Backus who had reluctantly promised to alert his fire patrol to the two missing guests.

"I think," Ted Brown said, his smiling making seams in his face, "that Backus thought those two don't want to be found for a while. He said as much to Franciscus."

There were knowing laughs in answer to this, and listening, Harriet Goodman was glad that the Harpers had remained in their cabin rather than come to the lounge.

"That Backus sure didn't want to help out," Katherine Brown agreed with playful indignation. "He's worried about fire, not a couple of missing people."

Several diverse points of view were heard, and in this confusion, Ted Brown ordered drinks from the bar.

It was more than an hour later, when the noise in the lounge was greater and the talk was much less unguarded, that Franciscus appeared in the doorway. His black clothes were dusty and his face was tired. At the back of his dark eyes there was a cold wrath burning.

The conversation faltered and then stopped altogether. Franciscus came across the floor with quick, relentless steps, to where Jorry Fitzallen sat with Harriet Goodman. "I need you," he said to the doctor, and without waiting for a response, he turned and left the lounge.

The Kiowa made no apologies, but followed Franciscus, hearing the talk erupt behind him as he reached the front door.

On the porch, Franciscus stopped him. "We found her. She's dead."

"You're certain?" Jorry asked. "Laymen sometimes think that . . ."

Franciscus cut in sharply. "I've seen enough dead bodies to recognize one, Dr. Fitzallen."

Jorry Fitzallen nodded, chastened, though he was not sure why. "Where is she?"

"In cabin 19. Her parents are . . . distraught. If you have a sedative, a strong one, Mrs. Harper could use it." The words were crisp, and

Franciscus' ire was no longer apparent, though Jorry Fitzallen was sure that it had not lessened.

"I'll get my bag. Cabin 19 is on the eastern path, isn't it?"

"Yes. Second from the end on the right." He studied the physician's sharp features. "You will need to be very discreet, Jorry."

Jorry Fitzallen puzzled the meaning of that remark all the way from his car to cabin 19.

Madelaine de Montalia was seated beside Mrs. Harper, her arm around Doris Harper's shoulder, a barrier for the near-hysterical sobs that slammed through her like seismic shocks. Franciscus, who was pouring a third double scotch for the stunned Mr. Harper, gave Jorry Fitzallen a quick glance and cocked his head toward the women on the couch.

With a nod, the doctor put his bag on the coffee table and crouched before Mrs. Harper.

Doris Harper gasped at the newcomer, looking toward her husband in deep distress. "Howard . . ." she wailed.

Franciscus stepped in, letting Mrs. Harper see the full compelling force of his dark eyes. "Yes, you are very fortunate, Mrs. Harper. Dr. Fitzallen came as soon as our message reached him, and he's waiting to have a look at you."

"But Emillie . . ." the woman cried out.

"That will wait," was Franciscus' immediate reply. He laid one beautiful, small hand on her shoulder. "You must be taken care of first." Had that ever happened to this poor, faded, middle-aged woman before in her life? Franciscus thought. He had seen women like her, all his life long. They tried to buy safety and love and protection by putting themselves last, and it had never saved them. He sighed.

"I'm going to give you an injection, Mrs. Harper," Jorry Fitzallen was saying in his most professional tones. "I want you to lie down on the couch afterward. You'll stay with her, will you, Miss . . . ?"

"As long as you think is wise," Madelaine answered at once.

Mrs. Harper gave a little, desperate nod of thanks and gritted her teeth for the injection.

"I think she'll sleep for several hours," the doctor said to Franciscus and Mr. Harper. "But she's already under tension, from what Mr. Franciscus has told me, Mr. Harper, and it would be wise to get her back into familiar surroundings as soon as possible."

"But we sold everything when we moved and changed . . ." He stopped, glancing uneasily from one man to the other.

"Your name, yes," Franciscus said gently. "But now that doesn't matter, and you will have to make certain arrangements. If you have family in another part of the country . . ."

"God help me, the funeral," Mr. Harper said, aghast, and put his hands to his eyes.

Before either Franciscus or Jorry Fitzallen could speak, Madelaine came up beside them. "I think that Mr. Harper would like a little time to himself, gentlemen." With a deft move, she extricated the grieving father from the other two. "Let's see the body," Jorry Fitzallen said quietly, feeling that same disquieting fatigue that the dead always gave him.

Franciscus held the door and the two passed into the smaller bedroom.

Emillie was nude, and her skin was more mottled than before, though this time the marks were pale. The body had a waxy shine and looked greenish in the muted light.

"Jesus H. Christ," Jorry Fitzallen murmured at the sight of her. "Is there *any* post-mortem lividity?"

"A little in the buttocks. That's about it." Franciscus kept his voice level and emotionless.

"Exsanguination is your cause of death, then. Not that there could be much doubt, given her color." He bent to touch one of the many wounds, this one on the inside of her elbow. "How many of these on her?"

"Sixteen total. Seven old, nine new. It happened before, which is why you were called. She was unconscious." Franciscus had folded his arms and was looking down at the dead girl.

"If her blood loss was as heavy as I think it might have been, no wonder she was out cold." He bent over the girl and examined the wound at the elbow. "What kind of creature makes bites like this? Or is this one of the new torture cults at work?"

"The wounds were made by a vampire; a very sloppy and greedy one," Franciscus stated surely.

"Oh, for the love of God, don't joke!" Jorry Fitzallen snapped. "I'll have to notify the county about this at once. The sheriff and the medical examiner should be alerted." He was inspecting two more of the bites now, one on the curve of her ribs and one just above her hip. "They're not deep. She shouldn't have bled like this."

Franciscus was silent.

"This is going to take a while," Jorry said, rather remotely. "I'm going to have to be very thorough. Will you give the ambulance service in Red Well a call. Tell them it isn't urgent, but they better bring a cold box."

"Of course," Franciscus said, grateful for the dismissal. There were too many things he had to do for him to spend more time with the Kiowa physician.

The Harpers left the next morning, and so did the Barneses, though they had done little but sit in their cabin and play table tennis in the recreation hall.

"She was so close to us," said Mr. Barnes, who had been in the first cabin on the eastern trail. He looked about nervously, as if he thought that death might be lurking around the registration desk.

"I quite understand," Mr. Rogers assured him, and handed him the accounting of the elderly couple's brief stay.

"How many have checked out this morning?" Madelaine asked when the lobby was empty. She had been standing at the mezzanine, watching Mr. Rogers.

"Dr. Muller, the Barneses, the Harpers, Amanda Farnsworth and the Lindholms. As Martha so correctly pointed out, a man with a heart condition does not need to be distressed, and the events of the last two days are distressing." He had closed the huge, leather-bound register.

"But Lorpicar is still here," Madelaine said, her violet eyes brightening with anger.

"Apparently. No one has seen him. He hasn't checked out. He could have decamped without bothering to settle his account, and that would be quite acceptable to me," Mr. Rogers said austerely, but with an understated familiarity.

The lobby doors by the foyer opened and Jim Sutton strode into the room. "Have either of you seen Harriet?" he asked anxiously.

"No, not since breakfast," Mr. Rogers answered. "Miss Montalia?"

"Not this morning."

Jim sighed, tried to look irritated and only succeeded in looking worried. "She was talking some nonsense about that Lorpicar whacko. She said that she could figure out where he was hiding if she could only figure out what his guilt-patterns are. What a time to start thinking like a shrink!" He started toward the door and turned back. "If Franciscus comes in, ask him if he's seen her. It's crazy, I know," he went on in a voice that ached to be reassured. "It's because of that girl. You'd think

I'd be used to bizarre deaths by now, wouldn't you? But with Harriet trying to prove a point, damn her . . ." He pushed the door open and was gone.

"Where's the Comte?" Madelaine asked Mr. Rogers quietly.

"Searching the cabins on the north end of the lake. He's already done the southern ones." His face showed no emotion, but he added, "I thank you."

Madelaine tossed her head. "I'll tell him. He likes Harriet." She was down the stairs and almost to the doors. "So do I."

"Next we'll have Mrs. Emmons out skulking in the bushes!" Franciscus burst out when Madelaine had told him about Harriet. "Why couldn't she have waited a bit?"

"For the same reason you didn't, probably," Madelaine said with a sad, amused smile.

He touched her face, a gesture of infinite longing. "I do love you, my heart. The words are nothing. But now, they are all we can share." He took her in his arms briefly, his face pressed against her hair. She was only half a head shorter than he and she was so lonely for him that she gave a little cry, as if in remembered pain.

"Why not you, when I love you best?" she protested.

"You know the answer. It is not possible when you and I are of the same blood. Before, well, since we do not die, we must find our paradise here on earth, and for a time it was ours. My dearest love, believe this. We have had our heaven together. And our hell," he added, thinking back to the desolation of war.

Their kiss was brief and intense, as if each feared to make it longer. It was Madelaine who stood back. "We have not found Harriet," she reminded him.

"And we must do that, if we are to prevent another tragedy." He agreed promptly, taking her hand. "You know what we are looking for. Undoubtedly he will have his box of earth somewhere near."

"And if he has treated Harriet to the same brutality that he gave Emillie?" Madelaine asked gently.

Franciscus tried for humor. "Well, we won't be able to keep Jim Sutton from filing a story on it."

"Don't mock, Saint-Germain."

He sighed. "If he has, we must be very, very cautious. We must be so in any case." He stopped in the open door of the empty cabin. "I don't want to sell this place. I like it here. These mountains remind me of my home, and the life is pleasant. I suppose it is wisest, though."

Madelaine touched his arm. "She may be all right. And a girl like Emillie . . . there will not be too many questions asked. You need not give up Lost Saints Lodge."

"Perhaps." He shook off the despondency. "I'll take the west side of the trail and you take the east. We should be able to do all the cabins in half an hour."

Harriet was on the floor of a tool shed near the stable. There were savage discolorations on her throat and wrists, and one of the rips in her skin still bled sluggishly.

"Good God," Madelaine said in disgust. "Hasn't that man any sense?"

"The evidence is against it," Franciscus said wryly. He bent to pick up Harriet. "She'll come out of it, but I think we'd better hold her in the Lodge. There's a room behind my . . . workshop where I've got a bed. Jorry Fitzallen can check her over."

"And what will he say?" Madelaine asked, not able to conceal her anxiety.

"My dear, Jorry Fitzallen is a Kiowa. He will be very circumspect. Last year there was a shamanistic killing which he attributed to snakebite, which, if you stretch a point, was true." He carried Harriet easily, as if she were little more than a child. "You'd best make sure that there is no one on the trail. I would not like to have any more rumors flying than we already have to contend with."

Jim Sutton had turned first pale, but now his face was flushed and he stammered as he spoke. "If I get m-my hands on that b-bastard . . ."

"You will endanger yourself and Harriet needlessly," Franciscus said sharply. "It won't work, Jim. It's much better that you stay with Harriet—she will be grateful, you know—than that you waste your energy running around the hills looking for this man."

The room off what Franciscus called his workshop was spartanly simple. There was a narrow, hard captain's bed, a simple writing table, and a chair. On the wall were three paintings, two of unremarkable subjects and talents, one, clearly by a more skilled hand, showed a rough-visaged Orpheus lamenting his lost Eurydice.

"This is yours?" Jim Sutton asked as he glanced around. Now that the shock of seeing Harriet had lessened, he was intrigued by his surroundings.

"Yes."

"It's damned austere," he said uncomfortably.

"I prefer it," Franciscus responded.

"That *Orpheus* looks something like a Botticelli," he remarked after staring at it a little while.

"It does, doesn't it?" Franciscus drew the single chair up to the bed where Harriet lay. "Come, sit down. She'll be awake by sunset. I'll have Frank send in an occasional double Cruzan." He waited while Jim Sutton reluctantly sat down. "I would recommend that you open the door only to me and Mr. Rogers. It's true that Lorpicar hasn't been found, but there is a possibility"—he knew it was, in fact, a certainty—"that Lorpicar may try to find Harriet to . . . finish what he started."

Jim Sutton's eyes were too bright. "I'll kill him," he vowed.

"Will you." Franciscus looked at the reporter. "Harriet needs your help. Leave Lorpicar to me."

"You?" There was polite incredulity in his expression.

"I know what I am up against, my friend. You don't. And in this instance, a lack of knowledge might be fatal." He bent over Harriet, his dark eyes keen. "She will recover. I don't think there will be any serious aftereffects."

"God, I hope not," Jim Sutton said quite devoutly.

Franciscus almost smiled. "I'll send you word when we've found Lorpicar. Until then, if you want to stay here, fine. If you'd rather leave, it would be best if you let Mr. Rogers know so that someone else can stay with Harriet."

"Then she isn't safe yet?" he said, catching at Franciscus' sleeve.

"She, herself, is not in any great danger. But Lorpicar is another matter, and he may still try to reach her." He wanted to be certain that Jim Sutton did not underestimate the risk involved. "Harriet is all right now, but if Lorpicar has another go at her . . ."

"Oh, shit." Jim rubbed his face. "The world is full of psychos. I swear it is."

Franciscus said nothing, but before he closed the door, he saw Jim Sutton take Harriet's unresisting hand between his own.

There was little conversation at dinner, though Kathy had outdone herself with the food. Guests drank more heavily than usual, and Nick Wyler had offered to stand guard on the porch with a shotgun, but Mr.

Rogers had quickly put an end to that idea, much to the relief of the other guests. By the time the dining room was empty much of the fear had been dispelled, though Mrs. Emmons had declared that she would not sleep a moment for fear she would be the next victim.

Frank kept the bar open until eleven, and Mr. Franciscus sat at the harpsichord in the lounge, playing music no one noticed. But even the most intrepid guests were touched by fear, and the last group bought a bottle of bourbon and left together, taking comfort from the drink and familiar faces.

"You going to bed, Franciscus?" the bartender called as he finished closing out the register for the evening.

"In a while. Don't mind me." He was playing a Scarlatti sonata now. "Turn off the lights when you go."

The bartender shrugged. "Whatever you say."

Half an hour later, Franciscus sat alone in the dark. The harpsichord was silent. The last pan had rattled in the kitchen some time before and the tall clock in the lobby sounded oddly muffled as its St. Michael's chimes tolled the quarter hour.

An errant breeze scampered through the lounge and was gone. Franciscus waited, alert, a grim, sad curve to his lips.

There was a soft tread in the dining room, the whisper of cloth against cloth, the quiet squeak of a floorboard.

The lounge, at an oblique angle to the foyer and separated from the lobby by an arch, was not touched by the single light that glowed at the registration desk, and the soft footfalls turned to the lounge from the dining room, seeking the haven of darkness.

When the steps were halfway across the room, Franciscus snapped on the light over the keyboard. It was soft, dispelling little of the night around it, but to the black-cloaked figure revealed on the edge of its luminescence, it glowed bright as the heart of a star.

"Good evening, Mr. Lorpicar," Franciscus said.

"You!"

Franciscus watched the tall man draw back, one arm raising as if to ward off a blow. "You've seen too many Hammer films," he remonstrated gently.

Milan Lorpicar chose to ignore this remark. "Do not think to stand in my way."

"Far too many," Franciscus sighed.

Mr. Lorpicar had been treated with fear, with hysteria, with abject adoration, with awe, but never with amused tolerance. He straightened to his full, considerable height. "You cannot stop me."

"But I can, you know." He had not moved from the piano bench. His legs were crossed at the ankle and his neat black-and-white clothes were relieved by a single ruby on a fine silver choker revealed by the open collar of his white silk shirt. Short, stocky, compact, he did not appear to be much of a threat, and Mr. Lorpicar sneered.

"You may try, Franciscus." His posture, his tone of voice, the tilt of his head all implied that Franciscus would fail.

The muted sounds of the lobby clock striking the hour caught the attention of both men in the lounge.

"It is time. I cannot stay," Mr. Lorpicar announced.

"Of course you can," Franciscus replied. He had still not risen, and he had maintained an irritatingly civil attitude. "I can't permit you to go. You have been a reckless, irresponsible barbarian since you came here, and were before, I suspect. But you need not compound your mistakes." A steely note had crept into his voice, and his dark eyes regarded the tall man evenly. There was no trace of fear in him.

Mr. Lorpicar folded his arms. "I will not tolerate your interference, Franciscus."

"You have that wrong," Franciscus said with a glittery smile. "I am the one who will not tolerate interference. You've killed one person here already and you are trying to kill another. I will not allow that."

With a terrible laugh, Mr. Lorpicar moved toward the arch to the lobby. "The woman is in the building. I feel it as surely as I felt the power of night at sunset. I will have her. She is mine."

"I think not." Franciscus raised his left hand. He held a beautiful eighteenth-century dueling pistol.

"You think that will stop me?"

"Would you prefer crucifixes and garlic?"

"If you know that, you know that bullets cannot harm me," Mr. Lorpicar announced as he started forward.

"Take one more step and you will learn otherwise." There was sufficient calm command in Franciscus' manner that Mr. Lorpicar did hesitate, regarding the shorter man with icy contempt.

"I died," he announced, "in eighteen-ninety-six."

"Dear me." He shook his head. "No wonder you believe all that nonsense about garlic and crucifixes."

Now Mr. Lorpicar faltered. "It isn't nonsense."

Franciscus got to his feet. He was a full ten inches shorter than

Milan Lorpicar, but he dominated the taller, younger man. "And these last—what?—eighty-four years, you have learned nothing?"

"I have learned the power of the night, of fear, of blood." He had said it before and had always found that the reaction was one of horror, but Franciscus merely looked exasperated.

"God save us all," he said, and as Mr. Lorpicar shrank back at his words, he burst out; "Of all the absurdities!"

"We cannot say . . . that name," Mr. Lorpicar insisted.

"Of course you can." He sat down again, though he did not set the pistol aside. "You're a menace. Oh, don't take that as a compliment. It was not intended as one."

"You do not know the curse of this life-in-death." He made an effort to gain mastery of the situation, and was baffled when Franciscus laughed outright.

"None better." He looked at Mr. Lorpicar. "You've been so involved with your posturing and pronouncements that you have not stopped to think about what *I* am." He waited while this sunk in.

"You walk in the daylight . . ." Mr. Lorpicar began.

"And I cross running water. I also line the heels and soles of my shoes with my native earth." He saw the surprise on Mr. Lorpicar's features deepen. "I handle crucifixes. And I know that anything that breaks the spine is deadly to us, so I remind you that a bullet, hitting between the shoulderblades, will give you the true death."

"But if you're vampiric . . ." Mr. Lorpicar began, trying to frame an appeal.

"It means nothing. Any obligation I may have to those of my blood doesn't extend to those who do murder." It was said pragmatically, and for that reason alone Mr. Lorpicar believed him. "You're an embarrassment to our kind. It's because of you and those like you that the rest of us have been hunted and hounded and killed. Pray don't give me your excuses." He studied the tall cloaked figure at the edge of the light. "Even when I was young, when I abused the power, this life-in-death as you call it, I did not make excuses. I learned the folly of that quickly."

"You mean you want the women for yourself," Mr. Lorpicar said with cynical contempt.

"No, I don't take those who are unwilling." He heard Mr. Lorpicar's incredulous laugh. "It isn't the power and the blood, Mr. Lorpicar," he said, with such utter loneliness that the tall man was silenced.

"It is the touching. Terror, certainly, has a vigor, but it is nothing compared to loving."

"Love!" Mr. Lorpicar spat out the word. "You've grown maudlin, Franciscus." He heard the chimes mark the first quarter hour. "You can't do this to me." There was a desperate note in his voice. "I must have her. You know the hunger. I must have her!"

Franciscus shook his head. "It's impossible."

"I want her!" His voice had grown louder and he moved toward the arch once more.

"Stop where you are!" Franciscus ordered, rising and aiming.

Before he could fire there was the crack of a rifle and Mr. Lorpicar was flung back into the lounge to thrash once or twice on the floor.

Aghast, Franciscus looked toward the lobby, and saw in the dimness that Jim Sutton was standing outside the inconspicuous door to the workshop, a .22 in his hand.

"How long have you been there?" Franciscus asked after he knelt beside Mr. Lorpicar.

"Long enough to know to aim for the neck," was the answer.

"I see."

"I thought vampires were supposed to melt away to dust or something when they got killed," Jim Sutton said between pants as he dragged the body of Milan Lorpicar up the trail toward cabin 33.

Franciscus, who had been further up the trail, said quietly as he came back, "One of many misconceptions, I'm afraid. We can't change shape, either."

"Damn. It would be easier to lug the body of a bat up this hill." He stood aside while Franciscus picked up the dead man. It was awkward because Mr. Lorpicar was so much taller than he, but he managed it well. "I don't think I really accept this," he added.

"There aren't any more occupied cabins from here to 33," Franciscus said, unwilling to rise to Jim Sutton's bait.

"What are you going to do?" he asked, giving in.

"Burn the cabin. Otherwise there would be too many questions to answer." He wished it had not happened. As much as he had disliked Lorpicar himself, and abhorred his behavior, he did not want the man killed.

"Why's that?" The reporter in Jim Sutton was asserting himself.

"Autopsies are . . . inadvisable. There's too much to explain."

Jim considered this and sighed. "I know this could be the biggest story of my career, but I'm throwing it away."

They had reached the last, isolated cabin. "Why do you say that?" He shifted Mr. Lorpicar's body. "The keys are in my left hip pocket."

As Jim retrieved them, he said, "Well, what the hell? Who'd believe me anyway?" Then stood aside and let Franciscus carry Mr. Lorpicar into his cabin.

"How'd that fire get started in the first place—that's what I want to know!" Ranger Backus demanded as he and four volunteers from the Lost Saints Lodge guests stood around the smoking ruin of cabin 33.

"I don't know," Mr. Rogers said. "I thought that Mr. Lorpicar had been out of the cabin for two days."

"You mean this is the fellow you had us looking for?" The ranger was tired and angry and the last thing in the world he wanted on his hands was another mystery.

"Yes. Mr. Franciscus and Mr. Sutton saw him briefly earlier this evening. They suggested that he should avoid the Lodge for a time because of this unpleasant business with the dead Harper girl." He gave a helpless gesture. "The fireplace was inspected last month. The stove was checked out. The . . . remains—" he looked toward the cabin and the mass of charred matter in the center of it—"It appears he was asleep on the couch."

"Yeah," Ranger Backus said disgustedly. "Probably smoking, and fell asleep and the couch caught on fire. It happened in Red Well last year. Damn dumb thing to do!" He rubbed his brow with his forearm. "The county'll probably send Fitzallen out to check the body over. Lucky for you this fellow didn't die like the girl."

"Yes," Mr. Rogers agreed with sincerity.

"You ought to warn your guests about smoking in bed," Ranger Backus persisted.

"Yes." Then Mr. Rogers recalled himself. "Backus, it's almost dawn, and our cook will be up soon. If you'd give the Lodge the chance to thank you for all you've done, I'd be very grateful."

The big man looked somewhat mollified. "Well . . ."

It was Jim Sutton who clinched the matter. "Look, Ranger Backus, I'm a reporter. After what I've seen tonight, I'd like to get your impression of what happened."

Ranger Backus beamed through his fatigue, and admitted, "Breakfast would go good right now, and that's a fact."

Harriet Goodman was pale but otherwise herself when she came to check out the next morning.

"We're sorry you're leaving," Mr. Rogers said as he handed back her credit card.

"So am I, Mr. Rogers," she said in her forthright way, "but since Jim asked me to go to Denver while he covers the trial and there's that conference in Boulder . . ."

"I understand." He paused and asked with great delicacy, "Will you want cabin 21 next year?"

"I . . . I don't think so," she said slowly. "I'm sorry, Mr. Rogers."

"So are we, Ms. Goodman," he replied.

"I'll carry your bags, Harriet," Franciscus said as he stepped out of the library.

"You don't have to," she said bracingly, but with a slight hesitation. "Jim's . . ."

". . . waiting at the car." He came down the stairs toward her. "If nothing else, let me apologize for putting you in danger." He picked up the three pieces of luggage.

"You don't have to," she said, rather remotely. "I never realized that . . ." She stopped, using the opening door as an excuse for her silence.

Franciscus followed her down the steps. "Harriet, you have nothing to fear. This isn't rabies, you know. One touch doesn't . . . condemn you to . . ."

She stopped and turned to him. "And the dreams? What about the dreams?" Her eyes were sad, and though the questions were meant as accusations, they sounded more like pleas.

"Do you know Spanish?" He saw her baffled nod. *"Y los todos están sueños; Y los sueños sueño son.* I think that's right."

" 'And everything is dreams; and the dreams are a dream.' " She stared at him.

"The poet was talking about life, Harriet." He began to walk once more. "You have nothing to fear from me."

She nodded. "But I'm not coming back next year."

He was not surprised. "Nor am I."

She turned to him. "Where will you go?"

"Oh, I don't know. Madelaine wants to see Paris. I haven't lived there regularly for a while." He nodded toward Jim Sutton, who stood by his three-year-old Porsche.

"How long a while?" Harriet inquired.

He paused and waited until she looked him full in the face. "One hundred eighty-six years," he said.

Her eyes flickered and turned away from him. "Good-bye, Franciscus. If that's your name."

"It's as good as another," he said, and they came to the car. "Where do you want the bags?"

"I'll take care of them," Jim Sutton said. "You'll see that her rental car is returned?"

"Of course." He held out his hand to Harriet. "You have meant a lot to me."

She took it without reluctance but without enthusiasm. "But there's only one Madelaine." There was only disappointment in her words—she was not jealous.

Franciscus shook hands with Jim Sutton, but spoke to Harriet. "That's true. There is only one Madelaine." He held the car door for her as she got in. "But then," he added, "there is only one Harriet."

Then he slammed the door and turned away; and Jim Sutton and Harriet Goodman watched him go, a neat, black-clad figure moving with easy grace through the long slanting bars of sunlight.

SUZY McKEE CHARNAS *(born 1939) won a following, particularly among feminist readers, with her first science fiction novel,* Walk to the End of the World, *in 1974, and her second,* Motherlines, *in 1978. But it was her 1980 vampire novel,* The Vampire Tapestry, *that won her a wide audience.*

The Vampire Tapestry is actually a series of connected novellas, of which "Unicorn Tapestry" is one. The title's reference to the medieval tapestries, such as those of Cluny, depicting the hunt and capture of the mythical beast suggests her theme of the relationship of hunter and prey.

Unicorn Tapestry (1980)

BY SUZY McKEE CHARNAS

"Hold on," Floria said. "I know what you're going to say: I agreed not to take any new clients for a while. But wait till I tell you—you're not going to believe this—first phone call, setting up an initial appointment, he comes out with what his problem is: 'I seem to have fallen victim to a delusion of being a vampire.' "

"Christ H. God!" cried Lucille delightedly. "Just like that, over the telephone?"

"When I recovered my aplomb, so to speak, I told him that I prefer to wait with the details until our first meeting, which is tomorrow."

They were sitting on the tiny terrace outside the staff room of the clinic, a converted town house on the upper West Side. Floria spent three days a week here and the remaining two in her office on Central Park South where she saw private clients like this new one. Lucille, always gratifyingly responsive, was Floria's most valued professional friend. Clearly enchanted with Floria's news, she sat eagerly forward in her chair, eyes wide behind Coke-bottle lenses.

She said, "Do you suppose he thinks he's a revivified corpse?"

Below, down at the end of the street, Floria could see two kids skidding their skateboards near a man who wore a woolen cap and a heavy coat despite the May warmth. He was leaning against a wall. He had been there when Floria had arrived at the clinic this morning. If corpses walked, some, not nearly revivified enough, stood in plain view in New York.

"I'll have to think of a delicate way to ask," she said.

"How did he come to you, this 'vampire'?"

"He was working in an upstate college, teaching and doing research, and all of a sudden he just disappeared—vanished, literally, without a trace. A month later he turned up here in the city. The faculty dean at the school knows me and sent him to see me."

Lucille gave her a sly look. "So you thought, ahah, do a little favor for a friend, this looks classic and easy to transfer if need be: repressed intellectual blows stack and runs off with spacey chick, something like that."

"You know me too well," Floria said with a rueful smile.

"Huh," grunted Lucille. She sipped ginger ale from a chipped white mug. "I don't take panicky middle-aged men anymore, they're too depressing. And you shouldn't be taking this one, intriguing as he sounds."

Here comes the lecture, Floria told herself.

Lucille got up. She was short, heavy, prone to wearing loose garments that swung about her like ceremonial robes. As she paced, her hem brushed at the flowers starting up in the planting boxes that rimmed the little terrace. "You know damn well this is just more overwork you're loading on. Don't take this guy; refer him."

Floria sighed. "I know, I know. I promised everybody I'd slow down. But you said it yourself just a minute ago—it looked like a simple favor. So what do I get? Count Dracula, for God's sake! Would you give that up?"

Fishing around in one capacious pocket, Lucille brought out a dented package of cigarettes and lit up, scowling. "You know, when you give me advice I try to take it seriously. Joking aside, Floria, what am I supposed to say? I've listened to you moaning for months now, and I thought we'd figured out that what you need is to shed some pressure, to start saying no—and here you are insisting on a new case. You know what I think: you're hiding in other people's problems from a lot of your own stuff that you should be working on.

"Okay, okay, don't glare at me. Be pigheaded. Have you gotten rid of Chubs, at least?" This was Floria's code name for a troublesome client named Kenny whom she'd been trying to unload for some time.

Floria shook her head.

"What gives with you? It's weeks since you swore you'd dump him! Trying to do everything for everybody is wearing you out. I bet you're still dropping weight. Judging by the very unbecoming circles under your eyes, sleeping isn't going too well, either. Still no dreams you can remember?"

"Lucille, don't nag. I don't want to talk about my health."

"Well, what about his health—Dracula's? Did you suggest that he have a physical before seeing you? There might be something physiolog-ical—"

"You're not going to be able to whisk him off to an M.D. and out of my hands," Floria said wryly. "He told me on the phone that he wouldn't consider either medication or hospitalization."

Involuntarily she glanced down at the end of the street. The woolen-capped man had curled up on the sidewalk at the foot of the building, sleeping or passed out or dead. The city was tottering with sickness. Compared with that wreck down there and others like him, how sick could this "vampire" be, with his cultured baritone voice, his self-possessed approach?

"And you won't consider handing him off to somebody else," Lu-cille said.

"Well, not until I know a little more. Come on, Luce—wouldn't you want at least to know what he looks like?"

Lucille stubbed out her cigarette against the low parapet. Down below a policeman strolled along the street ticketing the parked cars. He didn't even look at the man lying at the corner of the building. They watched his progress without comment. Finally Lucille said, "Well, if you won't drop Dracula, keep me posted on him, will you?"

He entered the office on the dot of the hour, a gaunt but graceful figure. He was impressive. Wiry gray hair, worn short, emphasized the mas-siveness of his face with its long jaw, high cheekbones, and granite cheeks grooved as if by winters of hard weather. His name, typed in caps on the initial information sheet that Floria proceeded to fill out with him, was Edward Lewis Weyland.

Crisply he told her about the background of the vampire incident, describing in caustic terms his life at Cayslin College: the pressures of collegial competition, interdepartmental squabbles, student indifference, administrative bungling. History has limited use, she knew, since mem-ory distorts; still, if he felt most comfortable establishing the setting for his illness, that was as good a way to start off as any.

At length his energy faltered. His angular body sank into a slump, his voice became flat and tired as he haltingly worked up to the crucial event: night work at the sleep lab, fantasies of blood-drinking as he watched the youthful subjects of his dream research slumbering, finally an attempt to act out the fantasy with a staff member at the college. He had been repulsed; then panic had assailed him. Word would get out, he'd be fired, blacklisted forever. He'd bolted. A nightmare period had followed—he offered no details. When he had come to his senses he'd seen that just what he feared, the ruin of his career, would come from his running away. So he'd phoned the dean, and now here he was.

Throughout this recital she watched him diminish from the dignified academic who had entered her office to a shamed and frightened man hunched in his chair, his hands pulling fitfully at each other.

"What are your hands doing?" she said gently. He looked blank. She repeated the question.

He looked down at his hands. "Struggling," he said.

"With what?"

"The worst," he muttered. "I haven't told you the worst." She had never grown hardened to this sort of transformation. His long fingers busied themselves fiddling with a button on his jacket while he explained painfully that the object of his "attack" at Cayslin had been a woman. Not young but handsome and vital, she had first caught his attention earlier in the year during a *festschrift*—an honorary seminar—for a retiring professor.

A picture emerged of an awkward Weyland, lifelong bachelor, seeking this woman's warmth and suffering her refusal. Floria knew she should bring him out of his past and into his here-and-now, but he was doing so beautifully on his own that she was loath to interrupt.

"Did I tell you there was a rapist active on the campus at this time?" he said bitterly. "I borrowed a leaf from his book: I tried to take from this woman, since she wouldn't give. I tried to take some of her blood." He stared at the floor. "What does that mean—to take someone's blood?"

"What do you think it means?"

The button, pulled and twisted by his fretful fingers, came off. He put it into his pocket, the impulse, she guessed, of a fastidious nature. "Her energy," he murmured, "stolen to warm the aging scholar, the walking corpse, the vampire—myself."

His silence, his downcast eyes, his bent shoulders, all signaled a man brought to bay by a life crisis. Perhaps he was going to be the kind of client therapists dream of and she needed so badly these days: a client intelligent and sensitive enough, given the companionship of a professional listener, to swiftly unravel his own mental tangles. Exhilarated by his promising start, Floria restrained herself from trying to build on it too soon. She made herself tolerate the silence, which lasted until he said suddenly, "I notice that you make no notes as we speak. Do you record these sessions on tape?"

A hint of paranoia, she thought; not unusual. "Not without your knowledge and consent, just as I won't send for your personnel file from Cayslin without your knowledge and consent. I do, however, write notes after each session as a guide to myself and in order to have a record in case of any confusion about anything we do or say here. I can promise you that I won't show my notes or speak of you by name to anyone—except Dean Sharpe at Cayslin, of course, and even then only as much as is strictly necessary—without your written permission. Does that satisfy you?"

"I apologize for my question," he said. "The . . . incident has left me . . . very nervous; a condition that I hope to get over with your help."

The time was up. When he had gone, she stepped outside to check with Hilda, the receptionist she shared with four other therapists here at the Central Park South office. Hilda always sized up new clients in the waiting room.

Of this one she said, "Are you sure there's anything wrong with that guy? I think I'm in love."

Waiting at the office for a group of clients to assemble Wednesday evening, Floria dashed off some notes on the "vampire."

Client described incident, background. No history of mental illness, no previous experience of therapy. Personal history so ordinary you almost don't notice how bare it is: only child of German immigrants, schooling normal, field work in anthropology, academic posts leading to Cayslin College professorship. Health good, finances adequate, occupation satisfactory, housing pleasant (though presently installed in a N.Y. hotel); never married, no kids, no family, no religion, social life strictly job-related; leisure— says he likes to drive. Reaction to question about drinking, but no signs of alcohol problems. Physically very smooth-moving for his age (over fifty) and height; catlike, alert. Some apparent stiffness in the midsection—slight protective stoop—tightening up of middle age? Paranoic defensiveness? Voice pleasant, faint accent (German-speaking childhood at home). Entering therapy condition of consideration for return to job.

What a relief: his situation looked workable with a minimum of strain on herself. Now she could defend to Lucille her decision to do therapy with the "vampire."

After all, Lucille was right. Floria did have problems of her own that needed attention, primarily her anxiety and exhaustion since her mother's death more than a year before. The breakup of Floria's marriage had caused misery, but not this sort of endless depression. Intellectually the problem was clear: with both her parents dead she was left exposed. No one stood any longer between herself and the inevitability of her own death. Knowing the source of her feelings didn't help: she couldn't seem to mobilize the nerve to work on them.

The Wednesday group went badly again. Lisa lived once more her experiences in the European death camps and everyone cried. Floria wanted to stop Lisa, turn her, extinguish the droning horror of her voice in illumination and release, but she couldn't see how to do it. She found nothing in herself to offer except some clever ploy out of the professional bag of tricks—dance your anger, have a dialog with yourself of those days—useful techniques when they flowed organically as part of a living process in which the therapist participated. But thinking out responses that should have been intuitive wouldn't work. The group and its collective pain paralyzed her. She was a dancer without a choreographer, knowing all the moves but unable to match them to the music these people made.

Rather than act with mechanical clumsiness she held back, did nothing, and suffered guilt. Oh God, the smart, experienced people in the group must know how useless she was here.

Going home on the bus she thought about calling up one of the therapists who shared the downtown office. He had expressed an interest in doing co-therapy with her under student observation. The Wednesday group might respond well to that. Suggest it to them next time? Having a partner might take pressure off Floria and revitalize the group, and if she felt she must withdraw he would be available to take over. Of course he might take over anyway and walk off with some of her clients.

Oh boy, terrific, who's paranoid now? Wonderful way to think about a good colleague. God, she hadn't even known she was considering chucking the group.

Had the new client, running from his "vampirism," exposed her own impulse to retreat? This wouldn't be the first time that Floria had obtained help from a client while attempting to give help. Her old supervisor, Rigby, said that such mutual aid was the only true therapy —the rest was fraud. What a perfectionist, old Rigby, and what a bunch of young idealists he'd turned out, all eager to save the world.

Eager, but not necessarily able. Jane Fennerman had once lived in the world, and Floria had been incompetent to save her. Jane, an absent member of tonight's group, was back in the safety of a locked ward, hazily gliding on whatever tranquilizers they used there.

Why still mull over Jane? she asked herself severely, bracing against the bus's lurching halt. Any client was entitled to drop out of therapy and commit herself. Nor was this the first time that sort of thing had happened in the course of Floria's career. Only this time she couldn't seem to shake free of the resulting depression and guilt.

But how could she have helped Jane more? How could you offer reassurance that life was not as dreadful as Jane felt it to be, that her fears were insubstantial, that each day was not a pit of pain and danger?

She was taking time during a client's canceled hour to work on notes for the new book. The writing, an analysis of the vicissitudes of salaried versus private practice, balked her at every turn. She longed for an interruption to distract her circling mind.

Hilda put through a call from Cayslin College. It was Doug Sharpe, who had sent Dr. Weyland to her.

"Now that he's in your capable hands, I can tell people plainly that he's on what we call 'compassionate leave' and make them swallow it." Doug's voice seemed thinned by the long-distance connection. "Can you give me a preliminary opinion?"

"I need time to get a feel for the situation."

He said, "Try not to take too long. At the moment I'm holding off pressure to appoint someone in his place. His enemies up here—and a sharp-tongued bastard like him acquires plenty of those—are trying to get a search committee authorized to find someone else for the director-ship of the Cayslin Center for the Study of Man."

"Of People," she corrected automatically, as she always did. "What do you mean, 'bastard'? I thought you liked him, Doug. 'Do you want me to have to throw a smart, courtly, old-school gent to Finney or MaGill?' Those were your very words." Finney was a Freudian with a mouth like a pursed-up little asshole and a mind to match, and MaGill was a primal yowler in a padded gym of an office.

She heard Doug tapping at his teeth with a pen or pencil. "Well," he said, "I have a lot of respect for him, and sometimes I could cheer him for mowing down some pompous moron up here. I can't deny, though, that he's earned a reputation for being an accomplished son-of-a-bitch and tough to work with. Too damn cold and self-sufficient, you know?"

"Mmm," she said. "I haven't seen that yet."

He said, "You will. How about yourself? How's the rest of your life?"

"Well, offhand, what would you say if I told you I was thinking of going back to art school?"

"What would I say? I'd say bullshit, that's what I'd say. You've had fifteen years of doing something you're good at, and now you want to throw all that out and start over in an area you haven't touched since Studio 101 in college? If God had meant you to be a painter, She'd have sent you to art school in the first place."

"I did think about art school at the time."

"The point is that you're good at what you do. I've been at the receiving end of your work and I know what I'm talking about. By the way, did you see that piece in the paper about Annie Barnes, from the group I was in? That's an important appointment. I always knew she'd wind up in Washington. What I'm trying to make clear to you is that your 'graduates' do too well for you to be talking about quitting. What's Morton say about that idea, by the way?"

Mort, a pathologist, was Floria's lover. She hadn't discussed this with him, and she told Doug so.

"You're not on the outs with Morton, are you?"

"Come on, Douglas, cut it out. There's nothing wrong with my sex life, believe me. It's everyplace else that's giving me trouble."

"Just sticking my nose into your business," he replied. "What are friends for?"

They turned to lighter matters, but when she hung up Floria felt glum. If her friends were moved to this sort of probing and kindly advice-giving, she must be inviting help more openly and more urgently than she'd realized.

The work on the book went no better. It was as if, afraid to expose her thoughts, she must disarm criticism by meeting all possible objections beforehand. The book was well and truly stalled—like everything else. She sat sweating over it, wondering what the devil was wrong with her that she was writing mush. She had two good books to her name already. What was this bottleneck with the third?

"But what do you think?" Kenny insisted anxiously. "Does it sound like my kind of job?"

"How do you feel about it?"

"I'm all confused, I told you."

"Try speaking for me. Give me the advice I would give you."

He glowered. "That's a real cop-out, you know? One part of me talks like you, and then I have a dialog with myself like a TV show about a split personality. It's all me that way; you just sit there while I do all the work. I want something from *you.*"

She looked for the twentieth time at the clock on the file cabinet. This time it freed her. "Kenny, the hour's over."

Kenny heaved his plump, sulky body up out of his chair. "You don't care. Oh, you pretend to, but you don't really—"

"Next time, Kenny."

He stumped out of the office. She imagined him towing in his wake the raft of decisions he was trying to inveigle her into making for him. Sighing, she went to the window and looked out over the park, filling her eyes and her mind with the full, fresh green of late spring. She felt dismal. In two years of treatment the situation with Kenny had remained a stalemate. He wouldn't go to someone else who might be able to help him, and she couldn't bring herself to kick him out, though she knew she must eventually. His puny tyranny couldn't conceal how soft and vulnerable he was . . .

Dr. Weyland had the next appointment. Floria found herself pleased to see him. She could hardly have asked for a greater contrast to Kenny: tall, lean, that august head that made her want to draw him, good clothes, nice big hands—altogether, a distinguished-looking man. Though he was informally dressed in slacks, light jacket, and tieless shirt, the impression he conveyed was one of impeccable leisure and reserve. He took not the padded chair preferred by most clients but the wooden one with the cane seat.

"Good afternoon, Dr. Landauer," he said gravely. "May I ask your judgment of my case?"

"I don't regard myself as a judge," she said. She decided to try to shift their discussion onto a first-name basis if possible. Calling this old-fashioned man by his first name so soon might seem artificial, but how

could they get familiar enough to do therapy while addressing each
other as "Dr. Landauer" and "Dr. Weyland" like two characters out of
a vaudeville sketch?

"This is what I think, Edward," she continued. "We need to find
out about this vampire incident—how it tied into your feelings about
yourself, good and bad, at the time; what it did for you that led you to
try to 'be' a vampire even though that was bound to complicate your life
terrifically. The more we know, the closer we can come to figuring out
how to insure that this vampire construct won't be necessary to you
again."

"Does this mean that you accept me formally as a client?" he said.

Comes right out and says what's on his mind, she noted; no problem there. "Yes."

"Good. I too have a treatment goal in mind. I will need at some
point a testimonial from you that my mental health is sound enough for
me to resume work at Cayslin."

Floria shook her head. "I can't guarantee that. I can commit myself to work toward it, of course, since your improved mental health is
the aim of what we do here together."

"I suppose that answers the purpose for the time being," he said.
"We can discuss it again later on. Frankly, I find myself eager to continue our work today. I've been feeling very much better since I spoke
with you, and I thought last night about what I might tell you today."

She had the distinct feeling of being steered by him; how important
was it to him, she wondered, to feel in control? She said, "Edward, my
own feeling is that we started out with a good deal of very useful verbal
work, and that now is a time to try something a little different."

He said nothing. He watched her. When she asked whether he
remembered his dreams he shook his head, no.

She said, "I'd like you to try to do a dream for me now, a waking
dream. Can you close your eyes and daydream, and tell me about it?"

He closed his eyes. Strangely, he now struck her as less vulnerable
rather than more, as if strengthened by increased vigilance.

"How do you feel now?" she said.

"Uneasy." His eyelids fluttered. "I dislike closing my eyes. What I
don't see can hurt me."

"Who wants to hurt you?"

"A vampire's enemies, of course—mobs of screaming peasants
with torches."

Translating into what, she wondered—young Ph.D.s pouring out of the graduate schools panting for the jobs of older men like Weyland? "Peasants, these days?"

"Whatever their daily work, there is still a majority of the stupid, the violent, and the credulous, putting their feather-brained faith in astrology, in this cult or that, in various branches of psychology."

His sneer at her was unmistakable. Considering her refusal to let him fill the hour his own way, this desire to take a swipe at her was healthy. But it required immediate and straightforward handling.

"Edward, open your eyes and tell me what you see."

He obeyed. "I see a woman in her early forties," he said, "clever-looking face, dark hair showing gray; flesh too thin for her bones, indicating either vanity or illness; wearing slacks and a rather creased batik blouse—describable, I think, by the term 'peasant style'—with a food stain on the left side."

Damn! Don't blush. "Does anything besides my blouse suggest a peasant to you?"

"Nothing concrete, but with regard to me, my vampire self, a peasant with a torch is what you could easily become."

"I hear you saying that my task is to help you get rid of your delusion, though this process may be painful and frightening for you."

Something flashed in his expression—surprise, perhaps alarm, something she wanted to get in touch with before it could sink away out of reach again. Quickly she said, "How do you experience your face at this moment?"

He frowned. "As being on the front of my head. Why?"

With a rush of anger at herself she saw that she had chosen the wrong technique for reaching that hidden feeling: she had provoked hostility instead. She said, "Your face looked to me just now like a mask for concealing what you feel rather than an instrument of expression."

He moved restlessly in the chair, his whole physical attitude tense and guarded. "I don't know what you mean."

"Will you let me touch you?" she said, rising.

His hands tightened on the arms of his chair, which protested in a sharp creak. He snapped, "I thought this was a talking cure."

Strong resistance to body work—ease up. "If you won't let me massage some of the tension out of your facial muscles, will you try to do it yourself?"

"I don't enjoy being made ridiculous," he said, standing and heading for the door, which clapped smartly to behind him.

She sagged back in her seat; she had mishandled him. Clearly her initial estimation of this as a relatively easy job had been wrong and had led her to move far too quickly with him. Certainly it was much too early to try body work. She should have developed a firmer level of trust first by letting him do more of what he did so easily and so well—talk.

The door opened. Weyland came back in and shut it quietly. He did not sit again but paced about the room, coming to rest at the window.

"Please excuse my rather childish behavior just now," he said. "Playing these games of yours brought it on."

"It's frustrating, playing games that are unfamiliar and that you can't control," she said. As he made no reply, she went on in a conciliatory tone, "I'm not trying to belittle you, Edward. I just need to get us off whatever track you were taking us down so briskly. My feeling is that you're trying hard to regain your old stability.

"But that's the goal, not the starting point. The only way to reach your goal is through the process, and you don't drive the therapy process like a train. You can only help the process happen, as though you were helping a tree grow."

"These games are part of the process?"

"Yes."

"And neither you nor I control the games?"

"That's right."

He considered. "Suppose I agree to try this process of yours; what would you want of me?"

Observing him carefully, she no longer saw the anxious scholar bravely struggling back from madness. Here was a different sort of man —armored, calculating. She didn't know just what the change signaled, but she felt her own excitement stirring, and that meant she was on the track of—something.

"I have a hunch," she said slowly, "that this vampirism extends further back into your past than you've told me and possibly right up into the present as well. I think it's still with you. My style of therapy stresses dealing with the now at least as much as the then; if the vampirism is part of the present, dealing with it on that basis is crucial."

Silence.

"Can you talk about being a vampire: being one now?"

"You won't like knowing," he said.

"Edward, try."

He said, "I hunt."

"Where? How? What sort of—of victims?"

He folded his arms and leaned his back against the window frame. "Very well, since you insist. There are a number of possibilities here in the city in summer. Those too poor to own air-conditioners sleep out on rooftops and fire escapes. But often, I've found, their blood is sour with drugs or liquor. The same is true of prostitutes. Bars are full of accessible people but also full of smoke and noise, and there too the blood is fouled. I must choose my hunting grounds carefully. Often I go to openings of galleries or evening museum shows or department stores on their late nights—places where women may be approached."

And take pleasure in it, she thought, if they're out hunting also—for acceptable male companionship. Yet he said he's never married. Explore where this is going. "Only women?"

He gave her a sardonic glance, as if she were a slightly brighter student than he had at first assumed.

"Hunting women is liable to be time-consuming and expensive. The best hunting is in the part of Central Park they call the Ramble, where homosexual men seek encounters with others of their kind. I walk there too at night."

Floria caught a faint sound of conversation and laughter from the waiting room; her next client had probably arrived, she realized, looking reluctantly at the clock. "I'm sorry, Edward, but our time seems to be—"

"Only a moment more," he said coldly. "You asked; permit me to finish my answer. In the Ramble I find someone who doesn't reek of alcohol or drugs, who seems healthy, and who is not insistent on 'hooking up' right there among the bushes. I invite such a man to my hotel. He judges me safe, at least: older, weaker than he is, unlikely to turn out to be a dangerous maniac. So he comes to my room. I feed on his blood.

"Now, I think, our time is up."

He walked out.

She sat torn between rejoicing at his admission of the delusion's persistence and dismay that his condition was so much worse than she had first thought. Her hope of having an easy time with him vanished. His initial presentation had been just that—a performance, an act. Forced to abandon it, he had dumped on her this lump of material, too much—and too strange—to take in all at once.

Her next client liked the padded chair, not the wooden one that Weyland had sat in during the first part of the hour. Floria started to move the wooden one back. The armrests came away in her hands.

She remembered him starting up in protest against her proposal of touching him. The grip of his fingers had fractured the joints, and the shafts now lay in splinters on the floor.

Floria wandered into Lucille's room at the clinic after the staff meeting. Lucille was lying on the couch with a wet cloth over her eyes.

"I thought you looked green around the gills today," Floria said. "What's wrong?"

"Big bash last night," said Lucille in sepulchral tones. "I think I feel about the way you do after a session with Chubs. You haven't gotten rid of him yet, have you?"

"No. I had him lined up to see Marty instead of me last week, but damned if he didn't show up at my door at his usual time. It's a lost cause. What I wanted to talk to you about was Dracula."

"What about him?"

"He's smarter, tougher, and sicker than I thought, and maybe I'm even less competent than I thought, too. He's already walked out on me once—I almost lost him. I never took a course in treating monsters."

Lucille groaned. "Some days they're all monsters." This from Lucille, who worked longer hours than anyone else at the clinic, to the despair of her husband. She lifted the cloth, refolded it, and placed it carefully across her forehead. "And if I had ten dollars for every client who's walked out on me . . . Tell you what: I'll trade you Madame X for him, how's that? Remember Madame X, with the jangling bracelets and the parakeet eye makeup and the phobia about dogs? Now she's phobic about things dropping on her out of the sky. Just wait—it'll turn out that one day when she was three a dog trotted by and pissed on her leg just as an over-passing pigeon shat on her head. What are we doing in this business?"

"God knows." Floria laughed. "But am I in this business these days—I mean, in the sense of practicing my so-called skills? Blocked with my group work, beating my brains out on a book that won't go, and doing something—I'm not sure it's therapy—with a vampire . . . You know, once I had this sort of natural choreographer inside myself that hardly let me put a foot wrong and always knew how to correct a mistake if I did. Now that's gone. I feel as if I'm just going through a lot of mechanical motions. Whatever I had once that made me useful as a therapist, I've lost it."

Ugh, she thought, hearing the descent of her voice into a tone of gloomy self-pity.

"Well, don't complain about Dracula," Lucille said. "You were the one who insisted on taking him on. At least he's got you concentrating on his problem instead of just wringing your hands. As long as you've started, stay with it—illumination may come. And now I'd better change the ribbon in my typewriter and get back to reviewing Silverman's latest best-seller on self-shrinking while I'm feeling mean enough to do it justice." She got up gingerly. "Stick around in case I faint and fall into the wastebasket."

"Luce, this case is what I'd like to try to write about."

"Dracula?" Lucille pawed through a desk drawer full of paper clips, pens, rubber bands and old lipsticks.

"Dracula. A monograph . . ."

"Oh, I know that game: you scribble down everything you can and then read what you wrote to find out what's going on with the client, and with luck you end up publishing. Great! But if you are going to publish, don't piddle this away on a dinky paper. Do a book. Here's your subject, instead of those depressing statistics you've been killing yourself over. This one is really exciting—a case study to put on the shelf next to Freud's own wolf-man, have you thought of that?"

Floria liked it. "What a book that could be—fame if not fortune. Notoriety, most likely. How in the world could I convince our colleagues that it's legit? There's a lot of vampire stuff around right now— plays on Broadway and TV, books all over the place, movies. They'll say I'm just trying to ride the coattails of a fad."

"No, no, what you do is show how this guy's delusion is related to the fad. Fascinating." Lucille, having found a ribbon, prodded doubtfully at the exposed innards of her typewriter.

"Suppose I fictionalize it," Floria said, "under a pseudonym. Why not ride the popular wave and be free in what I can say?"

"Listen, you've never written a word of fiction in your life, have you?" Lucille fixed her with a bloodshot gaze. "There's no evidence that you could turn out a best-selling novel. On the other hand, by this time you have a trained memory for accurately reporting therapeutic transactions. That's a strength you'd be foolish to waste. A solid professional book would be terrific—and a feather in the cap of every woman in the field. Just make sure you get good legal advice on disguising your Dracula's identity well enough to avoid libel."

The cane-seated chair wasn't worth repairing, so she got its twin out of the bedroom to put in the office in its place. Puzzling: by his history Weyland was fifty-two, and by his appearance no muscle man. She should have asked Doug—but how, exactly? "By the way, Doug, was Weyland ever a circus strong man or a blacksmith? Does he secretly pump iron?" Ask the client himself—but not yet.

She invited some of the younger staff from the clinic over for a small party with a few of her outside friends. It was a good evening; they were not a heavy-drinking crowd, which meant the conversation stayed intelligent. The guests drifted about the long living room or stood in twos and threes at the windows looking down on West End Avenue as they talked.

Mort came, warming the room. Fresh from a session with some amateur chamber-music friends, he still glowed with the pleasure of making his cello sing. His own voice was unexpectedly light for so large a man. Sometimes Floria thought that the deep throb of the cello was his true voice.

He stood beside her talking with some others. There was no need to lean against his comfortable bulk or to have him put his arm around her waist. Their intimacy was long-standing, an effortless pleasure in each other that required neither demonstration nor concealment.

He was easily diverted from music to his next favorite topic, the strengths and skills of athletes.

"Here's a question for a paper I'm thinking of writing," Floria said. "Could a tall, lean man be exceptionally strong?"

Mort rambled on in his thoughtful way. His answer seemed to be no.

"But what about chimpanzees?" put in a young clinician. "I went with a guy once who was an animal handler for TV, and he said a three-month-old chimp could demolish a strong man."

"It's all physical conditioning," somebody else said. "Modern people are soft."

Mort nodded. "Human beings in general are weakly made compared to other animals. It's a question of muscle insertions—the angles of how the muscles are attached to the bones. Some angles give better leverage than others. That's how a leopard can bring down a much bigger animal than itself. It has a muscular structure that gives it tremendous strength for its streamlined build."

Floria said, "If a man were built with muscle insertions like a leopard's, he'd look pretty odd, wouldn't he?"

"Not to an untrained eye," Mort said, sounding bemused by an inner vision. "And my God, what an athlete he'd make—can you imagine a guy in the decathlon who's as strong as a leopard?"

When everyone else had gone Mort stayed, as he often did. Jokes about insertions, muscular and otherwise, soon led to sounds more expressive and more animal, but afterward Floria didn't feel like resting snuggled together with Mort and talking. When her body stopped racing, her mind turned to her new client. She didn't want to discuss him with Mort, so she ushered Mort out as gently as she could and sat down by herself at the kitchen table with a glass of orange juice.

How to approach the reintegration of Weyland the eminent, gray-haired academic with the rebellious vampire-self that had smashed his life out of shape?

She thought of the broken chair, of Weyland's big hands crushing the wood. Old wood and dried-out glue, of course, or he never could have done that. He was a man, after all, not a leopard.

The day before the third session Weyland phoned and left a message with Hilda: he would not be coming to the office tomorrow for his appointment, but if Dr. Landauer were agreeable she would find him at their usual hour at the Central Park Zoo.

Am I going to let him move me around from here to there? she thought. I shouldn't—but why fight it? Give him some leeway, see what opens up in a different setting. Besides, it was a beautiful day, probably the last of the sweet May weather before the summer stickiness descended. She gladly cut Kenny short so that she would have time to walk over to the zoo.

There was a fair crowd there for a weekday. Well-groomed young matrons pushed clean, floppy babies in strollers. Weyland she spotted at once.

He was leaning against the railing that enclosed the seals' shelter and their murky green pool. His jacket, slung over his shoulder, draped elegantly down his long back. Floria thought him rather dashing and faintly foreign-looking. Women who passed him, she noticed, tended to glance back.

He looked at everyone. She had the impression that he knew quite well that she was walking up behind him.

"Outdoors makes a nice change from the office, Edward," she said, coming to the rail beside him. "But there must be more to this than a longing for fresh air." A fat seal lay in sculptural grace on the concrete, eyes blissfully shut, fur drying in the sun to a translucent water-color umber.

Weyland straightened from the rail. They walked. He did not look at the animals; his eyes moved continually over the crowd. He said, "Someone has been watching for me at your office building."

"Who?"

"There are several possibilities. Pah, what a stench—though humans caged in similar circumstances smell as bad." He sidestepped a couple of shrieking children who were fighting over a balloon and headed out of the zoo under the musical clock.

They walked the uphill path northward through the park. By extending her own stride a little Floria found that she could comfortably keep pace with him.

"Is it peasants with torches?" she said. "Following you?"

He said, "What a childish idea."

All right, try another tack, then: "You were telling me last time about hunting in the Ramble. Can we return to that?"

"If you wish." He sounded bored—a defense? Surely—she was certain this must be the right reading—surely his problem was a transmutation into "vampire" fantasy of an unacceptable aspect of himself. For men of his generation the confrontation with homosexual drives could be devastating.

"When you pick up someone in the Ramble, is it a paid encounter?"

"Usually."

"How do you feel about having to pay?" She expected resentment.

He gave a faint shrug. "Why not? Others work to earn their bread. I work, too, very hard, in fact. Why shouldn't I use my earnings to pay for my sustenance?"

Why did he never play the expected card? Baffled, she paused to drink from a fountain. They walked on.

"Once you've got your quarry, how do you . . ." She fumbled for a word.

"Attack?" he supplied, unperturbed. "There's a place on the neck, here, where pressure can interrupt the blood flow to the brain and cause unconsciousness. Getting close enough to apply that pressure isn't difficult."

"You do this before or after any sexual activity?"

"Before, if possible," he said aridly, "and instead of." He turned aside to stalk up a slope to a granite outcrop that overlooked the path they had been following. There he settled on his haunches, looking back the way they had come. Floria, glad she'd worn slacks today, sat down near him.

He didn't seem devastated—anything but. Press him, don't let him get by on cool. "Do you often prey on men in preference to women?"

"Certainly. I take what is easiest. Men have always been more accessible because women have been walled away like prizes or so physically impoverished by repeated childbearing as to be unhealthy prey for me. All this has begun to change recently, but gay men are still the simplest quarry." While she was recovering from her surprise at his unforeseen and weirdly skewed awareness of female history, he added suavely, "How carefully you control your expression, Dr. Landauer—no trace of disapproval."

She did disapprove, she realized. She would prefer him not to be committed sexually to men. Oh, hell.

He went on, "Yet no doubt you see me as one who victimizes the already victimized. This is the world's way. A wolf brings down the stragglers at the edges of the herd. Gay men are denied the full protection of the human herd and are at the same time emboldened to make themselves known and available.

"On the other hand, unlike the wolf I can feed without killing, and these particular victims pose no threat to me that would cause me to kill. Outcasts themselves, even if they comprehend my true purpose among them they cannot effectively accuse me."

God, how neatly, completely, and ruthlessly he distanced the homosexual community from himself! "And how do you feel, Edward, about their purposes—their sexual expectations of you?"

"The same way I feel about the sexual expectations of women whom I choose to pursue: they don't interest me. Besides, once my hunger is active, sexual arousal is impossible. My physical unresponsiveness seems to surprise no one. Apparently impotence is expected in a gray-haired man, which suits my intention."

Some kids carrying radios swung past below, trailing a jumble of amplified thump, wail, and jabber. Floria gazed after them unseeingly, thinking, astonished again, that she had never heard a man speak of his own impotence with such cool indifference. She had induced him to talk about his problem all right. He was speaking as freely as he had in the first session, only this time it was no act. He was drowning her in more than she had ever expected or for that matter wanted to know about vampirism. What the hell: she was listening, she thought she understood—what was it all good for? Time for some cold reality, she thought; see how far he can carry all this incredible detail. Give the whole structure a shove.

She said, "You realize, I'm sure, that people of either sex who make themselves so easily available are also liable to be carriers of disease. When was your last medical checkup?"

"My dear Dr. Landauer, my first medical checkup will be my last. Fortunately, I have no great need of one. Most serious illnesses—hepatitis, for example—reveal themselves to me by a quality in the odor of the victim's skin. Warned, I abstain. When I do fall ill, as occasionally happens, I withdraw to some place where I can heal undisturbed. A doctor's attentions would be more dangerous to me than any disease."

Eyes on the path below, he continued calmly, "You can see by looking at me that there are no obvious clues to my unique nature. But believe me, an examination of any depth by even a half-sleeping medical practitioner would reveal some alarming deviations from the norm. I take pains to stay healthy, and I seem to be gifted with an exceptionally hardy constitution."

Fantasies of being unique and physically superior; take him to the other pole. "I'd like you to try something now. Will you put yourself into the mind of a man you contact in the Ramble and describe your encounter with him from his point of view?"

He turned toward her and for some moments regarded her without expression. Then he resumed his surveillance of the path. "I will not. Though I do have enough empathy with my quarry to enable me to hunt efficiently. I must draw the line at erasing the necessary distance that keeps prey and predator distinct.

"And now I think our ways part for today." He stood up, descended the hillside, and walked beneath some low-canopied trees, his tall back stooped, toward the Seventy-second Street entrance of the park.

Floria arose more slowly, aware suddenly of her shallow breathing and the sweat on her face. Back to reality or what remained of it. She looked at her watch. She was late for her next client.

Floria couldn't sleep that night. Barefoot in her bathrobe she paced the living room by lamplight. They had sat together on that hill as isolated as in her office—more so, because there was no Hilda and no phone. He was, she knew, very strong, and he had sat close enough to her to reach out for that paralyzing touch to the neck—

Just suppose for a minute that Weyland had been brazenly telling the truth all along, counting on her to treat it as a delusion because on the face of it the truth was inconceivable.

Jesus, she thought, if I'm thinking that way about him, this therapy is more out of control than I thought. What kind of therapist becomes an accomplice to the client's fantasy? A crazy therapist, that's what kind.

Frustrated and confused by the turmoil in her mind, she wandered into the workroom. By morning the floor was covered with sheets of newsprint, each broadly marked by her felt-tipped pen. Floria sat in the midst of them, gritty-eyed and hungry.

She often approached problems this way, harking back to art training: turn off the thinking, put hand to paper and see what the deeper, less verbally sophisticated parts of the mind have to offer. Now that her dreams had deserted her, this was her only access to those levels.

The newsprint sheets were covered with rough representations of Weyland's face and form. Across several of them were scrawled words: *"Dear Doug, your vampire is fine, it's your ex-therapist who's off the rails. Warning: Therapy can be dangerous to your health. Especially if you are the therapist. Beautiful vampire, awaken to me. Am I really ready to take on a legendary monster? Give up—refer this one out. Do your job—work is a good doctor."*

That last one sounded pretty good, except that doing her job was precisely what she was feeling so shaky about these days.

Here was another message: *"How come this attraction to someone so scary?"* Oh ho, she thought, is that a real feeling or an aimless reaction out of the body's early-morning hormone peak? You don't want to confuse honest libido with mere biological clockwork.

Deborah called. Babies cried in the background over the Scotch Symphony. Nick, Deb's husband, was a musicologist with fervent opinions on music and nothing else.

"We'll be in town a little later in the summer," Deborah said, "just for a few days at the end of July. Nicky has this seminar-convention thing. Of course, it won't be easy with the babies . . . I wondered if you might sort of coordinate your vacation so you could spend a little time with them?"

Baby-sit, that meant. Damn. Cute as they were and all that, damn! Floria gritted her teeth. Visits from Deb were difficult. Floria had been so proud of her bright, hard-driving daughter, and then suddenly Deborah had dropped her studies and rushed to embrace all the dangers that Floria had warned her against: a romantic, too-young marriage, instant breeding, no preparation for self-support, the works. Well, to each her own, but it was so wearing to have Deb around playing the empty-headed hausfrau.

"Let me think, Deb. I'd love to see all of you, but I've been considering spending a couple of weeks in Maine with your Aunt Nonnie." God knows I need a real vacation, she thought, though the peace and quiet up there is hard for a city kid like me to take for long. Still, Nonnie, Floria's younger sister, was good company. "Maybe you could bring the kids up there for a couple of days. There's room in that great barn of a place, and of course Nonnie'd be happy to have you."

"Oh, no, Mom, it's so dead up there, it drives Nick crazy—don't tell Nonnie I said that. Maybe Nonnie could come down to the city instead. You could cancel a date or two and we could all go to Coney Island together, things like that."

Kid things, which would drive Nonnie crazy and Floria too before long. "I doubt she could manage," Floria said, "but I'll ask. Look, hon, if I do go up there, you and Nick and the kids could stay here at the apartment and save some money."

"We have to be at the hotel for the seminar," Deb said shortly. No doubt she was feeling just as impatient as Floria was by now. "And the kids haven't seen you for a long time—it would be really nice if you could stay in the city just for a few days."

"We'll try to work something out." Always working something out. Concord never comes naturally—first we have to butt heads and get pissed off. Each time you call I hope it'll be different, Floria thought.

Somebody shrieked for "oly," jelly that would be, in the background—Floria felt a sudden rush of warmth for them, her grandkids for God's sake. Having been a young mother herself, she was still young enough to really enjoy them (and to fight with Deb about how to bring them up).

Deb was starting an awkward goodbye. Floria replied, put the phone down, and sat with her head back against the flowered kitchen wallpaper, thinking, Why do I feel so rotten now? Deb and I aren't close, no comfort, seldom friends, though we were once. Have I said everything wrong, made her think I don't want to see her and don't care about her family? What does she want from me that I can't seem to give her? Approval? Maybe she thinks I still hold her marriage against her. Well, I do, sort of. What right have I to be critical, me with my divorce? What terrible things would she say to me, would I say to her, that we take such care not to say anything important at all?

"I think today we might go into sex," she said.

Weyland responded dryly, "Might we indeed. Does it titillate you to wring confessions of solitary vice from men of mature years?"

Oh no you don't, she thought. You can't sidestep so easily. "Under what circumstances do you find yourself sexually aroused?"

"Most usually upon waking from sleep," he said indifferently.

"What do you do about it?"

"The same as others do. I am not a cripple, I have hands."

"Do you have fantasies at these times?"

"No. Women, and men for that matter, appeal to me very little, either in fantasy or reality."

"Ah—what about female vampires?" she said, trying not to sound arch.

"I know of none."

Of course: the neatest out in the book. "They're not needed for reproduction, I suppose, because people who die of vampire bites become vampires themselves."

He said testily, "Nonsense. I am not a communicable disease."

So he had left an enormous hole in his construct. She headed straight for it: "Then how does your kind reproduce?"

"I have no kind, so far as I am aware," he said, "and I do not reproduce. Why should I, when I may live for centuries still, perhaps indefinitely? My sexual equipment is clearly only detailed biological mimicry, a form of protective coloration." How beautiful, how simple a solution, she thought, full of admiration in spite of herself. "Do I occasionally detect a note of prurient interest in your questions, Dr. Landauer? Something akin to stopping at the cage to watch the tigers mate at the zoo?"

"Probably," she said, feeling her face heat. He had a great backhand return shot there. "How do you feel about that?"

He shrugged.

"To return to the point," she said. "Do I hear you saying that you have no urge whatever to engage in sexual intercourse with anyone?"

"Would you mate with your livestock?"

His matter-of-fact arrogance took her breath away. She said weakly, "Men have reportedly done so."

"Driven men. I am not driven in that way. My sex urge is of low frequency and is easily dealt with unaided—although I occasionally engage in copulation out of the necessity to keep up appearances. I am capable, but not—like humans—obsessed."

Was he sinking into lunacy before her eyes? "I think I hear you saying," she said, striving to keep her voice neutral, "that you're not just a man with a unique way of life. I think I hear you saying that you're not human at all."

"I thought that this was already clear."

"And that there are no others like you."

"None that I know of."

"Then—you see yourself as what? Some sort of mutation?"

"Perhaps. Or perhaps your kind are the mutation."

She saw disdain in the curl of his lip. "How does your mouth feel now?"

"The corners are drawn down. The feeling is contempt."

"Can you let the contempt speak?"

He got up and went to stand at the window, positioning himself slightly to one side as if to stay hidden from the street below.

"Edward," she said.

He looked back at her. "Humans are my food. I draw the life out of their veins. Sometimes I kill them. I am greater than they are. Yet I must spend my time thinking about their habits and their drives, scheming to avoid the dangers they pose—I hate them."

She felt the hatred like a dry heat radiating from him. God, he really lived all this! She had tapped into a furnace of feeling. And now? The sensation of triumph wavered, and she grabbed at a next move: hit him with reality now, while he's burning.

"What about blood banks?" she said. "Your food is commercially available, so why all the complication and danger of the hunt?"

"You mean I might turn my efforts to piling up a fortune and buying blood by the case? That would certainly make for an easier, less risky life in the short run. I could fit quite comfortably into modern society if I became just another consumer.

"However, I prefer to keep the mechanics of my survival firmly in my own hands. After all, I can't afford to lose my hunting skills. In two hundred years there may be no blood banks, but I will still need my food."

Jesus, you set him a hurdle and he just flies over it. Are there no weaknesses in all this, has he no blind spots? Look at his tension—go back to that. Floria said, "What do you feel now in your body?"

"Tightness." He pressed his spread fingers to his abdomen.

"What are you doing with your hands?"

"I put my hands to my stomach."

"Can you speak for your stomach?"

" 'Feed me or die,' " he snarled.

Elated again, she closed in: "And for yourself, in answer?"

" 'Will you never be satisfied?' " He glared at her. "You shouldn't seduce me into quarreling with the terms of my own existence!"

"Your stomach is your existence," she paraphrased.

"The gut determines," he said harshly. "That first, everything else after."

"Say, 'I resent . . .' "

He held to a tense silence.

" 'I resent the power of my gut over my life,' " she said for him.

He stood with an abrupt motion and glanced at his watch, an elegant flash of slim silver on his wrist. "Enough," he said.

That night at home she began a set of notes that would never enter his file at the office, notes toward the proposed book.

Couldn't do it, couldn't get properly into the sex thing with him. Everything shoots off in all directions. His vampire concept so thoroughly worked out, find myself half believing sometimes—my own childish fantasy-response to his powerful death-avoidance, contact-avoidance fantasy. Lose professional distance every time— is that what scares me about him? Don't really want to shatter his delusion (my life a mess, what right to tear down others' patterns?) —so see it as real? Wonder how much of "vampirism" he acts out, how far, how often. Something attractive in his purely selfish, predatory stance—the lure of the great outlaw.

Told me today quite coolly about a man he killed recently—inadvertently—by drinking too much from him. *Is* it fantasy? Of course —the victim, he thinks, was college student. Breathes there a professor who hasn't dreamed of murdering some representative youth, retaliation for years of classroom frustration? Speaks of teaching with acerbic humor—amuses him to work at cultivating the minds of those he regards strictly as bodies, containers of his sustenance. He shows the alienness of full-blown psychopathology, poor bastard, plus clean-cut logic. Suggested he find another job (assuming his delusion at least in part related to pressures at Cayslin); his fantasy-persona, the vampire, more realistic than I about job-switching:

"For a man of my apparent age it's not so easy to make such a change in these tight times. I might have to take a position lower on the ladder of 'success' as you people assess it." Status is important to him? "Certainly. An eccentric professor is one thing; an eccentric pipe-fitter, another. And I like good cars, which are expensive to own and run." Then, thoughtful addition, "Although there are advantages to a simpler, less visible life." He refuses to discuss other "jobs" from former "lives." We are deep into the fantasy—where the hell going? Damn right I don't control the "games"—preplanned therapeutic strategies get whirled away as soon as we begin. Nerve-wracking.

Tried again to have him take the part of his enemy-victim, peasant with torch. Asked if he felt himself rejecting that point of view? Frosty reply: "Naturally. The peasant's point of view is in no way my own. I've been reading in your field, Dr. Landauer. You work from the Gestalt orientation—" Originally yes, I corrected; eclectic now. "But you do proceed from the theory that I am projecting some aspect of my own feelings outward onto others, whom I then treat as my victims. Your purpose then must be to maneuver me into accepting as my own the projected 'victim' aspect of myself. This integration is supposed to effect the freeing of energy previously locked into maintaining the projection. All this is an interesting insight into the nature of ordinary human confusion, but I am not an ordinary human, and I am not confused. I cannot afford confusion." Felt sympathy for him—telling me he's afraid of having own internal confusions exposed in therapy, too threatening. Keep chipping away at delusion, though with what prospect? It's so complex, deep-seated.

Returned to his phrase "my apparent age." He asserts he has lived many human lifetimes, all details forgotten, however, during periods of suspended animation between lives. Perhaps sensing my skepticism at such handy amnesia, grew cool and distant, claimed to know little about the hibernation process itself: "The essence of this state is that I sleep through it—hardly an ideal condition for making scientific observations."

Edward thinks his body synthesizes vitamins, minerals (as all

our bodies synthesize vitamin D), even proteins. Describes unique
design he deduces in himself: special intestinal microfauna plus
superefficient body chemistry extracts enough energy to live on
from blood. Damn good mileage per calorie, too. (Recall observable tension, first interview, at question about drinking—my note
on possible alcohol problem!)

Speak for blood: " 'Lacking me, you have no life. I flow to the
heart's soft drumbeat through lightless prisons of flesh. I am rich, I
am nourishing, I am difficult to attain.' " Stunned to find him positively lyrical on subject of his "food." Drew attention to whispering voice of blood. " 'Yes. I am secret, hidden beneath the surface,
patient, silent, steady. I work unnoticed, an unseen thread of vitality running from age to age—beautiful, efficient, self-renewing, self-
cleansing, warm, filling—' " Could *see* him getting worked up. Finally he stood: "My appetite is pressing. I must leave you." And he
did.

Sat and trembled for five minutes after.

New development (or new perception?): he sometimes comes
across very unsophisticated about own feelings—lets me pursue
subjects of extreme intensity and delicacy to him.

Asked him to daydream—a hunt. (Hands—mine—shaking now as
I write. God. What a session.) He told of picking up a woman at
poetry reading, 92nd Street Y—has N.Y.C. all worked out, circu-
lates to avoid too much notice any one spot. Spoke easily, eyes shut
without observable strain: chooses from audience a redhead in
glasses, dress with drooping neckline (ease of access), no perfume
(strong smells bother him). Approaches during the intermission,
encouraged to see her fanning away smoke of others' cigarettes—
meaning she doesn't smoke, health sign. Agreed in not enjoying the
reading, they adjourn together to coffee shop.

"She asks whether I'm a teacher," he says, eyes shut, mouth
amused. "My clothes, glasses, manner all suggest this, and I emphasize the impression—it reassures. She's a copy editor for a publishing house. We talk about books. The waiter brings her a
gummy-looking pastry. As a non-eater, I pay little attention to the
quality of restaurants, so I must apologize to her. She waves this
away—is engrossed, or pretending to be engrossed, in talk." A
longish dialog between interested woman and Edward doing shy-
lonesome-scholar act—dead wife, competitive young colleagues

who don't understand him, quarrels in professional journals with big shots in his field—a version of what he first told me. She's attracted (of course—lanky, rough-cut elegance plus hints of vulnerability all very alluring, as intended). He offers to take her home.

Tension in his body at this point in narrative—spine clear of chair back, hands braced on thighs. "She settles beside me in the back of the cab, talking about problems of her own career—illegible manuscripts of Biblical length, mulish editors, suicidal authors —and I make comforting comments, I lean nearer and put my arm along the back of the seat, behind her shoulders. Traffic is heavy, we move slowly. There is time to make my meal here in the taxi and avoid a tedious extension of the situation into her apartment— if I move soon."

How do you feel?

"Eager," he says, voice husky. "My hunger is so roused I can scarcely restrain myself. A powerful hunger, not like yours—mine compels. I embrace her shoulders lightly, make kindly-uncle remarks, treading that fine line between the game of seduction she perceives and the game of friendly interest I pretend to affect. My real purpose underlies all: what I say, how I look, every gesture is part of the stalk. There is an added excitement, and fear, because I'm doing my hunting in the presence of a third person—behind the cabbie's head."

Could scarcely breathe. Studied him—intent face, masklike with closed eyes, nostrils slightly flared; legs tensed, hands clenched on knees. Whispering: "I press the place on her neck. She starts, sighs faintly, silently drops against me. In the stale stench of the cab's interior, with the ticking of the meter in my ears and the mutter of the radio—I take hold here, at the tenderest part of her throat. Sound subsides into the background—I feel the sweet blood beating under her skin, I taste salt at the moment before I—strike. My saliva thins her blood so that it flows out, I draw the blood into my mouth swiftly, swiftly, before she can wake, before we can arrive . . ."

Trailed off, sat back loosely in chair—saw him swallow. "Ah. I feed." Heard him sigh. Managed to ask about physical sensation. His low murmur, "Warm. Heavy, here—" touches his belly—"in a pleasant way. The good taste of blood, tart and rich, in my mouth . . ."

And then? A flicker of movement beneath his closed eyelids: "In time I am aware that the cabbie has glanced back once and has taken our—embrace for just that. I can feel the cab slowing, hear him move to turn off the meter. I withdraw, I quickly wipe my mouth on my handkerchief. I take her by the shoulders and shake her gently; does she often have these attacks, I inquire, the soul of concern. She comes around, bewildered, weak, thinks she has fainted. I give the driver extra money and ask him to wait. He looks intrigued—'What was that all about,' I can see the question in his face—but as a true New Yorker he won't expose his own ignorance by asking.

"I escort the woman to her front door, supporting her as she staggers. Any suspicion of me that she may entertain, however formless and hazy, is allayed by my stern charging of the doorman to see that she reaches her apartment safely. She grows embarrassed, thinks perhaps that if not put off by her 'illness' I would spend the night with her, which moves her to press upon me, unasked, her telephone number. I bid her a solicitous good night and take the cab back to my hotel, where I sleep."

No sex? No sex.

How did he feel about the victim as a person? "She was food."

This was his "hunting" of last night, he admits afterward, not a made-up dream. No boasting in it, just telling. Telling me! Think: I can go talk to Lucille, Mort, Doug, others about most of what matters to me. Edward has only me to talk to and that for a fee—what isolation! No wonder the stone, monumental face—only those long, strong lips (his point of contact, verbal and physical-in-fantasy, with world and with "food") are truly expressive. An exciting narration; uncomfortable to find I felt not only empathy but enjoyment. Suppose he picked up and victimized—even in fantasy—Deb or Hilda, how would I feel then?

Later: truth—I also found this recital sexually stirring. Keep visualizing how he looked finishing this "dream"—he sat very still, head up, look of thoughtful pleasure on his face. Like handsome intellectual listening to music.

Kenny showed up unexpectedly at Floria's office on Monday, bursting with malevolent energy. She happened to be free, so she took him—something was definitely up. He sat on the edge of his chair.

"I know why you're trying to unload me," he accused. "It's that new one, the tall guy with the snooty look—what is he, an old actor or something? Anybody could see he's got you itching for him."

"Kenny, when was it that I first spoke to you about terminating our work together?" she said patiently.

"Don't change the subject. Let me tell you, in case you don't know it: that guy isn't really interested, Doctor, because he's a fruit. A faggot. You want to know how I know?"

Oh Lord, she thought wearily, he's regressed to age ten. She could see that she was going to hear the rest whether she wanted to or not. What in God's name was the world like for Kenny, if he clung so fanatically to her despite her failure to help him?

"Listen, I knew right away there was something flaky about him, so I followed him from here to that hotel where he lives. I followed him the other afternoon too. He walked around like he does a lot, and then he went into one of those ritzy movie houses on Third that open early and show risqué foreign movies—you know, Japs cutting each other's things off and glop like that. This one was French, though.

"Well, there was a guy came in, a Madison Avenue type carrying his attaché case, taking a work break or something. Your man moved over and sat down behind him and reached out and sort of stroked the guy's neck, and the guy leaned back, and your man leaned forward and started nuzzling at him, you know—kissing him.

"I saw it. They had their heads together and they stayed like that a while. It was disgusting: complete strangers, without even 'hello.' The Madison Avenue guy just sat there with his head back looking zonked, you know, just swept away, and what he was doing with his hands under his raincoat in his lap I couldn't see, but I bet you can guess.

"And then your fruity friend got up and walked out. I did, too, and I hung around a little outside. After a while the Madison Avenue guy came out looking all sleepy and loose, like after you-know-what, and he wandered off on his own someplace.

"What do you think now?" he ended, on a high, triumphant note.

Her impulse was to slap his face the way she would have slapped Deb-as-a-child for tattling. But this was a client, not a kid. God give me strength, she thought.

"Kenny, you're fired."

"You can't!" he squealed. "You can't! What will I—who can I—"

She stood up, feeling weak but hardening her voice. "I'm sorry. I absolutely cannot have a client who makes it his business to spy on other clients. You already have a list of replacement therapists from me."

He gaped at her in slack-jawed dismay, his eyes swimmy with tears.

"I'm sorry, Kenny. Call this a dose of reality therapy and try to learn from it. There are some things you simply will not be allowed to do." She felt better: it was done at last.

"I hate you!" He surged out of his chair, knocking it back against the wall. Threateningly he glared at the fish tank, but, contenting himself with a couple of kicks at the nearest table leg, he stamped out.

Floria buzzed Hilda: "No more appointments for Kenny, Hilda. You can close his file."

"Whoopee," Hilda said.

Poor, horrid Kenny. Impossible to tell what would happen to him, better not to speculate or she might relent, call him back. She had encouraged him, really, by listening instead of shutting him up and throwing him out before any damage was done.

Was it damaging, to know the truth? In her mind's eye she saw a cream-faced young man out of a Black Thumb Vodka ad wander from a movie theater into daylight, yawning and rubbing absently at an irritation on his neck . . .

She didn't even look at the telephone on the table or think about whom to call, now that she believed. No; she was going to keep quiet about Dr. Edward Lewis Weyland, her vampire.

Hardly alive at staff meeting, clinic, yesterday—people asking what's the matter, fobbed them off. Settled down today. Had to, to face him.

Asked him what he felt were his strengths. He said speed, cunning, ruthlessness. Animal strengths, I said. What about imagination, or is that strictly human? He defended at once: not human only. Lion, waiting at water hole where no zebra yet drinks, thinks "Zebra—eat," therefore performs feat of imagining event yet-to-come. Self experienced as animal? Yes—reminded me that humans are also animals. Pushed for his early memories; he objected: "Gestalt is here-and-now, not history-taking." I insist, citing anomalous nature of his situation, my own refusal to be bound by any one theoretical framework. He defends tensely: "Suppose I became lost there in memory, distracted from dangers of the present, left unguarded from those dangers."

Speak for memory. He resists, but at length attempts it: " 'I am heavy with the multitudes of the past.' " Fingertips to forehead, propping up all that weight of lives. " 'So heavy, filling worlds of time laid down eon by eon, I accumulate, I persist, I demand recognition, I am as real as the life around you—more real, weightier, richer.' " His voice sinking, shoulders bowed, head in hands—I begin to feel pressure at the back of my own skull. " 'Let me in.' " Only a rough whisper now. " 'I offer beauty as well as terror. Let me in.' " Whispering also, I suggest he reply to his memory.

"Memory, you want to crush me," he groans. "You would overwhelm me with the cries of animals, the odor and jostle of bodies, old betrayals, dead joys, filth and anger from other times—I must concentrate on the danger now. Let me be." All I can take of this crazy conflict, I gabble us off onto something else. He looks up—relief?—follows my lead—where? Rest of session a blank.

No wonder sometimes no empathy at all—a species boundary! He has to be utterly self-centered just to keep balance—self-centeredness of an animal. Thought just now of our beginning, me trying to push him to produce material, trying to control him, manipulate—no way, no way; so here we are, someplace else—I feel dazed, in shock, but stick with it—it's real.

Therapy with a dinosaur, a Martian.

"You call me 'Weyland' now, not 'Edward.' " I said first name couldn't mean much to one with no memory of being called by that name as a child, silly to pretend it signifies intimacy where it can't. I think he knows now that I believe him. Without prompting, told me truth of disappearance from Cayslin. No romance; he tried to drink from a woman who worked there, she shot him, stomach and chest. Luckily for him, small-caliber pistol, and he was wearing a lined coat over three-piece suit. Even so, badly hurt. (Midsection stiffness I noted when he first came—he was still in some pain at that time.) He didn't "vanish"—fled, hid, was bound by questionable types who caught on to what he was, sold him "like a chattel" to someone here in the city. He was imprisoned, fed, put on exhibition—very privately—for gain. Got away. "Do you believe any of this?" Never asked anything like that before, seems of concern to him now. I said my belief or lack of same was immaterial; remarked on hearing a lot of bitterness.

He steepled his fingers, looked brooding at me over tips: "I nearly died there. No doubt my purchaser and his diabolist friend still search for me. Mind you, I had some reason at first to be glad of the attentions of the people who kept me prisoner. I was in no condition to fend for myself. They brought me food and kept me hidden and sheltered, whatever their motives. There are always advantages . . ."

Silence today started a short session. Hunting poor last night, Weyland still hungry. Much restless movement, watching goldfish darting in tank, scanning bookshelves. Asked him to be books. " 'I am old and full of knowledge, well made to last long. You see only the title, the substance is hidden. I am a book that stays closed.' " Malicious twist of the mouth, not quite a smile: "This is a good game." Is he feeling threatened, too—already "opened" too much to me? Too strung out with him to dig when he's skimming surfaces that should be probed. Don't know how to *do* therapy with Weyland—just have to let things happen, hope it's good. But what's "good"? Aristotle? Rousseau? Ask Weyland what's good, he'll say "Blood."

Everything in a spin—these notes too confused, too fragmentary —worthless for a book, just a mess, like me, my life. Tried to call Deb last night, cancel visit. Nobody home, thank God. Can't tell her to stay away—but damn it—do not need complications now!

Floria went down to Broadway with Lucille to get more juice, cheese and crackers for the clinic fridge. This week it was their turn to do the provisions, a chore that rotated among the staff. Their talk about grant proposals for the support of the clinic trailed off.

"Let's sit a minute," Floria said. They crossed to a traffic island in the middle of the avenue. It was a sunny afternoon, close enough to lunchtime so that the brigade of old people who normally occupied the benches had thinned out. Floria sat down and kicked a crumpled beer can and some greasy fast-food wrappings back under the bench.

"You look like hell but wide awake at least," Lucille commented.

"Things are still rough," Floria said. "I keep hoping to get my life under control so I'll have some energy left for Deb and Nick and the kids when they arrive, but I can't seem to do it. Group was awful last night—a member accused me afterward of having abandoned them all. I think I have, too. The professional messes and the personal are all related somehow, they run into each other. I should be keeping them apart so I can deal with them separately, but I can't. I can't concentrate, my mind is all over the place. Except with Dracula, who keeps me riveted with astonishment when he's in the office and bemused the rest of the time."

A bus roared by, shaking the pavement and the benches. Lucille waited until the noise faded. "Relax about the group. The others would have defended you if you'd been attacked during the session. They all understand, even if you don't seem to: it's the summer doldrums, people don't want to work, they expect you to do it all for them. But don't push so hard. You're not a shaman who can magic your clients back into health."

Floria tore two cans of juice out of a six-pack and handed one to her. On a street corner opposite, a violent argument broke out in type-writer-fast Spanish between two women. Floria sipped tinny juice and watched. She'd seen a guy last winter straddle another on that same corner and try to smash his brains out on the icy sidewalk. The old question again: What's crazy, what's health?

"It's a good thing you dumped Chubs, anyhow," Lucille said. "I don't know what finally brought that on, but it's definitely a move in the right direction. What about Count Dracula? You don't talk about him much anymore. I thought I diagnosed a yen for his venerable body."

Floria shifted uncomfortably on the bench and didn't answer. If only she could deflect Lucille's sharp-eyed curiosity.

"Oh," Lucille said. "I see. You really are hot—or at least warm. Has he noticed?"

"I don't think so. He's not on the lookout for that kind of response from me. He says sex with other people doesn't interest him, and I think he's telling the truth."

"Weird," Lucille said. "What about *Vampire on My Couch?* Shaping up all right?"

"It's shaky, like everything else. I'm worried that I don't know how things are going to come out. I mean, Freud's wolf-man case was a success, as therapy goes. Will my vampire case turn out successfully?"

She glanced at Lucille's puzzled face, made up her mind, and plunged ahead. "Luce, think of it this way: suppose, just suppose, that my Dracula is for real, an honest-to-God vampire—"

"Oh *shit!*" Lucille erupted in anguished exasperation. "Damn it, Floria, enough is enough—will you stop futzing around and get some help? Coming to pieces yourself and trying to treat this poor nut with a vampire fixation—how can you do him any good? No wonder you're worried about his therapy!"

"Please, just listen, help me think this out. My purpose can't be to cure him of what he is. Suppose vampirism isn't a defense he has to learn to drop? Suppose it's the core of his identity? Then what do I do?"

Lucille rose abruptly and marched away from her through a gap between the rolling waves of cabs and trucks. Floria caught up with her on the next block.

"Listen, will you? Luce, you see the problem? I don't need to help him see who and what he is, he knows that perfectly well, and he's not crazy, far from it—"

"Maybe not," Lucille said grimly, "but you are. Don't dump this junk on me outside of office hours, Floria. I don't spend my time listening to nut-talk unless I'm getting paid."

"Just tell me if this makes psychological sense to you: he's healthier than most of us because he's always true to his identity, even when he's engaged in deceiving others. A fairly narrow, rigorous set of requirements necessary to his survival—that *is* his identity, and it commands him completely. Anything extraneous could destroy him. To go on living, he has to act solely out of his own undistorted necessity, and if that isn't authenticity, what is? So he's healthy, isn't he?" She paused, feeling a sudden lightness in herself. "And that's the best sense I've been able to make of this whole business so far."

They were in the middle of the block. Lucille, who could not on her short legs outwalk Floria, turned on her suddenly. "What the hell do you think you're doing, calling yourself a therapist? For God's sake, Floria, don't try to rope me into this kind of professional irresponsibility. You're just dipping into your client's fantasies instead of helping him to handle them. That's not therapy, it's collusion. Have some sense! Admit you're over your head in troubles of your own, retreat to firmer ground—go get treatment for yourself!"

Floria angrily shook her head. When Lucille turned away and hurried on up the block toward the clinic, Floria let her go without trying to detain her.

Thought about Lucille's advice. After my divorce going back into therapy for a while did help, but now? Retreat again to being a client, like old days in training—so young, inadequate, defenseless then. Awful prospect. And I'd have to hand over W. to somebody else—who? I'm not up to handling him, can't cope, too anxious,

yet with all that we do good therapy together somehow. I can't
control, can only offer; he's free to take, refuse, use as suits, as far
as he's willing to go. I serve as resource while he does own therapy
—isn't that therapeutic ideal, free of "shoulds," "shouldn'ts"?

Saw ballet with Mort, lovely evening—time out from W.—talking, singing, pirouetting all the way home, feeling safe as anything
in the shadow of Mort-mountain; rolled later with that humming
(off-key), sun-warm body. Today W. says he saw me at Lincoln
Center last night, avoided me because of Mort. W. is ballet fan!
Started attending to pick up victims, now also because dance puz-
zles and pleases.

"When a group dances well, the meaning is easy—the dancers
make a visual complement to the music, all their moves necessary,
coherent, flowing. When a gifted soloist performs, the pleasure of
making the moves is echoed in my own body. The soloist's absorption is total, much like my own in the actions of the hunt. But
when a man and a woman dance together, something else happens.
Sometimes one is hunter, one is prey, or they shift these roles
between them. Yet some other level of significance exists—I suppose to do with sex—and I feel it—a tugging sensation, here—"
touched his solar plexus—"but I do not understand it."

Worked with his reactions to ballet. The response he feels to pas
de deux is a kind of pull, "like hunger but not hunger." Of course
he's baffled—Balanchine writes that the pas de deux is always a
love story between man and woman. W. isn't man, isn't woman,
yet the drama connects. His hands hovering as he spoke, fingers
spread toward each other. Pointed this out. Body work comes easier to him now: joined his hands, interlaced fingers, spoke for
hands without prompting: " 'We are similar, we want the comfort
of like closing to like.' " How would that be for him, to find—
likeness, another of his kind? "Female?" Starts impatiently explaining how unlikely this is— No, forget sex and pas de deux for now;
just to find your like, another vampire.

He springs up, agitated now. There are none, he insists; adds at
once, "But what would it be like? What would happen? I fear it!"
Sits again, hands clenched. "I long for it."

Silence. He watches goldfish, I watch him. I withhold fatuous
attempt to pin down this insight, if that's what it is—what can I
know about his insight? Suddenly he turns, studies me intently till

I lose my nerve, react, cravenly suggest that if I make him uncomfortable he might wish to switch to another therapist—

"Certainly not." More follows, all gold: "There is value to me in what we do here, Dr. Landauer, much against my earlier expectations. Although people talk appreciatively of honest speech they generally avoid it, and I myself have found scarcely any use for it at all. Your straightforwardness with me—and the straightforwardness you require in return—this is healthy in a life so dependent on deception as mine."

Sat there, wordless, much moved, thinking of what I don't show him—my upset life, seat-of-pants course with him and attendant strain, attraction to him—I'm holding out on him while he appreciates my honesty.

Hesitation, then lower-voiced, "Also, there are limits on my methods of self-discovery, short of turning myself over to a laboratory for vivisection. I have no others like myself to look at and learn from. Any tools that may help are worth much to me, and these games of yours are—potent." Other stuff besides, not important. Important: he moves me and he draws me and he keeps on coming back. Hang in if he does.

Bad night—Kenny's aunt called: no bill from me this month, so if he's not seeing me who's keeping an eye on him, where's he hanging out? Much implied blame for what *might* happen. Absurd, but shook me up: I did fail Kenny. Called off group this week also; too much.

No, it was a *good* night—first dream in months I can recall, contact again with own depths—but disturbing. Dreamed myself in cab with W. in place of the woman from the Y. He put his hand not on my neck but breast—I felt intense sensual response in the dream, also anger and fear so strong they woke me.

Thinking about this: anyone leans toward him sexually, to him a sign his hunting technique has maneuvered prospective victim into range, maybe arouses his appetite for blood. *I don't want that.* "She was food." I am not food, I am a person. No thrill at languishing away in his arms in a taxi while he drinks my blood—that's disfigured sex, masochism. My sex response in dream signaled to me I would be his victim—I rejected that, woke up.

Mention of *Dracula* (novel). W. dislikes: meandering, inaccurate, those absurd fangs. Says he himself has a sort of needle under his tongue, used to pierce skin. No offer to demonstrate, and no request from me. I brightly brought up historical Vlad Dracul— celebrated instance of Turkish envoys who, upon refusing to uncover to Vlad to show respect, were killed by spiking their hats to their skulls. "Nonsense," snorts W. "A clever ruler would use very small thumbtacks and dismiss the envoys to moan about the streets of Varna holding their tacked heads." First spontaneous play he's shown—took head in hands and uttered plaintive groans, "Ow, oh, ooh." I cracked up. W. reverted at once to usual dignified manner: "You can see that this would serve the ruler much more effectively as an object lesson against rash pride."

Later, same light vein: "I know why I'm a vampire; why are you a therapist?" Off balance as usual, said things about helping, mental health, etc. He shook his head: "And people think of a vampire as arrogant! You want to perform cures in a world which exhibits very little health of any kind—and it's the same arrogance with all of you. This one wants to be President or Class Monitor or Department Chairman or Union Boss, another must be first to fly to the stars or to transplant the human brain, and on and on. As for me, I wish only to satisfy my appetite in peace."

And those of us whose appetite is for competence, for effectiveness? Thought of Green, treated eight years ago, went on to be indicted for running a hellish "home" for aged. I had helped him stay functional so he could destroy the helpless for profit.

W. not my first predator, only most honest and direct. Scared; not of attack by W., but of process we're going through. I'm beginning to be up to it (?), but still—utterly unpredictable, impossible to handle or manage. Occasional stirrings of inward choreographer that used to shape my work so surely. Have I been afraid of that, holding it down in myself, choosing mechanical manipulation instead? Not a choice with W.—thinking no good, strategy no good, nothing left but instinct, clear and uncluttered responses if I can find them. Have to be my own authority with him, as he is always his own authority with a world in which he's unique. So work with W. not just exhausting—exhilarating too, along with strain, fear.

Am I growing braver? Not much choice.

Park again today (air-conditioning out at office). Avoiding Lucille's phone calls from clinic (very reassuring that she calls despite quarrel, but don't want to take all this up with her again). Also meeting W. in open feels saner somehow—wild creatures belong outdoors? Sailboat pond N. of 72nd, lots of kids, garbage, one beautiful tall boat drifting. We walked.

W. maintains he remembers no childhood, no parents. I told him my astonishment, confronted by someone who never had a life of the previous generation (even adopted parent) shielding him from death—how naked we stand when the last shield falls. Got caught in remembering a death dream of mine, dream it now and then—couldn't concentrate, got scared, spoke of it—a dog tumbled under a passing truck, ejected to side of the road where it lay unable to move except to lift head and shriek; couldn't help. Shaking nearly to tears—remembered Mother got into dream somehow—had blocked that at first. Didn't say it now. Tried to rescue situation, show W. how to work with a dream (sitting in vine arbor near band shell, some privacy).

He focused on my obvious shakiness: "The air vibrates constantly with the death cries of countless animals large and small. What is the death of one dog?" Leaned close, speaking quietly, instructing. "Many creatures are dying in ways too dreadful to imagine. I am part of the world; I listen to the pain. You people claim to be above all that. You deafen yourselves with your own noise and pretend there's nothing else to hear. Then these screams enter your dreams, and you have to seek therapy because you have lost the nerve to listen."

Remembered myself, said, Be a dying animal. He refused: "You are the one who dreams this." I had a horrible flash, felt I was the dog—helpless, doomed, hurting—burst into tears. The great therapist, bringing her own hangups into session with client! Enraged with self, which did not help stop bawling.

W. disconcerted, I think; didn't speak. People walked past, glanced over, ignored us. W. said finally, "What is this?" Nothing, just the fear of death. "Oh, the fear of death. That's with me all the time. One must simply get used to it." Tears into laughter. Goddamn wisdom of the ages. He got up to go, paused: "And tell that stupid little man who used to precede me at your office to stop following me around. He puts himself in danger that way."

Kenny, damn it! Aunt doesn't know where he is, no answer on his phone. Idiot!

Sketching all night—useless. W. beautiful beyond the scope of line —the beauty of singularity, cohesion, rooted in absolute devotion to demands of his specialized body. In feeding (woman in taxi), utter absorption one wants from a man in sex—no score-keeping, no fantasies, just hot urgency of appetite, of senses, the moment by itself.

His sleeves worn rolled back today to the elbows—strong, sculptural forearms, the long bones curved in slightly, suggest torque, leverage. How old?

Endurance: huge, rich cloak of time flows back from his shoulders like wings of a dark angel. All springs from, elaborates, the single, stark, primary condition: he is a predator who subsists on human blood. Harmony, strength, clarity, magnificence—all from that basic animal integrity. Of course I long for all that, here in the higgledy-piggledy hodgepodge of my life! Of course he draws me!

Wore no perfume today, deference to his keen, easily insulted sense of smell. He noticed at once, said curt thanks. Saw something bothering him, opened my mouth seeking desperately for right thing to say—up rose my inward choreographer, wide awake, and spoke plain from my heart: thinking on my floundering in some of our sessions—I am aware that you see this confusion of mine. I know you see by your occasional impatient look, sudden disengagement—yet you continue to reveal yourself to me (even shift our course yourself if it needs shifting and I don't do it). I think I know why. Because there's no place for you in world as you truly are. Because beneath your various façades your true self suffers; like all true selves, it wants, needs to be honored as real and valuable through acceptance by another. I try to be that other, but often you are beyond me.

He rose, paced to window, looked back, burning at me. "If I seem sometimes restless or impatient, Dr. Landauer, it's not because of any professional shortcomings of yours. On the contrary —you are all too effective. The seductiveness, the distraction of our —human contact worries me. I fear for the ruthlessness that keeps me alive."

Speak for ruthlessness. He shook his head. Saw tightness in

shoulders, feet braced hard against floor. Felt reflected tension in my own muscles.

Prompted him: " 'I resent . . .' "

"I resent your pretension to teach me about myself! What will this work that you do here make of me? A predator paralyzed by an unwanted empathy with his prey? A creature fit only for a cage and keeper?" He was breathing hard, jaw set. I saw suddenly the truth of his fear: his integrity is not human, but my work is specifically human, designed to make humans more human—what if it does that to him? Should have seen it before, should have seen it. No place left to go: had to ask him, in small voice, Speak for my pretension.

"No!" Eyes shut, head turned away.

Had to do it: Speak for me.

W. whispered, "As to the unicorn, out of your own legends— 'Unicorn, come lay your head in my lap while the hunters close in. You are a wonder, and for love of wonder I will tame you. You are pursued, but forget your pursuers, rest under my hand till they come and destroy you.' " Looked at me like steel: "Do you see? The more you involve yourself in what I am, the more you become the peasant with the torch!"

Two days later Doug came into town and had lunch with Floria.

He was a man of no outstanding beauty who was nevertheless attractive: he didn't have much chin and his ears were too big, but you didn't notice because of his air of confidence. His stability had been earned the hard way—as a gay man facing the straight world. Some of his strength had been attained with effort and pain in a group that Floria had run years earlier. A lasting affection had grown between herself and Doug. She was intensely glad to see him.

They ate near the clinic. "You look a little frayed around the edges," Doug said. "I heard about Jane Fennerman's relapse—too bad."

"I've only been able to bring myself to visit her once since."

"Feeling guilty?"

She hesitated, gnawing on a stale breadstick. The truth was, she hadn't thought of Jane Fennerman in weeks. Finally she said, "I guess I must be."

Sitting back with his hands in his pockets, Doug chided her gently. "It's got to be Jane's fourth or fifth time into the nuthatch, and the others happened when she was in the care of other therapists. Who are you to imagine—to demand—that her cure lay in your hands? God may be a woman, Floria, but She is not you. I thought the whole point was some recognition of individual responsibility—you for yourself, the client for himself or herself."

"That's what we're always saying," Floria agreed. She felt curiously divorced from this conversation. It had an old-fashioned flavor: Before Weyland. She smiled a little.

The waiter ambled over. She ordered bluefish. The serving would be too big for her depressed appetite, but Doug wouldn't be satisfied with his customary order of salad (he never was) and could be persuaded to help out.

He worked his way around to Topic A. "When I called to set up this lunch, Hilda told me she's got a crush on Weyland. How are you and he getting along?"

"My God, Doug, now you're going to tell me this whole thing was to fix me up with an eligible suitor!" She winced at her own rather strained laughter. "How soon are you planning to ask Weyland to work at Cayslin again?"

"I don't know, but probably sooner than I thought a couple of months ago. We hear that he's been exploring an attachment to an anthropology department at a Western school, some niche where I guess he feels he can have less responsibility, less visibility, and a chance to collect himself. Naturally, this news is making people at Cayslin suddenly eager to nail him down for us. Have you a recommendation?"

"Yes," she said. "Wait."

He gave her an inquiring look. "What for?"

"Until he works more fully through certain stresses in the situation at Cayslin. Then I'll be ready to commit myself about him." The bluefish came. She pretended distraction: "Good God, that's too much fish for me. Doug, come on and help me out here."

Hilda was crouched over Floria's file drawer. She straightened up, looking grim. "Somebody's been in the office!"

What was this, had someone attacked her? The world took on a cockeyed, dangerous tilt. "Are you okay?"

"Yes, sure, I mean there are records that have been gone through. I can tell. I've started checking and so far it looks as if none of the files themselves are missing. But if any papers were taken out of them, that would be pretty hard to spot without reading through every folder in the place. Your files, Floria. I don't think anybody else's were touched."

Mere burglary; weak with relief, Floria sat down on one of the waiting-room chairs. But only her files? "Just my stuff, you're sure?"

Hilda nodded. "The clinic got hit, too. I called. They see some new-looking scratches on the lock of your file drawer over there. Listen, you want me to call the cops?"

"First check as much as you can, see if anything obvious is missing."

There was no sign of upset in her office. She found a phone message on her table: Weyland had canceled his next appointment. She knew who had broken into her files.

She buzzed Hilda's desk. "Hilda, let's leave the police out of it for the moment. Keep checking." She stood in the middle of the office, looking at the chair replacing the one he had broken, looking at the window where he had so often watched.

Relax, she told herself. There was nothing for him to find here or at the clinic.

She signaled that she was ready for the first client of the afternoon.

That evening she came back to the office after having dinner with friends. She was supposed to be helping set up a workshop for next month, and she'd been putting off even thinking about it, let alone doing any real work. She set herself to compiling a suggested bibliography for her section.

The phone light blinked.

It was Kenny, sounding muffled and teary. "I'm sorry," he moaned. "The medicine just started to wear off. I've been trying to call you everyplace. God, I'm so scared—he was waiting in the alley."

"Who was?" she said, dry-mouthed. She knew.

"Him. The tall one, the faggot—only he goes with women too, I've seen him. He grabbed me. He hurt me. I was lying there a long time. I couldn't do anything. I felt so funny—like floating away. Some kids found me. Their mother called the cops. I was so cold, so scared—"

"Kenny, where are you?"

He told her which hospital. "Listen, I think he's really crazy, you know? And I'm scared he might . . . you live alone . . . I don't know—I didn't mean to make trouble for you. I'm so scared."

God damn you, you meant exactly to make trouble for me, and now you've bloody well made it. She got him to ring for a nurse. By calling Kenny her patient and using "Dr." in front of her own name without qualifying the title she got some information: two broken ribs, multiple contusions, a badly wrenched shoulder, and a deep cut on the scalp which Dr. Wells thought accounted for the blood loss the patient had sustained. Picked up early today, the patient wouldn't say who had attacked him. You can check with Dr. Wells tomorrow, Dr.—?

Can Weyland think I've somehow sicked Kenny on him? No, he surely knows me better than that. Kenny must have brought this on himself.

She tried Weyland's number and then the desk at his hotel. He had closed his account and gone, providing no forwarding information other than the address of a university in New Mexico.

Then she remembered: this was the night Deb and Nick and the kids were arriving. Oh, God. Next phone call. The Americana was the hotel Deb had mentioned. Yes, Mr. and Mrs. Nicholas Redpath were registered in room whatnot. Ring, please.

Deb's voice came shakily on the line. "I've been trying to call you." Like Kenny.

"You sound upset," Floria said, steadying herself for whatever calamity had descended: illness, accident, assault in the streets of the dark, degenerate city.

Silence, then a raggedy sob. "Nick's not here. I didn't phone you earlier because I thought he still might come, but I don't think he's coming, Mom." Bitter weeping.

"Oh, Debbie. Debbie, listen, you just sit tight, I'll be right down there."

The cab ride took only a few minutes. Debbie was still crying when Floria stepped into the room.

"I don't know, I don't know," Deb wailed, shaking her head. "What did I do wrong? He went away a week ago, to do some research, he said, and I didn't hear from him, and half the bank money is gone— just half, he left me half. I kept hoping . . . they say most runaways come back in a few days or call up, they get lonely . . . I haven't told anybody—I thought since we were supposed to be here at this convention thing together, I'd better come, maybe he'd show up. But nobody's seen him, and there are no messages, not a word, nothing."

"All right, all right, poor Deb," Floria said, hugging her.

"Oh God, I'm going to wake the kids with all this howling." Deb pulled away, making a frantic gesture toward the door of the adjoining room. "It was so hard to get them to sleep—they were expecting Daddy to be here, I kept telling them he'd be here." She rushed out into the hotel hallway. Floria followed, propping the door open with one of her shoes since she didn't know whether Deb had a key with her or not. They stood out there together, ignoring passersby, huddling over Deb's weeping.

"What's been going on between you and Nick?" Floria said. "Have you two been sleeping together lately?"

Deb let out a squawk of agonized embarrassment, "Mo-*ther!*" and pulled away from her. Oh, hell, wrong approach.

"Come on, I'll help you pack. We'll leave word you're at my place. Let Nick come looking for you." Floria firmly squashed down the miserable inner cry, How am I going to stand this?

"Oh, no, I can't move till morning now that I've got the kids settled down. Besides, there's one night's deposit on the rooms. Oh, Mom, what did I do?"

"You didn't do anything, hon," Floria said, patting her shoulder and thinking in some part of her mind, Oh boy, that's great, is that the best you can come up with in a crisis with all your training and experience? Your touted professional skills are not so hot lately, but this bad? Another part answered, Shut up, stupid, only an idiot does therapy on her own family. Deb's come to her mother, not to a shrink, so go ahead and be Mommy. If only Mommy had less pressure on her right now—but that was always the way: everything at once or nothing at all.

"Look, Deb, suppose I stay the night here with you."

Deb shook the pale, damp-streaked hair out of her eyes with a determined, grown-up gesture. "No, thanks, Mom. I'm so tired I'm just going to fall out now. You'll be getting a bellyful of all this when we move in on you tomorrow anyway. I can manage tonight, and besides—"

And besides, just in case Nick showed up, Deb didn't want Floria around complicating things; of course. Or in case the tooth fairy dropped by.

Floria restrained an impulse to insist on staying; an impulse, she recognized, that came from her own need not to be alone tonight. That was not something to load on Deb's already burdened shoulders.

"Okay," Floria said. "But look, Deb, I'll expect you to call me up first thing in the morning, whatever happens." And if I'm still alive, I'll answer the phone.

All the way home in the cab she knew with growing certainty that Weyland would be waiting for her there. He can't just walk away, she thought; he has to finish things with me. So let's get it over.

In the tiled hallway she hesitated, keys in hand. What about calling the cops to go inside with her? Absurd. You don't set the cops on a unicorn.

She unlocked and opened the door to the apartment and called inside, "Weyland! Where are you?"

Nothing. Of course not—the door was still open, and he would want to be sure she was by herself. She stepped inside, shut the door, and snapped on a lamp as she walked into the living room.

He was sitting quietly on a radiator cover by the street window, his hands on his thighs. His appearance here in a new setting, her setting, this faintly lit room in her home place, was startlingly intimate. She was sharply aware of the whisper of movement—his clothing, his shoe soles against the carpet underfoot—as he shifted his posture.

"What would you have done if I'd brought somebody with me?" she said unsteadily. "Changed yourself into a bat and flown away?"

"Two things I must have from you," he said. "One is the bill of health that we spoke of when we began, though not, after all, for Cayslin College. I've made other plans. The story of my disappearance has of course filtered out along the academic grapevine so that even two thousand miles from here people will want evidence of my mental soundness. Your evidence. I would type it myself and forge your signature, but I want your authentic tone and language. Please prepare a letter to the desired effect, addressed to these people."

He drew something white from an inside pocket and held it out. She advanced and took the envelope from his extended hand. It was from the Western anthropology department that Doug had mentioned at lunch.

"Why not Cayslin?" she said. "They want you there."

"Have you forgotten your own suggestion that I find another job? That was a good idea after all. Your reference will serve me best out there—with a copy for my personnel file at Cayslin, naturally."

She put her purse down on the seat of a chair and crossed her arms. She felt reckless—the effect of stress and weariness, she thought, but it was an exciting feeling.

"The receptionist at the office does this sort of thing for me," she said.

He pointed. "I've been in your study. You have a typewriter there, you have stationery with your letterhead, you have carbon paper."

"What was the second thing you wanted?"

"Your notes on my case."

"Also at the—"

"You know that I've already searched both your work places, and the very circumspect jottings in your file on me are not what I mean. Others must exist: more detailed."

"What makes you think that?"

"How could you resist?" He mocked her. "You have encountered nothing like me in your entire professional life, and never shall again. Perhaps you hope to produce an article someday, even a book—a memoir of something impossible that happened to you one summer. You're an ambitious woman, Dr. Landauer."

Floria squeezed her crossed arms tighter against herself to quell her shivering. "This is all just supposition," she said.

He took folded papers from his pocket: some of her thrown-aside notes on him, salvaged from the wastebasket. "I found these. I think there must be more. Whatever there is, give it to me, please."

"And if I refuse, what will you do? Beat me up the way you beat up Kenny?"

Weyland said calmly, "I told you he should stop following me. This is serious now. There are pursuers who intend me ill—my former captors, of whom I told you. Whom do you think I keep watch for? No records concerning me must fall into their hands. Don't bother protesting to me your devotion to confidentiality. There is a man named Alan Reese who would take what he wants and be damned to your professional ethics. So I must destroy all evidence you have about me before I leave the city."

Floria turned away and sat down by the coffee table, trying to think beyond her fear. She breathed deeply against the fright trembling in her chest.

"I see," he said dryly, "that you won't give me the notes; you don't trust me to take them and go. You see some danger."

"All right, a bargain," she said. "I'll give you whatever I have on your case if in return you promise to go straight out to your new job and keep away from Kenny and my offices and anybody connected with me—"

He was smiling slightly as he rose from the seat and stepped soft-footed toward her over the rug. "Bargains, promises, negotiations—all foolish, Dr. Landauer. I want what I came for."

She looked up at him. "But then how can I trust you at all? As soon as I give you what you want—"

"What is it that makes you afraid—that you can't render me harmless to you? What a curious concern you show suddenly for your own life and the lives of those around you! You are the one who led me to take chances in our work together—to explore the frightful risks of self-revelation. Didn't you see in the air between us the brilliant shimmer of those hazards? I thought your business was not smoothing the world over but adventuring into it, discovering its true nature, and closing valiantly with everything jagged, cruel, and deadly."

In the midst of her terror the inner choreographer awoke and stretched. Floria rose to face the vampire.

"All right, Weyland, no bargains. I'll give you freely what you want." Of course she couldn't make herself safe from him—or make Kenny or Lucille or Deb or Doug safe—any more than she could protect Jane Fennerman from the common dangers of life. Like Weyland, some dangers were too strong to bind or banish. "My notes are in the workroom—come on, I'll show you. As for the letter you need, I'll type it right now and you can take it away with you."

She sat at the typewriter arranging paper, carbon sheets, and white-out, and feeling the force of his presence. Only a few feet away, just at the margin of the light from the gooseneck lamp by which she worked, he leaned against the edge of the long table that was twin to the table in her office. Open in his large hands was the notebook she had given him from the table drawer. When he moved his head over the notebook's pages, his glasses glinted.

She typed the heading and the date. How surprising, she thought, to find that she had regained her nerve here, and now. When you dance as the inner choreographer directs, you act without thinking, not in command of events but in harmony with them. You yield control, accepting the chance that a mistake might be part of the design. The inner choreographer is always right but often dangerous: giving up control means accepting the possibility of death. What I feared I have pursued right here to this moment in this room.

A sheet of paper fell out of the notebook. Weyland stooped and caught it up, glanced at it. "You had training in art?" Must be a sketch.

"I thought once I might be an artist," she said.

"What you chose to do instead is better," he said. "This making of pictures, plays, all art, is pathetic. The world teems with creation, most of it unnoticed by your kind just as most of the deaths are unnoticed. What can be the point of adding yet another tiny gesture? Even you, these notes—for what, a moment's celebrity?"

"You tried it yourself," Floria said. "The book you edited, *Notes on a Vanished People.*" She typed: ". . . temporary dislocation resulting from a severe personal shock . . ."

"That was professional necessity, not creation," he said in the tone of a lecturer irritated by a question from the audience. With disdain he tossed the drawing on the table. "Remember, I don't share your impulse toward artistic gesture—your absurd frills—"

She looked up sharply. "The ballet, Weyland. Don't lie." She typed: ". . . exhibits a powerful drive toward inner balance and wholeness in a difficult life situation. The steadying influence of an extraordinary basic integrity . . ."

He set the notebook aside. "My feeling for ballet is clearly some sort of aberration. Do you sigh to hear a cow calling in a pasture?"

"There are those who have wept to hear whales singing in the ocean."

He was silent, his eyes averted.

"This is finished," she said. "Do you want to read it?"

He took the letter. "Good," he said at length. "Sign it, please. And type an envelope for it." He stood closer, but out of arm's reach, while she complied. "You seem less frightened."

"I'm terrified but not paralyzed," she said and laughed, but the laugh came out a gasp.

"Fear is useful. It has kept you at your best throughout our association. Have you a stamp?"

Then there was nothing to do but take a deep breath, turn off the gooseneck lamp, and follow him back into the living room. "What now, Weyland?" she said softly. "A carefully arranged suicide so that I have no chance to retract what's in that letter or to reconstruct my notes?"

At the window again, always on watch at the window, he said, "Your doorman was sleeping in the lobby. He didn't see me enter the building. Once inside, I used the stairs, of course. The suicide rate among therapists is notoriously high. I looked it up."

"You have everything all planned?"

The window was open. He reached out and touched the metal grille that guarded it. One end of the grille swung creaking outward into the night air, like a gate opening. She visualized him sitting there waiting for her to come home, his powerful fingers patiently working the bolts at that side of the grille loose from the brick-and-mortar window frame. The hair lifted on the back of her neck.

He turned toward her again. She could see the end of the letter she had given him sticking palely out of his jacket pocket.

"Floria," he said meditatively. "An unusual name—is it after the heroine of Sardou's *Tosca?* At the end, doesn't she throw herself to her death from a high castle wall? People are careless about the names they give their children. I will not drink from you—I hunted today, and I fed. Still, to leave you living . . . is too dangerous."

A fire engine tore past below, siren screaming. When it had gone Floria said, "Listen, Weyland, you said it yourself: I can't make myself safe from you—I'm not strong enough to shove you out the window instead of being shoved out myself. Must you make yourself safe from me? Let me say this to you, without promises, demands, or pleadings: I will not go back on what I wrote in that letter. I will not try to recreate my notes. I mean it. Be content with that."

"You tempt me to it," he murmured after a moment, "to go from here with you still alive behind me for the remainder of your little life— to leave woven into Dr. Landauer's quick mind those threads of my own life that I pulled for her . . . I want to be able sometimes to think of you thinking of me. But the risk is very great."

"Sometimes it's right to let the dangers live, to give them their place," she urged. "Didn't you tell me yourself a little while ago how risk makes us more heroic?"

He looked amused. "Are you instructing me in the virtues of danger? You are brave enough to know something, perhaps, about that, but I have studied danger all my life."

"A long, long life with more to come," she said, desperate to make him understand and believe her. "Not mine to jeopardize. There's no torch-brandishing peasant here; we left that behind long ago. Remember when you spoke for me? You said, 'For love of wonder.' That was true."

He leaned to turn off the lamp near the window. She thought that he had made up his mind, and that when he straightened it would be to spring.

But instead of terror locking her limbs, from the inward choreographer came a rush of warmth and energy into her muscles and an impulse to turn toward him. Out of a harmony of desires she said swiftly, "Weyland, come to bed with me."

She saw his shoulders stiffen against the dim square of the window, his head lift in scorn. "You know I can't be bribed that way," he said contemptuously. "What are you up to? Are you one of those who come into heat at the sight of an upraised fist?"

"My life hasn't twisted me that badly, thank God," she retorted. "And if you've known all along how scared I've been, you must have sensed my attraction to you too, so you know it goes back to—very early in our work. But we're not at work now, and I've given up being 'up to' anything. My feeling is real—not a bribe, or a ploy, or a kink. No 'love me now, kill me later,' nothing like that. Understand me, Weyland: if death is your answer, than let's get right to it—come ahead and try."

Her mouth was dry as paper. He said nothing and made no move; she pressed on. "But if you can let me go, if we can simply part company here, then this is how I would like to mark the ending of our time together. This is the completion I want. Surely you feel something, too —curiosity at least?"

"Granted, your emphasis on the expressiveness of the body has instructed me," he admitted, and then he added lightly, "Isn't it extremely unprofessional to proposition a client?"

"Extremely, and I never do; but this, now, feels right. For you to indulge in courtship that doesn't end in a meal would be unprofessional, too, but how would it feel to indulge anyway—this once? Since we started, you've pushed me light-years beyond my profession. Now I want to travel all the way with you, Weyland. Let's be unprofessional together."

She turned and went into the bedroom, leaving the lights off. There was a reflected light, cool and diffuse, from the glowing night air of the great city. She sat down on the bed and kicked off her shoes. When she looked up, he was in the doorway.

Hesitantly, he halted a few feet from her in the dimness, then came and sat beside her. He would have lain down in his clothes, but she said quietly, "You can undress. The front door's locked and there isn't anyone here but us. You won't have to leap up and flee for your life."

He stood again and began to take off his clothes, which he draped neatly over a chair. He said, "Suppose I am fertile with you; could you conceive?"

By her own choice any such possibility had been closed off after Deb. She said, "No," and that seemed to satisfy him.

She tossed her own clothes onto the dresser.

He sat down next to her again, his body silvery in the reflected light and smooth, lean as a whippet and as roped with muscle. His cool thigh pressed against her own fuller, warmer one as he leaned across her and carefully deposited his glasses on the bedtable. Then he turned toward her, and she could just make out two puckerings of tissue on his skin: bullet scars, she thought, shivering.

He said, "But why do I wish to do this?"

"Do you?" She had to hold herself back from touching him.

"Yes." He stared at her. "How did you grow so real? The more I spoke to you of myself, the more real you became."

"No more speaking, Weyland," she said gently. "This is body work."

He lay back on the bed.

She wasn't afraid to take the lead. At the very least she could do for him as well as he did for himself, and at the most, much better. Her own skin was darker than his, a shadowy contrast where she browsed over his body with her hands. Along the contours of his ribs she felt knotted places, hollows—old healings, the tracks of time. The tension of his muscles under her touch and the sharp sound of his breathing stirred her. She lived the fantasy of sex with an utter stranger; there was no one in the world so much a stranger as he. Yet there was no one who knew him as well as she did, either. If he was unique, so was she, and so was their confluence here.

The vividness of the moment inflamed her. His body responded. His penis stirred, warmed, and thickened in her hand. He turned on his hip so that they lay facing each other, he on his right side, she on her left. When she moved to kiss him he swiftly averted his face: of course —to him, the mouth was for feeding. She touched her fingers to his lips, signifying her comprehension.

He offered no caresses but closed his arms around her, his hands cradling the back of her head and neck. His shadowed face, deep-hollowed under brow and cheekbone, was very close to hers. From between the parted lips that she must not kiss his quick breath came, roughened by groans of pleasure. At length he pressed his head against hers, inhaling deeply; taking her scent, she thought, from her hair and skin.

He entered her, hesitant at first, probing slowly and tentatively. She found this searching motion intensely sensuous, and clinging to him all along his sinewy length she rocked with him through two long, swelling waves of sweetness. Still half submerged, she felt him strain tight against her, she heard him gasp through his clenched teeth.

Panting, they subsided and lay loosely interlocked. His head was tilted back; his eyes were closed. She had no desire to stroke him or to speak with him, only to rest spent against his body and absorb the sounds of his breathing, her breathing.

He did not lie long to hold or be held. Without a word he disengaged his body from hers and got up. He moved quietly about the bedroom, gathering his clothing, his shoes, the drawings, the notes from the workroom. He dressed without lights. She listened in silence from the center of a deep repose.

There was no leavetaking. His tall figure passed and repassed the dark rectangle of the doorway, and then he was gone. The latch on the front door clicked shut.

Floria thought of getting up to secure the deadbolt. Instead she turned on her stomach and slept.

She woke as she remembered coming out of sleep as a youngster—peppy and clearheaded.

"Hilda, let's give the police a call about that break-in. If anything ever does come of it, I want to be on record as having reported it. You can tell them we don't have any idea who did it or why. And please make a photocopy of this letter carbon to send to Doug Sharpe up at Cayslin. Then you can put the carbon into Weyland's file and close it."

Hilda sighed. "Well, he was too old anyway."

He wasn't, my dear, but never mind.

In her office Floria picked up the morning's mail from her table. Her glance strayed to the window where Weyland had so often stood. God, she was going to miss him; and God, how good it was to be restored to plain working days.

Only not yet. Don't let the phone ring, don't let the world push in here now. She needed to sit alone for a little and let her mind sort through the images left from . . . from the pas de deux with Weyland. It's the notorious morning after, old dear, she told herself; just where have I been dancing, anyway?

In a clearing in the enchanted forest with the unicorn, of course, but not the way the old legends have it. According to them, hunters set a virgin to attract the unicorn by her chastity so they can catch and kill him. My unicorn was the chaste one, come to think of it, and this lady meant no treachery. No, Weyland and I met hidden from the hunt, to celebrate a private mystery of our own. . . .

Your mind grappled with my mind, my dark leg over your silver one, unlike closing with unlike across whatever likeness may be found: your memory pressing on my thoughts, my words drawing out your words in which you may recognize your life, my smooth palm gliding down your smooth flank . . .

Why, this will make me cry, she thought, blinking. And for what? Does an afternoon with the unicorn have any meaning for the ordinary days that come later? What has this passage with Weyland left me? Have I anything in my hands now besides the morning's mail?

What I have in my hands is my own strength, because I had to reach deep to find the strength to match him.

She put down the letters, noticing how on the backs of her hands the veins stood, blue shadows, under the thin skin. How can these hands be strong? Time was beginning to wear them thin and bring up the fragile inner structure in clear relief. That was the meaning of the last parent's death: that the child's remaining time has a limit of its own.

But not for Weyland. No graveyards of family dead lay behind him, no obvious and implacable ending of his own span threatened him. Time has to be different for a creature of an enchanted forest, as morality has to be different. He was a predator and a killer formed for a life of centuries, not decades; of secret singularity, not the busy hum of the herd. Yet his strength, suited to that nonhuman life, had revived her own strength. Her hands were slim, no longer youthful, but she saw now that they were strong enough.

For what? She flexed her fingers, watching the tendons slide under the skin. Strong hands don't have to clutch. They can simply open and let go.

She dialed Lucille's extension at the clinic.

"Luce? Sorry to have missed your calls lately. Listen, I want to start making arrangements to transfer my practice for a while. You were right, I do need a break, just as all my friends have been telling me. Will you pass the word for me to the staff over there today? Good, thanks. Also, there's the workshop coming up next month. . . . Yes. Are you kidding? They'd love to have you in my place. You're not the only one who's noticed that I've been falling apart, you know. It's awfully soon—can you manage, do you think? Luce, you are a brick and a lifesaver and all that stuff that means I'm very, very grateful."

Not so terrible, she thought, but only a start. Everything else remained to be dealt with. The glow of euphoria couldn't carry her for long. Already, looking down, she noticed jelly on her blouse, just like old times, and she didn't even remember having breakfast. If you want to keep the strength you've found in all this, you're going to have to get plenty of practice being strong. Try a tough one now.

She phoned Deb. "Of course you slept late, so what? I did, too, so I'm glad you didn't call and wake me up. Whenever you're ready—if you need help moving uptown from the hotel, I can cancel here and come down. . . . Well, call if you change your mind. I've left a house key for you with my doorman.

"And listen, hon, I've been thinking—how about all of us going up together to Nonnie's over the weekend? Then when you feel like it maybe you'd like to talk about what you'll do next. Yes, I've already started setting up some free time for myself. Think about it, love. Talk to you later."

Kenny's turn. "Kenny, I'll come by during visiting hours this afternoon."

"Are you okay?" he squeaked.

"I'm okay. But I'm not your mommy, Ken, and I'm not going to start trying to hold the big bad world off you again. I'll expect you to be ready to settle down seriously and choose a new therapist for yourself. We're going to get that done today once and for all. Have you got that?"

After a short silence he answered in a desolate voice, "All right."

"Kenny, nobody grown up has a mommy around to take care of things for them and keep them safe—not even me. You just have to be tough enough and brave enough yourself. See you this afternoon."

How about Jane Fennerman? No, leave it for now, we are not Wonder Woman, we can't handle that stress today as well.

Too restless to settle down to paperwork before the day's round of appointments began, she got up and fed the goldfish, then drifted to the window and looked out over the city. Same jammed-up traffic down there, same dusty summer park stretching away uptown—yet not the same city, because Weyland no longer hunted there. Nothing like him moved now in those deep, grumbling streets. She would never come upon anyone there as alien as he—and just as well. Let last night stand as the end, unique and inimitable, of their affair. She was glutted with strangeness and looked forward frankly to sharing again in Mort's ordinary human appetite.

And Weyland—how would he do in that new and distant hunting ground he had found for himself? Her own balance had been changed. Suppose his once perfect, solitary equilibrium had been altered too? Perhaps he had spoiled it by involving himself too intimately with another being—herself. And then he had left her alive—a terrible risk. Was this a sign of his corruption at her hands?

"Oh, no," she whispered fiercely, focusing her vision on her reflection in the smudged window glass. Oh, no, I am not the temptress. I am not the deadly female out of legends whose touch defiles the hitherto unblemished being, her victim. If Weyland found some human likeness in himself, that had to be in him to begin with. Who said he was defiled anyway? Newly discovered capacities can be either strengths or weaknesses, depending on how you use them.

Very pretty and reassuring, she thought grimly; but it's pure cant. Am I going to retreat now into mechanical analysis to make myself feel better?

She heaved open the window and admitted the sticky summer breath of the city into the office. There's your enchanted forest, my dear, all nitty-gritty and not one flake of fairy dust. You've survived here, which means you can see straight when you have to. Well, you have to now.

Has he been damaged? No telling yet, and you can't stop living while you wait for the answers to come in. I don't know all that was done between us, but I do know who did it: I did it, and he did it, and neither of us withdrew until it was done. We were joined in a rich complicity—he in the wakening of some flicker of humanity in himself, I in keeping and, yes, enjoying the secret of his implacable blood hunger. What that complicity means for each of us can only be discovered by getting on with living and watching for clues from moment to moment. His business is to continue from here, and mine is to do the same, without guilt and without resentment. Doug was right: the aim is individual responsibility. From that effort, not even the lady and the unicorn are exempt.

Shaken by a fresh upwelling of tears, she thought bitterly, Moving on is easy enough for Weyland; he's used to it, he's had more practice. What about me? Yes, be selfish, woman—if you haven't learned that, you've learned damn little.

The Japanese say that in middle age you should leave the claims of family, friends, and work, and go ponder the meaning of the universe while you still have the chance. Maybe I'll try just existing for a while, and letting grow in its own time my understanding of a universe that includes Weyland—and myself—among its possibilities.

Is that looking out for myself? Or am I simply no longer fit for

living with family, friends, and work? Have *I* been damaged by *him*—
by my marvelous, murderous monster?

Damn, she thought, I wish he were here, I wish we could talk
about it. The light on her phone caught her eye; it was blinking the
quick flashes that meant Hilda was signaling the imminent arrival of—
not Weyland—the day's first client.

We're each on our own now, she thought, shutting the window and
turning on the air-conditioner.

But think of me sometimes, Weyland, thinking of you.

This story was written while I was working on my 1982 anthology, Perpetual Light, *which contained stories of science fiction, fantasy, and horror dealing with the religious experience.*

*The "revelation" of the story perhaps loses some effect here by its
inclusion in a volume of stories about vampires. Even so, I think the
particular question that "Following the Way" raises of the link between
vampirism and Christianity remains an interesting one.*

*Following the Way
(1982)*
BY ALAN RYAN

Twenty years ago, in my senior year at Regis High School—a very fine
and very private Jesuit preparatory school on the upper east side of
Manhattan—vocations to the priesthood were the order of the day. As I
recall, twenty-five or so of the one hundred and fifty members of my
graduating class entered the seminary, most of them, not surprisingly,
choosing the Society of Jesus. Not all of them are priests today. (For
that matter, not all of the Jesuits who taught me at Regis are priests
today.) But vocations were in the air in that school, then half a century
old already, and I suspect that, even today, few boys pass through their
four years of study without at least considering, however briefly, the
possibility of the priesthood. I did. I think we all did. We had behind us,
though immediate in our thoughts, a long and impressive tradition.
And before us we had some very powerful male role models: priests
whom we respected as teachers and scholars, men who had devoted
their lives to God, to an ideal, and to us, men who were clearly happy in
their work, and who were, at the same time, interesting. The exceptions
—sadly and most notably, the headmaster of the school during my four
years there—only emphasized the union of humanity and spirituality in
the others. For a boy with the inclination, the lure was hard to resist.

Those boys who were so inclined naturally sought and found willing advisers among the priests and scholastics on the faculty. But the
rest of us—a spiritually silent majority—were not overlooked by the
ever-thorough Jesuits—oh, no—and, sometime during the first half of
our senior year, each of us was invited into the office of the Jesuit
student counselor for a private chat. (I should stress that there was no
coercion here. At Regis we were seldom "ordered" to do things; rather,

we were "invited.") I remember that, in my case, the priest—a kind, charming, very learned, and often sickly man named William Day—who will figure prominently in this chronicle of my vocation—engaged me in polite conversation for some minutes without raising the question that I knew very well was at hand. The idea was that, if I had been reluctant to acknowledge interest in the priesthood before now, this would be my golden opportunity. I said nothing, and the poor man—as he had no doubt done a hundred times in the previous two weeks—had to broach the subject himself. Had I, he wondered casually, ever considered becoming a priest? Yes, Father, I answered, I had. Ah ha, he said, nodding gently. You've thought about it? Oh, yes, I said. And what conclusion have you reached? It's not for me, I said. Oh, he said, I see, and stopped nodding. And why is that? he asked. Sex, I said. Apparently I said it with such conviction that he was thoroughly convinced of my thinking on the subject and ended the conversation there and then.

But times and people change.

I went from four years with the Jesuits at Regis High School to four years with the Jesuits at Fordham University. The Lincoln Center campus was then only in the planning stage, and I was always glad I missed it. (Leave it to the Jebbies, we joked in the cafeteria, to luck into expensive real estate and a good address.) Like my classmates who accompanied me from Regis, I was happy to exchange East 84th Street for the Rose Hill campus in the north Bronx. The Third Avenue El still rattled past the campus then and the traffic was heavy and noisy on Fordham Road and Webster Avenue, but the campus itself was an island, a green and peaceful island apart from the world outside, firmly anchored in bedrock by the pylons of handsome Kéating Hall, its gray fieldstone blocks and clock tower so quintessentially representative of American college architecture that fashion photographers and TV crews filming commercials were often to be found on its steps. It was a lovely place: the green expanse of Edwards Parade, the rose-covered trellis in the square beside Dealy Hall, the musty antique air of Collins Theatre, the richly detailed chapel that sang aloud to God, all of it peaceful and lovely.

The Jesuit priests there were much the same as those at Regis—a little more worldly, perhaps, a little wittier, a little more acerbic, a little more eccentric, but, in all that mattered, essentially the same. I admired them, admired the wit and the learning and the grace with which they moved through the world, the casual self-assurance, the *flair*. My father had died when I was a child and there were no other male relatives close by, so, lacking a model at home, and primed by four years at Regis, I naturally turned toward these men and sought to emulate them. It was not a bad choice.

I spent most of my time in college—intellectually, at least, and psychologically, I suppose—as a young gentleman in a nineteenth-century novel might have spent his time at Oxford. I wrote some poetry, submitted some stories to *The New Yorker* and the *Atlantic Monthly,* and spent a great deal of time pursuing women. I read—in Greek— Plato and Aristotle and Euripides and, to lighten the mood, Sappho and the poets. (Xenophon and Homer had been amply translated at Regis.) Horace, Catullus, and Livy held sway in Latin class. Ronsard, Racine, Flaubert, Camus, Ionesco, were read in French; Dante in Italian; Chaucer in Middle English. I majored in French for three of the four years, studied linguistics and the gothic novel and early American literature and European history and "gentlemen's biology" and did some Russian on the side, in addition to the equivalent of full majors in philosophy and theology that were required of all undergraduates at the time. Most of my teachers were Jesuit priests.

One afternoon in the spring of my junior year, I was coming down the steps of Keating Hall when I met that same Jesuit who had offered me my golden opportunity to confess a vocation at Regis. I had heard through the Jesuit grapevine that he'd been unwell and was now at Fordham, taking courses and regaining his strength. It was a warm day —not warm by summer standards, but warm for April after winter's chill—but the priest was buttoned up tight in a black raincoat that obviously still had its winter lining in place. I knew him to be in his early forties, but a casual observer might have guessed him ten years older than that. Looks can be deceiving.

"Hello, Father Day."

He slowed his already slow progress up the shallow steps of Keating and mumbled the half-smiled greeting teachers offer former students whom they no longer recall. But I had stopped where I was and apparently something compelled him to raise his eyes to my face, and when he did so, he halted too. Eyes momentarily alive, he scrutinized my face.

"Regis," he said.

I smiled and said yes.

"Three years ago?"

"Yes."

"Of course," he said. His eyes narrowed, and before I could remind him myself, he told me my name, as casually as if I'd last been with him yesterday.

These Jesuits, I thought.

I was about to ask him how he was, but he spoke before I could.

"Sex," he said, and we laughed together, remembering. "Most succinct answer I ever had," he said, "and a good one, a good one."

We stood on the steps, chatting easily and pleasantly. He seemed eager to know how I was doing at Fordham, what I was studying, who my teachers were, what plans I had for the future. In high school there had been much talk about "the Regis spirit," one manifestation of which was the invisible but substantial tie that links alumni whenever they encounter each other in the world in later years. It can make confidants of strangers, this common baggage of shared learning, assumptions, attitudes. Father Day, I knew, was a Regis man himself, and I was warmed by this tangible evidence of the Regis spirit in action. After a few minutes, he suggested that we go to the Campus Center for coffee—his treat—and since I had been heading there myself when we met, I readily agreed.

We sat for two hours, happily telling stories about mutual acquaintances at Regis, stories that often made us laugh as we compared quite different versions of the same events as seen from the sides of students and faculty. Then the conversation gradually drifted back to me and my life at Fordham and my future and I wasn't even surprised when Father Day inquired casually if I had ever thought again about the possibility of a priestly vocation. I had, of course. In a setting like that—spiritual, intellectual, psychological—one does. It was—and here I measure my words with extra caution—a not unattractive possibility. But, still, it was not attractive enough to win me over. My interest in that direction was based primarily on practical and pragmatic considerations, and definitely not on any "call from God to His service" that I had felt. He smiled understandingly when I told him I had thought about it but my conclusion remained the same.

"No harm in asking," he said, and maintained his slight smile.

I agreed.

"And no harm in thinking about it further," he said, the smile unchanged.

I agreed again.

"Will you?" he asked.

"Think about it further?"

"Yes."

"All right," I said, my smile matching his. "Couldn't hurt."

"Right," he said. "Couldn't hurt. Which is the punch line of an old vaudeville joke." He leaned back in his chair. "Ten minutes before he's going on stage, see, this famous comedian dies in his dressing room and the stage manager has to . . ."

We talked another twenty minutes or so before I had to leave for a late class. Even then, as I rose and gathered my books, it did not occur to me that Father Day, when we first met on the steps of Keating Hall, had been heading into the building and had changed his direction entirely to spend two and a half hours talking with me in the cafeteria.

When we parted at the front doors of the Campus Center, we assured each other how good it had been to talk and sincerely wished each other well. We both felt it, I was certain: the Regis spirit, made flesh.

It was three years later and I was twenty-four, a graduate student at UCLA, before I saw him again. Either because I had promised or because it was inevitable, I had indeed been thinking further about the priesthood.

Los Angeles, UCLA, Westwood Village, and Santa Monica (where I had a furnished apartment just off Wilshire Boulevard, about ten blocks from the beach), seem unlikely places to be thinking about withdrawing—to a degree, at least—from the world and devoting one's life to the service of God. I did, however, and although I was aware of the contrast between my own thinking and that of those around me, I continued to consider, if only in a pragmatic way, the possibility of becoming a priest.

The idea had much to recommend it. I was alone in the world now, my mother having died in an automobile accident in Switzerland during the summer following my graduation from Fordham. I went to California an orphan, lacking even brothers, sisters, aunts, uncles, cousins, to form a family. There was, in that regard, no one to take into account but myself. On the other hand, a religious community could readily fill the need for a structure and a sense of purpose and continuity in my life.

Furthermore, my mother's death had left me financially independent as well, thanks to her firm belief in large amounts of travel insurance, and my independence and self-sufficiency made me, I think it fair to say, rather more mature in my judgments than others in their early twenties, and rather more than I might have been myself in different circumstances.

As for the "sex" I had mentioned to Father Day half a dozen years earlier as an overriding factor in my negative decision, it had proved, as I grew older, less of a problem. To speak the truth, I was no virgin, and I think my needs and appetites at the time, during those years, were as normal as anyone else's, which may prove a mystery to laymen who think that priests and future priests are sometimes spared the hunger. They are not; I can vouch for it. But I did find, through necessity of time and circumstance, that the urge can be controlled, not through any secret vice, which is most often only a form of self-torture, serving merely to remind us of what we lack, but through a careful discipline of the will.

In a practical sense, my life was right for the priesthood. In a psychological sense—and a practical one—I was comfortable with the idea; I would teach in any case. In a spiritual sense, it meant nothing at all; I felt no infusion of God's spirit, no call to His service, and began truly to wonder if that last were really needed.

And then, once again, I ran into Father Day.

It was early May, the end of the academic year, the oral exams for my master's degree successfully completed, and nothing before me but a summer of travel. I had driven back to the campus to return some books and was sitting near the entrance to Royce Hall, enjoying the California sun, reading a newspaper, and listening to the noon carillon concert from the undergraduate library. I had nothing to do for the afternoon, nothing to do, in fact, for a week until my plane left for Europe.

I heard a voice speak my name and say, "Well, hello."

I raised my head and there was Father Day.

He looked much the same as he had three years before. In fact, we might almost have been back on the steps of Keating Hall at Fordham, amid the elms and the dogwood, rather than here beside the Spanish architecture of Royce Hall, amid the bird of paradise plants and the palms. He still looked older than his years—the same observation I had made at Fordham, the last time I'd seen him. And he was still somewhat overdressed. The sun was warm, with only a gentle breeze blowing across the campus, but Father Day wore black woolen slacks and a black turtleneck shirt under a battered gray tweed sport jacket. Even discarding the standard clerical garb, as Jesuits feel so free to do, he had not indulged in any great license. He looked, as he had before, like a man recovering from a long illness, which indeed he was. Thin blood, I thought, meant to thicken in the sun. I said it was good to see him and that he was looking well.

We satisfied each other's curiosity and quickly provided basic information. He told me he had been on campus the whole spring term. Nominally, he was here to take courses in comparative religion. Actually, he was in California for a rest to build up his strength. He spent part of his time helping out with light duties—mass and confession—in a parish church in North Hollywood, where he was living now. He was thinking of accepting a teaching position he'd been offered at Loyola University. I told him that, unless a decent teaching position came along for me, I planned to start work on my doctorate in the fall term and, in that case, would no doubt turn into the archetypal perennial student. He smiled a little ruefully and said that it wasn't such a bad life, and then we were laughing together.

And before I realized it, we were once again talking about me and I was, once again, admitting that thoughts of the priesthood were still in my mind. And, again before I realized it, we had strolled from the campus out to Westwood Village and had found a quiet booth in a bar near the Bruin Theatre.

"You keep turning up in my life," I said when we had beers in front of us.

"Twice," he said.

"Twice is almost a pattern."

"Almost," he agreed.

"Maybe you're haunting me."

"Maybe," he said and took a long drink from his glass. "Or maybe God is haunting you through me."

I thought of all the practical reasons I had for taking Holy Orders, and of all the spiritual reasons I lacked. "Not bloody likely," I said.

"Oh?" It's a Jesuit habit to say that; it offers nothing but elicits much.

So I told him, told him all the wide range of my thoughts on the subject, told him how, although I had not reached a definitive conclusion, the inevitable answer, born of inertia, seemed certainly negative. He listened patiently, his face without expression, until I finished.

"So, then, you feel no call to the priesthood, no compulsion. Is that right?"

I shook my head. "None."

"The call can come in any variety of ways," he said. "The path to God is not a straight one."

"And there are many doors in the castle, yes, I know, Father."

"Don't be impatient."

"Sorry."

"Maybe I'm your call."

I looked at him then and, for a long moment, and for the first time, seriously wondered if perhaps he was right, perhaps he was truly haunting me.

"The path to God is not a straight one," I said, and we both smiled and relaxed, the moment of tension gone.

"If we run into each other like this again," he said, "it will definitely be a pattern."

"Indeed," I said.

"Patterns like that must be considered."

"All right," I said, "if we run into each other like this again, I'll grant you it constitutes a pattern."

"And you'll consider it?"

"The pattern?"

"The priesthood."

"Ah," I said. And a moment later: "All right."

"Good," he said. "I think this calls for another beer."

It was not three years this time, but six weeks, before I saw him again.

I took a place in the queue for tickets to the Royal Ballet at Covent Garden and there he was just in front of me. Neither of us realized it until he'd bought his ticket and turned away from the counter. Suddenly there we were. I quickly purchased my own ticket and followed him outside into Floral Street. A minute later, we were established in the Nag's Head a few doors away, two pints of lager before us.

"You're following me," I said. "It's beginning to look slightly sinister."

"Is it?" Jesuits love to ask questions.

"A bit. What are you doing here? I thought you were in Los Angeles."

"I was. Actually, in a way, I still am. I took the faculty position at Loyola and then rather lucked into a university travel grant. It was none of my doing, actually."

"I'll bet," I said lightly.

"Actually," he replied.

He looked, it hardly seems necessary to mention, quite the same as before. The weather in London was cool and damp even in summer, but he was still overdressed. It seemed a permanent feature of his appearance. Apparently the California sun had not succeeded in thickening his blood. I didn't imagine the chilly air of London would accomplish much in that line, but the thought seemed not to have occurred to him.

"Did you follow me here?"

He shook his head, a gentle smile on his lips. "Impossible," he said.

That, of course, was the truth, and I knew it already. Apart from the obvious reasons, if he'd appeared just behind me in the queue, I might have doubted, but he had been there in front of me when I arrived, no question about it, and I did not.

"Then you're haunting me," I said.

"So it appears," he replied. He lifted his glass and in one long drink finished off the beer. "I have to be on my way," he said. "Let's meet for dinner."

We agreed on seven-thirty at Romano Santi in Soho, and a moment later he was gone. I stayed longer in the Nag's Head, ordered another pint and drank it as slowly as the first. After that, I walked over to Charing Cross Road and spent the rest of the afternoon in the National Portrait Gallery. I barely saw the faces in the paintings. I could see only the face of Father Day, haunting me wherever I went.

During the meal, we limited the conversation to general topics. Afterward, he invited me back to his house for drinks. As we rode in the taxi the length of Oxford Street from Soho to Notting Hill Gate, and then pulled up in front of a lovely home in Kensington Park Road which he was renting for the summer, I wondered what sort of travel grant provided that sort of living allowance. These Jesuits, I thought. They're like some fine old family, ripe with old money.

"Shall we sit in the sitting room?" he said as he gestured me inside. "It seems only proper."

By that point, I was half expecting servants, but the house was empty. We'd had chianti with the meal and he suggested a lighter burgundy now. He poured the wine himself. When we were settled in easy chairs, he wasted no time.

"I think you have a vocation," he said. "Perhaps you feel no call, nothing of the sort you've thought all along you ought to feel, but a vocation nonetheless."

"Why?" I asked. I tried to sip my drink calmly.

"Why do you have a vocation or why do I say that?"

"Both." These Jesuits, I thought again. They never stop. It comes with long practice.

"Both," he repeated, in a tone that reminded me of the classroom. "As for the first, why you have a vocation, I couldn't begin to tell you. I almost hate to say it because it sounds entirely too pat, but it's not for us to question the ways of God."

"Just lucky, I guess." I said it as much to provoke him as for anything else.

"I guess," he said, and studied me curiously, as if wondering at the oddness of God's dealings among men. While he studied me, I had the opportunity to do the same with him, and realized that, at least for the moment, he no longer looked as sickly as he had before. He looked, rather, like a man with a definite job to do, a man with a clear purpose.

"As for the second point," he said, "why I'm telling you this, remember that Christ taught us to be fishers of men."

"The wise fisherman doesn't cast his net at random," I said.

"Nicely put."

"Why me, Father?"

"You're the type."

"*What* type?"

"Why, the priestly type, of course."

"That's a tautology."

"You'll make a splendid Jesuit," he laughed. "Here, let me top up your glass."

We sat together in silence for a while, with only the wine and our thoughts.

"Have you not noticed," he said at last, "that I seem to keep recurring in your life? Oh, never mind, of course you have." He leaned forward in his chair. "Answer a question. The Church will last forever, will it not? Until, would it be safe to say, the end of time, at least? Agreed?"

I nodded.

"Why?" he snapped. "How can that be?"

I hesitated, answers that had once seemed so clear—or at least so thoroughly assumed—now failing me.

"I've forgotten a lot of my catechism," I said to cover my hesitation.

"You haven't forgotten *this* catechism," he said. "These are answers you never knew. What is the central fact in your belief?"

"That Christ was the Son of God."

"And?"

"That He died on the cross. The sacrifice of the cross."

"The sacrifice of the cross," he repeated. "And what is the central practice, the central event, of your worship?"

"The Eucharist," I said. "The sacrifice of the mass."

"The sacrifice of the mass. Can you live forever?"

"Yes."

"How?"

"My soul is eternal. Listen, I—"

"You can live forever," he said.

I looked at him.

He said it again, more slowly. "You can live forever."

It was my turn. "How?" I said.

He raised his wine glass toward me. It reflected the light from a lamp and glowed ruby red.

"This is the cup of my blood," he said. "Take and drink of it." He was smiling.

I looked from his face to the glass of wine, held aloft as it might be held above the altar, offered to God and displayed to the faithful, with the words of consecration transforming it to blood.

Of course. At last. Here was the epiphany I'd sought, the obvious thing, long regarded but never seen till now: the realization, revelation, moment, insight, the ancient sacred secret of the Church. I was surprised only in that I felt no surprise.

I thought of all the priests I'd known, thought of all the times I'd been at mass and heard a priest murmur those words, transforming wine into the blood of Jesus Christ. Thought of the cross. Thought of the ages the Church, alone of all institutions, had lasted already. Thought of the ages ahead. And, again very practical, thought of myself standing before an altar, speaking those very same words, ordained with the power of transforming ordinary wine into sacred blood, an endless supply for an endless lifetime. I held my breath a moment, then looked back at Father Day.

"Do the others know?" I asked. "Or is it only the Jesuits?"

When he was done laughing, he caught his breath and said, "Oh, this is definitely not a perfect world. Yes, the others know." And he was off again into gales of laughter.

When he'd caught his breath a second time, he raised his glass in a silent toast. Then he set it down, rose from his chair, and came and stood beside me. He bent forward and gently—very gently—placed his lips against my neck.

This was all some years ago.
What follows is forever.
I am a priest and shall remain so. I rest eternal in the bosom of the Lord. I am following the way. I am satisfied.

RAMSEY CAMPBELL *(born 1946) is generally regarded by both readers and critics as one of the foremost contemporary writers of short horror fiction. As a teenager, he began writing stories in imitation of the style and themes of H. P. Lovecraft. August Derleth, director of Arkham House, published a collection of these stories,* The Inhabitant of the Lake, *in 1964 when Campbell was only eighteen.*

In recent years, Campbell has won wide attention for his novels, which include The Doll Who Ate His Mother *(1976),* The Face That Must Die *(1979; revised edition, 1982),* The Parasite *(1980, published in Great Britain as* To Wake the Dead*),* The Nameless *(1981),* Incarnate *(1983),* Night of the Claw *(1983, published in Great Britain as* Claw *by Jay Ramsey),* Obsession *(1985), and* The Hungry Moon *(1986).*

Still, it is Campbell's short fiction on which his reputation rests. His stories, starkly modern in their focus on gritty urban terror, often set in his native Liverpool, have an uncanny ability to raise goose bumps. Reviewing his collection, Dark Companions, *in the Washington* Post *in 1982, I said that for the characters in Campbell's stories, things are pretty bad to start with . . . and then they get worse.*

The Sunshine Club
(1983)
BY RAMSEY CAMPBELL

"Will this be the last session?" Bent asked.

I closed his file on my desk and glanced at him to detect impatience or a plea, but his eyes had filled with the sunset as with blood. He was intent on the cat outside the window, waiting huddled on the balcony as the spider's cocoon like a soft white marble in one corner of the pane boiled with minute hectic birth. Bent gripped my desk and glared at the cat, which had edged along the balcony from the next office. "It'll kill them, won't it?" Bent demanded. "How can it be so calm?"

"You have an affinity for spiders," I suggested. Of course, I already knew.

"I suppose that ties in with the raw meat."

"As a matter of fact, it does. Yes, to pick up your question, this may well be the last session. I want to take you through what you gave me under hypnosis."

"About the garlic?"

"The garlic, yes, and the crosses."

He winced and managed to catch hold of a smile. "You tell me, then," he said.

"Please sit down for a moment," I said, moving around my desk and intervening between him and the cat. "How was your day?"

"I couldn't work," he muttered. "I stayed awake but I kept thinking of how it'd be in the canteen. All those swines of women laughing and pointing. That's what you've got to get rid of."

"Be assured, I will." I'll have you back at the conveyor belt before you know, I thought: but there are more important fulfilments.

"But they all saw me!" he cried. "Now they'll all look!"

"My dear Mr Bent—no, Clive, may I?—you must remember, Clive, that odder dishes than raw meat are ordered every day in canteens. You could always tell them it was a hangover cure."

"When I don't know why myself? I don't want that meat," he said intensely. "*I* didn't want it."

"Well, at least you came to see me. Perhaps we can find you an alternative to raw meat."

"Yes, yes," he said hopelessly. I waited, staring for a pause at the walls of my office, planed flat by pale green paint. Briefly I felt enclosed with his obsession, and forced myself to remember why. When I looked down I found that the pen in my hand was hurrying lines of crosses across the blotter, and I flipped the blotter onto its face. For a moment I feared a relapse. "Lie down," I suggested, "if it'll put you at your ease."

"I'll try not to fall asleep," he said, and more hopefully, "It's nearly dark." When he'd aligned himself on the couch he glanced down at his hands on his chest. Discovered, they flew apart.

"Relax as completely as you can," I said, "don't worry about how," and watched as his hands crept comfortingly together on his chest. His sleeves dragged at his elbows, and he got up to unbutton his jacket. He'd removed his hat when he entered my office, though with its wide black brim and his gloves and high collar he warded off the sting of sunshine from his shrinking flesh. I'd coaxed his body out of its blackness and his mind was following, probing timidly forth from the defences which had closed around it. "Ready," he called as if we were playing hide and seek.

I placed myself between the couch and the window in order to read his face. "All right, Clive," I said. "Last time you told me about a restaurant where your parents had an argument. Do you remember?"

His face shifted like troubled water. Behind his eyelids he was silent. "Tell me about your parents," I said eventually.

"But you know," said his compressed face. "My father was good to me. Until he couldn't stand the arguments."

"And your mother?"

"She wouldn't let him be!" his face cried blindly. "All those Bibles she knew he didn't want, making out he should be going to church with her when she knew he was afraid——"

"But there was nothing to be afraid of, was there?"

"Nothing. You know that."

"So you see, he was weak. Remember that. Now, why did they fight in the restaurant?"

"I don't know, I can't remember. Tell me! Why won't you tell me?"

"Because it's important that you tell me. At least you can remember the restaurant. Go on, Clive, what was above your head?"

"Chandeliers," he said wearily. A bar of sunset was rising past his eyes.

"What else can you see?"

"Those buckets of ice with bottles in."

"You can't see very much?"

"No, it's too dim. Candles——" His voice hung transfixed.

"Now you can see, Clive! Why?"

"Flames! F—— The flames of hell!"

"You don't believe in hell, Clive. You told me that when you didn't know yourself. Let's try again. Flames?"

"They were—inside them—a man's face on fire, melting! I could see it coming but nobody was looking——"

"Why didn't they look?"

His shuddering head pressed back into the couch. "Because it was meant for me!"

"No, Clive, not at all. Because they knew what it was."

But he wouldn't ask. I waited, glancing at the window so that he would call me back; the minute spiders stirred like uneasy caviar. "Well, tell me," he said coyly, dismally.

"If you were to go into any of a dozen restaurants you'd see your man on fire. Now do you begin to see why you've turned your back on everything your parents took for granted? How old were you then?"

"Nine."

"Is it coming clear?"

"You know I don't understand these things. Help me! I'm paying you!"

"I am, and we're almost there. You haven't even started eating yet."

"I don't want to."

"Of course you do."

"Don't! Not——"

"Not——"

Outside the window, against the tiger-striped blurred sky, the cat tensed to leap. "Not when my father can't," Bent whispered harshly.

"Go on, go on, Clive! Why can't he?"

"Because they won't serve the meat the way he likes."

"And your mother? What is she doing?"

"She's laughing. She says she'll eat anyway. She's watching him as they bring her, oh——" His head jerked.

"Yes?"

"Meat——"

"Yes?"

It might have been a choke or a sob. "Guh! Guh! Garlic!" he cried, and shook.

"Your father? What does he do?"

"He's standing up. Sit down! Don't! She says it all again, how it's sacrilegious to eat blood—— He's, oh, he's pulling the cloth off the table, everything falls on me, everybody's looking, she comes at him, he's got her hair, she bites him then she screams, he smiles, he's smiling, I hate him!" Bent shook and collapsed in the shadows.

"Open your eyes," I said.

They opened wide, trustful, protected by the twilight. "Let me tell you what I see," I said.

"I think I understand some things," he whispered.

"Just listen. Why do you fear garlic and crosses? Because your mother destroyed your father with them. Why do you want and yet not want raw meat? To be like your father who you really knew was weak, to make yourself stronger than the man who was destroyed. But now you know he was weak, you know you are stronger. Stronger than the women who taunt you because they know you're strong. And if you still have a taste for bloody meat, there are places that will serve it to you. The sunlight which you fear? That's the man on fire, who terrified you because you thought your father was destined for hell."

"I know," Bent said. "He was just a waiter cooking."

I switched on the desk-lamp. "Exactly. Do you feel better?"

Perhaps he was feeling his mind to discover whether anything was broken. "Yes, I think so," he said at last.

"You will. Won't you?"

"Yes."

"No hesitation. That's right. But, Clive, I don't want you hesitating when you leave this office. Wait a minute." I took out my wallet. "Here's a card for a club downtown, the Sunshine Club. Say I sent you. You'll find that many of the members have been through something similar to what you've been through. It will help."

"All right," he said, frowning at the card.

"Promise me you'll go."

"I will," he promised. "You know best."

He buttoned his coat. "Will you keep the hat? No, don't keep it. Throw it away," he said with some bravado. At the door he turned and peered past me. "You never explained the spiders."

"Oh, those? Just blood."

I watched his head bob down the nine flights of stairs. Perhaps eventually he would sleep at night and go forth in the daytime, but the important adjustments had been made: he was on the way to accepting what he was. Once again I gave thanks for night shifts. I went back to my desk and tidied Bent's file. Later I might look in at the Sunshine Club, reacquaint myself with Bent and a few faces.

Then, for a moment, I felt sour fear. Bent might encounter Mullen at the club. Mullen was another who had approached me to be cured, not knowing that the only cure was death. As I recalled that Mullen had gone to Greece months before, I relaxed—for I had relieved Mullen of his fears with the same story, the raw meat and the garlic, the parents battling over the Bible. In fact it hadn't happened that way at all—my mother had caused the scene at the dining-room table and there had been a cross—but by now I was more familiar with the working version.

The cat scraped at the window. As I moved toward it, the cat's eyes slitted darkly and it tensed. I waited and then threw the window open. The cat howled and fell. Nine storeys: even a cat could scarcely survive. I stood above the lights of the city, lights clustering toward the dark horizon, and the tiny struggling red spiders streamed out from the window on threads, only to drift back and settle softly, like a rain of blood, on my face.

Nearly a hundred of STEVE RASNIC TEM'*s short stories have been published since his first work appeared in Ramsey Campbell's anthology*
New Terrors *in 1980. His poetic and allusive style has come to be a fine
instrument for creating terror. Already an outstanding writer of short
stories, he began writing novel-length horror fiction with* Excavations
(1986).

The first major showing of Tem's work was in my anthology, Night
Visions 1 *(1984), which contained seven new stories by Tem. "The Men
& Women of Rivendale," in which the word "vampire" notably does not
occur, was one of them.*

The Men & Women of
Rivendale
(1984)
BY STEVE RASNIC TEM

The thing he would remember most about his days, his weeks at the
Rivendale resort—had it really been weeks?—was not the enormous
lobby and dining room, nor the elaborately carved mahogany woodwork framing the library, nor even the men and women of Rivendale
themselves, with their bright eyes and pale, almost hairless, heads and
hands. The thing he would remember most was the room he and Cathy
stayed in, the way she looked when she curled up in bed, her bald head
rising weakly over her shoulders, the way the dark brocade curtains
hung so heavily, trapping dust and light in their intricate folds.

Frank thought he had spent days staring into those folds. He had
only two places to look in that room: at the cancer-ridden sack his wife
had become, her giant eyes, her grotesque, baby-like face, so stripped of
age since she had begun her decline. Or at the curtains, adrift constantly
with shadows. They were of a dark, burgundy-colored material, and he
never knew if they had darkened with dust and age or if they were
meant to be just that shade. If he examined the curtains at close range
he could make out the tiny leaf and shell patterns embroidered over the
entire surface. From a distance, when he sat in the chair or lay on the
bed, they looked like hundreds of tiny, hungry mouths.

Cathy had told him little about the place before they came—that it
was a resort in Pennsylvania, in the countryside south of Erie, and that

it used to have hot springs. He hadn't asked, but he wondered what happened to the spring water when it left such a place. As if somebody somewhere had turned a tap. It didn't make any sense to him; natural things shouldn't work that way.

Her ancestors, the family Rivendale, had run the place when it was still a resort. Now many, perhaps all of her relatives lived in the Rivendale Resort Hotel, or in cottages spotted around the sprawling grounds. Probably several dozen cottages in all. It had been quite a jolt when Frank walked into the place, stumbling over the entrance rug with their luggage wedged under his arms, and saw all these Rivendales sitting around the fireplace in the lobby. It wasn't as if they were clones, or anything like that. But there was this uneasy sort of family resemblance. Something about the fleshtones, the shape of the hands, the perpetually arched eyebrows, the sharp angle at which they held their heads, the irregular pink splotches on their cheeks. It gave him a little chill. After a few days at Rivendale he recognized part of the reason for that chill: the cancer had molded Cathy into a fuzzy copy of a Rivendale.

Frank remembered her as another woman entirely: her hair had been long and honey-brown, and there had been real color in her cheeks. She had been lively, her movements strong and fluid, an incredibly sleek, beautiful woman who could have been a model, though such a public display would have appalled her and, he knew without asking, would have disgraced the Rivendale name.

Cathy had told him that filling up with cancer was like roasting under a hot sun sometimes. The dusty rooms and dark chambers of Rivendale cooled her. They would stay at Rivendale as long as possible, she had said. She could hide from nurses and doctors there.

She wouldn't have surgery. She was a Rivendale; it didn't fit. She washed herself in radiation, and, after Frank met these other Rivendales with their scrubbed and antiseptic flesh, the thought came to him: she'd over-bathed.

She never looked or smelled bad, as he'd expected. The distortions the growing cancer made within the skin that covered it were more subtle than that. Sometimes she complained of her legs suddenly weakening. Sometimes she would scream in the middle of the night. He'd look at her pale form and try to see through her translucent flesh, find the cancer feeding and thriving there.

One result of her treatments was that Cathy's belly blew up. She looked at least six months pregnant, maybe more. It had never occurred to either of them to have children. They'd always had too much to do; a child didn't have a place in the schedule. Sometimes now Frank dreamed he was wheeling her into the delivery room, running, trying to get her to the doctors before her terrible labor ceased. A tall doctor in a brilliant white mask always met him at the wide, swinging doors. The doctor took Cathy away from him but blocked Frank from seeing what kind of child they delivered from her heaving, discolored belly.

Nine months after the cancer was diagnosed, the invitation from the Rivendales was delivered. Cathy, who'd barely mentioned her family in all the years they'd been married, welcomed it with a grim excitement he'd never seen in her before. Frank discovered the invitation in the trash later that afternoon. "Come to Rivendale" was all it said.

One of the uncles greeted her at the desk, although "greeted" was probably the wrong word. He checked her in, as if this were still a resort. Even gave her a room key with the resort tag still attached, although now the leather was cracked and the silver lettering hard to read. Only a few of the relatives had bothered to look up from their reading, their mouths twitching as if they were attempting speech after years of muteness. But no one spoke; no one welcomed them. As far as Frank could tell, no one in the crowded, quiet lobby was speaking to anyone else.

They'd gone up to their room immediately; the trip had exhausted Cathy. Then Frank spent his first of many evenings sitting up in the old chair, staring at Cathy curled up on the bed, and staring at the curtains breathing the breeze from the window, the indecipherable embroidered patterns shifting restlessly.

The next morning they were awakened by a bell ringing downstairs. The sound was so soft Frank at first thought it was a dream, wind-chimes tinkling outside. But Cathy was up immediately, and dressing. Frank did the same, suddenly not wanting to initiate any action by himself. When another bell rang Cathy opened the door and started downstairs, and Frank followed her.

Two places were set for them at one of the long, linen-draped tables. "Cathy" and "Frank," the place cards read. He wondered briefly if there might be someone else staying here by those names, so surprised he was to see his name written on the card in floral script. But Cathy took her chair immediately, and he sat down beside her.

There was a silent toast. When the uncle who had met them at the desk tapped his glass of apple wine lightly with a fork the rest raised their glasses silently to the air, then a beat later tipped them back to drink. Cathy drank in time with the others, and that simple bit of coordination and exaggerated manners made Frank uneasy. He remained one step behind all the others, watching them over the lip of his glass. They didn't seem aware of each other, but they were almost, though not quite, synchronized.

He glanced at Cathy; her cheek had grown pale and taut as she drank. She wasn't eating real food anymore, only a special formula she took like medicine to sustain her. Although her skin was almost baby-smooth now, the lack of fat had left wrinkles that deepened as she moved. Death lines.

After breakfast they lingered by the enormous dining room window. Cathy watched as the Rivendales drifted across the front lawn in twos and threes. Their movements were slow and languid like ancient fish in shallow, sun-drenched waters.

"Shouldn't we introduce ourselves around?" Frank said softly. "I mean, we were invited by someone. How do these people even know who we are?"

"Oh, they know, Frank. Hush now; the Rivendales have always had their own way of doing things. Someone will come to us in time. Meanwhile, we enjoy ourselves."

"Sure."

They took a long walk around the grounds. The pool was closed and covered with canvas. The shuffleboard courts were cracked, the cracks pulled further apart by grass and tree roots. And the tennis courts . . . the tennis courts were his first inkling that perhaps he should be trying to convince her of the need to return home.

The tennis courts at Rivendale were built atop a slight, tree-shaded rise behind the main building. He heard the yowling and screeching as they climbed the rise, so loud that he couldn't make out any individual voices. It frightened him so that he grabbed Cathy by the arm and started back down. But she seemed unperturbed by the noise and shrugged away from him, continuing to walk toward the trees, her pace unchanging.

"Cathy . . . I don't think . . ." But she was oblivious to him.

So Frank followed her, reluctantly. As they neared the fenced enclosure the howling increased, and Frank knew that it wasn't people in there making all the noise, but animals, though he had never heard animal sounds quite like those.

As they passed the last tree Frank stopped, unable to proceed.

Cathy walked right up to the fence. She pressed close to the wire, but not so close the outstretched paws could touch her.

The tennis courts had become a gigantic cage holding hundreds of cats. An old man stood on a ladder above the wire fence, dumping buckets of feed onto the snarling mass inside. Mesh with glass insulators attached—*electrified,* Frank thought—stretched across the top of the fence.

The old man turned to Frank and stared. He had the arched eyebrows, the pale skin and blotched cheeks. He smiled at Frank, and the shape of the lips seemed to match the shape of the eyebrows. A smile shaped like mothwings, or a bite-pattern in pale cheese, the teeth gleaming snow-white inside.

Cathy spent most of each day in the expansive Rivendale library, checking titles most of the time, but occasionally sitting down to read from a rare and privately-bound old volume. Every few hours one of the uncles, or cousins, would come in and speak to her in a low voice, nod, and leave. The longer he was here the more difficult it became to tell the Rivendales apart, other than male from female. The younger ones mirrored the older ones, and they were all very close in height, weight, and build.

When Cathy wasn't in the library she sat quietly in the parlor or dining room, or up in their own room catnapping or staring up at the ornate ceiling. She would say every day, almost ritualistically, that he was more than welcome to be with her, but he could see nothing here that he might participate in. Sitting in the parlor or dining room was made almost unbearable by the presence of the family, arranged mummy-like around the rooms. Sometimes he would pick up a volume in the library, but invariably discovered it was some sort of laborious tome on trellis and ornate gardening, French architecture, museum catalogs. Or sometimes an old leather-bound novel that read no better. It was impossible to peruse the books without thinking that whatever Cathy was studying must be far more interesting, but on the days he went he never could find the books she had been looking at, as if they had been kept somewhere special, out of his reach. And for some reason he hesitated to ask after them, or to look over his wife's shoulder as she read. As if he was afraid to.

This growing climate of awkwardness and fear angered Frank so that his neck muscles were always stiff, his head always aching. It was worse because it wasn't entirely unexpected. His relationship with

Cathy had been going in this direction for some time. Until he'd met Cathy, he'd almost always been bored. As a child, always needing to be entertained. As an adult, constantly changing lovers and houses and jobs. Now it was happening again, and it frightened him.

The increasing boredom that was beginning to permeate his stay at Rivendale, in fact, had begun to impress on him how completely, utterly bored he had been in his married life. He'd almost forgotten, so preoccupied he'd become with her disease. When Cathy's cancer had first begun, and started to spread, that boredom had dissipated. Perversely, the cancer had brought something new and near-dramatic into their life together. He'd felt bad at first: Cathy, in her baldness, in her body that seemed, impossibly, both emaciated and swollen, had suddenly become sensuous to him again. He wanted to make love to her almost all the time. After the first few times, he had stopped the attempts, afraid to ask her. But as she approached death, his desire increased.

Sometimes Frank sat out on the broad resort lawn, his lounge chair positioned under a low-hanging tree only twenty or so feet away from the library window. He'd watch her as she sat at one of the enormous oak tables, poring over the books, consulting with various elderly Rivendales who drifted in and out of that room in a seemingly endless stream. He'd heard one phrase outside the library, when the Rivendales didn't know he was near, or perhaps he had dreamed his eavesdropping while lying abed late one morning, or fallen asleep midafternoon in his hiding place under the tree. "Family histories."

The pale face with the near-hairless pate that floated as if suspended in that library window bore no resemblance to the Cathy he had known, with her dark eyes and nervous gestures and narrow mouth quick to twist ugly and vituperative. They'd discovered it was so much easier to become excited by anger, rage, and all the small cruelties possible in married life, then by love. They'd had a bad fight on their very first date. He found himself asking her out again in the very heat of the argument. She'd stared at him wide-eyed and breathless for some time, then grudgingly accepted.

Throughout the following weeks their fights grew worse. Once he'd slapped her, something he would never have imagined himself doing, and she'd fallen sobbing into his arms. They made love for hours. It became a delirious pattern. The screams, the cries, the ineffectual hitting, then the sweet tickle and swallow of a lust that dragged them red-eyed through the night.

Marriage was a great institution. It gave you the opportunity to experience both sadism and masochism within the privacy and safety of your own home.

"What do you want from me, you bastard!" Cathy's teeth flashed, pinkly . . . her lipstick was running, he thought. Frank held her head down against the mattress, watching her tongue flicking back and forth over her teeth. He was trapped.

Her leg came up and knocked him off the bed. He tried to roll away but before he could move she had straddled him, pinning him to the floor. "Off! Get off!" He couldn't catch his breath. He suddenly realized her forearm was wedged between his neck and the floor, cutting off the air. His vision blurred quickly and the pressure began to build in his face.

"Frank . . ."

He could barely hear her. He thought he might actually die this time. It was another bad joke; he almost laughed. She was the one who was always talking about dying; she could be damned melodramatic about it. She was the one with the death wish.

He opened his eyes and stared up at her. She was fumbling with his shirt, pulling it loose, ripping the buttons off. Maybe she was trying to save him.

Then he got a better look at her: the feverish eyes, the slackening jawline, tongue flicking, eyes glazed. Now she was tugging frantically at his belt. It all seemed very familiar and ritualized. He searched her eyes and did not think she even saw him.

"Frank . . ."

He woke with a start and stared across the lawn at the library window. Cathy's pale face stared back at him, surrounded by her even paler brethren, their mouths moving soundlessly, fish-like. He thought he could hear the soft clinking of breaking glass, or hundreds of tiny mouths trying their teeth.

The thing he would remember most was this room, and the Rivendales watching. They had a peculiar way of watching; they were very polite about it, for if nothing else they were gentlemen and ladies, these Rivendales. Theirs was an ancient etiquette, developed through practice and interaction with human beings of all eras and climes. Long before he met Cathy they had known him, followed him, for they had intimate knowledge of his type. Or so he imagined it.

Each afternoon there was one who especially drew Frank's attention: an old one, his eyebrows fraying away with the heat like tattered moth wings. He walked the same path each day, wearing it down into a seamless pavement, and only by a slight pause at a particular point on the path did Frank know the old man Rivendale was watching him. Listening to him. And that old one's habitual, everyday patterns were what made Frank wonder if the world might be full of Rivendales, assigned to watch, and recruit.

He was beginning—with excitement—to recognize them, to guess at what they were. They would always feed, and feed viciously, but their hunger was so great they would never be filled, no matter how many lives they emptied, no matter how many dying relationships they so intimately observed. Like an internal cancer, their bland surfaces concealed an inner, parasitic excitement. They could not generate their own. They couldn't even generate their own kind; they had to infect others in order to multiply.

Frank had always imagined their type to be feral, with impossibly long teeth, and foul, blood-tainted breath. But they had manners, promising a better life, and a cold excitement one need not work for.

He was, after all, one of them. A Rivendale by habit, if not by blood. The thought terrified.

The thing he would remember most was the room, and the way she looked curled up in bed, her bald head rising weakly over her shoulders.

"I have to leave, Cathy. This is crazy."

He'd been packing for fifteen minutes, hoping she'd say something. But the only sounds in the room were those of the shirts and pants being pulled out from drawers and collapsed haphazardly into his suitcase. And the sound the breeze from the window made pushing out the heavy brocade curtains, making the tiny leaf and shell pattern breathe, sigh, the tiny mouths chatter.

And the sound of her last gasp, her last breath trying to escape the confines of the room, escape the family home before their mouths caught her and fed.

"Cathy . . ." Shadows moved behind the bed. It bothered him he couldn't see her eyes. "There was no love anyway . . . you understand what I'm saying?" Tiny red eyes flickered in the darkness. Dozens of pairs. "The fighting is the only thing that kept us together; it kept the boredom away. And I haven't felt like fighting you for some time." The quiet plucked at his nerves. "Cathy?"

He stopped putting his things into the suitcase. He let several pairs of socks fall to the floor. There were tiny red eyes fading into the shadows. And mouths. There was no other excitement out there for him; he couldn't do it on his own. No other defense against the awesome, all-encompassing boredom. The Rivendales had judged him well.

Cathy shifted in the bed. He could see the shadow of her terrible swollen belly as it pushed against the dusty sheets and raised the heavy covers. He could see the paleness of her skin. He could see her teeth. But he could not hear her breathe. He lifted his knee and began the long climb across the bedspread, his hands shaking, yet anxious to give themselves up for her.

He would remember the bite marks in the cool night air, the mouths in the dark brocade. He would remember his last moment of panic just before he gave himself up to this new excitement. The thing he would remember most was the room.

TANITH LEE *(born 1947) began her career in England writing stories for young readers, but with the American publication of her first adult novel,* The Birthgrave *(1975), she won an instant reputation as a fantasist. A prolific author, Lee followed up her first success with a long list of novels that cover the range of science fiction, fantasy, horror, and sword-and-sorcery.*

Her short novel Sabella, or the Blood Stone *(1980) crosses genre categories as it tells the tale—erotic, colorful, and intense, like most of Lee's stories—of a female vampire on a future Mars.*

"Bite-Me-Not" is a good example of Lee's rich style and imagination and promises to be one of the most memorable vampire tales of the 1980s.

Bite-Me-Not
or, Fleur De Feu
(1984)
BY TANITH LEE

CHAPTER I

In the tradition of young girls and windows, the young girl looks out of this one. It is difficult to see anything. The panes of the window are heavily leaded, and secured by a lattice of iron. The stained glass of lizard-green and storm-purple is several inches thick. There is no red glass in the window. The colour red is forbidden in the castle. Even the sun, behind the glass, is a storm sun, a green-lizard sun.

The young girl wishes she had a gown of palest pastel rose—the nearest affinity to red which is never allowed. Already she has long dark beautiful eyes, a long white neck. Her long dark hair is however hidden in a dusty scarf and she wears rags. She is a scullery maid. As she scours dishes and mops stone floors, she imagines she is a princess floating through the upper corridors, gliding to the dais in the Duke's hall. The Cursed Duke. She is sorry for him. If he had been her father, she would have sympathized and consoled him. His own daughter is dead, as his wife is dead, but these things, being to do with the cursing, are never spoken of. Except, sometimes, obliquely.

"Rohise!" dim voices cry now, full of dim scolding soon to be actualized.

The scullery maid turns from the window and runs to have her ears boxed and a broom thrust into her hands.

Meanwhile, the Cursed Duke is prowling his chamber, high in the East Turret carved with swans and gargoyles. The room is lined with books, swords, lutes, scrolls, and has two eerie portraits, the larger of which represents his wife, and the smaller his daughter. Both ladies look much the same with their pale, egg-shaped faces, polished eyes, clasped hands. They do not really look like his wife or daughter, nor really remind him of them.

There are no windows at all in the turret, they were long ago bricked up and covered with hangings. Candles burn steadily. It is always night in the turret. Save, of course, by night there are particular *sounds* all about it, to which the Duke is accustomed, but which he does not care for. By night, like most of his court, the Cursed Duke closes his ears with softened tallow. However, if he sleeps, he dreams, and hears in the dream the beating of wings. . . . Often, the court holds loud revel all night long.

The Duke does not know Rohise the scullery maid has been thinking of him. Perhaps he does not even know that a scullery maid is capable of thinking at all.

Soon the Duke descends from the turret and goes down, by various stairs and curving passages, into a large, walled garden on the east side of the castle.

It is a very pretty garden, mannered and manicured, which the gardeners keep in perfect order. Over the tops of the high, high walls, where delicate blooms bell the vines, it is just possible to glimpse the tips of sun-baked mountains. But by day the mountains are blue and spiritual to look at, and seem scarcely real. They might only be inked on the sky.

A portion of the Duke's court is wandering about in the garden, playing games or musical instruments, or admiring painted sculptures, or the flora, none of which is red. But the Cursed Duke's court seems vitiated this noon. Nights of revel take their toll.

As the Duke passes down the garden, his courtiers acknowledge him deferentially. He sees them, old and young alike, all doomed as he is, and the weight of his burden increases.

At the furthest, most eastern end of the garden, there is another garden, sunken and rather curious, beyond a wall with an iron door.

Only the Duke possesses the key to this door. Now he unlocks it and goes through. His courtiers laugh and play and pretend not to see. He shuts the door behind him.

The sunken garden, which no gardener ever tends, is maintained by other, spontaneous, means. It is small and square, lacking the hedges and the paths of the other, the sundials and statues and little pools. All the sunken garden contains is a broad paved border, and at its center a small plot of humid earth. Growing in the earth is a slender bush with slender velvet leaves.

The Duke stands and looks at the bush only a short while.

He visits it every day. He has visited it every day for years. He is waiting for the bush to flower. Everyone is waiting for this. Even Rohise, the scullery maid, is waiting, though she does not, being only sixteen, born in the castle and uneducated, properly understand why.

The light in the little garden is dull and strange, for the whole of it is roofed over by a dome of thick smoky glass. It makes the atmosphere somewhat depressing, although the bush itself gives off a pleasant smell, rather resembling vanilla.

Something is cut into the stone rim of the earth-plot where the bush grows. The Duke reads it for perhaps the thousandth time. *O, fleur de feu—*

When the Duke returns from the little garden into the large garden, locking the door behind him, no one seems truly to notice. But their obeisances now are circumspect.

One day, he will perhaps emerge from the sunken garden leaving the door wide, crying out in a great voice. But not yet. Not today.

The ladies bend to the bright fish in the pools, the knights pluck for them blossoms, challenge each other to combat at chess, or wrestling, discuss the menagerie lions; the minstrels sing of unrequited love. The pleasure garden is full of one long and weary sigh.

"Oh flurda fur

"Pourma souffrance—"

Sings Rohise as she scrubs the flags of the pantry floor.

"Ned ormey par,

"May say day mwar—"

"What are you singing, you slut?" someone shouts, and kicks over her bucket.

Rohise does not weep. She tidies her bucket and soaks up the spilled water with her cloths. She does not know what the song, because of which she seems, apparently, to have been chastised, means. She does not understand the words that somehow, somewhere—perhaps from her own dead mother—she learned by rote.

In the hour before sunset, the Duke's hall is lit by flambeaux. In the high windows, the casements of oil-blue and lavender glass and glass like storms and lizards, are fastened tight. The huge window by the dais was long ago obliterated, shut up, and a tapestry hung of gold and silver tissue with all the rubies pulled out and emeralds substituted. It describes the subjugation of a fearsome unicorn by a maiden, and huntsmen.

The court drifts in with its clothes of rainbow from which only the color red is missing.

Music for dancing plays. The lean pale dogs pace about, alert for tidbits as dish on dish comes in. Roast birds in all their plumage glitter and die a second time under the eager knives. Pastry castles fall. Pink and amber fruits, and green fruits and black, glow beside the goblets of fine yellow wine.

The Cursed Duke eats with care and attention, not with enjoyment. Only the very young of the castle still eat in that way, and there are not so many of those.

The murky sun slides through the stained glass. The musicians strike up more wildly. The dances become boisterous. Once the day goes out, the hall will ring to *chanson,* to drum and viol and pipe. The dogs will bark, no language will be uttered except in a bellow. The lions will roar from the menagerie. On some nights the cannons are set off from the battlements, which are now all of them roofed in, fired out through narrow mouths just wide enough to accommodate them, the charge crashing away in thunder down the darkness.

By the time the moon comes up and the castle rocks to its own cacophony, exhausted Rohise has fallen fast asleep in her cupboard bed in the attic. For years, from sunset to rise, nothing has woken her. Once, as a child, when she had been especially badly beaten, the pain woke her and she heard a strange silken scratching, somewhere over her head. But she thought it a rat, or a bird. Yes, a bird, for later it seemed to her there were also wings. . . . But she forgot all this half a decade ago. Now she sleeps deeply and dreams of being a princess, forgetting, too, how the Duke's daughter died. Such a terrible death, it is better to forget.

"The sun shall not smite thee by day, neither the moon by night," intones the priest, eyes rolling, his voice like a bell behind the Duke's shoulder.

"Ne moi mords pas," whispers Rohise in her deep sleep. "Ne mwar mor par, ne par mor mwar. . . ."

And under its impenetrable dome, the slender bush has closed its fur leaves also to sleep. O flower of fire, oh fleur de fur. Its blooms, though it has not bloomed yet, bear the ancient name *Nona Mordica*. In light parlance they call it Bite-Me-Not. There is a reason for that.

CHAPTER II

He is the Prince of a proud and savage people. The pride they acknowledge, perhaps they do not consider themselves to be savages, or at least believe that savagery is the proper order of things.

Feroluce, that is his name. It is one of the customary names his kind give their lords. It has connotations with diabolic royalty and, too, with a royal flower of long petals curved like scimitars. Also the name might be the partial anagram of another name. The bearer of that name was also winged.

For Feroluce and his people are winged beings. They are more like a nest of dark eagles than anything, mounted high among the rocky pilasters and pinnacles of the mountain. Cruel and magnificent, like eagles, the somber sentries motionless as statuary on the ledge-edges, their sable wings folded about them.

They are very alike in appearance (less a race or tribe, more a flock, an unkindness of ravens). Feroluce also, black-winged, black-haired, aquiline of feature, standing on the brink of star-dashed space, his eyes burning through the night like all the eyes along the rocks, depthless red as claret.

They have their own traditions of art and science. They do not make or read books, fashion garments, discuss God or metaphysics or men. Their cries are mostly wordless and always mysterious, flung out like ribbons over the air as they wheel and swoop and hang in wicked cruciform, between the peaks. But they sing, long hours, for whole nights at a time, music that has a language only they know. All their wisdom and theosophy, and all their grasp of beauty, truth or love, is in the singing.

They look unloving enough, and so they are. Pitiless fallen angels. A traveling people, they roam after sustenance. Their sustenance is blood. Finding a castle, they accepted it, every bastion and wall, as their prey. They have preyed on it and tried to prey on it for years.

In the beginning, their calls, their songs, could lure victims to the feast. In this way, the tribe or unkindness of Feroluce took the Duke's wife, somnambulist, from a midnight balcony. But the Duke's daughter, the first victim, they found seventeen years ago, benighted on the mountain side. Her escort and herself they left to the sunrise, marble figures, the life drunk away.

Now the castle is shut, bolted and barred. They are even more attracted by its recalcitrance (a woman who says "No"). They do not intend to go away until the castle falls to them.

By night, they fly like huge black moths round and round the carved turrets, the dull-lit leaded windows, their wings invoking a cloudy tindery wind, pushing thunder against thundery glass.

They sense they are attributed to some sin, reckoned a punishing curse, a penance, and this amuses them at the level whereon they understand it.

They also sense something of the flower, the *Nona Mordica*. Vampires have their own legends.

But tonight Feroluce launches himself into the air, speeds down the sky on the black sails of his wings, calling, a call like laughter or derision. This morning, in the tween-time before the light began and the sun-to-be drove him away to his shadowed eyrie in the mountain-guts, he saw a chink in the armour of the beloved refusing-woman-prey. A window, high in an old neglected tower, a window with a small eyelet which was cracked.

Feroluce soon reaches the eyelet and breathes on it, as if he would melt it. (His breath is sweet. Vampires do not eat raw flesh, only blood, which is a perfect food and digests perfectly, while their teeth are sound of necessity.) The way the glass mists at breath intrigues Feroluce. But presently he taps at the cranky pane, taps, then claws. A piece breaks away, and now he sees how it should be done.

Over the rims and upthrusts of the castle, which is only really another mountain with caves to Feroluce, the rumble of the Duke's revel drones on.

Feroluce pays no heed. He does not need to reason, he merely knows, *that* noise masks *this*—as he smashes in the window. Its panes were all faulted and the lattice rusty. It is, of course, more than that. The magic of Purpose has protected the castle, and, as in all balances, there must be, or come to be, some balancing contradiction, some fiaw. . . .

The people of Feroluce do not notice what he is at. In a way, the dance with their prey has debased to a ritual. They have lived almost two decades on the blood of local mountain beasts, and bird-creatures like themselves brought down on the wing. Patience is not, with them, a virtue. It is a sort of foreplay, and can go on, in pleasure, a long, long while.

Feroluce intrudes himself through the slender window. Muscularly slender himself, and agile, it is no feat. But the wings catch, are a trouble. They follow him because they must, like two separate entities. They have been cut a little on the glass, and bleed.

He stands in a stony small room, shaking bloody feathers from him, snarling, but without sound.

Then he finds the stairway and goes down.

There are dusty landings and neglected chambers. They have no smell of life. But then there comes to be a smell. It is the scent of a nest, a colony of things, wild creatures, in constant proximity. He recognizes it. The light of his crimson eyes precedes him, deciphering blackness. And then other eyes, amber, green and gold, spring out like stars all across his path.

Somewhere an old torch is burning out. To the human eye, only mounds and glows would be visible, but to Feroluce, the Prince of the vampires, all is suddenly revealed. There is a great stone area, barred with bronze and iron, and things stride and growl behind the bars, or chatter and flee, or only stare. And there, without bars, though bound by ropes of brass to rings of brass, three brazen beasts.

Feroluce, on the steps of the menagerie, looks into the gaze of the Duke's lions. Feroluce smiles, and the lions roar. One is the king, its mane like war-plumes. Feroluce recognizes the king and the king's right to challenge, for this is the lions' domain, their territory.

Feroluce comes down the stair and meets the lion as it leaps the length of its chain. To Feroluce, the chain means nothing, and since he has come close enough, very little either to the lion.

To the vampire Prince the fight is wonderful, exhilarating and meaningful, intellectual even, for it is colored by nuance, yet powerful as sex.

He holds fast with his talons, his strong limbs wrapping the beast which is almost stronger than he, just as its limbs wrap him in turn. He sinks his teeth in the lion's shoulder, and in fierce rage and bliss begins to draw out the nourishment. The lion kicks and claws at him in turn. Feroluce feels the gouges like fire along his shoulders, thighs, and hugs the lion more nearly as he throttles and drinks from it, loving it, jealous of it, killing it. Gradually the mighty feline body relaxes, still clinging to him, its cat teeth bedded in one beautiful swanlike wing, forgotten by both.

In a welter of feathers, stripped skin, spilled blood, the lion and the angel lie in embrace on the menagerie floor. The lion lifts its head, kisses the assassin, shudders, lets go.

Feroluce glides out from under the magnificent deadweight of the cat. He stands. And pain assaults him. His lover has severely wounded him.

Across the menagerie floor, the two lionesses are crouched. Beyond them, a man stands gaping in simple terror, behind the guttering torch. He had come to feed the beasts, and seen another feeding, and now is paralyzed. He is deaf, the menagerie-keeper, previously an advantage saving him the horror of nocturnal vampire noises.

Feroluce starts toward the human animal swifter than a serpent, and checks. Agony envelops Feroluce and the stone room spins. Involuntarily, confused, he spreads his wings for flight, there in the confined chamber. But only one wing will open. The other, damaged and partly broken, hangs like a snapped fan. Feroluce cries out, a beautiful singing note of despair and anger. He drops fainting at the menagerie keeper's feet.

The man does not wait for more. He runs away through the castle, screaming invective and prayer, and reaches the Duke's hall and makes the whole hall listen.

All this while, Feroluce lies in the ocean of almost-death that is sleep or swoon, while the smaller beasts in the cages discuss him, or seem to.

And when he is raised, Feroluce does not wake. Only the great drooping bloody wings quiver and are still. Those who carry him are more than ever revolted and frightened, for they have seldom seen blood. Even the food for the menagerie is cooked almost black. Two years ago, a gardener slashed his palm on a thorn. He was banished from the court for a week.

But Feroluce, the center of so much attention, does not rouse. Not until the dregs of the night are stealing out through the walls. Then some nervous instinct invests him. The sun is coming and this is an open place, he struggles through unconsciousness and hurt, through the deepest most bladed waters, to awareness.

And finds himself in a huge bronze cage, the cage of some animal appropriated for the occasion. Bars, bars all about him, and not to be got rid of, for he reaches to tear them away and cannot. Beyond the bars, the Duke's hall, which is only a pointless cold glitter to him in the maze of pain and dying lights. Not an open place, in fact, but too open for his kind. Through the window-spaces of thick glass, muddy sunglare must come in. To Feroluce it will be like swords, acids, and burning fire—

Far off he hears wings beat and voices soaring. His people search for him, call and wheel and find nothing.

Feroluce cries out, a gravel shriek now, and the persons in the hall rush back from him, calling on God. But Feroluce does not see. He has tried to answer his own. Now he sinks down again under the coverlet of his broken wings, and the wine-red stars of his eyes go out.

CHAPTER III

"And the Angel of Death," the priest intones, "shall surely pass over, but yet like the shadow, not substance—"

The smashed window in the old turret above the menagerie tower has been sealed with mortar and brick. It is a terrible thing that it was for so long overlooked. A miracle that only one of the creatures found and entered by it. God, the Protector, guarded the Cursed Duke and his court. And the magic that surrounds the castle, that too held fast. For from the possibility of a disaster was born a bloom of great value: Now one of the monsters is in their possession. A prize beyond price.

Caged and helpless, the fiend is at their mercy. It is also weak from its battle with the noble lion, which gave its life for the castle's safety (and will be buried with honour in an ornamented grave at the foot of the Ducal family tomb). Just before the dawn came, the Duke's advisers advised him, and the bronze cage was wheeled away into the darkest area of the hall, close by the dais where once the huge window was but is no more. A barricade of great screens was brought, and set around the cage, and the top of it covered. No sunlight now can drip into the prison to harm the specimen. Only the Duke's ladies and gentlemen steal in around the screens and see, by the light of a candlebranch, the demon still lying in its trance of pain and bloodloss. The Duke's alchemist sits on a stool nearby, dictating many notes to a nervous apprentice. The alchemist, and the apothecary for that matter, are convinced

the vampire, having drunk the lion almost dry, will recover from its
wounds. Even the wings will mend.

The Duke's court painter also came. He was ashamed presently,
and went away. The beauty of the demon affected him, making him
wish to paint it, not as something wonderfully disgusting, but as a kind
of superlative man, vital and innocent, or as Lucifer himself, stricken in
the sorrow of his colossal Fall. And all that has caused the painter to
pity the fallen one, mere artisan that the painter is, so he slunk away.
He knows, since the alchemist and the apothecary told him, what is to
be done.

Of course much of the castle knows. Though scarcely anyone has
slept or sought sleep, the whole place rings with excitement and vivacity. The Duke has decreed, too, that everyone who wishes shall be a
witness. So he is having a progress through the castle, seeking every
nook and cranny, while, let it be said, his architect takes the opportunity to check no other windowpane has cracked.

From room to room the Duke and his entourage pass, through
corridors, along stairs, through dusty attics and musty storerooms he
has never seen, or if seen has forgotten. Here and there some retainer is
come on. Some elderly women are discovered spinning like spiders up
under the eaves, half-blind and complacent. They curtsy to the Duke
from a vague recollection of old habit. The Duke tells them the good
news, or rather, his messenger, walking before, announces it. The ancient women sigh and whisper, are left, probably forget. Then again, in
a narrow courtyard, a simple boy, who looks after a dovecote, is magnificently told. He has a fit from alarm, grasping nothing; and the doves
who love and understand him (by not trying to) fly down and cover him
with their soft wings as the Duke goes away. The boy comes to under
the doves as if in a heap of warm snow, comforted.

It is on one of the dark staircases above the kitchen that the gleaming entourage sweeps round a bend and comes on Rohise the scullery
maid, scrubbing. In these days, when there are so few children and
young servants, labor is scarce, and the scullerers are not confined to
the scullery.

Rohise stands up, pale with shock, and for a wild instant thinks
that, for some heinous crime she has committed in ignorance, the Duke
has come in person to behead her.

"Hear then, by the Duke's will," cries the messenger. "One of
Satan's night-demons, which do torment us, has been captured and lies
penned in the Duke's hall. At sunrise tomorrow, this thing will be taken

to that sacred spot where grows the bush of the Flower of the Fire, and here its foul blood shall be shed. Who then can doubt the bush will blossom, and save us all, by the Grace of God."

"And the Angel of Death," intones the priest, on no account to be omitted, "shall surely—"

"Wait," says the Duke. He is as white as Rohise. "Who is this?" he asks. "Is it a ghost?"

The court stare at Rohise, who nearly sinks in dread, her scrubbing rag in her hand.

Gradually, despite the rag, the rags, the rough hands, the court too begins to see.

"Why, it is a marvel."

The Duke moves forward. He looks down at Rohise and starts to cry. Rohise thinks he weeps in compassion at the awful sentence he is here to visit on her, and drops back on her knees.

"No, no," says the Duke tenderly. "Get up. Rise. You are so like my child, my daughter—"

Then Rohise, who knows few prayers, begins in panic to sing her little song as an orison:

"Oh fleur de feu
"Pour ma souffrance—"

"Ah!" says the Duke. "Where did you learn that song?"

"From my mother," says Rohise. And, all instinct now, she sings again:

"O flurda fur,

"Pourma souffrance

"Ned ormey par

"May say day mwar—"

It is the song of the fire-flower bush, the *Nona Mordica*, called Bite-Me-Not. It begins, and continues: *O flower of fire, For my misery's sake, Do not sleep but aid me; wake!* The Duke's daughter sang it very often. In those days the shrub was not needed, being just a rarity of the castle. Invoked as an amulet, on a mountain road, the rhyme itself had besides proved useless.

The Duke takes the dirty scarf from Rohise's hair. She is very, very like his lost daughter, the same pale smooth oval face, the long white neck and long dark polished eyes, and the long dark hair. (Or is it that she is very, very like the painting?)

The Duke gives instructions and Rohise is borne away.

In a beautiful chamber, the door of which has for seventeen years been locked, Rohise is bathed and her hair is washed. Oils and scents are rubbed into her skin. She is dressed in a gown of palest most pastel rose, with a girdle sewn with pearls. Her hair is combed, and on it is set a chaplet of stars and little golden leaves. "Oh, your poor hands," say the maids, as they trim her nails. Rohise has realized she is not to be executed. She has realized the Duke has seen her and wants to love her like his dead daughter. Slowly, an uneasy stir of something, not quite happiness, moves through Rohise. Now she will wear her pink gown, now she will sympathize with and console the Duke. Her daze lifts suddenly.

The dream has come true. She dreamed of it so often it seems quite normal. The scullery was the thing which never seemed real.

She glides down through the castle and the ladies are astonished by her grace. The carriage of her head under the starry coronet is exquisite. Her voice is quiet and clear and musical, and the foreign tone of her mother, long unremembered, is quite gone from it. Only the roughened hands give her away, but smoothed by unguents, soon they will be soft and white.

"Can it be she is truly the princess returned to flesh?"

"Her life was taken so early—yes, as they believe in the Spice-Lands, by some holy dispensation, she might return."

"She would be about the age to have been conceived the very night the Duke's daughter d— That is, the very night the bane began—"

Theosophical discussion ensues. Songs are composed.

Rohise sits for a while with her adoptive father in the East Turret, and he tells her about the books and swords and lutes and scrolls, but not about the two portraits. Then they walk out together, in the lovely garden in the sunlight. They sit under a peach tree, and discuss many things, or the Duke discusses them. That Rohise is ignorant and uneducated does not matter at this point. She can always be trained. She has the basic requirements: docility, sweetness. There are many royal maidens in many places who know as little as she.

The Duke falls asleep under the peach tree. Rohise listens to the lovesongs her own (her very own) courtiers bring her.

When the monster in the cage is mentioned, she nods as if she knows what they mean. She supposes it is something hideous, a scaring treat to be shown at dinner time, when the sun has gone down.

When the sun moves towards the western line of mountains just visible over the high walls, the court streams into the castle and all the doors are bolted and barred. There is an eagerness tonight in the concourse.

As the light dies out behind the colored windows that have no red in them, covers and screens are dragged away from a bronze cage. It is wheeled out into the center of the great hall.

Cannons begin almost at once to blast and bang from the roofholes. The cannoneers have had strict instructions to keep up the barrage all night without a second's pause.

Drums pound in the hall. The dogs start to bark. Rohise is not surprised by the noise, for she has often heard it from far up, in her attic, like a sea-wave breaking over and over through the lower house.

She looks at the cage cautiously, wondering what she will see. But she sees only a heap of blackness like ravens, and then a tawny dazzle, torchlight on something like human skin. "You must not go down to look," says the Duke protectively, as his court pours about the cage. Someone pokes between the bars with a gemmed cane, trying to rouse the nightmare which lies quiescent there. But Rohise must be spared this.

So the Duke calls his actors, and a slight, pretty play is put on throughout dinner, before the dais, shutting off from the sight of Rohise the rest of the hall, where the barbaric gloating and goading of the court, unchecked, increases.

CHAPTER IV

The Prince Feroluce becomes aware between one second and the next. It is the sound—heard beyond all others—of the wings of his people beating at the stones of the castle. It is the wings which speak to him, more than their wild orchestral voices. Besides these sensations, the anguish of healing and the sadism of humankind are not much.

Feroluce opens his eyes. His human audience, pleased, but afraid and squeamish, backs away, and asks each other for the two thousandth time if the cage is quite secure. In the torchlight the eyes of Feroluce are more black than red. He stares about. He is, though captive, imperious. If he were a lion or a bull, they would admire this 'nobility.' But the fact is, he is too much like a man, which serves to point up his supernatural differences unbearably.

Obviously, Feroluce understands the gist of his plight. Enemies have him penned. He is a show for now, but ultimately to be killed, for with the intuition of the raptor he divines everything. He had thought the sunlight would kill him, but that is a distant matter, now. And beyond all, the voices and the voices of the wings of his kindred beat the air outside this room-caved mountain of stone.

And so, Feroluce commences to sing, or at least, this is how it seems to the rabid court and all the people gathered in the hall. It seems he sings. It is the great communing call of his kind, the art and science and religion of the winged vampires, his means of telling them, or attempting to tell them, what they must be told before he dies. So the sire of Feroluce sang, and the grandsire, and each of his ancestors. Generally they died in flight, falling angels spun down the gulches and enormous stairs of distant peaks, singing. Feroluce, immured, believes that his cry is somehow audible.

To the crowd in the Duke's hall the song is merely that, a song, but how glorious. The dark silver voice, turning to bronze or gold, whitening in the higher registers. There seem to be words, but in some other tongue. This is how the planets sing, surely, or mysterious creatures of the sea.

Everyone is bemused. They listen, astonished.

No one now remonstrates with Rohise when she rises and steals down from the dais. There is an enchantment which prevents movement and coherent thought. Of all the roomful, only she is drawn forward. So she comes close, unhindered, and between the bars of the cage, she sees the vampire for the first time.

She has no notion what he can be. She imagined it was a monster or a monstrous beast. But it is neither. Rohise, starved for so long of beauty and always dreaming of it, recognizes Feroluce inevitably as part of the dream-come-true. She loves him instantly. Because she loves him, she is not afraid of him.

She attends while he goes on and on with his glorious song. He does not see her at all, or any of them. They are only things, like mist, or pain. They have no character or personality or worth; abstracts.

Finally, Feroluce stops singing. Beyond the stone and the thick glass of the siege, the wing-beats, too, eddy into silence.

Finding itself mesmerized, silent by night, the court comes to with a terrible joint start, shrilling and shouting, bursting, exploding into a compensation of sound. Music flares again. And the cannons in the roof, which have also fallen quiet, resume with a tremendous roar.

Feroluce shuts his eyes and seems to sleep. It is his preparation for death.

Hands grasp Rohise. "Lady—step back, come away. So close! It may harm you—"

The Duke clasps her in a father's embrace. Rohise, unused to this sort of physical expression, is unmoved. She pats him absently.

"My lord, what will be done?"

"Hush, child. Best you do not know."

Rohise persists.

The Duke persists in not saying.

But she remembers the words of the herald on the stair, and knows they mean to butcher the winged man. She attends thereafter more carefully to snatches of the bizarre talk about the hall, and learns all she needs. At earliest sunrise, as soon as the enemy retreat from the walls, their captive will be taken to the lovely garden with the peach trees. And so to the sunken garden of the magic bush, the fire-flower. And there they will hang him up in the sun through the dome of smoky glass, which will be slow murder to him, but they will cut him, too, so his blood, the stolen blood of the vampire, runs down to water the roots of the fleur de feu. And who can doubt that, from such nourishment, the bush will bloom? The blooms are salvation. Wherever they grow it is a safe place. Whoever wears them is safe from the draining bite of demons. Bite-Me-Not, they call it; vampire-repellent.

Rohise sits the rest of the night on her cushions, with folded hands, resembling the portrait of the princess, which is not like her.

Eventually the sky outside alters. Silence comes down beyond the wall, and so within the wall, and the court lifts its head, a corporate animal scenting day.

At the intimation of sunrise the black plague has lifted and gone away, and might never have been. The Duke, and almost all his castle full of men, women, children, emerge from the doors. The sky is measureless and bluely grey, with one cherry rift in the east that the court refers to as "mauve," since dawns and sunsets are never any sort of red here.

They move through the dimly lightening garden as the last stars melt. The cage is dragged in their midst.

They are too tired, too concentrated now, the Duke's people, to continue baiting their captive. They have had all the long night to do that, and to drink and opine, and now their stamina is sharpened for the final act.

Reaching the sunken garden, the Duke unlocks the iron door. There is no room for everyone within, so mostly they must stand outside, crammed in the gate, or teetering on erections of benches that have been placed around, and peering in over the walls through the glass of the dome. The places in the doorway are the best, of course; no one else will get so good a view. The servants and lower persons must stand back under the trees and only imagine what goes on. But they are used to that.

Into the sunken garden itself there are allowed to go the alchemist and the apothecary, and the priest, and certain sturdy soldiers attendant on the Duke, and the Duke. And Feroluce in the cage.

The east is all 'mauve' now. The alchemist has prepared sorcerous safeguards which are being put into operation, and the priest, never to be left out, intones prayers. The bulge-thewed soldiers open the cage and seize the monster before it can stir. But drugged smoke has already been wafted into the prison, and besides, the monster has prepared itself for hopeless death and makes no demur.

Feroluce hangs in the arms of his loathing guards, dimly aware the sun is near. But death is nearer, and already one may hear the alchemist's apprentice sharpening the knife an ultimate time.

The leaves of the *Nona Mordica* are trembling, too, at the commencement of the light, and beginning to unfurl. Although this happens every dawn, the court points to it with optimistic cries. Rohise, who has claimed a position in the doorway, watches it too, but only for an instant. Though she has sung of the flue de fur since childhood, she had never known what the song was all about. And in just this way, though she has dreamed of being the Duke's daughter most of her life, such an event was never really comprehended either, and so means very little.

As the guards haul the demon forward to the plot of humid earth where the bush is growing, Rohise darts into the sunken garden, and lightning leaps in her hands. Women scream and well they might. Rohise has stolen one of the swords from the East Turret, and now she flourishes it, and now she has swung it and a soldier falls, bleeding red, red, *red*, before them all.

Chaos enters, as in yesterday's play, shaking its tattered sleeves. The men who hold the demon rear back in horror at the dashing blade and the blasphemous gore, and the mad girl in her princess's gown. The Duke makes a pitiful bleating noise, but no one pays him any attention.

The east glows in and like the liquid on the ground.

Meanwhile, the ironically combined sense of impending day and spilled hot blood have penetrated the stunned brain of the vampire. His eyes open and he sees the girl wielding her sword in a spray of crimson as the last guard lets go. Then the girl has run to Feroluce. Though, or because, her face is insane, it communicates her purpose, as she thrusts the sword's hilt into his hands.

No one has dared approach either the demon or the girl. Now they look on in horror and in horror grasp what Feroluce has grasped.

In that moment the vampire springs, and the great swanlike wings are reborn at his back, healed and whole. As the doctors predicted, he has mended perfectly, and prodigiously fast. He takes to the air like an arrow, unhindered, as if gravity does not any more exist. As he does so, the girl grips him about the waist, and slender and light, she is drawn upward too. He does not glance at her. He veers towards the gateway, and tears through it, the sword, his talons, his wings, his very shadow beating men and bricks from his path.

And now he is in the sky above them, a black star which has not been put out. They see the wings flare and beat, and the swirling of a girl's dress and unbound hair, and then the image dives and is gone into the shade under the mountains, as the sun rises.

CHAPTER V

It is fortunate, the mountain shade in the sunrise. Lion's blood and enforced quiescence have worked wonders, but the sun could undo it all. Luckily the shadow, deep and cold as a pool, envelops the vampire, and in it there is a cave, deeper and colder. Here he alights and sinks down, sloughing the girl, whom he has almost forgotten. Certainly he fears no harm from her. She is like a pet animal, maybe, like the hunting dogs or wolves or lammergeyers that occasionally the unkindness of vampires have kept by them for a while. That she helped him is all he needs to know. She will help again. So when, stumbling in the blackness, she brings him in her cupped hands water from a cascade at the poolcave's back, he is not surprised. He drinks the water, which is the only other substance his kind imbibe. Then he smooths her hair, absently, as he would pat or stroke the pet she seems to have become. He is not grateful, as he is not suspicious. The complexities of his intellect are reserved for other things. Since he is exhausted he falls asleep, and since Rohise is exhausted she falls asleep beside him, pressed to his warmth in the freezing dark. Like those of Feroluce, as it turns out, her thoughts are simple. She is sorry for distressing the Cursed Duke. But she has no regrets, for she could no more have left Feroluce to die than she could have refused to leave the scullery for the court.

The day, which had only just begun, passes swiftly in sleep.

Feroluce wakes as the sun sets, without seeing anything of it. He unfolds himself and goes to the cave's entrance, which now looks out on a whole sky of stars above a landscape of mountains. The castle is far below, and to the eyes of Rohise as she follows him, invisible. She does not even look for it, for there is something else to be seen.

The great dark shapes of angels are wheeling against the peaks, the stars. And their song begins, up in the starlit spaces. It is a lament, their mourning, pitiless and strong, for Feroluce, who has died in the stone heart of the thing they prey upon.

The tribe of Feroluce do not laugh, but, like a bird or wild beast, they have a kind of equivalent to laughter. This Feroluce now utters, and like a flung lance he launches himself into the air.

Rohise at the cave mouth, abandoned, forgotten, unnoted even by the mass of vampires, watches the winged man as he flies towards his people. She supposes for a moment that she may be able to climb down the tortuous ways of the mountain, undetected. Where then should she go? She does not spend much time on these ideas. They do not interest or involve her. She watches Feroluce and, because she learned long ago the uselessness of weeping, she does not shed tears, though her heart begins to break.

As Feroluce glides, body held motionless, wings outspread on a downdraught, into the midst of the storm of black wings, the red stars of eyes ignite all about him. The great lament dies. The air is very still.

Feroluce waits then. He waits, for the aura of his people is not as he has always known it. It is as if he had come among emptiness. From the silence, therefore, and from nothing else, he learns it all. In the stone he lay and he sang of his death, as the Prince must, dying. And the ritual was completed, and now there is the threnody, the grief, and thereafter the choosing of a new Prince. And none of this is alterable. He is dead. Dead. It cannot and will not be changed.

There is a moment of protest, then, from Feroluce. Perhaps his brief sojourn among men has taught him some of their futility. But as the cry leaves him, all about the huge wings are raised like swords. Talons and teeth and eyes burn against the stars. To protest is to be torn in shreds. He is not of their people now. They can attack and slaughter him as they would any other intruding thing. *Go,* the talons and the teeth and the eyes say to him. *Go far off.*

He is dead. There is nothing left him but to die.

Feroluce retreats. He soars. Bewildered, he feels the power and energy of his strength and the joy of flight, and cannot understand how this is, if he is dead. Yet he *is* dead. He knows it now.

So he closes his eyelids, and his wings. Spear swift he falls. And something shrieks, interrupting the reverie of nihilism. Disturbed, he opens his wings, shudders, turns like a swimmer, finds a ledge against his side and two hands outstretched, holding him by one shoulder, and by his hair.

"No," says Rohise. (The vampire cloud, wheeling away, have not heard her; she does not think of them.) His eyes stay shut. Holding him, she kisses these eyelids, his forehead, his lips, gently, as she drives her nails into his skin to hold him. The black wings beat, tearing to be free and fall and die. "No," say Rohise. "I love you," she says. "My life is your life." These are the words of the court and of courtly love songs. No matter, she means them. And though he cannot understand her language or her sentiments, yet her passion, purely that, communicates itself, strong and burning as the passions of his kind, who generally love only one thing, which is scarlet. For a second her intensity fills the void which now contains him. But then he dashes himself away from the ledge, to fall again, to seek death again.

Like a ribbon, clinging to him still, Rohise is drawn from the rock and falls with him.

Afraid, she buries her head against his breast, in the shadow of wings and hair. She no longer asks him to reconsider. This is how it must be. *Love* she thinks again, in the instant before they strike the earth. Then that instant comes, and is gone.

Astonished, she finds herself still alive, still in the air. Touching so close feathers have been left on the rocks. Feroluce has swerved away, and upward. Now, conversely, they are whirling towards the very stars. The world seems miles below. Perhaps they will fly into space itself. Perhaps he means to break their bones instead on the cold face of the moon.

He does not attempt to dislodge her, he does not attempt any more to fall and die. But as he flies, he suddenly cries out, terrible lost lunatic cries.

They do not hit the moon. They do not pass through the stars like static rain.

But when the air grows thin and pure there is a peak like a dagger standing in their path. Here, he alights. As Rohise lets go of him, he turns away. He stations himself, sentry-fashion, in the manner of his tribe, at the edge of the pinnacle. But watching for nothing. He has not been able to choose death. His strength and the strong will of another, these have hampered him. His brain has become formless darkness. His eyes glare, seeing nothing.

Rohise, gasping a little in the thin atmosphere, sits at his back, watching for him, in case any harm may come near him.

At last, harm does come. There is a lightening in the east. The frozen, choppy sea of the mountains below and all about, grows visible. It is a marvelous sight, but holds no marvel for Rohise. She averts her eyes from the exquisitely penciled shapes, looking thin and translucent as paper, the rivers of mist between, the glimmer of nacreous ice. She searches for a blind hole to hide in.

There is a pale yellow wound in the sky when she returns. She grasps Feroluce by the wrist and tugs at him. "Come," she says. He looks at her vaguely, as if seeing her from the shore of another country. "The sun," she says. "Quickly."

The edge of the light runs along his body like a razor. He moves by instinct now, following her down the slippery dagger of the peak, and so eventually into a shallow cave. It is so small it holds him like a coffin. Rohise closes the entrance with her own body. It is the best she can do. She sits facing the sun as it rises, as if prepared to fight. She hates the sun for his sake. Even as the light warms her chilled body, she curses it. Till light and cold and breathlessness fade together.

When she wakes, she looks up into twilight and endless stars, two of which are red. She is lying on the rock by the cave. Feroluce leans over her, and behind Feroluce his quiescent wings fill the sky.

She has never properly understood his nature: Vampire. Yet her own nature, which tells her so much, tells her some vital part of herself is needful to him, and that he is danger, and death. But she loves him, and is not afraid. She would have fallen to die with him. To help him by her death does not seem wrong to her. Thus, she lies still, and smiles at him to reassure him she will not struggle. From lassitude, not fear, she closes her eyes. Presently she feels the soft weight of hair brush by her cheek, and then his cool mouth rests against her throat. But nothing more happens. For some while, they continue in this fashion, she yielding, he kneeling over her, his lips on her skin. Then he moves a little away. He sits, regarding her. She, knowing the unknown act has not been completed, sits up in turn. She beckons to him mutely, telling him with her gestures and her expression *I consent. Whatever is necessary.*

But he does not stir. His eyes blaze, but even of these she has no fear. In the end he looks away from her, out across the spaces of the darkness.

He himself does not understand. It is permissible to drink from the body of a pet, the wolf, the eagle. Even to kill the pet, if need demands. Can it be, outlawed from his people, he has lost their composite soul? Therefore, is he soulless now? It does not seem to him he is. Weakened and famished though he is, the vampire is aware of a wild tingling of life. When he stares at the creature which is his food, he finds he sees her differently. He has borne her through the sky, he has avoided death, by some intuitive process, for her sake, and she has led him to safety, guarded him from the blade of the sun. In the beginning it was she who rescued him from the human things which had taken him. She cannot be human, then. Not pet, and not prey. For no, he could not drain her of blood, as he would not seize upon his own kind, even in combat, to drink and feed. He starts to see her as beautiful, not in the way a man beholds a woman, certainly, but as his kind revere the sheen of water in dusk, or flight, or song. There are no words for this. But the life goes on tingling through him. Though he is dead, life.

In the end, the moon does rise, and across the open face of it something wheels by. Feroluce is less swift than was his wont, yet he starts in pursuit, and catches and brings down, killing on the wing, a great night bird. Turning in the air, Feroluce absorbs its liquors. The heat of life now, as well as its assertion, courses through him. He returns to the rock perch, the glorious flaccid bird dangling from his hand. Carefully, he tears the glory of the bird in pieces, plucks the feathers, splits the bones. He wakes the companion (asleep again from weakness) who is not pet or prey, and feeds her morsels of flesh. At first she is unwilling. But her hunger is so enormous and her nature so untamed that quite soon she accepts the slivers of raw fowl.

Strengthened by blood, Feroluce lifts Rohise and bears her gliding down the moon-slit quill-backed land of the mountains, until there is a rocky cistern full of cold, old rains. Here they drink together. Pale white primroses grow in the fissures where the black moss drips. Rohise makes a garland and throws it about the head of her beloved when he does not expect it. Bewildered but disdainful, he touches at the wreath of primroses to see if it is likely to threaten or hamper him. When it does not, he leaves it in place.

Long before dawn this time, they have found a crevice. Because it is so cold, he folds his wings about her. She speaks of her love to him, but he does not hear, only the murmur of her voice, which is musical and does not displease him. And later, she sings him sleepily the little song of the fleur de fur.

CHAPTER VI

There comes a time then, brief, undated, chartless time, when they are together, these two creatures. Not together in any accepted sense, of course, but together in the strange feeling or emotion, instinct or ritual, that can burst to life in an instant or flow to life gradually across half a century, and which men call *Love*.

They are not alike. No, not at all. Their differences are legion and should be unpalatable. He is a supernatural thing and she a human thing, he was a lord and she a scullery sloven. He can fly, she cannot fly. And he is male, she female. What other items are required to make them enemies? Yet they are bound, not merely by love, they are bound by all they are, the very stumbling blocks. Bound, too, because they are doomed. Because the stumbling blocks have doomed them; everything has. Each has been exiled out of their own kind. Together, they cannot even communicate with each other, save by looks, touches, sometimes by sounds, and by songs neither understands, but which each comes to value since the other appears to value them, and since they give expression to that other. Nevertheless, the binding of the doom, the greatest binding, grows, as it holds them fast to each other, mightier and stronger.

Although they do not know it, or not fully, it is the awareness of doom that keeps them there, among the platforms and steps up and down, and the inner cups, of the mountains.

Here it is possible to pursue the airborne hunt, and Feroluce may now and then bring down a bird to sustain them both. But birds are scarce. The richer lower slopes, pastured with goats, wild sheep and men—they lie far off and far down from this place as a deep of the sea. And Feroluce does not conduct her there, nor does Rohise ask that he should, or try to lead the way, or even dream of such a plan.

But yes, birds are scarce, and the pastures far away, and winter is coming. There are only two seasons in these mountains. High summer, which dies, and the high cold which already treads over the tips of the air and the rock, numbing the sky, making all brittle, as though the whole landscape might snap in pieces, shatter.

How beautiful it is to wake with the dusk, when the silver webs of night begin to form, frost and ice, on everything. Even the ragged dress —once that of a princess—is tinseled and shining with this magic substance, even the mighty wings—once those of a prince—each feather is drawn glittering with thin rime. And oh, the sky, thick as a daisy-field with the white stars. Up there, when they have fed and have strength, they fly, or, Feroluce flies and Rohise flies in his arms, carried by his wings. Up there in the biting chill like a pane of ghostly vitreous, they have become lovers, true blind lovers, embraced and linked, their bodies a bow, coupling on the wing. By the hour that this first happened the girl had forgotten all she had been, and he had forgotten too that she was anything but the essential mate. Sometimes, borne in this way, by wings and by fire, she cries out as she hangs in the ether. These sounds, transmitted through the flawless silence and amplification of the peaks, scatter over tiny half-buried villages countless miles away, where they are heard in fright and taken for the shrieks of malign invisible devils, tiny as bats, and armed with the barbed stings of scorpions. There are always misunderstandings.

After a while, the icy prologues and the stunning starry fields of winter nights give way to the main argument of winter.

The liquid of the pool, where the flowers made garlands, has clouded and closed to stone. Even the volatile waterfalls are stilled, broken cascades of glass. The wind tears through the skin and hair to gnaw the bones. To weep with cold earns no compassion of the cold.

There is no means to make fire. Besides, the one who was Rohise is an animal now, or a bird, and beasts and birds do not make fire, save for the phoenix in the Duke's bestiary. Also, the sun is fire, and the sun is a foe. Eschew fire.

There begin the calendar months of hibernation. The demon lovers too must prepare for just such a measureless winter sleep, that gives no hunger, asks no action. There is a deep cave they have lined with feathers and withered grass. But there are no more flying things to feed them. Long, long ago, the last warm frugal feast, long, long ago the last flight, joining, ecstasy and song. So, they turn to their cave, to stasis, to sleep. Which each understands, wordlessly, thoughtlessly, is death.

What else? He might drain her of blood, he could persist some while on that, might even escape the mountains, the doom. Or she herself might leave him, attempt to make her way to the places below, and perhaps she could reach them, even now. Others, lost here, have done so. But neither considers these alternatives. The moment for all that is past. Even the death-lament does not need to be voiced again.

Installed, they curl together in their bloodless, icy nest, murmuring a little to each other, but finally still.

Outside, the snow begins to come down. It falls like a curtain. Then the winds take it. Then the night is full of the lashing of whips, and when the sun rises it is white as the snow itself, its flames very distant, giving nothing. The cave mouth is blocked up with snow. In the winter, it seems possible that never again will there be a summer in the world.

Behind the modest door of snow, hidden and secret, sleep is quiet as stars, dense as hardening resin. Feroluce and Rohise turn pure and pale in the amber, in the frigid nest, and the great wings lie like a curious articulated machinery that will not move. And the withered grass and the flowers are crystalized, until the snows shall melt.

At length, the sun deigns to come closer to the earth, and the miracle occurs. The snow shifts, crumbles, crashes off the mountains in rage. The waters hurry after the snow, the air is wrung and racked by splittings and splinterings, by rushes and booms. It is half a year, or it might be a hundred years, later.

Open now, the entry to the cave. Nothing emerges. Then, a flutter, a whisper. Something does emerge. One black feather, and caught in it, the petal of a flower, crumbling like dark charcoal and white, drifting away into the voids below. Gone. Vanished. It might never have been.

But there comes another time (half a year, a hundred years), when an adventurous traveler comes down from the mountains to the pocketed villages the other side of them. He is a swarthy cheerful fellow, you would not take him for herbalist or mystic, but he has in a pot a plant he found high up in the staring crags, which might after all contain anything or nothing. And he shows the plant, which is an unusual one, having slender, dark and velvety leaves, and giving off a pleasant smell like vanilla. "See, the *Nona Mordica*," he says. "The Bite-Me-Not. The flower that repels vampires."

Then the villagers tell him an odd story, about a castle in another country, besieged by a huge flock, a menace of winged vampires, and how the Duke waited in vain for the magic bush that was in his garden, the Bite-Me-Not, to flower and save them all. But it seems there was a curse on this Duke, who on the very night his daughter was lost, had raped a serving woman, as he had raped others before. But this woman conceived. And bearing the fruit, or flower, of this rape, damaged her, so she lived only a year or two after it. The child grew up unknowing, and in the end betrayed her own father by running away to the vampires, leaving the Duke demoralized. And soon after he went mad, and himself stole out one night, and let the winged fiends into his castle, so all there perished.

"Now if only the bush had flowered in time, as your bush flowers, all would have been well," the villagers cry.

The traveler smiles. He in turn does not tell them of the heap of peculiar bones, like parts of eagles mingled with those of a woman and a man. Out of the bones, from the heart of them, the bush was rising, but the traveler untangled the roots of it with care; it looks sound enough now in its sturdy pot, all of it twining together. It seems as if two separate plants are growing from a single stem, one with blooms almost black, and one pink-flowered, like a young sunset.

"Flur de fur," says the traveler, beaming at the marvel, and his luck.

Fleur de feu. Oh flower of fire. That fire is not hate or fear, which makes flowers come, not terror or anger or lust, it is love that is the fire of the Bite-Me-Not, love which cannot abandon, love which cannot harm. Love which never dies.

APPENDIX I
VAMPIRE NOVELS

Following is a selected list of novels about vampires, organized by author. It is intended only as a guide to further reading in vampire literature, and is limited to contemporary titles. Taken as a group, these novels, even those with historical settings, demonstrate the many ways in which writers are adapting traditional vampire lore and using it for their own modern literary purposes.

SUZY MCKEE CHARNAS

The Vampire Tapestry (1980)

Charnas takes a psychological approach here, examining the idea of the vampire as predator in five related novellas. ("Unicorn Tapestry" is included in this volume.)

LES DANIELS

The Black Castle (1978)
The Silver Skull (1979)
Citizen Vampire (1981)

In this trilogy of novels, Daniels places the vampire Don Sebastian de Villanueva in a variety of historical settings, including the Spanish Inquisition, sixteenth-century Mexico, and the French Revolution. Daniels's work bears favorable comparison with the historical novels of Chelsea Quinn Yarbro.

CHARLES L. GRANT

The Soft Whisper of the Dead (1983)

This is a short novel in which Grant tells a deliberately "old-fashioned" vampire tale, set in New England, with appropriate Victorian trappings.

STEPHEN KING

'Salem's Lot (1975)

'Salem's Lot, King's second novel, is considered by many to be his best. Outstanding in structure, pacing, and characterization, it is both powerful and frightening in its depiction of ordinary people compelled to battle a monstrous force of evil that is taking over their small Maine town.

TANITH LEE

Sabella, or the Blood Stone (1980)

Part science fiction, part fantasy, dark, bloody, and erotic, *Sabella, or the Blood Stone* is the powerful story of a female vampire on a future Mars.

GEORGE R. R. MARTIN

Fevre Dream (1982)

Fevre Dream is an attempt to create a new vampire mythology. In a tale set on Mississippi riverboats in the 1850s, Martin presents a vampire who wants to be cured—and to help cure others—of what he regards as an affliction.

RICHARD MATHESON

I Am Legend (1954)

Matheson's major novel depicts a frightening future world in which everyone, with the exception of the narrator, has become a vampire.

ROBERT R. MCCAMMON

They Thirst (1981)

McCammon's venture into vampire lore is a lively and colorful story, filled with bizarre characters, among them an albino motorcyclist and an evil manufacturer of coffins, and even more bizarre scenes, including a nightmarish journey, dodging vampires all the way, through the sewers of Los Angeles.

MEREDITH ANN PIERCE

The Darkangel (1982)

This strange novel uses fairy-tale elements and those of gothic melodrama in a vampire tale set on the moon.

ANNE RICE

Interview With the Vampire (1976)
The Vampire Lestat (1985)

These are the first two volumes in Rice's "The Chronicles of the Vampires." Like Les Daniels and Chelsea Quinn Yarbro, Rice uses richly detailed historical settings, here the steamy, religion-haunted world of old New Orleans and the bizarre underworld of eighteenth-century Europe. *The Vampire Lestat* also employs opening and closing passages that, like S. P. Somtow's *Vampire Junction,* present the modern vampire as a rock star.

S. P. SOMTOW

Vampire Junction (1984)

S. P. Somtow is a pseudonym for science fiction writer Somtow Sucharitkul, who here creates a modern-day vampire as a young rock musician. (Anne Rice also uses this device in *The Vampire Lestat.*)

WHITLEY STRIEBER

The Hunger (1981)

The Hunger, without ever using the word "vampire," describes an alien vampiric race that inhabits the same world as humanity. Set in present-day New York City, it also looks back through history and creates a memorable character in the vampire Miriam Blaylock.

THEODORE STURGEON

Some of Your Blood (1961)

Sturgeon, one of the great modern fantasists, developed a shocking (and bloody) variation on traditional vampire lore in *Some of Your Blood.* Some readers are offended by its theme, but no reader ever forgets it.

PETER TREMAYNE

Bloodright (1977; published in Great Britain as *Dracula Unborn*)
The Revenge of Dracula (1978)
Dracula, My Love (1980)

Tremayne spins three colorful tales based on both Bram Stoker's treatment of vampire lore and legends of the notorious fifteenth-century ruler Vlad Tepes, known as Dracula ór "The Impaler." The first is presented as a manuscript by Mircea, son of Dracula; the second recounts a tale of Dracula's activities in Europe; and the third is a Victorian tale in which a young woman from Edinburgh takes a job as governess in Castle Dracula.

F. PAUL WILSON

The Keep (1981)

In a lively novel filled with tension and stirring personal combats, Wilson sets the ancient evil of vampirism against the modern evil of Nazism.

CHELSEA QUINN YARBRO

Hotel Transylvania (1978)
The Palace (1978)
Blood Games (1979)
Path of the Eclipse (1981)
Tempting Fate (1982)
The Saint-Germain Chronicles (1983)

Yarbro's le Comte de Saint-Germain is among the most memorable vampires in modern times. Deathless, dark, mysterious, and erotic, he moves through history, observing—through the unblinking eyes of an immortal—the continuing inhumanity of mankind. These are historical novels, using their settings—pre-Revolutionary Paris, fifteenth-century Florence, Nero's Rome, ancient China, and Europe during the rise of Nazism—as foils for a vampire who is sometimes deadly, often horrified at the behavior of mortals, and always charming and attractive. *The Saint-Germain Chronicles* contains five related stories, of which "Cabin 33" is included in this volume. (Les Daniels and Anne Rice also use historical settings for their vampire novels.)

APPENDIX II
VAMPIRE MOVIES

Vampires, from the melodramatic to the comic, have always been popular in the movies. Following is a selected list of some of the most interesting, showing the wide range of treatments vampires have received on film.

ABBOTT AND COSTELLO MEET FRANKENSTEIN (1948)

Bela Lugosi once again plays Dracula, very seriously, in the midst of the comedy team's antics.

ANDY WARHOL'S DRACULA (1974)

Directed by Paul Morrissey, this story of an aging Dracula seeking the blood of virgins in Catholic Italy has much to recommend it, including a light touch of humor in contrast to the frequently bloody events.

BLOOD AND ROSES (1961)

This is director Roger Vadim's fairly faithful adaptation of J. Sheridan Le Fanu's "Carmilla," starring Annette Stroyberg, Elsa Martinelli, and Mel Ferrer. Highly erotic, it has been cut and its impact much reduced by American censors.

BLOODSUCKERS (1971)

Patrick Macnee and Peter Cushing star in an uneven film that presents vampirism as a psychological perversion.

BRIDES OF DRACULA (1960)

Brides of Dracula features a vampire running amok in a girls' boarding school and stars Peter Cushing as Van Helsing. Interestingly, Christopher Lee turned down the vampire role in *Brides of Dracula*, fearing he would be typecast.

CAPTAIN KRONOS, VAMPIRE HUNTER (1974)

This excellent film (by writer-director Brian Clemens, best known for his television series "The Avengers") features humor, powerful visual imagery, and a vampire who robs his victims of youth rather than blood.

COUNT DRACULA (1970)

Christopher Lee as Dracula and Klaus Kinski (who has played the title role himself, in *Nosferatu the Vampyre)* as Renfield, plus a serious attempt to retell Stoker's novel, are nearly thwarted by an otherwise shoddy production.

DRACULA (1931)

This landmark film, directed by Tod Browning, was adapted from the stage play by Hamilton Deane and John L. Balderston, first presented in London in February 1927 and in New York in October of that year. Hungarian actor Bela Lugosi had played the title role on the Broadway stage and repeated it in the film, thus preserving his unforgettable characterization. Among the notable elements of his portrayal is his dreamy, balletic style of movement, creating an image that places the vampire in a world apart from that of mere mortals.

DRACULA (1979)

Frank Langella plays Dracula, with Laurence Olivier as Van Helsing, in this modern version of the play by Deane and Balderston. Langella had played the role in a 1977 Broadway revival of the play.

HORROR OF DRACULA (1958)

The first, and one of the best, vampire films from Britain's Hammer Films, *Horror of Dracula* boasts Christopher Lee in the title role and Peter Cushing as Van Helsing. Lee's portrayal of the vampire in this and later films came to embody the aristocratic, erotic, and evil Dracula for modern times.

THE HUNGER (1983)

Based on Whitley Strieber's novel, this film stars Catherine Deneuve as the lovely vampire Miriam Blaylock, who seduces first David Bowie and then Susan Sarandon. Beautifully filmed, it is relentlessly contemporary in its music and imagery, yet manages to convey the terrible loneliness of the immortal vampire.

LOVE AT FIRST BITE (1979)

George Hamilton plays Dracula in this parody, pursuing model Susan Saint James through modern New York, aided by Arte Johnson as Renfield.

MARK OF THE VAMPIRE (1935)

This is another exploration of the vampire myth by Tod Browning, who had earlier directed the classic *Dracula*.

MARTIN (1977)

Director George A. Romero's vampire film, considered by many to be his best, uses the vampire image for a frightening exploration of modern guilt and morality.

NOSFERATU (1922)

This silent film, subtitled "A Symphony of Horror" and directed by F. W. Murnau, was the first based on Bram Stoker's *Dracula*, even though, since the adaptation was unauthorized, the settings and characters' names were changed. It is one of the most powerful vampire films ever made, not least for actor Max Schreck's portrayal of the ratlike and repellent Dracula figure. This characterization was repeated years later by Klaus Kinski in director Werner Herzog's version, *Nosferatu the Vampyre*.

NOSFERATU THE VAMPYRE (1979)

German director Werner Herzog's film is slow, visually beautiful, and eerie. It stars Klaus Kinski in a memorable portrayal of Dracula that is reminiscent of Max Schreck's 1922 performance in *Nosferatu*.

THE RETURN OF THE VAMPIRE (1943)

Although the Dracula figure is given a different name here, this film marked Bela Lugosi's return to his greatest role.

'SALEM'S LOT: THE MOVIE (1979)

The shortened commercial version of this film is somewhat weaker than the original four-hour version made for television. Adapted from Stephen King's novel, it was directed by Tobe Hooper and stars David Soul.

THE SEVEN BROTHERS MEET DRACULA (1974)

This martial-arts film has Peter Cushing as Van Helsing helping a Chinese friend fight Dracula, who leads an army trained in kung fu.

THE VAMPIRE LOVERS (1970)

This film is loosely based on J. Sheridan Le Fanu's "Carmilla."

VAMPYR (1932)

This early sound film by Danish director Carl Dreyer is loosely based on Le Fanu's "Carmilla," and features a memorable scene in which a young Englishman is buried in a coffin with a glass window.